# THE COMPLETE SHAMBLES

## THE FOUR ONDINE NOVELS

EBONY MCKENNA

The Complete Shambles

The Four Ondine Novels

Print ISBN: 9781922486103

ebook ISBN: 9780648284239



**Previous Publishing History**

The Summer of Shambles

First edition published as Ondine in 2010 (paperback) by Egmont UK

Second edition published as The Summer of Shambles (ebook) 2013 by Ebony McKenna

The Autumn Palace

First edition published as Ondine: The Autumn Palace (paperback) in 2011 by Egmont UK

Second edition published as The Autumn Palace (ebook) 2013 by Ebony McKenna

The Winter of Magic

First edition published (ebook) 2014 by Ebony McKenna

The Spring Revolution

First edition published (ebook) 2015 by Ebony McKenna

# THE SUMMER OF SHAMBLES

$$1$$

_______

This is a great story, and like a good many great stories before it, it begins with a teenage girl. Her name is Ondine de Groot and she is fifteen. She has long dark hair past her shoulders, which is neat for about five minutes before it gets messy and stringy. Her eyes are dark brown and pretty, except when she's rolling them. She also adores small animals, of which you will hear more in a moment.

Ondine's story began exactly twelve years ago today, in a place called Brugel,[1] a pretty country in Eastern Europe, which is well known for its old buildings.[2]

On the day this story began, Ondine was nearing the end of her time at Psychic Summercamp. As the name suggests, Psychic Summercamp was a place for students to spend their summer holidays developing their psychic and other extra-sensory skills. In some countries, students spend their holidays at adventure camp, fat camp or mathletics. In Brugel, they do things differently.

Back to Ondine. She was in a dormitory with three other girls (who were asleep on account of it being so early in the morning) and she awoke with a jolt.

"Saturn's rings! It's six o'clock! I've slept through the astral projection exam." Ondine sat up and pushed the covers away. The bed's throw rug fell to the floor, smothering the furry black ferret that lay curled up beneath.

"Melody, wake up," she said, nudging the sleeping girl in the bunk above her. "What happened in the astral exam?"

It took Melody a few more nudges to wake up. Yawning, she swiped her mousy-blonde hair from her face, rubbed the sleep from her eyes and inspected it, then stopped as she realized she had an audience.

"Ah, sorry." Melody looked embarrassed as she blinked herself awake. "What's going on, what time is it? The sun isn't even up." The psychic lessons didn't seem to have worked very well on her either.

"Shh, you'll wake the others," Ondine said. "Now, quick, what happened in the astral?"

"I . . . I don't know. I must have slept through it!" Melody's face crumpled and she made ready to cry. "I'm going to fail, aren't I?"

"Don't worry, I'll fail more than you." As Ondine looked around the room, she spotted the handle of her suitcase poking out from under her bed. It gave her an idea. "This entire thing is a waste of time, and a waste of our summer holidays. We're supposed to be having fun with boys and falling in love, not studying. I'm going to run away to home."

A great many girls of Ondine's age would love to run away *from* home, but Ondine was the other way around. She'd had it up to here (hold your hand at eyebrow level) with the whole psychic thing and knew it was time to quit.

And another thing, how was she supposed to have fun and meet cute boys if she spent her school holidays in another kind of school?

While Melody watched the door for teachers, Ondine packed up her clothes and her gimgaws and doohickie whatsits and zipped the case closed.[3]

"Shouldn't you tell Mrs Howser you're leaving?" Melody asked.

"Pfft. She's the psychic one, why should I bother?" Ondine looked at the sleeping forms of her remaining roommates. "You can tell the other two when they wake up."

"How will you get home?" Melody asked.

Valid question. Psychic Summercamp was located on the outskirts of

Brugel's capital city, Venzelemma, and Ondine's family lived right over on the other side.

"There's a bus stop down the end of the street, so I'll take that to central station. Then I'll get the train the rest of the way home." Ondine sounded pleased with her plan as she lifted the faux-fur-throw off the ferret and folded it into a messy rectangle-ish shape on the end of her bed.

The throw, not the animal. Ferrets don't fold so well.

"What about Shambles?" Melody asked, looking at the sleeping animal on the ground.

Oh dear. Ondine hadn't given much thought to the ferret, because she didn't think the creature should be coming with her. Ondine was more your fluffy kitten-y type of girl, so she hadn't given much attention that morning to the long and skinny bundle of black. Turning up at home, unannounced, before Summercamp finished would give her family enough of a fright. Turning up unannounced with a weasel in her hands might finish her mother right off.

"He's a sweet thing, and he's really taken to you." Melody's eyes were bright with possibilities.

"You're right," Ondine agreed.

During the weeks at camp, Ondine and Shambles the ferret had become unlikely buddies. He'd turned up one day and made himself at home, following Ondine about.[4] He'd even come to classes with her. The thought of abandoning the little fella to the craziness of Summercamp and Mrs Howser made something twist in her tummy. Probably guilt. A bit of hunger too.

Then Shambles the ferret woke up, spun around a few times and stood up on his hind legs, looking like an elongated, begging puppy. If puppies had pointy noses, long whiskers and sharp teeth.

"And nobody else got a pet while they were here," Melody said. "You were really lucky."

Hmmm, what to do? It didn't sit right with her conscience to leave him.

"I'll take him with me and find him a good home," Ondine said, scooping up the creature and tucking him into the crook of her arm.

"Shambles, you're going to have to behave yourself or I'll leave you on the bus." It was her way of trying to sound stroppy. The little fella was pretty cute once you got to know him.

———

SO THAT's how Ondine came to leave Psychic Summercamp on that warm summer's morning, with a ferret wrapped around her neck like a scarf and the scent of geraniums and lavender in her nostrils as she walked along the flower-studded footpath to the bus stop.[5]

The wind blew her hair in wild directions, whipping at her lips and eyes. There was nothing she could do to prevent it; she needed both hands to carry her heavy case. Not even a spare hand for Shambles – he hung on to her collar.

It wasn't until Ondine got off the bus and reached Venzelemma's crowded central train station that the ferret spoke.

"Thank gooniss for tha–, I'm all bumpy and broke," Shambles said with a deep Scottish accent, then climbed on to her head to get a better view. "Progress! The train'll be here in a minute. When we get tae yer hoose we can eet, I'm fair starven."

Ondine gasped and dropped her case on the platform in shock. Because, make no mistake about it, there was definitely a man's voice coming from the ferret. Sure, summer was all about having fun and meeting boys, but not this kind!

Quickly, she found a place to sit down, then she hauled Shambles into her hands to have a good look at him, all the time wondering if she'd gone a bit . . . funny.

**-Interlude-: What and where is Brugel? (Source: Brugelwiki.org.bu)**

**BRUGEL** (pron. Broo-gl) Officially: The Serene Duchy of Brugel. Brugel is a small country in Eastern Europe. It is the only country in the world with a hexagonal flag. It has a single house of parliament, the Dentate (the place with teeth).

The First Minister is the head of government. The Duke of Brugel is the head of state.

Brugel is at the crossroads of old and new Europe. Previously part of the USSR, Brugel declared independence in 1991 and shares its northern and eastern borders with Slaegal, its western and southern borders with Craviç and holds on with its fingertips to an acreage of beach along The Black Sea. The capital and largest city is Venzelemma.

The Brugel language is derived from an earlier form of English. This came about after many Jutes, Angles and Saxons took a wrong turn in the fifth century and found themselves at the Black Sea. [Citation needed]

Brugel has survived through many hardships, having been annexed into the Constantine, Austro-Hungarian, Prussian and Holy Roman empires at various – and mercifully short – times in history. In the 1950s Soviet tanks often rumbled through the main streets of Venzelemma – on their way to somewhere else.

Any rumours you may have heard about Brugel are probably true. All psychics and mediums can trace their DNA to the foothills of Brugel. The countryside is the birthplace of gypsy folklore, and fairy tales and talking animals are interwoven in daily life. This is a country where the strange and unusual are not only tolerated, they are encouraged.


**-End interlude-**

"I've lost my mind," Ondine said. A furtive look around told her nobody else was paying them any attention. The station was full of gray-looking people heading off to work for the day, completely unaware of the teenage girl with scruffy brown hair holding a black ferret.

"Nae ye havnae, but ye can hear me," Shambles added in his thick brogue. "Looks like somethin' rubbed off at Summercamp."

Ondine rolled her eyes. "Ma will be so pleased. All that gypsy blood in my veins and all I can do is talk to rodents."

"I'm nae rodent, ye bampot, I'm a ferret. Completely different. Right then, hae comes the loco. Let me at yer neck."[6]

"But . . . but!" Ondine's brain turned to slurry as she tried to make sense of this talking animal. All the while heated embarrassment roared up her neck and face.

"No backing out now, lassie. I'm coming with ye. Now grab the case and on we get. And upon my honour, I promise to behave."

What could she do? It was still such a shock that her new furry friend could talk. And why could she only hear him now? At that moment the train pulled in and Ondine had no more time for prevaricating.[7]

It was a tense ride home on the train, what with the uncomfortable wooden seats, a talking ferret wriggling about her neck and passengers giving her very strange looks. As soon as the engine arrived at her home station, Ondine grabbed Shambles away from her throat and put him on her shoulder.

His little paws reached up to the top of her head. He stretched and had a good look around.

"Oh, so ye live in this part of town, how very la-de-dah! No wonder yer parents have money tae pish away on psychic dafties."

By this point you may have formed the opinion that Shambles was not your run-of-the-mill ferret, and you'd be right. You may have also formed the opinion

that he's saucy and cheeky, and you'd be right there too. But if you think he's nothing but trouble, you're wrong, although he does give that impression.

As keen as she was to race home, Ondine waited for the train to clear the station before she stepped off the end of the platform to walk across the tracks, looking both ways to make sure no other trains were coming. The pedestrian overpass would have been safer, but it was closed to the public until the official opening.

"Pinch me, I'm dreaming," Shambles said as he noted the direction Ondine was taking him. "The girl lives in a pub!"

The ferret spoke the truth. Ondine's parents ran a hotel and public bar on the main road in a pretty swanky part of Venzelemma. Three floors tall and painted bright blue and white, the hotel towered over the neighbourhood. Even the newer buildings looked like old buildings to help them blend in.

*The Station Hotel* prided itself on being a family business, where everyone pitched in and helped. Not yet old enough to serve alcohol in the bar, Ondine worked in the dining room and helped out behind the scenes. A lot.

Most people think if your parents run a restaurant, you eat delicious five-course meals every night.

You don't.

Ask anyone what it's really like and they'll tell you it's nothing but work. Washing dishes, ironing tablecloths, cleaning the floors, chopping wood for the fire, keeping the fire going all night, preparing food. Look, the list just goes on and on.

But for Ondine, working at home with her parents appealed more than howling at the moon or looking for omens in tea leaves or reading palms or any other great wastes of time that sucked away her precious summer holidays.

"Wait up, we cannae just walk in. Yer mother will fair faint," Shambles said, holding on to Ondine's shoulder.

That made Ondine stop for a moment and think about her plan of action.

"She'll be glad to see me," she said. "Although I don't know what she'll make of you. She's not the pet kind."

"I'm nobody's pet!" Shambles clenched his paws on his hips in frustration. "And dinnae tell no one about finding a new home for me, either. Yer the first person who's heard me in scores of years, mebbe more. I've lost count. I need ye tae stick around and help me, because I think I'm losing my social skills."[8]

Laughter caught in Ondine's throat. It had been a trying morning to say the least, and she wasn't used to lugging heavy things for long distances. Plates piled high with food were fine, because they only needed carrying from the kitchen to the dining-room tables. Heavy suitcases were another matter entirely.

"Are all ferrets like you? I mean, how come you can talk?"

"Because I'm nawt a real ferret. I'm Hamish McPhee, but I offended a witch and she turned me thus. I've bin like this for years. Powerful magic it was and all. Haven't a gray hair on me. Thank gooniss she used a staying spell."

Ondine's eyes widened in surprise. "You offended a witch? Wow!"

"Aye. She took it badly."

"You must have done something really awful to her." Her mind reeled as she wondered what sort of offensive thing might make a witch turn a regular man into a weasel. A regular man! Ondine's memory leapt back to her time in Summercamp, when she'd allowed Shambles to sleep in her dorm. Well, that was before she'd known what he really was. Now that she did know, there'd be no more of that!

"Aye, and I'm deeply ashamed," Shambles admitted.

"What did you do then? And is this witch about to descend on me and demand the return of her familiar?"[9]

"I'm no familiar! They're silly animals turned into fat-belly pets. I'll have ye remember I'm a regular man living in reduced circumstances."

"You're stalling. What did you do?"

"Aw, I was a right neep. I was supposed tae partner her at a debutante ball. Ye know the ones, where the girls get all dolled up and look like brides? And then they get presented to some fancy-pants man, like a mayor or a duke."[10]

"It must have been a while ago. Hardly anyone does a deb any more."

"This girl took it real serious-like. And I didnae. I wasnae yer ideal partner, on account of the fact I had ma first taste of plütz that night."[11]

His tone told Ondine he felt truly sorry for his actions, and she started to feel a bit sorry for him in return.

By now they'd reached the back door. Ondine fished around in her pockets for her key and made ready to let them in. The smell of fried breakfast foods wafted from the kitchen windows, making her tummy rumble.

"Aw, breakfast. I could murder some big fatty sausage," Shambles said, his tongue licking the fur around his mouth in anticipation.

"You're stalling," Ondine said. "Tell me what happened, and then we'll have food."

"Ooooh, listen to ye! All grown up and sophisticated, like," Shambles teased, then Ondine stared daggers at him and his voice dropped to a sombre tone. "I didn't know she was a real witch, otherwise I wouldnae called her one. But she was getting snippy with me, so I ducked off and had some more plütz. It's like peaches and rocket fuel that stuff, and I've nawt touched it since. Then she got really pished with me when I stepped on her feet and fell over. I ripped the lacy bit at the bottom of her skirt and then she got really mad. She called me pond scum. I called her a witch. She looked like her head might explode. She said, 'You're damn right I'm a witch. And you're nothing better than a low-down weasel,' and then she said I could stay like that."

"Wow. And she turned you into a ferret, right there in front of everyone?"

"Naw, she turned me into a donkey! Of course she turned me into a ferret! She was fair affronted."

Ondine gaped at him.

"Ferrets are smaller than weasels, but we're the same family, so maybe I am a low-down weasel after all. But between us, I prefer ferret."

Ondine giggled. "I think she did the right thing. Debutante balls take a lot of organizing, and a lot of rehearsals. I think you should apologize to this poor girl as soon as possible. Then you might be yourself again." The thought of Shambles becoming himself made her wonder what he might look like if he were a real man again? His accent alone made her grin.

Opening the back door, the pungent odour of fried meats and old beer greeted them.

"Aww, that's the good stuff." Shambles took a noisy sniff.

"Ondine! What are you doing home?" her mother called out from the hallway.

"Hi, Ma, you look great. Have you lost weight? I love your hair." Her mother looked as plump as ever, but her new burgundy-brown hairdo skimmed her face and made her look thinner. Flattery ought to put her in a good mood. Just to be on the safe side, Ondine adopted what she hoped was a pleading look on her face. "I . . . I got homesick so I came back."

Ma stopped mid-stride, mouth open, when she saw the ferret on her daughter's shoulder. "Heavens above! What is *that*?" She pointed to the ferret with one hand, while the other patted the ample bosom above her heart, as if the beating organ might leap from her chest.

It called for quick thinking on Ondine's part, because her mother could be either furious or happy about the situation.

"He's really tame. Please, Ma, let me keep him?"

But Shambles was having none of it. "That's the one!" he cried out, finally finding his voice. He scurried down the back of Ondine's vest. "That's the witch!"

# 2

"I am not a witch," her mother said. "Ondine, is there a man just out the back door? With a Scottish accent?"

A sick little feeling settled in Ondine's stomach as she took in her mother's pale, shocked face. "You heard him?"

"Yes, I did hear him, and he called me a witch." Then the crease in Ma's forehead relaxed and the tension in her shoulders fell away. "And, by the way, it's lovely to see you." She moved forwards to embrace her daughter. Around her neck she wore three gold rings with rubies set in them. They flashed in the light as they bounced and jiggled. Just as Ondine thought they might hug, her mother's shoulders hitched again and her eyebrows shot up. She must have seen the ferret. "Ondi, I didn't expect you back so soon, but you can tell me why later. We're run off our feet – I could use another pair of hands. Good thing school doesn't start back for a few weeks yet otherwise I'd be in real strife. You can fill me in on Summercamp later. Right now I need you to tell me what that ferret is doing down your back."[1]

"OK, Shambles, the jig is up, off you get." It wasn't easy, but Ondine contorted her body and pulled the reluctant critter away from the middle of her back. "Ma, meet Shambles. Shambles, this is my mother, Colette."

"Naw, lass, hide me!"

"What?" Ondine exclaimed.

"Run for yer life!"

"Stop wriggling, Shambles! What on earth's wrong with you?"

So much had happened in such a short time, Ondine felt sure she must be running on pure adrenalin.

It was left to Ma to break the tension. "Bless my soul, a talking ferret! Ondine, is this your familiar from Summercamp?"

Ondine then explained the true situation. Ma laughed loud and hearty, making the rings around her neck jiggle and jump.

"I know who you are, Shambles," Ma continued. "You're that weasel what slighted my auntie and ruined her presentation! Hamish McPhee, the Laird of Glen Logan."

Stunned amazement turned Ondine mute for a second.

Shambles piped up, "The witch who turned me is yer auntie? Nawt ye? But if yer all wrinkly, she must be double-wrinkly . . . or dead, no?"

"You're well suited to being a ferret, Shambles." Colette wiped tears of mirth from her eyes. "My auntie Col is eighty-five years young and in perfect health, I'll have you know."

It was a case of mistaken identity, on account of the fact Ondine's mother bore such a striking resemblance to Ondine's great-aunt (as Shambles remembered her). They both had the same short stature, plump faces that smiled a lot, deep brown eyes and dark hair.[2] Ondine too had inherited most of those features, except she was already taller than her mother (or perhaps Ma had started shrinking?). The fact that Ondine's ma and great-aunt had the same first name only added to the confusion.

"Aw naw, aw naw! I've lawst tha will tae live," Shambles bellowed. "If she's eighty-five, what does that make me? I must hae been a ferret half a century then!"

"You're old enough to know better, even if you haven't aged in ferret form. You're the same age now as you were when you were turned." Colette picked up Ondine's case and lugged it towards their family quarters. "My auntie warned me about boys like you, and she was right, you'll never learn. You're lucky you're still a ferret, otherwise I wouldn't let you near my daughters. Given your taste for the sauce, I shouldn't let you anywhere near the bar either."

Yikes! Ondine better not tell her Ma about how much time Shambles spent in her room at Summercamp. Then another thought flickered through her head – A laird, eh? *I wonder what lairds look like?*

"So, can we keep him?" Ondine asked. "I mean, it wouldn't be fair if we set him out on the street. He can sleep in the laundry. I'll make him a bed in there."

"Are you a good mouser?" Ma asked, as she gave Shambles a serious looking over.

"Sure, why d'ye ask? Have ye a wee gun and holster for me?"

"You'll keep," Ma said with one arched brow, then steered them towards the stairs. "Sorry, Ondi, we're full up and I've had to rent out your room on account I didn't think you'd be back for another fortnight. You can share with Cybelle for now."

"Oh, Ma, not again," Ondine said, unable to stop the whine in her voice. "Cybelle snores."

"And I'm sure she'll be delighted to see you too. Come down for breakfast and bring Hamish the Shambles with you when you're done. We'll have a family meeting to remember."

When Ma was out of earshot, Shambles whispered, "Why does she wear those rings around her neck?"

A dry grin crept over Ondine's face. "It's because she's working with food all day – it's not hygienic." The absolute truth? Her mother, having borne three children, had grown too big for her baubles.

---

WHAT MA PROMISED, she delivered. The entire family squeezed around the breakfast table, watching Shambles snaffle sausage after sausage. All the while he made lickety-sloppity-chompity noises as he ate.

"He's so ugly! He looks like a strung-out rat," said Marguerite, the eldest at twenty-one and a quarter. Marguerite would know about ugly, being so far removed from it herself. She had inherited the best of her parents' looks. Deep brown eyes framed with long lashes, tidy arched eyebrows and glossy brown hair that waved and curled in just the right way and always looked neat.

"But he has a . . ." Ondine nearly said "lovely", but even she couldn't bring herself to say that. Instead she settled for, "cute . . . personality."

"The health inspector won't like it, not after we had rats this winter," Ondine's father, Josef, said. "So you'd better keep him under wraps until you can find a new home for him." Josef stood out amongst the sea of brunettes, having turned completely grey. His eyebrows, however, had not. They remained stubbornly black and threatened to join in the middle like two furry caterpillars fighting over a leaf.

"But he's her assignment," Ma said. "He's Ondine's new familiar – it's all part of the program. He has to stay otherwise she'll fail the course."

Those comments – otherwise known as outright fibs – made Ondine's jaw fall open in shock, before she shut it in a hurry. If Da knew Shambles was a real lad, he would throw him out. Ma had also side-stepped the issue of Ondine quitting Summercamp two weeks early.

Da was annoyed. "I paid good money for that place, and they send them home as part of it? I want a refund."

"I'll look into it," Ma said in her most soothing tone.

"Go along with it. I'll nawt protest," Shambles whispered between mouthfuls.

The sight of wet food chunks falling out of Shambles's gob on to the table provided Ondine with an idea. She shovelled her meal into her mouth, to prevent having to talk or answer questions with anything more than a nod or shake of the head, lest she spray her family. If Ma did all the talking, Ondine didn't have to tell any lies . . . as such.

The middle daughter, Cybelle, who was nineteen, added to the fray. "He can sit on the piano while I play in the evenings. He can guard the tips jar with those nippy little fangs of his." As a performer, Cybelle also kept herself very neat. She was lucky enough to have dead-straight hair, cut in a bob with a thick fringe.

If Ondine hadn't had a mouth full of food, she would have told Cybelle she liked her new eyeliner, and could she borrow it please?

"Excellent. That settles it." Ma looked happy with herself. "OK, meeting's over, we all have work to do. Ondi, you and Belle are on laundry duty, Margi's in the kitchen with me on food prep, Josef, check the bar supplies. The Plütz Appreciation Society is coming to lunch."

The PAS was a band of men and women dedicated to damaging their stomachs, livers and kidneys in the most pleasurable way possible. They arrived as ladies and gentlemen and left as purple-lipped human debris, leaving an enormous mess behind them. However, they also left the hotel a sizeable pile of cash for their troubles, so they were always welcome to return.

"I'd better get a stiff broom too, so we can sweep them out before the dinner crowd turn up," Josef said, rising from the table. As he passed Ondine, he paused and kissed the top of her head. "It's lovely to have you back."

"So, ye cannae hear me then?" Shambles said to the man of the house, making Ondine hold her breath for the answer. But no answer came.

How odd that her mother could hear him, but not her father. Perhaps only women could hear Shambles – or maybe only relatives of Aunt Col? In that case, why hadn't Cybelle or Marguerite heard him either?

That's the trouble with ferrets. Just when you thought you had them figured out, they managed to surprise you.

After checking out his new digs in the laundry, Shambles had no intention of catching mice or rats or anything else that might bite him back. Instead, he spent the late afternoon hanging around the kitchen door, catching food scraps Ma and Ondine threw his way.

He was in a pub, and that meant there was beer to be had. But how? The family wouldn't let him near the ale taps and he couldn't very well sit in full view of the public, because – he remembered with a shudder – drunks loved to shove him down their trousers.

Ditching Cybelle's plans to sit him on the top of the piano in the dining room, he slunk through the shadows into the front bar. The noise hit him like a wall, with every table full, and everyone talking at once. In the far corner, people played darts and shouted out their scores. The scent of hops and barley filled his senses, making him light-headed. In places, the carpet was so sticky he had to wrench his paws up to keep moving. Another problem was avoiding clumping great human feet.

He hid under a table in the darkened far corner. It wasn't so noisy over here. Three men sat hunched over their frothy drinks. One squeezed lemon juice over a bowl of hot chips, then shook pepper over them. The powder went everywhere, falling like grey snow over Shambles's head, making his eyes water. It was a warm night, and he envied how people could take their jackets off to cool down. Being stuck with a fur coat, he didn't have that option. Instead, he licked his legs to cool down. The air felt so thick and humid, he could almost taste the beer with each grooming lick, along with plenty of pepper. All his efforts achieved was wet fur. There had to be a better way to cool down. A plan took shape in his head. When the drinkers at the table above him went to the bathroom, he'd dash up on to the table and help himself to their dregs. A nice drink would hit the spot.

Only, it didn't quite go to plan, because what the men talked about at that table made his insides scrunch up. The more Shambles heard, the more he wanted to crawl up the closest trouser leg and sink his fangs into soft flesh. That would teach them a lesson! But the longer he delayed any course of action, the more he heard, and it was damning stuff.

Which only made him want to hear more.

When the men did eventually get up, he saw their scuffed boots heading towards the front door. There was nothing for it, he had to follow.

---

It was good to be home, despite the work – or maybe because of it. Ondine loved feeling useful, and she felt very useful in the kitchen, helping make meals, taking food to tables and sharing jokes with the patrons. The more she smiled, the bigger the tips. Even the mean ones could usually come around – and if they didn't, no harm done, they'd be gone in a few hours.

Tonight, the dining room resounded with chatter and music, with Cybelle on piano taking requests and Marguerite in the bar pouring the beers with Josef. Their father kept track of the money and also made sure the tipsy patrons kept their hands off his daughters. With her shiny hair, previously mentioned deep brown eyes and not-previously-mentioned Cupid's bow lips, Marguerite was the looker of the family. Exactly why Josef kept her closest to him.

"It's not his fault he's so uptight," Ma said to Ondine in the kitchen.

"How did you know what I was thinking?" Sometimes she'd swear her mother was the psychic one. Maybe Ma should have gone to Summercamp instead?

"He thinks all men are lecherous drunks, but he can't help it because they are what he mostly sees. I try and tell him there are some good ones out there; that he's not the only decent man left in Brugel. But it's falling on deaf ears. Right, here are the meals for table eleven, out you get."

Many people would find the truncated and many-threaded conversations confusing but Ondine was used to them. She made her way to the table and placed the food down.

Across the dining room, a woman screamed. "Aaaaaaaaahhhhh! A rat!"

Not again! Ondine's heart sank at the thought of rodents infiltrating the rooms. Just as quickly, her spirits lifted when she saw the blur of long black fur.

"It's all right, everyone relax. It's just my pet ferret," she said, scooping Shambles off the floor and on to her shoulder. She stroked the top of his smooth head. "He's very clean and harmless. I apologize for the disruption."

Time to get away before things got out of hand. How stupid of Shambles to be scurrying around the dining room! They'd be sure to get another visit from the health inspector after this.

"You are in so much trouble, Mister!" Ondine hissed as they made for the family's private room on the other side of the kitchen.

"Hear me out, lass, there's *merdah* afoot and I came tae warn ye. I heard them plotting the whole thing. I followed one of them; man's got a head like a guiser's neep. We have tae warn the Duke."[3]

"What's going on?" The voice belonged to Ma, who'd heard the commotion and followed them out to the back room. "Why was Shambles running around the dining room?"

"He heard people plotting to kill someone."

"Aye, I did! They were in the front bar, drinking their courage and plotting their evil against the Duke of Brugel. I know where they live. We have tae take action, before it's too late."

Ma threw her hands skywards. "I can't abandon a full house!"

"But Ma, someone's going to get killed!" Ondine said.

"OK, OK. If what you say is true, Shambles, then you're right, the Duke needs to be warned. Ondine, I'll get your Da and the two of you can warn him."

"The three of us," Shambles corrected.

"What do you mean the three of us? I can't leave, we're only halfway through dinner," Ma said.

"Naw. I mean I'm goin' with Ondi and Josef. I'll tell them everything I heard as we go – it will save time," Shambles said.

"But what do we tell him?" Ondine asked. "How do we explain to royalty that a ferret told us about a murder plot?"

"We'll tell him *you* overheard the plot, Ondi, while you were tending tables in the bar," Shambles instructed.

"But . . . but . . ." Confusion bubbled in her veins and sapped her brain. Never in her life had she felt so out of control, and that was saying something for a girl with two older sisters who lived in a pub.

"Hurry lass, there's no time to lose. Do you want the Duke's blood on yer hands?"

**3**

_______

H_ow they reached the Duke of Brugel's city domain that night isn't important, but what they said to him when they got there is, so we'll pick up the story from there._[1]

"IT'S SO BIG," Ondine said as they approached the gates of the Duke's domain.

Big didn't even come close. Humongous would be more apt.[2]

Ondine let Josef do all the talking at the security gate, then a sentry walked them across the vast gravel expanse towards the side entry. The looming walls and dark shadows sucked all the warmth from the summer's evening. Ondine's breath came in short bursts and her feet ached. As they walked along the cavernous hallway, the echoes of their footsteps reverberated in her ears. No ordinary tiles on this floor. She marvelled at the intricate mosaic work and wondered how many years it had taken to make it. A cool chill settled in her neck, despite Shambles wrapping himself around her like a stole. For his part, Shambles remained as still as it was possible for a ferret to remain still, so the Duke wouldn't notice how alive he was.

They entered a large room and waited. The Duke cast an imposing figure as he arrived, dressed in a suit and tie, and took a seat at the other end of the room. Standing so far away from him, Ondine felt small and insignificant. The sentry put his hand out to let them know they were not allowed to step any closer. From such a distance, Ondine could see very little of the Duke, except his silvery white hair, which curled back in soft waves from a pronounced widow's peak. He had the classic Brugel split moustache, which is shaved at the philtrum, and a narrow goatee, which he stroked thoughtfully.[3]

"My Lord Duke," Josef began with a steady and loud voice. He bowed his head and very nearly tugged at a forelock of hair while he was at it.

Ondine was impressed that her father knew the correct way to address a duke. But then Da loved his tradition, so perhaps it wasn't so surprising.

"We apologize for the late hour and the interruption to your family, but time is against us. My name is Josef de Groot and my family owns *The Station Hotel*. Our clientele is well behaved and law-abiding, but tonight my daughter, Ondine, overheard people in our public bar plotting to do harm to your person. We came as quickly as we could. To warn you."

"Really?" The Duke's voice carried across the room. It was hard to tell from the distance, but he didn't seem that interested. He stroked his goatee again. "And why should I take your word for it? How do I know you're not scamming for money? You could be part of the plot, looking to be paid off."

"Yes, Your Grace, all good points. Your criticism does you credit. Perhaps my daughter could explain," Josef said, giving Ondine a nudge of encouragement.

From behind her ear, she heard Shambles's reassuring whisper, "Tell him what I told you about the plot, that they plan tae do him in at the railway station tomorrow morning, at the opening of the new overpass."

So Ondine did, trying to make her voice loud enough to be heard, but not shouting, which would be rude.

Then Shambles gave Ondine a detailed description of the men's faces, and told her to tell that to the Duke as well.

"One of them was also missing the top half of his index finger," Ondine relayed with due diligence.

"Aye, probably picking his nose when someone punched him in the face," Shambles whispered.

That bit did not bear repeating. Ondine needed all her strength to bite her tongue and stop the bubbling laugh in her throat from escaping. It didn't take Psychic Summercamp lessons to know the Duke would not appreciate comedy at this point. Not when people wanted to kill him in the morning. With an audience and everything.

"Hmm," the Duke said after thinking some more. "Step closer."

The sentry allowed them to take six paces before stopping them once again. They were closer, but far from intimate.

"You came upon this plot how?" the Duke asked.

Ondine repeated everything Shambles told her. "I was serving a table nearby, and overheard some of their conversation. I came back and cleared another table so I could keep listening."

For a while the Duke stopped stroking his goatee and pondered the information, as was his right. He'd just been delivered a huge shock. He was entitled to paranoia. This time somebody really was out to get him. He was well within his rights to pause and think.

After a few more moments of thought, in which Ondine shifted her weight from her left leg to her right and back again, the Duke motioned to the sentry to let them get even closer. Another six steps. They were about three meters apart.[4]

"How old are you, child?"

"Say you're eighteen, say you're eighteen," Shambles whispered furiously from behind her ear. The ferret was smart to remind her, because if she told the truth, the Duke might ask questions about a fifteen-year-old working in a pub. Not good at all.

"I'm nineteen, Your Grace," Ondine said, figuring if she had to lie, she might as well make it a good one. "And I think I'd like to stay nineteen for a long while to come."

A smile split the Duke's face. "I understand. My dear wife has been thirty-four for many years now."

Ondine dared not look at her father, in case he became confused and gave the game away. To his credit, he started making excuses about getting back to the hotel, lest the patrons take advantage of reduced staff numbers. The Duke had other ideas. He wanted more information, and it was clear from his expression that he wouldn't let them cross back over the threshold until he had it.

The sound of footsteps caught their attention. It came from the top of the curved timber staircase to their right. The conversation stopped.

An embarrassing heat crept up Ondine's neck and face as she looked at the handsome owner of the footsteps, with his tousled dark blond hair and deep brown eyes.

"Lord Vincent." Josef gave a diplomatic nod of his head, while at the same time his hand reached towards Ondine's. "We will not trouble your father a moment longer. Come along, Ondine, good girl."

*Good Girl?* Ondine cringed.

"On the contrary. You're no trouble," the Duke said.

But Ondine's father had other concerns. Naturally, he'd know the name of the Duke's son – his paternal radar knew the identity of every bachelor in the immediate three counties. Despite what her mother had said earlier in her father's defence, Ondine found it really hard to see things through Da's eyes. OK, a lot of men were drunks, but not all the men who came to the pub got roaring drunk, and not every man in the world spent time in pubs. Was he ever going to see things that way, or was he stuck in the Middle Ages?

Ondine wasn't looking at the master of the house any more, she could only look at the son, while her pulse started beating just that naughtily bit faster in her ears. He looked perhaps nineteen, maybe a little older, and his expression gave him an air of moneyed confidence. Like his father, he wore a suit and tie – an updated version, the kind that looked effortlessly expensive. Lord Vincent descended the staircase and walked deliberately towards her, a smile playing at the edges of his mouth. All of which gave Ondine the chance to appreciate his features.

"Vincent, is there something you want, boy?" The Duke's voice sounded terse.

The young lord's buoyancy dimmed a fraction. Ondine could see an annoyed look cross his face. A familiar pang took hold in Ondine.

Despite their differences in social status, they shared something in common – parents who expected them to behave as adults, but treated them like children.

"No, sir," Vincent said. In the blink of an eye he reset his features, giving him fresh confidence as if nothing could trouble him. "I was merely on my way out to an engagement."

"Right then. Be home by two, and don't bring any flotsam back with you this time," the Duke said.

A nod was all the Duke received in return. As Vincent walked past Ondine towards the door, she dared a glance and saw him roll his eyes. An inappropriate giggle formed, but she tamped it down.

"I don't like him," Shambles whispered.

If not for the Scottish accent, Ondine would have sworn the words had come straight from her father.

When the meeting with the Duke finally finished, Josef hustled them back to the hotel so they could resume work, all the while lecturing Ondine about the dangers of unruly boys.

"Don't fall for the first boy who pays you attention. Keep yourself nice," he said as they approached the back door.

"Da, give me a little credit, please, and stop treating me like a kid," Ondine whined, betraying her maturity.

"That's right, you're nineteen, aren't you? Trying to act all sophisticated to impress the little lord."

"I was not! I only lied about my age because the Duke asked how old I was, and if I'd told him the truth, then he'd wonder why an underage girl was serving alcohol. I was saving your skin."

"Hold your tongue," Josef said. "We're home now. Time for you to get back to work."

Just when Ondine thought she'd won the argument, Da had pulled the "I'm your father" routine, using it like a get-out-of-jail-free card. His timing, as always, was perfect, because he usually called an end to their debates just as Ondine thought of some great comeback lines. Like, "You were born old" and "You're just grumpy because it saves time being anything else." Words that would, for now, remain unspoken.[5]

Before Ondine could work up a full head of steam, she saw something that took her breath away.

It was a scene that made her appreciate her eldest sister more than cinnamon toast and marshmallows, because what they witnessed on that balmy summer evening made her father forget all about potential problems between Ondine and Lord Vincent.

There was her eldest sister Marguerite, in the darkened beer garden, all kissy-face with a young man.

"Margi, what is going on?" her father spluttered.

For a fleeting moment, Ondine felt sorry for her sister. In some respects, she could understand why Da raged at her about boys, because she was the youngest. But Margi was positively ancient and old enough to do whatever she liked in Ondine's eyes.

"This ought to be good!" Shambles said, positioning himself on Ondine's shoulder for a better view of the oncoming fireworks.

**4**

———

Marguerite and the lad sprang apart, their eyes round like golf balls, mouths open in shock. It must have been serious, because Marguerite's normally perfect hair looked tousled. For a long second, nothing happened, but Ondine knew it was only the kind of lull that heralded something ominous, like the stillness between a bolt of lightning and the resulting thunderclap.

The young man stood up first, ran his hand through his short brown hair, straightened his rumpled jacket, then extended his trembling palm towards Josef to shake his hand. Josef offered nothing in return.

The lad let his hand drop, along with the expression on his face. "Mr de Groot, this isn't what it looks like. I have nothing but the most honourable intentions towards your daughter."

"Good opening gambit," Shambles said. "It'll buy him five seconds before yer da runs him through."

"Who are you?" Josef asked. It sounded like he was talking through gritted teeth.

"Da, please, calm down. That's no way to treat your future son-in-law," Marguerite pleaded.

"My what?"

In the darkness, it was hard to tell, but Da's face was probably close to purple.

"Sir," the lad started again, holding his hand forward for the second time, which was a pretty gutsy gesture, given the circumstances. "My name is Thomas Berger and I would like your permission to marry your daughter Marguerite."

A sharp intake of breath was all Ondine could manage, such was her shock.

Marguerite? Engaged? *Already?*

"Aw, the nice!" Shambles said. "They're in looove."

Finally, Josef extended his hand to Thomas but it wasn't a shake. More like a death grip. Awkward silence ensued.

Everyone looked to the ground. Margi scrunched her hands in her lap.

"I don't appreciate being kept in the dark," Da said at last.

"Maybe if you didn't fly off the handle all the time, we wouldn't have to keep secrets," Margi said.

*Go Margi!*

"What are you doing out here?" The voice came from the back door, and they turned as one to see Ma standing on the threshold. "Back inside all of you, there's work to be done. Oh, hello there, Thomas dear, how are you?"

Another sharp intake of breath made Ondine's lungs fit to burst.

"Good thanks, Mrs G," the young man replied. His familiar tone with Ma told everyone this relationship with Marguerite must have been going on for a while. This latest revelation left Ondine light-headed with equal portions of excitement and confusion.

"Lovely." Ma turned to the rest of the party. "Josef? In here please, I need you to tap the next keg. Margi, when you're ready you can relieve Cybelle at the bar. Oh good, Ondine, you're here too. You can get started on the dishes piling up in the sink."

"This isn't finished, young lady," Josef warned Marguerite as she headed for the relative safety of the public bar. Her father wouldn't dare upset the patrons by arguing in front of them, but that didn't stop him from venting his anger in the relative quiet of the hallway. "This isn't finished by a long shot."

"Show's over, but nawt for long I bet," Shambles said as he and Ondine headed for the kitchen, where teetering towers of greasy plates awaited. "I'm really warming to Da. I've met plenty like him. Such good fun. Thought he'd pop a blood vessel."

"Hush up, Shambles, or I'll use you as a dishcloth," Ondine warned.

---

LATER THAT NIGHT – actually, it was early the next morning – after they'd guided the last patrons out, locked the doors, mopped the floors, wiped the bar, washed the dishes, locked the takings in the safe under the kitchen floorboards and turned out the lights, everything descended into quiet.

A tense kind of quiet, judging by the looks that had passed between Marguerite and Ma, and then from Ma to Da.

Cybelle tucked her straight bob behind her ears as she helped Ondine dry and polish the last of the cutlery. "Wouldn't mind being a fly on the wall tonight, eh, Ondi?"

"Brilliant idea." Shambles took his leave from Ondine's shoulder and disappeared in a blur of black fur up the back stairs towards their parents' quarters.

"For once, I'm glad I'm not the oldest," Ondine said. "Margi's really taking one for the team tonight."

"Da will get over it. He just has to get used to the fact we're not babies any more," Cybelle said.

"Lucky we're not Catholic, or he'd have shipped us off to the nunnery."

"Don't give him ideas. He'll convert us in a heartbeat," Cybelle said with a soft giggle.

The chink and clunk of silverware (not sterling silverware, this was the cheaper kind) muffled their conversation. In any case, Ma and Da would be too caught up in "the Marguerite situation" to pay them much heed, so they could keep talking.

"So, what's going on with you and Shambles?" Cybelle asked.

Ondine dropped her fork. "Wh-at do you mean?"

"Come on, Ondi. I've seen you listening to him. He talks to you, doesn't he? And you talk back." Cybelle's pale brown eyes looked so dramatic under all that eyeliner and thick fringe. They positively bored into Ondine's soul. Despite her earlier brush with deceit at the Duke's house, Ondine found it impossible to lie to her sister.

"So far only Ma and I can hear him. Ma knows who he is – he used to be a real man once. He was the Laird of Glen Logan, that's what Ma says anyway. He knew great-aunt Col, back when she was our age."

"You mean Witchy Woman?" Cybelle's eyes gleamed and her eyebrows disappeared under her fringe.

It was their secret name for their great-aunt, not that they ever said so within adult hearing.

"Shh, Auntie Col can get very upset when she's offended," Ondine said, then she relayed an abridged version of how Col the Older had treated Shambles, after the way Shambles had behaved at the debutante ball, which only made Cybelle's eyes gleam even more.

"So, how old is Shambles? He'd have to be eighty at least if he was around when Old Col was young."

"That's the lucky bit. Thanks to Old Col's spell, he hasn't a hair of grey on him, and he's so sprightly. He acts more like he's our age," Ondine said with a shrug of her shoulders as she dried the last spoon. She picked up the cutlery and clunked it all in the drawers. "Phew, that's it for the night. I'm fair knackered."

"You're what?" Cybelle asked.

"Just something Shambles says."

***

WHEN ONDINE and Cybelle tucked themselves into their beds later that night, Shambles leapt into the room and dived for Ondine, snuggling into the warmth of her neck.

"What are you doing, Shambles? You're supposed to sleep in the laundry," Ondine said as his soft warm fur caressed her skin. It wasn't right to have a man in her bed, but then Shambles wasn't really a real man as such, so perhaps that made it OK. What with all the shocks and revelations today, she barely knew what to think. And he wasn't really *in* the bed, it was more like sharing a pillow, and where was the harm in that?

"Aye, but the laundry's mockit. This is the nice."[1]

"He's talking to you, isn't he? What's he saying?" Cybelle whispered.

"I have no idea. He's reverted to Scottish."

"Aw, lass, I like ye, because ye feed me cold stovies. As a return favour, I'll tell ye everything your parents said about Marguerite when they thought no one was listening."[2]

In a few hours' time, after the sun came up, there would be an attempt on the Duke's life at the station. But right now Ondine was more interested in dramas closer to home.

"Yer da says she's too young, but he can't see that ye've all grown up and he can't control ye any more. Yer ma was more circumspect," Shambles said as he made himself comfortable on Ondine's pillow. "She says Thomas would move in and then they'd have an extra pair of hands at the bar, and Margi wouldnae work out front any more and be leered on by drunks. Sure and it would be better if she married and stayed close to home, than married and ran away. She also said she'd get a refund on the Summercamp, owing to the fact you'll be needed here now and won't be going back."[3]

Ondine shook her head as a wry smile crept over her lips. "Trust Ma to appeal to his practical side." Secretly she felt glad her mother wanted her back.

"What did he say?" Cybelle asked.

The wry smile turned into a huff. "I feel like a parrot, having to repeat everything. Shambles, how come Ma and I can hear you and Cybelle can't?"

A cheeky look crossed Shambles's face and he winked at Ondine. "Because you're the fairest in the land."

A giggle percolated in her tummy, but she held it in check. "Um, he's not sure," she said, feeling a little embarrassed at the compliment. High time to switch off the light – that way Cybelle wouldn't be able to see

Ondine grinning. Cybelle also wouldn't be able to see how furiously she was blushing, judging by the heat pouring through her neck and face as the man in ferret form cuddled against her skin.

"So, what next?" Cybelle asked.

Shambles relayed what he heard to Ondine, and Ondine relayed what she heard to Cybelle. "Yer ma wants the wedding to happen as soon as possible. They're planning an engagement party, and yer da will have to get used to having another man around the hoose."

For a moment Ondine wondered what it would be like having an older brother. Except it wouldn't really be like having an older brother, because Thomas would be much too polite to boss her around like a real older brother would.

"Yer Da's main concern is that all of this will give you and Cybelle ideas," Shambles added. "He thinks it will set a bad example, but Thomas isnae gonna stoat the ba' ". Your ma had an answer for that too – she said, 'How can it be a bad example if they're married?' She said it was only natural that married people should live together. It was either that or Margi and Thomas elope and live somewhere else, and then we'd be short one barmaid slash kitchen hand slash laundry girl. We'd have to bring in more outside help, and that would mean paying proper wages."[4]

They thought about this for a little while, until Cybelle said, "Don't you think it's strange? Da couldn't wait for us to grow up so we'd be able to help out more. But now that we are older he's treating us like babies."

"I *know*. It's driving me crazy. Was he always like this or am I just noticing it more?" Ondine asked the darkness.

Shambles piped up, "Dads are the same the world over. When their babies grow up and start getting interested in other people, they realize every other randy lad out there is just like they used to be. It's the circle of life."

Ondine didn't see it like that. "I think that's what they call hypocrisy. Da just wants it all his own way."

"Then you should let him think he's getting it," Shambles muttered.

Despite the late hour, Ondine couldn't stop her mind from racing. Injustice did that to a girl.

"Good on Ma for standing up for Margi," Cybelle said. "By the time they get round to me, it will be much easier, and when it's your turn, Ondi, they'll be so worn down they won't protest."

That caught Ondine by surprise. "What do you mean? What's going on with you?"

"Oh, um, you know, I was just talking hypothetically. Goodnight." And with that, the middle daughter rolled over to face the wall and pretended to sleep. Except she wasn't asleep because Ondine didn't hear any snoring.

"She's a dark horse, that one," Shambles said, having a chuckle. The giggly movement of his body tickled Ondine's neck. Margi had kept a big secret, and she'd kept it very well. Maybe Belle had a secret too. And what about Ondine's turn? Who would she fall in love with? she wondered. For some reason, Lord Vincent's handsome face popped into her mind.

The search for answers about her sisters' secrets kept Ondine awake for another few minutes, before she succumbed to a mixture of fatigue and the soporific effect of Shambles's warm, furry body against her and she fell asleep.

———

WHEN THE SUN CAME UP, there was little time to think about personal matters, as the Duke's impending doom sat heavily with Ondine and Shambles. Josef was at his overprotective fatherly best, refusing Ondine permission to attend the grand opening of the pedestrian overpass at the station.

"I need to know what happens, so I can see whether our warning helped the Duke. I mean, what's the point of us spending all those hours worried about him if we can't see the outcome for ourselves?" Ondine protested as she returned to the kitchen from the dining room. They were in the midst of the breakfast service for the hotel's guests, so they worked and talked at the same time. Something they were very good at.

Da was having none of it. "One, it's potentially dangerous. Two, you have a job to do. Look at all those dishes by the sink – they'll not clean themselves."

Nothing could be further from the truth, Ondine thought, as her hands clenched into angry fists at her sides. The bit about ditching work, that is. The rest of it was true. Dishes never cleaned themselves.

More plates of bacon, sausages, eggs and toast were ready, so Ondine took those out to a table. When she came back, her dad still looked cross.

"Let her go, Da," Cybelle interjected. "You go with Ondi if you're that worried about her safety. I'll stay and help Chef with food prep for the lunch crowds."

Chef, who had a real name but nobody used it, was the only true employee at the hotel. As such he was the only one who could be fired. He was tall yet light on his feet as he moved about the kitchen cooking meals and stirring sauces. He wore the same bleached-white uniform every day, although he would need a new one soon judging by the way his potbelly strained against the buttons. Under his white hat flecks of jet-black hair poked out, contrasting sharply with his pale skin.[5] All the while the family argued (although they'd deny it was an argument, they'd say it was just debating things, long and heartily, and a bit loudly), Chef stayed out of the line of fire and kept right on cooking.

A soft chuckle sounded on Ondine's shoulder. It came from Shambles. He must be enjoying himself, she thought, a little puzzled. Maybe Shambles liked a bit of argy-bargy?

Ondine cajoled her father again. At times she felt like exploding with frustration. "Please let me go, Da."

"We both know someone out there . . ." her father pointed in the direction of the train station, as if they didn't know where it was ". . . wants to kill the Duke. It's dangerous. What kind of father would I be if I exposed my daughter to that kind of peril? The safest thing for us to do is to stay here."

Was he being deliberately daft? If Ondine's eyes could roll any further into her head, she'd be looking into her brain. As much as she tried to keep a cool head, her pulse skipped up a notch and her clenched fists wanted to pummel something. "You've got it all wrong, Da. Nobody's going to be interested in us. We'll stay out of the way. I want to see the people who planned this get caught. I want to see them hauled away, and when that happens, it might be nice if the Duke perhaps caught sight of us and acknowledged our help."

"You mean if Lord Vincent caught sight of you," Josef countered.

"You're impossible!" Ondine clenched her fists in impotent fury. Up until this point, she hadn't even thought of Vincent. Well, not much anyway, and what chance he'd even be there? Pretty slim, she suspected.

"It's a fiddler's biddin' then," Shambles said behind her ear, which didn't help at all.[6]

"I thought you'd have a bit more natural curiosity about you." Ondine tried one more time to bend her father's will to her own. "We spent all that time last night warning him, and now you're not even interested to see how it turns out? What if by being there, we can stop it somehow? There could even be a reward in it for you."

"Aye, and then yer arse'll fall awf!" Shambles said, rumbling with laughter.[7]

A terse silence filled the kitchen, broken only by the sound of Chef cracking eggs into the poaching pan.

Her father practically glowered at her. "You're that keen, aren't you? Fine, we'll go, but we're not staying more than half an hour. Then it's straight back to work for you."

Tension fell away from Ondine's shoulders, making her feel taller and lighter. "Thank you, Da." She kissed him firmly on the cheek, and then gave him a huge hug, nearly knocking Shambles off her shoulder in the process. A broad smile split her face. "This is going to be so exciting!"

**5**

————

A huge crowd gathered that morning at the railway station, bringing a carnival atmosphere to something that was normally, well, *pedestrian*. The smell of fried onions and sausages at the fund-raising stalls filled the air, making Ondine's stomach rumble.

Buskers entertained the crowds and played violins and accordions. Women dressed as fairies did a roaring trade painting children's faces in lurid colours.

"I'm off to get me some sausage." Shambles leapt from Ondine's shoulder and disappeared into the milling crowd in a blur of black.

"No, Shambles, wait!"

Too late, the ferret was gone. Damn that impetuous bampot, she thought, borrowing one of his words to suit her means.

"Right then, let's get a good position so we can see the Duke cut the ribbon," Da said, holding Ondine by the hand. This only served to take her further from where she last saw Shambles.

"Hang on, Da, Shambles has run off. I need to find him," she said, trying to tamp down the rising sense of panic in her gut.

"He'll be fine. Come on." Squeezing through the crowd, Da found them a good vantage spot, where they could see the Duke standing at the podium, a pair of scissors in his hands. Standing beside him was a woman of indeterminate age. She had that caught- in-a-wind-tunnel look about her, with arched eyebrows that looked like they were trying to run away from her. Sunlight sparkled off the tiara that sat on her blonde head. Under her arm, she held a furry white dog.

"Is that the Duchess?" Ondine asked.

Da laughed out loud. "She wishes! No love, that's the Infanta, the Duke's oldest sister."

"She looks so fancy!" Ondine saw more sparkles of sunlight – even the little dog had jewels in its collar. The thought of the small animal having such a fancy collar made her wonder about Shambles, and whether he might look quite handsome with sparkles around his neck.

Another chuckle from her father. "Fancy is one way to put it. A bit overdone perhaps. She might have been Duchess if her little brother wasn't born."

The crowd milled about them and someone stepped on Ondine's foot. A ripple of worry rippled through her. Shambles could easily be trampled in the crush.

"Da, we need to find Shambles."

"He'll be wherever the food is. Now hush, let's listen to what the Duke –"

Shots rang out. Real gunshots that were so loud you'd swear someone had smacked you on the inside of your head with a brick.

People screamed.

"Get down!" Da yelled. With a jolt he pulled Ondine to the ground, shielding her body with his.

Confusion and turmoil took hold. Everyone around them crouched down, huddling in fear. Noise and screaming filled the sky. Police officers blew their whistles. From a gap under her father's arm, Ondine saw a man running away down the street.

People say that when a big, scary event happens, it takes place in slow motion. In this case, nothing could be further from the truth as it all took place at lightning speed. The police closed in, chased down the culprit for half a block, and then tackled him into submission.

"They got him!" Ondine said with relief.

The Duke must have taken their warning seriously. He must have organized more police. Ready to pounce at the slightest provocation.

For the next few minutes everyone stayed low to the ground as the police rounded up another two suspects. With her heartbeat hammering in her ears, Ondine heard her father say something. She couldn't make out the exact words because her ears were still ringing from the gunshots.

"I said, 'They've given the all-clear,'" Josef said even louder this time.

But still nobody moved. Well, why would they? Only moments ago shots had rung out above their heads. From their crouched position, Ondine looked around to where the Duke was, to see if the show would go on. The Infanta remained huddled behind a chair. The Duke was on his feet, looking perplexed. In his hand was his traditional three-cornered hat, only now it had a bullet-sized hole through the top of it.

"Ohmygosh! They nearly killed him," Ondine said, her heart still beating far too quickly.

Josef wrapped his arms around her and held her close, kissing the top of her head. "Now do you see why I didn't want you to come here? If anything happened to you, I'd never forgive myself."

"Thanks, Da." She wanted to say, "You worry too much," but in the present circumstances, his worries were perfectly justified.

"I love you so much, my darling girl. And I know you're all grown up now, but I can't help it. To me, you'll always be my baby and that's just how it is."

"It's OK." Ondine returned the hug, not caring that he'd called her a baby. At this moment, she'd forgive him just about anything. Trembles rippled through her body as she let the shock take hold. "I love you too, Da."

So much remained unsaid as they embraced. Ondine nearly suffocated in the crushing hug but she didn't care. As a father, he suffocated her in so many ways but right now she wasn't complaining.

To their surprise, the Duke indicated he'd carry on with the ceremony. The mere fact that he was bodily unharmed brought many more people to their feet. The cheers ringing in Ondine's ears told her they'd done the right thing. They'd warned the Duke, he'd organized police protection and the crowd had witnessed a nasty scare rather than an assassination.

"Right then," the Duke called out, gathering his composure and dusting himself off. He picked up the enormous ceremonial scissors and held the blades apart. "I declare this new pedestrian access open."

*What an amazing man.* Ondine marvelled at how quickly he'd recovered his senses. By now she and Josef were on their feet too. The Infanta, however, kept her distance from the podium.

With a gracious nod, the Duke cut the ribbon and the two halves of fabric fluttered to the ground. People applauded, probably with gladness but also a great deal of relief. A group of schoolchildren cheered and raced on to the overpass. They reached the highest point and threw coloured streamers into the crowd.

The Duke acknowledged the gathering. "Thank you, everyone, for coming. Now, if you'll excuse me, I need a drink!"

The crowd laughed and cheered again, and Ondine could only marvel once more at how well he'd recovered. His poise in the face of such danger seriously impressed her, and she couldn't stop smiling. If she'd been the one in the firing line, she would have been a gibbering mess like the Infanta. But that Duke, wow, what composure!

There was little time to think further about this, because at that moment Da spotted Lord Vincent standing near his father's entourage.

Josef grabbed his daughter's hand. "Time we got back." Without further explanation, he led her down the road towards their hotel.

Ondine stole a glance over her shoulder for Shambles and thought, *I hope he's all right.* In the next glance she saw the Duke and (oh goody!) Lord Vincent, following them to the pub. Something jumped in her chest, as if her heart suddenly had to beat double time to keep up with rapidly unfolding events.

"Hey, Da, when the Duke said he needed a drink, he was serious. They're right behind us."

"In that case, we'd better get straight back to the bar so they can have that drink."

"But where is Shambles? He won't know where we are if we run off and leave him," Ondine said, trying to hide the panic in her voice. How would one little ferret cope in such chaos? All on his own?

"I wouldn't worry about Shambles, he knows he's on to a good thing with you. He'll find his way home."

"But, Da, he could get trampled to death. Or worse. Someone could steal him!" A fluttering sense of panic took hold of Ondine. Wrenching her arm free, she turned away from Josef and scanned the streets for any sign of black fur.

"For goodness' sake! He's just a ferret. If he doesn't come home, I'll get you another one. Now hurry up before we're overrun by the mob." His firm hand gripped Ondine's upper arm, dragging her at a fast clip towards the pub's front door. They hardly ever entered by the main door. In this case her father made an exception, lest the patrons get into the pub before they did.

"But he's not just a ferret, Da, he's a real man! He's only in ferret form because Old Col turned him into one!" Ondine yelped as they stumbled across the threshold. "He needs me or he won't survive!"

"He's a what?" Josef's eyes grew into golf balls. If golf balls were lined with red squiggles from stress.

There was no moisture in her throat when she swallowed. Oh dear. Now she'd blown it. And she had his full attention so there was no getting out of it. A pulse trembled at her neck as Josef stared her down. The secret was out and she had nobody to blame but herself. Her sisters knew how to keep secrets; why couldn't she?

"Oh good, you're back," Ma said from the doorway, breaking the tableau.

A sigh of relief escaped Ondine's lips and she felt her shoulders sag. God bless Ma's incredible sense of timing!

"No, dear, you're not interrupting me this time," Da said sternly.

Caught in the spotlight of her father's stare, Ondine felt her tongue turn to sandpaper. A squeak came out instead of words.

"Well, she'd better be quick," Ma said, looking out through the large front windows. "Is that the Duke of Brugel heading this way, with about two hundred followers?" She turned and headed towards the kitchen.

"Chef! Cybelle! Margi! Thomas! All hands on deck – the whole city's coming for lunch."

"I thought that ferret was a ferret, pure and simple," the head of the de Groot household said. Only moments earlier he'd been cuddling Ondine and telling her how much he loved her. Now he looked like he could happily have her sectioned.[1]

"I'm sorry, Da. Shambles was a man once, and Old Col turned him into a ferret because he got drunk at her debutante ball."

"And what? You forgot to tell me?"

A confusing sickness took hold of Ondine, spreading out from her heart and filling her body, right down to her boots. Before she could respond, they heard multiple footsteps on the path outside.

Time was against them and Da had to let the situation drop so he could make ready with the beer. Any relief Ondine could have felt from her reprieve was quickly replaced by concern for Shambles. Then her concern for Shambles was quickly replaced by excitement at the appearance of the Duke of Brugel and his son Lord Vincent in the hotel's doorway.

Something light and fizzy stirred inside Ondine. Just from looking at Vincent. Because he was so very lovely to look at.

No time to gaze, they had work to do. To help with the crowd, Margi, Thomas and Josef all tended bar, and Ondine felt seriously impressed at how well they worked together. Like they'd been doing it for years. She had to hand it to Margi, the older girl had held her ground – as had Thomas from the looks of things. But as much as Ondine thought she should be worrying about her sister and her prospective brother-in-law, she couldn't keep her mind from straying to thoughts of Shambles, and where he could be.

---

YOU MAY HAVE HEARD the expression "babe magnet", which is a term applied to a handsome man who draws women – or babes – to him. Just as a regular magnet attracts paperclips and iron filings, seemingly without any effort. Magnetism is one of the elemental forces of nature at work, and is one of the easier aspects of science to understand. Shambles the ferret was no babe magnet, but he was a *trouble* magnet, with an uncanny knack for attracting and finding trouble. You could say his knack for attracting trouble was also an elemental force of nature.

The moment he slipped away from Ondine's shoulder that morning, he followed his nose to the smell of frying sausages from one of the fund-raising stalls along the railway platform. The onions he didn't care for, but the sausages made his mouth water.[2]

A plan formulated in his head – stay close to people near the barbecue and hot plates and sausages will drop from the sky.

Soon, a suitable leg presented itself, with sturdy shoes and thick denim pants, making it easy for Shambles to get a grip. Before its owner could finish yelping, "What's on my leg?" he'd dropped his sausage, bread, onions and mustard on the ground. Shambles jumped free and launched himself towards his prize, grabbed it in his teeth and disappeared behind the stall. And oh, it was bliss, eating a sausage that was half as long as his body.

The hot fat dripped over his chin. Chunks of meat-ish mince slid down his throat and warmed his belly. In another few chomps, all that remained of the meal was a smear of grease on his black fur.

A clever person, perhaps even a not-so-clever person, might feel satisfied with that score and leave well enough alone. Not Shambles. Filled with confidence at how well his first attempt had gone, he reasoned a second attempt would be even more successful.

He didn't have to wait long for another mark. This man had pants made from a thick canvas-type material (Shambles hadn't studied fashion, so didn't know silk from sawdust) and a satchel on his side that made an excellent hitching post for a ferret to dig his claws and fangs into. In a heartbeat Shambles raced up his leg, grabbed on to the bag and opened his mouth to catch the sausage.

Then it all went horribly wrong.

The satchel opened and a gun fell out. Helpless, Shambles watched the weapon drop to the ground. It discharged on impact. His world split apart with the loudest sound he'd ever heard. Everyone screamed. Shambles hit a nearby wall with a thud and kept falling, his arms scrabbling for something to hang on to on the way down. His claws caught in a thick material – the man's pants – and he clung on hard, lurching back and forth with momentum as the man ran off. Nasty hot bile filled the back of his throat. His ears filled with screams. Then a whistle blew and heavy footsteps closed in. Several pairs of footsteps.

From the corner of his eye, Shambles saw a policeman lunge towards them. He let go of the leg, fell hard on the pavement, and his world turned black.

BACK AT THE PUB, things were so busy in the dining room the piano stood silent. Cybelle worked in the kitchen beside Chef, while Ondine and Colette took orders and served food.

"Ondi, take these meals to table twelve," Cybelle said, before she rushed back to the stove to remove a tray of savoury tarts.

Her arms loaded with food (two plates balanced on one arm, a third plate on the other), Ondine took her orders and walked to the designated table. That's when she saw Lord Vincent sitting at the head of it. Not that she was going to drop the plates or anything, but the sight of him nearly made her miss a step. He looked ruffled and gorgeous; his sun-kissed, dark blond hair was all messed up but his brown eyes were clear and bright, and trained on her.

Heat crept up Ondine's neck at the thought of him checking her out.

"It's Ondine, isn't it? That's a beautiful name," Vincent said, extending his hand in friendship.

Something turned to liquid inside her.

Being polite, Ondine served Vincent and his companions their meals, and then took his hand to give it a friendly shake. Her skin tingled at his warm touch. How long should they hold hands for? Would it be rude to pull away? Then he did something that made her insides go completely gooey. Eyes still locked with hers, Vincent turned her hand over and kissed the inside of her wrist.

The touch of his tender lips against her skin was the most erotic thing Ondine had ever experienced.

Heat shot up her arm, darted into her heart and pinged all around her body. Until this moment, she'd loved the feeling of just looking at him. Now he'd kissed her she felt something strange, wonderful and new lurch low in her belly.

Ondine wasn't really sure what it was, but she knew she liked it.

**6**

———————

A whole week later and no sign of Shambles. Not a skerrick. For a teenage girl with an overactive imagination, it was a complete disaster. Visions of Shambles lying dead in a city gutter filled Ondine's mind. That's if he was already dead. He might have been carried off by a hawk, his limbs ripped off while he yet lived, to be shoved down the hungry mouths of chicks. Or some revolting child might have found him and taken him home, where she'd be half strangling him to death with affection, then putting a bonnet on his head so that he matched the rest of her dollies! Ondine found herself thinking of Shambles far too much. Thinking how vulnerable and small he was. Other times she found herself wondering what he might look like as a proper man. If she could find a way to turn him human again, would she like the end result? Would he be as handsome as Lord Vincent?

All the anxiety meant her appetite paid the price – she could barely eat for worry at breakfast. Then she became ravenous around lunchtime and found herself eating scraps off people's returned plates.[1]

It had also been a week of astonishing busyness and flat-out-edness. Business had never been so good, all because the Duke and his dishy son had come to their pub after the ballyhoo at the station.

*I'll never wash my wrist again.* Ondine cast her mind back to that lush kiss on her tender skin. How she'd blushed furiously in front of Vincent and his gang, and the way he'd looked at her with an unreadable but unquestionably exciting-and-a-little-bit-dangerous expression. That promise to protect her wrist vanished after she had to roll up her sleeves and get stuck into the washing-up.

Laundry duty washed away another layer of skin, so really, all she had were memories.

But oh, what lovely memories. His soft, warm lips brushing her skin, his walnut-brown eyes fixed on hers, her heart racing nineteen to the dozen. Even now, as she thought of him, her pulse increased. While folding sheets and tablecloths and pillowcases, Ondine kept seeing the lovely Lord Vincent's smiling eyes. Finishing with the folding, she made sure no one was looking and dared to kiss herself in the same spot.

What a let-down! No sensations at all, just the feeling that she must look like an idiot. Thank goodness nobody had seen her. Not even Shambles, to make her feel like a twit for entertaining such thoughts.

And Lord Vincent hadn't been back to their dining room all week, which was such a shame. Ondine felt sure that he'd be back in a day or two. Three at the most.

A sudden cry of anguish echoed through the kitchen, which sounded suspiciously like Ma having a conniption.

"I don't believe it! They can't write such things! How dare they publish this! Josef, get a lawyer, let's sue them! This is all lies. Lies, lies, lies! Call themselves a newspaper? This is a rag. It's not fit for the toilet!"

"Ma, what's wrong?" Ondine called out, as she hot-footed her way towards the centre of the family storm. When she reached the kitchen, she found everyone standing around the island bench, reading an article from the *Weekend Hacienda Leisure Guide*.

Somebody had written a review of their hotel. And it wasn't very nice. The food and wine critic, known by the pseudonym Dee Gustation, had gone to town on them.

"But when was she here?" Cybelle asked. "I never saw anyone with a notebook in the dining room. Did you, Ondi?"

"Nope, and everyone's been really nice as well. Nobody's even sent any food back, which is a good thing, right?" Ondine asked.

"We haven't seen anyone in the bar who might be a critic, have we, Thomas?" Marguerite added. Thomas shook his head.

Thomas was crowding around the table along with the rest of the family, his paler brown hair contrasting sharply with the family of dark brunettes. Everyone kept talking, so Ondine bent her head at a funny angle (the page was upside down, so it took all her concentration) to read the article.


### Dangerous Dining Adventures


*A* NIGHT *at* The Station Hotel *is a true adventure in dining, where the faint-hearted need not apply.*

*Let's begin with our first brush with death – the table wine. Called such because its only true use should be for cleaning the tables at the end of the night.*

*This is a hotel with a family atmosphere, which extends to the guests – in such a way that those in the dining room can easily become caught up in domestic disputes emanating from the kitchen.*

*Despite this, the food – when it does eventually arrive – is edible. That is what little you can find under the sea of gravy.*

*The beer is suitably cold, chilled from the frosty stares of the publican/over-protective father who has no issue with using his beautiful daughters for slave labour. In many museums, you can look but not touch – here, don't even look at the daughters lest the father turns you into a block of ice with just one glance.*

*Towards the end of the evening, the rousing music from a talented but frustrated concert pianist is a fitting way to end the night. The raucous clamour from the piano and singing elder sister distracts everyone from the noises made by patrons in gastric distress outside in the gutter.*


"OH, I CAN'T BEAR IT!" Ma said as she wiped tears from her cheeks with the back of her hand. "Who could be so cruel to us?"

"Someone who is jealous of our success," Da said.

From where Ondine stood, she figured her father's guess was as good as anyone else's.

A sad quiet descended in the kitchen, which was pretty remarkable considering there were seven people all hunched around the table, reading the newspaper.

"I'll go to the paper's office and find out who wrote this," Marguerite said. "I'll explain that they're wrong. I'll invite the reviewer back so she can write something positive about us."

"Or make up something worse!" Josef said.

"Hey, look, Da," Ondine said, trying to change the subject. "Here's a story about the people who tried to shoot the Duke. They've written a fair bit . . . they've charged three men and . . . what does "diplomatic immunity" mean?"

"It means they've got a good lawyer," Josef said with a sniff of disgust.

The telephone rang, making them all jump. For a moment nobody wanted to answer it, then Ma straightened her posture, brushed her hair back, and picked it up.

"*Station Hotel*, good morning . . . Yes . . . I see . . . Yes, of course . . . No, no problem at all, thank you for calling and letting us know. Have a lovely day."

Ma put the receiver down on to the cradle and shuddered. "That was the van Nyuus booking, cancelling for tonight.[2] Cybelle, you're better on the phone than me, can you take the rest of the calls? I'm going to lie down for a mo–"

A streak of black fur barrelled into the kitchen, ran under the table and up Ondine's leg.

"Shambles! Oh, Shambles, my darling, you're alive!" Ondine cried, scooping the bundle of bedraggled fluff into her arms and kissing the top of his messy head. Sparks of joy danced around her heart. He was back!

"As much as I appreciate a kiss from a fair maiden, there's no time for that," Shambles said as he panted for breath. "Everyone get to work, the halth inspecta is coming!"

Ma turned white and her chin wobbled in distress. "Can this day get any worse? Who cares if the health inspector comes? We're done for anyway!"

Josef, Chef, Thomas and Marguerite all turned to Ma, asking variants on the "what did you say?" theme. Because, of course, they hadn't heard Shambles say anything. Only Cybelle remained looking at Ondine. The middle daughter instinctively knew, from her mother's screeching reaction, that Shambles had come back with bad news.

Ignoring them all, Ondine cuddled her returned friend. "Shambles, you stink. Where have you been? You must be starving. Here, have some sausages. Chef, can you grab some bones out of the stockpot?"

Shambles found his voice. "It's that ungrateful Duke's family. This is all their doing. They're hell-bent on running us out of town! And I'll say yes to the meat too, I'm fair starven."

Confusion reigned at the table while Shambles virtually inhaled his snack. Ondine patted his back, feeling the corrugated ribs through matted fur.

All eyes turned to Ma, waiting for an answer.

She gave it to them, revealing Shambles's true identity and communication skills.

Da shook his head. "Now you're saying he can talk? Then why can't I hear him?"

Confusion aplenty. Thanks to the newspaper review, they were already in a state of shock. It was only natural that the news that their ferret could talk and was in fact a real man would completely bowl them all over.

*You'll understand a certain need for brevity at this stage, what with everything being so exciting – plus, you already know the whole story up to now, so you don't need to hear it again. Let's pick this up after the half hour of "whats?" and "hows?" to the point where people started to make sense again.*

Chef shook his head and said, "Now I've heard everything."

Marguerite and Thomas gave each other surprised looks.

Da's jaw clamped shut and Ondine could tell, just from his expression, that his mind was already moving on to more important matters: white-hot indignation. "But we saved that miserable Duke's life!" he spat.

Cybelle chimed in, "What could he have against us? He came over here after the incident, bringing half of Venzelemma with him. He was having a great time, wasn't he, Ondi?" Heat seared Ondine's cheeks as she thought about what a great time she'd had, with Lord Vincent kissing her wrist. Her skin still tingled just thinking about it.

"Right then, no time to waste. Let's close the place ourselves and then there's no reason to let the health inspector in," Ma said, rising from the table and fetching the clutch of keys.

"But we've got guests, and a full house tonight!" Da said, then corrected himself. "I mean, a nearly full house."

"We cancel everything, just for a week, and we'll work like stink and get it all sparkling from floor to ceiling. Cancelling the bookings buys us some time and when we re-open, the inspector will be so dazzled by everything he won't be able to find anything to fault. Margi, you and Thomas make up some signs for the front windows to say we're closed for renovations. Belle, you and Chef put on a slap-up lunch for everyone who's still here, as a way of saying thanks and goodbye, for the moment. Ondi, give Shambles a bath, he stinks, then both of you join your da in the bar. We'll start at the front and work our way through the entire place."

"Colette, my love," Da said, finally breaking his wife's string of orders, "how are we to pay for this?"

"We'll find a way. Something will turn up."

As Shambles finished his third sausage, Ondine offered him some water, which he happily accepted. "I'm going to give you that bath, Shambles," she said, and kissed the top of his head again. The acrid stench of dead things flew up her nose. "Pee-yew, you reek!"

A rumbly laugh escaped Shambles. "Care to rub me back, lass?"

From across the table, Ma gave the ferret a stern look. "Shambles, that's not appropriate!"

Shocked, Ondine looked at her mother, face aghast. Jupiter's moons,

Ma had good hearing! Then she saw her father's icy cold glare – created not from hearing Shambles, but from guessing what he must have said. A smile formed at the corner of Ondine's mouth. The newspaper article was right in one respect: her dad could chill a whole room with a single glance.

As much as she should feel angry because of her father's mood swings, Ondine felt happy. Shambles was alive and in one (smelly) piece, and for that she was grateful. In a few hours, her father would be over the shock of the news and would return to normal. The best thing for Ondine to do was stay out of his way.

"Thank ye for the food, and for yer concern. It's nice to be missed. I missed ye too," Shambles whispered as they left the kitchen. "And by the way, I noticed Cybelle and Chef were touching knees under the table." The fresh information sent a bolt of shock through Ondine.

"Belle and Chef? What?"

"That sister of yers is a dark horse," Shambles chuckled. Ondine's mind went blank. Not that Belle couldn't have a love interest, but that it would be with Chef. "I can't get my head around it. But – but he's nearly twice her age. Belle and Chef?"

"Sure, and I'm older than ye, but yer about to get me fair nekked in a bath, eh lass?"

Heat scorched Ondine's neck and face again. Thank goodness nobody else was in earshot of the ferret. As much as she'd like to make verbal repartee with him, there was little time for mucking about. Ondine knew they'd be needed for renovations, whatever that entailed, so it was straight up to the bathroom for both of them.

Upon reaching the basin, Shambles came over all shy. "Ah, I'll take it from here if ye don't mind."

"Don't be silly, you won't even be able to turn on the taps," Ondine said.

Shambles looked at his options. "Right then. Well. Close yer eyes."

"We don't have time for this. You need a bath and I'm giving you one." Ondine placed the plug in the plughole and set about filling the basin with warm water.

"Right . . . but it's just that . . . I've never had a bath with anyone else before. It's well confronting if ye think aboot it."

Ondine laughed. "But Shambles, come on, you're only . . ."

"Only what? A ferret? Thanks a lot."

"I didn't mean that."

Shambles shook his head, "Thank you. I think. Now, I have to warn ye," he dipped his front paw in the water, "oh no, that's too hot, more cold water please." Ondine did so. "That's better. Now, I have to warn you about that Duke and his family. Especially Vincent. He's got it in fer us."

Ondine dropped the soap, "Lord Vincent? But he was here with his friends and they had a great time." She blushed furiously at the memory. The wrist he'd kissed now propped up the black ferret in the basin. He leant against it for support, and she could feel his small heart hammering away.

"He was here? Then it's worse than I thought. Stay away from them, Ondi, They're bad news. They're the ones setting the halth inspecta on to us. They want to close us down."

Ondine retrieved the soap and scrubbed Shambles's furry back. Time to change the subject.

"Shambles, before you became a ferret, how did you like to do your hair?" He'd look so cute with a big curl on his forehead.

"Eh? I dunno, lass, I jest brushed it. Why d'ye ask?"

"Just wondering," she said, wondering how he might have done his hair, wondering what colour it had been, wondering whether he was as handsome as Lord Vincent. "I mean, was it really long so you had to tie it back or did you cut it short?"

"Short like Lord Vincent's?"

"Yeah," she said before thinking.

"Aha! So you're thinking of him while you're bathing me, lass?"

Mercury's wings! "No, it's not like that."

"Really now?"

"Shambles, please. I was actually wondering what *you* looked like."

"And why might that be? So ye can compare me to Vincent?"

Yes. "No, not like that. Just that it would be nice if I knew who I was talking to." Phew, that was a close call!

"All right. I used to be fit, like. I had short hair, and all the bits of my face were where they're s'posed to be."

The description helped. A bit. "You're lucky I didn't know who you really were, otherwise I might have left you at Psychic Summercamp."

A stray thought came unbidden – thank goodness she'd come home early from Summercamp, otherwise who knows what might have happened?[3]

After Ondine finished washing and drying Shambles, and he looked and smelled like a proper clean ferret should, she made for the dining room and got to work. She carried chairs and tables out to the rear garden – as soon as guests vacated them – so she could scrub them down in daylight. It was impressive how quickly guests chose to leave the premises once she removed their capacity to remain sitting.

Shambles ducked under a chair. "What are you doing?" Ondine asked.

"Gnawing awf tha gobs of chewing gum," he replied, sounding like he had a mouth full of the goo already. "Folks have such filthy habits."

In the harsh light of day, the timber furniture looked hideous. Many pieces were scratched and dented and some refused to stop wobbling.

"Let's do some sorting," Shambles said. "The worst of them go by the back shed. We'll take the wee stoppers off the feet and use them on the good stuff."

"Good idea, Shambles."

"Aw, thanks, lass. It's nice to feel useful."

Ondine beamed at the compliment. "So, you haven't filled me in on where you've been. Care to elaborate?"

"I was fair traumatized by the whole thing. I woke up in the Duke's place. Big and echoey and full of people wearing stompy boots. If I ever go back there, it will be too soon. I found a place to hide and waited for the Duke to return. He did, with Vincent, and all the time I was there, Vincent was saying how they needed to close us down."

"But . . . that doesn't make sense. If they hated it, why didn't they say something when they were here?"

"I don't know what their motives are either, lass, but I know what I heard, and it was Vincent leading the charge. Hey, how come every time I say his name ye get that funny look on yer face?"

"I don't get a funny look."

"Yes ye do. *Lord Vincent.*"

Ondine kept her expression as stern as possible.

"I know ye don't want to listen to me, but it's the truth. Lord Vincent is nawt to be trusted."

"I've heard enough," Ondine said. "We have work to do." She spent the rest of the day scrubbing down timber, polishing the good items and fixing what she could, with Shambles directing her. Ma came out to inspect their work, a beaming smile spreading across her satisfied face.

"I thought I'd have to buy a whole new set, but you've done a marvellous job, you two. Right, when you're finished, come and help us carry out the carpet."

Just as her mother had ordered, the family was scrubbing their way through the entire building. It meant tearing up the ancient, smelly carpet and exposing the floorboards. Considering the flooring was old, stained and reeked of beer, the renovations were long overdue. By the end of the day they'd done a lot of work, but the place didn't look exactly clean. If anything, they'd stirred up such huge amounts of fetid dust they'd created yet more mess. It was only one day; they were sure to make more mess tomorrow.

Rolling up the carpet had exposed a thick layer of old newspapers. Not the underlay most people had in their homes to create a soft cushion to walk on, contributing to a lovely, homey atmosphere. Like the carpets before them, the newspapers stank of beer and other weird things, so they had to go as well.

"Load them all into the fireplace. We'll have a ritual burning and cleansing ceremony tonight. I hope Auntie Col gets here in time – she'll have some good spells," Ma said.

"Is yer Auntie Col coming here tonight?" Shambles asked. "Could she turn me back?"

Ondine froze. Shambles wanted to be a real man again. Which meant she'd finally get to see what he looked like. In her mind, she'd begun giving him features she found pleasing. But what if the end result fell short? What if he was – gulp – gobsmackingly ugly? In her heart, she knew that was a selfish way of looking at things. Shambles was entitled to his former life. He should be allowed to be himself again no matter what he looked like.

*It's the personality, not the package that counts.*

Another sad thought popped into her head. If Shambles became human again, there would definitely be no more snuggling in bed.

She shook the imaginings from her mind in the same way she shook the dust from the old curtains.

"Becoming human again is a good idea, Shambles. We could do with the extra manpower," Ma said.

Typical Ma.

"Hey, look at this," Marguerite interrupted. She held up a sheet of old newspaper. Because it had been protected from sunlight, the paper had retained its original off-white colour. The contrasting black text was easy to read. "It's an obituary of the old Duke of Brugel. Must be the current Duke's father. Oh, and it's a juicy one too. Listen to this: it says he died without having to answer to charges of embezzlement."

"Keep hold of that. It might come in handy," Da said.

"So might this," Thomas said, lifting up a section of floorboard. "There's something down here."

Working together, Da and Thomas pulled up another two boards. All of them were cut into short lengths, as if designed to come away together. In the cobwebby recesses beneath the barroom floor lay a large metal box. It reminded Ondine of the deposit box in the kitchen, where they put all their money for safekeeping until the banks opened.[4]

The mysterious box was so heavy they called in Chef to help them lift it out. The men grunted and groaned, pulled it free with an 'oomph', then dropped the box at their feet. More dust billowed.

A tingle of excitement crept into Ondine's throat – along with the dust – as she began to imagine what might be in the box.

"What's in it?" Marguerite asked the hushed room.

In a flash, Shambles dropped down from Ondine's shoulder and clambered on to the box, chewing at its leather straps until they came free.  Thomas and Josef lifted the lid.  Their mouths fell open.  So did Ondine's.  And Ma's, and Marguerite's. Even Shambles's wee furry mouth, full of nippy fangs and a little pink tongue, gaped in shock.

"Saturn's rings!" Ondine gasped.

"Looks like we've found a way to pay for the renovations," Da said.

"What did I tell you? I knew Shambles would bring us good luck," Ma said.

**7**

The contents of the box gleamed in the afternoon sunlight shining through the front windows. Gold rings. Bracelets. Fine threads of necklaces studded with diamonds. Brooches. Earrings with drop pearls. A tiara with red gems that might have been rubies – Ondine couldn't tell. Not a tangled mess, as you might expect, but all sorted and segmented into neat little compartments. Underneath the tray of gleaming jewellery they found wads of banknotes, stamped with faces and places on them, which Ondine didn't recognise. They must have been made before the currency changed.[1]

"Do pirates come this far inland?" Cybelle held up a necklace with a delicate anchor-shaped charm at the clasp. The anchor spun back and forth, catching the light. Strange that the main feature of the necklace should be at the back, until Ondine realised it was designed to be worn with your hair up.

Marguerite stepped closer to admire the booty. "Do we invoke the international treaty of 'finders keepers'?"

Unable to stop herself, Ondine reached forward and picked up a couple of elegant necklaces. One looked as delicate and complicated as a crocheted doily, if you could make a doily from spun silver, then BeDazzle it with diamonds.[2]

Ma sounded out of breath. "Let's just think about this for a minute. Think about where all of this may have come from."

Ondine could have sworn she saw a gob of spittle dart from her mother's mouth, as if she were salivating over their new-found riches. Nobody else took any notice of her – they were too busy making strange "ooh" noises and admiring piece after piece.

"Let's move it to the back room for the moment, so we can keep working on the clean-up," Ma said at last.

"Er, no, my love, I think this means work stops for the day," Da said, rubbing his hand over his chin in thought.

Ondine found herself caught in the web of admiration. The next object she picked up was a simple bracelet made from braided gold. She couldn't help testing the latch to see if it would fit around her wrist.

"Have ye all lawst yer minds?" Shambles said, climbing Ondine's shoulder. "There's a halth inspecta coming."

Ondine shook her head to try and grab hold of her senses again. "Um, everyone, Shambles just made a good point: we need to hide the loot before the health inspector comes." With reluctance she put the fine piece back in the box.

Ma took a deep breath and stepped back. "Chef, Thomas, Josef, get that box out the back somewhere safe. We'll keep going with the cleaning up in here."

A heavy creak of timber provided an immediate stop to the discussion, as the front door pushed open to reveal a suit-clad woman (and not the man they'd been expecting) holding a clipboard. A pair of soda-bottle thick, tortoiseshell-rimmed glasses sat on the bridge of her thin nose, making her deep grey eyes appear much larger than they should.

In a flurry of movement, everyone tossed their jewels into the box. The men made themselves look busy. Ma and her daughters stood in front of the box to hide it.

Something about the woman looked odd to Ondine. It wasn't her short, salt-and-pepper hair or her enormously wide bottom and thighs, barely reined in by her too-tight skirt, although that did look weird. For a moment longer Ondine found herself staring, before she worked it out. The woman had no eyelashes at all.

"Quick, make a distraction," Shambles ordered.

Extending her hand in greeting, Ondine walked towards their visitor. "Hello, you must be the health inspector. My name's Ondine and I've just come back from Psychic Summercamp. May I please read your palm? Oh, thank you," she said, taking the woman's hand before she had time to refuse. All the while, Ondine's heart hammered behind her ribs, shocked at her own audaciousness.

"You have a rodent on your shoulder," the woman said, her eyelashless eyes widening even more.

"Grrrrr," Shambles said.

*Lurch* went Ondine's stomach. Perhaps the ferret on the shoulder wasn't such a good idea, hygiene-wise? "Oh please, pay him no mind – he's my familiar, and he's also my assignment from Summercamp. And he's a ferret, not a rodent. Member of the stoat and otter family; completely different species to rodents. They're very clean animals, ferrets. Can't speak for rats or mice though. Well, look here at your life line." Ondine channelled her mother's skill of jumping from one subject to the next without pausing for breath.

It wasn't a case of seeing anything in the palm, because Ondine didn't have a clue what to look for. It didn't matter – all she had to do was distract the woman, not divine her future. Which meant saying the first thing that popped into her head.

"You have three grown sons. The youngest is a teenager who is still at school, but the other two are older and have careers now."

"How did you know that?" the woman said, her steely grey eyes softening at the information. She still hadn't introduced herself, but that opportunity seemed to have passed.

*Keep going, that's the best diversion.*

"You don't like what the eldest is doing. It's not that you disapprove; it's just that you worry about him. He is really happy because he's following his dream. The middle son is a bit of a plodder. He's good, but he's coasting along, isn't he? You know he can do better but he won't apply himself. The youngest is your baby, and always will be, but you need to let him grow up and make his own mistakes."

"Well, I'll be!" the woman said. "If you tell me what my name is then I'll really believe you're psychic."

Something tingled inside Ondine, a mixture of full-blown pride at her success so far and adrenalin at how daring she had become. "It's Wilma Klegg, but that doesn't make me psychic, merely observant. It's written on the top of your clipboard." A smile of satisfaction spread over her face. A buzz of confidence filled her soul.

*Hey, I can do this.*

"Ondine, please leave the health inspector alone, she has a job to do," Ma said as she approached them. Her mother's voice sounded annoyed and imperious. To an outsider, it would seem like the mother was rescuing a visitor from a precocious child. However, the de Groot women knew Ondine had just saved them from a whole heap of trouble.

As Ma led Mrs Klegg towards the kitchen, she turned back to Ondine and mouthed the words, "Thank you."

"Ye did well, lass. That was inspired, like." Shambles gave her a wet, whiskery kiss on the cheek. "I'm really proud of ye."

A little thrill of excitement raced through Ondine. "I just said whatever popped into my head. I guessed she had kids, because you don't get thighs like that on a spinster. I took her right hand, and I saw the ring on it, with three sapphires, so I figured that she'd had three boys."

"Eh? Jewellery marks children?"

Ondine beamed. Who'd have thought she'd enjoy pretending to be psychic? "Why yes, Shambles. When a woman gives birth, the very least her devoted husband can do is to shower her in jewellery to mark the occasion. It's a very strong tradition in my family. Haven't you seen Ma's rings, with the rubies set in them? One ruby for each of us."

"Top marks for being observant. But what about all that guff about her boys and how she treats them?"

A chuckle escaped Ondine's lips as she bent down to the floor to scoop up mouldy newspapers for the fire, checking them first in case they contained anything juicy about the former Duke. "I just thought about the way Da thinks of us. I think I'm starting to work out why he's so strict with me. I'm his baby; he doesn't want me growing up too soon. When the first child leaves the nest, the parents fall over themselves with worry. I just figured that if Mrs Klegg had three boys, and we're three girls, how different could it be? I just told her what she wanted to hear."

"Well then, yer truly psychic. The old lady Howser would be proud of ye."

"Mrs Howser?" Ondine thought of her Psychic Summercamp instructor. "I bet she hasn't even noticed I'm gone."

With a pang she thought of her friend Melody, and how much she missed her.

"Did I ever tell ye how I came to be at Mrs Howser's?" Shambles asked.

"I don't believe you have," Ondine said, not really paying him much attention because she felt too nervous about what the health inspector might find.

"It's a funny story, really. After Old Col cast her spell I was all adrift, ye might say. She was friends with Mrs Howser at the time, ye see. But they weren't really friends because they weren't very nice to each other. More what you call frenemies. Are ye even listening to me, Ondi?"

*What?* "Yes, of course." Ondine watched Mrs Klegg and Ma disappear into the kitchens and heard lots of *tisking* noises of disapproval.

"Ye know lass, I never did meet Mr Howser. I don't think he lasted the distance. But Mrs Howser took a shine to me and stole me right from under Colette Romano's nose. I thought Colette would come for me, once she got over her fit of pique, but she never did."

"That's nice," Ondine said, barely hearing a word of it.

---

AN HOUR LATER, Wilma Klegg's scowl deepened into a dark furrow. The more her lips thinned and pressed together like closed book pages, the more Ma's painted-on smile looked ready to crack. Wilma pulled on a white glove and ran her finger over the kitchen benches. She sighed with disappointment. Something heavy fell in Ondine's stomach. A sense of foreboding clamped around her heart.

"We are closed for renovations, so it's natural the building is not up to correct specifications," Ma explained, her hands clasped in front of her stomach so that just her thumbs had room to wriggle – which they did, putting the world's best fidget to shame. "Furnish us with a list and we'll comply with everything on it."

"Yes, you will," Mrs Klegg said.

"It's all mince," Shambles said from Ondine's shoulder.[3]

They were both watching from a safe distance, so Ma and Mrs Klegg wouldn't hear them. "The Duke would run ye out of town, so he would. More than likely that box of bangles under the floor is at the centre of it all."

An idea percolated in Ondine's mind, so she re-read the newspaper obituary about the Duke's father and made a note of the newspaper's date.

"I reckon those jewels are the old Duke's secret stash," Shambles said.

Ondine wondered if her parents were thinking along the same lines. "Maybe you're right about the old Duke, Shambles," Ondine said, although she found it very hard to believe Vincent had anything to do with this. "Let's go to the city library and see if we can find out more." She grabbed her tattered school bag and headed for the door.

The warm sun and fresh air cleared the dust from Ondine's brain as she walked to the train station. Shambles clung to her shoulder. She might not be able to help the family any further with the health inspector, but if she could find some more information about the former Duke, it might give them a way to get the present Duke off their case.

"Yer a good lass, and I like the view from here," Shambles said with a saucy chuckle. Blushing furiously, Ondine looked down to see his point of view – the open 'V' in the neck of her shirt. The day felt hot already, but she quickly did all her buttons up.

Would there be no end to this blushing?

*To think I actually missed you!*

The ancient bluestone library building frightened Ondine at first. It was so tall and dark it blocked out the sun. Her legs felt a little wobbly as she scaled the steps. With the ferret moving about on her shoulder, she felt sure someone would stop her at the door.

"Keep still," she whispered, but it was no use.

A librarian approached, looked a bit startled, then settled his features and gave Ondine a smile that made his eyes crinkle all the way to his temples. "You'll find pet care and animals in six-three-six. It's the second row on the right."[4]

"Thank you, but I'm not here for that. I'd like to look at some newspapers from about thirty years ago, please. Where would they be?"

"They're in the archive room, but you won't be able to take animals in there, I'm afraid. It's a controlled environment."

"Um, what about if I sat outside the archive room, and you brought the papers to me? Would that be OK?"

"Good thinking, lass," Shambles whispered.

The librarian shook his head. "I'm sorry, we can't do that either. Have you got a box you could put your pet in for the time being? Otherwise you could put her in a locker."

"I'll naw go in a box!" Shambles protested, but it fell on deaf ears as Ondine accepted the compromise and took a locker key. Ondine felt no compulsion to correct the librarian, because she didn't want him paying any closer attention to her "pet" passenger.

"Hush up. It's for your own good." A tingle of delight raced up Ondine's spine. She was enjoying this.

"Dinnae put me in the locker!" he pleaded, as she opened the ventilated door.

"Stop whining. Just pretend you're going in, then at the last second get in my bag and stay absolutely still."

Shambles had the choice – shut in a metal box or crammed into the bag. He chose the latter and kept quiet.

The archive room smelt of naphthalene, making Ondine's eyes water and the inside of her nose freeze.[5] Shafts of light poured through from the small windows up on high, giving the room an ethereal feel. She found the pile of newspapers and worked backwards from the date of the old Duke's obituary, scanning for anything mentioning his name. In the months prior to his death, she found a page of court reports, and one short item that outlined a failed criminal case against the old Duke. There were lots of quotes from the old Duke's lawyer saying they were "always confident the unconstitutional charges would be dropped". Hope and a little bit of confusion surged in Ondine's chest. They were on to something.

Turning the pages back in time, they found an earlier court report.

"It says here the lawyers for the Duke are challenging the 'constitutional validity' of the charges. Can you make sense of this?"

Shambles peered at the newsprint, his head turning left and right as he scanned the column of text. "Aye, he's saying he can't be brought to trial because he's the Duke. They're quoting the ancient law of 'nascut regulum'."[6]

"What's that supposed to mean?"

"I don't know, but I think it worked."

Turning the pages yet further back in time, they found few mentions of the Duke, apart from the regular fortnightly list of visiting dignitaries. Almost as if the newspaper was pointedly ignoring him.

But of course, they were looking at this with hindsight – nobody at the time knew he was about to pop his clogs. For a while Ondine became distracted with other news events, and all the photographs highlighting the bizarre fashions of the day made her snort.

Then something caught her eye – a photograph of the old Duke and Duchess at an opening night at the theatre. The Duchess was wearing a diamond necklace that at first looked like a triangle of lace. Ondine got out her notepad and drew a picture of the necklace and the rest of the jewellery the Duchess wore. It was an old photograph, and although Ondine was no jewellery designer, she felt sure she'd seen that same piece in the box they'd uncovered under her family's floorboards.

"Eh, lass, didya read the rest of it?" Shambles said. "Says here the Duchess's jewellery is on loan from the Hera Collection. Have you heard of them?"

"Can't say I have. Stay quiet and I'll get the librarian to help me look it up."

Before Shambles could protest, she shoved him back into her bag.

That old familiar, tingling feeling of excitement started to course through her veins. Ondine knew she was on to something, and it felt great. Now to find the librarian and gather more information.

To Ondine's surprise, her questions weren't something the man had to look up. He'd heard of the Hera Collection before, and knew where the best book on the subject could be found.

"It's famous, but a bit before your time," he said, reaching for an enormous book filled with colour-plate images of some of the finest jewellery Ondine had ever seen.

"Have a look at these and try to keep your eyes in your head," the librarian added.

Drooling in a public library was not the done thing, so Ondine kept her mouth closed and swallowed several times in an effort to stop salivating. Page after page of incredible designs made her want to weep. There were clusters of choker necklaces, strings of pearls, glistening tiaras and stunning multi-jewelled earrings with matching necklaces. There were delicate rings for young debutantes, along with gaudy big monsters for fat old ladies with chubby fingers.

When she turned the page her breath hitched. It was the same necklace the Duchess had worn in the old newspaper photo. Ondine put the picture she'd sketched beside the photograph and her heart started beating way too fast at the discovery. Then she took out her pencil and altered her drawing, rubbing a bit out here and there, sketching it again, and so on, until her drawing was perfect.

Look, she had a good brain, but she just didn't have the artistic bent Marguerite possessed, so the drawing and re-drawing took a while.[7] Eventually, she was done.

"Thank you so much for your help," Ondine said to the librarian as she packed her things and shoved them into her bag. A muffled "ooof" sounded from inside it, but she coughed to smother Shambles's grunts.

She couldn't get home fast enough with the exciting news.

---

"ONDI, THANK GOODNESS FOR YOUR PERCEPTION," Ma said when Ondine returned home, Shambles riding high on her shoulder. "Mrs Klegg would have seen that entire box of jewels if you hadn't acted as fast as you did. And your psychic gift kicked in at just the right time. She was really very impressed with your vision, which made up for what she saw around here. Look at this: she's given us a list of repairs and changes to make, and then we can re-open next week."

*I was guessing*, Ondine wanted to say, but she held her thoughts for a moment so she could explain what she'd learned in the library. "I need to see the jewellery. Ma, have you heard of the Hera Collection?"

"Of course I have, every woman's heard of it."

"Well, I hadn't. Until today, that is."

"It was before your time, dear," Ma said.

A disappointed sigh escaped Ondine. Why did older people have to be so patronising about things and events taking place "before their time"? That complaint would have to wait until another day though – right now she had more pressing matters.

"The Duke. The one before the one we've got. Shambles and I have been to the library, and we've got the goods on him. The old Duchess borrowed pieces from the Hera Collection. One of them looks like this," Ondine said, showing her mother the drawing she'd made of the necklace.

They didn't waste any time heading to Ma and Da's bedroom, where they found Cybelle and Marguerite sitting on the bed, trying on jewels and giggling like toddlers.

"Margi, stand up now," Ma commanded.

The eldest obeyed, her eyes downcast in shame at their discovery. The glittering jewels on her neck practically danced in the sunlight. Excitement bubbled in Ondine as she took in the delicate necklace around her sister's neck.

"It's the same one all right," Shambles said. "Looks good on her, too."

8

A few days later, Ondine was none the wiser about the fate of all those lovely jewels. "Tell me again why the Hera Collection won't go public?" Ondine asked her mother as they rolled out the new carpet for the dining room.

It had been a crazy time. In the last week Ma had taken it upon herself to make contact with the Hera Collection and organise the safe return of the jewels. The cash, on the other hand? Nobody needed to know about that, so it found its way into the deposit box under the kitchen floor.

"They didn't want to go public because the old Duke and Duchess are no longer with us, and the present Duke's family is one of their best customers," Ma declared.

"Haaalp!" Shambles yelled as he fell over backwards under the carpet roll.

"But the Duke *stole* from them, or at least, his dad did," Ondine said as she grabbed Shambles out of harm's way. A good thing she'd acted so quickly, otherwise he would have ended his days as a nasty lump under the new carpet.

Only a few metres of carpet to go and they'd be finished. In this room at least.

"That's very true," said Ma. "But the present Duchess is

photographed wearing their jewels, just as the old Duchess was, and by doing that she becomes a walking advertisement for them. They still make their money selling to people who aspire to be like the Duchess. By returning the jewels on the quiet, we've spared Hera a public scandal."

*Spared the Duke's family from messy criminal charges more like*, Ondine privately fumed.

"Did they let us keep any of it as a reward?" Cybelle asked, hammering the carpet tacks into the corners of the room to keep the new flooring steady. "Surely not all of it was theirs?"

"Surely it was," Ma said, adding a heavy sigh for emphasis.

Tears pricked the back of Ondine's eyes. All that beautiful jewellery, gone just as fast as it had come into their lives.

"But that's not fair! They could have left us some of it, as thanks for saving their reputation," Marguerite complained as she and Thomas moved another table into position. Despite the hard work, Marguerite's long dark hair looked glossy and wavy. Cybelle's bob looked neat and tidy. Ondine? Her hair hung in messy string-tails and the top of her scalp felt greasy.

"I'm afraid not. They couldn't risk somebody recognising the pieces on any of us. Imagine if we wore them to a public event. We'd be in jail for theft faster than you could say 'that's not fair'."

"Because we're not the kind of people who are allowed to wear it. Are we?" Ondine said, clenching her hands in frustration.

That's all life seemed to be lately. One frustrating event after another.

"But why did you have to give it all back then?" Cybelle moaned, doing a very good job of sounding coherent considering she had a dozen carpet tacks in her mouth.

"Pfft! I didn't give it *all* back. D'you think I'm stupid?" Ma said, having a good chuckle at her daughters' expense.

Anger and jubilation roiled in Ondine. Anger that their mother had told them a whopping great fib. Jubilation that there were still a few nice pieces somewhere in safe keeping.

"You were winding us up, weren't you, Ma?" Ondine finished rolling the carpet out. Then she trimmed off the extra length with a sharp knife.

A few more tacks from Cybelle and they'd be done for the afternoon. Not much left on Mrs Klegg's list now.

In unison, Marguerite and Cybelle rolled their eyes in frustration. Getting a straight answer out of their mother would be impossible now, because Ma knew how much they'd wanted to keep some of those trinkets and baubles for themselves.

"On to important business," Da said as he entered the room. He and Chef manoeuvred the piano into its corner in the dining room. Everyone moved out the way to let them get it into place. Shambles leapt onto Ondine's shoulder.

Ma brushed down her skirts. "We re-open tomorrow for lunch. I'm thinking perhaps with the new opening, we could give the place a new name."

"What's wrong with the old one, Mrs G?" Thomas asked.

"Nyeh, it's too dull," Ma said. "It doesn't do anything for me any more. What do you think, Josef?"

"I think the present name is fine," said Da. "Everyone knows where *The Station Hotel* is – it's across the road from the station."

"How about The Jewel?" Cybelle said with a wicked gleam in her eye.

"Or The Crown?" Marguerite said.

"I know. What if we call it *The Duke and Ferret*?" Ondine said.

They all laughed at that.

"You know what? That has a pretty good ring to it," Ma said. "And it could prove a handy insurance policy. The Duke wouldn't dare close down a pub named in his honour. Good thinking, Ondi. You truly have the gift."

With that, her mother kissed her affectionately on the forehead and surveyed the improvements. "It all looks grand. Well done, everyone."

---

LATER THAT NIGHT, Ondine tried to sleep, but her brain would not switch off. Back in her own room again, she had no one to talk to. She took a walk down the darkened hall to see if Cybelle was awake. Judging from the rollicking snores, her sister was deeply out of it. There was nothing for it but to chat with Shambles, simply because he would be up for a natter when nobody else would. But where was he? The kitchen seemed the logical place, and indeed, that was where she found him, licking cold fat off a dirty frying pan.

"Ye've come to take me to bed, lass?"

Did he have to be so cheeky all the time? "You should be in the laundry. Everyone else is asleep."

"So why are you up?"

A heavy weight pushed her shoulders down. "It's Ma. I'm trying to work out how to tell her I don't have the gift."

"Sure you've got the gift, so you do," Shambles said.

Maybe some warm milk would help. Ondine set about making herself something comforting. *The drinking chocolate's around here somewhere.* "I don't have the gift," she protested, her head starting to throb with confusion. It wasn't right to mislead her mother. If Ma got the idea into her head that Ondine really was psychic, she might send her back to Summercamp and Mrs Howser. "I've just been saying the first thing that comes into my head. That's not being psychic, it's just blurting things out."

"But they're the right things, so they are," Shambles said.

Frustration made Ondine clench her teeth, but she resisted the urge to grind her back molars into powder. "Well, maybe I'm just ... smart. I mean, is that so far-fetched? Why does it have to be some extra power? Why can't I be the smart one instead of the psychic one?"

"It really bothers you, doesn't it, lass?"

Taking a few breaths, Ondine sorted her thoughts out. Too right it bothered her, for more reasons than she could say. Perhaps because the entire psychic concept left her feeling like a liar and a scam artist. She knew plenty of people who had the gift for real, but she wasn't one of them. And another thing. If people said she was psychic, they'd want more of it, and eventually it would all unravel because they'd find out there was no more to give. They'd find out she was a fraud.

It didn't feel right to foster a lie.

"You're a smart girl. You'll work it out," Shambles said.

THERE WAS no time to think about anything the next morning, as the entire family – which now encompassed Thomas – set about readying for the lunchtime re-opening. Chef and Cybelle were little more than a blur of work in the kitchen; Thomas and Da polished the new beer glasses and steins; Margi, Ondine, Shambles and Ma made up the guests' beds on the second floor.

In a flash of black, Shambles darted under the bed they were working on.

"You've run under every bed up here. I didn't put the jewels anywhere you could find them, you know," Ma said.

"I'm checking for Oose. They breed under beds and frighten folk."[1]

Ahead of her mother's question, Ondine shrugged. "I have no idea what he's on about."

"You knew what I was going to ask? I told you, you're psychic," Colette said.

A muscle twitched in Ondine's jaw. "Ma, please. Drop it, OK?"

"We're done here," Marguerite interrupted. Apart from the soft red in her cheeks, she still looked neat. You'd never know she'd been doing so much work. "We'd better get downstairs before the doors open, or we'll be overrun."

"Thank you, Margi, that's very *smart* of you," Ondine said with deliberate emphasis. Then she looked at her mother. "Or maybe Margi's the psychic one?"

"You'll keep," Ma said.

They made it down the stairs just in time to see Thomas open the door to half a dozen thirsty people, who made straight for the bar and ordered drinks. In a couple of seconds Da had his hands full of beer steins and the till started ringing with sales. Cybelle walked into the bar carrying a plate of savoury morsels, offering them around.

"You're not giving food away, are you?" Ma whispered to her middle child.

"They're samples, Ma, as a re-opening special. It's Chef's idea. Isn't he clever? He has some really good ideas to update the menu and –"

"Right, I'll have a good talk to Chef."

From her position in the doorway Ondine watched the exchange, and her heart ached for her middle sister. If she were older, she could walk into the bar and offer her moral support. Being only fifteen, she didn't dare set foot in it, just in case someone dobbed her in to the Duke or Mrs Klegg. Instead, she waited until she caught Cybelle's attention and gave her the thumbs-up, because that was all she could do for now.

Cybelle shot her back a confused look.

*So much for being psychic.*

The lunch crowd kept them busy all afternoon. The kitchen roared back into life with a host of new and delightful smells, courtesy of Chef's additions. Lunchtime grew into late afternoon and another of Chef's ideas – afternoon tea – brought in more people for scones, jam and cream, with tea or coffee. This time, Ma beamed at Chef's innovation, because it created a profitable time of the day where previously none had existed. And scones are scones the world over, so nobody needed free samples.

As Ondine served the guests, Cybelle took to the piano and Marguerite joined her. From out the back, Shambles raced through the dining room and scurried up on top of the piano to join in. Ondine held her breath, waiting for calamity, but this time nobody screamed. The girls laughed as the animal wailed and carried on, holding his little ferrety paws over his chest as he squeaked his heart out.

It had been an excellent idea renaming the pub *The Duke and Ferret*. If anyone saw Shambles, they'd know he was the hotel mascot and not a rat.

Above the melody, Ondine heard the chink and clunk of coins piling into the tips jar on top of the piano. A beaming smile cracked her face.

*This is brilliant!*

"Shy little thing, isn't he?" Ma joked, then she too started singing on her way back to the kitchen, her arms full of dirty plates.

"He just wants to get out of work," Ondine said. With a sigh she bade the piano farewell and made for the pile of dirty plates by the sink. She pushed her sleeves up and plunged her arms into the hot, soapy water.

Late afternoon rolled into early evening. Ondine sat in the private room behind the kitchen with Shambles, Cybelle and Chef. They were eating from a platter of food Chef had brought out for them, resting and recharging before the evening crowd arrived. As far as Ondine was concerned, Shambles had done the least real work out of the lot of them, but that didn't stop him eating his bodyweight in cold meats and cheeses.

"Born and bred salad dodger, aren't you, Shambles?" Chef said.

"I used to love potatoes and fresh fruit, but I cannae handle it no more," Shambles confessed, talking with his mouth full.[2]

"You probably used to love table manners too," Ondine said.

Ignoring them, Cybelle made a large "O" with her mouth so she could properly reapply her eyeliner.

Through the sound of munching and slurping water, Ondine heard her mother's voice rise an octave in delight, all the way from the dining room.

"Sounds like someone's turned up for Margi's engagement party tomorrow," Cybelle said, as they heard their mother's voice grow louder on approach.

Wait, what? Margi's engagement party was tomorrow? How had Ondine missed that?

"It's lovely to see you again. Come through. Oh, you must see the girls, they've grown so much," Ma said as she walked towards them.

There in the doorway stood their great-auntie Col.

Food dropped from Shambles's mouth. "It's the witch! It's really her this time!" he shrieked.

Nobody said anything for what felt like ages, but in reality was probably only five seconds, as the elderly but sprightly woman creased her eyes and scrutinised Shambles.

A tiny bit of sick burnt the back of Ondine's throat, such was her shock and surprise. Old Col was here, the Witchy Woman who'd turned Hamish the lad into the animal he was today. Ondine swallowed hard and stared up at her elderly relative, her heart beating faster in anticipation of what might come.

"Hamish McPhee, you haven't changed a bit," her great-aunt Col said.

"Aye, ye cursed me good, so ye did."

"Not one of my better ones, but it seems to have stuck."

"Aye. Come here and give me a kiss." Shambles held his furry arms wide for a hug.

A cold spike of jealousy stabbed Ondine's heart. What if Auntie Col returned Shambles to his Hamish-ness, and he up and left them?

Another cold spike, this time of fear. What if it was even worse? What if Auntie Col returned Shambles to his Hamish-ness, and he was ugly?

*Don't be so superficial.*

But once the thought took hold, she couldn't *unthink* it.

**9**

---

They'd been talking for more than two hours, Shambles and Old Col, but Ondine had no idea what they were discussing. Every time she returned from the dining room with empty plates, she looked in on the private room behind the kitchen. There they were, Shambles jittering about on the table and Old Col nodding her head from time to time. They spoke in hushed tones, their backs to the doorway so Ondine couldn't even read their expressions.

The old lady and the ferret. What could they be talking about?

"No slacking off, go take table twelve's dessert order," Ma said. "Leave Hamish and Aunt Col alone. When they're ready to talk to you, they'll let you know."

A spark raced up Ondine's spine. Her mother had called him Hamish instead of Shambles. Would that mean her great-aunt had decided to release the enchantment so he could become human again? Yet again Ondine wondered whether Hamish might be as handsome as he sounded. Or at the very least, as handsome as Lord Vincent.

*I shouldn't compare them, but I can't help it.*

It was impossible for Hamish to sit still. Being a human with ferret qualities (although by now perhaps it was the other way around) he did his best to listen quietly and "sit nice" as his mother used to say.[1]

It was a losing battle. The mixture of excitement and fear coursing through his body had him trembling from nose to tail-tip.

"Ye understand how completely sorry I am," he started, knowing it barely touched the sides of the cavernously bad feeling existing between them.

"You offended me mightily, you know that," Aunt Col said, and from the look on her face – as wrinkly and "of a certain age" as it was – she'd kept hold of her pain for many, many years.

"Aye, I know, and I am deeply sorry. And at first I was angry with ye for doin' it, but I've come to understand why ye did it. Ye've taught me a lesson, one I'll nawt likely forget," Hamish said, taking a deep breath (for a ferret anyway) and trying to move the conversation forwards. "I didn't realise yer debutante ball was so important to ye. But I know I ruined it for ye, and I'm very sorry. If you change me back, I'll partner ye again and we'll get it right this time."

They both sat there for a moment, as Hamish looked at Old Col, and she looked back at him. All the while Hamish's tiny Shambles-heart whirred like a drum roll.

"Eh, lass? Now that we're older and wiser, is there any chance ye can forgive me?"

The papery skin on Old Col's face made a concertina on her cheeks as she smiled. "You're half right. I'm certainly much older, and I do believe I am somewhat wiser. You did hurt me, Hamish, for many reasons – but you're right, it was a long time ago, and holding a grudge is so terribly ageing."

Hamish held his breath, waiting for the next bit.

"I forgive you," Old Col said, her eyes sparkling behind their stubby lashes. In those few words, Hamish felt his spirits soar.

Then just as quickly they crashed as he surveyed his furry body. "But, I'm still a ferret!"

"So you are. Which means it must be up to you now. Perhaps you like being a ferret because it means you are excused from life's obligations."

"So you're saying I'm still a ferret because . . . because I *like* it?"

The grin she gave him sent a heavy, sinking feeling into the pit of his stomach. "That must be it. *Weasel* your way out of that one!"

<hr>

THE MINUTES DRAGGED LIKE HOURS, until towards the end of the evening, Ondine finally heard her great-aunt Col summon her to sit beside them at their table. The wrinkles on her face and her gnarled, arthritic fingers may have given the woman an appearance of age, but her mind still cracked as fast as a whip.

"Ondine, come here, child. Hamish has something he wishes to say to you," Aunt Col said, motioning to the ferret, who sat near the edge of the table with his head bowed.

"Aye, lass, I do. But before I go on, I want to tell ye how much I appreciate everything ye've done for me. Ye've taken me in and provided for me. I couldnae asked for more."

Fear gripped Ondine's heart and gave a good squeeze. His words sounded so ominous. Her hands wobbled, so she clasped them together to hold them still.

"Aunt Col has lifted the spell, but I think I've been a ferret so long I've forgotten what I used to be. She says it's up to me now, but I'm nawt sure I know how to be me again. Ye've shown me what it means to be part of a family, to work together and make a real go of it."

Ondine pleaded with Aunt Col. "Change him back!"

"I already have. He's responsible for his life now."

"But you were the one that turned him into a ferret in the first place," Ondine protested.

"That's true, but spells only work on willing recipients. I did call him a weasel for being so horrible to me and ruining my big night, but he must have believed it to make the spell work."

"So why isn't he changing back then?"

A sad little voice piped up, "Because ah'm nawt worthy of ye."

Ondine noted the drawl in his accent, proving just how deeply embarrassed he must be feeling.

"Don't be silly. Of course you're worthy. You're helping out around the pub and you prevented the Duke's assassination, for goodness' sake. They're pretty worthy things in my book."

The little ferret gave a sigh and said, "Yeah, I guess so." But he didn't sound convinced.

A tear trickled down Ondine's cheek at the thought of Hamish living the rest of his life trapped in that little body.

"Ach, dry yer eyes," Shambles said, his accent thick with remorse. "Ah know ye were looken forward to me being human again, but ye'll have to wait a bit until I get mah heed right."[2]

*Now who's the psychic one?*

---

LATER THAT NIGHT, when all was quiet, Shambles sneaked into Ondine's room. In automatic response to seeing the ferret near her bed, Ondine patted the pillow and made room for him.

"Nay, lass, I just came to bid you goodnight. Now get yer sleep. I'm for the laundry."

Heaviness tugged Ondine's heart. As if she were missing him already. "You don't have to sleep down there, Shambles. Ma knows you're here anyway."

"All the more reason to stay in the laundry. It's nawt appropriate for me to be in yer room. I've taken advantage of yer . . . *hospitality* . . . enough."

Ondine heard the emphasis on the word and chose to ignore it. She opened her mouth to speak, but nothing came out because her mind had gone blank. Not completely blank, obviously, otherwise her vital functions like breathing would stop. But the thinking part of her brain shut down. Possibly because all she could do was imagine how lonely she'd be without him snuggled in beside her. For a while Ondine sat there in her bed, while Shambles stood there in the middle of the floor, neither saying anything for what felt like the longest time.

Finally, Shambles sighed. "I think yer great-auntie's right. I have to behave like a man. I think mebbe if I go with her we might be able to find some spells that might help."

He was leaving? How would that help anyone?

"Sham– no, Hamish?" Ondine cleared her throat. "You're the only one here who doesn't treat me like a child. Please don't start now."

"Yer nawt a child, that's for sure." The ferret shook his furry head. "You're the smartest one here. And that's why I have tae go. I'll only drag ye down if I remain."

Nothing he said made any sense. "You'll at least stay for Margi's party tomorrow night, won't you?" Ondine tried to sound reasonable, while in her heart she felt very close to begging. Only she wouldn't beg, and she wouldn't whine, because that would betray how mature she was trying to appear.

"One last party, eh? Well, OK, if it means that much to ye."

Ondine's shoulders sagged in relief. She hadn't realised how tense she'd become during the course of their conversation, but now she sighed out loud with the reprieve. Maybe she could convince Aunt Col and Shambles to stay with them? After all, they had room for plenty more under their roof.

Shambles made for the door, but stopped before he left.

"Is there something else?" Ondine asked.

"Yeah, there is. Yer ma told me about Lord Vincent. She said he was making puppy eyes at you in the dining room the other day."

"Thanks, Ma." Ondine flushed at the memory.

Shambles shrugged. "Big families are short on privacy."

"What about Lord Vincent?" she asked, as a fresh wave of tingling spread across her wrist at the memory of his kiss.

"You're a smart one. I think you already know."

"And if I wasn't smart? If I was only a child. What would you tell me?"

"I'd tell ye to stay away from him, because he reminds me too much of me."

With that, Shambles walked out of her room, leaving Ondine with a sinking, empty feeling inside.

<hr>

THAT NIGHT, as Ondine slept, she tried to dream of Lord Vincent, but her subconscious wouldn't let her. Instead, Melody, her friend from Psychic Summercamp, appeared. Pang! Ondine had meant to keep in touch with her friend, but things had become so busy she hadn't found the time. In the dream, they were sitting in a field of flowers, at dusk on a balmy summer's evening. Fireflies danced around them. It was a lovely, calm scene, and Shambles appeared (eating a sausage, of course, because any time Ondine thought of Shambles it was associated with eating). It all felt so peaceful, Ondine wanted the dream to last for ages.

"Mrs Howser wants to see you," Melody said. Her friend's words brought a change of scene. It became dark and a cold draught played around her legs, yet a bright spotlight shone on her. Shambles stopped eating and cried out in pain, clutching his belly.

"We're coming," Melody said.

"Aw naw! I'm dying," Shambles said.

Ondine sprang awake, dripping with perspiration while her heart thundered behind her ribs, threatening to burst free.

"I'm not psychic, it was just a dream," she said to the empty room.

So why couldn't she convince herself?

<hr>

NOT SLEEPING PROPERLY MADE Ondine grumpy. When Melody and Mrs Howser arrived in the dining room late the next afternoon, her heart sank and she became even grumpier. Not because she didn't like them, but the fact that they were here in person meant perhaps the rest of last night's dream might come true as well. The bit that didn't end well for Shambles. Still, she hugged Melody hello.

"Hey, Ondi, it's good to see you! Did you get my message in your dream?" Melody beamed. "I've cracked astral projection at last. Mrs Howser's been so helpful. Is Shambles still here?"

"Th-that was you?" Cold dread snaked through her system.

"Yes! I'm still not sure how much came through. I used a new technique, but I was in your dream last night, wasn't I? I can tell because you've gone pale. Oh dear, I didn't go overboard, did I?" Melody blurted.

Ondine wanted to be sick.

"Aren't you going to show us to a table?" Mrs Howser asked as she hitched a multitude of coloured shawls over her shoulders. High summer, but the woman acted like she had a chill. "You can tell us how you're getting along with Shambles. I've actually missed him."

Remembering her manners just in time (and taking a deep breath so she could rein in her nausea), Ondine invited them to take a seat, then dashed to the kitchen and returned a few minutes later with a pot of steaming tea.

"We're flat out, to tell the truth. We have a pretty full dining room tonight, and it's Margi's engagement party to Thomas as well, out in the garden. Hi, Thomas," she added, as the topic of conversation walked in, bringing a decanter of wine to the patrons on a nearby table.

"I know it's your sister's engagement party," Mrs Howser said with a haughty tone. "Your mother invited us, in exchange for me graciously waiving the remainder of your tuition fees. Even though I was under no obligation, due to you leaving in somewhat *hurried* circumstances."

Gulp.

"Hey, Ondi. Thanks for stringing up the fairy lights in the garden – they'll look great in the dark," Thomas said.

Ondine felt eternally grateful for Thomas's interjection. She was really starting to like her future brother-in-law, and felt a little glow of extra love for her eldest sister. Margi had chosen well.

Melody piped up, "Fairy lights? But in the dream they were fireflies."

Something staggered behind Ondine's ribs and her throat turned to ash. Everything about her dream was coming true.

"Where is Shambles?" Mrs Howser asked.

"H-he's around here somewhere. He's fitting in really well," Ondine said, making bland conversation while she tried to work out whether Melody and Mrs Howser appearing today and the fireflies, no, *fairy lights* in the garden meant everything else in the dream would happen. The moment she had some free time, she'd take down those horrible lights. Surely, if they weren't there, the rest of the dream couldn't come true?

At that point, Ma and Great-Auntie Col came in. Ondine took the initiative and made introductions, pulling up more chairs to accommodate them, all the while trying to find an excuse to leave. As soon as she could get out to the garden, she could sabotage her earlier work.

"We've already met," Old Col said, giving Mrs Howser a stern look. "Been a while, Birgit. Still glomming round the camp, gazing at tea leaves?"

"Hello, Col. Still spitting acid, I see?" It was physically impossible for Ondine's eyeballs to pop out of her head, but it felt like they were about to, such was her shock.

"Um, Melody, why don't we go out to the beer garden and help with the decorations?" If these two old biddies wanted to trade insults down memory lane, she'd rather not be around to see it.

"Oh, it's just like the dream!" Melody said with delight as she saw the lights strung up between the trees. In twilight, the effect wasn't very good, but when the sun set in a hour or so, they would look just like fireflies.

A heavy sense of dread choked Ondine's throat as she pulled up a chair and removed a strand of lights from the nearest tree branch. "No, it's not going to be like the dream! Melody, what did you do? I woke up and nearly puked, I was so sick with fear. Why did you put that bit in about Shambles dying?"

Now it was Melody's turn to pale, leaving nothing but contrasting brown freckles on her face. "But I didn't. We were in a field of fireflies and I said we were coming to pay a visit. Shambles wasn't even in it. He's not sick, is he?"

Confusion time. "Are you sure?" Ondine rolled up the cables.

"Yes, absolutely positive, I promise," Melody said.

Ondine took a few deep breaths to steady her nerves. There was no point even trying to think with all this adrenalin racing around her body. It made her tremble and want to cry and yet she felt strangely hungry all at the same time. She needed a clear head so she could think about a rational answer, not turn into an emotional wreck.

So Melody had not dreamt of Shambles? At last, a positive sign! Things were looking up. If all of Melody's side of the dream came true, no dramas there. Just as long as Shambles's part didn't come true. That was the critical bit.

"It's OK. I've got my wires crossed. Let's get the rest of this set up. We should keep busy out here so we can stay well clear of the two witches inside, don't you think?"

Melody giggled.

There were tablecloths and piles of plates and cutlery to set out for that night's party, so they set to it. Ma had planned the evening to coincide with the full moon, so they'd have plenty of natural light to add to the mood.[3]

Work proved a welcome distraction, and before long they had the place looking inviting.

"Ondi, maybe . . . maybe I crashed the dream you were already having," Melody suggested as she placed knives and forks at each setting.

"Yeah, that could work. I mean, hey, it was just a dream, right?"

"Well, of course. Sometimes a dream is just a dream. It doesn't have to mean anything," Melody said.

The object of their concern came bounding out into the beer garden in a streak of dark fur, his mouth full of food. "Ondi, ye've got to try Chef's new meatballs, they're to die for," Shambles said.

Actually, what he really said was "O-fi, oof ot oo iy eff's ew eetaaals, ere o ie or" because he had a mouth full of food.

"Weh hey!" In a blaze of black fur, he leapt on to the top of the last un-set table and skidded along the surface, the tablecloth bunching up at his feet.

The girls laughed at Shambles, even though Ondine should have been cross with him. But she couldn't be, not when he might be leaving soon with Aunt Col. She wouldn't let them end things on an argument.

"Aw, I messed up yer table," Shambles said, surveying the damage. "I'll fix it up for ye." With that, he gripped the edge of the fabric in his teeth and walked backwards across the surface, dragging the cloth with him.

From the other end, Ondine held the edges in place, smoothing it out and making it ready. "Thanks, you're a great help," she said.

Suddenly, with a yelp of shock, the ferret dropped backwards off the edge of the table, dragging the tablecloth down with him.

"Shambles!" Ondine screamed, racing towards him.

He lay there, a lump underneath the fabric, moaning in pain.

"Oh, my darling, I'm so sorry!" Ondine cried. She didn't need to look around to know Melody was standing behind her, probably just as freaked out as she was. Ondine pulled the tablecloth back to reveal Shambles's head and give him some fresh air.

Shambles groaned even louder. "Oh, the pain!"

"He can talk! Great heavens! Shambles can talk!" Melody said, amazed.

"You heard that?" Ondine's heart picked up speed at the revelation, yet there was little time to explain it all. If she thought Melody being able to understand Shambles was a shock, she had an even bigger one coming.

As he lay groaning and writhing on the ground, twisting and turning under the tablecloth, Shambles grew to twice his size and his face fur matted together, forming skin. The long whiskers retracted and his head began to bulge.

"I'm dying!" he cried out to Ondine. "Bring me whisky, I'm dying!"

The dream. That horrible dream!

"Mercury's wings!" Ondine cried as great wet tears splashed down her face and on to Shambles's writhing, deformed body. "You can't die, Shambles! I won't let you!"

"I'll get Mrs Howser," Melody said, and ran back inside.

"Oh God, oh God," Shambles groaned, "I'm goin' tae boak."[4]

"No, Shambles, you'll be OK. Melody's getting help," Ondine said, although what help anyone could be at this present moment escaped her. On the other hand, a witch had got him into this mess; maybe a witch could get him out of it?

Confusion scrambled her brain. She couldn't think what to do – she'd never seen anything like this before and didn't even know how to start helping him. All she could do was stand back as Shambles kept growing and expanding under the tablecloth. Moaning and groaning about the state of his gelatinous body. All the while his face pulsed and wobbled. A horrible thought made Ondine feel ashamed for even thinking it.

What if his face set like that?

"There's the light," he said. "It's calling me, I have tae go tae the light."

Fear making her tremble, Ondine looked in the same direction. Her horrible dream was about to become reality.

As she turned her head, she felt her stomach lurch as a white light shone on her face. A moment later, blessed relief coursed through her. "That's not the light, Shambles. That's just the full moon, you bampot."

When she turned to check on Shambles, her breath hitched. He'd stopped thrashing about, stopped moaning and groaning. Now he was shivering.

And completely human.

The next surprise came straight after the first, as Shambles looked up at Ondine. Far from looking like a bucket of twisted shoes, his face could have belonged to a movie star. He was even more handsome than Lord Vincent. With a shock of black hair and a dangerous gleam in his green eyes.

He was glorious!

Heat coursed through her body and her tongue turned to sandpaper as she tried to swallow. Something flip-flopped in her belly. Thank heavens for the tablecloth, because from the looks of things, he didn't have a patch of clothing on. Ondine's pulse hammered freshly in her ears.

*I'm going to have a heart attack before I make sixteen.*

"I'm nawt dead," he said at last.

Despite her concern for some modicum of decorum, a smile broadened her face and happiness bubbled in her veins. Heavens above, her dream had been wrong. Way wrong.

Those devilish green eyes stayed fixed on hers, while a lopsided grin added a mischievous gleam. Suddenly she averted her gaze and dropped her lashes so she could study the ground.

"I'm nawt dead," Shambles said again, louder this time as he turned his hands back and forth in the moonlight. Then he wrapped the tablecloth around his middle, stood up and shook his head in amazement. He took a step closer and cupped Ondine's cheek in his palm. Heat seared her face. "The dream didn't come true."

"The . . . the . . ." The dream? He knew about it?

"You're not dead by a long shot," Old Aunt Col said from the doorway, making Ondine and Shambles-Hamish turn quickly to see they had company.

"But if you lay a finger on my grand-niece, you'll wish you were."

Indeed, they had an audience, including Ondine's mother who, from the shocked look on her face, had seen quite a bit too.

**10**

———

It was Ma who came to her senses first, ordering Shambles-we-should-call-him-Hamish-now to go inside and get dressed. She gave him some of Josef's old clothes so he could dress properly.[1]

Tablecloths are only fashionable for attending a toga party, and this was not such an occasion.

"I look like a waiter," he said, as he came back to the beer garden.

At the sound of his voice, Ondine turned and looked to the ground because she'd become used to Shambles approaching from a low vector and racing up her leg. But of course he wasn't a ferret any more, he was a real man.

A real man who made her heart do stupid things because she'd spent so much time fantasising about what he might look like, and now he was even better than she'd imagined.

Old black leather shoes, scuffed and somewhat curled up at the toes, came into view, then an expanse of black socks capped by the hems of his pants. Something made her stall over the hem, because she didn't want to look up any further, knowing what a furious blusher she could be.

"Sure, the pants are too short, but they're better than the tablecloth," he said, taking a step closer to Ondine. "Ye can look up, lass, ye won't turn to stone. Yer ma says she's made me look nice."

If she'd known the word "smitten", Ondine would have used it to describe herself when she looked into Hamish's face. Those green eyes glistened in the moonlight, giving him a dangerous look, while his shock of black hair lay flat on his head, smoothed down into submission with gel. Ondine's palms itched to mess it all up again, as her face burned with fresh embarrassment.

What a man! If she'd thought Lord Vincent was attractive, Hamish was off the scale. To her deep, cringe-inducing embarrassment, nothing came out of Ondine's mouth, because she found herself thinking, *You look gorgeous*. But she didn't know if she'd said it out loud or not.

At that point, Cybelle walked past and made kissing noises as she headed back to the kitchen, shattering Ondine's illusion that they were the only two people on the planet. Everyone else in the garden looked at the two of them as well: Mrs Howser, Old Col, Melody, Ma and Marguerite.

Then Ma spoke up, "It's all hands on deck tonight, people will be arriving for dinner soon. Hamish, head to the kitchen and help Chef and Josef, they're run off their feet. Ondi, it's not your engagement party, it's Margi's. Roll your sleeves up and get to the sink."

Just like her mother to double-book the night. She probably figured with all the extra guests at the engagement party, she could rope some of them into waiting tables.

"Yes, ma'am," Hamish said, and gave Ondine a look she couldn't read – although she felt something flip over in her belly – before he turned and left.

---

OF COURSE they wouldn't get a moment alone, Ondine privately fumed as she followed him to the kitchen and pulled on an apron and an enormous pair of gloves. Sure, they were standing near each other, but at the rate the dishes piled up, there wasn't a chance to say any more than, "Pass me another tea towel, this one's soaked." And even though they had obviously been psychically linked in the dream she'd had, it didn't seem to work when they were awake. A few times she tried to psychically ask him to pass a towel, but he didn't.

*Can you hear my thoughts*? Ondine silently asked.

Hamish made no reaction, so she took that as a "no". She felt frustrated at her lack of psychic progress, but at the same time a little bit glad he couldn't read her mind right now.

Da kept looking askance at them, and shook his head a few times. Ondine could have sworn he chuckled too. Every now and then, Ondine caught her parents quickly discussing things in hushed tones, then they'd throw a glance her way. Probably just to make her feel paranoid.

Chef barely had time to acknowledge the new member of staff, because he was busy cooking a dozen steaks five different ways from rare to well done.[2]

Then another thought struck Ondine: with the new year of school starting at the end of summer, she would be away all day and writing assignments all night. They'd have to keep Hamish on to help out while she was busy studying. Surely her parents wouldn't put her education at risk?

Perfect logic.

The thought sent a glimmer of excitement through her system as she plunged her hands into the scalding water to scrub one of Chef's particularly nasty stockpots.

"Right you two, stop mooning at each other," Ma said as she approached. They'd been washing dirty dishes for nearly an hour by this stage. "You're both on front of house for the rest of the night, so do your best. Whoever gets the most tips earns a day off tomorrow."

The thought of a day off – sleeping in, reading her favourite book, lounging about in her pyjamas until noon – held serious appeal. That and not being up to her armpits in greasy water.

Ondine turned to Hamish and pulled her hand from the glove with a noisy squelch. "May the best one win."

"You're on," he said, giving her hand a friendly shake.

She should have been confident, but when his hand took Ondine's, her bones turned to mush and the intensity of his gaze made her forget what they were supposed to be doing. Then another thought occurred to her: perhaps she should throw the competition and make sure Hamish won?

"Stop making eyes, go clean up and get out the front. Dinner won't serve itself," Ma said.

Ondine ducked out of the kitchen for a moment and returned wearing fresh, clean, dry clothes. It hadn't taken her long, but she was already running behind. According to Ma, Hamish was out there charming everyone.

She took the plates of food to a family with four children and sighed. With a large family, there wouldn't be much money left over for tips. On the other hand, it would help Hamish get ahead in the race, so that wouldn't be such a bad thing.

Her competitive spirit kicked in when she saw the group of ladies at her next table.  One look at their pastel blue hair told her they were retirees, most likely widows, possibly with a bit of cash to splash. She took their orders and they all said yes to dessert, plus tea and coffee. Turning back to the kitchen, she caught sight of Hamish as he fare welled an earlier group – all well-dressed and aged around thirty. They should have plenty of spare change. The resigned look on his face indicated otherwise.

"What's wrong?"

"Teachers. Lousy tippers," he said.

"Why don't you take my table that just came in? Charm their socks off."

Hamish cast a glance at the new group of women. From the look of their showy earrings and manicured hands, they had plenty of cash to spare. "You'd do that for me?"

"Sure, what are friends for?"

Hamish grinned, then stalled for a second as he gazed into Ondine's eyes. "You're letting me win?"

A wicked smile split Ondine's face. "No, I'm giving you an even chance. You'll make them feel young and pretty again; I'll just remind them of their long-lost youth." Then she pretended to blow on her nails and shine them on her shirt.

*Game on. Gimme your best shot.*

*Great Pluto's ghost, I'm reduced to thinking in clichés.*

---

PICTURE THE FOLLOWING: two old glass jars that once held industrial amounts of artichoke hearts and pimento-stuffed olives (which were very tasty, thank you) sitting on a shelf. As Hamish accepted the tips from one table, he dropped the coins and the occasional note into his jar on the right with a satisfying tinkety-clunk.

As Ondine accepted tips from her tables, she returned to the kitchen and placed half her tips in her jar on the left (again, with a satisfying tinkety-clunk) and the other half in Hamish's jar on the right. A person with nothing more to do than watch the tips jars all night would see the coins and notes clunketing and tinketing left and right, a few more for Hamish, then a few more for Ondine, who gave yet more to Hamish.

Anyone would think she was trying to throw the game.

In this case, absolutely true.

"Ondine, what are you doing?" Ma asked, arms crossed tightly over her ample bosom.

A large invisible rock formed in Ondine's throat as she tried to swallow. When she opened her mouth, nothing came out.

Hamish walked towards them with a spring in his step, his hands full of money, his voice a sing-song. "Mrs G, here's the receipt and money from table ten for you, and the tips for me."

Ma had to uncross her arms to take the money, but as soon as she took the notes she re-folded them. Holding her mother's eye contact proved too much like confrontation, so Ondine turned to check on Hamish.

On his face she saw the smile of a man with no troubles.

"Righto, let's count them, shall we?" He lifted a jar with each hand. "Och, it's so nice to have thumbs again!"

Time moved slowly as Ondine found herself unable to move her feet. Ma had her in some kind of suspension glare that kept her fixed to the spot. The complete opposite of what she should do, which was to get out of there and join the rest of the engagement party in the rear garden.[3]

Hamish seemed oblivious to all of it as he hefted the jars to the table. "Let's see who's the winner."

Ondine felt sure she saw a gleam in his eye. Sure enough, the gleam became a full-blown twinkly glisten as he emptied both jars at once on to the table. The entire contents mushed and tinkled together in one messy coin pile.

Ondine's mouth fell open. He'd done it deliberately! Didn't he want to win?

"Oh dear, I guess I should have given that more thought." He gave a nonchalant shrug.

A giggle escaped Ondine's open mouth. Despite her best efforts, she couldn't make it stop.

Ma uncrossed her arms, but only so she could put her hands on her hips. "You two. You're incorrigible!"

Ondine snorted.

Ma conceded defeat. "Fine, call it a draw. Enjoy your morning off tomorrow."

Hamish grinned and sent Ondine a look that made things dart around inside her in an altogether quite lovely way. Then his face fell. "Morning off? I thought the winner got the day off?"

"Yes, but it's a draw, so a day off for one person becomes a morning off for two. Now, Margi's lot are still out the back, go join them."

Typical Ma, Ondine thought, always one step ahead.

* * *

As THEY WALKED out to the back garden, Ondine stayed a few paces behind Hamish.[4]

Soon she found herself under the full attention of her great-aunt.

"He must be mending his ways," Old Col volunteered as she took a seat under a tree to settle in for the night. "Although from the way he looks at you, Ondi, I can't vouch for how long it will last. Praise the heavens for a full moon, for there's nowhere to hide when Luna is watching us."

"How come he's not a ferret any more?" Ondine asked the question she'd been dying to know the answer to ever since Shambles changed into Hamish.

Her great-aunt gave a theatrical sigh and shook her head. "He must have found the motivation to break the spell. Let me think. What did I curse him with . . . "

*As if you could forget something like that.*

" . . . Clearly, he wants to be human again. What do *you* think is happening?"

"I have no idea."

"Surely you do. He's bonding with you, I'm positive. Which leads me to wonder, what powers do you have that you can reverse one of my spells?" Great Aunt Col fixed Ondine with a beady eye.

*Lurch* went something inside her belly.

Margi spotted them and came over. "Ondine, what happened to the fairy lights?" She pointed to the bundles of globes bunched up in a tree.

"Oh, sorry about that, I'll fix it," Ondine said, grateful for something to do other than be subjected to Old Col's inquisition. Bless Margi, she'd rescued Ondine just in time.

But when she made to climb up the stepladder, she wobbled and nearly fell off.

Help was at hand. Melody came to her aid and held the ladder steady. "Ondi, he's gorgeous," she whispered.

The bundle of fairy lights tangled in her hands. "Um, if you say so."

"Are you blind? He's absolutely divine," Melody said, fanning her face with her hand, pretending she'd become flustered.

"Cut it out!" Ondine hissed, desperately trying to stem the shaking in her hands and failing.

"He really likes you, too. I can tell by the way he looks at you. Do you think your mother will let him stay with you?"

"Oh, Melody, let it drop!" Ondine became even more anxious, but from the mischievous look in Melody's eyes, there was no way her friend would comply. As much as she loved thinking about Hamish, the thought of everyone else thinking about her and Hamish only added to her frustration. Her only chance of reprieve was to change the subject entirely. "So, Mrs Howser, yeah?"

It worked. Melody looked confused and crinkled her forehead. "What about her?"

"She and Old Col obviously go way back – they were less than pleased to see each other today." Ondine felt giddily pleased with herself for so successfully moving the topic on to something much safer.

"Oh yeah, way back. They were good friends, but I found out from Mrs Howser that they had a huge falling-out at a debutante ball of all places. By the way, are you thinking of doing your deb? My mother wants me to, but they're sooo last century. All those dance lessons just for one night of dressing up. I guess that's what they did before television."

Something sprigged Ondine's memory. Had Hamish, when he was Shambles, told her something like this? Except, more fool her, she hadn't been paying attention because her mind was full of Lord Vincent. "Mrs Howser told you all of that?" Now it was Ondine's turn to press for answers and watch Melody squirm.

"Not in so many words. I, um, sort of found out during an, uh, astral exercise."

That was seriously impressive. "Astral, eh? You're really doing well in that. And Mrs Howser has no idea you know all this?"

The conversation should have ended in them giggling, but what Melody said next made Ondine wish she'd never gone down this path.

"I think it was over Hamish. They each wanted the same man to partner them at the deb, but Old Col won out. But . . . I guess Col lost in the end, because Hamish got drunk and it all ended badly. You wouldn't think to look at them now, but those witches were both really pretty when they were our age."

"Talk about carrying a grudge. Just for a stupid dance," Ondine said.

"But if it was over Hamish, and he looked like that," Melody fanned her face with her hand again, "I can understand it!"

Ondine rolled her eyes. "Promise me we won't have a falling-out over something as silly as a dance?"

"Of course not. And we won't have a falling-out over Hamish either, because he's so taken with you nobody else could get a look-in."

Ondine's hands trembled with nerves and she dropped the bundle of lights on the ground.

## 11

Despite the late hour, Marguerite and Thomas's engagement party kept going strong. In between duties in the kitchen, Colette and Josef made regular appearances in the garden and were on their best behaviour around Thomas's folks.

All night Ondine fought hard to keep her focus on the party when the whole time her thoughts strayed to Hamish in human form. If only he'd stayed back in the kitchen, it would have been bearable, but he had to keep walking around with trays of food, making nice with everyone. Like this for instance:

"Can I tempt you?" he asked a group of Margi's friends, offering a tray of canapés.

The dirty flirt! The girls all smiled and giggled and took the morsels of food. As soon as his back was turned they huddled their heads together and tittered with suppressed laughter. The same thing happened to the next group he approached.

Frustrated, Ondine deliberately looked away from Hamish and saw Mrs Howser sitting at a table, with a mixed group of Thomas's friends. What could they have in common? Then she saw it: Mrs Howser upended a teacup on to her saucer and turned it back.

Inching closer, she heard the old lady's predictions. " . . . a carriage. You are going on a journey."

*Pfft, isn't everyone on a journey?* Ondine restrained her scorn but couldn't help rolling her eyes. Something she seriously had to stop doing, because it was starting to hurt the sockets.

"Read mine," a girl enthused.

"You'll need to drink the tea first. Infuse it with your aura."

"But I don't like tea."

Stifling a snort, Ondine made to leave, but her mother, who just happened to be passing at that moment, had other ideas. "Ask Ondi for your future – she'll read it in your palm."

A trickle of fear entered Ondine's soul. Expectant eyes turned to her. She felt trapped. She mouthed "no" to her mother in protest, but the woman ignored her.

*Is this Gang Up On Ondine Day?*

"But, Ma, I'm not –"

"You should have seen her the other day! She had the health inspector nailed, right down to how many children. We passed the inspection with flying colours, by the way."

"Read mine then." The same young woman who didn't like tea sprinted towards Ondine with her palm out. "Tell me what I'm in for."

"She has the gift, it's in her blood," Ma gushed.

Ondine didn't know what matricide meant, but she was having thoughts of it all the same.[1]

The window of opportunity to protest closed with a thud in her ears. The eager teenager held her palm out for inspection. The face that greeted Ondine looked so happy, so expectant. It would really sour the party mood if she refused. Promising to growl at her mother later, she set to work making stuff up.

"I'll need both hands. One palm is what you were born with, the other is what you make of it." She sensed Mrs Howser's eyes on her as she looked over the two palms. Scant weeks earlier, she'd fled Psychic Summercamp. Unfortunately it had followed her home. Time stretched. Nothing came into her head to help her out. Her own palms began to sweat. Her customer's palms were just soft mounds of flesh with lines on them. Pale, with a few blotches of red near the juncture of her fingers.

Eczema?

"You really need to watch out for allergies," Ondine blurted.

"Ohmigosh you're right! I get terrible hay fever and eczema. What else?"

When Ondine looked up at the girl's face, she saw her smile, and noticed the very pale gums around her teeth.

"Are you a vegetarian?"

"Not normally, but I've just started this new regime to see what sets me off. Wow. You're good!"

No, she wasn't good, if anything she'd just insulted her by insinuating she was low in iron. Hardly a sign from the heavens. The guesswork should have put her customer off, but all it did was make her eager for more "divine" instructions.

"You have a kind heart and like looking after people," Ondine said. Nobody in their right mind would disagree with that.

The girl withdrew her hands. "I nearly forgot," she said. "I need to cross your palm with silver, don't I? Otherwise it's bad luck." She drew a few coins from her purse and gave them to Ondine.

Money.

So that's why her mother was so keen to foster the psychic connection. They could make money from it! The realisation made her sick to her boots. It was one thing to engage in some harmless entertainment as a party trick, but when money was involved, it became outright fraud. "No, please, this is just for fun. Keep your money."

"Hardly." The girl protested. "Last thing I want is a gypsy curse hanging over me. I heard about what happened to your boyfriend."

Whoa, *boyfriend*?

"If you don't want the money, put it towards Margi's wedding." She told Ondine, "Now, tell me how I meet my husband, and how many children we'll have."

"I'm next," Ondine heard to her left. "Then me," another said. "Start a queue then," she heard her mother say.

Lurch went her stomach.

Fizz went her brain.
She was done for.

———

ASIDE FROM HER PALM-READING SWINDLE, the rest of the party was excellent. Less than half a dozen beer glasses broken, nobody came to blows, people laughed a lot, the police only came around twice to check on the noise and Margi and Thomas danced whenever the music played. The best part of the night – as far as Ondine was concerned – was Mrs Howser and Aunt Col retiring earlier than everyone else, both claiming "a headache". They'd probably sneaked into the front bar to continue bickering. Or raid the plütz supply more like. On the minus side, Hamish had spent the rest of the night walking among everyone. Correction, *flirting* among everyone, tempting people with plates of food. Whenever Ondine saw him, she had to fight the growing hunger pains in her tummy against the prospect of having her family see her talking with Hamish and making a fuss. It was best to keep clear of him completely and go hungry.

Da made a speech that started maudlin and got worse, lamenting about losing his oldest daughter, his first baby who would always be his baby. Funny, that – he'd told Ondine she'd always be his baby, that day at the train station. Surely by now he had to accept his three "babies" were allowed to grow up?

"It's difficult for me, with three daughters," he continued, looking at everyone through beer goggles.[2] "When I was Thomas's age, I could never understand why the girls I liked had such strict fathers. Now I do. It's because every young man out there is just like I used to be!"

People howled with laughter and thumped Thomas on the back.

"But seriously," Da continued, "Thomas, you're a real surprise package. You're one of the good ones, and I'm pleased as plütz to welcome you to the family."

To Ondine's complete surprise, the two men embraced in a manly hug. Her father was softening. Hooray for Margi!

Da's speech was tame compared to those made by Thomas's friends, which started in the gutter and ended up in the sewer. Margi blushed scarlet and Thomas yelled out, "Who invited you?"

"You did!" they yelled back.

"I don't know these people!" Thomas buried his head in his hands.

Poor Margi, she winced and cringed so much during the ribald speeches Ondine felt sorry for her. Although just for a moment it was a relief to have someone else become the centre of embarrassment. When the speeches were over, it was time for more dancing, so Ondine and Melody joined in with a large group of Margi and Thomas's friends. During one of the old-style progressive dances, Ondine twirled around the group and caught sight of Hamish standing in the doorway, watching her.

Of course, she had to trip right at that moment. Stupid shoes. When she looked up, Hamish was gone, thank goodness. She could get on with ignoring him properly.

"I see him looking at you," Marguerite said as she sidled up to Ondine. "Reminds me of the way Thomas used to look at me. He's working up the courage to ask you out."

"I doubt it." *I hope so.*

"Count on it." Margi gave her a warm hug, then cast her eyes back to her fiancé. "Would you look at that. Da and Thomas are into the plütz like old friends."

"Who would have thought it?" Ondine said. "Da's really coming round to the idea of Thomas joining the family."

"You can thank Ma for that, she brought him round. And Thomas too – he's been the perfect gentleman." Of course her sister would say that, being so madly in love with Thomas. Ondine tried to smile and be happy for her sister – truly she was – but sadness seeped in.

"Oh, Ondi, cheer up." Margi noticed right away, of course. "It may not seem so now, but one day you will be as happy as me. I know it."

---

Wʞᴇɴᴠ ᴛʜᴇ ʟᴀᴀ... When the last of the guests left around three in the morning, Ondine hobbled to a bench under the fairy lights and rubbed her aching feet. It felt good to soothe the knots and aches. As she massaged the sore skin, she felt as if someone were watching her.

"Yer family puts on a fine ceilidh."[3]

Hamish approached with a plate of hors d'oeuvres.[4]

Ondine tucked her feet underneath her skirts to hide how ugly her toes looked from being squished and mashed all night. She made to speak but her mouth went dry.

"Ye havnae eaten all night. If I didn't know any better, I'd say ye've been avoiding me, lass."

"Don't be silly," she said, surprised that she managed three words when her throat felt so parched.

"Here, eat." Hamish grabbed Ondine's hand, making her hold the plate of food. At his touch, heat shot up her arm and she stared at the food, her appetite nowhere to be found.

"I like being human again," Hamish said, tilting his head down so he could make eye contact with her lowered gaze.

A lock of dark hair fell over his forehead. An ache started in Ondine's heart. Heavens above, he was so handsome a girl could completely lose her head. As if to deny her feelings, she picked up a slice of savoury tart and shoved it into her mouth. It didn't matter that only moments ago she'd been touching her feet and her hands were probably covered in germs. All she wanted to do was stuff her mouth with food so that she didn't say something stupid.

Ordinarily she loved Chef's food. No wonder Cybelle had fallen for him – the man cooked like an angel! Yet right now, Ondine couldn't taste anything because the presence of this Scot had invaded all her senses and turned the food to dust.

---

HAMISH VERY much wanted to kiss Ondine, there and then. She'd suddenly gone shy, and that wasn't like her. But then, he'd also gone a bit shy, and that wasn't like him at all.

"Ondi, do ye still like me?" She couldn't still be thinking about Lord Vincent, could she?

Before the lass could answer, Chef and Cybelle walked out, each with one of those pull-along shopping trolleys grannies love so much.

"There you are. Time for market," Cybelle said.

"Wh-ut?" Ondine's voice didn't come out the right way to Hamish's ears. He was having trouble working out how to make words as well. They were under some kind of new, restricting spell that handicapped regular speech. Normally he had no problem on the chatty front. What was the point of being himself again if he talked gibberish with the girl he wanted to impress?

"We always go to market at this time," Chef said, "Seeing as you're both up, you can help."

"Happy to help," Hamish managed. He had to start repaying their hospitality somehow.

As if sharing an unspoken thought, Cybelle nodded at Chef and took his hand. Then they walked together out the side gate. It gave Hamish an idea. He held his hand out for Ondine. For a moment he wasn't sure if she got the clue, until she blinked and slipped her hand in his. Warmth surged up his arm and into his heart at the contact. Her soft, small hand in his felt absolutely perfect, as if it belonged there. Then she smiled and he beamed back, his brain momentarily at a loss for something sensible to say.

So unlike him.

They walked, hand in hand, a few paces behind Cybelle and Chef, in the dark pre-dawn morning. The streets were quiet, broken only by the sounds of their footsteps.

Their paces fell into a natural rhythm as they reached the market, and found themselves looking upon a hidden world of traders and businesses that were never seen by everyday people. The kind of people who valued their sleep.

Lanterns of every shape and colour hung from the rafters to light the way. Even at this early hour, the markets were teeming with people like ants around a banana skin.

They crossed the street where Belle and Chef had already gone, falling further behind. Ondine leaned closer to Hamish, "Stick close to me, it can get pretty crowded. If you get lost, we'll meet back at this corner, OK?"

"Not a problem," holding her hand just that little bit tighter.

For someone used to seeing the world from ankle height, the early morning market proved an exciting and daunting place for Hamish. It was something like a mixture between a madhouse and a stockyard. Stalls filled with chickens squashed up beside grocers selling mountains of fresh vegetables and fruit. And the smell! Animals, fresh fruit, bruised fruit, vegetables, flowers and spices all mixed in his nostrils. How nasty would it be to get here any later? The heat of the day would stink the place right up.

"How much for the box of oranges," Ondine asked one of the traders.

"For a beautiful girl, only five schlips," the grocer said with a beaming smile.

"Five! Do I look like I'm made of money? I'll give you three," Ondine haggled.

"I have five daughters to marry off, be gentle with me. Four and a half."

"They're all mushed underneath the top layer, I bet. Three and a half, and that's my final offer."

Hamish stood there, trying to keep his jaw from falling as he watched Ondine beat the price down, all the while she kept smiling and being so very nice about sending the grocer broke.

With pantomime agony, the grocer said, "Take it, please, before I leap into the river."

"Done! Hamish, grab that box please," Ondine handed over the money.

The grocer cast a look at Hamish, "This man, he is your husband?"

"Oh no, he's just here for the muscles."

"In that case, Muscles, come back later and meet my daughters, you'll have to marry one of them as I can no longer afford to feed them."

Ondine dismissed his banter. "Follow me Hamish."

In another lifetime, Hamish wouldn't have been seen dead in a market, haggling with people. Shopping just wasn't his thing. Yet, here, with Ondine as his guide, he found himself happily following her around the stalls, carrying all her goods without complaint.

Smiling, no less! What was wrong with him?

He'd never felt this… strange and yet comforting sense of … domestic life. Perhaps it was the effects of being human again, of experiencing life as it should be. Or maybe the joy came from being around Ondine.

The next sight made his insides clench tight for all the wrong reasons.

Ferrets. In cages. Piled five high. It was too much to bear and he shut his eyes. Acid burned his gut. Nasty things moved in his throat so he swallowed hard.

"Oh dear." Ondine said as she saw the caged animals.

The girl had the good sense not to make a scene. "Can we move on?" Hamish looked away, mind reeling at the thought that it could well be him going stir crazy in one of those the tiny cages.

*There but for Old Col go I.*

"Why don't we buy them and set them free?" Ondine asked.

In his heart he knew she was trying to be helpful. Setting ferrets free? Where would they go? He'd been lucky, he'd landed on his feet when he'd met Ondine.

He thought about talking to them, asking what they wanted. Then he realised he couldn't. The noise they made was just that, noise. He couldn't understand them any more than Ondine could.

"Let's get out of here," he hefted the boxes of fruit and vegetables and moved them away.

"Are you all right? You're looking mockit."

Hearing one of his words with her accent sounded twee, but it had a serendipitous effect in that he momentarily forgot the nausea brought on from seeing his fellow ferrets in a cage.

"It's OK. I just wasnae expecting to see that. They won't be sold for food or fur, if that's what yer worried about. They'll be sold for rabbit hunting."[5]

Ondine gave him a sympathetic look, before she moved towards a display of pumpkins the colour of the morning sun. It was clear to him she hadn't bought his explanation, but she wasn't pressing him on it either.

A woman who left a man alone to his thoughts. What a marvel. The tension eased from his shoulders and he fell in line behind Ondine.

After an hour more of shopping and haggling, Ondine and Hamish carried their boxes of food to the street corner, where they waited for the others.[6]

"Chef and Belle should be back soon," Ondine craned her neck to see above the milling crowd. The sun was coming up, but the extra light didn't help find her sister. "I'm too short. Help me stack these boxes."

Doing as he was told, Hamish piled the boxes on top of each other, so she could climb up and see over people's heads. He held her hand steady; enjoying the warm buzz from touching her skin.

*Errant thoughts eh? What can you do about them?*

With a shudder, Ondine's balance failed and she wobbled on the top box. His heart lurched. In a flash he grabbed her around the waist and pulled her close. "It's OK, I've got you," he said.

She slipped further down in his arms and they were nose to nose. "So you have," she said, sounding breathless.

From behind his ribs, Hamish's heart came alive as he held this feisty young woman in his arms. "Did ye see Chef or Belle while you were up there?"

"No, I didn't."

"So they could be a while then?" He was fascinated by how much Ondine's eyes were dilating.

"Yes," it came out as a breath. "Could be."

A voice inside his head said, "I've lost my mind. I've gone and fallen in love." And then a moment later, another voice in his head said, "Good for me, then."

If he kissed her now, would she kiss him back?

A new – female – voice, piped in from the sidelines. "Are you right there?" It was Belle, standing beside Chef, both of them dragging their filled trolleys behind them. "We have to get all of this back into the cool room."

Although they'd pulled away at the rude intrusion, Hamish found himself unable to wipe the smile off his face. And from the flushed look of Ondine, perhaps his feelings would be reciprocated.

Something lurched behind Hamish's ribs.

*One spell broken, another taking its place?*

Pulling the trolleys behind them, Belle and Chef were able to hold hands on the walk back. No such luck for Ondine and Hamish, they hefted their boxes of food and couldn't relax until they got back to the hotel.

If her sister hadn't interrupted them at the market, Ondine felt sure Hamish would have kissed her. Would he try again? She hoped so as she made her way out to the garden to wait for the sunrise.

"I need to tell ye something, Ondi." Hamish's hand touched the back of hers.

Ondine's heart started racing in her chest and the skin on her arm puckered into goosebumps.

"Yer cold." He took his jacket off and placed it around Ondine's shoulders. "There, fits ye better than me anyway."

A nod was all she could manage.

"Ye don't like me anymore?"

Ondine gulped as her throat constricted. "No, that's not true," she replied, but she didn't say anything else because her brain had stopped working properly. She didn't say, "Hamish, I like you too much," or "Hamish, you're the most handsome man I've ever met," or "Hamish, you'd better ask me to marry you or I'm going to die right now." Although her thoughts took her exactly along those lines.

"I'm no psychic, so I can't read yer mind. But I'll tell ye what's on mine," he started.

Ondine forgot how to breathe.

"I've taken Old Col's advice to heart. I need to mend my ways. Tonight has shown me that. I have it in me, I can reclaim my life, and make it a good life too."

Hamish shifted on the garden bench, and angled himself towards her. "Ondi, can ye please look at me? I want to know ye don't hate me."

It took an almost superhuman effort, but somehow she managed to get her head to turn enough, and her eyelids to lift enough, so she could look him in the face. Not his twinkling eyes, which would hurt her heart too much if she looked deeply into them. She settled for his lips. That was a mistake, because the moment she looked at his mouth she wanted to kiss it.

*Stupid hormones. Turning me into an idiot.*

"You've shown me that it's noble to be useful. To be part of a family. I've never had that before . . ."

What he said didn't make sense, because she barely heard half of it over her hammering heart. Was he saying he wanted to stay with her family, or was he about to return to his in Scotland?

"I've asked yer ma and da if it's all right if I can stay here. Just until I find me feet, like."

*Yippee! Hamish is staying. Hamish is staying. Hamish is staying. Oh dear, did I say that out loud?*

"I've relied on other people's charity for too long. I need to find my own way."

Hey? Had she missed a segue? One moment he was talking about staying, then he talked about leaving. She wished he'd make up his mind!

Then he seriously overstepped the mark and took Ondine's hands completely in his. "Do me a favour and keep away from Lord Vincent."

Fury took hold and her breath hitched. She pulled her hands away and felt her palms grow itchy. Oh, how she wanted to slap his smug face! It was bad enough that he was so beautiful, that she was sure he was about to kiss her in the market, that he said such lovely things right now . . . before ruining it all.

"You sound just like Da."

"I want you to be happy, and I don't think Lord Vincent would make you happy."

"So I'm not even allowed to have some fun?" she blurted out.

Hamish looked into her eyes and a lopsided grin changed his face from serious to gleeful. "Aye, a girl like you should have some fun."

The reprieve gave Ondine a chance to collect herself. Anyone else would have patronised her, treated her like a child, but not Hamish. Guilt stabbed her heart. She owed him the same courtesy.

"Hamish?" She hesitated, not knowing what to say next. It was right that he couldn't stay indefinitely. Her parents were pretty generous, coping with everything that had transpired, but generosity has its limits.

He leant closer, his eyes focused on her lips. Closer. Closer, his lips descended towards hers. His eyes closed, hers followed suit, her heart hammering with anticipation and belly turning flip-flops as she waited for his lips to touch hers.

To her utter dismay, his lips touched her cheek instead.

"Jupiter's moons!" she exclaimed. If this was to be their first kiss (hopefully of many), she wanted it to be a good one. Seizing her chance, she held Hamish's face in her hands and pressed her lips directly to his.

An arrow-fast jolt of lust shot through Ondine and her breath caught. His lips felt so warm and inviting, the pressure not much more than chaste but the contact made her whole body buzz and fizz. Time locked around the two of them, extending the moment, filling her heart with a strange mixture of elation and pride. She'd kissed him, really kissed him, and hadn't botched it up.

Hamish pulled back, his shining eyes locked with hers. The smile he gave her sent warm flurries all around her.

"Ye shouldnae done that," he said, sounding like he, too, was short of breath.

"Why not?"

"Because now I have tae do this," he said, parting his lips and pressing them back to Ondine's, coaxing her to open to him. She nearly lost her mind at the intimate contact and the swathe of sweet and strange sensations roaring through her body. The kiss deepened and she heard a soft moan escape from Hamish. Tiny electric shocks danced over her lips.

His chin felt prickly against her plump skin. Beard whiskers grazed her.

"Ouch." She pulled back and rubbed her fingertips over her inflamed skin.

A half-embarrassed grin spread over her face. Her first pash-rash? Expecting to see the same delight in his expression, she met his eyes just as they were turning from green to black.

Matching black fur spread over his face.

"Oh no, not now!" A heavy weight grabbed at her heart.

"What?" Hamish managed before he doubled over in pain, clutching at his belly. He reached to Ondine for support, and the skin over the back of his hand turned black and furry.

The sun rose for the new day, casting the beer garden into pink-orange light. The full moon was gone. A pile of second-hand clothes sat lifeless on the ground. Where Hamish the man had been, now sat Shambles the ferret.

**12**

---

Swearing. Some people are good at it, some people trip over their tongues. Take the not-yet-sixteen Ondine, for example. Her swearing wasn't very advanced, because she'd had a reasonably protected life so far – as protected as a person can be while living in a pub.

For example, when she becomes frustrated or shocked, she will just as likely say "Jupiter's moons!" as "Clutterbuck!" (or something sounding very much like that). On the other hand, Shambles, who up until now had managed not to swear too much in front of the de Groot family, proved himself proficient in profanity.

"Ye chanty wrassler, A'll dun't ye!"[1]

His accent came back thick and strong. "A'll gar ye claw whaur it's no yeukie!"[2]

"A'll saut yer brose, Old Col!"[3]

"Ma tongue isna unner yer belt!"[4]

Despite the accent, some of his further swearing required no translation, which only made Ondine's face burn with shame. Those lips she'd just kissed spewed forth the most fearsome curses.

"Shambles, please calm down!" Her heart ached for the man he'd been not a moment ago. How horribly unfair that he should revert like this. Could the timing be any worse?

Despite her pleas, Shambles would not be stopped. He swore some more, with a few new expressions. After he'd exhausted his repertoire, he went back to the start and repeated the tirade all over again.

It was too cruel, watching him writhe about on the ground, her handsome young man reduced to ferret form again. Ondine felt her heart constrict, tied up like one of Chef's string roasts. Heat seared her face and eyes. Something wet splashed on her cheeks. Oh for shame, she was crying! What was the point of trying to behave – and be treated – like an adult, if she ended up blubbering like a child who'd just found out Santa wasn't real.[5]

"What's all the racket?" Ma said, as she came out to the garden and took in the scene of Ondine crying with a black ferret at her feet. "What did he do to you?"

"It's yer mad auntie, she's struck me down again, and I didnae do anything!" Shambles complained, rubbing his furry paws over his head in anguish.

"We only kissed," Ondine said, surprised to hear her words come out as a croak.

"That's highly inappropriate, Ondine de Groot," Ma said.

It's a sure sign of trouble when parents use your full name. Ondine knew better than to argue with her parents when they were in a foul mood.[6]

Actually, arguing with them at any point often proved a waste of time because she seldom emerged the winner. But all good sense had flown because their Beautiful Kiss had ended too soon, as had Hamish's human form. "It was just a kiss," she found herself repeating in a tone that implied it didn't really matter, when in reality it really, really did matter. It mattered a whole lot.[7]

She'd become good friends with Shambles the ferret, but Hamish the young man seemed the answer to her dreams. How long had she imagined what he'd be like as a real person? Then to get a glimpse of his true self, to let him into her heart – only to have it taken away so soon. Could life become any crueller?

Shambles resumed swearing. Loudly and lustily.

"Get inside, Ondine. I'd like to speak to Shambles alone," Ma said.

"You're so unfair." Ondine wiped the tears off her face with the back of her hand. "I'm not a baby, so stop treating me like one!"

"We'll stop treating you like one when you stop behaving like one," Ma shot back.

In frustration, Ondine's hands balled into fists. This was an argument she couldn't win, but she'd try anyway. "You were my age when you and Da got together, so that makes you a hypocrite as well!"

"It was different then –" Ma started.

"Oh, blow it out your ear!"

Things went very silent. Ondine slapped her hand over her mouth in shock. She'd never spoken to her mother like that before, and the power of it made her heart hammer against her ribs.

Ma stood there, mouth agape. Even Shambles stopped swearing and moaning on the ground.

With lips pressed into two straight lines of fury, Ma straightened her shoulders and drew herself up to her full height, which was a couple of centimetres short of her youngest child. When had her mother shrunk so? Ondine wondered about this for a nanosecond before they resumed the mother–daughter showdown.

Her voice low and dangerous, Ma said, "Show some respect for your elders."

"Is that the best you can come up with? Speaking to me like I'm a child? Ma, I'm nearly sixteen. I'm allowed to kiss whoever I like!"

"It wasnae her fault," Shambles piped up. "It was all me doing. I took advantage of her, and that must be why I'm a ferret again. I had lusty thoughts and didnae feel worthy of her."

Confusion knotted Ondine's brain. Their encounter had been nothing like Shambles described. The way she remembered it, Hamish had given her a chaste kiss on the cheek, and she'd demanded more. Her cheeks flushed with heat.

"It's "whomever". Now get inside, Ondine – you're overtired."[8]

It must have been pure aggravation that made Ondine say what she said next, because no rational person would have blurted it out.

"Oh yeah, fine, send me to my room. But while you've been so busy spying on me, you haven't even noticed that Cybelle and Chef are making eyes at each other."

"She's just saying things. Don't listen to her," Shambles said, but his intervention made no impact.

The colour drained from Ma's face and for the first time in Ondine's memory, her mother was at a loss for words.

A huge theatrical yawn escaped Shambles's little mouth, as if he'd given up on both of them. Or he just wanted to clear the area for the oncoming catfight. "I did me best, ye wouldnae listen. I'm for the laundry. Goodnight, ladies."

Heavy, nasty guilt sank into Ondine's feet. She couldn't move. She'd just dropped her sister right in it, and Cybelle had done nothing to deserve it. If Ondine believed she was entitled to happiness, weren't her sisters entitled to the same?

Which made her a hypocrite of the highest order.

Between clenched teeth, her mother said, "Go. To. Your. Room."

Something made Ondine's feet move, although her brain felt so fogged she had no idea how she managed to find the way to her bedroom and crawl under the covers.

Sunlight pierced daggers through the curtain gaps. She feared sleep because of the frightening dreams that might come her way. Should she stay awake and feel miserable, or fall asleep and have her subconscious make her feel worse?

In the end, the choice was not hers to make. Despite the beams of early morning light in her room, Ondine passed into unconsciousness, just before the worst few hours of her life unfolded.

**13**

———

Ondine had the strangest sensation of having had a particularly awful dream. Shambles had become a real man, and a stunningly handsome one at that, but then some force took it all away and he was back to being a ferret.

As her brain clicked and whirred into wakefulness, she knew it was no dream. Waking up further, she sprang out of bed and clutched her stomach. She wanted to be sick, and for so many reasons. Last night, she'd made a fool of herself in front of Hamish and in front of her mother. Topping it off, she'd robbed her middle sister of any privacy she might have enjoyed while her parents were distracted with Margi and Thomas.

There was a choice to be made. Get out of bed and face her mother and sister or stay in her room forever.

A staccato rap on the door put paid to any notion that the choice was hers to make.

"Ondi, get up, family meeting," Da said.

"I want at her first," Cybelle said. With an angry look that could strip paint, Cybelle burst into her room and slammed the door behind her. Black panda smudges circled her eyes where the neat eyeliner used to be.

Nasty, heavy things tumbled around in Ondine's stomach.

"How dare you!" Cybelle's face was red with fury. "Do you have any idea what you've done? Henrik's going to get the sack because of you!"

"I'm . . . I'm sorry," Ondine blurted. Hot tears sprang into her eyes and blurred her vision. Who was Henrik again? Oh yeah, that's what Chef's name used to be, before he was Chef. "I'm so sorry, Cybelle. I didn't mean it. I was so angry with Ma . . . it . . . it . . . just came out."

Cybelle stood there with her hands on her hips, her lips pressed white in a hard, straight line. Just as her mother's had been the night before.

"Sorry's not good enough! You've just ruined my life. I hope you're happy!"

With that, Cybelle slapped her hard on the cheek.

Pain seared Ondine's face, but she didn't put up a fight. "I deserved that." Tears welled again. "Belle, I'm so sorry, I really a –"

Cybelle slapped her other cheek, spreading the pain. Behind Cybelle, Da charged in and grabbed his middle daughter in a bear hug.

"That's enough!"

Cybelle flailed her arms, kicked her legs out and screamed so hard bits of spit flew out of her mouth, "I hate her, I hate her! She's not my sister!"

"Calm down, love. It's all right, I'll not sack Chef."

A new batch of tears sprang from Ondine, and she covered her face in shame. Heavy guilt roiled in her stomach and curdled her brain. All she wanted to do was stay in her room and cry. Her father would have none of it, demanding her attendance downstairs.

Not caring what she looked like, Ondine shrugged on a dressing gown and trudged down to the gathering. Old Col sat regally at the top of the table, while Shambles stood before her, pleading his case.

"What did ye do to me, Col? I thought ye lifted the spell."

"I did," the elderly woman said with a tired shrug. "I'm as much in the dark about this as you. My only guess is the full moon must have played some part. We all know there's nowhere to hide on the night of a full moon."

"Spare yer epithets," Shambles said.

Da's mouth fell open in surprise. "Ondi, I can hear him talk now."

If her father could hear Shambles, it would save time with translations. It also eroded any last vestiges of privacy she might have had with him. Not that she deserved any privacy after what she'd blurted out about Cybelle last night.

Shambles nodded to Ondine to acknowledge her entrance, then resumed his pleading to Old Col, throwing his short arms around as he talked.

"But I didnae do anything wrong. We all know that. I was being responsible for the first time in my *life*. It was just a kiss, it was never going tae go any further. Why would that make me turn back into . . . into this?"

Just a kiss had been the same words Ondine had used. They were a lie so she could save face. But hearing Hamish-as-Shambles say it to someone else, with everyone listening, well, that was a different matter entirely. Maybe to him it was just a kiss, but to her it was everything.

Old Col looked at the ferret. "Ah, but you see, Hamish, maybe this isn't a punishment after all. Maybe the full moon shone a light on the kind of man you could be." Her eyes glistened with confidence.

Ondine had no idea what the old woman was banging on about. Forget sage advice, this was more like scratching around for answers like a chicken in a compost heap.

"Enough of that," Da said, taking his seat at the other end of the table and pulling Ondine down beside him. Cybelle sat across from them so she could shoot her sister filthy looks. The fact that Cybelle also sat beside Chef was not lost on anyone, particularly Josef.

Incredibly, Ma stayed quiet as Shambles approached Ondine and climbed on to the crook of her arm. If this had been last night, if he'd been a man again, his touch would have sent searing heat into her bloodstream.

But it was the morning. He was a ferret again. What a passion killer!

"I am sorry about last night. I'm sorry I made ye cry," Shambles said.

"It's not your fault," Ondine managed, giving him a wan smile that didn't reach her eyes. Maybe he was a ferret again because she didn't want him to leave. Wasn't that what she'd been turning over in her head yesterday? If he became human again, he'd probably leave. If he remained a ferret, he'd stay with her.

The head of the household cleared his throat and directed his comments to Chef. "I have a blinding headache from last night, so excuse my lack of manners. Henrik, I want to know what your intentions are with Cybelle."

They could all tell by Da's clipped tone that it was not a request. And he'd called Chef by his real name for the first time in ages. Ondine's heart sank. Their father had been softening so nicely lately – now he seemed to have reverted to caveman mentality.

Cybelle kept her head bowed, her hands clenched into fists on the table. Every now and then she lifted her eyes to shoot Ondine a greasy look of utter contempt, before resuming her sulk.

Nobody said anything for a few seconds as everyone else's eyes fell on Henrik.

When Henrik spoke, his voice was quiet but determined. "No, Josef. It's private. This is something between me and Cybelle, no one else."

In shock, Cybelle lifted her head and smiled as she looked with pride at her paramour. Henrik glanced back at Cybelle, and traced his fingers over her white knuckles.

Nothing came out of Da for a moment, such was his surprise. He swallowed and started again. Like a spluttering lawn mower, it took a while before he got a good spin going. "You will tell me, because it concerns my daughter, and your tenure here as an employee," he demanded.

So he was about to sack him? Ondine couldn't believe how nasty her father sounded.

"Remind me never to play poker with your da," Shambles whispered.

"I heard that," Josef said, turning his now-famous frosty stare towards Ondine, which nailed her to the spot. After he'd turned her blood to ice, he looked over everyone at the table. "Who else heard him? Show of hands."

Gradually, everybody raised a hand to about shoulder height, even Henrik.

"All of you?" Ondine blurted.

They nodded. Her heart sank. There really was no privacy in a large family. Judging by the extra people sitting around the table, hers was about to get larger.

Shambles piped up, "That's great news! If ye can all hear me, it must mean the spell is breaking."

Da turned to Henrik, waiting for an answer from his earlier question.

Henrik kept his voice low and steady as his eyes locked with Josef's. "Mr de Groot, if you sack me, you'll be minus a chef. I'll go and find another job. But it won't stop me seeing Cybelle. Only Cybelle can decide that."

A strange icy feeling spread through the room. "That's right," Cybelle said in little more than a whisper as she touched Henrik's arm for support. "If Henrik goes, I'll go too. Then you'll be short one chef and one daughter."

Blotches of red bloomed on Da's face, while the veins on his neck doubled in size and threatened to burst. Ondine felt she might be sick from all the excitement.

"What he means is, he wants what's best for Belle," Ma interrupted. "We want you to be happy, sweetheart."

"My head is killing me," Da said by way of explanation. "I know this is coming out wrong, but this is all a big shock to me."

Henrik spoke again, "It's only an hour till lunch, so if you want to sack me, better do it now, otherwise I've got work to do." At that he rose from his seat.

Josef said nothing more.

Henrik kissed the top of Cybelle's head, not gloating in victory, just confirming that he and Cybelle were united. A team.

A stab of jealousy pierced Ondine's heart as she watched her mother wrap her arms around Da's shoulders in comfort, while Margi rested her head on Thomas's shoulder.

Hope sank like a stone as she sat there with a talking ferret instead of the real man he should be, a real man she could fall in love with.

Things then took a turn for the worse as Ma looked towards her.

"Ondine, you may give me that apology now."

It would have been so convenient if Melody or even Mrs Howser had come in at that point, to break the tension. No luck – they were sleeping off the party. As they weren't family, they'd been spared the meeting. A hard lump formed in Ondine's throat as she swallowed. She'd never shouted at her mother like she had last night, and it called for a grovelling apology. Everyone was looking at her, and it made it that much harder to deliver when all she wanted to do was crawl into a cave. Preferably one with a big rock she could shove over the entrance. Life as a hermit held tremendous appeal.

"I'm sorry, Ma." Ondine's voice was barely above a whisper as she bowed her head.

"Didn't quite catch that," Ma shot back.

Ondine tried to swallow again. "I'm sorry, Ma." This time it came out like a squeak, but it was louder and at least her mother would hear it.

"For what?"

Ondine lifted her head and looked directly in her mother's eyes. "I'm sorry, Ma, for being rude to you last night, and for answering back, and for implying you talk out of your ear." Tears blurred her vision.

Ma smiled and said, "Thank you, I appreciate that. Now you may apologise to Cybelle."

Oh great, she had to go through it all over again.

"I'm so deeply sorry, Belle, for betraying your trust and telling Ma about something I shouldn't have."

"I don't accept it. You had no right to say anything, you –"

"Belle, that's enough," Da interrupted.

An uncomfortable silence descended around the table.

Ma cleared her throat. "Good. Now go to your room, Ondine. You're grounded until I say so. I'll let you say goodbye to Melody and Mrs Howser, but that's it. And then we'll talk about changing your electives for school. Joining the ski team is no longer an option."

Something heavy drained out of Ondine. It could have been her fighting spirit, or perhaps her sense of justice. Had her parents just taken her choices away from her? For what? Gossiping about her sister? She couldn't move her legs. Shock rooted her to the spot.

"You're going to take my ski lessons from me because I was rude?"

Da spoke up. "No, we'll need to change your electives because we can't afford them any more. You'll need to choose classes that have the least number of excursions and the cheapest textbooks. We now have two weddings to plan and they cost more than your education."[1]

"What?" Cybelle looked shocked. "Why should I get married? I'm not getting married! Nobody gets married any more."

"I don't care how modern you think you are, there are some traditions I insist on. You are getting married. That is one argument you will not win," Ma said.

Forget her sister not wanting to get married, Ondine was still reeling about her curtailed studies. "But what about all the jewellery and money you kept?"

It was Ma's turn to blush. "It's gone, Ondi. We spent it on renovations. That's why we couldn't afford to close the dining room last night. We need everything we can get."

Shame and frustration made Ondine's chin wobble out of control. To add to her misery, she felt hot splashes of unrestrained tears on her cheeks.

*Just kill me now, my life is over.*

"And leave Shambles here. He's not to be in your room again."

"I'm sorry, lass," Shambles said, leaning up to give her a cold, wet and a little bit whiskery kiss on her neck.

There was nothing for Ondine to do but trudge up to her room and rot.

**14**

---

A couple of hours after the horrible and soul-destroying family meeting, somebody tapped lightly at Ondine's bedroom door.

"What?" she moaned, not even bothering to disguise the misery in her voice.

"It's only me," Melody whispered. "Can I come in?"

"I'm grounded. I'm not allowed to have friends anymore."

Melody came in anyway, and closed the door behind her with a soft click. "I heard about what happened. It's awful."

As she stepped closer, Ondine noticed the girl had a floppy, leather-bound notebook in her hand.

"You'll have to narrow it down. It's *all* awful," Ondine said, wiping her nose on her sleeve. "Hamish turned back into a ferret, Cybelle hates me, I'm grounded, and my parents can't afford to pay for the classes I want to do because they want Belle and Chef to get married. Be careful Ma doesn't find you in here – she'll ground you too."

"She can't ground me," Melody said.

"Nah, you're right, she'll just ground me twice." Ondine sighed. Pitifully, with all the pathos she could muster, she said, "I know why they call it grounding – because it grinds you into the dust and makes you give up hope."

"Then I came just in time. Look what I found." Melody held out the book for Ondine to see.

It looked soft and old on the outside, and inside the pages had handwritten notes, except for the ones at the back that were left blank.

"It's someone's diary. But it's hard to read because the writing's all scrunched up," Ondine said.

The diary pages had a well-preserved feel about them, as if it had been sealed up in the dark somewhere for a long time.

"I think it's Old Col's," Melody offered, her eyes opening wide with wonder.

"Where did you find it?" Ondine tried to make out the scrawled handwriting. Squinting didn't work. She held the pages further away from her face. That didn't work either. "It's all just scrawl, page after page of it."

They looked at the pages in silence, trying to make sense of the bunched-up lettering. "Where did you find it, Mel?" Ondine asked again.

"Um . . . Look at this page, I think I can make out what it says."

Avoiding the question confirmed Ondine's suspicion. "Did you steal it?"

"Oh no, I would never steal," Melody said, making a crossing movement over her right breast.

"The heart's on the left side."

Hastily, Melody made a crossing motion over her left breast before confessing, "It came to me in a dream."

Ondine's jaw fell open in shock. "You went into Old Col's dreams? How did you do that without her knowing?"

For a moment Melody found something interesting to look at on the bedspread. "I'm getting pretty good at it," she admitted.

"Not good enough," a strong voice said from the doorway.

They both looked up to see Old Col standing there.

"You really must be more careful with your dream-catching, young lady," Old Col said, walking in. "Honestly, it was all I could do not to burst into a fit of giggles. I haven't seen anyone that cack-handed since . . . well, Howser never was any good at it, and now she's passing on her mistakes to you. Come on, make room on that bed for an old lady, I need to rest my bones."

Too shocked to question their instructions, the girls moved apart and made room for Old Col between them. The woman took her sweet time lowering her frame to the bed.

"If you knew Mel was in your dream, why didn't you hide the diary?" Ondine asked.

"Because this way was much more fun," her great-aunt said, and added a wicked laugh. "For a girl who's grounded, you sure got a lot of company. Shambles, you can get out from under the bed now."

Confused and stunned, Ondine picked her feet up and folded them under herself, then peered over the edge of the bed to see Shambles slink out from underneath. "When did you get in there?"

"Sorry, Ondi. I was going to say something . . . but . . . well . . . it would have been rude to interrupt," he said. For a ferret, he looked a bit sheepish.

"Right, Mel, pay attention," Old Col said. "This is my diary, and I let you find it, because I am old and I get my fun when I can. Naturally, you can't read it because I wrote it in code. Shambles, Ondi, this concerns you both because I've got the spell I used on Hamish in here somewhere. Right, let's find the page I'm after . . ." She licked a wrinkled finger and stabbed at the page corners to turn them over. "Getting close now, hmm, no, can't read that out, that's private, OK, next page, no, that's private as well."

This went on for some time, and Ondine couldn't help fidgeting and wondering whether anyone else would walk past and notice all the people in her room. She darted a quick look at Melody and saw that she, too, was fidgeting.

"Now it gets interesting, I've just met a handsome young laird called Hamish McPhee, and he's utterly charming." Old Col lifted her eyes from the diary and glanced at the ferret. "That would be you then."

A weird feeling overcame Ondine. She wanted to know everything that had happened between Hamish and Old Col at that fateful debutante ball, but at the same time she wasn't sure she really wanted to know. Or at least, she knew she wanted to know, but it felt awkward knowing that Old Col would know that she knew. And Melody too.

"Found it. I thought Hamish wanted to court me, but he's not interested, just like all the oth– . . . um, let's see what else I've written."

Ondine could have sworn her great-aunt was blushing. What had she nearly said? It sounded suspiciously like "all the others", which meant exactly what?

Maybe she hadn't been an old prude her whole life. Then another, scarier thought pinged across her brain. If she'd turned Hamish into a ferret for messing up her debutante ball, what else was she capable of?

"What others?" Hamish stood up to his full height (which wasn't very tall) and put his hands on the equivalent of where his hips should be if he were a man. "How much others have you turned into like me?"

A tingling sensation stole over Ondine's skin and she silently thanked Hamish for asking the question she dared not utter. This could get very juicy. They just had to stay quiet and let it unfold. Now, if she could just find a way to let Melody know about shutting up, they could –

"You mean there are others like Hamish?" Melody blurted out.

Too late!

"Do you want to hear the curse or not?" Old Col said, her voice sounding testy as she scanned through the pages. "Because I can very well take the diary and go."

"Please stay, Aunt Col," Ondine begged. "We need to hear the curse so we can figure out how to reverse it permanently."

"You girls remind me so much of how we used to be, Birgit and I. We were good friends – we used to do everything together. I'm not sure how, but as we got older, we started to get pretty competitive. I had my gifts, she had hers. When Hamish came on the scene, our competitive streak turned to jealousy. We should have known Hamish had a mind of his own, but each of us thought we could control him. I . . . gosh, I can't believe I did this, but I cast a spell on him just to drag his sorry self to the debutante ball in the first place. He was such a handsome man. Quite turned my head. Ah dear, the things we do. It seemed so important then, but in hindsight, vanity got the better of me. Just once, I wanted to feel like a princess. Birgit was so much better looking than me, y'see. But I had Hamish on my arm for the ball."

For a moment the old woman batted her eyes as if she might be crying, then she righted herself and kept going.

"Everybody was looking at me, and I felt wonderful. Birgit was furious and said she'd never speak to me again. But it didn't matter at the time because I had Hamish. Only, the enchantment started to wear off because alcohol and free will have a stronger pull than magic. I wasn't to know that at the time, having never touched the stuff until that point in my life.[1] If I'd just let Hamish have his say beforehand, he might have partnered me anyway. But you see, I was too jealous of Birgit. I wanted to make sure I had the best date. So I made him think he wanted to dance all night with me. Except he came to his senses soon enough and knew I'd tricked him.

"Not even the strongest magic in the world can make people do something they really don't want to do. Hey, Hamish?" Col looked at the ferret on the floor.

"Sorry, Col. I wes pretty young an' stupid meself at the time."

Old Col wiped her eyes and flicked through the book. "Right, the curse, let's see . . . oh, here it is . . ."

*"You revolting little weasel. How dare you break my heart?"*

"It's not one of my better ones." Old Col absently scratched her face.

Melody looked confused. "It doesn't even rhyme. I thought all spells had to rhyme."

"That's just what Birgit Howser would have you think. Don't worry, it gets worse." Old Col cleared her throat to read the next part of her curse.

*"You can stay like that for all I care. You're all the same, you lot."*

•  •  •

"See, I completely destroyed the metre as well. Put that down to the heat of the moment, I guess," she said with a shrug.

"That's it? That's the curse?" Melody asked.

"Told you it wasn't one of my better ones, although it's lasted longer than I thought it would," Col said.

Ondine rubbed the patch of skin between her eyebrows to help her think. "So, if he's been a ferret all this time, does that mean you don't care? Is that what it would take to get him back?"

Old Col closed the book. "I'd best get out before your ma finds me in here and I get grounded too."

"I'm still in the room ye know, ladies. Can we get back to the issue of how I get back to me regular self?"

They all looked at Shambles.

He cleared his throat. "I hev a theory. For most of the years I've bin like this, nobody could hear me. But now people can. The curse is wearing off, so it is. I've reformed since Ondi took me in, truly I have. Surely that's enough to make ye care?"

"I do believe you have changed, Hamish," Old Col said. "I swear to you, I do care, and I have lifted the curse. You've had a glimpse of the man you once were, and can be again. The rest is up to you."

At her great-aunt's words, Ondine couldn't help thinking about the glimpse she'd had of the man Hamish could be. And That Beautiful Kiss. It was the kind of sense-memory that stayed with you.

Shambles looked up at Ondine and their gazes locked.

*Please be human again, Hamish. Please kiss me again, Hamish.*

**15**

———

As it transpired, Ondine's "grounding" was not the usual kind. She was isolated in her room for most of the day, but her parents allowed her out for kitchen duty when they had customers. Considering they had customers nearly all day long in the bar and dining room, things didn't feel that much different from her normal life.

For the rest of the day, Shambles kept his distance, but she told herself that was because he didn't want to cause more problems or get her into trouble. To add to her punishment, hardly anyone talked to her or even looked at her; the dark glares Cybelle gave her notwithstanding.

They were incredibly busy that night. Ma set Ondine to work in the front dining room instead of scrubbing greasy dishes. There she stood, pencil and paper in hand, ready to walk into a room full of people.

With a quick pep-talk to bolster her spirits, she stepped out into the public arena and took the orders from table six. It was Mrs Howser's table, and she'd invited some friends to dine with her. They wanted the set menu. Too easy. "I can do this," Ondine said to herself as she headed back to the kitchen to give Chef the details. The beautiful smells of the busy kitchen invaded her senses, but she ignored her growling tummy as she gave her table's order to Chef.

Her voice cracked, making the word "six" sound a lot ruder than it should have. "Four sit meals for table sex," she said.

Any moment now searing heat would pour up her neck and face.

Huh? Nothing. How strange.

For a man who had every right to be furious with Ondine, Chef Henrik looked pretty calm. "Thanks." He took the note and stuck it to the metal stove-hood with a magnet.

"Right." *Keep going on with work and act as if everything is completely normal.* Down the other end of the kitchen, Melody stood with her sleeves rolled up, washing plates![1]

Ooompfh. She turned and walked straight into Cybelle, whose arms were filled with dirty plates.

Arms filled no longer.

The load crashed to the floor with a clang of cutlery and a smash of breaking plates.

"I'm so sorry." Ondine scraped up the mess with her hands and threw the pieces in the bin. "I didn't see you."

Through clenched teeth, Cybelle said, "You did it deliberately."

With her usual, uncanny sense of good timing, Ma appeared. Their mother knelt down with a dustpan and brush to sweep up. "Happens to the best of us. Ondi, get back out front of house and take table seven's order. Belle, everything's OK."

Straightening herself out, Ondine stood at the kitchen door and drew a steadying breath before she faced the public. Just as she took her first step, she felt a hard push in her back and she sprawled forwards, arms whirling. For a sickening moment she thought she'd land face-down on the carpet. At the last nanosecond her feet came forward. With a wobble she righted herself, and ran a nervous hand through her hair. The push in the back had to be Cybelle's doing, but having an argument in full view of the public would only prove that restaurant reviewer correct.

Pasting on a smile, even though she wished for the ground to swallow her whole (something she knew would never happen, but that didn't mean she stopped wishing it), Ondine headed to table seven.

"Did you enjoy your trip?" Lord Vincent asked. His face split with a smile.

*Omistars he's here! He's here and Ma sent me out deliberately to his table when she could have sent Belle.* "Er, yeah, not used to the new carpet."

Again she waited for the furious blushing. Again it didn't come.

Did that mean she was getting better at handling boys? Confidence returning, Ondine stood poised with pencil and paper. "Are you ready to place your orders?" she asked.

Lord Vincent gave her a devastatingly gorgeous smile that made her insides go flippy-floppy. To keep on the task at hand, she turned to the rest of the people in his group. She had to do something to stop naughty thoughts invading her senses. If Lord Vincent tried that inside-wrist-kiss again she'd melt into a puddle.

Only the night before, she'd seen the true Hamish and decided he was far more handsome – and attainable – than Lord Vincent. But that was because she never thought she'd see Vincent again. Now Vincent was here and Hamish was a ferret once more, and she couldn't help losing her head a little.

She mentally told herself off for being so inconsistent with her affections.

Lord Vincent said, "Thank you Ondine," after she took their orders – top-range stuff too, none of this we're-only-students-we'll-order-the-cheapest-thing-on-the-menu-and-then-share-a-dessert stinginess.

With Vincent's smile fixed in her mind, Ondine's feet barely touched the floor on the way back to the kitchen, although she kept a keen eye out for Cybelle to avoid another collision.

"How is table seven?" Ma asked as she walked past, her arms full of plates of delicious, steaming food.

"Dreamy," Ondine murmured, then gave a mental shake of her head as she heard her mother chuckle.

For the rest of the night, Ondine kept her distance from Cybelle and had only necessary conversation with Chef and the odd sly smile from her mother. Lord Vincent, on the other hand, seemed keen to talk every time she delivered food or took their plates away or refilled their carafe of water. His friends had excellent manners, Ondine noted – knife and fork placed together in the centre of the plate when they were finished, instead of a scrunched-up napkin.[2]

"That was delicious," Vincent said, locking eyes with Ondine and making her heart skip a beat.

Delicious indeed. "I'll pass your compliments on to the chef."

"Is the beer garden open tonight? We might take our coffee out there." His gorgeous eyes burned into hers. The noise of the restaurant died away, making Ondine feel like the world only existed for the two of them. Her brain felt woozy and sluggish under his attentions, as if she'd been at the cooking sherry. All the while, her pulse beat loudly in her ears.

"Let me set up a table for you. Give me a couple of minutes and I'll come back and get you."

"That sounds promising," Lord Vincent said with a saucy grin.

This time Ondine did blush, as that familiar bothersome heat seared her skin, but she turned away before he could see how much he'd affected her.

Outside, they still had the fairy lights in the trees from Margi and Thomas's party, so she turned them on and set to work, flicking the tablecloth into the air and laying it down on to a table. The last time she'd done this, Shambles had raced in and skidded along the top, before turning into a very handsome man who'd delivered Ondine her first real kiss.

And then he'd warned her about Vincent.

Jealousy did strange things to people, Ondine thought. But she missed Hamish all the same. Yes, he was still around (judging by the copious sausages Chef kept turning over on the stove), but the rules of her grounding meant they weren't to talk to each other.

But oh, how she missed him. Seriously missed him, which was more than she thought was good for her. What was the point of falling in love with a man if he turned back into a ferret when the moon went down?

Falling in love! Oh no, that's not what she meant to think at all. Not when she thought she might have the attentions of Lord Vincent. Admittedly, he was completely out of her reach socially, but a girl could dream, couldn't she? And he'd asked to be seated outside and was flirting so outrageously with her, he must be interested, surely?

Then why were her thoughts filled with the delicious Hamish?

Gah! Ondine shook the images from her mind as she straightened out the wrinkles in the tablecloth, all the while chiding herself for such foolishness. If a person looked up "confused" in the dictionary, it would say "Ondine de Groot".

"Beautiful," Vincent said, strolling outside. There were no clouds tonight and the moon along with the bud lights cast small amounts of magic over the garden.

Ondine kept straightening out the tablecloth, even though it didn't need doing. Anything to keep busy. To keep from falling under Vincent's spell.

"It is a beautiful garden," she managed. Something tugged at her, reminding her to keep thinking of Hamish.

"Not the garden, you." He closed the distance between them.

How did a girl respond to that? A sensible girl would say, "You're very kind. Now I'll bring out the tea and coffee orders for your table of friends," but by this point "sensible" and Ondine had long parted company. She giggled.

Like a twit.

Burning heat spread from her neck all the way to her forehead. If only her feet would work, then she'd walk out of here and back into the kitchen. Even with her shove-in-the-back sister, the kitchen was a much safer prospect right now.

No such luck. Vincent took a step closer while Ondine stood mute. Another step, and he was only a metre away. Less now as he took another step.

One more step and they were almost touching. His hand cupped her chin. Tingling heat spread over her skin and down her body, making her pulse hitch in her throat and her mouth turn dry.

*Quick, find something to say, or this is going to get way out of hand.*

Her brain fled as Vincent's lips slowly closed the distance between them. Closer, closer, almost touching.

*Jupiter's moons, he's going to kiss me!*

She tried to swallow, but her tongue stuck to the roof of her mouth. Her voice croaked as she blurted out, "How come your da wants to close us down?"

Vincent paused a centimetre from his target. His voice sounded smooth and hypnotic. "Don't talk about my father. I don't want to be thinking of him when I'm with you."

When his lips came down on hers, Ondine expected to swoon, but she didn't. Instead her eyes flew open while his cold, wet tongue darted into her mouth in an altogether uncomfortable and completely baffling experience.

There was even a bit of slobber. Ondine's hands came up and pressed against Vincent's chest, keeping their bodies apart, but only just.

"Stop fighting it, you know you want it." His lips continued to make a mess of her face.

"This isn't going to happen," Ondine said, surprised at how confident she sounded. A girl of her years should have been revelling in the intimacy, but instead it felt . . . not wrong, because that would mean she felt something. No, this was more of a sad hollowness, a disappointing sequel to their earlier encounter.

How quickly her emotions had changed. She would have sworn she'd heard birds singing in her head when she'd first laid eyes on Lord Vincent. Now she felt a bit grubby as he continued his Braille conversation.

"That's enough." Ondine pushed Vincent backwards, so that their faces were a good few centimetres apart and she could breathe properly without having him pressed so tightly against her.

"Now you're going shy on me? Take what you can get, honey, I won't offer again."

Anger bubbled in Ondine's veins. "And I won't accept either. I'm going back inside."

She took a sideways step to get past him, but he blocked her exit, his nostrils flaring. "No you don't. Not until I get what I came for."

Cold, horrible, paralysing fear glued Ondine to the spot.

Her words came out as a squeak. "L-leave me alone." She said it again, hoping it would come out stronger. Nope, still a squeak.

"Where is it?" Vincent said, closing the distance again so they were almost nose to nose, body to body. Each time Ondine took a breath, her breasts touched his chest.

No more squeaks. All she could do was whisper, "Where's what?"

"Don't play dumb with me. Where's the money?"

"I d-don't know what you're –"

Slap! Lord Vincent's palm came down hard across her face. His voice took on a growling demand. "Where's the money?"

Jupiter's moons her cheek burned! But it didn't hurt as much as her heart, which felt like it could shatter into a million pieces.

Ondine whispered, "I'm going to scream," but her squeaky voice made the threat completely pathetic. All the while her pulse hammered in her ears.

"You have one sister damaging the piano and the other's howling at the moon. Nobody will hear you out here. Now tell me where the money is."

Trapped. Utterly trapped. In the quiet, between the thudding of her own heart, Ondine could hear loud music from inside the pub. Vincent was right; they wouldn't hear a thunderbolt out here, let alone one sad girl's screams.

Her face stung from his slap, but it was more a pain of disappointment. She thought she'd been a fairly decent judge of character until now.

"We've spent it," Ondine confessed.

For a second Lord Vincent's face fell, before a nasty sneer took hold. "Nice try. I almost believed you. Tell me where it is."

"I've told you we sp –"

His hand flew up, ready to smack her again.

"– It's inabox underthefloorboards inthepub," Ondine blurted. With a burst of strength she didn't know she had, she pushed him away and made a run for it.

A hard hand gripped her arm, swinging her back so sharply her shoulder felt like it would pop out of the socket.

A growl came from deep within Ondine. "Get your hands off me!"

The back door swung open and a murderous scream erupted. "Arrrrgggghhh! Hands off what's nawt yers!"

Familiar black fur blurred past Ondine. Relief washed over her at Shambles's timely intervention.

"What the . . ." Vincent stumbled backwards in shock as something raced up the leg of his trousers. A howl of pain sprang from his throat as he fell down with a thud, hard on his bottom. Then he battered madly at his leg with his hands. "Get off!"

"Nowt until ye leave her alone!" Shambles cried out.

"I am, I am." Lord Vincent swatted at the rapidly moving lump under his trousers. He managed to hit himself a few times, which made him wince. Changing tactics, he stood up, crazily shaking his leg to free him of the demon possessing it.

With a battle cry of victory, Shambles rolled away from Vincent's leg. Then he rounded on his victim and gave him a nasty swipe against the ankle. It drew blood.

"Stitch that, Jimmy!"

"It talks!" Vincent gasped at the sight of his pint-sized enemy.

"I don't just talk, pal," Hamish said, swiping at Vincent's ankle again and making another cut.

Vincent made to stomp on his attacker, but Shambles darted out of the way, then doubled back and charged up Vincent's leg.

"A ferret?!" Vincent tried to shake him away before he could reach anything sensitive. "You set a *ferret* on to me? Say goodbye to the hotel, I'm going to close this place down!"

With her heart beating a tattoo in her chest, Ondine's body trembled all over from fear and indignation.

"Yer all pish and wind," Shambles said as he leapt free of Vincent and then made for the safety of Ondine. When he reached her shoulder, he made ready to launch himself at Vincent's stricken face.

"That's enough, Shambles. I think he's got the message."

"You're finished, witch!" Vincent said. "I'll have you charged with treason."

"Oh really?" Shambles asked. "Exactly how're ye gonna explain what ye were doin' when ye got cut, eh?"

The colour drained from Lord Vincent's face. The shock value was priceless. Courage stirred in Ondine. "Everyone knows Shambles is always with me, and I'm happy to tell people what you tried to do to me. So go ahead, tell everyone you came off second-best to a ferret."

They stared at each other for a moment, but it was Vincent who blinked first.

"Watch your back," he said and made to leave. The words carried a veiled threat, but his voice cracked in the middle, exposing it as nothing but bluff.

"I'd watch yours if I were you, and your legs," Ondine said as Vincent walked out of the side gate of the garden. "We'll send the dinner bill to your da."

Shambles yelled out, "And ye'll need ten rabies shots, all of them in the a–"

Ondine slapped her hand over Shambles's mouth. "No need to be rude."

"Ah, yer a feisty one! I'm real proud of ye." Shambles gave Ondine a wet, whiskery kiss on the cheek.

Proud of her? Well, that was about the best thing she'd heard all night. "Thanks, Hamish. I can't thank you enough for arriving when you did."

What a mess she'd made of things! Why, when she had someone as beautiful and funny as Hamish to look forward to, did she even contemplate an idiot like Lord Vincent?

*Because*, said a scared little voice said in her head, *he may never be proper Hamish again!*

"Did he hurt ye, lass?"

There were so many different levels of hurt a person could feel. "I guess not, but . . . oh, Hamish, you tried to warn me about him, but I wouldn't listen. Go on, say 'I told you so'."

"Nay, hen, you don't need to be told anything. You're far smarter than me."

"You're just saying that." Ondine brushed off the comment as she made to return to the kitchen. She was still grounded; any prolonged absences would make her mother suspicious.

"No, I'm nawt just saying that. It's true. And thanks for calling me Hamish, it's nice to be treated like a person again, even if I'm living in reduced circumstances."

Something made Ondine stop at the back step. Here she was, growing older by the day, feeling frustrated because everyone treated her like a kid. All the while the adult male on her shoulder fared little better because of his present ferrety incarnation.

"If it helps any, you're a real person to me. And I hope the spell wears off permanently soon so you can be yourself again."

*Please be you again, Hamish.*

Shambles gave a wickedly deep chuckle as they walked down the hall. "Sure, yer just saying that, lass, cos ye want another kiss. I wouldn't mind another meself. Yer very good at it."

No heat of embarrassment this time, but a wide grin split her face at the thought.

Shambles chuckled, then stopped suddenly. "What are we doing in the laundry?"

"I'm pretty sure this is your room and, as I'm grounded, I'm not allowed to have anyone in mine. That includes you."

"Nobody will notice. And you can't expect me to stay down here, it's all reekie."[3]

For a moment Ondine stood still, wondering what to do, but then Shambles made her mind up for her. "Ye were giving it laldy on that eejit, but yer still in shock and I think someone should keep an eye on ye, and as I was there, it may as well be me."[4]

"Why am I regretting this already? You're sleeping on the end of the bed, OK? Above the covers."

"I wouldnae have it any other way."

As they approached the kitchen, Shambles peeled off Ondine's shoulder and begged Chef for leftovers. Things were winding down for the night, with only a few tables left to receive their desserts.

"Lord Vincent had to leave," Ondine told her mother. It wasn't exactly a lie. "We're to send the bill to the Duke."

Her mother's face took on an air of concern. "What happened out there? You don't look so good."

"And I don't feel so good either. Da was right, Vincent's a total pain in the . . . neck." She wanted to say worse, but good manners turned up in the nick of time.

"You should go to bed," Ma said, touching the back of her hand to Ondine's forehead.

"Vincent knew about the jewellery, and the money. I don't know how, but he did."

"Oh dear."

"Exactly."

"Right." Ma was quiet for a while, as she thought what to do next. At the same time, she put the coffee on and set up cups and saucers. Not only could she talk about five things at once, she could practically do them as well. "Things won't settle down out front for another hour at least, and you look ready to drop. Your father's retired early for once, Thomas is doing a great job at the bar. You get some sleep, then we'll talk about it in the morning."

No second invitation needed. Ondine was only too glad to head to her room and collapse.

SOMETIME DURING THE NIGHT, Shambles arrived and made good on his promise to stay at the end of the bed.

"Settle, lass. I cannae sleep with yer feet kicking me all the time."

"Stop fidgeting then."

A knock came on the door. "Ondi, are you in there?"

"Quick, Hamish – under the bed, Ma's coming in," Ondine whispered, then called out to the door in a louder voice, "Where else would I be?"

Instantly she wished she'd kept her mouth shut. Already in enough trouble, answering back to her parents again could make things worse. Especially if Ma walked in and found she had company. Ondine couldn't think of a worse punishment than being stuck in her room whenever she wasn't needed for work, but her mother had no such lack of imagination and would be bound to come up with something more heinous. The furry black streak disappeared under the bed, his claws skittering on the floorboards as Ma opened the door. Thank goodness for creaky hinges drowning out the sound!

"Ondi, I'm sorry things went so badly with Vincent tonight. I thought your father was overreacting about him. Turns out his instincts were spot on," Ma said, positioning her well-cushioned self on the end of the bed, right where Hamish had been. "I told your da everything that happened —"

"But nothing happened!" Ondine protested.

"Sweetheart, it's not your fault, and you have nothing to feel embarrassed about. Vincent's the one with the problems, not you."

"But . . . how do you know what happened?"

"Hamish told me, because he was concerned for you." Ma embraced Ondine in a hug and gently rubbed her back. "We all think you've been very brave and Vincent's going to get what's coming. Aunt Col's looking into it. She could turn him into a toad or a slug. Which would you prefer?"

Ondine smiled in relief. And hey, Ma had called Shambles "Hamish" again.

"It's good to see you smile. I have some more good news. I was going to wait until the end of your grounding to let you know about school, but you need cheering up. Ondi, we do have the money. You can take the classes you want."

Hope sparkled in Ondine's veins; she would have a life again! Then confusion made her head turn fuzzy. "But . . . but why did you say we didn't?"

"Because I wanted you to think about your actions, and to realise that they have consequences," Ma said.

After the altercation with Lord Vincent, Ondine hardly needed a reminder about consequences, but she was also intrigued by their sudden return to wealth. "So . . . how much money do we have?"

Ma gave her a knowing smile, then kissed her on the forehead. "Enough. Not enough to be silly with, but enough. It's getting late, you should go to sleep," she said, closing the subject.

Part of Ondine wanted to give her mother a good old-fashioned yelling at for scaring her so much. Another part wanted to wrap her arms around her and hug her till they both dissolved into tears. The second idea won out.

Tears poured out. "I love you, Ma."

"I love you too, sweetheart. But better save your tears for the morning, Ondi. Aunt Col is leaving and she'll be taking Shambles with her, so they can work out a way to reverse the spell for good."

Cold dread snaked around Ondine's heart and gave a squeeze. "Tomorrow?" she croaked.

"I'm afraid so. Just as well he's back to being a ferret, otherwise I'd be worried you might try something stupid. And then I'd have three weddings to plan instead of two. I'd best be getting back to the kitchen. Goodnight, dear." With that Ma closed the door behind her, leaving Ondine feeling confused and frustrated.

Old Col would be taking Hamish with her? Then another thought smacked her. *Three* weddings? Her parents were so stuck in the past!

The minute you're interested in a boy they want to marry you off.

From underneath the bed, she heard, "Want to try something stupid?"

To her shock and delight, she saw Hamish looking up at her. The real Hamish McPhee, not the ferret but the man. With a devilish grin on his face.

## 16

-----

"You're . . . you're you again!" Ondine said, although she fought to keep her voice down in case she alerted anyone else to Hamish's sudden change in circumstances.

A roguish smile split his face. "Aye, and I'm all skin and no fur, so throw me a coat, will ye? And ye might want one for yerself, yer looken peely-wally."[1]

Ondine leapt from the bed, half in shock, half in excitement. Her mind ran through several scenarios.

"You're human again, so that means you don't have to leave with Old Col tomorrow. You can make your own decisions. I mean, you can still go with her if you want, but you could just as easily stay. I'm sure Ma would appreciate the extra labour."

"Draw breath, lass. Yer sounding just like yer mither, jumping from one thing to the next. Now give me a coat, I don't intend to spend the night under yer bed with fluff bunnies in me jacksie."

Ondine trod softly to her wardrobe to fetch her biggest coat. The last thing she needed now was her mother back at the door, wondering who she was talking to.

Except her mother would say "to whom she was talking". Gah! Even in her thoughts she could hear the corrections.

"You look ridiculous," Ondine whispered, as she covered a giggle with her hand. Her biggest coat barely fit over Hamish's broad shoulders. Two long, hairy legs poking out underneath completed the silliness.

"We'll need to get yer da, borrow his clothes for a while until I can get some more of me own."

"At this time of night? I don't want to be the one to wake him. It's his first night off in ages. You've seen him grumpy. If you rouse him now it'll be like poking a wasps' nest. I'll find you a spare room for the night and we can see him in the morning."

At that, Ondine reached into her jacket pocket for her bunch of keys and found them missing. She checked the other pocket as a rising sense of panic made her hands tremble. "I can't find my keys! I must have dropped them outside or left them in the kitchen or something."

"Or that toerag took them." Hamish practically spat the words out. He stripped the bed covers, grabbed the top sheet and wrapped it around himself like a bad kilt. In the process he gave Ondine a quick flash of firm upper thigh. Just how a girl was supposed to concentrate with such a distraction was beyond her.

"Think about it," he said, tucking the fabric around his waist. "Why else would he want to get ye alone?"

Picking her ego up off the floor, Ondine wondered why else indeed? Her heart staggered at how completely stupid she'd been.

"I didnae mean to say it like that," he added.

So he could read minds now? Ondine shook her head. The man was blunt, but he was also right. The whole thing with Lord Vincent smacked of a set-up, perhaps from the night she first laid eyes on him.

"The night we warned the Duke . . ." she started.

"Eh?" Hamish interrupted.

"Vincent was there in the palace – he was listening to us when we spoke to his father. And now he knows about the jewellery and the money. Maybe he knew all along?"

"Aye, nawt much gets past ye."

Ondine slumped on to the side of her bed, and Hamish sat close beside her. Too close, making the hairs on her arms stand up.

"Be honest with me. You saw all of this coming, didn't you?" she asked.

For a moment he was quiet, then he turned to face her, taking her chin in his fingers. "I didn't know at first, but I knew I didn't like him. He told his da his friends had been sick after eating here, and the Duke believed him, and that's when he set the health inspector on to us."

A furrow crept over Ondine's brow. "You told me to be careful, and I didn't listen."

Hamish swallowed as his gaze bored into Ondine. "There was a lot going on. We've all been pretty busy."

"It's sweet of you to say that." Ondine knew if she'd had the time again, she still wouldn't have listened to sense because she'd been so smitten with the handsome lord. Someone had paid her attention and she'd ignored the warning signs. "And there I was thinking it was all because you were jealous."

Hamish gave her another comforting smile. "Aye, I *was* jealous. How could I compete with the son of a Duke?"

*You were competing with the son of a Duke? For me?* The thought cheered Ondine immensely until she directed her thoughts back to the problem at hand.

"And now that son-of-a-Duke has stolen my keys. We'll have to get new locks in the morning. Da will be furious," Ondine said.

"Unless he breaks in tonight."

"Oh dear." Ondine made for the door. "Grumpy or not, I'd better get Da."

"No, wait. I have a better idea." A warm hand landed on Ondine's shoulder, sending more whirly things through her system. "If Lord Vincent's planning on making a return tonight, let's give him a welcome to remember."

He gave her a grin hot enough to melt her slippers.

---

"ALL SET?" Hamish asked as they huddled in their hiding place, in the darkened dining room.

"I think so," Ondine said, trying – and failing – to stop her hands from shaking as she oh-so-carefully laid a single strand of fake pearls across the top of the jewellery box. "You're sure this will work?"

"Nope, nawt at all. He may nae even come tonight, and tomorrow we'll change the locks so after that we won't have to worry. But he'd be a fool if he didn't send someone over before he thinks you've noticed the keys are gone. Ach, this coat is too tight."

When Ondine turned, she saw Hamish pulling the coat off with a fair amount of force, giving her a magnificent display of his lean chest and arms. If her hands were shaking before, they were full-on trembling now.

Thank goodness it was dark, he wouldn't see how much she was staring at him. The one saving grace in all this was the complete lack of searing heat up her neck. She'd finally stopped blushing. Although in the darkness he wouldn't have noticed. Stupid hormones. What was the point of not blushing if nobody was around to witness it?

The shard of moonlight through the window exposed his marvellous bare chest only an arm's length away, sapping her concentration.

"I'll make some coffee, to help us stay awake," she offered. Partly to help them out, but mostly so she could clear her head for a moment and get away from him, to catch her breath. Drinking the coffee was not an option – she felt jittery enough thank you very much.

Suddenly she heard a noise.

"Hawd yer wheesht." Hamish's strong hand grabbed her arm and pulled her down to the floor, where they hid behind an upturned table.[2]

No translation needed for Ondine. She clamped her mouth shut and breathed as silently as she could manage, while the close contact with that male flesh made her pulse hammer in her ears. It made so much noise she was sure Hamish – or their intruder – could hear it.

In the many books that Ondine had read, she'd often come across descriptions of men. They could be brutal or whiny, fat or scrawny, nervous or domineering, have funny gaps between their teeth or nervous tics. But nothing had prepared her for the reality of being this close to . . . the real thing. The real flesh and blood, the very masculine scent of him invading her senses, how he could be so naughty and charming and then so confident all at once. A girl could easily lose her head. Just as Old Col must have.

And then he'd let Old Col down in a very public way, embarrassing her in front of her friends. How could one person be so much fun, but such a liability?

In silence, they heard a key turn in the lock. The front door made a soft shudder as it came away from the jamb. Footsteps padded on the new carpet. From their hidden position behind the table, they watched the legs move about. At first they walked over to the fireplace, checking inside it and among the ashes, then over to the piano, where they heard the lid lift up and close down with a soft "tunk". Ondine thought they'd put the jewellery box in a really obvious place, but it still took an agonisingly long time for the intruder to get anywhere near the goodies. Come on, come on, Ondine prayed silently. At that moment Hamish's warm hand pressed over hers in unspoken support, as if he'd heard her. She looked at his face. He held his index finger over his lips to indicate their need for absolute quiet.

The pulse coursing through her system had other ideas as it banged away in her ears.

In the silence, something made a horrible – and loud – snap.

"AARRRRGGGHH!" the thief cried out. He pulled his hand from the jewel box and shook it all around, their pre-set rattrap clamped over his fingers.

Hamish pushed the table back and they came out of hiding. All the while the thief kept screaming in agony, in between torrents of swearing.

In a blur of movement, Hamish grabbed him by the collar, forced the man to the ground and sat on him.

"Ye right there?" Then he grabbed a bottle of blue food dye out of his pocket and squirted it over the man's head and down the neck of his shirt, staining his skin good and proper. Ondine grabbed the thief's free hand (the one not turning red from the rat trap) and held it steady, so Hamish could douse that with more food dye.

Hamish cried out with victory, "Ha ha! Caught red-handed, or blue-handed in this case."

"Need a hand?" Ondine asked, as she turned the restaurant lights on to reveal the identity of their thief.

Ondine's father, with his stubbly face and messy, sticky-up hair, chose that moment to stagger into the restaurant. "Oh dear heavens," he blurted as he took in the scene.

It couldn't have looked good. In fact, it was any wonder the old man's heart didn't give out on the spot. His daughter wearing pyjamas, a man who used to be a ferret wearing nothing more than a bed sheet around his middle, and the son-of-a-Duke lying screaming on the floor, with a blue face and his hand caught up to the knuckles in a rat trap.

"We caught him in the act, Da, he was trying to break in and steal all that money we found. So me and Hamish set this trap and –"

"Hamish and I," Josef corrected.

"He stole my keys earlier tonight, so Hamish and I were waiting for him. We thought he'd send a lackey but he was stupid enough to come himself."

It would have been a heavy silence passing between them if not for the whimpering Vincent on the ground trying to budge the rattrap off his hand.

Josef looked down at him. "I'm calling your father," he said.

Several furtive looks passed between Ondine and Da, as well as Hamish and Da, and then back to Vincent.

"Get the old man in then, and let's get this over with," Vincent said, blowing air on his swollen knuckles. They looked red and cracked. For a moment – but only a moment – Ondine felt sorry for him as she removed the metal trap from his joints. Would his hand recover?

"Sit tight, Hamish," Da said as he turned to leave the room. "I'll call the Duke."

*Da has his number? Interesting.*

When Ondine turned back to look at Vincent, she could have sworn she saw a smile playing over his face.

Strange that he should smile when the shock of the events might give his old man a heart attack.

"Mercury's wings!" All the pieces fell into place. "You wanted to get caught so the trauma would give the Duke a heart attack. You can't wait for him to show up and die of shame. You were there that night when we came to warn the Duke about the attack at the station. You were there at the station, and you knew what was coming because you organised the whole thing. How dare you! You ought to be ashamed of yourself."

"Good luck trying to prove it," Vincent said, sounding more confident than he had any right to, considering the circumstances.

"You're forgetting one thing. I'm a witch," Ondine said, overcome with a fresh bout of shakes at how daring she sounded. "I'm from a long line of witches and I can read your thoughts. You want your father dead so you can inherit. Right now you'd pretty much like me dead as well but that's beside the point."

A snarl grew on Vincent's face. "Nice try. As soon as my father turns up with his lawyers I'm out of here."

"He's on his way," Da said.

And now Ma, Old Col, Melody, Mrs Howser, Cybelle, Chef, Thomas and Marguerite all appeared in the dining room, in various stages of wakefulness. For the first time in Ondine's memory, Marguerite's hair looked messy.

Another thought raced through her head: since when did Chef and Thomas start spending the night in the hotel?

"Hamish!" Ma, Mrs Howser and Old Col said together.

"Evening, ladies," Hamish said back, still sitting on the disgruntled Lord Vincent.

Everyone looked at Vincent and then back to Hamish, then they all started asking questions at once.

"What's going on?" Margi asked.

"What's he doing here?" Cybelle asked.

"When did Hamish come back?" Ma asked.

"Is that Ondine's bed sheet?" Old Col asked.

"Oh, he's gorgeous!" Melody said.

It took a while to explain everything. Ondine felt grateful when the Duke finally turned up and they'd be able to bring the crazy evening to an end.

Then things got ugly.

**17**

———————

W ho broke the silence first? Vincent, of course. "Father, thank God you're here. They've kidnapped me and are holding me for ransom," he said. "They're all in on it – they planned the attack on you at the railway station too. Look what they've done to me! Charge them with treason."

It took all of Hamish's strength to hold Vincent down on the floor.

"That's complete rot. He stole my keys earlier tonight so he could break in and burgle us," Ondine said in their defence.[1]

"Don't listen to them, they'd say anything," Vincent countered. "Ring the police!"

Sickness threatened to overwhelm Ondine. Who would the Duke believe? Or should that be whom?

*Ack! This is no time to worry about grammar.*

"Shut up, prat!" Da thundered, then he turned to the Duke and modulated his voice. "I apologise for being the bearer of bad news once again, Your Grace. It is hard to believe your flesh and blood can be anything less than perfect. However, Vincent was attempting to steal our takings from tonight. From what I understand, he may well have been attempting to steal the virtue of my youngest daughter as well."

Embarrassment pinged through Ondine. Now everyone would know.

For a moment the Duke looked at Vincent with concern on his face, and Ondine felt something twist in her gut.

"If I may make a suggestion," Hamish said, still sitting on top of their would-be burglar. "We're all in our pyjamas, and he's come dressed to steal."

Brilliant! Ondine beamed a smile at Hamish. He beamed one right back at her, making her insides feel all funny. She felt embarrassed at the intensity of his smile, but Hamish had just saved their collective skins. She had every right to beam with pride at how clever and quick he'd been.

"And if we wanted to kidnap your son, we'd have stayed anonymous. So why would we call you here?" Ondine added.

Hamish beamed at her again and she liked it.

The Duke looked mightily annoyed as he glared at his wayward son. "I warned you, you stupid boy. I've signed the papers for Fort Kluff. You're shipping off tomorrow."[2]

Veins bubbling with happiness, Ondine grinned at Hamish while little things fluttered and flip-flopped inside her tummy.

"Ondine," the Duke began, "lately it seems, whenever there's trouble in my life, you're there to stop it. Your information saved my life at the station and now you've saved my family's reputation. I don't think we could have survived the scandal if this had gone public. Thank you."

She beamed with happiness and curtsied, then realised the unsaid "between the lines" kind of implication – everything that happened here tonight must be kept private.

The Duke continued. "Mr and Mrs de Groot, I apologise for the grief I caused your family in sending the health inspector. That was Vincent's idea and I should have checked things out for myself before acting. Two of my best advisors have retired in the last year and I find myself lacking . . . *information* . . . from people I can trust."

Then he looked at Ondine and a puzzled expression flashed across his face. "How old are you, Ondine, really?"

"Your Grace, I'm fifteen."

"Good. I appreciate your honesty. Now, where is that ferret I saw you with?"

Her eyebrows shot up into her hairline. He'd remembered that? Perhaps the hotel's new name had jogged his memory?

"Aye, that would be me," Hamish said.

Now it was the Duke's turn to lose his eyebrows into his greying hair.

Squashed beneath Hamish, Vincent let out a groan of misery.

"I got yer son a good one earlier tonight," Hamish said. "On the leg."

Time slowed down for a moment as the Duke digested the information. A pang of sympathy in Ondine felt completely appropriate. After all, a man wearing a bed sheet, with a foreign accent, had just claimed to be a ferret.

The Duke's mouth opened and closed a few times. Perhaps he needed to unlock his jaw so his ears could open more?

To add to the general confusion, some of the hotel's paying guests, wearing dressing gowns and sleeping caps, turned up to check out what was going on.

"Nothing to worry about," said Da. "We'll provide complimentary breakfast to compensate for your disturbed sleep." He encouraged the rest of his children and soon-to-be in-laws back to their respective rooms, and told Melody and Mrs Howser, "It's all under control."

Out of the corner of her eye, Ondine saw her mother lingering in the kitchen, listening in on the conversation.

The Duke's eyes twitched as he looked over Hamish. "You say you are the ferret? In that case, change into one."

Gulp went Ondine. *What if he can't? It's all my fault. I spent so long wishing him to be a real man, maybe he won't be able to change back. Then the Duke will think we're liars. And if he thinks we lied about a man being a ferret, he'll start to think we've lied about everything else.*

Still sitting on Lord Vincent, Hamish adjusted his toga. "I'll do what I can." A look of concentration crossed his face and his eyes rolled back under his eyelids.

It was a tense time for Ondine. As much as she loved seeing Hamish in his human form, if he couldn't become a ferret again on command, they'd be in a whole world of trouble. Relief washed over her as Hamish groaned and clutched at his stomach. He started to shrink and grow dark. His face – that handsome face – turned furry. It was painful to watch, but Hamish must have been in even more pain.

While everyone stood dumbfounded in wonder, Vincent bucked the suddenly reduced weight off his back and sprang up to make his escape.

"Hold it!" Flinging his arm out, Da leapt forward and clotheslined Vincent, sending him sprawling.

"Khaaak!" Vincent coughed. "That's assault!"

"I didn't see anything," The Duke said with a shrug. He didn't take his eyes off Hamish as he reverted to his Shambles form. You could tell by the way he stroked his goatee with his pinky and ring finger that he was thinking really, really hard about what he'd just seen.

Panting, Shambles looked up at the Duke, then across to Ondine. The tip of his nose looked pale and he swallowed a lot.

"Well, I'll be." The Duke clapped his hands. "I've seen some magic in my time, but that's mighty powerful. How do you do it?"

Shambles the ferret panted on the ground, gathering his strength. "It's a lawng story."

The Duke turned to Ondine. "You are too young to serve alcohol. You could not have been working in the bar that night. It wasn't you who overheard the plot against me, was it?"

Twist, lurch, flip went her belly. "You are right, Your Grace, I wasn't in the bar. It was Hamish . . . I mean, Shambles. That's what we call him when he's a ferret. He was under a table and he overheard the whole thing. He was the one who encouraged us to warn you of the plot against your life."

"I've never seen anything like it. What an incredibly convenient talent to have!" the Duke said, still shaking his head as he looked at the ferret on the ground.

Ondine didn't think it was very convenient at all.

"I wouldnae call it that," Shambles echoed her thoughts as he clutched his stomach.

The Duke stood there. All the while a smile played over his face. "You must tell me, Ondine, how does he do it?"

"It's a strong enchantment," Ondine said. "My great-aunt, Colette

Romano, cursed him, and only recently he's been able to rediscover his human form."

"Hmm, how very interesting," the Duke said.

Ondine blushed furiously. Mercury's wings, what an inconvenient time to start blushing again. She managed a squeaky, "Hamish is very glad to be human again."

"You'd make a good politician." The Duke winked at her. It had a strange effect in that it should have been friendly, but it creeped her out.

*This doesn't feel right.*

"Your great-aunt is the one with the magic?" the Duke asked. "She sounds like she'd make a wonderful ally. Would she be here by any chance?"

Something prickled in Ondine's conscience. If the Duke had Old Col under his command, how far would he take things? Sure, the old woman had acted in frustration against Hamish, but that was a one-off. At least, Ondine hoped it was a one-off. But what if someone like the Duke ordered her to turn other people into animals? Would her great-aunt be able to refuse?

"Did somebody ask for me?" Old Col appeared at the kitchen doorway, her eyes wide and innocent. Like she just *happened* to be nearby.

Listening in, more like.

"Your Grace, this is my great-aunt Colette." Ondine made the introductions.

"May I congratulate you on your good work, madam," the Duke said. He took her hand and kissed the back of it.

"Why thank you, Your Grace."

The Duke's face looked younger, brighter. Like he was having a Very Good Idea. Or even a Great Idea. At that point, one of the Duke's drivers came in and whispered something in his ear. The Duke whispered something back. The driver nodded, then clamped his hand on Vincent's shoulder and marched him outside.

On the floor, Hamish was still a ferret. The Duke stared at him and shook his head again. "I've seen so many things . . ." The man used to making speeches seemed temporarily lost for words. Turning to Old Col, he said, "I have need for talent in my employ, and you have that. What else can you do apart from turning men into ferrets?"

Old Col did a slow blink, then said, "I can keep secrets."

"An excellent quality."

Metal screeched inside Ondine's head. Did the Duke of Brugel just offer Old Col a job? What kind of job would it be?

On the floor, Shambles began changing back into Hamish. Much to Ondine's relief. Seriously much. It looked painful, though, as if someone were punching him in the belly. From the inside.

It caused another look of wonder to cross the Duke's face. "Bravo!" He clapped. "That's very, very good. When I came here tonight I thought I would be in for a bad night indeed. Shambles and Ms Romano, you have cast a silver lining on events, wouldn't you agree?"

"Thank you, Your Grace," Old Col said.

"Aye," Hamish said.

The Duke played with his goatee again. "Like I said, I have need of good talent, and you fit the bill. Shambles, you're brave and . . . adaptable. You're not afraid to tell me the truth and you think on your feet. I value that. How would you like to work for me?"

*Oh no, this is not good at all. Hamish is supposed to stay here with us, not go off and work for the Duke.*

Buzzing filled Ondine's ears as she waited for Hamish to politely refuse the offer. Surely he'd want to stay with them?

"In what capacity?" The voice belonged to Ma, who had been standing quietly behind them.

*Thank goodness for Ma, she'll make it easier for Hamish to say no.*

The Duke smiled and looked far too self-assured. The more in control the Duke looked, the more unsteady Ondine felt.

Pure confidence filled the Duke's being. Steady shoulders, non-twitching face, hands palm-outwards. "Shambles, in your ferret form, you could provide me with invaluable information. You see, the Duchess lunches on a regular basis with her . . . friends. She needs a companion with a clear head and an eye for detail. Many people take advantage of our hospitality, whether at court here in Venzelemma or at the country estate in Bellreeve. It pains me to admit it, but valuables are going missing. I will be run off my feet when parliament resumes in autumn. Having someone looking out for me will prove most useful."

It sounded like spying. Ondine was sure Hamish would want nothing to do with that.

"Go on," Hamish said, making a mockery of Ondine's thoughts.

"Nothing so hard as working here, I dare say, and you will be well compensated," the Duke said.

*But . . . but . . . Hamish wants to stay here.*

"Sounds tempting," Hamish said, putting Ondine's old coat back on.

All the while Ondine's pulse roared in her ears because she wanted to stop and ask a dozen questions but felt too terrified to speak.

"You want him to spy on your guests?" Old Col crossed her arms over her chest.

Instead of denying it, the Duke laughed. "You are right, my dear woman, that is exactly what I need you to do. In a nice way, of course. Ms Romano, Shambles, what do you say to joining my employ?"

*Say no, say no, say no. Say you want to stay here. I don't like this. He calls you Shambles when you're Hamish.*

"You'll pay me to make sure nothing gets nicked? I say a big yes to that. I could do it with my eyes closed," Hamish said.

Ondine looked at Hamish and back at the Duke. Why did Hamish accept so quickly? Didn't he realise if he went to work for the Duke, they'd hardly see each other? Maybe on weekends . . . but that was when the hotel was busiest and then Ondine wouldn't have any time to see him.

The more Ondine thought about it, the sadder she felt. Why, they'd hardly see each other at all!

What counter-offer could she have that would make him stay at the hotel? Judging by the silence from her parents behind her, they had nothing to suggest.

Old Col smiled (a bad sign) and said, "Your Grace, I humbly accept."

The Duke beamed with happiness. "I am in your debt. You will begin the first week of September."

One word echoed through Ondine's head. No. No, no, no, no!

**18**

---

The worst thing in the world had just happened right in front of her eyes, and nobody realised! If Hamish worked for the Duke, Ondine might never see him again! What a disaster! He'd be so busy, he might forget about her! He might even fall in love with someone else!

Ondine's head hurt from all the exclamation points!

After the Duke had gone, sleep proved impossible. Apart from the fact that she didn't have her bed sheet (Hamish had taken that for his toga), everything felt wrong. Tossing and turning held no appeal at all, so she made her way down to the kitchen for some warm milk. Maybe that would help?

She didn't see Melody until she nearly crashed into her.

"Can't sleep?" Melody asked.

"Got that right." Ondine gave a dramatic sigh to prove her point, then set about raiding the fridge. "You neither, huh?"

"Um . . . yeah."

A troubling thought scudded through Ondine. "You weren't trying to read my dreams, were you?"[1]

Melody looked at the ground, as if there were something very interesting in the tiles. "I'm sorry, Ondi. It's just that I know something big happened here tonight with the Duke, but Mrs Howser pulled me away before I could find out. And I really want to know."

No privacy during her waking hours, now Melody wanted in on her private thoughts in her sleeping ones. "You don't need to read my dreams. Just . . . ask yourself, what's the worst that could have happened tonight? Because that's exactly what did happen."

"Vincent got away?"

"That too, but it was worse. The Duke offered Hamish a job."

"But that's great!"

Frustration made Ondine slam the refrigerator door. "No it's not, it's terrible!"

"It is?"

Ondine wanted to scream. "Of course, it is. Hamish will be ages away and I'll never get to see him."

"But . . . he'll still be around. I mean, it's not like he's going all the way to . . . I dunno, New Zealand or something."

"New Zealand? Where's that?"

"Not sure, but I think it's really far away."[2]

"Oh." Ondine poured herself a mug of milk and put it in the microwave. "It's just . . . I thought Hamish liked it here."

"He likes you, that's for sure."

A smile stole through, despite her pitiful mood. "You think so?"

Melody laughed. "Ondi, stop hunting for compliments. Hamish really does like you. And I know you like him."

"So why is he leaving?" She nearly added the word "me" at the end of the sentence, but reined it in just in time.

Melody shrugged so hard her shoulders nearly smacked her ears. "Go ask him that."

That's the problem, Ondine thought. She couldn't ask him because she wasn't sure she wanted to know the real answer. Cold dread weighed her down. What if he was leaving because he wants to get away?

She didn't let her thoughts add the words "from me" at the end of that sentence either.

"You're scared, aren't you?"

"Melody, stop reading my thoughts." It was so annoying when her friend was right.

"I'm not, but it's pretty obvious what you're thinking. Ondi, you're going to have to ask him why he's leaving. If you do, you'll know why. If you don't, you never will."

A heavy and overly-dramatic sigh worked its way out of Ondine. "You're right."

The toothiest grin split Melody's face. "Course I am. Anyway, your dreams aren't the only ones I visit."

"No! You don't go into Hamish's dreams, do you?"

"I know he dreams about you." Melody smiled even more, then seemed to realise how inappropriate it was and had the grace to look chastened.

"That's a terrible invasion of privacy!" Ondine grinned. "What were they about?"

Ping! went the microwave.

"Your milk's ready." Melody fidgeted for a bit. "Why don't you take it to Hamish? I think he's having trouble sleeping tonight as well."

It was a good idea. All the excitement of the night would make it hard for anyone to sleep. Taking him a cup of warm milk would make her appear thoughtful and considerate of Hamish's situation. And if anyone saw her near his room and asked her what she was doing there, she'd have a believable excuse.

"Thanks, Mel. Now, no more sneaking into people's dreams." Ondine made for the door, then wondered which way to turn. The ferret Shambles might be somewhere cosy, but where would the man Hamish be?

"Your Ma's got him sharing a room with Thomas and Chef down the hall in number thirteen," Mel said without needing to be asked.

"Thanks."

Stepping quietly so she didn't wake anyone else, Ondine made her way to room thirteen. Another problem stacked on to the already teetering tower of problems – how would she speak to him in private if Chef and Thomas were in there as well?

Or worse. What if the three of them were sound asleep and she woke the wrong person in the dark?

She stood outside the door for a good minute, working out whether she should knock or just try and open the door as quietly as she could.

"What are you doing here?"

Gulp! It was Cybelle walking towards her. "I just . . . I need to speak to –"

"Get back to bed or I'll tell Ma you were down here," Cybelle said.

Great, so her sister was still cross with her. "I'll tell her you were down here too. Then we'll both be in the same amount of trouble."

"Except you're still grounded, so you'll be worse off."

Gulp! *She's right!*

They were so busy trading quips Ondine didn't notice the door open. "Evening, ladies." Hamish stood there, wearing Da's old pyjamas and the wickedest grin she'd ever seen. It made her insides go all melty.

"*Kh.*" Cybelle made a disparaging sound. "You two are hopeless. Is Henrik in there?"

"Aye." Hamish may have been answering Cybelle as he stepped aside to let her through the door, but he kept his eyes firmly on Ondine.

Melty, melty, melty.

"I, um." *Why is this so hard?* "I couldn't sleep."

"Can't blame ye really. Neither can I."

"I have hot milk." She held up her cup to show him.

Hamish beamed. "Yer a thoughtful lass." He tilted his head, indicating they should take a walk up the hallway to the lounge.

Miracle! Ondine's legs worked and she followed him. As they neared the private room by the kitchen, Hamish stepped back and whispered, "This one's taken."

Ondine craned her neck. "Oh." Marguerite and Thomas were talking quietly in there.

"The garden?" Hamish said with a shrug.

Still holding her cup of milk, Ondine followed him outside. The balmy summer night wafted the scent of evening jasmine around them.

"This looks like a good spot," Hamish said.

How sweet that he chose the same place where they'd shared That Beautiful Kiss. There was another part of the garden she didn't care for, where Lord Vincent had been such a pig. As if reading her thoughts, Hamish guided Ondine to sit with her back to the offending place so she wouldn't have to look at it. He took the cup of milk from her hand and placed it on the ground, then held her hands in his. Warmth spread through her at his touch.

The lovely surroundings should have given the ensuing conversation a dreamlike quality, but when she spoke, it all came out in a rush. "Please don't go and work for the Duke."

Seconds passed. All he did was look at her in that way of his and her heart felt like it was breaking against her ribs.

"Why not?"

"Because . . . because you don't have to. I'm sure Da would give you a job here if you asked him."

"And take advantage of his hospitality? Nah. I've done that long enough."

"But you're good. I mean, you won the tips competition easily. You charm the customers and everyone."

"I appreciate the vote of confidence, but working for the Duke would be a great opportunity for me. Surely ye see that?"

"Yes, but . . ." Things twisted inside her, and it hurt to breathe. In her head, she played out a few scenarios. Things in her favour – the darkness and the fact that Hamish would be leaving. Things not in her favour – the darkness and the fact that Hamish would be leaving. If she told him she loved him, and he stayed, it would be wonderful. If she told him she loved him and he left anyway, she'd die from a broken heart.

But if she didn't tell him she loved him, he would definitely leave.

She didn't even want to think about what she'd tell her school friends when the new term began. They'd ask about how she spent her summer holidays and she'd burst into tears.

Heat raced up her neck. "Hamish . . . I . . . I think I love you."

Hamish leant forward and pressed his warm lips against hers, sending flurries through her. That bashing sound in her head was her pulse roaring into life. When he pulled away, her eyes were still closed.

"Ondine, I love you right back."

"Oh, Hamish!" She threw her arms around his neck and hugged him. What bliss, everything was going to be OK after all.

"But I have to leave."

"What? No!" With a thud Ondine fell back into her seat and stared at him. This was not going the right way! "That's not how it works! I just bared my soul to you. I've never done that *ever*, and you say you're leaving anyway?"

"Aye." He tucked a stray hair behind her ear and caressed her cheek with his palm. "But knowing ye love me makes it easier. Gives me something to look forward to when I get back."

"But . . . you don't need to leave in the first place. I know it's treason to say this," she lowered her voice on the off-chance someone might overhear, "but I've gone right off the Duke. I don't like the sort of job he's offering you."

"What's nawt to like? I get to ferret around and make sure no trinkets end up in the wrong people's pockets."

"It just doesn't sound right, that's why. He's a Duke. He's loaded. Why doesn't he install security cameras instead?"

Hamish cupped Ondine's cheek again. "It's nawt really about the job description, is it? More the fact I'll be away that's upsetten ye."

"I suppose so." His warm hand felt so good she almost forgot her own mind.

"Ondi, I do love ye. Taking a job with the Duke is the perfect way for me to show ye how much."

"What?" It made no sense at all. He loved her so he was leaving?

"Hear me out. It's been a long time since I was a real man. I want to get it right. That means being responsible. Getting a real job. Staying here, by the grace and favour of yer parents . . . that's nawt being responsible. Taking a real job with the Duke of Brugel will prove to yer parents that I'm worthy of ye. I'll be a man for the first time in me life."

"But . . . the Duke wants you to be a ferret."

"Aye, Ondi, we all have to make sacrifices."

Heat burned the back of her eyes. Her vision blurred and a hot tear splashed down her cheek. *Jupiter's moons, now I'm crying like a nine-year-old.*

"Ach, dry yer eyes. I'll nawt leave tomorrow. He doesn't need me until September. We've still got the rest of the summer, and then I'll only be across town. I'll come and visit whenever I can."

"Promise?"

"Promise."

Ondine threw her arms around Hamish and hugged him tightly. The thought of having to separate shredded her heart, so she wound her arms that bit tighter round him.

In the east, the faint glow of dawn broke the murky night sky.

"It's morning already," Hamish said, noticing the change in the light.

"Maybe we should get inside?" An uneasy little flip began to flop inside Ondine's belly. Last time they'd been here in the garden, as dawn had broken, Hamish had reverted to ferret form.

"No. Let's see what happens." Hamish cupped her chin, pulled Ondine closer and kissed her again, making her brain fizz and crackle. Every time their lips met her mind went all fuzzy and she loved it. She loved him. Even better, he loved her.

They pulled apart for a little bit, and checked the sky.

So far so good.

The sun cleared the horizon, bathing the air with the warming rays and colours of a new summer's day.

"You're still you," Ondine beamed.

"Aye. See, being responsible is paying off already."

"Good. Kiss me again then."

He did as he was told and her whole body buzzed with the joy of it.

"Hamish? Promise me when you're working for the Duke that you'll come back as often as you can?"

"As long as ye promise to welcome me back like this each time."

Ondine beamed. "That's a very easy promise to make."

As they kissed into the morning, Ondine banished thoughts of how soon autumn would be upon them. Instead, she focused on the precious few weeks of summer remaining, and the promises they'd made to each other.

Especially her promise about welcoming him back.

– The End –

# THE AUTUMN PALACE

**1**

———

Let's get one thing clear from the outset. Ondine de Groot is not now, nor will she ever be, psychic.

Smart? Yes.

Prone to blurting out the wrong thing at the wrong time? Certainly.

But psychic? Hardly.

However, as she held Hamish's warm hand in hers and walked towards the train station in West Venzelemma, she felt something momentous might happen.

Very soon.

Possibly in the next few pages.

Hamish was about to take on a job with the Duke of Brugel, who lived two boroughs away in the poshest part of Venzelemma.[1]

It would take nine train stops to get there, which meant the next hour could be their last together for a long, long time. In fact, Ondine might not see him again for a whole week! That was far too long to go without seeing the boyfriend she'd only just found.

Giving his hand a squeeze, she steadied her bubbling emotions. In return Hamish gave her his trademark lopsided grin, making her insides go squishy.

"Yer up tae something, lass, I can tell."

"I was just thinking we might not have to say goodbye, once we reach the Duke's place." Naughty flurries spun in her head as a plan to stay together began to form.

"I thought ye looked crafty."

Ondine grinned. "You know how I promised my parents I'd see you to the Duke's, then come home. And then I also had to promise I wouldn't ask the Duke for a job . . ."

"Och, hen, there's a 'but' coming any minute now."

"But!" And here Ondine beamed with how cleverly she could get around the promises she'd made to her parents without actually breaking them. "It doesn't mean *you* can't ask the Duke for a job on my behalf."

"Yer sure yer nae stretching yer arm farther than yer sleeve'll let ye?"

A few cranks and cogs shifted in Ondine's head before she figured out what he was getting at. "I'm not overreaching. We'll be fine. What could possibly go wrong?"

"I wouldnae want tae get yer parents off-side. When they find out they'll be fair affronted."

Ondine's hopes crumpled. "You don't want us to be together?"

"Ye cannae look at me like that, it breaks me wee heart. Ye know I love ye more than anything and I'll do what I can for ye, lass."

The tenseness in her shoulders eased. "I love you so much. If the Duke says 'no,' then I'll wear it. But if he says 'yes,' then we can stay together."

The cool autumn breeze blew her brown hair over her eyes, spoiling her view. Hamish tucked a stray tendril behind her ear. He gave her such a loving smile she forgot how to breathe.

"Yer sure this is what ye want?" he asked. "I'll be right busy, what with all the important things the Duke has planned for me. Havtae admit, I'm right jumpy about ma first real gig."

Ondine could have sworn his chest puffed out with pride. Fair enough, too. The Duke wanted Hamish – and his particular talents – to spy for him.

"I am absolutely sure. Oh, Hamish, we're going to have such an adventure."

"Aye. I cannae wait." He grinned at her again and she felt lightheaded with relief.

Fresh emotions bubbled in her heart. "Hamish, you are the best thing that's ever happened to me."

"Aw, hen, yer all that and more tae me." He gave her a quick kiss. "But time's wasting, let's nawt keep the Duke waiting."

Just as they were asking for a couple of City Saver tickets a familiar voice called out, "Yoo-hoo".[2]

Turning around, Ondine saw five suitcases cludder into a neat pile on the ground, as if they'd been levitating not a moment earlier.[3] A lead weight dropped in her stomach at the sight of her Great-Aunt Colette Romano standing beside the luggage. How on earth had she packed it, then carried it, then caught up with them so quickly? Oh, that's right, she was a witch.[4]

"What's she doing here?" Ondine said to Hamish behind gritted teeth.

"There you are! Hamish, help me with these? There's a good boy." Old Col bustled up to the counter in front of them.

Ondine saw Hamish's brows rise in confusion.

"Col, we are just paying for our tickets," Hamish said, putting money on the counter. The older woman's hand slammed down hard on his. He winced. Ondine winced in sympathy. For an old bird, she sure packed a wallop.

Old Col grew stern. "Put your money away, I do not travel second."[5]

"I'm not asken ye to."

"Then how am I to be Ondine's chaperone if we are not all in the same carriage?" She made a tisking sound, shook her head and turned her attention to the confused ticket clerk. Then she said in a too-loud voice, "Three first tickets to Bellreeve, thank you."

Ondine thought, *Chaperone? For a train ride across town?*

Hamish said, "That is very generous of you, but . . ."

The sound of rusty brakes screeched inside Ondine's head. "Bellreeve? What are we going all the way out there for? The Duke's right here in Venzelemma."

"We are going to Bellreeve because that is where the Autumn Palechia is."[6]

"But –" started Ondine.

"But –" started Hamish.

Old Col breathed in deeply and squared her shoulders. "Enough!" Just in case they didn't get it, she held her palm up in a stop sign.

Silently, Ondine gave Hamish's hand another squeeze to let him know, *We're in this together, we'll be OK.* Judging by Hamish's pale face, he wasn't so sure. Col had a way of messing up his life. He'd be numpty to think she'd go easy on him now.[7]

"Come, children." Old Col had that air of command about her.

Ondine and Hamish could only shrug and follow. All the while Ondine kept wondering about the sudden change of plan. Then Old Col turned and glared at them, which had the effect of chilling the air by five degrees. "The suitcases aren't going to carry themselves, are they?"

An empty feeling stole over Ondine as Hamish let go of her hand and retrieved Old Col's cases. They looked back-breakingly heavy and there were five of them. Why didn't Old Col levitate them instead?

"Aunt Col, I appreciate your concern for my welfare, but you really don't need to come. I know the way to the Duke's city palace, it's not that far from here," Ondine said. "Hamish and I have been there before, you know."

"You would say that, child."

Patronising old . . . It didn't make sense to travel all the way to Bellreeve when the Duke lived so close by. If Ondine were honest with herself, she would also admit that the thought of travelling to the country and being so far away from home made her nervous. Having grown up in the bustling streets of Venzelemma, the city felt familiar. The country-side was another matter entirely. With its dark spooky woods and big noisy animals lumbering about, travelling there felt a bit scary and intim-idating.

"Clearly you have not thought beyond your hormonal urges, Ondi. There is a bigger picture here and you are blind to it. You may recall that when the Duke of Brugel graced your parent's hotel several weeks ago,[8] he asked me to work for him, and I accepted.[9] He also invited Hamish into his employ, and Hamish accepted. He has not, however, extended any such invitation to you. Were the two of you to arrive at his city doorstep together, you, Ondine, would be returning alone."

The luggage weighed Hamish down. Ondine's back hurt in sympathy and she grabbed one of the cases to lighten his load. A few paces on, her shoulder felt ready to give out, plus she had a burning strain in her lower back, but she bore it.

Ondine said, "The Duke will find something for me to do. I'll work for free if I have to."

"Don't debase yourself like that!" Old Col tisked for good measure. "Clearly I arrived just in time, before you made a total fool of yourself. If you followed politics at all, you would know the Duke and his family always spend the autumn in Bellreeve before parliament opens. He'll be there soon enough, so we'll be spared the hassle of relocating. If anything, we could scout the area for anything untoward."

"Oh!" That threw an entirely new light on things.

"When the three of us arrive in Bellreeve tonight, we will have travelled so far and for so long that our gracious host will feel obliged to offer you some kind of employment. No decent person would send a young girl on such a long return journey alone."

It was almost as if Great-Aunt Col was going out of her way to help Ondine. The thought should have been reassuring, but instead it made her uneasy. A few moments ago she and Hamish had been in charge of their destiny. Or as in charge as you can be when you're relying on a duke to give you a job. Now her great-aunt had taken over and Ondine didn't like it one bit.

The train's first-class carriage was at the very end of the platform, directly behind the engine. Negotiating the crowd involved lots of "sorrys", "s'cuse mes" and "did you have that bruise alreadys?" as they squeezed their way through. Finally they arrived and Hamish dumped the cases on the ground with a satisfying cludder. Joints clicked and creaked as he stretched his back.

"Oh, look, there's a trolley. Hamish, why didn't you use that?" Old Col put her hand to the side of her mouth and laughed. It was supposed to come out as a giggle, but it sounded more like a cackle.

Although it would be impossible to be inside two people's heads at the same time, Ondine knew she and Hamish shared a thought: *That was deliberate.*

A porter arrived and began loading the cases into the luggage van. It would have been nice if the porter had been somewhere near the ticket counter when they'd first arrived – he could have saved them a lot of backache.

"In you get, children." Old Col pointed to the carriage door and they climbed aboard.

Inside looked like a plush lounge room. Correction, a series of plush lounge rooms, with leather recliner chairs and nifty little tables by the windows. It smelled like money.

When Ondine touched the nearest headrest, she felt the soft leather squish beneath her hand.

"It's so lush!" she said. No rubbish on the floor, no graffiti on the walls, no missing light fittings or torn seats. The carpet was so thick she left dents in it as she walked.

"Aye, it's Barry!" Hamish said as he walked behind her.[1]

The aroma of walnuts filled the air. Ondine could also smell coffee, honey and a sprinkling of nutmeg. Further up the carriage a passenger sipped a steaming mug of coffee and nibbled a delicate pastry.

They sank into their chairs – no hard bench seats in here – and Hamish smiled at Ondine. Fresh bursts of warmth flurried across her skin.

"Ahh, young love," Great-Aunt Col said, giving them a stern look. "May I remind you, Ondine, you are only fifteen and not an adult, no matter how much you pretend to be one. Hamish would do well to remember that."

Defying her great aunt, Ondine planted a kiss on Hamish. Zap! Electricity arced between them as their lips touched.

"Wow!" Ondine shook her head in astonishment.

Hamish pulled away and gave her a wicked grin. He rubbed his old borrowed shoes against the carpet a few times and kissed Ondine again.

Ping!

Static crackled across Ondine's skin and made the fine hairs on her arm stand up. Every little kiss jolted her with bursts of electricity.

"Behave yourselves," Old Col said, but she didn't sound all that serious.

The electric kisses proved addictive and Ondine rubbed her shoes against the carpet again. She licked her lips and moved in for a kiss.

Pow!

"Ouch!" Hamish said. "That was really strong!"

"I'm so sorry!" Had she hurt him?

"Och, that's all right. Kiss me better, then." She received another delicious electric shock for her troubles.

"That's enough now, both of you. Remember, you're in public," Old Col said.

Buildings moved past the window at increasing speed, taking them away from the city at an alarming rate. The summer with Hamish had been truly wonderful, but all too brief. Memories tugged Ondine into backstory, to the time when she and Hamish met. She'd been leaving Psychic Summercamp.[2]

He'd been a ferret. A talking ferret who, after an exasperating series of events, finally became a gorgeous lad. Which everybody, especially Ondine, agreed was a rather excellent turn of events. Ondine was happiest when Hamish was his handsome self instead of his animal incarnation. Over their summer together, the curse had pretty much worked itself out. Hamish could be human as long as he was near Ondine, which suited her just fine. Yet they were about to work for the Duke, and the Duke would probably prefer Hamish to remain a ferret as much as possible.

"This is going tae be so exciting I cannae wait tae make a start," Hamish said. "And Col, at first I didnae like yer interfering, but now I can see ye'll help Ondi get a job and then we'll be working together and having adventures, so we will."

Ondine loved hearing him talk. There was something magical and a little bit naughty in the way he spoke. Just thinking about how they could stay together and work together made her glow. It really felt like everything would turn out wonderfully.

The afternoon tea trolley arrived. Col ordered a pot of Darjeeling for herself and some nibbles for Ondine and Hamish.[3] The waiter made a few deft moves and extracted side tables from within the armrests.

"This is tha good stuff, eh, lass?" Hamish gave Ondine another of his lopsided smiles. The ones that made her go all silly in the head. The next moment he cut a small piece off his marinated artichoke and offered it to her.

There was something so tender and touching about the action, Ondine felt overcome. She accepted the morsel and chewed it as delicately as she could. "It's heavenly." She shut her eyes to savour the moment. When she opened them, she found Hamish gazing at her with adoration. They were lost in a bubble of love as she returned the favour, feeding him a tidbit from her plate.

"Easy on tha salad, hen."

"Oh, sorry, I forgot you're still not used to it." Ondine picked the leafy greens off her fork and replaced them with chunks of chicken and ham.

"It's taking a while tae adjust, like," he said.

It sure was. As a ferret he ate nothing but protein and fat. Not through choice but necessity, because carbohydrates could put him in a coma. But now he was human, surely he could vary his diet?

As if reading her mind, he added, "Old habits die hard."

"They certainly do," Old Col said, interrupting them. At which point Col tipped the remains of her tea into the saucer and then studied the tealeaves. "Oh, look, we're going on a journey."

Ondine rolled her eyes – a safer option than going "Pfffft", because she had another mouthful of scrumptious food. Since when did her great aunt look for signs in a teacup? Col had scorned her old friend Mrs Howser for doing just that at Thomas and Margi's engagement party.

"No, really, look." Old Col held out the teacup for Ondine to see.

To Ondine's surprise, she saw the clear outline of a locomotive in the wet leaves. "That's a . . . it really looks like a train. Mercury's wings, I never thought you'd be into reading tealeaves. It's even got a carriage and everything."

"Really?" Old Col knitted her brows and had another look in the cup. She turned the cup this way and that, then shook her head. "That's not a carriage, dear, it's a coffin. What a shame, that means somebody's going to die."

# 3

As much as Ondine didn't want to believe in the power of tealeaves, she couldn't shake the image of that small coffin outlined in Darjeeling in Aunt Col's cup.

On their train chugged, through the valleys of Novorsk Kallun[1] and the dramatic Lake Obski, where sunlight glittered on towers of crystalline rocks.[2]

As the sun headed for the hills, they arrived in the northern borough of Bellreeve, where the air smelled like wet leaves. Judging by the puddles on the road, it had been raining. Judging by the dark clouds above, it would rain again soon. There were rows upon rows of buildings, but none of them over two storeys high. It looked like the kind of place that called itself a city, but was barely more than a town. Aunt Col waved a fan of banknotes at the porters to have their cases brought to the palechia.

Ondine wondered how Col had so much money. First-class travel and flashing the cash to get help had never entered Ondine's mind. Not that her parents were poor, but with three children and a business to run, Ma and Da kept a firm hand on finances. Her great-aunt on the other hand must have pillows of gold.[3]

"It's not far, we shall walk from here," Old Col said in her best school-marmish tone.

With no bags to carry, Ondine slipped her hand into Hamish's. In return, Hamish gave her a smile that made her knees go squishy. They walked through the quiet streets as shop owners packed up and closed their businesses for the day.

"I cannae wait fer our adventures tae begin," he said.

Ondine squeezed his hand. Apprehension niggled at her as she silently hoped she could stay with Hamish and not be sent home.

Old Col led them up a tree-lined road that climbed a hill.

"Well, here we are." She stopped at the top, where the landscape opened out before them. Ahead stood the centuries-old gatehouse with its cobblestone path. Ondine sighed as she took in the velvety green meadows, sprinkled with tiny white flowers. Towering trees dropped their yellow and orange leaves like confetti on the ground. In the middle of the loveliness sat an enormous mansion fit for a . . . well, a duke. Three storeys high and forty-five huge windows across, it dominated the estate.[4]

It had a pale yellow façade and manicured creepers wound around white columns.

"It's beautiful," Ondine said with a breathy sigh. On impulse, she leaned towards Hamish and rested her head on his shoulder.

"Aw, nawt this, Col, ye goiven!" Hamish said.[5]

"What?" Ondine couldn't believe her ears. How could someone gaze upon such a pretty scene and not feel at peace with the world?

When Col turned back to look at them, her face was all innocence. "You don't like it?"

Hamish glared at Old Col and said, "Out of all the places in Brugel, ye had tae bring me here, din't ye?"

With a sinking feeling Ondine looked from Hamish to her great-aunt and then back again. "What is this place?"

"It's the Duke's autumn palace." Col laughed and winked. The woman was having far too much fun at Hamish and Ondine's expense.

"You've been here before," Ondine said, "both of you."

Old Col shrugged. "Why, you're right! We have been here, many years ago." Then she turned and set off towards the gatehouse.

"A great many," Hamish said, shaking his head. "Only it wasnae called Bellreeve then. If I'd known, I wouldnae come."[6]

Figuratively, the twig snapped. Ondine rolled her eyes. "This is where the debutante ball took place, isn't it?"[7]

"Aye. You're a smart lass." He gave her a smile but it looked tight and strained and his nostrils were flared.

"I didn't realise it was here. I guess I never thought about where it happened," Ondine said, taking slower steps to create distance between themselves and Old Col, who walked towards the imposing building, giggling to herself.

Ondine whispered to Hamish, "Do you think she knew all along?"

"Aye, I do."

Ondine didn't ask more, because she knew it would upset Hamish very much to speak of those horrible events. She wound her arm around his waist and gave him a hug. He returned it but without the intensity she needed. Despite the picture-postcard scene, her happy mood evaporated. Somewhere in this vast palace was a ballroom, where, decades ago, Great-Auntie Col had lost her dental-floss-thin grip on her temper and cast Hamish into ferret form. And in that form he'd stayed for years and years, until he'd met Ondine. The only good to come from his being trapped as a member of the weasel family was that his human physical form had not changed since that day.[8]

They walked to the gatehouse and Ondine let Col do all the talking. The guard looked at the three of them and asked for identification.

Oh dear, Ondine had none, neither did Hamish. "They are with me," Old Col said, "The Duke is expecting us."

"Wait one moment," the guard said, picking up an intercom and pressing a button.

"By the time you do that, we could be inside already. Come children," Col said, breezing past him.

Eeek, that felt a bit naughty. Hamish took Ondine's hand and they followed Col.

Click clack went her feet on the cobble stones, which had fleur-de-lis carved on them.

Wind suddenly howled through the trees. Ondine's dark hair whipped across her face and stung her eyes. A gust pushed her from behind and she lost her footing.

"Steady, lass." Hamish held her hand as the trees around them twisted and thrashed. His lips kept moving, but the wind stole the rest of his words.

Old Col staggered, then turned and pointed.

Ondine looked behind them to see a tornado sucking up everything in its path – buildings, plants and earth. It was heading right for them! The guard fled his post, just before the twister ripped up the gatehouse.

"Run!" Hamish yelled, grabbing her and racing towards the safety of the palace.

The wind clawed at them. Ondine screamed as something exploded beside her and slate tiles flew through the sky.

*Bang!*

The twister sucked the doors off the stables and half a dozen terrified horses bolted out. The next second Col had Ondine by the other hand. The three of them ran towards the palace portico.

Just as someone slammed the enormous doors in their faces.

**4**

———————

"Let us in!" Ondine banged her fists on the timber door.

"Stand back," Old Col commanded. She drew her hands up to the sky and then pushed them towards the door handle.

Nothing happened.

*I wonder if Old Col's as magic as she used to b–*

The doors burst open to reveal half a dozen terrified staff huddling against the wall.

The wind was howling. Ondine turned to see if the twister was following them in. To her enormous relief it changed course at the last second and zig-zagged down the hill towards the lake.

"Phew, that was close."

The tornado kept vacuuming up everything in its path, becoming a waterspout as it crossed the lake. Then, just as fast as it had sprung up, it lost its power and vanished into the dark clouds.

All was still.

"Was that your doing, Col?" Hamish asked, his voice burning with anger.

"Most certainly not. But if you'll pardon the pun, it sure put the wind up me. I've never seen anything like it."

The nervous staff broke their huddle. One of them stepped forward and held out his hand to Col.

"Pyotr Nillinskovic at your service. I am the seneschal."[1]

"Colette Romano. Here at the Duke's pleasure."

Pyotr walked to the door and had a look outside at the damage. "The school roof's gone and the stables are a mess." He quickly issued orders to the rest of the staff. "Find the horses – and find new homes for them, then relocate the school to somewhere with a roof."

Without missing a beat, or even checking if they had recovered from the shock, Old Col said, "This is Hamish McPhee, he is also here at the Duke's invitation. And this is Ondine, my grand-niece."

The ground slipped a little beneath Ondine's feet. Not literally, for that would be an earth tremor and Brugel is not in a quake zone. The ground slipped figuratively, making her feel a bit wobbly on the inside. She shook Pyotr's hand and with a shaky voice said, "Pleased to meet you."

"And I you," Pyotr said with a welcoming smile that made Ondine start to feel at ease.

Pyotr turned to Hamish and welcomed him calmly with a handshake. Ondine had an inkling she was going to like this man as the colour returned to his lined face. He had the most obvious comb-over she'd ever seen. The wide parting began just above his ear and stretched his slick brown hair right over to the other ear. She had to give herself a mental kick to stop staring at it.

"How old are you, Ondine?" Pyotr asked.

"Fifteen, sir."

"I see. Then you can work in the afternoons, and attend the palechia school in the mornings. Once we find a new home for the school, of course. Please come with me."

She couldn't believe how quickly Pyotr had recovered his composure.

The moment Pyotr turned away, Hamish squeezed Ondine's hand. Not to demonstrate his love – it was all about keeping a straight face while they gazed at that astonishing head of hair. Or not-hair. As much as she loved looking at Hamish, it took all her effort not to look at him right now, because if she did, she'd collapse in a fit of giggles.

Their feet clacking on the mosaic-tiled floor, the three of them followed Pyotr inside. Delicious aromas of roasting meat and vegetables wafted through the air. They must be somewhere near the kitchens.

"Do you have any work experience?" Pyotr asked Ondine.

"My parents run a pub and I help out a fair bit," she said.

"You know your way around a kitchen, then?"

"Of course."

Hamish squeezed her hand again. She kept her giggles in check as she answered more of Pyotr's questions while politely looking him in the eye and trying very hard not to look at his hair. Odd that the seneschal wasn't asking Old Col or Hamish any questions. Then another twig snapped – Hamish and Col already had jobs. She, however, was at a loose end and the kind man was trying to find her something to do.

"If the three of you would come this way, I'll take you to your lodgings. Then I shall inform the Duke of your attendance."

"He's here already?" Ondine asked.

"Yes. A last-minute change of plans," Pyotr said.

Aunt Col's brows shot up in surprise. "A good thing we came directly, then, otherwise we would have been cooling our heels in Venzelemma."

Ondine couldn't help thinking her great-aunt knew a lot more than she was letting on. Pyotr's acceptance of them was so fuss-free that Ondine began to wonder if something was afoot. Ondine might lack a lot of what might be called "life experience", but she trusted her instincts, and those instincts were telling her to be very careful. Which meant no gasping at the priceless paintings, no ooh-ing and ah-ing at the intricate decorations and the luxurious furniture as they walked past open sitting rooms. She kept her eyes firmly fixed on the middle of Pyotr's back – not looking down in case he turned around and thought she was acting sullen. She dared not look up because of that tantalisingly bad hair.

"This will be your room, Ondine," Pyotr said, as they stopped outside door 404.

It was smaller than her bedroom at home. There were two narrow, single beds, one made up with a well-loved teddy bear sitting on the pillow and a crocheted blanket on the top. The other bed – which would be Ondine's – had plain white sheets and a beige quilt. Each bed had a matching white side table and a small white chest of drawers at the foot of the bed. The window looked out to a narrow, cobbled courtyard where washing flicked and flapped on the clotheslines.

*Drab-tastic!*

Pyotr continued, "Your bags are yet to arrive. We'll walk to the laundry, where I'll introduce you to Miss Matice. She is the Master of Domestic Services, which is one of the most important jobs we have here."

Nice that he tried to talk up the job description, but Ondine wasn't fooled. As they walked away from the kitchens and headed towards the laundry, those lovely cooking aromas faded away, replaced by strong smells of bleach, floral detergent and something that might almost pass for green apples.

"I'm very happy to do laundry," Ondine said, because she didn't want to seem ungrateful. OK, laundry was a drudge, but Pyotr could have given her plenty of worse things to do, like scrub floors or toilets. "But, if you don't mind me asking, how come you wanted to know about my kitchen experience?"

"Because, if you've worked in a kitchen, you'll know all about wine and food stains, and how to get them out." Pyotr gave her a big grin.

Old Col snickered into her hand.

Hamish looked despondent and slightly worried. "You'll be OK." He leaned forward and gave her a kiss on the cheek, which had the temporary effect of making her forget all about her imminent menial work. The drudgery would be worth it if she and Hamish could be together.

"Young love. Bless," an unfamiliar voice said. Ondine felt heat rising in her face as she turned. Pyotr introduced her. "Miss Matice, this is Ondine, she will be starting here today. Would you be so kind as to take her under your wing?"

Miss Matice's hair was pulled into a tight blonde ponytail that made her head look alarmingly thin, like the rest of her reed-thin body, which almost disappeared when she turned sideways.

"Delighted," Miss Matice said, extending her bony hand to Ondine. "Please, call me Draguta, we friends now, yes?"

"Y-yes." With a mental hiccup, Ondine shook hands and tried to keep a straight face. Honestly, what kind of parents burdened their kid with such a horrible name? An uncharitable thought arrived – maybe she'd been a really ugly baby.

"Bye, then," Hamish said, giving Ondine a lopsided smile.

She wanted to throw her arms around him and kiss him silly, but that would not go down so well with her new employer. And she really needed to make a good impression so they would see how useful she was and allow her to stay.

With a small wave, she bid him farewell and made ready to face up to her new job.[2]

Pyotr, Old Col and Hamish turned and walked away.

"Start with baskets. Is about to rain, get washing off line," Draguta said in her strangely clipped style of talking. Ondine wondered if perhaps Brugelish was her second language.

Through the open doorway, Ondine looked out at the courtyard and saw a small team of workers removing washing from the line. She walked out and reached up to the first peg.

Something wet and smelly slapped on her hand. Urgh! It was a fish! A woman next to Ondine screamed and came running inside, dropping her basket of laundry in the process. "It's raining fish!"

Plop! Flop! Splat!

Like some bizarre dream, fish fell all around Ondine, landing with wet spluds on her head and shoulders and the ground. Some of them kept wriggling and flipping. And oh, the putrid smell!

Argh! Horrified, yet compelled to stay on task, Ondine grabbed the washing from the line and threw it into the basket. Wet projectiles kept hammering her. Ooof, her head. Ouch, her shoulder. Biff, her face.

All around people were screaming and crying and huddling under the eaves to get away from the hideous rain.

Ondine picked up her laundry basket and charged inside.

"Where is laundry?" Draguta demanded.

Looking down, Ondine gasped. Her basket was full of fish. "It must be underneath!"

"Is crazy! Crazy!" Draguta threw her hands up in the air in frustration. "Will have to wash all over again!"

"Or, looking on the bright side, I've caught us dinner," Ondine said.

"Ha! I like you!" Draguta slapped her on the back. "Now, get rid of fish and get washing. Here, take basket and sort for colours."

In the next breath, Draguta caught the attention of another laundry worker and told her to take all the fish to the kitchens.

Feeling bewildered by the strange turn of events, Ondine could only shrug and get to work, sorting clothes. Draguta tended to an industrial-sized machine that had just finished spinning. Not for the first time, Ondine wondered whether she would ever get used to calling Draguta by that harsh name. Strong veins popped out on Draguta's sinewy arms as she pulled wet bath sheets and towelling robes from the machine. At the same time, another laundress moved towards a small door set into the wall. Dirty clothes spilled on to the floor.

"A laundry chute! That's cool," Ondine said.

"Not nearly," Draguta said. "They be lords and ladies, but live like slobs. They put down chutes in one day what regular people use in week. Get used to it."

"Draguta, do you have a middle name?" Ondine asked as she separated the dirty clothes into their respective piles.

The laundry master's face turned to a scowl. "Elena. Named after grandmother, may she rot in hell!" Draguta turned to her right and spat on the floor.

A slither of fear slid up Ondine's spine and she mentally ruled out ever mentioning the name Elena again.

Should she try another tack? Why not. "Do you have a nickname?"

"No."

Ondine gulped. "Well . . . most people call me Ondi for short, so feel free to call me that, I don't mind."

"My name is Draguta. Is strong name." Draguta hefted a basket of wet washing on to where her hips would be if she had a gram of fat on her. A strong name for a strong woman.

It took two workers to heft each of the remaining baskets of washing out to the courtyard, where the rain had stopped just as fast as it began. Draguta managed a whole basket on her own. Ondine stayed inside, sorting the remaining dirty clothes.

"You need to go through pockets," Draguta instructed, as she came back into the laundry. "They filthy, leave tissues behind. Lost count of times to rewash dark pants because of shredded tissue. Don't be shy, shove hand in there. Ferret around."

*Ferret?*

Panic surged through Ondine. She'd forgotten all about Hamish and what might happen if they were separated. "Jupiter's moons! Ferret!"

                                  **5**

                          ___________


H ow far had Hamish gone? What if he transformed into a ferret in front of the seneschal?

"I have to go!" Ondine shot up, knocking over a pile of silk blouses. Charging down the hallway, she yelled out, "Hamish, wait!"

On she ran, hoping she wasn't too late. All that time on the train and they hadn't spent one moment discussing how they were going to manage Hamish's . . . *issue.* They had been together so much during summer, she'd become used to him being human whenever she was around. What if he'd lost the ability to control his transformations?

A familiar groan of pain and a filthy Celtic curse carried up the hall. Ondine's vision blurred as tears threatened to leak out. Skittering around the corner, she saw Shambles the ferret lying on the floor. Clothes everywhere. Old Col cast Ondine a dark look, as if this were all her fault. Pyotr merely cocked one eyebrow and swallowed, waiting for an explanation. Ondine herself struggled to find a reason.

For a moment she opened and shut her mouth, but nothing came out. Pyotr had just witnessed a terrifying weather event and now a man turning into a ferret. She wondered if she should tell him about the fish rain? It would be a lot to take in. Dread crawled through her body. She didn't have to be psychic to know they were in serious trouble if she didn't think of something quickly.

The something she thought of was: "You've never seen a man turn into a ferret before?"

"Can't say that I have." Pyotr scratched his temple.

"You have now," Ondine ploughed on. "You can see what a great asset he'll be to the Duke. After all, Shambles is the one who foiled the assassination attempt against him. The Duke wouldn't even be here if not for him. That's why he offered him a job, because he saved his life. And if Duke Pavla goes under, Lord Vincent would take control, and who wants that?"

"Thank you, yes." Pyotr nodded slowly, closing his eyes as he did so, indicating he'd heard – and possibly seen – quite enough.

"If ye could all turn around for a wee bit, I need tae straighten meself out," Shambles said, wincing as he budged and fudged his way into a sitting position to become humanly Hamish again. Ondine felt a fresh pang of longing for him. He looked like he was in so much pain.

They turned their backs to give him privacy.

"I have seen many things in my years . . ." Pyotr started.

Ondine waited for him to finish his sentence, but after a few breathy pauses with nothing between them, she realised he wouldn't.

"Great-Aunt Col did it to him, in the ballroom here at the palechia. Years ago when she made her debut." Ondine turned to see how the seneschal was taking it. A flicker on Pyotr's face, a raised eyebrow, then his features were back in place, as if they were discussing nothing more than the weather.

Well, not the weather they'd just had, obviously, but regular weather.

With a small cough Old Col said, "You are the epitome of discretion, sir, and we are in your debt."

Once he had his trousers on the right way, Hamish stood up. He sat down again straight away and looked a bit woozy.

Ondine knelt beside him and put her hand on his shoulder, "You're hurting."

"Naw lass, I'll be fine."

She didn't buy it, and gave him a tender kiss on the forehead to salve the pain.

Pyotr spoke up. "I think it would be best if he returned to his animal form."

"But –" Ondine started.

Pyotr said, "As much as it appears to pain him, I believe the Duke would prefer him to remain a ferret."

"Dinnae fuss, it will just be for a wee while," Hamish said.

Ondine began to fret. They were at the Duke's palechia because they wanted to be together. But the Duke only wanted the ferrety Shambles side of Hamish. It hurt to know the only way they could be together was to be apart.

Ondine flung her arms around Hamish's neck and hugged him, hard. "We'll work something out," she said, and kissed him again.

Pain lanced Ondine as she watched him revert to his animal form, but it was nothing compared to the physical pain he must be feeling.

Pyotr said, "By the way, what is that smell?"

"It's trout," Ondine said. "Lots of them fell from the sky as we took in the laundry."

Pyotr stopped and stared at Ondine. "Do you mean to say it has rained fish?"

"Yes, sir. But we've cleaned most of it up."

"Just a moment," he said as two men walked down the hall towards them. Pyotr asked them to remove any stray fish from the lawns, trees and rooftops. "And see that you clean out any debris that may have fallen through the school roof." They looked startled.

"I meant what I said," Pyotr added, dismissing the workmen. He returned his gaze to Col, Shambles and Ondine, his face showing no sign that he'd asked the workers to perform anything out of the ordinary. "Come this way. The Duke does not like to be kept waiting."

6

"Delighted to see you!" Duke Pavla said as he took Old Col's hand in his. They were standing in his gleaming study. The leather chairs looked so shiny Ondine thought she'd slide right off them. Not that she had permission to sit down yet. The Duke – and the Duchess Kerala was here too – hadn't invited them to do so. The Duke looked the same as he always did – dressed in an expensive, dark suit, his hair swept back from his widow's peak. His high-maintenance split moustache looked so neat it might have been stencilled on. "Dare I say you have arrived just in time. Somebody tried to poison me with seafood," he said.

"My Lord Duke, you have no cause for alarm. Falling fish are a natural phenomenon, caused by the twister turning into a waterspout over the lake," Old Col said. Then she added, "It vacuumed the fish and water into the clouds. A completely natural, albeit startling, event."

For a palpable few seconds Duke Pavla stared at her as if she had said something really strange. Well, she had.

"Falling fish?"

"As a result of the twister, Your Grace."

It took him a few moments to compose himself. "I was referring to earlier events at the fish markets," he said.

Now Ondine was really confused.

With a wave of his hand the Duke invited them to sit. He also dismissed Pyotr, so it was just the five of them in the room. Ondine did her best not to fidget. To her dismay, Shambles climbed on to Col's shoulder, not hers.

The Duke sat behind his desk. The Duchess remained standing behind him. She looked immaculate, as only the seriously rich can. Perfectly applied make-up, shiny mahogany hair, a tailored suit that complimented her hourglass frame and soft dainty hands. She wore an imperious look on her face, a mixture of revulsion and concern. Obviously not a small-animal lover.

It was hard to explain why, but Ondine had the feeling the Duchess was one of those people who preferred her animals without a pulse and covered in Béarnaise sauce.

Duke Pavla said, "This is too much of a coincidence. You've heard about what happened at the fish markets yesterday?"

Old Col coughed softly. "No, Your Grace."

The Duke looked bewildered. Ondine felt incredibly uncomfortable. Surely at some point things would start making sense. Wouldn't they?

The Duchess placed a comforting hand on Pavla's shoulder.

"I was due to open the new sushi bar," Pavla said. "They would have made me eat the stuff, too. A good thing I changed my schedule. I sent my dear wife to the markets in my place. They had a listeria outbreak but thank the stars she was unharmed. If anything had happened to you, my love . . ." his voice trailed off as their eyes locked.

A pang gripped Ondine. They looked so very much in love. Would she and Hamish ever have that? Impossible if he remained a Shambles-ferret.

"I'm fine. I have an iron constitution," the Duchess said.

"I can't help thinking someone has cursed me. Yesterday bad food. Today a twister, now you're saying there was fish rain? If this is the result of dark magic, I'm glad to have you as an ally, Miss Romano," the Duke said. He turned to Shambles, who was still on Old Col's shoulder. "And you, Shambles, I can see you will be a valuable asset."

"Aye. Ready, willing and able. Where would ye like me tae start?" Shambles said.

"I think you should begin with the most obvious. The kitchens," the Duke said. "Watch them closely for the next week and report anything unusual directly back to me."

"Or me. If the Duke is unavailable," Kerala added.

"Yes, good idea, my love." The Duke still hadn't addressed Ondine, which made her feel insignificant. Then again, maybe if he ignored her, she could slip under the radar? If he didn't directly send her home, did it mean she could stay?[1]

Unexpectedly, the Duke winked at Shambles, which was not endearing. If anything, Ondine felt even more unsettled. The Duke moved towards a pile of letters, picked up a gold paper knife and began slicing the envelopes open. He talked the whole time, reading one thing while discussing another. Meanwhile, the Duchess walked over to a side table and poured herself a glass of wine.

The Duke opened the next envelope. Brown powder fell from the papers it contained.

*Poison?*

"Get back!" Shambles yelled. "Dinnae breathe it in!"

The Duke coughed and reeled away in shock.

Instinctively Ondine grabbed a rose bowl off the side table, tipped the flowers on to the floor, then slapped the upturned bowl over the envelope and powder.

The Duchess's mouth fell open as she stood in mute shock. Her eyebrows shot up and stayed there. Inside the bowl water dripped on to the powder, turning it into a dark brown liquid that oozed across the desk.

"What is it?" the Duke said.

Confusion made Ondine feel dizzy. "Looks like coffee," she suggested.

"We don't know that for sure," Col said.

"I feel so terribly foolish," the Duke said, wiping his brow. Perhaps they'd all overreacted.

What a mess Ondine had made of the Duke's study. The brown liquid stopped oozing and started sinking into the table, eating right through the veneer.

"Not so foolish after all," Col said. "It's some kind of acid."

"Who sent it?" Shambles asked.

"There is no return address on the envelope," Col said, picking it up. "Your Grace, call the police, this needs to be tested."

"Wait," the Duchess said, stepping closer to the table. "Let me see it."

Great-Aunt Col handed the envelope to the Duchess, who held it up to the light as if she might make out something the others had missed.

"The stamp has not been franked, so we do not know which sorting office it came from. Maybe if I try this . . ." She took out a pack of matches from her handbag and lit one, holding it beneath the envelope. "Saw it in a movie once, there was a secret message written in – ouch!" The envelope caught fire and she dropped it hastily.

"Are you all right, my love?" Pavla rushed to his wife's side and checked her hand. "You'll need a cold compress."

As the burning envelope fluttered to the ground, Shambles raced down Col's shoulder and stomped his paws on the glowing paper to put it out. "Weil, there goes that," he said.

"I was trying to help," Kerala said.

The Duke's skin turned grey. He took a small breath, then adjusted his tie. "Colette, you and Shambles – and Ondine, it seems – have arrived just in time. I want you to be my eyes and ears here in the palechia. From now on you will open all my correspondence. If there is no return address, incinerate it immediately."

Uneasiness morphed into dismay in Ondine. When she'd set out with Hamish, she'd had visions of being with him and having a great time. Not for a moment did she think they'd have to work that hard. Not harder than she already did at her parents' pub in Venzelemma. Now she felt as if they were responsible for the Duke's very survival. And she didn't have a clue how they would do that.

"You wouldn't credit it, but I used to think I was paranoid," Pavla said. "However, I have come to accept that somebody really is out to get me. As much as Vincent knows he will one day succeed me, he is far from ready. As they say, 'Fate chooses our relatives, we choose our friends'."[2]

The mention of Vincent's name sent fresh ripples of worry through

Ondine. Lord Vincent was the Duke's teenage son and heir, but he was also a total prat and had tried to bring on his father's heart problems so he could inherit the title ahead of time. At least he was now in a military academy fifty kilometres away and couldn't do anything directly. But what if he had spies in the palace?

"Your safety and continuing good health are my paramount concern," Old Col said to the Duke.

"Ondine." Duke Pavla turned his full attention to her. Worry filled her stomach with concrete. "I appreciate your swift action, but you are so young. You should be with your parents."

"I –" Ondine made a start, but she couldn't finish.

"She has the gift of sight, Your Grace," Col said. "She will prove very useful."

"Really, now?" Pavla's eyes widened.

Not really, she wanted to say, but Col had dropped her in it and the Duke was interested. If the Duke wanted to believe in it, then why not? What some people called psychic powers, others called "cold reading" or "being really observant".[3] If he thought she could be useful, she'd get to stay.

"Aw, yeas, she's brilliant at it," Shambles added, climbing back on to Col's shoulder.

The Duchess moved to stand beside her husband, placing her hand on his arm. Her knuckles turned pinky white as she squeezed him that little bit too much. Ondine thought Kerala wanted to say something, but she kept silent.

"How very useful," Pavla said. In the next breath he summoned Pyotr back into his study to show him the mess. Pyotr nodded and ushered them into the anteroom while he cleaned it up.

The Duchess murmured, "Are you sure about this?" in Pavla's ear.

Despite her low voice, Ondine heard everything she said: "They turn up in a storm, then it rains fish and now you have a toxic letter. It's too much of a coincidence."

Old Col coughed into her closed hand. "Please forgive my rudeness, Your Grace, but this really should be a matter –"

"For the police? Of course it is. I will put Brugel's finest on the case.

They are continuing the investigation of the attempt on my life at the railway station. But from all accounts the scallions under arrest are taking the blame upon themselves and refusing to implicate anyone further. They will, in time. Given the right motivation, everybody talks."

A disconcerting look crossed his face. He dropped his voice low. "Here, among family, friends and staff, I need something . . . less overt. Men and women in uniform won't loosen tongues. If anything, it would make the schemers behave impeccably and make everyone else miserable. I need whoever is out to get me to feel as if the authorities' attentions are otherwise . . . diverted. Are we on the same page? Good. The three of you will gather information on everyone at the palechia and report back anything you see, hear or suspect."

"We'll get started right away, so we will," Shambles said.

With a pang of longing, Ondine looked at Shambles. As a ferret, he could slip into rooms and listen to conversations without anyone noticing. He'd be the perfect spy.

"Do you have a list of suspects?" Old Col asked.

"Hand over the phone book," Shambles said.

Ondine clamped down a grin. This was not the time for jokes.

To their credit, the Duke and Duchess ignored the quip. Pavla said, "A couple come to mind. Lord Vincent is all too eager to assume the reins of power. Or should that be reigns?"

Crickets chirped in Ondine's head, because the Duke's pun only worked in print form.

Pyotr walked past them with a trolley full of boxes and lumpy plastic bags. Evidence, Ondine guessed, as Pyotr nodded to them that his work was done.

"No matter," the Duke said as he ushered them back into his study. "My son and heir has learnt his lesson. His supporters, on the other hand, could well be plotting my downfall. Another I suspect is my eldest sister, Anathea."

"The Infanta?" Old Col asked.

The Duchess coughed as she sipped her wine.

Looking about the study, Ondine could see no trace of their recent drama. Only a notebook lay on the table to conceal the burn in the wood.

She gave a mental shudder. That coffee, or whatever it was, could have burned through the Duke.

Duke Pavla continued: "All this would have been hers, you see. But fate intervened and I was born. She begrudges me the right that is mine by birth. Words are her poison of choice. Makes mischief. Most right-thinking people take anything she says with a slice of lemon."[4]

The Duchess made a moue with her mouth and wrinkled her nose at the mention of her sister-in-law.

"Miss Romano, you and Shambles shall attend dinner tonight, ostensibly as my guest, but privately I want you to be on the alert for signs of discontent. Ondine, you will be needed in the laundry."

*Oh, thanks, I get sent to work and Col gets a free meal.*

"Yes, Your Grace," Col said.

"The entire family is in residence. It should provide ample opportunity to observe the various personalities at play."

After they were ushered out, Ondine checked to make sure nobody could overhear them before she spoke. "I can't believe he's making the three of us responsible for his safety! He should bring in the experts."

"Thank you for your vote of confidence," Old Col said.

"I didn't mean it like that."

"Of course not. What you really mean is you're only fifteen and you have the burden of a nation on your shoulders."

An invisible weight descended on Ondine as she let the truth of Col's statement settle. "How much does he really expect us to do? We're not trained detectives." *What we are is a scared girl, a ferret and an old witch.*

"Ah, my dear, that is why we shall be so effective. I am the batty old lady with a pet on her shoulder, and you are an innocent girl. Nobody will suspect a thing."

"Right." Ondine mulled it over. "You're being quiet, Shambles."

"Aye, I was thinking about Pyotr. Nothing seems to faze him."

"Hmmmm," Ondine said.

Col gave a most disarming smile. "You're thinking like detectives already. Nobody should be above suspicion."

"In that case, Vincent is still at the top of my list," Ondine said. "Mercury's wings, I've just realised something. Pavla said Vincent had learnt his lesson, past tense. Does that mean he's not at the academy any more?"

"Oh dear," Hamish said.

"Oh double dear," Col said. "He won't be happy that we're here either. We'll have to try our best not to antagonise him. Right, Ondine, you should get back to the laundry. Shambles, we need to dress for dinner."

Shambles leaned over and gave Ondine a whiskery wet smudge on the cheek, but it didn't comfort her at all. If anything, it made her wonder when she'd next see him as proper Hamish again.

7

Hamish wanted to be human all the time, but he knew the only way to make progress in their hunt for suspects was to remain a ferret and allow people to call him Shambles. He'd much rather be with Ondine in the laundry, but that wasn't an option. He'd also love to be able to talk more, but he exercised extreme control and stayed mute as Pyotr announced Old Col's arrival at dinner.

"Your Graces, honoured guests, ladies and gentlemen, I present Miss Colette Romano."

Perched on Col's shoulder and blinking away tears from her strong perfume, Shambles was able to check out the room from human eye-level. Over to one side he noticed two small boys. They were well-dressed for their age, wearing cut-down suits like mini-gentlemen.

The boys exchanged sly looks and Shambles instinctively knew they were up to no good.

A waitress offered drinks to some adults near them. One of the boys stuck out his foot and tripped her up. She yelped in surprise, her face filled with horror. Then the most bizarre thing happened. Pyotr, who was standing close by, turned around at exactly the right moment, put his hands out and caught the falling tray. Some of the drink sloshed out, but the glasses didn't fall.

Everyone around them looked momentarily stunned. Pyotr kept his composure and handed the tray back to the grateful waitress. She then carried on serving guests as if nothing had happened, but Shambles could tell by her rapid breaths that she hadn't fully recovered.

No sign of the Duke, which was odd – he'd invited them, so surely he'd be here by now? The Duchess, holding a glass of red wine, approached Col. Suddenly the world dropped from beneath Shambles, and he hung on for dear life.

What the?

Old Col was curtseying! After her graceful bob, things righted themselves and he was back to eye-level again.

"My Lady Duchess, it is an honour," Col said.

The Duchess enunciated her words far too carefully as she said, "You. Are. Too. Kind."

Duchess Kerala wore her dark hair in a neat helmet shape. Light bounced off her hair, it was that shiny. The hand holding the glass of wine looked soft and fleshy, as if she'd never performed a manual task in her life.

The waitress appeared and asked the Duchess, "Your Grace, may I offer your guest an aperitif?"[1]

"Thank you, but soda water is fine," Old Col said.

Surprise jolted Shambles. He felt sure Col would help herself to the best of whatever was on offer. The twig snapped – Col wanted to keep a clear head.

The two young boys who had tripped up the waitress were now eyeing Shambles with undisguised glee. Thank goodness he was out of their reach. Oh great! Old Col decided to walk towards them. In the time it took the thought 'I'm still safe up here' to travel from one side of his ferret-sized brain to the other, Col had bent down to the boys' level.

"Hello, there," Col said, "This is my pet ferret, Shambles. He's very friendly. Would you like to pat him?"

Wrong on so many counts, but if he uttered a word to them it would blow his cover. He turned his head towards Col's ear and murmured, "If they pull my tail, I'm out of here."

"He's funny looking," one of the boys said.

One of the little snipes pulled his tail, while the other clonked him on the head with a forceful pat. The impact was so great his teeth crashed together.

From across the room, Duchess Kerala said, "Boysh, be gentle." She didn't take a step closer to intervene; instead another woman stepped in and calmly directed the boys away. Shambles rummaged around in his brain: had the Duchess slurred her words? When she spoke again, he was sure of it.

"Thank you, nanny. The boysh can have their dinnersh now," the Duchess said. Looking at the boys, Shambles could see them growing into little Lord Vincents, attitude and all. He made a mental note to keep clear of every one of the Duke's offspring, even if he was supposed to be a docile "pet". Nervously, he scanned the room, but saw no sign of Vincent. He didn't know if that was a good thing or not. If he were here, he could keep an eye on him, but Vincent also knew he was a ferret who could turn into a man, and might blow his cover.

At the other end of the room, the double doors opened. A woman wearing a starched white apron over black trousers and a black shirt nodded to the Duchess. The Duchess handed her empty wine glass to the nearest member of staff and announced to the room, "Dinner is sherved."

Shambles licked his chops. Wonderful aromas of caramelised onions, roast meat and crispy potatoes wafted in.

The dining room looked decidedly blue. Blue walls, and in the middle of the room, a long table with a blue-and-white table cloth. A swift team of waiters, all dressed in black with starched white aprons, placed several bowls of salad at intervals along the table. The bowls were filled only with green leaves, thin slices of spring onion, shavings of Parmesan cheese and white beans.[2]

Shambles saw the table was set for eighteen. A quick headcount told him there were a couple of spare seats. Hope sprang inside him as he wondered if he might get fed. He'd be extra nice to Col. She'd give him some food. He might even charm some of the guests into feeding him as well. With so many people, and such large silver domes over all the plates, surely there would be plenty of leftovers?

Duke Pavla entered from another set of doors. Everyone bowed their heads as he walked in. He stepped towards Kerala and kissed her tenderly on the cheek. A lump formed in Shambles's throat. They made such a lovely couple. He hoped he and Ondine would still be as affectionate when they were that old.

They stood waiting for the Duke to be seated. To Shambles's surprise, the Duke did not sit at the head of the table. Instead, he chose the centre of one of the long sides, opposite the Duchess. The seat beside the Duchess was empty, and Shambles wondered who would sit there, if not the Duke?

"Good evening," Pavla said. "As of now, fish will no longer be on the menu. Be seated."

As soon as the Duke sat down, everyone else followed. The waiters lifted the domes off the plates to reveal the banquet beneath.

Shambles's stomach did a double take. What tiny amounts of food!

Even for a man the size of a ferret it was a measly serving. Half a boiled egg, sliced. Two slivers of roast chicken, so thin you could see through them. A tiny clump of fried onions. Sautéed zucchini and more of those white beans.[3] Oh yes, and three thin scallops of potato. All arranged in the middle of a large white plate with a thick band of blue around the edge.

"This better be the entrée," he murmured to Col as his stomach grumbled.

Old Col coughed, then lifted him off her shoulder and placed him on her lap. It got him out of sight, so he could slip under the table, unnoticed, and report back on anything he overheard. Despite the small portions, Old Col came through for him and let a chunk of egg fall from her fork. With a leap he met the food mid-flight and swallowed it before he landed.

Somewhat recharged, he set to work, ears on alert. Avoiding people's feet became his main priority. Above the table, the dinner guests looked composed and serene, but underneath there was a fair amount of fidgeting and fenudging going on.[4]

Heading for the end of the table, Shambles saw a pair of legs crossing nervously back and forth at the ankles. He strained his ears to snapping point.

"murmur, murmur, food, murmur, right, murmur, murmur, tennis."

Not much help there, so Shambles decided to walk behind the twitching feet and sit directly under the speaker's chair.

"murmur, murmur, rule out murmur the food," one male voice said. "murmur, never enough of it."

A person sitting beside him gave a low chuckle. "murmur, murmur, Infanta."

It sounded promising. Shambles listened some more and heard someone whisper, "running out of time" and "need to move soon" but nothing that made a cohesive whole. A staccato march announced the return of the waiters, who removed the empty plates. He strained to hear more conversation but the sound of feet drowned it out.

Moving about under the table, he searched and listened for more interesting conversations. Someone arrived late and took the remaining empty seat. He recognised the smarmy voice say, "Good evening, Mother," and heard him kiss her on the cheek.

Vincent! Shambles scurried back over the parquet to get away from Vincent's heavy boots. The last thing he needed was to get too close. All the same his ears stayed on high alert as he heard the Duchess mutter to her son, "One day, all this will be yours."

Really now? That was interesting!

Without warning, pain seared Shambles's insides. Panic shot through him. He silently cried out for Ondine to take away his agony. In his mind, he fixed an image of her sweet face to help him focus. How had this come on so quickly? His black furry arms buckled and bleached and turned into skin. His legs grew and grew. Just in time he pulled himself away from someone's twitching foot. Any moment now, Vincent might drop a fork or a napkin, reach down to get it and see him lying on the floor, bare as the day he was born.

He kept thinking of Ondine. When he angled his head so he could see through the forest of legs, he thought he'd died and gone to heaven. There she was, his beautiful Ondine, standing by the door with a tray of steaming hot hand towels. Her proximity must be why he'd changed. Slapping his forehead – silently! – he felt like a silly wee daftie! He could be a ferret any time he liked, but when she came near him, he turned human. Or, if he were already human, and she walked off, he reverted to ferret. If he didn't start controlling it soon, he'd be in serious trouble!

Ondine caught a glimpse of him and momentary shock played over her lovely features. Just as quickly, she reset her face, as if she hadn't seen anything at all. Hamish felt a fresh surge of pride at how well she handled herself, considering the crazy circumstances.

"Your Grace," Ondine said, walking towards the Duke. Galloping agony pummelled Hamish from the inside, but now his biggest worry was fear of discovery. He had to change back or he'd be exposed. All the time he said not a peep, made not a single groan or even a loud panting noise.[5] Watching her feet move around the table and stop at each person was another form of torture. But the motivation to remain undetected overrode all else. Revisiting the pain, he willed his body back to ferret form.

Through blurry vision, he saw Ondine's feet approaching the Duchess and Vincent and nearly miss a step. Oh no, this was hardly the quiet sneaky start he'd hoped they could all make. Vincent now knew Ondine was here, so they'd have to be extra careful.

Staggering on to his four paws, Shambles wobbled and hobbled back to the safety of Old Col. Lovely meaty aromas assailed his senses. When he looked up, he found a tiny lamb cutlet dangling from her fingers.

"Aye, yer a good woman." He kept his voice quiet, so that only Col could hear.

He buried his face in the meat, biting off chunks and swallowing them without chewing. He heard rather than saw Ondine leave via the servant's door. A pang gripped his heart at her departure, but he knew she'd want to get as far away from Vincent as possible.

Safely back in his ferret shape, and feeling better for having eaten, Shambles thought some more about how he might control his magic. With another pang he realised something awful: in order to do his job properly without detection, he'd have to keep his current form.

And that meant keeping away from Ondine.

A furious barking sound came from the guests' entrance. Two of the waiters opened the double doors. In stepped the Infanta Anathea holding a white ball of fluff under her arm. It barked and yapped like a lunatic.

(The dog, not the Infanta.) With the frozen expression of a woman caught in a strong wind, the ash-blonde Infanta looked around at everyone seated at the table. For a while Shambles tried to work out what was wrong with her face. Everybody knew the Infanta was at least a decade older than the Duke, but her eyebrows were up near her hairline and her forehead looked ironing-board flat.

Keeping that imperious look on her face, perhaps because she was incapable of any other expression, Infanta Anathea turned to the Duke and snarled, "You started dinner without me?"

Everyone stopped talking. The room reverberated with clunks and clangs as they put their cutlery down. A flash of silver caught Shambles's eye – he turned to see someone dropping a small fish knife into a clutch bag and clicking the top closed. Shambles snuck over to the patent-leather bag. It was so shiny he could see his furry reflection in it.

The Duke rose from his chair. "Dear sister. Dinner is at seven sharp. Just as it always is. Your seat is waiting."

"You're so rude," the Infanta said.

Shambles used the distraction to his advantage, the Infanta's voice drowning out the quiet "snick" as he opened the clutch bag. He grabbed the stolen knife with his teeth and brought it to an empty spot under the table, well clear of anyone's feet.

At that moment the Infanta's little dog spotted Shambles under the table. The dog wriggled and spasmed like he'd been struck with an electric prod.

"No, Biscuit," the Infanta said.[6]

Biscuit paid the Infanta no mind. With a blood- curdling "ru-ru-ru-ru" the white hairy thing launched itself into the air. He landed on the ground and charged for Shambles.

"Biscuit! Heel!" the Infanta commanded, but Biscuit had another master – blood lust!

For a terrifying quarter of a second Shambles considered transforming into a human to save his skin. But he could only do it if Ondine were still here, and she'd gone.

Panic surged through his furry body as he looked up to see Old Col's worried face.

With a lunge he shot up the leg of the chair, but his claws tangled on the hem of Col's skirt.

"Ru-ru-ru-ru," Biscuit barked.[7]

Quick as a flash, Old Col's hands grabbed Shambles around the middle to pull him to safety. Biscuit hurled himself into the air, his mouth open, white teeth and red gums bared.

The pretty white dog sank his fangs into Shambles's ferrety neck and chomped down hard.

Three people screamed at once, Shambles wasn't sure who.

Old Col began muttering something.

Forty-two teeth *skrittled* onto the floor.[8]

Shambles's world went fuzzy and he passed out.

										8

						___________

$B$eing neither a witch nor a woman possessed of supernatural powers to see into rooms without being in them at the time, Ondine remained oblivious to Shambles's current plight. To her credit, she had realised her presence in the Duke's dining room during the evening meal had been a huge mistake. She knew Hamish and Old Col would be at the dinner, but she couldn't refuse Draguta's request to take the hot hand-towels in. Guilt spread through her at the huge amounts of pain it must have caused Hamish for her to appear like that and make him transform. It didn't help that Vincent had been there too. Thankfully he only gave her a greasy look and had kept his mouth shut. The moment she'd done her job, Ondine had nodded to the Duke and Duchess and quickly scarpered out of there. Her assumption being that Hamish would revert to ferret form and remain safe and undetected, if a little green around the gills.

Not knowing Hamish was bleeding from the neck after Biscuit's attack, Ondine followed Draguta to the staff lounge and ate a bowl of vegetable soup and a multi-grain dinner roll. Unaware that the Infanta was screaming profusely at Old Col about the chance "that revolting thing" had given her champion rabies, Ondine accepted a second bowl of soup.[1]

She was also completely insensible to the next development, where Old Col made an incantation to the powers of the earth, stars and moon, at which point Biscuit's teeth fell out.

But the Infanta's high-pitched screams that could open a can? Yes, Ondine heard them loud and clear. Just about everyone in the palechia heard them. They ripped through the halls and the thin plaster walls like daggers of foul temper. The piercing noise reached the staff lounge, where Ondine's second bread roll beckoned, but ultimately lay untouched.

In a heartbeat Ondine took flight and ran towards the horrible sounds of chaos and terror.

Only to find herself face to face with her worst nightmare. OK, her second worst nightmare. Her first worst nightmare was being separated from Hamish. But her second worst nightmare was Lord Vincent.

He was standing right in front of her. His eyes glinted with anger as he scraped his blond highlights back from his forehead. A gleam of satisfaction stole through her as she saw remnants of a blue stain on his hand, left over from the night they'd caught him robbing the family hotel. Did he not wash, or was it sheer guilt keeping the stain there? Not for the first time, Ondine wondered what she'd ever seen in him. He might have been handsome if he weren't so ugly on the inside.

"What are you doing here?" she asked.

"What are you doing here?" he asked straight back. "And don't stand there like an idiot. Bow to your betters."

*Just because you've got a title it doesn't mean you're better than me.* The memory of the night he slapped her hard on the face came flooding back.[2] In defiance, she kept her back ramrod straight. "Aren't you supposed to be in Fort Kluff?"

"It didn't take." He examined a fingernail and said, "Why are you here?"

"I'm working."

Vincent mimicked, "I'm working." He made no sideways movement to let her pass.

Frustration surged through Ondine. "May I pass?"

Silently he stepped to the side and made room.

Ondine took a step but something smacked her hard in the shins. A lurching, falling sensation lasted all of half a second before she hit the floor with a thud. She looked up and saw a smirk on his face.

"Not quite a bow, but it will do."

Picking herself up, Ondine brushed away the hurt in her palms. "You're a –"

"– tut tut! When I'm Duke, you'll show me more respect."

"When you're Duke I'll emigrate to Slaegal!"[3] Ondine stomped off as best she could, head high, limping slightly, but all the same savouring the victory of getting the last word in.

Just as she turned the corner Vincent yelled out, "Witch!"

His tone carried such a sting she was sure he used it in the derogatory sense. Indignation on behalf of her great-aunt surged through her. A retort sprang to her lips just as Old Col arrived, carrying a prone Shambles in her arms. Around his neck she'd wrapped a white linen napkin.

Correction, some of it was white but mostly it was covered in deep burgundy stains.

"Shambles!" Ondine cried.

Lurch. Her stomach did that horrible sinking-with-fear thing as she looked at him. Then lurched again as another nagging, awful, this-is-not-right feeling took hold. She was standing right next to him, close enough for her to touch his head and say, "Oh, you poor darling."

*So why hadn't he changed back into a man now that they were close again? Did he not want to? Gasp. Was he too injured?*

"Quick, let's get to my room," Old Col said. They ran up the stairs and rushed down the hall, then shut the door behind them for privacy.

Ondine grabbed a couple of towels and placed them on the bed, so they could lie Shambles down without staining the duvet.

With a waver in her voice, Ondine asked, "How did it happen?" All the while she gently stroked Shambles's soft ferrety head and even kissed him twice. Did his eyelids flutter open? Did he mutter even one saucy comment about kisses? No. Which made Ondine worry even more. "Jupiter's moons, he's dying."

"He's not dying," Old Col said, unwrapping the cloth to reveal Shambles's matted wet neck. His furry body gently rose and fell with his breathing.

"But there's so much blood," Ondine said.

"That there is. Fortunately, most of it belonged to Biscuit. That's the Infanta's crazy dog, by the way. Thank goodness the dog bite missed anything vital, otherwise Shambles would have bled to death."

Fresh pain seared Ondine and her tummy curdled like lemon juice in milk. She felt like she might stop breathing. Her strapping, handsome lad was simply lying there in his fragile ferrety state and there was nothing she could do about it.

Old Col related the entire sorry tale to Ondine. About how the champion show dog had gone the full-beserker on Shambles and how she had used ancient magic and ripped the little mutt's teeth out. Every last one of them.

Old Col looked ashamed. "In the panic of the moment, I wanted Biscuit's teeth out of Shambles. I must have said the spell not quite right. Maybe I had a senior moment?"

Hope surged in Ondine. If that nasty dog had no teeth left, Shambles would be safe from future attacks. "Will he make a full recovery?" Thinking of only Shambles, not the Infanta's dog.

"Undoubtedly. He's sleeping it off. When the dog attacked, Shambles was about to let fly with enough profanities to strip the wallpaper. There wasn't time to think. I cast a spell to make him appear dead, so that I could get him out of the dining room."

Relief washed over Ondine like a tidal wave. But there was one more unknown factor in the sorry adventure, not counting all the unknown unknowns.[4]

"Aunt Col, why is he still a ferret?"

Col shook her head, pursed her lips as if in deep thought and said, "We'll have to wait and see."

---

WAITING IS AWFUL. There's the waiting for a meal to arrive when you can smell it cooking, and your stomach is saying "hurry up". There's the butterflies-in-the- tummy waiting for a gymnastics score from the fussy judges who are not sure if they should deduct half a point or a whole point for stepping outside the white lines. Then there's the hopeless I-feel-completely-sick kind of waiting, as a young girl looks upon the hopeless shape of an injured ferret waiting to see if he'll ever become handsomely human again.

An hour dragged by. When Ondine looked at Old Col's watch, it lied and said only eight minutes had passed. Fifteen more of Ondine's hours passed over the next two real hours. There was no change from Shambles at all, just the rise and fall of his furry little tummy as he breathed in and out. Every now and then his paws twitched. At one point, his eyelids flickered and seemed ready to spring open, but it was just his eyes quivering. Dreaming.

"You need sleep yourself, you've got school in the morning," Old Col said.

"But it's got no roof."

"Pyotr told me they'll make do with one of the barns."

"Do I have to go?"

"Of course you do. If you don't, the Duke will send you home. By the way, your parents are furious with me for letting you stay and work here."

Gulp. Hamish had taken up so much of her headspace she hadn't given a thought to her parents. "It didn't go down well?"

"You should have heard your mother scream when I phoned her and told her where we were. They wanted you to go home immediately. I told them you'd get a better education here. So you'd better prove me right or we're all in strife. And another thing, make sure you call them every now and then, just so they know you're safe and well."[5]

Rubbing her eyes and finding gritty things in the corners, Ondine agreed to return to her room.

Some people have worried so much about another's fate they have lain awake all night with the stress of it. Ondine was not such a person. Yes, she fully planned to worry all night about Shambles and whether he would ever be Hamish again. The new bed felt strange and cold; a recipe for further fretting. Her body, however, had other ideas and she fell asleep two pico-seconds after pulling the covers up.

Tasting a mouthful of dust, Ondine half-woke and prised her eyes open. It was dark – hardly surprising as it must have been the middle of the night. The true surprise was trying to swallow. Her tongue felt dry enough to leave splinters in her cheeks.

*I must have fallen asleep with my mouth open*, she thought. Quickly followed by another important thought: *I need a drink*.

Eyes adjusting to the low light, Ondine saw no refreshing glass of water on her side table. She attempted to swallow again and felt the ash-dry results. Wincing at the night chill, Ondine pulled her top blanket over her shoulders and did her best to be as quiet as possible so she didn't wake Draguta the laundry boss, who was asleep in the bed beside hers. She closed the door with a soft click and made her way to the kitchen.

At this time of night, she expected to be alone. No such luck. There in the kitchen, standing at the central galley bench, was a woman dressed in a shimmery satiny nightgown, with a whimpering fluffy white dog. A white dog with soft red gums, full of gouges where his teeth used to be.

The Infanta! Ondine tried to work out the correct form of address to use. Your Grace? My Lady? Her father would have known, but he wasn't here to help.

"Your Highness." Ondine quickly dropped into a curtsey. In any case, she couldn't say much more because her mouth was as dry as week-old bread. The woman smiled and Ondine felt a surge of relief at getting it right.[6]

At first Ondine thought she'd surprised the woman, judging by the Infanta's shocked expression, but after a while it became obvious the woman's eyebrows sat up like that permanently.

"Why were you sent to the kitchens at this late hour, child?"

Croak, rasp. "No one sent me. I need a drink of water, Your Highness."

The Infanta nodded her head towards the taps and put a spoon in the dog's mouth. For the smallest moment Ondine felt sorry for Biscuit. Straight after that she thought the dog deserved everything he got for attacking her beloved Shambles.

Glass of water safely in hand, Ondine decided to get out of there before she said anything stupid. When she turned around, she saw the Infanta make a quick movement away from the large stockpot bubbling over a low flame.

"What?" The Infanta's gaze bored into her.

Ondine was hardly going to say she thought the Infanta had put something in the soup. A queef of disgust spread through her at the thought that the Infanta was feeding the dog with the soup spoon. Or was the soup just for the dog? In which case it would be all right, if a little unconventional. However, if it was the communal soup, she should probably warn everyone it had Biscuit slobber in it.[7]

Hot on the heels of that internal soliloquy, Ondine had another thought that pushed disgust aside and let fear in. Maybe the Infanta didn't put the spoon back in the soup. Maybe she put something else in the soup?

"Sorry, I just . . . my eyes are still half shut. Please excuse me, Your Highness, I must get back to bed."

Those imperious raised eyebrows made Ondine uneasy. Somehow, Ondine felt sure the Infanta had put something in the soup and she had to tell Old Col the moment she got the chance.

"What are you named, child?"

"Ondine, Your Highness."

"And what did you see, Ondine, hmm?"

"I . . ." She took a gulp of water and thought desperately for something convincing to say. The dog provided inspiration as it licked the offered spoon. "I'm so sorry to stare, but I saw that your puppy has no teeth. I really wasn't expecting that."

No change at all in the Infanta's expression. It was hard to know if this was deliberate. "No. Earlier this evening I wasn't expecting my dog to be mauled either," she said. "It was my baby brother's new friend who did it. This had better be set to rights or there'll be trouble."

Something else Ondine wasn't expecting – the Infanta paid no attention to her audience and put that licked doggy spoon back in the soup, confirming her earlier guess at the slurry of dog bacteria swilling in the pot.

Ondine's face must have betrayed her disgust, because the Infanta said, "He has a better pedigree than anyone else under this roof."

Yes, but his mouth is still teeming with germs, Ondine thought. How unfair that the Duke had set the health inspector on her parents' hotel, when all along he should have been paying closer attention to his own kitchen![8]

Again and again, the Infanta spooned soup from the pot to the dog. The dog stood on the galley bench, licking away. A few drops of soup landed on the bench, right where the kitchen staff would be preparing food in the morning. The dog licked that up as well.

The Infanta stopped spooning and looked at Ondine. "You are new here, aren't you?"

"Yes."

"Far too many people are being hired of late. I don't approve, but the Duke won't listen to me. Work hard and keep out of trouble. Plenty of people think they know what is going on but they don't. You think you might know something, so you go and tell the Duke. Save yourself the bother. He isn't interested. If you see anything or hear something strange and you want to know what it means, you come to me instead, you hear?"

Ondine gulped and gave a meek, "Yes," all the while wondering how she was going to survive living in this crazy place.

9

———————

Morning? Isn't that when it's light? No such luck. Ondine woke to find Draguta giving her a gentle nudge on the shoulder and saying, "Time for get up." [1]

In the distance Ondine could hear people stirring and getting ready for the new day. There were noises of feet scuffing down the hall, the hiss of showers and the scrape of cutlery on crockery in the staff lounge as people had breakfast.

Hamish! Ondine's mind sprang into action. Some teenage slugabeds cannot get themselves right in the head or body before midday. Ondine surprised herself and her generation by getting dressed, cleaning her teeth and brushing her hair into a tight ponytail in record time. All the while she fretted. What if he had woken in the night and she wasn't there? Would he think she'd abandoned him?

When Ondine arrived in Col's room, she found her great aunt looking fresh and lively, ready for a new day. Unfortunately, when she clapped eyes on Hamish, he was still a Shambles-ferret.

"Shambles, you're awake. Are you OK?"

"All the better fer seeing your beautiful face," Shambles said as he climbed up on Col's shoulder so he could be eye-to-eye with a blushing Ondine.

"You two, you're incorrigible," Col said.

"Then stop incorriging us," he said.

Ondine giggled. Even though she was looking at a ferret, in her mind she could see Hamish's devilish grin and imagined his sparkling green eyes full of fun.

Old Col made a scoffing noise, then said, "I'm glad you're here. We need to confab."[2]

"You've found out who's trying to kill the Duke?"

"I'm good, dear, but not quite that good. However, Shambles has discovered that people are helping themselves to silverware and probably anything that can fit in your hand. So please take care when you're doing the laundry to go through people's pockets and remove anything valuable."

"Of course I will," Ondine said, gazing longingly at the ferret-that-should-be-her-sweetheart and wishing he'd become human again. "And you're sure you're feeling OK?"

"Aw yeas, all ticketeyboo. Best sleep in ages."

He certainly sounded confident. "But, you're still a ferret, even though I'm right here."

"Aye, yer a smart lass. Isnae she a smart one, Col?"

Aunt Col rolled her eyes. "Quite."

Shambles gave the widest grin in a ferret's arsenal and winked at Ondine. "Sheer willpower. I've *goat* it in spades. Worked it out while I was under the table and ye walked in at dinner. Had tae think on me feet. And it feels bettah staying like this instead of changing back and forth all the time. Sure and the Duke needs me tae be like this on account of being able tae do me job, lass."

Niggling worries started niggling and worrying Ondine. "But . . . you like being human, don't you?"

"Aw, I *loave* being human." He winked again. "But ye know I have so many responsibilities now, and I cannae very well sneak aboot if everyone can see me. Now, as much as I love tae see yer smiling face, it's past seven, lassie. Classes start at quarter past. Ye'd best make yer feet yer friends."

Giddy hope and confusion churned in Ondine's heart, which wasn't difficult considering the stress of the previous day, the earliness of the current hour and her bizarre conversation with the Infanta during the night. Which reminded her.

"Don't drink the soup." Keeping things short and simple, she explained her encounter with the Infanta, the spoon, the dog and the soup pot.

With a shudder, Old Col said, "I will inform the Duke. Now, best you get to school. I will be taking a stroll near the arch of crepe myrtle trees on the western lawn around three this afternoon. Meet me there."

"OK. I'll see you then." Ondine gave her great aunt a kiss on the cheek and gave Shambles a peck on the top of his head. They walked off in different directions – Old Col and Shambles towards the conservatory for breakfast, Ondine to her new classes. More nagging worries followed Ondine all the way to the school barn. Worries that went along the lines of, *I know Shambles needs to be a ferret most of the time, but when nobody else is around, he really ought to be my Hamish.*

The barn showed all the signs of a hurried conversion into a classroom. It had a portrait of the Duke on the wall, dusty windows, creaky floorboards and tables and chairs. Enough for a teacher and a dozen students aged between eleven and fifteen. One large, portable white board stood at the head of the room.

A woman who looked about the same age as Ondine's oldest sister Marguerite came up to her. "Good morning, you must be Ondine. The seneschal has told me all about you. I'm Ms Kyryl. You can take a seat next to Hetty if you like. Let's begin."

Ms Kyryl had dark hair pinned tightly at the back of her head. She wore conservative pleated blue trousers, flat black shoes and a buttoned-up white shirt under a v-neck jersey, which matched her trousers. On her hips she wore an intricately braided leather belt, with tassels at the ends and tiny brass bells that tinkled musically as she walked.

Ondine sat down next to the smiling Hetty. Hetty had ramrod-straight black hair, tied in pigtails either side of her head, which made her look about ten, although she was clearly Ondine's age. Hetty had the tiniest little button nose. When she smiled, her cheeks turned into round cushions and her scimitar eyes almost closed.[3]

"I shouldn't be glad about the storm, but I am," Hetty said. "The thing is, I've always wanted a pony and now I've got one. Just looking after it, of course, until they rebuild the stables. But I've finally got a pony!"

"A horse is a lot of extra work," Ondine said. "Where do you keep it?"

"In our lounge. We've moved all our furniture out and laid down straw and it's so wonderful."

Ondine's jaw nearly hit the table.

"Ha ha, got you! We're keeping it in our barn for the meantime. Sorry to tease you! I'm so glad to finally have a friend my age." Hetty then fired off a series of questions: "Have you moved here with your parents? What jobs do they have? Are you staying permanently or is it a seasonal contract?"

"I'm here with my great-aunt . . ." Ondine started. She nearly added that she'd also come with Hamish, but she wasn't sure what to call him. She thought 'my boyfriend who turns into a ferret at the most inconvenient times' was a bit of a mouthful. And hard to explain. She didn't know how to answer the rest of the questions because she didn't want to reveal Old Col's job description, nor how long they would be staying. Hopefully not for that long because she wanted to go home with Hamish and resume her normal life. Hetty looked so pleading, Ondine didn't want to dash her hopes by saying they wouldn't be here for long.

"Good morning, class," Ms Kyryl said.

"Good morning, teacher," the students said as one.

"I was born here and the whole time there have only been two other children who were my age." Hetty rolled her eyes as she added, "And they were both boys, who came and went. I've always gone to school here. Well, not here in the barn, back in the proper schoolhouse. My parents run the chicken farms. They supply the palechia and most of Bell-reeve with poultry. My brothers and sisters were all born here too. I have two older brothers and one older sister. My sister does the accounts for a toy factory in Norange and my brothers are at Venzelemma University."

Ms Kyryl interrupted them. "Hetty, I know you're excited, but it's class time now. Everyone, please stand for the national anthem."

Scraping chair noises echoed around the room as they all stood, hands on heart as the teacher pressed a button on the portable CD player. The opening strains of *Oh Brugel, My Heart* rang out.[4]

Everyone sang, even Ms Kyryl (who sounded off- key). Despite the stirring words and rampant patriotism of a people whose spirit yearned to be free, whenever Ondine sang the words "my heart", she thought of Hamish rather than her country. When she sang about the "young and the strong" she also thought of Hamish. When she sang about "hallowed fields" and "wealth for toil" she had no idea what they meant, so she thought about Hamish for good measure.[5]

Once the anthem finished, they recited the Pledge of Brugel. Ondine ran the words together in a light drone: "I love God and Brugel. I honour the flag. I serve the Duke. I cheerfully obey my parents, teachers and the law."

Ms Kyryl said, "Thank you, children. Once they fix the roof we'll move back to our old rooms, but this will do for now. This is always a lovely time of year, because we have the Harvest Festival to look forward to. Once again the Duke has asked us to stage a pageant in the ballroom, to entertain the visiting dignitaries. The great and the good of Brugel will all be there, so I know you will do your very best on the night."

Ms Kyryl handed out sheets of paper with a list of characters, including Farmer One, Farmer Two, Cabbage, Turnip, Apple, Setting Sun and Harvest Moon.

Ms Kyryl continued, "It's traditional for the festival to follow the full moon, which this year will begin on Thursday the twenty-ninth of October. The Harvest Ball and pageant will be on the Saturday. Now, children, who would like to play the role of Harvest Moon?"

Ondine worked out the dates. The Saturday would fall on October the thirty-first, Halloween.[6]

Several hands shot up in the air. Ms Kyryl's eyes alighted on Hetty and she gave her the role. Hetty looked delighted and beamed with pride. Ondine felt a bit silly that she hadn't raised her hand fast enough.

Ms Kyryl cast more speaking roles. Each time, Ondine shot her hand up, only to miss out. Until it came to Cabbage. Nobody wanted to be Cabbage.[7]

Ondine sighed, raised her hand and felt the sting of defeat. "I'll be Cabbage if you like," she said.

The boys sitting across from them giggled.

"Hush, class," Ms Kyryl said. "Thank you, Ondine, you are very gracious."

They read through the play. Each time Ondine came to do her lines the boys sitting on the other side of the classroom made squelching noises with their hands in their armpits.

Hetty murmured, "Don't let them get to you. They are just snotty boys."

"Thanks." Ondine hadn't known Hetty for long, but already she began to feel she had an ally in this strange palace.

Miss Kyryl said, "Very good everyone. OK, put your scripts away and we'll have a history lesson."

Ondine and Hetty took out their notebooks.

Ms Kyryl smiled to the class. "Now, children, who can tell me when Brugel was founded?"

Everyone's hands went up. Not to be overlooked, Ondine shot hers in the air too because she knew the answer.

The teacher's eyes alighted on Ondine and she answered with satisfaction, "Brugel was declared an independent state in twelve sixty-four."[8]

Giggles rippled through the classroom. What? How could the answer be wrong?

"Not to worry," Ms Kyryl said. "Who can tell us the real answer?"

Looking bright and perky, Hetty responded with, "Brugel was the first land found after the flood."

"Correct."

WHAT! Ondine felt her eyebrows nearly shoot off her forehead. Keeping her voice low, she murmured to Hetty, "There was a flood? When?"[9]

"Who founded Brugel?" Ms Kyryl asked.

Ordinarily Ondine knew the answer, but she kept her hand down this time.

Another student said, "The four mountain tribes joined together to defeat the barbarians."

Ms Kyryl said, "That's right. And the leader of the tribes?"

Another child this time: "Became the first Grand Duke."

"Very good. And how many Grand Dukes and Dukes have we had?"

"Two hundred and seven," another child said.

"And have we ever had a Duchess lead Brugel?" This time the students kept their hands down, but after a bit of thought, Hetty raised her hand and answered, "Elmaree the First became Grand Duchess in seventeen forty."

"Very good," Ms Kyryl said. "And during her reign the Russian empire annexed the Grand Duchy of Brugel. After Elmaree, what happened? Anyone?"

No hands went up, so the teacher supplied the information: "Her son Leopold led a rebellion to secure autonomy for Brugel. After that, Brugel lost its status and became a Duchy instead of a Grand Duchy, but it regained its independence. Have we had any more Duchesses?"

Some of the children shook their heads, not entirely sure.

The teacher supplied the answer. "In nineteen eighteen we had Duchess Yalene. During her reign, can anyone tell me what happened?"

Ondine's hand rose in the air, because she had a fair idea of the answer. Not from the name of the ruler, but from the date. It was ingrained in Brugelish DNA.

"Yes, Ondine?"

"Brugel became part of the Soviet Union."

"Very good!"

Relief crashed through Ondine at finally getting something right.

"We nearly had another Duchess more recently, can anyone tell me?"

All hands shot in the air. "The Infanta Anathea," Hetty said.

"Correct. She was heir presumptive and would have been Duchess . . . until what happened? Can anyone tell me?"

Just about every child recited, "Lord Pavla was born and Brugel rejoiced."

"That's right. Lord Pavla the Fourth is Duke of Brugel."

"And we've got our independence," a boy across the room said. "And that's why Brugel is always better off with a Duke."

Ondine blurted, "That's hardly fair."

Ms Kyryl's eyebrows shot up in surprise. "Quite a statement. Andreas?" She looked at the boy who had just spoken. "Care to elaborate?"

Andreas looked smug and arrogant. He had to be at least two years younger than Ondine, but that precocious look on his pale, lean face told the world he knew everything.

"The facts speak for themselves. The times Brugel had a Duchess, we lost our autonomy."

"But . . ." Heat roared through Ondine. "They just happened to be Duchesses during really difficult times."

Andreas gave her a look of utter superiority and scratched the side of his nose. Ondine could have sworn he sneaked the edge of his thumb inside and had a pick as well. "We have had Grand Dukes and Dukes during very difficult times as well, but they didn't lose their country."[10]

His smugness reminded Ondine so much of Lord Vincent that she couldn't help wondering if they might be related. No sooner had the thought crossed her mind than she pushed it aside. She would not let Vincent unsettle her, she'd put all that behind her.

"An interesting debate," Ms Kyryl said, "but there were also times when Duchesses, although not ruling in their own right, acted as regents to their sons who became Grand Dukes. Brugel did not lose its autonomy then."

"Doesn't change the facts," Andreas said with the self-satisfaction of someone who was too young to know anything but already knew everything.

Ondine thought about her encounter with the Infanta the previous night. Maybe some people thought Brugel was better off with the Duke at the helm, but she knew Anathea didn't see it that way and wanted her rightful place on the throne.

But how far would she go to claim back her birthright?

## 10

———————

That afternoon Ondine's ears rang with censure as she put another coin in the payphone to keep the call going.

"You will come back on the first train, young lady." Her mother's voice ripped into her.

The coin-warning light on the soviet-era phone flickered again. It wanted more money or it would cut out. How unfair that she had to pay to listen to Ma scream at her.

"Everything is fine, really. And I have an important job to do, and Col is taking very good care of us."

"I don't care. You get back here this instant!"

"I'm sorry, but I can't." Who would want to go home with such a screaming reception waiting for her? Besides, she needed to be with Hamish. "Sorry, Ma, the light's flashing again and I've run out of money. Can you send me some?"

"I'm not going to fund your escapades!"

"Well, then, I'll have to keep working so I can save up enough to get the train ticket back. Sorry, Ma, but the phone –"

The line went dead. Light-headed with relief, Ondine replaced the receiver and headed to the laundry. She worked hard with Draguta, washing and then hanging clothes and sheets on the lines. The fishy smell had almost gone from the courtyard, which was a definite plus. The sun gave some warmth but the wind had a cool bite to it. When it was time for her tea break at three o'clock, she dashed off towards the crepe myrtle trees, her skirts whipping at her legs. The papery flowers were in their last flush of bloom. Their pink, white and red petals looked so beautiful against the green leaves and marble grey of the trunks. Dried petals sprinkled the ground like confetti. The trees were so old and well looked after, they formed a flowery tunnel to walk under. More importantly, they offered a secluded place to meet.

As she walked under the trees, Ondine's heart caught in her throat. Standing there like a groom at the altar was Hamish.

Not the ferret, but proper Hamish, wearing freshly pressed black trousers and a white shirt. Sunlight filled her as she raced to him and threw her arms around his neck.

"I'm so glad to see you," She whispered into his ear.

"And it's always so lovely tae see ye, lass," he said as she pulled away to get a good look at his gorgeous face. He stroked her cheek with the pad of his thumb. "Although I see yer face every time I close me eyes."

Ondine felt herself beaming all over at the compliment. For a moment she didn't know what to say. All she wanted to do was gaze adoringly into his sparkling green eyes for a while. So she did. Then she touched the delicate skin on his neck where last night she'd seen only matted fur and dried blood. To her surprise, his skin looked unharmed.

"It doesn't have a scratch!"

"Aye."

"Did it heal when you changed?"

"It must hae." Hamish gave a shrug. "There's got tae be an upside tae all of this."

Ondine kissed the spot anyway. "Now you're all better."

She felt his muscles tighten under her lips and he gave a soft groan. "Don't be so sure. If ye do that again, I'll fall apart at the seams."

She giggled and kissed him again in the same spot.

"All right, you two, that's enough." Aunt Col suddenly made her presence known, her words mentally dousing Ondine with cold water. In the cool autumn air, Aunt Col looked pale, her hair a little more salt than pepper, and was that a wattle forming at her neck? A pang of sadness gripped Ondine. Every time her great aunt looked at Hamish he reminded her of her lost youth. Would the same happen to Ondine? Would Hamish stay young as she grew old?

Col cleared her throat. "We need to compare notes about last night. Vincent is not happy we're here, so let's do our best not to antagonise him."

Ondine rubbed her shin at the memory.

Hamish's hand slipped into hers behind her back. The contact made it hard for her to think straight.

"So, let's report," Aunt Col said.

"Um." Ondine had a think. "Apart from the soup incident with the Infanta, nothing else so far. Everyone here seems to have a lot of work to do. I think they're too busy to plot the Duke's downfall."

"Yes." Col chewed at her bottom lip and her forehead seemed to develop more wrinkles. "All the same, disgruntled staff can bear a grudge." Col yawned. "Oh, bless me. I need more coffee. Now, what was I saying?"

Behind Ondine's back, Hamish entwined his fingers in hers and she felt her brain go fuzzy.

"It's early days yet, but keep your eyes and ears open," Col said. "I'd hazard a guess there's no love lost between Duchess Kerala and Anathea. You were under the table at the time, Hamish, but I saw them look daggers at each other at dinner."

"Aye, I was busy liberating silverware from someone's handbag. Who was sitting down towards the kitchen door by the way?"

"They would be Anathea's daughters." Old Col rubbed her temple in frustration. "Which is another black mark for the Infanta."

"I will be extra vigilant in the laundry and keep a lookout for stolen things too," Ondine said. Meanwhile Hamish kept playing with her hand and she came over all silly.

Old Col huffed in frustration. "Stop it, you two. We're not getting very far just yet, but I think it's important to compare notes as often as we can. Ondine, you should get back to work before you are missed. Hamish, we need to check the Duke's mail."

"Yes, Col." Ondine made to move away, but Hamish gently tugged her hand and brought her back to him. Despite her great-aunt watching. Ondine kissed Hamish firmly on the lips. The contact sent jolts of electricity through her.

"Love ye. See ye soon, lass." Hamish winked at her.

Ondine's tummy turned to jelly and she giggled. Then reality crashed through. "Wait. You're opening mail?"

"Yes, and the afternoon post has just arrived," a commanding voice said.

The three of them looked up to see Duke Pavla himself approaching, arm in arm with Duchess Kerala. They were taking an afternoon stroll in the gardens together. As they stopped, Kerala tilted her head to rest it on Pavla's shoulder.

Just in time Ondine remembered to make a quick curtsey.

"My Lord Duke, Lady Duchess," Col said.

Remembering she wasn't supposed to speak unless spoken to, Ondine kept quiet and let Old Col do the talking. All the same, fear poured down her spine. She hadn't had a chance to think about this the day before, but surely professionals in a secure facility should screen the mail, not her great aunt and the man she adored. But she also knew the Duke wanted everything to appear completely normal so that whoever was out to get him would not realise anyone was on to him. Or her.

Oh dear. Another worry wormed into her brain. Last time they'd met, Hamish had been his Shamble-ferretyness. Now he was a man. Did Kerala even recognise him?

It was completely bonkers.

The Duke looked at the three of them and said, "What news, Miss Romano?"

"We are continuing with investigations, Your Grace," Col said.

The Duchess asked, "Have you found anything?" Her eyes not quite as focussed as they should be. Ondine wondered if she'd had a drink or two at lunch?

"Not yet," Col said.

"Shambles, you look well enough," Pavla said.

Ondine wished the Duke would call him Hamish when he was in proper Hamish form. It seemed demeaning.

"Aw yeas, much better thanks, Yer Graces."

"Good. I was worried for a moment there. You're not . . . stuck as a human, are you?"

Ondine watched the Duchess's face intently, but her expression betrayed no curiosity at all. How strange.

"Aw naw, I can change back whenever I need tae."

"Then please do so. I do not want people to see you like this. The fewer people know about your presence, the better. When you're finished with surveillance in the kitchens, I want you to focus on the gardeners and farmers. Make sure the produce is safe. If there is something untoward happening in the food chain, I need to know."

The Duke took his Duchess for the rest of their walk.

Col exhaled with relief the moment they left. "Holiday's over, we have serious work to do."

"Aye," Hamish said.

Fear constricted Ondine's chest. Her breaths came in staggered jumps. "Please, be careful."

Hamish tucked a stray lock of hair behind Ondine's ear and gave her the softest kiss on the tip of her nose. "I wasnae going tae, but now ye've said it, I'll take extra care."

"You're making fun of me."

He kissed her again, this time on the lips and her heart staggered behind her ribs. "Dinnae fuss yerself, although it warms me wee heart tae know yer thinking of me."

As he let go of her hand, Ondine shivered. Hamish could be seriously hurt. If anything happened to him, she'd never forgive herself.

## 11

As the days went by things settled into something of a pattern for Ondine. Lessons in the morning, half an hour for lunch, then laundry in the afternoon with Draguta. A good amount of Ondine's work consisted of going through every pocket for snot rags, snuff boxes and stolen silverware, before putting the clothes in the cavernous washing machines.

*I wonder what Hamish is up to*, Ondine thought as she pulled out a small key from a jacket's inside pocket one afternoon. No sooner had this thought formed in her head than the man himself appeared. Except her heart sank, because he was only the ferret of the man.

"Come here, little fella, the laundry's no place for you." What she really wanted to say was, "Oh, Shambles, I'm so glad to see you. Every time I see the post van arrive I can't stop the panic rising in me."

In a blur of dark fur, Shambles raced up Ondine's side and stood on her shoulder. He gave her a whiskery wet kiss on the cheek. "Aye, lass, I missed ye and I wanted to see how ye were gettin' on," he said in a low voice. "The Duke's goat me checking up on laundry now."

Draguta dropped her bundle and stared at them. *Gulp*, gulped Ondine. Had the laundress heard him? Shambles shifted his weight from left to right. A difficult thing to do considering he had two of each foot, and Ondine's shoulders were hardly large.[1]

Draguta found her voice: "No dirty animals here! Out! Now!"

Relief engulfed Ondine – Draguta had said "animals" not "talking animals". She hadn't heard him speak. Their secret was safe. "He's my aunt's pet. He's perfectly harmless. And clean."

"No break rules. Duchess strict on that. You get me in trouble when bring animals in here." Draguta shook her head and picked up the most enormous load of wet washing. The bottom of the basket bowed under the weight, but Draguta didn't even grunt. Instead, she looked at Shambles with a steady eye and kept her voice stern. "Don't shed fur on the clean linen."

"She's good value, that one," Shambles murmured as Ondine got back to work.

More workers brought clean washing in from the line and then set to the industrial machines, ironing the creases out.

"Ondine, take to Duchess's suite," Draguta said.

Ondine gathered the neat stacks of freshly laundered sheets and towels. They were so heavy she had to use both hands. There was no room for Shambles, so he had to run along beside her.

With a grunt of frustration Ondine said, "If you were Hamish again, you could help carry some of this."

"Good idea, lass. Let's go past Col's room and I'll get some clothes."

Thank goodness, she'd see her lovely Hamish again. And her arms wouldn't feel like they were about to drop off.

When he emerged from Col's room as his handsome self, her heart flipped over. He took half the load but the linen formed a big white barrier preventing them from sharing a proper kiss. Instead he leaned over and kissed her cheek. It would do. For now.

They walked towards the palechia's south wing.

"I've been so busy, lass," Hamish said with a grin on his face. "I found out the farmers hae cheated on cleaning the vegetables. All sorts of manure and muck on them by the time they reach the kitchens. The Duke was right pleased with me help."

"Nice one," she said. At least cleaning vegetables was hardly a dangerous pursuit.

"Aye, and I checked tae make sure the only fertiliser they were using was the stuff from a cow's belly."

"Fertiliser? How can that be dangerous?"[2]

"Aw, lass, yer so innocent." He gave her a smile and a wink.

Boggled for a moment, Ondine felt he was patronising her. "What about the mail?"

"Aw yeas, that's settled right down, but still very important."

The pride on his face told Ondine how much he loved his job. Which was good, but it also niggled at her in ways she didn't want to examine too closely.

"And now you're spying on the laundry?" Did it mean she'd get to see more of him? Perhaps yes. But perhaps it meant she'd only see him as a ferret.

"*Goat* it in one," Hamish said.

When they arrived at the Duchess's chambers, the opulence took Ondine's breath away.

Incredible, magnificent, ornate, overblown and fabulously expensive were the first thoughts that came to mind.

Breakable was the next.

They took extra care negotiating the sitting room – specifically the narrow path between all the polished tables and desks with their curvy legs. Not being an expert on timber, Ondine didn't know they were made from Bruge-loak, but her nose tingled at the overpowering scent of furniture polish.[3]

The furniture itself wasn't the problem, just everything on it. Every display table and bureau had tall vases filled with fresh flowers, while the desks were overflowing with photo frames and antique inkpots and silver boxes of all shapes and sizes. There were so many things Ondine didn't even know what to call them. All she could do was hold on to her tower of linen and make sure she didn't knock anything over.

A series of gilded photographs of Kerala and Pavla on their wedding day adorned the wall. The Duchess had the same dark, shiny helmet of hair she wore now, and a serene, confident expression on her face. The

Duke's hair was darker and his face younger and more hopeful. In most of the photographs, their posture looked regal and stiff, but in one the photographer had captured them in an unguarded moment. Their bodies were angled together and they gazed adoringly at each other.

"It's well posh, eh, lass?" Hamish said.

"Mercury's wings, I've never seen anything like it." Every wall had niches for yet more antiques. Along the length of one wall were more books than a person could read in a lifetime. Along another wall stood wine racks filled with more bottles than a person could drink in a lifetime. Scattered around the room were a dozen fancy chairs that looked far too old and expensive to ever sit on.[4]

Every window overlooking the south lawn had the thickest curtains, held back with rich twists of gold-coloured cord.

"But no tassels?" Hamish winked at Ondine. "I do love tassels, they really complete the look and add that wee touch of grandeur."

"What?" Ondine stared at Hamish for three pico-seconds before he cracked up and she started laughing too. It was so nice simply to be with him, she almost didn't mind the drudgery of work.

"Come awn lass. Let's stop gawking and get the beds made."

The bedroom raised the opulence bar another notch. Of course the Duchess would sleep in a four-poster bed with heavy curtains. Of course she would have more tables stacked with framed photographs and antiques and more of those elegant vases that would break the moment you touched them. Fresh flowers stood tall in each vase, filling the air with a heady aroma that reminded Ondine of cloves and apples.

Arms aching from carrying the stack of sheets, Ondine dumped them on a footstool and rolled her shoulders. "Right, which one of these enormous wardrobes is a linen press?"

A door Ondine opened revealed fabulous clothes hanging on padded wooden hangers. All were the same colour.

"She must like wearing yellow," Hamish said, scratching his head.

Ondine opened the next door. "Or blue. Saturn's rings, look at this." Each door she opened revealed a new colour. Taking a closer look, she saw each hanger had a tag with a date and event written on it. One had several dates on it, all but the last crossed out.

"Jupiter's moons, she keeps track of when she last wore something and what she wore it to. That's very organised."

"Organised or anally retentive?" Hamish said.

Ondine opened the door of the next wardrobe, still hoping to find where to put all the clean linen. This door revealed shelves and a pull-out desk, complete with an old-style ledger. Did she dare look at it?

Of course she dared. They were here to spy, weren't they? With shaking fingers she opened the ledger. Each page contained lines and lines of information about staff. The day they started and how much they earned each month.

"Saturn's rings, look how little I earn." At least she wouldn't be lying to her parents about not being able to afford a train ticket home. Amazed, she sat down on the floor to continue reading the ledger.

A strained squeak escaped her mouth.

"What, no planets this time?" Hamish knelt beside her.

"She's got everyone here. The chefs take home a pittance but look how much Ms Kyryl earns. That's a lot for a teacher." Ondine scratched her head. "Great Pluto's ghost, here's a column dated a few months ago that shows how much everyone weighs. Why would she do this?"

"She likes tae keep track of everything?"

"Yeah, everything." She flicked through the pages and found some recent diary entries.

*Ondine de Groot. Arrived with Colette Romano and a ferret.*

Ondine's jaw fell open. "That's it?"

"Ye havenae been here long," Hamish reminded her.

They both read the lines about Colette Romano.

Her arrival date, her job description as "advisor" and her staggeringly huge wage. Beside those notes, the Duchess had written, *Overpaid and overfed.*

Ondine laughed, then stopped to listen for footsteps. No, just her imagination and racing heartbeat making her feel guilty. "We really shouldn't be reading this."

"Yes, we should. The Duke wants us tae get information, this is information."

"But surely he knows what's in here? I mean, she's his wife, she's probably written all this down for his benefit?"

"Mebbe she's keeping secrets from him." Hamish flicked a few pages back and found an entry for Draguta Matice. Because she'd worked at the palechia for so many years, there were several notes. One of them said:

APPROACHING SECOND LONG-SERVICE LEAVE. *If we don't get rid of her soon she'll cost us a fortune.*

"OH, Hamish, how could she say that? It's so unfair. You can't just sack someone because they've got holidays coming up."

Hamish turned on the sarcasm. "But the Duchess is always right, Ondi."

"I have to warn Draguta." Ondine stood up to leave. In the process, she tipped over the ledger and a piece of paper fell out from the back of it. The handwriting was so small Ondine had to squint. It had columns of dates and details of cash deposited, adding up to a steadily growing balance.

"Ye've hit the jackpot, lass, the Duchess has a secret bank account!"

"But . . ." It didn't make any sense. "If this is a bank account, why is it all hand-written?"

Hamish scratched his forehead. "Mebbe it's not a real bank? Mebbe she's stashing it under the mattress for a rainy day?"

"We have to tell the Duke," Ondine said.

"But we'll havetae be careful how we do it. Ye've seen how loved-up they are. It would break his heart tae find out she's keeping secrets from him."

Something went a bit woozy in Ondine's head. The bank balance was enough to buy half the country. How nice of Hamish to start rubbing her back. She felt instantly soothed as he gently massaged her shoulders.

They heard footsteps in the hall and froze until they faded off into the distance.

"We'd better pack this up before someone walks in," she said.

In a blur of papers, Ondine tucked the piece of paper into the ledger and shoved it back in its rightful home. Then Hamish resumed rubbing her shoulders.

"Left a bit, lower . . . oh, nice! But Hamish, how do we know if we've put it all back the right way?"

"Eh . . . too easy. We'll put a half glass of wine in there with it."

"What's that going to achieve?"

Hamish's eyes narrowed with a glint of mischief. "When she next looks at it, she'll think she put it away in a hurry. She won't remember because the wine glass will remind her she was drinking at the time."

"Or she'll know someone else has been here, going through her things."

"Time will tell."

While Ondine chewed her bottom lip in apprehension, Hamish left the bedroom, then came straight back with a clean glass and a bottle of sauvignon blanc. He unscrewed the cap. They only needed a little wine for the bottom of the glass. Hamish replaced the cap and put the bottle beside the ledger as well.

Ondine wasn't so sure it would work. "Would she do that?"

"Mebbe. Mebbe not. Mebbe she'll open the cupboard door and be so distracted by the bottle she won't care."

"There were far too many 'maybes' in that."

They closed the wardrobe and Ondine made for the door. She didn't want to spend another minute up here.

"Aren't ye forgetting something? We have tae change the sheets."

Ondine slapped her forehead. Not changing the sheets was a sure-fire way to make the Duchess angry. Plus, she'd probably blame Draguta for the mistake and sack her.

Working together, they stripped the old sheets, making sure not to knock the antiques over in their haste, then grabbed new sheets and remade the bed, taking extra care to straighten out creases. Hamish lifted up the top mattress and shook his head. "No money under here. Just thought I'd check."

In the bathroom – more marble everywhere and gold taps, for goodness' sake – Ondine bundled up the used linen and shoved it down the laundry chute, then did the same with the old towels. In a few minutes, there were clean towels hanging over the rails where they should be.

"Here it is," Hamish said from the bedroom.

Ondine stuck her head out of the bathroom door and saw Hamish standing next to a bureau. Marble-topped, of course. He'd found the linen press.

"Good one." She grinned. He'd already stacked the rest of the clean linen in there.

"I think our work here is done," Hamish said, giving Ondine a smile that made her feel a bit wonderful all over. "Now, hen, whatever we saw in that book has tae stay between us. I mean, we'll tell Col and she'll be fair astounded, but nobody else."

"But I have to warn Draguta, she needs to know Kerala has it in for her."

"But if we tell her, she might change her behaviour and then the Duchess will think she knows more than she does. She might even think it was Draguta looking at the secret bank account."

"Which will give her a reason to sack her."

"Exactly."

"Even though Draguta would be completely innocent," Ondine explained.

"Aye."

"But if we don't warn her, the Duchess will sack her anyway. And she doesn't deserve that."

This whole spying caper gave Ondine a headache. On top of that, keeping secrets from people she regarded as friends had set up a nasty ache in her heart.

**12**

———

Another day. Another pile of laundry. Hamish was off somewhere else, spying on staff. Ondine's job stayed the same. Going through people's clothes for lost objects felt wrong to Ondine, but the Duke wanted her to work in here and report anything suspicious. Surely it was an invasion of privacy? On the other hand, it had to be done. Ondine pressed her fingers into a pocket and felt something small and chunky. Urgh! In her hand lay a crusted tissue that had something wrapped inside it. A voice in her head said, Look away, look away! but she couldn't.

Teeth. Several of them. All small, off-white, some triangular, some a little more like molars. The exact sort of teeth Biscuit the dog no longer had in his mouth.

"I'm going to be sick!" Ondine said, dropping the dirty parcel on the floor with a soft *fwob*.[1]

Draguta came back at that point. "You have Infanta's basket. She is worst. Never know what you pull out of pockets. Last week, I found dirty spoon and sticky lid from medicine bottle."

Ondine nearly placed her hand over her mouth to stop herself queefing. In the nick of time, she remembered her hand had touched the gritty tissue. The laundry trough, soap and hot water beckoned.

"She's really winning me over, that Infanta," Ondine said to Draguta. "I met her one night, in the kitchen. She was spoon-feeding her dog soup, and I swear to Pluto and back she kept putting the dog spoon in the pot."

"Excuse, please." Draguta pushed Ondine out of the way and promptly vomited in the trough. "You should told me before ate soup. So much leftovers. I have double helpings."

Mentally, Ondine filled in Draguta's speech with all the definite and indefinite articles the laundress had left out.

"I'm so sorry, I didn't think." Guilt ebbed through Ondine as she took in Draguta's pale grey face. "You must be on a hair trigger. I only just said it and you puked, yet you've been eating the soup every day."

"Urgh." Draguta wiped her face with a cold wet towel, then draped the cloth over the back of her neck for good measure. "Feeling rancid last couple days. Thought coming down with something. Now I know. Dogs have more bacteria in mouths what are people in Brugel. I surprised more are not sick."[2]

Draguta's words proved truly prophetic. For the next few hours, a great many people in the palechia were sick, most of them staff, who regularly ate soup because there wasn't much variety on offer. Of those who were sick, most were caught completely by surprise and nowhere near a laundry trough or basin at the required moment. This in turn translated into an increased number of dirty towels, sheets, pillow cases, blankets and rugs arriving in the laundry. Another problem with so many people being sick? Fewer able-bodied staff to do the cleaning up.

Old Col appeared at the doorway, her face drawn and pale. "Ondine, I need clean towels and bedsheets."

"What's wrong?"

"Nothing," Col said, noting all eyes in the laundry were on her.

"Are you sick?" Ondine asked.

"Of course not. Whatever gave you that idea?" Col said as beads of sweat appeared on her top lip.

Panic sliced through Ondine and she ushered her great aunt out of the laundry and into the hall so they could grab a word in private. "You look terrible."

"I'm only pretending it's for me. I was trying to tell you that, using ESP, but you're mentally deaf."

Smackdown! "Gee, thanks." Ondine rolled her eyes. "So why do you need linen? Is Hamish sick?"

"Ixnay on the icksay, it's the ukeday."

Confusion creased Ondine's face. "What on earth are you talking about?"

Old Col kept her voice to a low murmur: "We're pretending the Duke has only lost his voice so that nobody panics. He's here, confined to bed. Tell nobody."

Oh dear!

Oh dear, oh dear, oh double dear! Checking the hall to make sure nobody was within earshot, Ondine asked, "Is the Duchess here too?"

"No. She left for the city yesterday evening, and will be back tomorrow. She took Vincent with her, he's going to stand in for the Duke at the Opera."

"But that's terrible!"

"I know. It's a three-hour-show."[3]

"Not that! I mean Vincent's acting as if he's the Duke already!"

"Keep your voice down. I'm sure this is one of those twenty-four-hour things and Pavla will be all right again. Now get me the clean linen."

Ondine did Col's bidding, then quickly told her what they'd seen in the Duchess's ledger. As she got back to the laundry she couldn't help wondering if they'd completely failed in their mission already. Vincent wanted to take over; standing in for his ill father was the first step.

Back at work in the laundry, Draguta scolded her. "If told more people about dog soup, we not have such mess."

Ondine felt chastened, even though it wasn't exactly her fault. "But it was the first night I was here. And people are suddenly sick now? It doesn't make sense."

"Infanta making dog soup each night I bet."

That could be it. One night of bad food might not make too many people sick, but night after night, week after week? Then again, Hamish had said the farmers hadn't been cleaning the vegetables properly, so perhaps that was part of it? When she swallowed, she felt something niggling in her throat, like the start of a cold. Definitely the time of year for it at any rate.[4]

Draguta hauled wet washing into a basket. "No chatty-chat with me, not in mood."

As Ondine hosed the sick off yet another rug, she hoped the mess and illness would all be over soon. Lost in thought, she very nearly hosed the blur of fur as it ran towards her. "Shambles, what are you doing here?" she cried.

Draguta stared daggers at Ondine. "I said no pets!"

Gulp. Ondine grabbed Shambles and took him outside, so they could chat in private.

"Is it the Duke? Is he all right?"

"Aw, lass, ye've never seen so much sick. Col's doing her very best tae get him through it."

"And Kerala's not here while everyone else is throwing their guts up."

A thoughtful look crossed the little ferret's face. "Now that ye mention it . . ."

"Do you think – but no. It can't be her. Do you think? I mean, why would she harm him? She loves him. And if anything happened to him, it would all go to Vincent anyway. She's not in line. Maybe . . ." Ondine kept thinking out loud. "Maybe it's Vincent making the Duke sick?"

Just thinking about Vincent turned Ondine's stomach. She had once fallen for his charm. What if Vincent was working his charm on someone here at the palechia? Someone young and naive like Ondine had been.

"Aye, Vincent's a dirty wee bast –"

"H'hem!" Ondine cleared her throat as she saw laundry workers approaching with clean washing from the line.

Shambles kept his voice low. "And another thing, the teacher is giving ye a test first thing tomorrow. Overheard her the day before yesterday at afternoon tea with the Duchess."

"You're taking afternoon tea with the Duchess? Half your luck." Ondine looked at the laundry flapping in the breeze and wondered what had happened to her plans for a grand adventure with Hamish.

"Dinnae be angry with me, lass. I would have told ye earlier only I've been busy with all me responsibilities."

Ondine couldn't help thinking Hamish loved having such an interesting job, with all those responsibilities.

Shambles gave Ondine a scratchy kiss on the cheek. "I know ye'll give it yer all. It's maths and yer a big win at that."

*If only it were proper Hamish, not ferret Shambles, kissing me,* Ondine thought with a sigh. "Thank goodness it's not a history test. I'd suck at that."

"I thought ye liked history?"

"Not any more." Ondine felt guilty taking a break while everyone else was working so hard. "Sorry, Shambles, I need to get back to work."

Shambles gave her another hurried kiss.

"Thanks for the warning, I'll swot up tonight," she said.

"Yer welcome. Oh, and I nearly forgot another thing. So much going on, so little time. Tomorrow, yer invited tae afternoon tea."

"Really?" Ondine felt the rush of excitement. Finally, something more interesting than laundry! "Wow, that is such an honour to get an invite. Oh dear! I've nothing to wear."

"Col has something for ye. It will look well on ye, too."

## 13

The next morning, Ondine arrived a few minutes early at the school barn door. Hetty was already there, smiling as Ondine approached.

"It's so nice to have another girl my age at school. I'm so glad to have a best friend again. Someone to share my secrets. You'll share all yours too, won't you?" she said, smiling, her cheeks plump and round.

Something caught in Ondine's brain. Sharing secrets reminded her of lazy summer afternoons with Melody, pretending to read their futures in a pack of cards as they divulged all sorts of family stories. Now with Hetty, the rules were different, but she had to pretend everything was normal. Putting on her best secret-sharing grin, she said, "Sure."

"I probably sounded a bit desperate just then. Sorry about that. It's so weird, this place." Hetty gave a hesitant smile. "There are so many people, but it's still lonely at times."

Ondine found herself nodding to the truth of it, but then wondered if Hetty had some kind of agenda. Immediately she slapped that thought away. Since coming here she'd been off-kilter. Hetty was just being friendly, in an anxious, lonely kind of way.

Ms Kyryl arrived and opened the barn door for the students. Hetty talked all the way to their desk. She seemed so desperate for friendship. A bit naive. What if Vincent had convinced Hetty to do his bidding?

Ondine mentally shook the thought away. Hetty might be immature, but she wasn't silly. Or at least, not as silly as Ondine had once been. *Then again, she lives on a chicken farm*, Ondine thought. Chickens were a fine source of salmonella if they weren't handled with the utmost care. Perhaps the illness ripping through the palechia originated with the chickens?

Ms Kyryl said good morning and announced the maths test. The class groaned. Ondine groaned, too, because she had to pretend she was just as surprised as everyone else. In fact it was a convincing groan, because she'd studied into the night and still felt half-asleep.

The test itself hurt her brain, but she felt pretty confident she'd done a good job. There were a few questions where she didn't have a clue. The ones involving parabolas. They always turned her brain to concrete.[1]

It was over soon enough and they took out their textbooks to work though the next chapter of maths problems while Ms Kyryl marked the papers.

"I love maths," Hetty said to Ondine. "When my sister was at home, she used to help me with my homework and I really got the hang of it. I'll definitely be doing things with maths when I'm older. How about you?"

When Ondine thought about her future, she suddenly realised she hadn't given it much consideration. "I'm not sure what I want to do. I guess I . . ."

"Don't leave me hanging. What is it? You can tell me. I'll keep your secrets."

There was that word again, secrets. Secrets Ondine couldn't share, no matter how relieved she'd feel if she could unburden herself. Ondine couldn't deny the bond developing between them. Hetty was the only other girl her age in the whole palechia. They had to be friends, otherwise she'd have nobody. And perhaps if they became really good friends, Ondine could find out if Hetty was working for Vincent.

"OK. The thing is, I'm not really sure what I want to do. Probably work in my family's hotel and then maybe later I'll branch out. I guess as long as I'm with Hamish I know I'll be happy."

Hetty's eyes grew round in surprise and she made a little squeak. Just as suddenly, her voice dropped lower. "You've got a boyfriend already? Oh, my gosh. You city girls grow up fast!"

An opportunity revealed itself. "What about you? Any handsome boy caught your eye?"

Hetty blushed furiously and lowered her head in embarrassment. "I don't know the first thing about boys."

"But there must be one you like?"

Hetty shook her head.

At that moment, Ms Kyryl handed back the test results. There in the top right corner of Ondine's paper was "D+" in green pen, followed by the number fifty-eight.

That sinking feeling of failure pulled her down into her seat.

"Dee plus? But I –" Just in time, Ondine reeled in the words that threatened to fly out. She couldn't admit she'd studied, because it was supposed to be a surprise test. But to get less than sixty per cent? What a burn. All that studying for nothing.

"But you what?" Ms Kyryl asked.

"But . . . I thought I got most of them right," she said. Oh, how embarrassing, her voice sounded so whiny.

"You did very well considering your lack of formal education. Your great aunt tells me you attended a psychic camp during your summer holidays, which I understand was not a great success."

Giggles rippled through the classroom. Embarrassment raced up Ondine's neck and face. Even her ears burned.

"It was Ma's idea," Ondine started. Sure, she'd thought it a great waste of time, too, but now the class was laughing at her, she felt strangely protective of her family's choice. After all, regular school terms are mandatory, but surely what you do in your holidays is free choice? Otherwise why call them holidays?

Ms Kyryl asked the students to open their textbooks to a set page and they embarked on a new set of quadratic equations.[2]

Hetty leaned over and whispered, "Don't feel bad. We went to maths camp over the summer."

"Oh." That would explain why they were all so good at it.

"But I bet you had more fun," Hetty said.

After school Ondine dashed to Old Col's room in the hope of seeing Hamish. To her continuing disappointment, she found him in Shambles form, sitting atop a small table crammed with platters of food. Old Col sat beside him, making notes.

"Smells great, I'm starving." Ondine reached for a slice of cheese.

"Not so fast." Old Col's hand slapped her on the wrist. "We haven't approved it yet."

Shambles piped up, "Hullo, lass. Pavla's goat us taste testing. Best job in the world. That lamb's tae die for."

"You're tasting his food now? But what if someone really is out to get him and they put something in it!" Fear twisted her tummy.

"That is the whole point, dear child," Old Col said. "Considering how sick the Duke is, we should have done this earlier. He's turned the corner now, thanks for asking. Although he's a long way from being at his best."

"I meant to but . . . I'm glad he's feeling better. That's such a relief."

Col said, "He's banned all seafood since it rained fish and he's banned coffee. He very nearly banned soup as well, but then they'd have nothing to feed the staff."

"There's sandwiches," Ondine said, wishing she had something solid to eat. Then the reality of the situation hit home. "But what if you get really sick?"

"Aye, goat it worked out too," Shambles said with his ferrety mouth full. "Ye noticed how me neck injuries all healed when I changed. If there's anything wrong with the food, I'll change intae meself and I'll be all better."

"Does this mean you don't have time to open his mail anymore?"

"Not in the slightest," Col said, then laughed. "We're very busy, keeping the Duke hidden in his sickbed, opening mail and eating all day." Taking up a knife and fork, she cut a morsel from the edge of the hard cheese and gave it to Shambles. The two of them chomped away happily.

Squelch. A cramp of hunger twisted Ondine's tummy. The need for food overrode her fear of what might be in it. She snatched a hunk of cheese and wolfed it down.

"There you are! Where have my teeth gone?" a voice demanded from the doorway.

The three of them turned to see Infanta Anathea standing there with that ironing-board-smooth face of hers, holding no-teeth-Biscuit under one arm.

"That spell must be reversed," Anathea said. She had a look on her face that was hard to read. "And that thing on the table needs to be put down."

Calm as you like, Col said, "Do you have the teeth?"

Guilt made Ondine gulp. She'd had the teeth. But she'd thrown them away.

The Infanta said, "Do I look like the kind of person who has a set of dog teeth in her bag?"

Ondine thought she looked like the kind of person who carried around all sorts of crazy things in her bag. And a fair bit of it had to be emotional baggage.

"I can't do much without the teeth," Col said.

Was she baiting the Infanta? Surely her great aunt would not be so rude.

"Fix it, now, or so help me something will be done!"

"Yes, yes." Col held her hands out. "Give me the dog."

"Ru-ru-ru-ru," Biscuit wailed.

Shambles tensed.

Anathea held on to Biscuit tightly. "No, he will not be abused again."

With a resigned voice, Col said, "I'm not going to abuse him. I'm going to help him. I'm sure he has more teeth in his gums that can come through soon –"

"He's a champion breed, not a shark!" Anathea protested, handing the dog over.

Col said, "Ondine, will you get my travelling bag, it has some nifty potions in there."

Doing her great aunt's bidding, Ondine fetched the carpetbag. The medicine bottles clinked and rattled as she picked it up. She handed the bag to Col, who passed her Biscuit. Ondine really didn't want to hold the dog who'd nearly killed her dearest love, so she gave him back to Anathea.

"Ru-ru-ru-ru."

In a flash of fur, Shambles dashed off the table, raced over to the bed and climbed to the top of the bedhead. Then he leapt even higher and balanced on the lampshade. Ondine didn't blame him wanting to be out of reach when Biscuit got his teeth back.

"It's all right Shambles, his bark's worse than his bite," Ondine said.

"How dare you!" Anathea said.

"Ooops, sorry." Ondine found something interesting on the floor to look at.

"Let's have a look," Col said, taking Biscuit back into her arms and not caring that he snarled and wriggled. "There, there. Kleine denta wachsen, kleine denta wachsen."[3]

"What is being said?" Anathea demanded.

"I'm encouraging his little teeth to grow. Now, Ondine, my hands are full. Grab me the tin marked 'salamander'."

Rifling through the bag Ondine found bottles and boxes and an assortment of strange things. "Found it."

Tucking the dog under one arm, Col flicked open the tin and shook a little powder into Ondine's palm. She dabbed the tip of her finger in the powder and proceeded to rub it on the dog's gums.

A wince of disgust creased Ondine's face. "It's not real salamander, is it?"

"It's their dried eggs. Right, that should do it."

"The teeth have been fixed now?" Anathea said as she took her dog back.

"I'm a witch, not a dentist. You'll have to wait and see."

Anathea held Biscuit close to her chest. "I will not be made fun of! You mark my words, make an enemy of me and you will never know a moment's peace!"

With that, she stormed out.

Shambles leapt off the lamp and landed on the bed. "She's going tae the top of me list of suspects."

"Agreed," Col said. "I've been looking at the line of succession. Vincent is too young to succeed but if anything happened to the Duke, Anathea could make a play for power."

"Is that such a bad thing?" Ondine said. "Surely anyone's better than Vincent?"

"No argument here," Shambles said, climbing back on to the table, where he helped himself to a bite of roast lamb. He swallowed it in one gulp. "Mmmpfh, aw, very good, yeas."

"What about the salad?" Ondine asked. "Aren't you going to try that?"

"Aw no, lass. Ye know us ferrets cannae stand it," he said.

"Then perhaps you should be Hamish again, and then you could eat a bit of everything and –"

Old Col chimed in. "I know what you're getting at, child. You'd like to see more of Hamish, because you can't think beyond your own needs. But we've got it worked out. He eats fat and protein, I eat the fruit and veg, and together we have all the bases covered." Col picked up a leaf from the salad then took some red powder from a small metal box and sprinkled it over the food.

"Is that a magic antidote?" Ondine asked.

"Paprika. I love it. Mmm, interesting . . . I thought that was spinach but it must be something else. In any case, it's fine, if a little bitter."

"Can you please take this more seriously!" Ondine wanted to stamp her feet. They were eating potentially poisonous food. When they weren't eating they were opening potentially explosive mail. They didn't seem the slightest bit worried.

"Oh dear." Shambles ducked away from the table and scurried into the bathroom. In a few moments he returned as Hamish, dressed in a shirt and dark trousers. "Bad news. I think the lamb is off."

Fear turned Ondine's tummy to lead at the thought that her darling Hamish could be sick. But it was so good to see Hamish as his human self again. "Are you feeling OK?"

Beads of sweat broke out on his brow but he smiled anyway. "All the better fer seeing ye."

"I worry about you." She reached forward and gave him a hug.

"Oh dear, that's turned," Col said behind them as she sniffed the left-over lamb. "Hamish, I'm surprised you couldn't smell it."

"Aye, weil, I could, only it smelled good because I was hungry."

"Hamish, you must be more careful," Ondine said.

Col pushed the offending pieces onto a side plate. "Not even the Infanta deserves that. Looks like lamb's off the menu now as well."

Ondine hugged Hamish more tightly. "I can't believe it, someone really is trying to poison the Duke."

"Perhaps," Col said.

Ondine turned to her. "You've got a bit of . . ." She touched her tooth.

"Thank you." Col removed the stray greenery from between her teeth. "But I hope it's not as sinister as that. Maybe some well-meaning idiot in the kitchen has served up something they should have thrown out a few days ago."

Despite Hamish's arms holding her close, a cold shudder rippled through Ondine. "This place is giving me the creeps."

Col folded her napkin and got up from the table. "No time for that, child. We must all ready ourselves for afternoon tea with the Duchess. Hamish, you know what to do."

It broke Ondine's heart to watch him change into a ferret again. Maybe when afternoon tea was over, they might find some time to be themselves again?

*There I go again, wanting the impossible.*

# CHAPTER 13-A

This book has two chapter thirteens because there is so much bad news.

Ondine felt like she had to pass another test as she and Hetty took their seats at one of the small tables in the conservatory that afternoon. She felt like a princess wearing the dress Old Col had picked out for her. It was made from floaty peach-coloured layers, which twirled and swished with each step. Her great aunt had even bought her the sweetest pair of low-heeled slippers, all sparkly and lovely.  They were strapless shoes, so walking in them took a bit of getting used to, because they nearly slipped off her feet each time she took a step.

Sunlight streaked through the conservatory windows. Outside, the autumn wind flickered through the row of liquid amber trees, making their orange and yellow leaves twist and spin into the air as they fell from their boughs.[1]

There were about twenty small tables here, all made from lace-iron.[2] Ondine recognised the tablecloths from her time in the laundry. It didn't take a psychic to know most of them would be covered in wine and tea stains by the end of the day and she'd have to wash them again.

Old Col and Shambles sat at a different table, closer to the Duchess.

The Duchess, her glossy mahogany hair perfectly coiffed, sat at the head of a longer table in the centre of the room.

Nobody made any introductions to Ondine or Hetty, but Ondine didn't mind. It was enough to be all dressed up, sitting in such lovely surroundings, eating delicate sandwiches and crisp, sweet biscuits, washed down with tea.

"We're seat filling," Hetty said in a soft voice. "It happens from time to time. The Duchess can't stand to have an empty table, so she lets us come as long as we behave ourselves."

"Why not move the empty tables and seats out?"

"Because they are screwed to the floor."

Ondine placed her hand on the edge of the table and tried to move it. Not even a slight budge. She tried the same with her chair, with the same result. "Who screws furniture to the floor?"

Hetty leaned closer and kept her voice low. "A few years ago, some tables and chairs went missing. My parents helped search the farmhouses and barns to try and find them. They never showed up. The Duchess ordered the rest of the furniture to be bolted down. It's been that way ever since."

"Lucky us, then," Ondine said as she helped herself to a cheese finger sandwich from the neat little display tower in the middle of her table. Glancing across the room, Ondine saw Hamish-as-Shambles appearing to sleep on Col's lap. His ears strained back and forth like a radar dish, listening for morsels of information.

"We don't get the fancy sandwiches either," Hetty said, "just cheese or jam for us, but it's nice all the same to be here. It's a bit like playing dressing-up, don't you think?"

Ondine smiled. "Quite!" She took another cheese sandwich and pretended it was chicken and avocado. A tuft of white fluffy mould clung to the side of the cheese. Back at her family's pub, she'd eaten mouldy cheeses all the time – but they were proper mouldy, with a mottled blue coating. This was hard yellow cheese and all kinds of wrong.

Out of the corner of her eye, she saw a guest at another table slip a dessert fork into her handbag. Stealing cutlery? Ondine picked up one of the spoons at her place setting and turned it over. The maker's stamp indicated sterling silver. The good stuff.

As politely as she could, Ondine tried to get her great aunt's attention. She coughed a little into her closed hand. That did nothing. So she made a "psst" sound, which also achieved nothing. Finally she threw caution to the wind and said, "Aunt Col, may I give your pet ferret some cheese?"

That got her attention. And Shambles's. Ondine quickly excused herself from Hetty, and took the slice of the expired cheese to Shambles. When she reached them, she murmured to him, "Show the mouldy bit to Col. Meanwhile, there's a nicked fork in the blue bag."[3]

Ondine quickly made her way back to Hetty, whose eyes were as round as the saucers beneath their teacups. "The Duchess doesn't normally allow pets in here. Your great aunt must be very special."

"You have no idea," Ondine said and added a giggle.

Across the room, Shambles disappeared under the tables. A few moments later, he appeared at Ondine's feet with a silver fork in his mouth. Ondine leant down and held out her hand as he deposited the cutlery in her palm. He disappeared again and a few moments later reappeared with a teaspoon. Ondine cast a glance around the room, pretending to admire all the finery. What she really did was check nobody was looking her way, then she snuck the extra items beside her cake plate.

The side doors opened to announce a new arrival. Hetty gave a high-pitched shriek as Lord Vincent walked in.

Ondine hissed, "Calm down."

Such was her excitement, Hetty sat there and silently vibrated in her chair. Try as she might, Ondine couldn't stop her eyes rolling towards the ceiling.

Looking relaxed and charming, Vincent made the rounds of the room, shaking hands with guests and making small talk. Between Hetty's gasps, Ondine made out a few words. Something along the lines of Vincent standing in for his father, who was unavailable.

More squeaking from Hetty. "He's coming over here," and, "Ohmygosh I'mgoingtodie."

"Good afternoon, ladies," he said, his face showing no sign of upset at the fact that Ondine had scored a seat in here. If anything, he seemed almost . . . pleasant. It had to be an act, especially considering the way he'd treated her last time.

Hetty giggled.

Knowing all eyes were on them, Ondine played along. "Good afternoon, My Lord."

"I have a pony!" Hetty gushed.

Ondine slapped her palm to her forehead.

Vincent turned the charm on full blast. "Really now? Are you kindly taking care of one of my father's horses?"

"Eeeee –" Hetty said, furiously nodding her head.

"Then I thank you for your troubles. I hope we can have the stables repaired soon."

*Please pull yourself together*, Ondine silently begged. It reminded her of how she'd lost her head over Vincent way back when, but surely she hadn't acted quite as silly as Hetty.

Hetty grinned and made a weird sound in the back of her throat.

Vincent smiled again and said, "It was a pleasure meeting you," then he moved on.

It was impossible to get anything coherent out of Hetty while Vincent was in the room. After what felt like half an hour, but was probably only a few minutes, he finished his circuit of the room, spoke a few words to his mother and left.

"Ahhhhh," Hetty said with a too-loud sigh. "Isn't he amazing?"

Ondine coughed water into her nose and grabbed her napkin. By the time she finished, Hetty still wore a double-glazed expression.

"Come on, snap out of it," Ondine said.

As if her words had done the trick, Hetty suddenly remembered where she was and her hand came up to her mouth. "I have no idea what I just said then. Tell me I didn't say anything stupid."

"He seemed impressed you had a pony."

Hetty buried her face in her hands. "I want to die." At that moment, the Infanta walked in with Biscuit tucked under her arm. Try as she might, Ondine couldn't see if the dog's teeth were growing back yet.

The Infanta wore a sky-blue tailored suit, several years out of date, and eye shadow to match. On her face she wore an imperious, you-started-without-me look.

The Duchess put down her glass of wine. "Anathea, you're not in the diary. To what do we owe thish unecshpected shurprise?"[4]

It was only mid-afternoon, but Ondine heard the slur in Duchess Kerala's words and wondered how much she'd had to drink.

The Infanta kissed the top of one of the female guests' heads and said, "Hello, dear."

It must be one of her daughters, Ondine thought. It also happened to be one of the women stealing cutlery. Then the Infanta looked at the Duchess. "Since when do I need an appointment to see my sister-in-law?"

Ondine had been thinking the same thing. Afternoon tea was a regular event, and they seemed to have spare tables – or at least enough spare seats to invite school children. So why was there no spare seat for Anathea?

Unless the distaste for each other ran so deep Kerala went to extraordinary lengths to make sure there were no spare seats?

An uncomfortable silence cloaked the room. Nobody wanted to say anything, probably because nobody knew what to say. The Duchess drained her wine glass and touched a hand to her hair, as if to set it in place. A stalling tactic – there was no way her dark lacquered hair had come the slightest bit loose. She turned to her social secretary, who handed over a leather-bound diary. The Duchess flicked a few pages forwards and backwards, pursed her lips and frowned.

"I have shpace at three tomorrow afternoon. Can it wait until then?"

"After midday? What's the point?" the Infanta said.[5]

The cold look between the Duchess and the Infanta dropped the temperature in the room by ten degrees. Biscuit wriggled in the Infanta's arms and made a "ru-ru-ru-ru" bezerker bark, trying to get at Shambles.

Ondine feared for her beloved.

Shambles stood up on Old Col's lap and made his own, "ru-ru-ru-ru" sound back at the dog. Biscuit yelped and tried to burrow into the Infanta.

Everyone, including Ondine and Hetty, laughed. The distraction helped break the icy tension in the room. The Duchess accepted another glass of wine from the waiter.

Old Col spoke up, "Did I mention, Your Grace, that I can read tea leaves? I'm very good."

The Duchess smiled and appreciated the diversion for what it was. The Infanta still didn't have a seat and nobody offered her one. While the waiters brought out pots of freshly brewed tea, Anathea and her crazy dog took their leave.

Old Col poured tea and the conservatory regained the atmosphere of a garden party.

"My niece is proficient at reading palms," Old Col said. "Ondine, would you be so kind as to share your gift?"

"Really?" Hetty said. "Wow, you should have told me! I'll get you to read mine later."

"I'm not that good," Ondine said.

With a flagging heart, Ondine approached the Duchess. "I will need both hands, Your Grace." Inside, she trembled, but she did her best to control it.

The Duchess put down her glass of wine and gave her palms to Ondine. The nail on her left pinkie finger was so long it had started to curl inwards. It mildly grossed Ondine out to see the yellow stains underneath it. This close, she could see Duchess Kerala's blue eyes, but they didn't shine. If anything, they looked cold and calculating.

"Thank you. You're right-handed." Ondine had seen the Duchess make a note in her diary with her right hand, so it wasn't guess work. "That means your left is the life you were given, and the right is the one you've made for yourself."

Then Ondine made the mistake of looking at those soft, pampered palms. Instantly she regretted it, because she didn't like what she saw. Clean, simple lines on the left hand, but a right hand filled with complicated scribbles, slashes and crossings out. As if her present life was trying to scratch out the past. The words "secret", "deceit", and "danger" immediately came to mind.

Looking up, Ondine saw Old Col give her a satisfied nod.

Ondine summoned every ounce of diplomacy she possessed and

began the reading. "You are so generous, Your Grace, and so concerned for the welfare of others it almost reduces you to tears."

The Duchess smiled and said, "Go on."

Complete mince, as Shambles might say, but it seemed Ondine's kind words met with approval. She really wanted to say, "I think you're as cunning as a sewer rat," but that would do her no good at all. Meanwhile, others at the table drank their tea, swilled their cups and turned them upside down on their saucers. Old Col looked for omens in the mush.

Out of the corner of her eye, Ondine saw one of the guests offering Shambles the last piece of mortadella from her plate.[6]

Ondine felt even more uncomfortable as she continued with the reading. "I see your marriage continuing happily, for a great many years into the future."

The Duchess gave Ondine an unreadable look, as if she'd told her something she hadn't wanted to hear. Her tone stayed deadpan. "A charming divershion, I'm shure."

Ondine's stomach dropped to the floor. Old Col must have read the distress in her face because she made a timely interruption: "Some tea, Your Grace?"

*Thank you, Aunt Col.*

Ondine looked about the room and saw Hetty serving tea to several women seated nearby. It seemed everyone here wanted to know their futures. From under the table, Shambles liberated a cake fork from another handbag. It was going to be a long afternoon.

---

The early evening chill teased Ondine's skin as she dashed towards the crepe myrtles. Her feet came loose in the pretty shoes, so she kicked them off on the grass and ran in bare feet, her skirts swishing and swooshing around her knees like an unfurled hibiscus flower. The swirling wind blew leaves and petals off the branches, making her feel like she was inside a snow-globe.

Joy burst through the gloom the moment she saw Hamish standing there. "Oh, sweetheart!" she cried and wrapped her arms around her beloved.

He felt stilted as he hugged her. Worry wormed through her. This was not the warm welcome she'd expected.

"It's g-good to s-see you."

She was wearing a gorgeous dress, but Hamish's smart clothes felt damp and stuck to his skin. The twig snapped. "You're freezing!"

"I'm a wee bit wet, lass."

"Oh, my stars, what happened?"

"I left me clothes behind the trees fer next time, but they goat smothered in dew."

"Oh, you poor darling. I should have brought you a coat or something. Or a mug of soup."

"Not the d-dog soup, I hope," Hamish said.

When Ondine kissed him, his lips felt so cold it shocked her. She trailed kisses over his cold cheeks, doing her level best to warm him up.

Old Col interrupted. "We'd best keep this brief, the Duke will be wanting information soon. Ondine, what news do you have?"

"I've been thinking about how sick everyone was after eating the soup. It couldn't all be dog germs. If the Infanta is in the kitchens at night, maybe she's putting something else in the food, not just the dog spoon."

"Aye." Hamish held Ondine close to him, as if she were a hot-water bottle. "The Infanta is bonkers."

Old Col nodded. "The Duke is right to think she is up to something. But we have no proof yet. Afternoon tea today provided more information. The tealeaves were very good. The Infanta's eldest daughter has not lodged her income tax for the past seven years. One of the Duchess's friends and the Infanta's other daughter are stealing silverware and selling it on Bee-Bay.[7] The visiting ladies from the hospital charity lie about their age, but that's a small thing. They're also terrible gossips and tell all their friends at the bowls club about who has come in for what type of surgery and how often."

Surprise jolted through Ondine. "You got all that from tea leaves?"

"No. But I have excellent hearing. Eavesdropping is one of my hobbies," Old Col said. "Now, Ondine, what did you really see in the Duchess's palms?"

Ondine gulped. "I didn't like it one bit. I mean, I was just telling her what she wanted to hear, but at the same time, I felt she was hiding something. This horrible feeling came over me and I felt a bit sick."

"That could be the alcoholic fumes from her breath," Hamish said.

Ondine laughed. Hamish was still cuddling her and it felt wonderful.

"The Duchess certainly likes the sauce," Old Col said. "But I'm fairly sure the Duke is aware of that. We should keep an eye on her, but my gut feeling is to hold off saying anything about her to the Duke at this point. If we sully the reputation of the woman he loves, without real proof, we'll be out of here faster than you can sneeze."

"But surely the ledger I told you about, surely that's proof she's up to no good," Ondine said.

"Aye, lass, but mebbe he doesn't want us to know she's goat a savings account. I think he wants us snooping intae other people's affairs, nawt his."

The cool wind blew around Ondine and the warmth from Hamish evaporated. She turned to find him transformed into Shambles, standing on top of a pile of crumpled clothes.

"But I was enjoying that," Ondine said.

"Me, too, lass, but Col's right. We need more proof, and I'm going tae get it."

Did he need to get it right now? She'd been so happy to see him as himself again.

Col smiled with approval. "Excellent idea, Shambles. Follow the Infanta and see what she's up to in the kitchens."

"Be careful," Ondine added, "Biscuit's teeth may be back."

"Aye, lass. I shall blend intae the shadows." He gave her a ferrety wink and dashed off.

"Don't be sad, dear," Col said as Ondine headed back across the lawn to pick up her shoes. "He's doing his job."

"Yes, but does he have to enjoy it quite so much?"

<h1 align="center">14</h1>

At this point in time, the chances of the words "model student" and "Ondine de Groot" being used in the same sentence were slim. However, when it came to laundry work, she excelled. Growing up in her family's hotel had given her all the training she needed for long working hours and little free time.

"Thank you, Ondine, you doing great job," Draguta said as they folded the clean clothes into neat bundles.

Ondine grinned. "You're welcome."

"Here. Take sheets and towels to Infanta and make up room."

Ondine accepted the bundle of linen and headed up the stairs to the Infanta's wing.

"You took long enough," the Infanta said as Ondine arrived.

"My apologies, My Lordship," Ondine said, using the correct form of address this time. She looked around the Infanta's rooms for an empty surface so she could put down her linen, but there were none. It looked like burglars had ransacked the place, but surely if they had, the Infanta would have been screaming the house down and calling for the police? Then Ondine realised the Infanta had opened the door her herself.

"Ma'am, where is the butler?"

"She quit. Rude girl."[1]

"I see," Ondine said, looking around.

In his basket, Biscuit lay on his back, paws akimbo, snoring contentedly. A pang of jealousy shot through Ondine at how much she'd love to trade places with the dog. She spotted a small patch of clear space on the floor and put her linen down. Then she headed for the bed and began stripping it.

"You needn't take that 'high and mighty' attitude with me, girl," the Infanta said. "I know what you're thinking."

"Ma'am, I'm thinking I have a lot of work to do today."

"Don't answer back."

Great Pluto's ghost, no wonder the last butler quit!

Without prompting, the Infanta said, "You don't know what it's like to have your life ripped away from you. To have your hopes and dreams dashed."

Ondine kept busy changing the bed sheets. Last time she was stuck listening to the Infanta, in the kitchen, she'd had had nowhere to avert her eyes.

"I was going to be married to a prince, you know. Not one of those Slaegal princes, they're a schlip a dozen.[2] In Slaegal you lift up a rock and you find a prince. My prince was a real one, from the house of Hollenstotder-Betansk. The arrangement was already made. The date set for the week after my sixteenth birthday."

The Infanta gave a noisy sigh. "Am I going to have to pour the tea myself?"

Far from finished with her present task, Ondine stopped making the bed and walked to the serving table where a teapot sat beside some empty cups.

She lifted the lid and found the teapot empty. Great, she'd have to start from scratch. On the dresser she found the kettle, also empty, so she walked to the Infanta's kitchenette and filled it. When it boiled, she tipped some of the water into the pot, swirled it round to warm the porcelain, then poured the water out.

With a note of surprise in her voice, the Infanta said, "You know what you're doing."

"Thank you, ma'am." Ondine put two teaspoons of leaves in the warm pot. The moment the kettle boiled again, she poured the scalding water over the leaves and the water turned a satisfying dark brown.

"How do you like it, ma'am, weak or strong?"

"Strong and stewed."

Ondine nodded and checked the milk jug. The leftover milk in the bottom had formed a thick band of dried scab around the inside wall. Ick!

Scrub, scrub, nearly done. Just for a cup of tea!

"At this time of day, I take it with lemon. I only like milk first thing in the morning."

*You could have told me that before I wasted my time scrubbing the jug!*

In the fruit bowl she found three lemons. She chose one, washed the skin and cut it into thin slices. Then she put a slice in the teacup, grabbed the strainer and poured the Infanta her cup of tea.

"May I return to making your bed, ma'am?"

"Of course. You know, if things had been different, I would have been in the south wing, instead of up here on the draughty north face."

Ondine got straight back to work and finished with the bed, then carried all the dirty linen to the laundry chute in the bathroom. The fabric made soft *dadud* noises as it fell against the chute's angled walls.

"When they thought I'd be the ruling Duchess, I used to have my linen changed every day. Now I'm lucky if it's changed once a week," the Infanta said.

*My heart bleeds*, Ondine thought as she scooped the Infanta's used towels off the floor and dropped them down the chute. All she had to do next was put the clean towels on the rails and get out of there. Being around Anathea made her twitchy and nervous. If she stayed too long, the Infanta would make her clean the bathroom. As far as Ondine was concerned, her job was done.

"And another thing. This is a fine cup of tea, Ondine. Thank you."

"You're welcome, ma'am." The batty old cow had said something nice! Ondine decided to return the favour as she made her way to the door. "I hope you have a lovely day."

"Come back here, I haven't finished with you. Here, let me pour you some tea."

To Ondine's surprise, the Infanta poured her a cup. "Do you take sugar?"

"Yes, two please." Why didn't she just excuse herself and walk out? Her job here was done. Draguta needed her back in the laundry.

"Do you know what it's like to have to bow, scrape and curtsey to someone you despise, Ondine?"

Lord Vincent appeared in her mind. "Yes, ma'am."

"I believe you do." The Infanta looked at her for a while, then a slow, knowing smile spread over her face. "You've met Vincent, haven't you?"

"Wow, you're good."

"He's a piece of work, let me tell you. Far too eager to take over. Thinks he's got it all worked out. With Vincent, the fire's burning but the cow's still in the field."[3]

A giggle escaped Ondine's lips. She couldn't think of anything sensible or non-committal to say, so she drank her tea.

"I was thirteen years old when it was all taken away," the Infanta said. "Thirteen! Old enough to understand my duties, my obligations and my destiny. Old enough to know that when people bowed and curtseyed to me, it was because of my God-given birthright. I was *someone*. They called me 'Duchetta Anathea', the little duchess. I would have been only the third ruling duchess in all of Brugel's history. Oh, I had such lovely plans for making Brugel truly great."

The Infanta's top lip curled in contempt as she said, "Then he was born. The mewling snotty-faced brat. A sickly child by all accounts. Not that they'd let me see him at first. My mother had been ordered bed rest for months before he was born. I was forbidden to see her. I hadn't even known she was pregnant when the orders for her bed rest came. But I knew what was being done. They must have known a boy would be born, otherwise there would not have been such a fuss."

The Infanta looked at the ceiling before she continued. "I knew it was a boy the morning I was not called Duchetta. My father the Duke arrived to tell me the news. He called me 'Infanta'. After that, I was called Infanta by all the staff, and bows were not made. Only nodding heads. When I was finally allowed to meet my baby brother, I was ordered to curtsey to *him.* A few weeks later, news arrived that my engagement was broken. Thirteen years old and my life was over. How do you like that?"

It was hard to know if the Infanta was asking a rhetorical question or a real one. Either way, Ondine didn't have an answer.

A resigned look came over Infanta Anathea's face. "You're a good listener, and you make a fine pot of tea. Your talents are wasted in the laundry. How would you like to work for me? I need a new butler."

Warning bells went off inside Ondine's head. "Ma'am, I'm honoured but –"

"You will be paid double the money."

That made things interesting! "Can I think about it?"

"What is there to think about? You are a smart girl, although from what I hear you need to pay attention in class. A good word can be said to Ms Kyryl."

Jupiter's moons! If the Infanta could put in a "good word" with her teacher, she could probably put in a bad word too.

"Your timetable, what is it?"

Ondine drew a mental picture of her school and laundry schedule, then she explained it to the Duchess.

"I see," she said. "From now on, you will fetch my breakfast before school, then work for me in the afternoon from Wednesday to Friday and then mornings at the weekends."

"But that –"

"– Still leaves you with Tuesday afternoons off. Now go and tell that wafer-thin washer-woman that you will be working for me. Then return here with morning tea, I'm feeling peckish."

No choice at all, then. "Yes, Ma'am. Would you like fruit or cake?"

"Cake? Good luck finding that! Unless you plan on making some yourself? Now that's a handy skill to have."

"We could . . . make a cake together? It might be fun."

Anathea laughed and slapped the table. "Me? Bake?" She wafted her hands in front of her, mimicking the actions of cooking. "I don't do baking."

"Maybe you should?"

"Don't push it."

Head buzzing with confusion, Ondine made her way downstairs to see Draguta and tell her of her change in circumstances.

"I didn't want to take the job but she kind of made it hard for me to say 'no'," Ondine said.

"Of course she did. You watch that woman, she all charm and cheer, then strikes and you never see it coming. You get whiplash keeping up."

"I know. She gave me a compliment and it scared me."

"Be careful, OK?"

"Thanks, Draguta. I'll be very careful."

**15**

The next morning Ondine woke with a jolt. Hunger made strange noises in her belly. She barely had time to bolt down a bowl of Toots Wheat before darting off to the Anathea's rooms to start cleaning.

"I would like a cooked breakfast brought to me as well," the Infanta said.

Ondine silently groaned at the extra workload, although she did her very best not to roll her eyes. She was used to carrying plates of food to customers in her parents' pub, but trudging up two flights of stairs with a tray of bacon and eggs and a pot of tea was difficult and potentially messy.[1]

With each step the tea made lolloping noises and threatened to slosh out of the pot. Her arms ached, her calves burned, her breath came out in loud puffs as she carried the heavy tray up the stairs. At last she reached the Infanta's rooms.

"Was this cooked by you?" the Infanta asked as she lifted the silver dome off the plate.

Fried-bacon smells pervaded the room. Biscuit the gummy dog stirred in his basket.

"No, ma'am, the chefs cooked it," Ondine answered.

Without touching the food, the Infanta placed the dome back over the plate and said, "Take it back."

*What*? "But it's perfectly good," Ondine protested.

The Infanta's expression remained impassive, possibly because her face just didn't move all that much, but her voice brooked no argument. "Don't back chat! I want this thrown out. I want a new breakfast cooked. I want no other hand but yours to touch my food. Is that understood?"

No! Ondine thought, but with a small voice said, "Yes."

Trudging back down the stairs, Ondine reached the kitchen and put the tray down on a side bench near the bins. Lifting the dome, she grabbed the fork the Infanta hadn't even touched and ate everything on the plate. A few minutes later she'd made a new breakfast and it was time to climb the stairs again and present the food to the Infanta, who looked none too please at the delay in her meal service.

With a snap of Anathea's fingers, Biscuit shot out of his basket and sat on his mistress's lap. The Infanta lifted the dome off the plate and said, "You vouch that this was cooked by no one but you?"

"Yes, ma'am."

"Good." She picked up the fork and stabbed at a quivering pile of scrambled egg, then ate it. Her steely eyes blinked slowly. "It's good," she said at last. To Ondine's horror, she scooped more food with her fork and fed it to Biscuit. Then she put the Biscuit-slobbered fork back into the egg on her plate and ate another mouthful.

"You think I'm being difficult, don't you, child?" the Infanta asked.

*I'm thinking a lot of things*, Ondine thought.

"I trust you, Ondine. That is why I want all my meals prepared by you. The kitchen staff cannot be trusted. Corners are cut. Mistakes are made."

Pangs and pings went off inside Ondine's head in frustration. The Infanta was sharing food with her dog, yet she worried about germs from the kitchen staff?

The Infanta went on: "Everyone was made sick recently. I know it came from the kitchen. They are lazy and poorly trained. It's not their fault, of course. Proper staff were not hired. They were not screened prior to working here. Students are cheaper than people who are qualified."

"Yes, ma'am." Ondine tucked a stray hair behind her ear and did her best not to fidget. She had her own theories about how everyone became sick and it centred around the dog with no teeth.

"My bed will be made now and the room will be tidied," the Infanta said.

"Of course," Ondine replied, feeling as if she'd snapped out of a spell. She set to making the bed and tidying the room. All the while, she kept catching glimpses of Infanta Anathea and her dog eating from the same plate. Heaven help her, she just couldn't seem to look away.

"Ma'am, if I may . . ." Ondine said after she'd cleared the floor, "I must get to class."

"Yes, of course. Go. When you finish school, you may make lunch. I would like poached fish."

"But the Duke has banned fish," Ondine said.

"From his plate, not mine. And it will be fresh. If you can find the gamekeeper, see if there are any trout left in the lake."

Silently Ondine groaned at the ever-tightening squeeze on her free time. She'd been cross with Hamish for enjoying his job a little too much and now she'd gone and taken on a second job. They'd be lucky to see each other at all at this rate.

———

THE DAYS GREW COLDER and the shadows grew longer. Fewer guests arrived at the palechia, making the normally bustling estate feel cavernous and eerie. The one short break Ondine had from the palechia was when she joined the school children in the main street of Bellreeve to hang up bunting for the coming Harvest Festival at Halloween.

All week she juggled school and the Infanta. At the weekend she spent her afternoons in the laundry rummaging through clothes for stolen chotskys.[2] And she hadn't seen Hamish, proper Hamish, in so long, she wondered if he might be liking his job more than her.

She barely had five minutes to call her mother, who sounded terse down the line.

"But things are fine, Ma."

"I don't care. You went behind our backs and now you're halfway across the country. You need to be home with us, you –" Oh, thank goodness, the phone started to bleep.

"I'm running out of coins, I have to go."

"Don't you dare hang up on me! Put more coins in. Your sister is trying to organise her wedding and she doesn't know when you'll be home. Your father is furious. You come home right –"

Merciful heavens, the phone went dead. Worn out from the strain, Ondine staggered back to her room, to find Hamish asleep in it. Or rather, Hamish waking up with a smile on his face.

"Yer a sight fer sore eyes," he said, giving her his charming lopsided grin that made her insides melt.

Relief made her feel as bright as sunshine. "It's great to see you, too." Ondine threw herself against Hamish and hugged him with all her heart.

Neither of them said anything for a while, revelling in the rare moment of privacy, content simply to gaze at each other. There are times when things need to be said, and other times, like this, when no words are needed.

In . . .

. . . a . . .

. . . book . . .

. . . it . . .

. . . might . . .

. . . look . . .

. . . a . . .

. . . bit . . .

. . . like . . .

. . . this.

They kissed, too. Lovely kisses that made her feel such utter contentment she couldn't believe she could be this happy. How silly she was so think he didn't love her enough. Everything would be fine.

Eventually, the kissing ended and they tried talking to each other instead.

"How is school?" Hamish asked.

Ondine gave a dramatic sigh. "Awful. Well, not awful the whole time, just most of the time."

"What do ye mean?"

"Remember a while back, you told me we'd have a test? Well, I studied really hard for it, but I only scraped through. And now I'm doing double-duty with Anathea and the laundry, I hardly have any time to study."

"Ye know I'll help out as much as I can."

"Can you do my homework?" she joked.

"I'll think of something," he said, just before kissing her again.

"Shh," Ondine said, her ears straining for sounds in the hallway.

Hamish raised his eyebrows as if to ask, "What"?

Big exhale. "Sorry, I thought I heard Draguta coming." More than anything, Ondine wanted to spend time with Hamish, but their respective workloads in the palechia were making that nigh impossible.

"How about I do the next test for ye?" Hamish winked and kissed her again.

Ondine nearly lost her head, but managed to say, "Yes, please."

"I'm serious. I could sneak intae the teacher's office and get the answers fer ye."

"If only." Ondine wanted him to be quiet and enjoy the kisses. Something in the back of her mind niggled and naggled. "But . . . you're not serious, are you?"

"I'm very serious. If ye fail at school, the Duke might send ye home."

Home to her furious parents? No, thanks. "But I don't like the idea of cheating." He kissed her again but she pulled away. "I mean it. I don't want to cheat."

"I know ye don't want tae, lass, but ye might need tae."

"But it's wrong," she said, feeling sick at the thought. "You really shouldn't be thinking like that."

Hamish softly touched his nose against hers, making her tummy flip in the most delicious way. It made Ondine wonder whether he'd listened to her at all. When she kissed him again, her heartbeat thumped in her ears like hard shoes on parquet. Mercury's wings, someone was coming this way. The parting kiss Hamish delivered before scarpering off in his ferrety incarnation was almost her undoing.

---

Taking her seat next to Hetty the next morning, Ondine rubbed her eyes. So very tired! It had been lovely to see Hamish in private last night. A grin formed. Little zings of joy danced in her head.

"What are you smiling about?" Hetty asked.

The smile grew, but Ondine shook her head and said, "Nothing." She had to bite her tongue and say as little about Hamish as possible. Especially to Hetty, whose tongue ran faster than a startled gazelle. They had so little privacy here. Keeping those few stolen kisses to herself made them all the more precious.

"Good morning, class," Ms Kyryl said as the last couple of students came into the room.

Ondine, Hetty and the rest of the class stood up, sang the national anthem way off key, recited the pledge of allegiance to the Duke and resumed their seats.

"We have a science test this morning," Ms Kyryl said.

A groan escaped from Ondine's throat. "Ms Kyryl, how come you're giving us another test?" she asked.

"Because there's no point teaching you things you already know. I need to know what you don't."

*That's everything.*

"Ten minutes' reading time and half an hour for the test," Ms Kyryl said.

Scanning the exam pages, Ondine tried to make sense of the questions. Multiple choice gave her a one-in-four chance of getting it right, but it also gave her a three-in-four chance of getting it wrong.

Something tapped at her foot. Looking down, Ondine saw a dark ferret grinning up at her. A ferret with a wedge of paper in his mouth.

Once again she had to restrain her natural reaction. Ordinarily she would have given a bit of a squee.[3]

Sharp but not unwelcome claws latched on to her leg and climbed up.

Shambles reached her lap and spat out the paper. It was damp in a few places, but what did Ondine care for a bit of ferret phlegm in this situation? Especially when she looked at the note and understood its power.

Answers.

Thrilled and terrified all at once, something churned in her stomach and she thought she might be sick. They'd talked about cheating, but only in the hypothetical sense and she'd been so distracted by his kisses she hadn't been thinking straight.

At any moment Hetty might see Shambles and scream, blowing his cover. Her teacher then might spot the crumpled paper in her hand and demand to know why she was cheating – which surely would result in expulsion or at the very least a hideous form of punishment.

She cast a furtive look at Hetty. Had her desk-mate seen the ferret?

Yes.

Hetty's mouth fell open and her eyes became as round as glistening marbles. Then she shut her mouth and blinked furiously. Pricks of panic spiked through Ondine. Everything rested on Hetty's reaction. Slowly – horribly slowly – Hetty's face moved through some strange emotions. As if she couldn't work out whether she should laugh or scream. Bold as brass, Shambles crawled on to Ondine's shoulder where everyone could see him. Well, they'd all know about the ferret now. She was about to move him off when he murmured into her ear, "Ye must lift yer grade or yer teacher will send ye home."

Yes, but cheating? Maybe she could lift her grades by studying even harder? It wasn't impossible. She'd just have to give up sleep for a while. Cold dread radiated from her tummy. Being sent home didn't bear thinking about. Hetty was still looking at her strangely as well.

Ondine whispered, "He's absolutely harmless."

Hetty swallowed a few times. "Is that your great aunt's ferret? The one who came to afternoon tea?"

"I'll take that." Yoink! Ms Kyryl's slender hands wrapped around Shambles's belly and ripped him off Ondine's shoulder.

Powerless, Ondine watched as Ms Kyryl plonked Shambles in a cardboard box and tucked the lid closed. "This is a school, not a zoo." From her handbag, Ms Kyryl took a small bottle of disinfectant, squirted the liquid into her palm and rubbed her hands together. Frustration and fear of Hetty discovering more about Shambles threatened to swamp Ondine.

Surely Hetty hadn't heard him speak? "He must have escaped from his cage," she whispered to Hetty, who looked like she was calming down a fair bit now. Thank goodness.

"Back to your tests, children," Ms Kyryl said.

The answers lay in Ondine's hand. Casting a glance around the room, she made sure nobody was looking her way. Did she give in to temptation and cheat? Giving it another moment's thought, Ondine vowed to try her best first, and only cheat as a last resort.

Question one: What element oxygenates human blood?

A: copper

B: gold

C: iron

D: zinc

Too easy. She circled "C" and moved on to the next question. Confidence radiated through her at the thought that she might not need to cheat after all. The next few questions were tricky, but she knew the answers. When she turned the next page things came a little unstuck. How many bones in the human body? Name the muscle group between the shoulders. The same muscle group presently tensing up the more she tried to work out the answers. For the next two minutes she held off looking at the answers, to see if she could get any more questions right for herself first. Of the remaining twenty questions, she knew at least half the answers. But only getting half right wouldn't be enough. Hamish had just warned her she needed to lift her grades. The damp paper made hardly a sound as she opened it.[4]

Andreas across the room coughed and sniffed.

A few people looked his way. It gave Ondine the chance to peek at Shambles's note without anyone else noticing.

*Of course! I knew that really,* Ondine thought as she looked at the answers and finished the test.

By the time Ms Kyryl called, "Pens down," Ondine felt she'd scored at least seventy-five per cent, maybe eighty. Some of her answers were pure guesses, because Hamish's spit had smeared the note. They handed back the test papers and the air whooshed out of her lungs in relief.

For the next half hour they read about how white blood cells work in the body, how they recognised germs and defeated them. Ondine copied the diagram from the textbook into her school notebook.

Hetty leaned over and whispered, "Did you hear about the Duke?"

Fear jabbed at Ondine's nerves. How did Hetty know about that? Last she'd heard, Col had said something about him being on the mend. Could he still be sick?

"He was due to visit my parents' farm at the weekend to Pardon the Chicken, but he sent the Infanta instead.[5] I was there, because, well, I thought maybe Vincent might come in his place. Anyway, it all went badly. I don't think the Infanta likes handling poultry. And her dog ran through the barns and ruffled their feathers. It could have been a blood-bath, except it turns out the dog has no teeth, so he just gummed them a bit and they ended up pecking him and chasing him away. You should have seen it –"

"Girls. Quiet please," Ms Kyryl said.

Ondine should have laughed at the thought of the chickens turning the tables on the dog, but all she could think about was the Duke being sick again.

Ms Kyryl handed back the papers – all except Ondine's and Hetty's. The two of them sat at their desk, wondering why the teacher hadn't given back their tests. Meanwhile, Ms Kyryl pulled the television trolley towards the centre of the room and slotted a disk into the player.

"You two can see me in my office," Ms Kyryl said to Hetty and Ondine. "The rest of the class can watch last year's performance of the Harvest Pageant. Please take note and use this as a chance to memorise your lines. I want an even better performance this year."

Guilt rooted Ondine to her chair. Hetty stood up and obeyed her teacher. The rest of the class all looked at Ondine with suspicion. Somehow she found the will to get to her feet. Walking to the teacher's office, she cast a glance at Shambles's cardboard prison. He'd managed to get one claw through the thick wall. With the television on, nobody heard his gnawing escape.

Ms Kyryl took a seat behind her desk and made a gesture for the girls to sit down. Then she showed them their test papers. They'd both scored one hundred per cent. Ordinarily Ondine would feel elated, but she didn't because she hadn't earned it.

"You may explain yourselves now," Ms Kyryl said.

Hetty croaked, "I've been studying really hard."

"You let Ondine copy from your paper." Ms Kyryl's tone dripped with accusation.

"No, I didn't!" Hetty said.

"Hetty didn't let me copy," Ondine protested, "I've been studying too."

"Ondine, you are a plodder. If you'd scored eighty per cent, I'd be proud of you for buckling down. Full marks, on the other hand, makes me suspicious."

Ondine needed to think of something, fast. "Why is it so hard to believe I'd be good at science? I love science."

"Come now, Ondine. You spent your summer on dream analysis and inventing horoscopes. That is about as far from science as you can get."

"Which is exactly why I left early. I really do like science."

An uneasy quiet rippled through the room. Hetty sniffed and wiped her nose on her sleeve. Then she looked at Ondine with tears in her eyes and asked, "You didn't copy from me, did you?"

"No, Hetty, I promise I didn't." At least that wasn't a lie.

Ms Kyryl twisted her mouth to one side, deep in thought. "I'm going to give you the benefit of the doubt. This time. But I'm also going to split you up. From now on, Hetty, you will sit with Andreas. Ondine will sit on her own."

Panic spread across Hetty's face. "But Andreas picks his nose and . . . wipes it on the desk!"

"I know," Ms Kyryl said, handing over a small bottle of disinfectant. "You'll need this."

A shudder of revulsion rocked Ondine. "Please don't punish Hetty, she didn't do anything wrong. All she's done is be nice to me. I'll sit next to Andreas."

"Interesting," Ms Kyryl said, twisting her mouth in thought again.

Something flickered in Ondine. Silent understanding crossed between herself and the teacher. Taking the worse punishment was tantamount to an admission of guilt. She hadn't copied from Hetty. What she'd really done was read notes from a ferret, but how did she explain that?

Hetty gave the bottle of disinfectant to Ondine.

They walked back into the classroom and Ondine took her seat by Andreas. She tried to take an interest in the rest of the play, but couldn't help watching Shambles chew his way out of the box. Once free, instead of scurrying away to freedom, he sneaked back into Ms Kyryl's office.

Ondine silently pleaded, *Don't get more answers for me. This whole cheating thing makes me feel sick.*

**16**

---

Funny how life turns out. One moment you're madly in love and setting out on an adventure. The next it's a beautiful Sunday after-noon in autumn and you're up to your armpits in dirty laundry.

"Not what you thought it would be?" Draguta lifted enormous bath sheets out of the machine and into the waiting basket without so much as a grunt.

Ondine shook her head. "Am I that easy to read?"

"Yes."

A dramatic sigh rushed out of her. "I'm sorry, Draguta. I'm grateful for the job, but somehow I just . . ."

"You in slump."

Ondine continued separating red socks from a pile of whites. Despite all the work, it beat staying at home in the family pub, because this way she could still see Hamish from time to time. "I think it's the food that's been the real surprise. Somehow I thought it might be a bit more grand."

"Everyone thinks same. Duchess sets meal budgets. Her purse tight as fish's bum."

Ondine laughed and said, "But they're so rich."

"Exactly. Want to stay that way."

Ondine plunged her hands into a shirt pocket and pulled out a crumpled tissue. "Draguta, how long have you been here?"

Draguta rolled her eyes, mentally counting. "In four months, will be twelve years."

"Wow. That's amazing! I would have been three years old when you started here."

"Ack! Don't make me feel old."

"Sorry." Ondine sorted some more clothes into piles and began loading them into the washing machines. "How come you've stayed so long?"

"Did not plan to. Like said, I lasted few months and found work suited me. And there are pay-offs. Coming up to second long-service leave. Going to have well-deserved break."[1]

Ondine already knew about the long-service leave because of the note she'd seen in the Duchess's ledger. She managed a polite, "Good for you," before changing the topic to the ball and pageant for the Harvest Festival and Halloween.

Which meant loads more washing of costumes and curtains ahead of the production.

<hr>

"SHAMBLES, I don't think it's such a good idea to give me the answers to the tests any more," Ondine said that night. The ferret had snuck into her room and she'd already told him about the Infanta taking the sick Duke's place at the chicken farm.

"But it's important ye keep up yer good marks," Shambles said. "If ye score badly from now on, she'll know ye must hae been cheating. If yer consistently good, it's proof of yer improvement. Just make sure ye don't score one hundred per cent again."

"I didn't mean to! I must have guessed right, that's all."

Shambles gave her a friendly nudge. "So mebbe ye are psychic."

"Urgh!" Ondine rolled her eyes so high her sinuses hurt. Her ear hurt a bit too. Maybe she was coming down with a virus from sitting next to Andreas the snot-robber?

"How is Pavla? Is he feeling better?" she asked.

"Nawt really. Col thinks he's caught something. There are a few going round. Chills and all that, what with the cold weather moving in. We're checking his food and the meat is fine. Col said the salad is a bit weird, but they must be moving on to winter veg, so it's turning bitter."

Ondine couldn't help feeling some of that bitterness herself. Here she was, working harder each day doing four jobs at once – butler, laundress, student and spy – and she didn't seem to be doing very well at any of them.

WHEN ONDINE ARRIVED at school the next morning, she found Ms Kyryl and Pyotr the seneschal deep in conversation over some paperwork. For a moment Ondine's stomach lurched. What could they be talking about? Pyotr remained in the classroom as the students took their places and sang the national anthem. In key.

Beautifully!

Even Ms Kyryl, whose singing voice usually sounded like a rusty saw, reached the high notes.

*How bizarre*, Ondine thought.

When they recited their pledge of allegiance to the Duke, they all tried to sound a little more enthusiastic about it.

Ms Kyryl said, "Thank you, class, now if you would line up, tallest to shortest, in front of the whiteboard."

Nobody asked any questions, but Hetty sidled up to Ondine and whispered, "It's worming day. Everyone gets a dose."

"Whose idea is this?" Ondine asked.

"The Duchess's."

"No need for chatting," Ms Kyryl said. "The sooner we get this done, the sooner we get back to our studies."

One by one they lined up and stood on the scales.

Pyotr wrote notes on his clipboard. Ondine couldn't help thinking her weight would make its way into the Duchess's ledger.

"You're a little heavy, better take two doses to be on the safe side," Ms

Kyryl said as Pyotr jotted down Ondine's weight. Ondine had never considered herself 'heavy' before, but, compared to the rest of the children, she did look a little taller and better filled out. More to the point, they all looked reed thin. Probably on account of their meagre diet.

The medicine tasted like chalky bananas. "Not bad . . ." Ondine said to Hetty as she resumed her place in the line up.

Hetty shook her head slowly, a look of defeat on her face. "Wait four hours, then you'll change your mind."

"Right children, grab your scripts for the Harvest Pageant, we'll do a read-through of the whole thing from start to finish. In the next few days I want you to know your cues and get your lines word perfect."

"I'm so excited," Hetty bubbled as she reached for her script. "My parents are so pleased I'm the Harvest Moon this year."

Dread sank a hole in Ondine's stomach. Everyone was happy about the pageant except her. Because everyone else had a decent role. She'd be the one up on stage, in front of everyone, dressed as a cabbage.

---

THAT AFTERNOON, Ondine was hard at work in the laundry. There were piles and piles of washing to get through.

"Not more vomiting?" Ondine groaned, not feeling too great at the sight of all the extra work.

"No, this precautionary," Draguta said, sounding thoroughly annoyed. "Every sheet, mattress protector, pillow slip, towel, hand towel, bathmat and dressing gown get washed today."

"And every single pair of underpants by the looks of it," Ondine said, wincing at the teetering tower of smalls.

"Hate worm day," Draguta said. "As if not busy enough!"

Pain suddenly buckled in Ondine's stomach, "Excuse me. I need to go to the toilet." She made it just in time. Damn that medicine, it ripped right through her! It took a few moments to get her breath back and she felt a little light-headed.

"You taken worse than most," Draguta said.

"Ms Kyryl gave me a bit extra to be on the safe side."

Draguta slapped her hand over her stomach and laughed, "Did she? Have you been wriggling and fidgeting in seat?"

"No, I haven't!"

"Feeling more hungry than usual? Lately I have appetite of ravenous beast!"

"Of course I'm hungry, but that's because the meals here are so small!" Ondine had eaten very well in her family's hotel. Not three-course meals every night (there wasn't time), but a healthy range of fruit and vegetables and plenty of protein.

"Now you see reason for worming day. I tell you secret." Draguta stepped closer so that none of the other laundry workers overheard them. "Duchess in charge of catering budget. Think we eat too much. Must be riddled with worms. Every six months on dot, worm day comes and every single person in palechia must to take medicine."

"Has anyone ever actually had worms?"

"The dogs . . ." Draguta trailed off as a visitor came into the laundry. A number of other people also turned to check out the new arrival.

Despite her roiling stomach, sunshine spread through Ondine's veins at the sight of the gorgeous man walking in. It was exactly the medicine she needed to cure her bout of malaise.

"Hello, Hamish," she said.

A few people looked at Ondine and then back at Hamish. They said nothing, but Ondine could tell they were all dying to know who this strapping young man was. He looked effortlessly handsome, with a lock of dark hair flopping across his forehead. His clothes looked new, judging by the sharp creases down the front of his navy trousers and the starched shirt.

"Col thought ye might need an extra pair of hands tae help out, on account of it being worm day and all," he said, smiling at Ondine.

Good Old Col. She thought how very lax her great aunt had been at the whole chaperone caper. She made a mental note to thank her, next time they had a pow-wow.

"All help appreciated," Draguta said as Hamish walked towards them. "Here, fold sheets."

"Aye, ma'am," Hamish said.

Pyotr the seneschal came in with his satchel full of medicine in one hand and a clipboard and pen in the other. As usual, his long hair was plastered across his bald scalp. "Good afternoon, everyone. If I could have your attention," he said.

Ondine shot her hand up. "I've been dosed already. In school this morning."

"Ah, yes, Ondine. I have you marked down." Then he looked up and saw Hamish. He frowned. "Hamish, you haven't been dosed yet. I'll just add you in here." Pyotr wrote something on his paper. "Good, now if I can get everyone to line up, please, you can step on the scales one at a time."

Ondine watched as everyone stopped what they were doing and obeyed the seneschal. When it was Hamish's turn to step on the scales, Pyotr wrote down his weight, then gave him a single spoonful of worming medicine. The face Hamish made caused a new roiling in Ondine's tummy and she quickly excused herself. When she came back, Pyotr was finishing the dosing. Even the used spoons went back into a bag.

"Fun time over, everyone back in work." Draguta mopped her brow. "On worming day, all sheets must dry in sunshine. Gardeners put up lines. Here, take baskets out and hang up."[2]

It took all Ondine and Hamish's efforts to heft one basket out of the door. They walked through the courtyard (which hardly got any sun, as it was on the north side of the palechia) and along the gravel paths towards the south lawn. In the skies above them, shafts of sunlight streaked through the tiny gaps between the clouds. Clouds that looked dark and a bit ominous. Ondine silently hoped the rain would hold off long enough for the sheets to dry.

Turning the corner, they saw a sea of white sheets flapping in the breeze. It had a sort of modern-art-installation aesthetic and Ondine found herself smiling. In between the flapping sheets, they could see workers' heads and arms moving, hanging up yet more sheets.

Further down the lawn a team of workers hammered in temporary poles and strung lines between them. Ondine and Hamish carried the basket down to the new line and launched the sheets over them. It was hard work, yet Ondine felt strangely calm and ever so domestic. The scent of freshly mown grass mingled with the lemony fragrance of washing. They both reached for the same pillowcase and Hamish's hands wrapped around Ondine's.

"Ye look so pretty with the sun in yer hair." He curled a loose tendril around his finger and Ondine felt herself all overcome. When he brushed her cheek with his thumb, she couldn't stop the grin.

The snap and flap of sheets filled her ears. Hamish leaned closer. Her eyelids fluttered shut as he pressed his lips to hers. Ondine dropped the wet towel and held his face in her hands. The gentle rasp of his cheeks on her palms made her pull back in shock.

"What's wrong, lass?"

Relief flooded through her. "Sorry, I thought for a moment there you were changing back."

Hamish rubbed his cheek and smiled. "Aye. I'll havetae shave."

Heat raced up Ondine's neck. Shaving? That made Hamish seem so much older in her eyes. She leaned forward for another kiss and felt stubble against her chin. A giggle escaped – she'd get pash-rash for sure.

Another lovely kiss made Ondine's heart kick behind her ribs and her breath started to quaver into little puffs and pants. She could never get enough of those melting kisses. They lost all track of time, standing together between the fluttering white sheets, Hamish trailing kisses all the way down her neck and collarbone. It felt so wonderful and a little bit naughty into the bargain.

"Aw nae!" Hamish pulled back and grabbed at his belly.

Ondine wailed, "Are you all right?"

Hamish turned so pale he almost looked blue. Dismay and despair filled Ondine as she watched him collapse on the ground. Moans and groans followed.

His clothes fell in a heap. After a few choice curses, Shambles the ferret poked his head out.

"Oh, why now of all times?" Frustration took hold. Ondine screamed and kicked the washing basket while Shambles looked up at her with a wretched expression.

**17**

———————

Apart from the sheer aggravation of having the man you love transform into a ferret at the very moment you least want it to happen, Ondine had no idea *why* it had happened. She no longer had Hamish's help to hang out the washing either. They'd done very little of it because they'd been so distracted. And she'd kicked the washing basket so hard the clean sheets had *flomped* out on to the grass.

She picked up a white bed sheet and threw it as best she could over the line. Brushing off the blades of grass only made it worse: the beautiful, white, one-thousand-thread-count cotton now had natty green smudges. The sheets would have to be washed again.[1]

Draguta would be furious.

Walking back to the laundry, her foot hurt, her arms hurt from carrying the basket by herself, and her heart hurt because their kissing had ended way too soon.

"I'm sorry, Draguta. These sheets fell on the grass, I'll redo them. I'll stay back late if I have to."

Draguta put her fists on her hips. "Yes, you will. Where is helper Hamish?"

"Um . . . he had to go." Her vision started to blur, which meant tears wouldn't be far behind. She couldn't very well expose his secret by saying he'd turned into a ferret.

Pyotr chose that moment to make another appearance. "Ondine, there you are. Your great aunt is asking for you. She's had a bad reaction to the medicine."

"She should call for a doctor, not me," Ondine said. It was an uncharitable thing to say, but she wasn't in a charitable mood.

"Go. You are needed," Draguta said.

"But there's so much work to do here." Ondine wiped her sleeve over her face and sniffed.

Draguta shrugged in resignation. "There is. Sooner you see your great aunt, sooner you come back and help."

---

"As if I have worms!" From her bed, Old Col looked furious. Shambles had made his own way back and was sitting on the bedside table.

Two pink lips pressed into a thin line dominated Col's pale, wrinkled face. "That woman has a nerve, lumping me in with the rest of the staff. I'm here as the Duke's guest! This is not how a hostess should treat her guests. I've a good mind to turn her into a –"

"Col! No!" Ondine had to interrupt before her great aunt cursed Duchess Kerala into something awful and irreversible. The image of No-Teeth-Biscuit's raw, red gums popped into her head.

"Relax, Ondine, I can't do her any harm here. The Duke and Duchess are in the south wing. As much power as I have, I can't curse people by remote control."

Ondine said, "Please tell me Vincent had a dose of medicine, too? It would make me feel so much better."

"I hope so," Shambles said.

Ondine took in the sight of her great aunt properly. She looked so old and frail. "Is the Duke feeling better?"

"His specialist is here from Venzelemma. We've cancelled all his appointments and have to pretend he's tied up with paperwork."

"Is he getting worse?" This was all getting so horrible and serious and not at all like the escapade she thought she'd be having with Hamish.

"Not worse, exactly. But not any better either." Old Col made a face and breathed in hard against the pain. Ondine felt sorry for her great aunt.

"Pyotr said you needed me?"

"Did he? That's odd, I don't remember speaking to him." She sucked her breath in as another pang took hold. "Shambles, if this is anything like your pain at transformation, I am truly sorry."

"Thanks. Yer a fine woman." His furry face crinkled in what Ondine could only assume was somewhere between shame and sympathy. "If ye'll excuse me." Shambles made for the bathroom. In a few moments, to Ondine's pure relief, he reappeared as his most gorgeous human self again, clothed and complete with a shy grin.

"That's much better," Ondine said, finding herself smiling again.

Hamish's forehead crinkled like a concertina. "Aye. I think I know how it happened. The medicine hit me hard and sudden. It made me feel like the pain I get when I'm changing back, and so I did. Sorry about the lousy timing."

Ondine shut her eyes and counted to ten.

"Oh yes? And what were you and Ondine doing at the time?" Old Col asked.

"Nothing. Can I get you something to settle your tummy?" Ondine changed the subject as fast as she could.

"Ha ha, you must have been up to no good. Maybe Hamish felt guilty and that's why he turned back?"

"Some antacid perhaps, Aunt Col?" Ondine tried again.

"That would help. And a bowl of Toots Wheat with full-fat milk," she said, smoothing the bed covers. "I always find that helps bind things together and move them along."

"I'll get some from the kitchen. I wish I'd thought of it earlier, it might have helped," Ondine said, thinking back to her own reaction to the medicine.

Old Col breathed hard against the next intestinal spasm. "This is so annoying. I have a very important meeting this afternoon with the CovenCon organisers and I must be well. We have a lot to discuss."

"What's CovenCon?" Ondine asked.

"It's our annual witches' convention. It's in Norange this year, of all places, so I'll have to update my passport. Birgit Howser is organising it. There's an oxymoron if ever I heard one. She couldn't organise a you-know-what in a you-know-where. Oh, come on, you two, stop swooning at each other and get me some medicine!"

"You know, maybe we should all get out of here and go home." Ondine huffed out a pent-up sigh. "The whole lot of them are wonky in the head. The Duchess is stashing money, the Duke thinks his eldest sister should be sectioned. Not to mention the way Vincent turned out. What makes people behave like that?"

"Generations of inbreeding," Hamish said.

Ondine laughed. "He's a balloon, that Vincent," he added.[2]

From the smile on his face, Ondine could tell he was really warming to the subject.

Old Col gave a slow shake of her head. "Ondine, our family is far from perfect. Those who live in glass houses and all that."

"We might have a few fights, but at least my family all love each other. I remember that night at the pub, the way the Duke looked at Vincent, as if he were nothing more than a huge disappointment. Vincent has everything he could ever want, but he's a total pain."

"Too much money can do that to you," Old Col said.

Hamish slapped his hands together. "Right, weil, enough tongues flapping like lambs' tails. We've goat a job tae do here and I fer one plan tae get it done."

"Oh, look at you, sounding all in charge," Ondine said, teasing.

"I was trying tae be more polite than saying "atspish", but ye forced me hand."[3]

"Yes, yes," Col said, "I know we haven't achieved much, but we'll get there."

"I dinnae mean tae rush ye, hen, but the Duke's in trouble and we're standing round jabbering. Let's get back tae work, like."

A wince of regret stole across Ondine. Why did Hamish have to like it here so much?

## 18

It was the end of another long day of school, butlering and homework. Ondine felt all warm and dozy as she settled into bed. Sleep embraced her like a welcoming hug. Scratching noises on the floor heralded the arrival of something small and furry.

"Pssst," he said.

"Whah?" Ondine murmured, not keen to open her eyes because it felt so good to keep them closed. Even though it was Shambles in the room and she should make the effort. But she was so tired. Couldn't he come back later?

"PSST!" he said, louder this time.

Through the fog of half-sleep, Ondine pulled the cover over her head. But then she heard his voice say:

"I'm me again. And ye need more blankets because I'm fair freezing."

She opened one eye and saw the man of her dreams, wrapped in two blankets he'd stolen from the end of her bed. "Oh, Hamish, it's you."

"Hush, don't wake Draguta," he said.

"Fine, but you're the one making all the noise."

"Ye have tae come with me, lass. There's something going on that ye should know aboot."

"But I'm all warm."

"It's the Duchess. She's not happy."

The warmth of the bed evaporated. She wobbled out and wrapped her quilt around her shoulders to stave off the chill. Her feet prickled with cold, so she reached for her shoes.

"Naw, lass, ye need tae be quiet, like."

"Righto." She pulled her socks on and her feet slid on the parquet floor.

"Aye, good," Hamish said as they padded down the hallway, making barely a noise.

"Why are we going to the laundry?" Ondine asked once she realised the direction he was taking her.

"Because the chutes have ears," Hamish said, leading her to one of the gaping black cupboard doors. "They're like a periscope fer sound." Hamish crouched on the floor and waved Ondine to sit beside him. She leaned into his embrace and felt freshly warmed and cared for. If they weren't having to spy on people in such a drab location, it might almost be romantic.

Voices carried down the chute.

"It's the Duchess and Ms Kyryl!" Ondine said.

"Smart lass." Hamish kissed her on the forehead.

Duchess Kerala and Ms Kyryl were chatting – complaining, really – about some kind of problem.

"I tell you, no good can come of them being here," the Duchess said. "Things turned strange the moment they arrived. I've never seen a storm like it. And then fish fell from the sky. I mean, don't you think that's fishy? And they have done nothing for my dear husband's health."

Turning to Hamish, Ondine saw him make a face that said, "I know". Understanding and worry passed between them – they were trying to help the Duke but the Duchess seemed convinced they were to blame for his failing health.

"The old woman is paid far too much for doing nothing. And the girl – I tell you, cuz, there was something in her eyes when she looked at me and read my palm. As if she had nothing but bad intent towards me."

"That's not true," Ondine whispered to Hamish. "She's got it in for me and I haven't done anything."

"Ye dinnae have tae convince me," he whispered back.

Hamish hugged her harder as the voices carried down the chute.

"I can get her expelled for you, would that make you feel better?" Ms Kyryl said. "Set her a test she'll fail. Or catch her cheating, which I already suspect at any rate."

"That would remove the child, but what about the old woman?" Kerala asked.

"We're done for!" Ondine exclaimed.

"Hush." Hamish kissed her again to console her. "At least now we know what we're up against."

They listened harder and did not like what they heard one bit.

"The old lady has to go, Dionysia. I don't like the influence that woman has. I can't help thinking she's poisoning Pavla's mind against me."

"Really?" Ms Kyryl asked the very question Ondine was thinking.

"He promoted her to personal secretary pretty fast. I'm suspicious. She made him stay here while I went to Venzelemma with Vincent. Who knows what she slipped into his food or whispered into his ear in my absence."

Ondine's brows rose in surprise. Her great aunt had become Pavla's secretary? *Way to go, Col!*

"You told me he was too sick to travel."

"That's what she said."

"I see. Well, I can't do much about the old lady, but I can do something about the girl. Set her exams to fail, make it seem like going home is a better option, that sort of thing."

Ondine shivered. "We're in so much trouble. We have to tell the Duke about what she's saying."

"Aye, but ye've seen them together. He's totally in *loave* with her. If we say she's a bad egg, then we really will be poisoning his mind against her."

"We're trying to help him. Can't she see that?" Fear and dread twisted in Ondine's gut. "I've just noticed, the Duchess isn't slurring her words like she normally does."

"Mebbe she's on the wagon?" Hamish said, giving her a reassuring hug.[1]

"First time for everything," Ondine said, trying to make light of the situation.

Ms Kyryl said, "It's getting cooler in the mornings. I can see the children's breath as they speak. Can I press you to ensure the renovations at the school are completed soon?"

"Surely it's not that cold yet? Anyway, if we want that girl gone, no point making her comfortable. Oh, would you look at the time? I must get my beauty rest."

"Yes, of course. I'll let myself out."

---

HUDDLED TOGETHER after hearing such a damning conversation, something pricked the back of Ondine's mind. "I just realised something," she said. "Kerala called her "cuz". I didn't know they were related."

"It explains why the teacher is on such a good wicket. It also means ye'll have tae be on yer best behaviour in school."

"Which means I can't cheat any more. She's already suspicious about me. She'll catch me for sure and expel me."

"But if ye fail, she'll send ye home. I need ye here with me, Ondi, I can't do this without ye."

His kiss made Ondine feel warm all the way through. It affected her brain like amnesia potion, making her forget everything except him.

Which is why it took them so long to get back to the room she shared with Draguta.

After another of his sweet kisses, Hamish pulled back and said, "Is school so horrible that ye'd want tae leave me?"

"Of course not. Did I tell you we're doing a play for the Harvest Ball at Halloween?" They had to keep their voices low, so as not to wake her room-mate. It had the effect of making Hamish even more delectable when everything he said sounded like sweet nothings in her ear.

"No, ye didnae. Yer in a play? Sounds like fun."

"It only lasts for five minutes, no biggie."

"What's your role? Queen of the Harvest?"

"Er, no. Promise you won't laugh."

"I solemnly swear." Hamish made the sign of an "x" over his heart. Then he did the sweetest thing, he leaned in and tenderly rubbed his nose against Ondine's.

Ondine gave a quiet sigh. "I'm the Cabbage."

Hamish smiled, but kept his honourable promise and didn't laugh. "Is that so bad? Is it a speaking role?"

"I have one line."

"That's Barry. I can't wait tae see it. I'll tell Old Col, we'll be cheering for ye."

Ondine gave Hamish a kiss. "Thanks."

"What fer?"

"For not making fun of me."

"I wouldnae do that. But lass, ye still look sad."

Another dramatic sigh. "I am. If I want to stay here, I have to study even harder. I'd better hit the books . . . and you'd better go."

Even though she'd been the one to say he had to leave, it hurt to see him walk away. Her textbooks beckoned.

---

AT SCHOOL THE NEXT MORNING, Ondine tried not to look at the teacher. All that eavesdropping made her feel guilty. Could she look Ms Kyryl in the eye without giving away what she knew?

They sang the national anthem. To Ondine's surprise they sounded like a well-rehearsed choir.

For once, things went Ondine's way. Andreas was sick and Ms Kyryl allowed her to sit with Hetty again.

"Hetty, your voice is amazing this morning," Ondine whispered as they took their seats. "Are you having extra lessons or something?"

Hetty blushed and her cheeks turned into little apples. "No, I'm not, but thank you for the compliment."

"Seriously, you should audition for Brugel's Best."[2]

A naughty look crossed Hetty's face. "My parents would die! They want me to become a financial advisor."

"A what?"

"An accountant."

"Oh!" Ondine felt slightly sorry for Hetty. She had such a chirpy, bubbly way about her. Ondine couldn't see her sitting behind a desk crunching numbers all day.

"Girls, please," Ms Kyryl said. "Don't make me split you up again. Open your history books to chapter eleven."

Ms Kyryl told them off three more times for talking before they finished history. Then it was time to rehearse the Harvest Pageant. It was so nice chatting with Hetty again, Ondine forgot to hate her Cabbage role and began to enjoy herself.

---

AFTER SCHOOL ONDINE grabbed a mortadella sandwich from the kitchen and dashed off to wait for Hamish and Old Col by the crepe myrtle trees. She had about five minutes before Anathea would start wondering where she was. The chill wind bit at her ears and blew the last of the leaves away – the trees were bare now except for their nobbly little seed pods. Ondine felt cold and exposed.

"Ondine, how lovely to see you here," Old Col said as she approached. She said it loudly enough that if anyone else heard or saw them, it would look like a chance encounter. Old Col had come dressed for this early taste of winter, wearing a faux-fur hat and muff.

For a moment Ondine wondered where Hamish could be. To her deep disappointment, Shambles the ferret poked his head out from inside the muff. The wind whipped at his head, parting the fur to reveal fragile skin beneath.

"It's right freezing, so it is, and me winter coat hasnae come in yet," he said.

A little ping of panic shot through Ondine. "Hamish, why aren't you being you?" The last time they'd met here, he'd been his beguiling self, all lopsided grin and mischievous eyes. Now he just looked like a bundle of trouble. And not the fun sort she might enjoy either.

"Sorry, lass, havetae work," Shambles said, with a ferrety grimace.

Another little ping went off in Ondine's chest.

Old Col coughed and looked about. "We can't stay long, we're due at afternoon tea presently. Ondine, do you have any news?"

Ondine stopped gazing at her sweetheart-stuck-as-a-ferret and turned to Old Col. The cool wind had added some rosy colour to her cheeks, and she looked much recovered from the worming medicine. Ondine could have sworn her great aunt was enjoying herself. Getting paid to attend afternoon teas, early dinners and late soirées – who wouldn't love it? Meanwhile, she was working too hard and studying late and generally feeling as if life wasn't fair.

"The Infanta is cracked like a dropped egg. And Vincent's total pain in the rear."

Shambles laughed. "No change there, then. Although, now ye mention him, he has nae given up me secret, so mebbe he's not all bad."

"That'll be the day," Ondine said.

Old Col's face became stern. "Don't speak too loudly, my dear. You never know who is listening. But well done on moving through the ranks, I'm sure you'll learn a great deal from Anathea. Hamish told me your teacher is giving you a hard time. You'll have to work extra hard there."

"Yes, Col. What little spare time I have will be spent studying."

A fresh blast of wind ripped through the trees and Shambles burrowed back inside the muff. Right now Ondine needed Hamish to be himself. The wind whipped her dark hair around and stung her eyes. She looked away and wiped her face. It was the cold wind making her eyes water, nothing more.

"I have to go," she said sadly. "Anathea wants trout for supper again."

Col tilted her head in thought. "Interesting that she should have a taste for it. I wonder if this is her way of defying the Duke?"

"Do I get a kiss?" Shambles stuck his head out from the muff.

"Of course." Ondine gave a sniff as she remembered how very much she adored kissing Hamish. Today all she could give him was a peck on the top of his furry head. She turned and ran towards the lake before the tears of frustration burst free.

**19**

---

Things did not improve for Ondine. Every morning she rose extra early to fix the Infanta's breakfast. Which, to her continued horror, Anathea shared with the dog. Then she made it to class and did her best to concentrate, then it was back to the Infanta and her bizarre demands for the rest of the afternoon. At the weekend it was laundry in the afternoons. At the end of each day, she had about an hour to cram in homework before she staggered off to bed and it all started again the next morning. There just weren't enough hours in the day to study properly, so although she did her best, it wasn't good enough.

On one cold and dark night, after everyone had gone to bed, Ondine woke to find herself asleep on her desk, a trickle of dribble blurring her notes.

"Psst, lass, there's another test in the morning."

Groggy, she rubbed her eyes to find Shambles under her desk. She was so tired, she didn't even have the energy to wish he was his wonderful self instead of the little animal. "There's a test every morning."

"I have the answers for ye, just in case ye need them, like."

No energy to fight, Ondine took the folded sheet of paper from Shambles and staggered into bed, fully clothed.

The next morning, as classes finished and they broke for lunch, Ms Kyryl asked Ondine to go into her office. Ondine wasn't thinking particularly psychic thoughts, but she knew it couldn't be a good thing to have to stay behind. When she yawned, it only made things worse.

"Ondine, please sit."

Tightness gripped her belly. Ms Kyryl wasn't even twisting her mouth in thought – did that mean she'd already made her mind up?

Shambles scurried out from under the teacher's desk and Ms Kyryl frowned.

"I'm so sorry," Ondine said. "Ha–Shambles, come here, please." She patted her knee and noticed her hand was trembling. Questions flooded her. What was he doing here? Had he broken his cover? To her relief, Shambles climbed up to her shoulder and gave her a scratchy nuzzle just below her ear.

*Schh-makkk!*

When would she see Hamish again, properly, with meltathon kisses and swoonworthy cuddles?

Ms Kyryl said, "I'll get to the point. I'm not sure how you're doing it, but your marks are phenomenal. You can't be copying from Hetty because most of the time you're sitting across the class from her. I doubt Andreas is any help."

The good grades should have been welcome news, except the teacher looked puzzled and unhappy. A nasty weight pulled at Ondine's shoulders and it wasn't because of Shambles sitting there.

"Can you tell me how you're doing it?"

It called for stalling tactics. "Um, doing what?"

"Doing so well. When you first came here, you had trouble settling in and your work was well below the class average. When I asked you questions, your answers were generally off the mark. Now your test results are leading the pack. What's going on?"

*Swallow.* "I'm studying really hard. That's why I'm so tired." That was the true, but not the whole truth.

Ms Kyryl looked unimpressed. "Is there something you want to tell me?"

*Double swallow*. Shambles gave her a kiss. Ondine didn't know what to say.

Mr Kyryl gave up waiting. "OK, let's try another way. In all my years of teaching, I have never seen a student improve so much in such a short space of time. I am good, but not that good. Which leads me to one conclusion. You are getting help."

A very small truck poured concrete into the pit of Ondine's stomach. She wasn't proud of having cheated, in fact, she was downright ashamed, but she'd done it because she loved Hamish so much she'd do anything to stay with him. And she'd worn herself down from studying every night.

Ms Kyryl folded and unfolded her hands. "Can you please tell me how you are getting help and who is giving it to you?"

Ondine looked at her blankly, because her brain had gone so very blank. It was also very quiet in there. If Shambles tried to help with a suggestion, Ms Kyryl would hear the ferret talking, and then Ondine would have a whole heap more explaining to do.

"Fine, I'll spell it out." Ms Kyryl rubbed a spot on the bridge of her nose. "I take cheating very seriously. I am on the verge of making a recommendation to the Duke that you leave the palechia school and return to your parents in Venzelemma. Do you have anything to say that might make me change my mind?"

Mercury's wings! Dry mouth, check. Tight tummy, check. Strange hazy wobbly feeling through her limbs. Checkeroony.

"I . . ." Ondine's pride shrivelled as she tried to think her way out of this mess. All she could come up with was the one excuse she really, really didn't want to use. But it was the only one that had any chance of working. "The reason I'm doing so well . . . is because I'm psychic."

"You're what?" Ms Kyryl burst out laughing. "Now I've heard everything."

"But it's true. I spent my summer holidays getting better at it." Or at least getting better at telling whopping great fibs.

"Oh, really?" Ms Kyryl wiped her eyes, as if the very idea could make her cry with laughter.

*Zoing*! An idea popped into Ondine's head. "I can prove it. I can talk to animals. I can talk to Shambles right here. And I can help you talk to him as well. Give me your hands and I'll show you." A surge of confidence came over her. So long as Shambles played his part, they'd bluff their way out of this mess.

"I suppose you're going to put me in a trance?" Ms Kyryl asked, one eyebrow darting up with suspicion.

"No, not needed." Tell the truth, she had thought of doing just that. For about a tenth of a second. She'd never tried – just observed trances at Psychic Summercamp. They'd looked a bit fake, too. Something in the back of her mind told Ondine her best chance of convincing Ms Kyryl of her psychic abilities was to play things very straight.

Shambles crawled on to the table and stood up on his back legs. He looked at Ms Kyryl, then back at Ondine.

Ms Kyryl's mouth did that side-twisty thing, indicating she was deep in thought.

"Hold my hand, Ms Kyryl, then you'll be able to hear Shambles through me."

The teacher's cool hand clasped Ondine's and the game was on. It had to be utterly convincing and completely accurate. Her future at the school and at the palechia – and therefore her time with Hamish – depended on it.

"Ms Kyryl, this is Shambles. He is my animal guide to the spirit world." Oh, how easily the false words came to her tongue!

Ms Kyryl twisted her mouth in a 'humour me' kind of way. Shambles stepped forward and put his paw on the back of Ms Kyryl's hand.

"It is lovely to meet you, Dionysia," Shambles said. He spoke with barely a trace of his Scottish accent. He sounded so formal, so believable. So clever!

Ms Kyryl blinked and looked from Shambles to Ondine. Slowly, she shook her head and looked at the little ferret. A Greek curse slipped from her lips.

"Yassou to you as well!" Shambles said.[1]

Ms Kyryl looked daggers at Ondine. "This is some kind of trick."

"No, nothing of the sort. Ms Kyryl, I am sorry to upset you, but this is completely real. Even I find it hard to take sometimes. I know I professed my love for science to you. Now I'm asking you to believe in magic. But . . . do you not think it's entirely possible for science and magic to co-exist?"

Shambles gently rubbed his paw on Ms Kyryl's turning-white knuckle. "You can use this to tell the bairns all about irony. Aye, it's a good one."

Panic burrowed in when Ondine heard Shambles's accent slip.

"Ms Kyryl, what would you like to know?" Ondine asked, keen to keep things moving.

The teacher drew a long, slow, breath, shaking her head. Ondine felt a bit sorry for her. This whole talking-animal caper was a lot to dump on someone.

Ms Kyryl exhaled. "You're the psychic one, why don't you tell me?"

"OK." It would have been easier with a bit of a hint, just so she knew where to start. As they were holding hands, Ondine figured she may as well start with them. She turned over her teacher's palms to look at the lines.

"You're left-handed, which I already know because I've seen you with a pen in your hand," Ondine said. A little internal voice reminded her to keep this as straight-down-the-line as possible. "In your case, the right hand is the life you were born with, and the left hand is the life you have made for yourself. Now if we look at the . . . this is really interesting."

The lines on the right hand were curved and swirly, the lines on the left were angular and straight. On both palms the lifeline cut deep and true, but on the left hand the fate line stopped short, then started again, slightly to one side of the first line.

"Ms Kyryl, you were born a creative, dramatic and emotional person, but you've carved a whole new life for yourself. It's like your parents wanted you to follow one path, but you've made a determined effort to become something else. Emotions aren't a weakness, but for you they might have been."

"This is all very general," the teacher said, chewing the inside of her cheek. "I fail to see how any of this applies directly to –"

"Ambition burns at the core of your being and you pine for a lost love," Shambles interrupted.

*Zoing*!

"How dare you!" Ms Kyryl withdrew her hands. "Ondine, if this is some kind of sick joke, you can stop it now."

Cold, clammy dread snaked through Ondine's heart. "I apologise, Ms Kyryl. Shambles can be too blunt at times, but he calls it as he sees it. You are very, very good at your job, but the lines on your hands say you yearn for something more creative. I've noticed, lately, when we sing the national anthem, you have a beautiful voice. Did you want a musical career instead of a teaching post? Perhaps you had a patron who might have supported you if not for some twist of fate?" Ondine felt like she was grasping for ideas, but it all seemed to fit. And if she hinted at the patronage angle, her teachers' relationship with the Duchess might come to light.

"I've had enough!" Ms Kyryl glared at Ondine. "I called you in here to give you one last chance to stay. This is not the way to do it."

Panic exploded into full-blown fear. A strange numb feeling spread over Ondine. "I am very sorry, Ms Kyryl. I didn't mean to be so blunt. I promise you I will never say a word of this to anyone."

"That point is moot. As of this moment, Ondine, you are no longer a student at the palechia. I will recommend to the Duke that you return to your parents in Venzelemma."

"Stop pretending ye only just decided that," Shambles said, "Ye were gointae do that anyway."

Something swirly happened in Ondine's head and she thought she might pass out.

Ms Kyryl folded her arms across her lean chest. "Why are you still here? Go!"

Feeling utterly wretched, Ondine dragged her feet from the converted barn and made straight for the privacy of her room.

"Great Jupiter's moons, I'm finished!"

**20**

———————

Panic and fear made it impossible for Ondine to think straight as she slumped back on her bed. Ms Kyryl's words kept swirling in her head and all she could focus on was her imminent expulsion from the palechia.

"Aw, I'm so sorry, me love," Hamish said.

Hot tears spilled down Ondine's cheeks. "This is hopeless." She was so enveloped in her grief, she barely paid attention to the man transforming beside her. He helped himself to her beige bedspread to keep warm. His strong arms embraced her and rocked her gently.

"It's all right, lass. I'll explain it tae the Duke and ye'll be able tae stay."

How she'd yearned to see Hamish again, but she felt so angry and shocked, she couldn't bring herself to look at him. She'd been doing a pretty good job of bluffing Ms Kyryl until Shambles had blurted out the "lost love" angle. But then, he'd also been right in that her mind was already made up to send her home, and nothing they could say could sway that.

"I should never have cheated. I should have studied harder from the start and then she wouldn't have been suspicious and none of this would have happened. You shouldn't have done it, Hamish. You knew she had it in for me. You should never have made me cheat."

"Studied harder? Nobody studies more than ye. Sometimes I think ye love school work more than me because ye spend so much time on it. Even so, she would have sent ye home, we had tae do something."

Coils of dread tightened the muscles in Ondine's shoulders. Going home meant facing her parents, who were still furious that she'd disobeyed them in the first place and run off with Hamish.

"Then why didn't we come up with something else?" she wailed. "If we're so smart, how come there wasn't some other way apart from cheating? Now look what's happened – she's expelled me!"

"Nawt yet she hasnae. We'll work something out."

"Saturn's rings, are you even listening? You were there, you saw how annoyed she was with the whole psychic thing! I should have admitted I cheated at the beginning and begged her forgiveness. Now all I've done is made her angrier."

"It's nawt that bad. We'll work it out. Old Col will help."

No amount of soothing words from Hamish made the slightest dent in Ondine's mood. "I should never have looked at that answer sheet in the first place and now look where it's got me. I never wanted to cheat, it always felt wrong, but I let you talk me into it because I trusted you." Drawing in a staggered breath, she continued her rant: "It's this stupid palace! It's done something to your head and now you love spying and sneaking around so much you think cheating is normal."

"So it's all me fault, is it?"

Ondine shouted, "Yes, it is!" As soon as the words were out she both wished she'd never said them and felt glad she'd blurted them out. Shaking her head at how hopeless everything had become, her breath came in painful gasps.

A stricken look of betrayal crossed Hamish's face, followed by utter despair. Palpable silence cloaked the room. They'd never had a problem with silences before, but now it felt horrible. The longer the silence lasted, the harder it became to break it. Try as she might, Ondine was afraid to say anything more because in her present state of anger and confusion she might make things even worse.

Hamish removed his arm from her shoulder. Ondine felt the chill.

"I was only trying tae help," he said. Then he shut his eyes and his body shrivelled away into his ferret shape.

A fierce ache ripped Ondine's heart open. "No, Hamish, please don't go." Not when they were still fighting, not when they hadn't sorted it out.

It was too late. He'd already reverted. "I think I havtae." His little ferret body waddled out of the room.

Alone, Ondine gave in to her misery and let the tears fall. She threw herself on her bed, face down in the pillow. After a few minutes of cathartic bawling, she turned the soaked pillow over to continue the marrow-deep sobs.

"What is such noise?" Draguta came in and saw Ondine on her bed. Ondine felt a bony hand rubbing her back. "There, there, what is upset you so?"

"Nothing," Ondine lied.

"Nothing? Then stop crying when is nothing."

Ondine couldn't stop. She'd lost her place in the palechia school, and even worse, she'd just lost Hamish.

"So, is something?" Draguta was too smart for her own good.

It all came out in a rush. "Hamish and I had a fight, and he walked out and now I think Ms Kyryl's going to kick me out of school because I've been cheating. I really tried hard but it wasn't enough and now it's too late because I messed it all up."

"You have the PMT," Draguta said. "Need chocolate."

With a loud sniff, Ondine wiped her eyes. Hormones would explain part of it. All the same, she'd been dealt a massive blow, which entitled her to a big cry.

Draguta opened a drawer and snapped off some squares of chocolate, then handed it to Ondine. "Here, eat. Best medicine."

"Thanks." Ondine took a bite. The cocoa-and-sugar hit triggered something in her brain and she started feeling better. Draguta held her arms wide for a hug, and Ondine accepted.

It was like hugging a lamppost.

The laundry mistress had been so kind, Ondine owed her some

honesty. "Draguta, I have to tell you something. You know how you're coming up to long-service leave?"

"Yes?" Draguta looked apprehensive as she sat down on her bed.

"Well, I found out – please don't ask me how – that the Duchess is being a total miser and she'll find a way to sack you before she has to pay you your leave."

Draguta reached for her teddy bear and hugged it to her chest. "Ptah! She did that last time. Thinks I stupid! Appreciate warning, but I prepared this time."

"I'm so relieved." Ondine wiped her eyes and took the last bite of chocolate. She kept her voice low. "I thought the Infanta was bonkers, but the Duchess is something else."

"It all be fine. I get back to work now," Draguta said, fetching another cardigan to wear over her existing warm clothes. "Infanta will be wanting you soon."

"I know." Ondine felt the chill in the air and reached for another jumper. "I just need to get myself together before I can face her."

Draguta left and Ondine felt misery seep into her skin. It was probably the cold as well, because the staff dormitory had no heating. She'd been sitting still for so long her muscles had started to stiffen. The little teddy on Draguta's bed offered a morsel of comfort. Ondine picked up the teddy and gave it a hug. Something jabbed her in the chest. It was like hugging Draguta again, all sharp angles and bones.

Since when did furry teddy bears have corners?

Ondine looked but she couldn't see anything amiss. She hugged the toy again and felt another jab. She gave the teddy's belly a squish for good measure and felt something hard beneath the stuffing.

Curiosity got the better of her. She turned the teddy upside down and began to look for signs of something not right. It felt a bit rude as she probed for holes. That's the problem when you're in the grip of curiosity. Even when it's rude, you still can't hold back.

Running her fingers along the seams, she found a tiny hole. She stuck her finger through and poked about – roughly where one of his kidneys would be, if stuffed toys had kidneys.

This stuffed toy had solid objects inside. Ondine tried to pull them out with her finger, but the hole was too small and the objects were too big.

If I can just ... rip! She tore a gaping hole in the side. *Ba-dump, ba-dump*, her heart began racing at the thought of what lay inside. *Badump-badump-badump*, her heart charged faster at the thought of Draguta walking back in and finding her violating the teddy.

Mercury's wings! Trinkets, keys, earrings, brooches and even a decorative spoon tumbled out of the toy and on to the bed. Quick as a flash, she stuffed them all back into the bear and tugged on the loose threads to close up the hole.

Staring at the toy, she couldn't help a worrying thought: *Oh, Draguta, what have you done?*

## 21

S hambles felt lower than a cockroach. A cockroach who'd walked into a deep pit, picked up a shovel and started digging the pit even deeper. Ms Kyryl was sending Ondine home for cheating and it was his fault. How had his well-meaning attempts to help his sweetheart back-fired so badly? When they'd met in the summer she didn't have classes or exams. He hadn't realised school and studying were so important to her, but clearly they were and he'd stuffed things right up.

He needed somewhere to think, but his stomach rumbled so loudly he had to find food first. Taking care not to get under anyone's feet, he scarpered down the hall and followed the cooking smells. Judging from the pungent caramelised onion, meat and rosemary aromas, roast lamb was on the menu. His mouth watered in anticipation. He should try and take some slices to Ondine, as a peace offering. The poor hen had eaten little more than soup and bread for the past few weeks, perhaps something solid might fix her right up?

On his brain went, telling him how clever he was to be able to think of Ondine when he was fair starving. Not that he'd given any thought as to how he might deliver such a meal to her in his present state. Perhaps he might find a wee bag or box he could carry the food in. What it lacked in presentation, he could more than make up for in affection and perhaps a grovelling apology, if that's what it took to get back in her good books.

As he neared the kitchen, a strident female voice echoed through the hall: "I've never sheen such wanton washtage!"

The kitchen noises stopped. No chopping, no washing, no sounds of blenders or grinders. Mindful that people might run out of the kitchen at any moment and step on him, Shambles kept to the edges and poked his furry head around the doorway to see what was going on.

It was Duchess Kerala in full rant. She made quite a sight, her head moving madly from side to side, all without so much as a hair breaking free from her shiny helmet-do. One hand held a glass of white wine, while the other gesticulated wildly to Emphasise! Every! Word!

"Look at that pile of perfectly good food you're about to throw out! All those potato shkins can go into shoups, not the composht bins. You're throwing out the bread crusts when any chef with half a gram of shense can make croutonsh with them. And I can't believe you're throwing out half the shelery! Shelery tops taste just like parshley and you've brought that in by the truckload.  And I can't believe you're throwing out the parshley shtalks instead of putting them in the casheroles! The washtage! It beggarsh belief!"

At this point, some people might draw breath, but the Duchess seemed beyond such mortal constraints.[1]

"What's thish? A ton of rhubarb leaves? You cannot throw thish out. I've told you before, it makesh a perfectly good subshitute for spinach!"

Nobody said anything in response. Shambles looked around the room at the trembling, pale-faced kitchen staff. They looked so young, barely older than Ondine. None dared answer back.

No chance of snaffling even a morsel of roast lamb while the Duchess kept storming around the kitchen, finding more and more things to complain about, her voice growing ever more shrill with each discovery.

Tummy rumbling even more loudly, Shambles turned tail and ran back to Old Col's room. Drat, her bed was empty. She must be out somewhere. The only thing to eat was a bowl of cat food one of the staff had set out in a bowl.

"Ah, weil, when in Brugel." Shambles took a deep breath and a small bite.

After a few mouthfuls, he started to feel better. But then he thought past his hunger and a fresh pang of regret hit him. He needed to make it up to Ondine, but huffing fish-breath all over her wouldn't help if he wanted to kiss and make up.

It was imperative he find some mouthwash to get rid of the lingering fishiness. He trotted into the bathroom and jumped on to the sink. Not in one leap – even a ferret has his limits – but two leaps. Floor to toilet seat – ooops, nearly fell in, must remember the lid's not always down! – then to the edge of the sink. He found a tube of toothpaste and managed to chew the flip-top lid off.[2]

Stepping on the tube, he forced out a neat white pipe of minty paste. A few licks later, his mouth filled with foamy freshness and he felt really pleased with the results.

At that moment, Draguta Matice walked into the bathroom with arms full of fresh towels and screamed, "Aaaaaah! Rabies!"

"Hnnnngggggff!" He tried to respond but he had a mouth full of foam. In desperation he spat out as much as he could into the sink, but the white bubbles coming from his mouth only made Dragutta scream louder. Draguta dropped her bundle on the bathroom floor and ran out of Old Col's room, shouting all the way,

"Pyotr! Pyotr! Rabies!"

No, no! Shambles forgot about the height and leapt to the ground. Crack! He landed hard on the floor, smacking his chin. Pain lanced through him. His head went all fuzzy and wobbly. If he'd had a chance to think, he would have descended in two stages, back to the loo seat, then the floor. Desperation had made him forget how small he was and how far he'd fall. Trying to shake out the pain only made it worse.

*Ye daftie wee bampot, ye've broken ye jaw!*

Still not thinking – he seemed to be doing a lot of that – Shambles ran after Draguta to make her stop. She didn't know he was really Hamish, but if he could explain himself, she might realise her mistake and stop screaming. He called out, "Wait!" but his jaw hurt so much it came out like "waaaad" and even he barely understood it.

People came rushing towards Draguta's screams, adding to the commotion. Maids, visitors, Pyotr the seneschal and, worst luck of all, Lord Vincent.

"I'll handle this," Lord Vincent said, raising his booted foot.

*Arrggghhh!* The blood froze in Shambles's veins as the size eleven sole filled his vision. Pain or no pain, he bolted sideways to avoid certain death and scarpered back into the safety of Old Col's room.

Not safe for long! Everyone from the hall poured into the room and began talking at once.

"Where did it go?"

"Over there, look!"

"It's under the bed."

"Is that it over there?"

"Throw a blanket on it."

"Someone get the dog-catcher!"

"Someone get a gun!"

Trembling with fear, Shambles cowered under the bed. He wiped his mouth with his furry front paw to clear away the foam. Not gentle enough! Fresh pain speared his jaw. A little bit of sick burned his throat as he feared for his life. Any second now one of them would look under the bed and it would be goodnight Shambles.

Wiping his mouth again – gently! – he managed to get rid of the remaining gobs of toothpaste. It still looked bad because his front legs were streaked with saliva. If anyone saw him, they could mistake his wet limbs for profuse sweatiness. The only option left to him was transforming into his human shape. If he concentrated hard enough and fixed Ondine's smiling dark eyes in his mind. Sure, he'd have a mountain of explaining to do when he crawled out from under the bed without a scrap of clothing on. But at least he'd be their size, and he'd be able to take on Lord Vincent on a level playing field.

"What's going on?" a woman said.

He knew that voice. It wasn't Ondine, but Old Col. Maybe her presence could bring him round? He anticipated the maelstrom of lurching and twisting as he willed himself to become human. But nothing happened.

"Your ferret has the rabies," Draguta said. "We must capture, before he bites anyone."

"He hasn't got rabies," Old Col said. "Whatever gave you that idea?"

From his hiding place under the bed, Shambles saw Lord Vincent's heavy boots stamp about the floor.

"How do you know it's not full of disease?" Vincent said.

"It had foaming mouth!" Draguta added.

"Nobody has rabies," Old Col said. "That ferret is my pet. He is vaccinated and in perfect health. I have the vet bills to prove it. Now if you don't mind, you're in my room and I'd like some privacy."

Lord Vincent snorted contempt. "You're a guest in this palace and you'll do what you're told."

"Hold your tongue!" Old Col snapped right back.

"Abwath –" A strange noise came from Lord Vincent's mouth.

Shambles peeked out from his hiding place to see the Duke's eldest son holding his tongue between his thumb and two fingers. In fact, he didn't seem able to let it go.

"Wha-hab-oo-dundame?" Lord Vincent cried.

"I told you to 'hold your tongue'. You're lucky it wasn't 'shut your face', then you'd be in real strife," Old Col said. "It will wear off when you reach the other side of the palechia."

It took all Shambles's willpower not to burst out laughing. It was probably a good thing, because laughing would hurt his jaw like crazy.

Vincent looked furious and stomped out of the room.

"Show's over, may I have some privacy please?" Old Col said.

When everyone else had left the room, Shambles craned his head out from under the bed. It hurt to speak, but he needed to thank her. "Tha' was goo' magic, Col."

Old Col grinned. "Yes. I rather think it was. Now, why are you even more difficult than usual to understand today?"

## 22

Melancholy cloaked Ondine as she tidied the Infanta's rooms. For some reason, Anathea wasn't being a total cow and had refrained from telling her off every minute.

"Where is my happy Ondine?" the Infanta asked after half an hour of heavy silence.

Ondine wiped her face, trying really hard not to bawl in front of her employer. But her chin wobbled and her vision started blurring. "I had a fight with my boyfriend and now I don't think he ever wants to talk to me again."

"You have time for a boyfriend?"

"Apparently not." Would this horrible pain behind her ribs ever go away?

"You love him?"

"With all my heart."

"And he walked away?" The Infanta's face softened.

"Yes."

"He let you down. Now you know how I felt," she said. "It won't be the first time. Mark my words, you will be let down time and time again." Imperceptibly, the Infanta's chin wobbled, but then she turned away.

It felt so strange to be sharing this moment of honesty with Anathea. Something shifted between them, Ondine could feel it. For the first time, she saw things from the Infanta's point of view. Fate had taken her fiancé, the man she might have grown to love and spend the rest of her life with. Yet the moment she'd lost her title, he'd given her the flick.

Steeling herself for some kind of rebuttal that would put her back in her place, Ondine asked the question that had nagged her for some time. "I know your first engagement fell through, but what about later on?" she ventured.

An icy glare greeted Ondine. "He was no better. I do not even say his name. I was young. My head was lost. We had three beautiful daughters together, but it wasn't enough." The Infanta shook her head and ground out the next sentence: "He wanted a boy."

"History repeated itself," Ondine said.

"That would have been preferable." Anathea drew breath and Ondine could only wait, and wait a bit more, to hear the rest of it.

"There was a boy born, but it was not by me. A week later I was served with divorce papers. And that is all that will ever be said of it. If you bring this up again, you will be dismissed immediately. Is that clear?"

Stricken with equal amounts of fear and sorrow, Ondine only nodded and hastily got back to work.

Soon after, Pyotr arrived at the Infanta's door. "Ondine, the Duke will see you now," he said.

The bottom dropped out of Ondine's world. Not that she was feeling particularly psychic, but she knew being summoned to the Duke's rooms couldn't be good news. But then a little spark of hope surged – if the Duke had asked to see her, he must be feeling well enough to see people. That had to be good, surely?

Feeling wretched for herself, Ondine followed Pyotr to the Duke's office. The Duke looked a bit strange, as if he hadn't completely recovered from whatever previously ailed him. Perspiration sprang from Ondine's face, neck, armpits and elbows. Not from nerves but because of the temperature – it was roasting hot in here, with four heaters on full blast. As Ondine removed her scarf and fingerless gloves, she noticed

Old Col looking calm but flushed in the face. Hamish was there too, in Shambles form, on her shoulder. Guilt spread through her at the sight of Shambles, because he looked so utterly pitiful. Oh, how she wished she could apologise to him and take back everything she had said. But this was not the place for domestic reconciliations. That's if reconciliation was on offer. Judging by the way he kept his ferrety gaze away from her, there might not be. Which set off another fresh burst of guilt and sorrow.

Ms Kyryl the teacher was also there, her face firm and set, like a ... well, like a disapproving teacher, really.

Resentment towards Shambles sliced through Ondine. If she hadn't cheated – if he hadn't encouraged her to cheat by taking advantage of how tired she was – she wouldn't have given Ms Kyryl enough ammunition to bring this situation to the Duke.

"Ondine, thank you for joining us," the Duke said.

Pyotr fetched a chair for Ondine and put it beside Ms Kyryl. Ms Kyryl nodded as Ondine sat down and cast another of those disconcerted looks at Shambles, her soft Adam's apple bobbing up and down.

The Duke spoke in a thin, wavering voice, which indicated he had a fair bit of recovering to do. "Ms Kyryl, Colette and I have been discussing your scholastic performance and I have several concerns. All things considered . . . you might be better off returning home to live with your parents and attending your local school."

"But I . . . I'm working so hard, please don't make me go." It felt so stuffy in here Ondine thought she might gag. She loosened the top button of her shirt but it made no difference. Without being asked, Pyotr walked around the room and switched off the heaters.

The room fell silent for a moment, except for the suddenly noticeable ticking of the wall clock. Tick, tick, tick, tick.

Not only was Shambles not even looking at her, he said absolutely nothing to help her. Every tick of the clock counted down the moments until Ondine's expulsion.

The Duke got to the point: "Ondine, you have been here several weeks, but it's not such a long time that your education would suffer if you returned to your previous school."

Tick, tick, tick, tick. Her mind raced. Naturally, they couldn't talk about spying in front of Ms Kyryl, so she tried very hard to come up with some other way of explaining how she could still be useful here.

The Duke continued, "Pyotr tells me you have been working in the laundry. I have heard no complaints and in fact Miss Matice sings your praises. You have been a credit to your great-aunt in that regard. However, a laundry position can easily be filled, so it would put the palechia at no disadvantage if you were to leave."

Ondine automatically nodded agreement, then blinked as she realised something important. "Um . . . Your Grace . . . I recently began butlering for the Infanta."

"Oh, really?" With an effort, the Duke sat a little straighter in his chair.

Ding! went Ondine's brain. The door of opportunity creaked open a fraction. Maybe that mad Infanta had saved her skin? "Yes, Your Grace. The Infanta requires me to prepare all her meals myself. She says I'm the only one she trusts."

"Does she now? How very interesting." The Duke stroked the edges of his split moustache before turning his steely gaze to the teacher. "Ms Kyryl, thank you for your time."

"Yes, Your Grace." Ms Kyryl bowed her head and walked out.

A cool gust of air from the corridor wafted in, helping to clear Ondine's head for just a moment.

After the door clicked shut, the Duke looked at Old Col, then at Ondine.

"Do go on," he said.

"Um." Ondine knew she had to say something good. Her future at the palechia depended on it. But what had she seen or heard from the Infanta that might prove useful to the Duke? A dreadful thought took hold. Perhaps Shambles refused to say anything because he thought she should be going home?

The Infanta's words rang in her ears: *You will be let down.* Ondine couldn't stand it. She didn't want to credit Anathea with foresight, but Shambles's silence seemed to confirm it.

Maybe everyone would be better off if she went home? If only she had some kind of sign she hadn't completely stuffed things up with Hamish and he would eventually return to her in Venzelemma.

Duke Pavla locked eyes with Ondine and leant forward, which served to accentuate his widow's peak. "You must tell me everything. Even the things you think might not be important. Little things that go unnoticed can sometimes turn out to be very important."

"Um," Ondine said again, as her mind reeled back to her first meeting with the Infanta. "Well, I think Aunt Col told you about the dog soup."

"Yes, and thank you for the warning."

"My pleasure. Well, we got talking. Or rather, she kind of lectured me. She said she didn't like so many new people being here in the palechia. I mean, all the new employees who don't seem to have much training. Maybe they aren't very good at handling food and that's why we're getting sick?"

"Interesting theory. Anything else?"

"She asked me to tell her everything. You know, if I saw or heard anything strange. So I said I would. And now I'm working for her and cooking all her meals."

"I see. Anything else?"

The full intensity of the Duke's attention gave Ondine an idea. She might be able to secure Draguta's continued employment. And she would be able to tell Draguta she'd spoken up for her. Maybe then her friend might explain what all those expensive trinkets were doing stuffed inside her teddy bear.[1]

"Your Grace, just before I tell you about Anathea, I have to ask about my friend Draguta Matice. She is due for long-service leave and I think the Duchess wants to sack her before the leave is due so she can save money."

She thought she'd been really clever, because she hadn't said anything about the ledger or the secret bank account. Unfortunately, she'd hadn't been clever at all, because Pavla's face creased, like he'd just smelt something horrible.

"Do not bring my wife into this, it will get you nowhere." He turned to Col, "I heard about what happened with Vincent earlier today. Just between us, I was quite grateful for your intervention, but my dear wife was inconsolable. I'd be most grateful if you would do your best not to upset her any further."

"The Duchess objects to me using magic?" Col said.

"That is putting it mildly. She was tremendously upset and would rather the three of you were gone. I made it clear you were here for a very important purpose, but I fear if she is upset again, I may have to ask you to leave."

"Yes, Your Grace," Old Col said.

Ondine's mind creaked and snapped and whirred and clicked at this new piece of information. They would have to be extra-extra careful about saying anything to the Duke about his wife, because he'd most likely take her side. If they wanted to keep their jobs, they might have to keep stump.[2]

A look of frustration crossed Duke Pavla's face. "Do you have any useful information about my sister that might be linked to my declining health?"

Ondine thought she might be sick with fear. "I'm sorry, Your Grace. I haven't noticed anything else. Yet."

"Then you'd better notice. Stay close to Anathea and tell me everything you see or hear. Is that understood?"

His words filled Ondine with fear and hope. Fear that she'd better come up with something, and hope that she might be able to stay on a bit longer and repair things with Hamish.

"And you, Shambles and Miss Romano, had better come up with something soon, other than my nieces stealing silverware, or I'll reconsider your employment."

*Gulp!*

As they left the Duke's office with his threat ringing in their ears, Ondine felt completely overwhelmed by the task at hand. "We are really up against it, Col," she said.

"You don't say," Col replied.

"What happened with Vincent, by the way?"

"I shut him up."

"Nice one." Ondine wanted to give her great-aunt a high five. Her feeling of quiet triumph soon evaporated as she waited for Shambles to say something to her. Anything would do. Despair wound itself through her system, growing more palpable with each passing minute of silence.

By the time they reached Old Col's room, Ondine's nerves were strung out.

Col placed Shambles on the end of her bed. Then she turned to Ondine. "So, what happened between you two? Did you have a fight?"

"No," Ondine lied.

"Nnn," Shambles mumbled.

The first noise to come from his lips and it wasn't even a proper word. To Ondine, he was completely out of sorts. When he started gesticulating with his paw in front of his face, she wondered if he was making a "go-away" gesture.

Old Col put her hands on her hips. "You're uncharacteristically quiet, Shambles. What gives?"

"Ah oke eye aw." He didn't really speak, it was more a case of the words sliding out sideways.

"Are you sick?" Ondine reached down to touch his furry face and he recoiled. *Oh no! Now he doesn't even want me touching him.* "I'm so sorry about everything I said. I take it all back. Please talk to me again."

"You did have a fight," Col said. "I knew it."

Feeling utterly wretched, Ondine's vision went blurry with fresh tears. "Yes, we did."

"Ondine, you'd best be running along. The Infanta will be waiting," Col said gently.

"In a minute." She dragged her sleeve over her eyes to dry them. If Shambles would just say something reassuring she would feel so much better.

With a groan of pain, Shambles began transforming into a human. Blessed relief filled Ondine's heart and she quickly grabbed a blanket to keep him warm. Then she ripped the cover off the bed to make another layer of warmth for him. In this part of the palechia, Hamish would freeze.

Hamish looked like he might be sick as he finished transforming. "Aw, thanks hen," he said, pulling the blanket around him. Despite the cold, beads of sweat dotted his brow. "I ken talk again, thank goodness fer that." He tenderly rubbed his jaw, "Aww, that's handy to know, eh, Col? I broke me jaw leaping awf the basin but it's all fixed now."

"You broke your jaw?" It didn't seem possible, but Ondine felt even worse than before. She and Hamish were supposed to have a *connection*. All this time, she thought he'd been ignoring her. Instead, he'd been in so much pain he couldn't even talk. And she hadn't even realised!

"I'm so sorry, Hamish," she said again. He still hadn't said any of the soothing words she needed right now, like 'It's fine, I love you', or 'I'm sorry too, I hope you can forgive me'. Maybe he didn't forgive her. Maybe he preferred being a ferret because it was becoming too painful to be a man? Then shouldn't he avoid the pain by staying human all the time instead? There was so much demanded of them. And Ondine didn't have the benefit of changing into an animal, yet she was still expected to work the espionage angle just as much as Hamish. It was exhausting.

"The Infanta is not known for her patience, child," Old Col said. "You two can make up some other time. Hamish, you need to keep an eye on Lord Vincent. He and Kerala are up to something, I can feel it in my waters."

Ondine didn't want to leave, she'd much rather stay and talk things through with Hamish. But instead of asking her to stay, Hamish gave her a sad look and said, "Ye'd best be going then."

Which Ondine took to mean he didn't want her with him. She turned to leave before she started a fresh bout of bawling.

**23**

———

"I would like some biscuits made," the Infanta said, as Ondine prepared her pot of tea and slices of lemon. The way the woman spoke made Ondine want to roll her eyes. Everything the Infanta said implied someone else had done it, or should do it. And whenever she spoke about something bad happening she had that knack of making it seem like someone else's fault.

"Yes, ma'am. I'll go down to the kitchen and do it." The thought of spending a bit of time in the kitchen, away from the Infanta, held great appeal.

"You know something? They could be made here." Anathea raised her hand and pointed vaguely to the left. "I've been told there's a kitchen next door."

"Next door? You're kidding?" Ondine still found it hard to guess the Infanta's mood, because her face remained so immobile. But from the woman's tone, she sounded serious.

"See for yourself. I think there is a connecting door somewhere – oh, look, if that table is moved, there's a latch to be found.  It's either a kitchen or a storage room. It's never been used."

How bizarre! Ondine grunted as she shifted the table and found the latch. It was easier to see the doorframe now, because she knew what to look for. But if you didn't, you might think it was a shoddy join in the wallpaper.

She turned the handle in the top of the dado and pulled the door towards her. It opened with a groan, as if waking from a hundred-year sleep. Beams of light streaked in through the dusty windows. Ondine found a light switch near the door. Sleepy fluorescent tubes buzzed and flickered into life. The air smelled musty and dry, as if the room had lain undisturbed for decades.

"Mercury's wings! What a great kitchen!" Ondine walked around, her footsteps stirring up dust motes on the terracotta tiles as she assessed the room. The old electric oven belonged in a museum. It looked like it had never been touched. When Ondine opened the refrigerator, she held her nose in anticipation of biohazard, but it was empty. The freezer door put up a fight. When it finally came free, Ondine discovered the inside was completely iced up. She leant down and switched it off at the power point.

"Has anyone ever used it?" she called out to the Infanta.

"Probably not. Certainly not by me."

Ondine would be able to prepare the Infanta's meals here instead of down in the kitchens. She set to wiping dust off the counters.

The Infanta said, "About those biscuits?"

*Saturn's rings, does she never let up?* "Yes, ma'am?"

"I was thinking. Perhaps the biscuits should be made by me?"

Double-take time. "Um, have you ever made them before?"

"There's a first time for everything."

*Oh dear!* "OK, then. First thing, take all your rings off and wash your hands. I'll find us some aprons." Sure enough, the kitchen had several pantries. Inside one, Ondine found everything she needed except ingredients. Probably just as well, because any food remains would have been supporting new ecosystems by now.

"I'll head downstairs and get the food."

In the kitchens she very nearly collided with the Duchess.

"Ondine? What in heavensh name are you doing here?"

That's right, the Duchess wanted her gone. In her peripheral vision,

Ondine saw pale, trembling people who looked as if they'd just been thoroughly told off. Ooops, very bad time to arrive.

"My Lady Duchess." She made a quick bow of respect. "I came to collect ingredients so I can cook for the Infanta."

"Really? She's not happy with the copioush free meals I shupply her?"

Oh dear, the slurring was back and it wasn't even that late in the day. Ondine didn't know where to look, so she kept her eyes lowered. "Your Grace, I can come back later if you like."

"You've got one minute."

Ondine wasted the first ten seconds of that minute in mute shock, before she sprang into action and grabbed a tray. Despite the Duchess's tight rein on food supplies, she at least found enough ingredients to make biscuits and pancakes. A small bag of flour, some butter, sugar, salt – they were easy to find but she needed more. Where was the chocolate and crystallised ginger? The pantry was so neat and ordered, with everything labelled – it was an obsessive-compulsive's dream. She found the ginger but no sign of chocolate. The Duchess hadn't kicked her out yet, so she reached for the refrigerator and grabbed a bottle of milk and a couple of eggs.

"I'm glad I didn't give you two minutesh, you would have cleaned me out," the Duchess said.

"Thank you, Your Grace," Ondine said, before making a hasty bow and an even hastier exit.

"Was there trouble?" Anathea asked when she returned.

"Just your sister-in-law keeping an eye on the food supplies."

"That woman." Anathea rolled her eyes and shook her head, making Ondine giggle in shared sympathy.

For the next half hour, she and the Infanta got their hands dirty making pancake batter and biscuits.

"This is good fun," The Infanta said.

They had flour all over the counter top and themselves, but they didn't care. Ondine couldn't get over the change in the Infanta. "I'll start cooking the pancakes," she said. "Now, the rule is, the first one is always a bit of a mess."

"Hah! Just like marriages!" Anathea said.

Ondine laughed, marvelling at this new Infanta and how friendly she could be when the mood suited her. Which sent a little ping of worry through her, because Duke Pavla had instructed her to report everything back to him. What could she say? *Your sister's not such a bad old sort after all?*

They rolled the biscuit dough into balls and flattened them on the trays with their fingers. They pressed the ginger pieces in, making patterns and smiley faces.

"Would you like to lick the bowl?" Ondine wondered if she'd gone too far in this new, informal atmosphere developing between them. How confusing that she should be having such a sweet time with the Infanta while her relationship with Hamish felt like it was falling apart.

"No, but a cup of tea wouldn't go astray."

"I'll get right on it, once I've put the tray in the oven," Ondine said.

"No need." The Infanta placed her hand lightly on top of Ondine's. "The pot of tea shall be made by me." Ondine wasn't sure if she could cope with any more surprises. The Infanta washed her hands, removed her apron and walked back to her rooms. Ondine remained in the kitchen, humming a quiet tune as she scraped the messy pancake off the pan and started a new one. Giving in to temptation, she had a bite. Ugly but delicious!

The sound of footsteps in the other room was followed by Duchess Kerala's strident voice: "Why are you not bowing to your bettersh?"

The demand for obedience had Ondine recalling her hideous encounter with Lord Vincent. Although she couldn't see the Infanta, Ondine assumed Anathea made some kind of bow, because she heard the Duchess say, "Thash better."

"Your Grace, by what honour do I have the privilege of our meeting today?" the Infanta said.

"The Duke has inshtructed me to invite you to the Harvesht Ball," the Duchess said in a tone that could only be described as pained.

"My brother is the very milk of human kindness," Anathea said.

Ondine remained in the kitchen. Hiding away seemed the safest bet as she listened to the women trying to be civil to each other.

"I trusht you will behave yourself this year," the Duchess said.

"I shall be the model of gracious behaviour."

"Good. That is all."

When the Infanta came back to the kitchen, she had a scowl on her face. An actual scowl! Her neatly plucked eyebrows were clamped down and there were ridges in her forehead. "Oh, that woman! Comes in here soaked to the gills and tells me to behave myself! She should be pushed down the stairs. She's so drunk everyone would think it an accident."

"Mmm," Ondine said as non-committally as possible. All the while uncharitable thoughts criss-crossed her head. She found herself completely agreeing with Anathea about how painful the Duchess was.

On the other hand, the Infanta wanting to cause harm to the Duchess meant she finally had something useful to tell the Duke. Even if it was only an empty threat. But what should she do? Save her skin or save this new-found friendship?

When the biscuits and pancakes were ready, they sat down together and ate them, with the pot of tea the Infanta made. The tea wasn't awful, as such, but Ondine knew she could make better. Not that she said so, because Anathea looked really pleased with herself.

"Come here, Biscuit," the Infanta called to the dog. He bounded on to her lap. She dipped her biscuit into her tea and fed it to the dog.

A biscuit for Biscuit.

Ondine couldn't help recoiling when Anathea dunked the rest of the Biscuit-sucked biscuit into her tea a second time.

---

When Ondine woke up the next morning in her cold dormitory, Draguta was already up and dressed, and about to leave. Ondine had to act quickly.

"Wait. I need to tell you something," she said.

"Oh yes?" Draguta's shoulders slumped. "Don't make me late. Duchess is more horrible than usual."

"Try not to be upset," Ondine said.

"Impossible. I upset."

Oh dear. Ondine gulped. Taking a deep breath, she said, "I know about your teddy."

The woman's eyes turned to ice. "Why you say 'teddy'?"

There seemed little point in pretending ignorance. "I didn't mean to pry. I found out by accident. I was feeling really fragile after I'd had that fight with Hamish and I gave your teddy a cuddle because he looked soft and warm. But he was all lumpy."

"You snoop!" Draguta leapt back to her bed and grabbed the stuffed toy, giving it a squeeze to make sure its contents were in place.

"No, it wasn't like that!" This was all going so badly! Ondine wrapped a thin dressing gown around herself to keep out the early morning chill. "I found out by accident . . . but . . . I couldn't help wondering . . ."

"Why I am thief?" Draguta placed the teddy under her pillow.

"I won't tell anyone."

"Hah! Have not lasted years in palace by trusting sweet-face girls."

If Draguta had smacked her she couldn't have hurt her more. "But we're friends," Ondine said, caught in confusion.

"I have no friends," Draguta said.

"But that's terrible!"

"Ack! Don't look full of sorrow." Draguta shook her head, put her hands on her hips and paced the room a bit. She threw her hands in the air and said, "Ack! I grow soft. Kerala sacked me before. One month before last long service. She found me . . ." she looked up, as if asking the heavens for guidance. Or forgiveness. " . . . Was private. Duchess found me. She said instant dismissal. I left, no savings. Came back two weeks later and begged for old job. Ha! Thought Duchess kind to let me back. At first. Then people talk. I put it all away in here," Draguta tapped the side of her head. "It was set-up, Duchess sacked me to save money. I know she will do again, I waiting for axe to fall. Teddy is compensation."

"Oh, Draguta, I'm so sorry." Ondine moved in for a hug, fully expecting a rebuff. Instead, Draguta threw herself into Ondine's arms. All sharp angles and pointy bits.

Draguta wiped her face. "Looks bad, but I never steal. I draw line at that. Never take money what isn't mine. But if Duchess and silly friends leave things in pockets when throw out washing, I keep. Not big things. Little bits and bobs they not notice. Is not stealing. Is collecting."

They stood on shaky ethical ground. On the one hand the Duchess had schemed to sack someone to save money – stealing Draguta's entitlements with a workplace loophole. Draguta was stealing by way of opportunity, but they were items that had gone unnoticed by their owners.

*Is it theft if it falls in your lap and the previous owner doesn't even realise?*

"I promise I won't tell a soul," Ondine said, thinking about all the people she couldn't tell. It made her heart ache that little bit more to think she couldn't even tell Hamish, because he wasn't even talking to her.

**24**

———

Ondine sat down on a rickety chair in the ballroom wearing her Cabbage costume for the Harvest Pageant. It was an ugly meringue of a dress, which sapped her confidence. However, it succeeded brilliantly at being a fabric cabbage – all layers of green lace and padded foam built around a succession of hoops. Even the ruffles around her neck looked just like a cabbage's outer leaves.

Ms Kyryl was on stage, directing the rehearsal. In one hand she held a banana. The moment she finished eating it, she called for a lunch break.[1]

Ondine nibbled on a cheese sandwich made from crusts of rye loaf. She looked over to see Ms Kyryl peel her jam sandwich apart and add anchovies and potato crisps to it.

Ondine lost her appetite.

Over by the doorway, a small ferrety shape darted behind the curtains. The shape moved to a quiet corner behind the stage. Any moment now, he'd dive into the costume trunk and transform into his lovely self.

"Oh, there ye are, lass," Shambles said from behind a prop tree.

*Why didn't he want to grab some clothes and become human?* Ondine gave thanks for small mercies that at least he was talking to her again.

Keeping her voice low so as not to attract attention, Ondine murmured, "Hamish, I'm sorry for everything I said before. I really am." Perhaps using his proper name would encourage him to be his proper self?

He shifted back and forth on his paws and looked at the ground. "Aye, ye cut me good. I was only trying tae help ye, lass."

"I know, but . . . I was really upset." Ondine fidgeted with her cabbage costume. "I thought maybe you might say sorry for making me so upset."

With possibly the worst timing in the world, Lord Vincent stepped into view. Looking his usual smug self, he said, "That costume suits you."

"Watch it, caramel yoghurt," Shambles said.[2]

"How very gallant of the ferret to defend your honour," Vincent said with a sneer.

Sickness spread through Ondine at the sight of him. As far as she was concerned, the less she had to do with him the better. "What do you want?" she asked.

"It's, 'What do you want, My Lord', to you."

Ondine closed her eyes hard, but they rolled behind her lids anyway. "Fine. What do you want, my lord?" She said it in such a way that Vincent would know she hadn't capitalised the letters.

"I want you gone. From the moment you arrived we've had nothing but bad magic. The storm, the fish rain, outbreaks of food poisoning, and now the seneschal seems to know what I'm about to say before I say it. He's always been good at anticipating people's needs, but he's never been able to read minds before."

"How can any of that be my fault?" Ondine said.

"Because you're a bad egg and you're spreading bad magic wherever you go." Vincent said, glaring at her.

"Watch it," Shambles said, rearing up on his hind legs and exposing his nippy wee teeth.

Across the room, Ondine saw Hetty whisper something to Ms Kyryl. Fear spread through her at the thought that they might have overheard Shambles. Instead, Hetty and Ms Kyryl both stood up and got all fidgety. A blush stole across Hetty's face. Nope, it wasn't Shambles making them pay attention, it was Vincent. Hetty was ga-ga for the Duke's son. *If only she knew what he was really like!*

Vincent stood his ground. "Because of you, an entire coven of witches is demanding an audience with my father to discuss all this messy magic. Why don't you save everyone the hassle and just leave?"

Oh, he made her cross! "Because he wants us here, OK? You probably haven't noticed, because you only think of yourself, but your dad's sick and we're trying to find out why."

"He was fine before you lot arrived, so if you want him to get better, you should get lost." He looked her up and down and sneered at her costume. "If you're not gone by the first of November, I'll have you arrested for trespassing."

With that, he sneered again and marched off. Not a moment too soon as far as Ondine was concerned. Out of the corner of her eye, she saw Hetty giving a dramatic sigh, as if the world's most famous movie star had just walked by.

"We have a saying in Scotland about people like him," Shambles said.

"I hope it's rude."

"Waste of time if it's not."

Ondine laughed and tried to look on the bright side. "Maybe he's right? Maybe we should go home."

"And leave all this? I don't know about ye Ondi, but I'm *loaving* it. First real job I've had in years. I've never felt so useful or important. Each week I'm on a different watch, it's so exciting."

"But . . . my parents would give you a job just like that." She clicked her fingers. She also thought, *And you're important to me,* but couldn't say it over the lump in her throat.

"But that wouldnae be a proper job, not really. More like a family obligation. And I thought ye liked me being responsible?"

Mist covered Ondine's eyes.

"Aw, naw, hen, dinnae cry. I'm truly sorry fer upsetting ye. And I know the teacher is giving ye a hard time, but I'm not sorry fer getting ye the answers. It was the only way tae save ye from being sent home."

"But . . . we should have thought of something else."

"I know. But there wasnae time. I felt lower than a worm when I saw how much I'd let ye down."

"Thank you." Ondine wiped away a tear of gratitude.

"Now the Duke knows yer working fer the Infanta, Ms Kyryl can't bother ye no more. I'm proud of ye, hen. There's bound to be plenty ye can tell the Duke about his mad sister, no?"

"No. That's the problem." Ondine felt her spirits sagging. "There's nothing to tell."

"Sure, there must be. That Infanta, she's always up tae something."

"I wish I shared your confidence."

Some reassuring kisses would have come in handy at this point, but her true love remained a Shambles-ferret.

"As much as we cannae stand Vincent, he had a point. There has been some strange magic round these parts," Shambles said.

"Strange doesn't begin to cover it. This place is off-the-scale weird. And have you heard the children sing? They used to sound like mangled cows, but now they're amazing."

"Aye, true. And have ye seen what Ms Kyryl's having fer lunch?"

"It's disgusting."

Across the room, Ms Kyryl finished eating her sandwich and began wrapping slices of salami around wedges of apple. Nearby, the rest of the school children scoffed their lunches. They sure were eating plenty. Maybe the cold weather made them hungry? If they hadn't all had their dose of worming medicine, the Duchess would be convinced they were infested with parasites. Hetty held her bowl of food up to her mouth and shovelled it in like she was starving.

Everyone ate so noisily Ondine and Shambles could continue their conversation without being overheard.

"I bet you've been giving the Duke plenty of information about Vincent," Ondine said to him.

Shambles shifted on his paws, as if the floor were made of lava. He looked up and swallowed, his accent full of remorse. "Apart from the obvious, that he's a total pillock, I goat nothing."

"You can't have 'nothing'?"

Shambles climbed on to her lap, but kept his voice low. "I know, I'm shocked as weil. It was a total bust. I snuck around fer ages, listening as hard as I could. I tried going through diaries, but there was nothing. I thought I might get something when the Duchess arrived in his rooms. She talked with him for a while, but I swear they said nothing incriminating. The most she's ever said is, "One day all this will be yours, ye need tae be ready", but that's it. I thought she'd say more, but she didnae."

"They know we're on to them. Tell me, Shambles, when you were listening, did you see them, or were you hiding?"

"I was hiding, of course."

"Right. So maybe they were saying one thing, but it meant something else. Or maybe they were passing notes and you didn't see it?"

"Yer a smart girl. Ye can see why I need ye here to help make sense of all this. Nice costume by the way."

Ondine ignored the compliment, because she felt so ungainly. "He must be planning something." She wondered if she were being suspicious merely because she couldn't stand Vincent, or if something really was going on. "If you've got nothing, what are we going to tell the Duke? You're going to have to find out something."

The Duke had threatened that they would all be sent home if they didn't get more information. A gleam of hope flickered in Ondine's mind – she would go back to her old school, where the lessons made sense and they wouldn't make her dress as a lumpy vegetable. Except then Hamish wouldn't be happy working for her parents in the pub. Why could nothing be simple?

"Eh ... we might have tae tell him about the Duchess's secret stash," Shambles said.

"I'd hold off on that. He doesn't like to hear bad things about her. Did you see his face when I talked about Draguta? If it came down to it, he'd take his wife's side over ours. And there's no point telling him Kerala drinks too much because everyone knows it, he just can't see it," Ondine said.

"Aye, it's a real shame when people can't see what's right in front of them," Shambles said.

"Children, places, please," Ms Kyryl called out.

Ondine swayed to her feet and flumped out her costume to get it back into proper cabbage shape.

"Unless," Shambles piped up, "yer sure ye havenae goat anything on the Infanta? Sure and she'd be worth something?"

Heavy guilt weighed her down. "The Infanta declared she'd love to push the Duchess down the stairs. But I'm sure she was only wishing out loud."

"Aye, there's bad blood between those two."

"You've got that right. But . . . I want to keep that between us for now," Ondine said.

"Aw nae! Don't tell me yer starting tae like her now?"

How could she explain her feelings when she didn't even understand them herself? "Kind of. I mean . . . she's not all that bad once you get to know her."

"Not that bad? She could be the one behind the Duke's troubles, and yer sticking up fer her! Ondi, love, ye have tae tell the Duke. If ye don't give him something, he could send ye home."

"Shambles, maybe that would be for the best," she said heavily. Sure her parents would ground her for the next month. Maybe the next year, but she knew where she stood with her family.

"Aw nae, dinnae think like that. I need ye here with me, Ondi."

"But everything's going wrong."

"Ye can't go!" Shambles's voice cracked. "Aw nae, ye look so sad, yer breaking my heart."

Ondine thought, *And you're breaking mine.*

**25**

———

The next day, Ondine and Infanta Anathea made fresh pasta together and cooked it with parsley, basil and butter. Ondine felt they'd forged some kind of bond, which only made her feel more wretched at the thought of ratting on her.

When they had finished eating, Pyotr came to the Infanta's rooms. Ondine's heart lurched behind her ribs.

"The Duke will see you now," he said to Ondine.

"Oh yes, and what's all that about?" the Infanta asked.

"I don't know," Ondine said, although she had a fair idea as guilt churned in her tummy.

When Ondine arrived at the Duke's office, Hamish was already there. Back in handsome human form in smart, clean clothes. He looked so lovely, standing tall as she walked in, with a lock of hair flopping over his forehead. Her hands itched to brush it away. Circumstances prevented it.

"Ondi, I'm a waiter again, I'll be working at the Halloween Ball. I'll be able to watch you in the play," he said.

*Oh dear.* "That's . . . nice," she replied.

"I don't have much time," the Duke said, his forehead creased in pain. Something scrunched behind Ondine's ribs at the sight of him – he should be getting better but instead he looked worse. This time, his office was freezing cold and she had to lock her jaw down to stop her teeth chattering.

"I need to be in four places at once," the Duke said. "Ondine, Hamish tells me you have some news?"

A cannonball to the gut couldn't have hurt more. Ondine looked at Hamish and couldn't believe he'd dropped her right in it.

A look of shame crossed Hamish's face and he said in a low voice, "I wouldnae be doing me job if I didnae tell him what ye told me."

Her mouth dry, Ondine swallowed.

"I'm waiting," the Duke said, rising from his chair and packing papers into an attaché case. A couple of times he winced and touched his side. One of the kitchen staff came in and delivered the Duke's elevenses – a tray of savoury pastries stuffed with spinach and feta. One of them was already cut in half. Old Col must have tasted it first.

The room felt so cold it was difficult to talk, but Ondine gave a small cough and spoke: "The Infanta admitted to me she would like to push your wife down the stairs." She wished the ground would open up and swallow her. "Actually, she didn't say she'd do the pushing, just that, you know, she wished it would happen."

The Duke shook his head and frowned. He didn't look cold. If anything, his cheeks were pink, as if he were hot. Annoyed, even. Did that mean he wasn't happy with the information? In which case she should have lied and said she had no information. Sweat broke out on Pavla's forehead and he breathed hard. Then he seemed to collect himself and gave Ondine a solemn look. "I am sorry you had to hear that. But I am grateful you told me. It's important to tell me these things. You may have saved my wife's life. Thank you, Ondine."

If it wasn't so cold, her jaw would have fallen open in shock.

---

THE NEXT DAY Ondine went to the kitchen to collect ingredients for lunch. Just as she was about to leave with her basket of vegetables, herbs, milk and eggs, Duchess Kerala arrived. At close range, Ondine could see the dark line around her face where the mask of make-up ended and her neck began.

"Where do you think you're going with that?" The Duchess pointed at Ondine's food with a plump finger. Her free hand held a glass of red wine, even though it was barely half-past breakfast.

"It's for the Infanta, Your Grace," Ondine said, bobbing a quick curtsey.

"Oh yesh, the woman who wants to push me down the shtairs! Well, she'll not have that." The Duchess pulled out the eggs. "Or that." She took away the parsley. "Or that." Removing the bottle of milk.

No chance of an omelette now.

"You may go." The Duchess dismissed Ondine with a wave of her hand, and although her head moved, her brown helmet remained stiff as a lump of wood. "And tell that woman she's lucky to have anything. All the support we give that freeloader and this is how she repaysh us."

Good thing the Duchess had not seen the rashers of bacon underneath the onions, otherwise she would have taken them too. Ondine got out of there as quickly as she could. When she reached the Infanta's rooms, things rapidly deteriorated.

The Infanta took one look in the basket and said, "Are you here to cook for me or poison me?"

*From one mad woman to the next.* "This is all I could get." The best way to deal with the Infanta's bad mood would be to get on with the cooking. It would at least keep her hands and mind busy.

"There are fifty dozen eggs produced in the chicken house each day. You are friends with the girl there. You're telling me none could be had?"

Ondine began slicing onions. "Your Lordship, I did get some, but Her Grace the Duchess took them from me. I was in no position to argue." They weren't even the nice red onions, which don't make you cry as much. These were the extra-thrifty white onions that burned your irises with the first cut.

"You seem to be on such good terms," the Infanta raised her voice and added a layer of sarcasm. "Because I was accused of wanting to push her down the stairs!"

The ground was never going to open up and swallow Ondine, so she should stop wishing for it. Her eyes burned and it wasn't the onions' fault. A horrible silence filled the kitchen. Ondine couldn't find the strength to look at Anathea.

"I am really, really sorry." She put the pan on the heat and slapped in a dob of butter. Anything to keep busy. "I really am. Really."

"I thought you could be trusted!"

The onions sizzled in the pan. Ondine wiped her eyes with her fingers, which only made her eyes sting more. "The Duke made me tell. He was going to send me home if I didn't say something." She made a start on the celery, stripping the string away as best she could.

"I will have my tea made now," the Infanta said, her voice cold and threatening.

Ondine turned off the hob to stop the onions burning and reached for the kettle.

"I am so disappointed in you," the Infanta said.

Something cracked in Ondine. "I said I was sorry!" She dropped to her knees and clasped her hands together in supplication as tears poured down her face. "Please find it in your heart to forgive me, Your Lordship. The Duke is paranoid, the Duchess is a drunk. They think you've got it in for them. I know that's not true, but they're crazy! I had to tell them something, because if they send me home, I'll never see Hamish again."

The Infanta took a step back to stop Ondine crying on her shoes. "Pull yourself together. I can't stand snivelling."

Ondine grabbed the edge of her apron and dried her face.

"Hamish is so important that for him you'd betray my trust?"

"I didn't think of it like that," Ondine said. "He works here in the palace, for the Duke. So if Pavla sends me home, I'll hardly ever see him." Would the Infanta notice Ondine was too much of a coward to answer her question?

"Why would you be sent home?"

Deep breath. "Because I was cheating on my school tests and Ms Kyryl told the Duke to expel me."

The Infanta shook her head. "You're a smart girl. Why would cheating be needed?"

"Because my marks were so low Ms Kyryl was going to send me back to my parents. And she's close to the Duchess and I think the Duchess hates me too. So Hamish got the answers for me but I did too well and she got suspicious."

A slow blink, as if the Infanta had to count to ten. "This Hamish thought he was helping, and instead you were let down. I told you. It is always the way with men. Hamish is just a man, and, as with all men, you will be let down by him."

Mind whirling, Ondine had no comeback. Because as much as she didn't want to believe her, the Infanta was right.

"He has already let you down. Trust me, he will again. I have been let down by all the men in my life. My daughters, too, were let down by the men in their lives. You will be let down by the men in yours."

*No. Not Hamish. He's not like that.* All the while a horrible thought nagged at her. Hamish had blabbed to the Duke about the Infanta and that should have stayed private. If he'd kept his mouth shut, she wouldn't be in this position. Oh, why did things have to get so messed up?

Anathea looked down at Ondine. "When will my cup of tea be made?"

## 26

The morning of Halloween felt so cold Ondine could see her breath as she got out of bed. Tonight she would be a cabbage on the stage. The thought should have filled her with dread and embarrassment, but she had far bigger things to worry about. Vincent had threatened to evict them tomorrow, which meant she and Hamish and Col had to find out who was making the Duke so sick, and how. They needed solid evidence. Today.

If they failed, Pavla might become so sick he could die. Then Vincent would step in and take over. They couldn't let that happen.

Pyotr knocked on her door. "Your great aunt needs you."

"What is it this time?"

"She is dying."

Bang! Ondine sat bolt upright. "What?" Immediately her mind returned to their journey on the train, when Old Col had spotted the shape of a coffin in the tealeaves. Had her great aunt seen her own death coming?

"Apparently," Pyotr said. "The doctor is with her now."

That's strange, Ondine thought. Pyotr seemed to answer the question she didn't even ask out loud. That might explain how he was always in the right place at the right time. Lord Vincent's accusations played in her head – maybe she was responsible for spreading bad magic? But for that to be true, she had to be a bit magic herself, and she didn't have a magic bone in her body. If she did, for starters she'd magic herself a nice warm coat.

Heart hammering with fear, Ondine followed Pyotr to Old Col's room and found her in bed. Her skin had a grey pallor. Beads of sweat gathered on her brow.

The doctor looked up, holding Old Col's wrist, and acknowledged Ondine and Pyotr as they walked in. "It's most likely kidney stones. They are very painful. It may also be some food poisoning at the same time," she said. "I will have to run some tests."

"Must be something I ate in Norange," Col whispered.

Ondine's eyebrows shot up. "You've been to Slaegal?"

"Yes. Nipped over for twenty-four hours but had to come straight back. I'm trying to help them organise the next CovenCon. They should bring it back here. There is some strange magic about." Col seemed exhausted by saying these few words. "A bunch of monkeys couldn't be less competent." Blurgle went her stomach.

The doctor interrupted them. "You need to stay hydrated and flush it out of your system. I'm recommending you drink a litre of cranberry juice per day. You'll also need to take charcoal pellets to help get the toxins out of your system."

Old Col's stomach made the strangest noises.

Ondine shared her worries with the doctor. "The Duke didn't look very well last time I saw him either. Like he was in pain. Do you think he might have kidney stones too?"

Shock played over the doctor's face. "Has he been eating foods rich in oxalic acid?"

"Ah . . . like what?" Ondine asked.

The doctor listed the ingredients, "Spinach, too much salt, too much meat?"

Pyotr nodded. "I will take you to him directly," he said.

"Good." The doctor picked up her bag.

"Wait." Old Col coughed and tried to sit up. "Stay, I need a witness."

The effort of sitting wiped her out. She closed her eyes as more sweat gathered on her brow.

Pyotr retrieved some papers from the nearby table. "Your great-aunt has made her will, she needs two non-beneficiaries to witness her signature." Pyotr then picked up a pen and placed it in Old Col's clammy palm. He grabbed a book off the side table to support the paper. Old Col opened her heavy eyelids and made a spidery signature on both papers.

Panic ate through Ondine. "But . . . Aunt Col, you're not dying. You just . . . probably feel like you are."

Pyotr handed the papers to Ondine. She couldn't help smiling when she saw Hamish would inherit everything.

"Um, I'm not eighteen. Am I even allowed to sign?"

"Good point." Pyotr gave the papers to the doctor instead.

A doctor in the midst of drawing up a needle full of clear liquid.

"What's that?" Ondine asked.

"Are you allergic to anything?" the doctor asked Col.

"Nothing gets to me, usually," Col said, beads of sweat growing over her top lip.

"Good," the doctor said. "This is a strong analgesic, which will treat the pain and give you some rest for a while. Now, I really must be attending the Duke."

"Is Aunt Col going to be OK?" Ondine asked, all the while wondering why Col and the Duke were sick but Hamish wasn't. At least, not last time she checked. Then it hit her – Hamish didn't eat green leafy things so he'd probably missed out on whatever was making Col and the Duke sick. Then she remembered something else – when Hamish transformed, he left his illnesses and injuries behind. Thank heavens he could change into a ferret, it had probably saved his life!

The doctor turned. "I expect your great-aunt will make a good recovery. But it depends on what she's ingested. Now, this is very important. If you hear of anything strange going on in the kitchens, you tell me, all right?"

"Oh yeah, sure." Great. Someone else who wants information. Just Ondine's luck. She really sucked at being a spy, because she knew nothing.

The moment the doctor and Pyotr left, Col murmured something. Ondine stepped closer.

"Sorry, Ondi," Col said, "This has all become very serious."

"You're telling me!"

"Must be Duchess doing . . . this."

"Now, Col, I don't want to stress you out, but we do need to get a move on." Ondine said. "If we don't get something on the Duchess or the Infanta tonight – and the way I see it, it has to be one of them – then Vincent's going to evict us tomorrow."

The doctor's needle was doing its work, because her great-aunt slumped back against her cushions and could barely put two words together.

Ondine said, "OK, don't talk, just two blinks for yes, one for no, OK?"

Two blinks.

"Right. So we know the Duchess is siphoning money into a secret account."

Two blinks.

"And we know the Duke probably doesn't suspect a thing."

Two blinks.

"And people are sick, including the Duke. So it's the Duchess slipping poison into the food?"

Two blinks.

"But what good would it do her to kill her husband? I thought they were in love? If she doesn't love him, why not get a divorce?" The twig snapped. "Ah, but if she got divorced, she'd be out of the palace and she'd have no money. But . . . Aunt Col, I'm really no good at this. If the Duke dies, it all goes to Vincent. But he's too young to – Mercury's wings, the Duchess would rule on his behalf, wouldn't she?"

Two blinks.

"So." Ondine sighed and felt a headache coming on. "How do we tell the Duke?"

Three blinks.

"What does three blinks mean?"

"Means . . . I don't know."

WHEN ONDINE RETURNED to her room, she found a furious Draguta cursing her name and the Duchess's under her breath.

"You!" Draguta made a spitting sound, her face full of fury. "Thought were friends, but friend stabbed me in back!"

"I haven't done anything!" Ondine splayed her palms out in surrender.

Draguta snatched her teddy and stuffed him inside a jumper, then squashed the jumper into her small suitcase. "Duchess seek me out. Makes example of me in front of whole staff! Call me snoop! Says I go through her things! I never touch her things. Everything fine until you come . . ." The rest of her words made no sense, as Draguta reverted to her mother tongue.

"But I didn't say anything! I even stuck my neck out with Duke Pavla so I could protect you!"

"Protect? Ptah!"

"I'm sorry." It came out as a squeak. Guilt turned Ondine's stomach into cement and her voice sounded thin and wobbly. "Why did she call you a snoop?"

"Something about wine glass and book few weeks ago. Said she waited to now so that all linen clean for Harvest Ball! Ptah! Not matter, Kerala never make sense at best of times. She want me gone, I gone."

It was Ondine's fault. And a bit of Hamish's as well. She played dumb but knew exactly what Draguta was talking about. The glass of wine they'd left when they first found the ledger, to confuse the Duchess into thinking she'd left it there herself. Clearly, it hadn't worked. Heart thumping, eyes misting, hands shaking, Ondine slumped on to her bed. Nasty, clanging clunks echoed around the room as Draguta snapped the locks on her case.

Silently, Ondine cursed her decision to follow Hamish to the palechia. Everything had gone so badly wrong, right from the start. Nothing in her life had ever been so messed up. She couldn't help thinking the entire palechia had to be cursed.

And then a horrible little voice in her head said it wasn't the palechia's fault, it was hers.

"Please, Draguta, don't be angry with me. I tried to help. Really, I did," she pleaded.

"Should have kept mouth shut."

Apologies were getting her nowhere. "The way I see it, the Duchess would have sacked you anyway. I know you're angry with her, but don't take it out on me!"

"Of course, is all about you!" Draguta hefted her suitcase and made for the doorway. "One day I come to your restaurant. I be big shot. I order best of everything. Then I puke all over floor!" With that, she stormed down the hall towards the servants' entrance.

Ondine dissolved into a flood of tears.

**27**

———

Ondine slipped away from the dress rehearsal for the pageant. Col had rallied in the past hour so she brought her a bowl of comfort food – mashed potato and gravy.

"I was poisoned," Col said to Ondine. "I'm entitled to feel sorry for myself."

"Have you thought of a way to warn the Duke?" Ondine asked.

"No." Old Col shook her head. "And the more I think about it, the more I'm convinced he can see no wrong in the Duchess. We're going to need irrefutable proof before he'll believe us."

Ondine felt frustrated. "But there's no time for that! We just have to explain and hope he'll listen." She reached for the box of charcoal pellets and shook ten of them into her palm. They left smudgy grey marks on her skin.

"Yes, yes." Old Col grabbed a glass of water, popped one pellet in her mouth and drained half the glass in one gulp. "Now it's your turn."

"I don't see why I have to –"

"– The doctor said this is the best treatment for this sort of thing. In your case, prevention is better than cure."

"Is Hamish all right?"

"Fit as a mountain goat. Lucky devil."

"Where is he?"

"Working in the kitchens, as a waiter. He's doing his best to find out the source of the food poisoning since it's not just me who's ill."

Ondine gagged as she tried to get the tiny pellet down her throat. It seemed to grow in size the closer it got to the back of her tongue. Would it go down or come flying back out?

"You're a good girl, taking care of me," Col said. "I'm sorry I haven't been around as much as I should have. And I haven't been nearly as good a chaperone as I promised your mother I'd be."

"That's OK, Aunt Col, you've had a lot to worry about." Ondine was quite glad her great-aunt had been so busy. Otherwise she would have had even less time with Hamish.

Col gave a knowing chuckle. "Are you nervous about the pageant tonight?"

Ondine grimaced. "No, just very embarrassed."

"Well, don't be. The Cabbage is a very important part. I'm sure you'll get a big cheer."

THAT NIGHT ONDINE took her place on the stage in the darkened wings, beside her fellow cast members. She sent a silent prayer of thanks that the play would be over in a few minutes.

A quick peek through the gap in the curtain revealed a packed ballroom. People were wearing the most amazing costumes. Grand ball gowns. High wigs with feathers. Baroque pantaloons. And that was just the men! Amongst the wide skirts were women dressed as monsters, sailors and soldiers. Vincent was in attendance, wearing an army uniform. There were also at least two dozen witches. Not classic movie-witches with long black skirts and pointy hats. These were true Brugel witches, who wore earth-coloured tunics with thick trousers and heavy travelling cloaks. On their backs they carried multi-pocketed backpacks. The rest of the costume consisted of warm hats with ear-flaps and on their feet, strong boots. Clothing designed for travel on foot or horseback, not broomsticks.

*Sure it was Halloween, but how unoriginal that so many women dressed as witches, Perhaps there was a special deal at the costume shop?*

Even Aunt Col had come as a witch. Judging by the way she virtually inhaled every passing canapé, she'd made a full and, quite frankly, remarkable recovery from her illness and was back to tasting every morsel of food before the Duke had any of it.

How Ondine wished this night would be over soon. Butterflies flipped in her belly at the thought of going on stage in front of so many people. She took a few deep breaths and steadied her nerves. That's when she heard two female voices, growing nearer. One of them sounded like Old Col, the other voice she didn't know. They were muttering something, trying to keep it private, but Ondine couldn't help straining her ears.

*I shouldn't. But I am here to spy*, she thought, as she took a step back and listened as hard as she could.

". . . need to move CovenCon to Brugel, this is where the weird magic is," Col said.

"Agreed," the other woman said. "... feels like epicentre . . . so strange."

"Doesn't begin to cover it."

". . . Growing stronger."

"You feel it too?" Col asked.

"Oh yes. It's this ballroom. Has anything strange happened here?"

Ondine couldn't help rolling her eyes. This ballroom was where Old Col had first turned Hamish into a ferret. It didn't surprise her that it could be a centre of strange magic.

"So strong," Old Col said.

Just as Ondine thought, *gee her voice sounds close*, her great-aunt stepped around the corner. Followed by the other woman. And Ondine found herself staring into the glistening round eyes of Brugel's First Minister!

Gulp!

No words came out. The two women – both dressed as witches – stared at her, boring holes right through her. Well, she had just been sprung listening to them. And she must look an absolute sight in her

Cabbage costume. Any nerves she'd had about going on stage were now completely overtaken by fear of what her great-aunt might do to her.

"It's her!" The First Minister said, her mouth dropping open in a most unparliamentary way.

Ondine looked behind her, but saw only the boy cast members. She turned around again. The First Minister kept staring right through her.

"Me?" Ondine felt sick right down to her frilly green socks.

"Yes, you! You're doing all this," the First Minister said.

"I rather think she is," Old Col said, making Ondine feel even more confused. Her great-aunt knew she didn't have any magic. Maybe she was just going along with it, like the time she'd made Ondine read the Duchess's palms?

Another gulp. "I haven't done anything."

"It is you." The First Minister was beginning to creep Ondine right out. "There is something about you. You have the strangest magic, it's seeping out of your pores. You don't even realise, do you? You're like a sieve."

"But I'm . . ." Ondine didn't know what she was, only that she didn't understand a word of what the First Minister was saying. Maybe she'd been at the plütz?

"You're due on stage, there's a girl," Col said. "Better get to it."

Head swirling in confusion, Ondine felt only too glad to take her leave. She found her position on stage behind the lowered curtain and tried to think straight. There was no argument that the palechia was full of strange things, but they weren't her fault. She hadn't made Pyotr psychic, or taught the children and Ms Kyryl to sing. Or caused the fish to fall out of the sky. Had she? Her great aunt must have been trying to impress the First Minister, that's all. Yes, that sounded completely reasonable and believable.

A hush fell as the curtain parted and Ms Kyryl walked to the centre of the stage, to make the opening announcement. "Your Graces the Duke and Duchess of Brugel, Madam First Minister . . ."

Glancing about the crowded room, Ondine saw the First Minister take her seat.

" . . . distinguished guests, ladies and gentlemen. Welcome to the

Harvest and Halloween Ball at the palechia. As is traditional, the night begins with the children's pageant. Without further ado, I present to you the Palechia School children."

Ondine quickly crouched into position and waited for her cue. All thoughts fled, including what she was supposed to be doing up there. A huge roar of applause filled the room as the curtain parted to reveal their colourful, cardboard set. Suddenly she didn't feel so bad. She could get through this!

Farmer One and Farmer Two strolled on to the stage with their tools. The crowd broke into applause.

"Our months of toil will soon be rewarded," Farmer One said as she hefted her cardboard hoe over her shoulder.

"That is true," Farmer Two said, enunciating clearly. "In fact, you could say our labours will soon bear fruit."

The audience roared with laughter and cheered. *Mercury's wings, what an easy crowd!*

"Here is the apple, so sweet and ripe," Farmer One said.

The boy playing Apple spun around and twisted himself from the branch of a cardboard tree, as if the farmers had just picked him. The audience broke into fresh applause.

Farmer Two moved over to the vegetable patch. "And here is the Turnip, here is the Cabbage!"

Andreas stood up and said, "I am Turnip," then gave a bow.

That was Ondine's cue to stand up and deliver her line, "I am Cabbage." As she leant forward to take her bow, her skirts flew up in the air behind her. The audience roared with laughter as Andreas the Turnip peeked behind Ondine and pretended to be shocked. Just as they'd rehearsed it.

As she did a little twirl, she cast a look at Sun and made a sweeping gesture with her hand. Cue Sun stepping sideways offstage.

"Oh no, we still have much work to do, but the sun is leaving us," Farmer Two said.

"It will soon grow dark," Farmer One said.

"The light is here," a voice said from offstage. Hetty, dressed in her silvery lunar costume, shimmied into position. "I am Harvest Moon. I will help you."

The crowd went crazy. Ondine couldn't get over what an enthusiastic audience they had. Making her way backstage as the play moved into the final scenes, Ondine found Hamish waiting for her.

"Lass, ye were great up there," he said, smiling at her.

Ondine shrugged away the compliment, too distracted by Hamish looking so gloriously dashing in his waiter's outfit.

"Ye did well tonight, lass," he said, stealing a quick kiss that made her feel beautiful despite her frumpy costume. "Here, I grabbed some food from the kitchen."

"Thanks," Ondine said as she took a pastry. "Oooh, these look nice, what's in them?"

Hamish shrugged. "Silver beet and feta. Well, it might be spinach, or it might be rhubarb leaves."

Ondine nearly choked. "Rhubarb leaves? You're kidding?"

Confusion swamped Hamish's face. "No, I'm not. I heard the Duchess tell them tae do it, tae save money, like."

"No way!"

"Sure. She told them to stop wasting food and use potato skins in the soup, rhubarb and celery leaves in the pastries. They've been following her orders ever since."

Ondine's body grew cold all over and she put the pastry back on Hamish's plate. "Rhubarb leaves are toxic!"

"They are? But . . . the food's full of them! It's the Duke's favourite snack!"

Ondine stared at the plate of pastries, each one a neat rectangle of tasty death. Instantly her memory reeled back to the time Old Col had upturned the teacup on the train and declared, *That's not a carriage, dear, it's a coffin. What a shame, that means somebody's going to die.*

"Great Pluto's ghost!" Ondine gasped. "Col didn't get sick in Slaegal, she was poisoned right here. Throw these in the bin. We have to stop people eating them."

Ondine charged into the ballroom and ran directly towards the Duke.

He was dressed as a Baroque dandy with a gold cane. She nearly lost her footing as her voluminous skirts buffeted the shocked guests.

The Duke looked pale as he leaned on his cane. In his other hand, he had a pastry.

"No!" Ondine screamed as she ran. "Don't eat the green ones!" All the while she kept begging, *He can't die. The tea leaves can't come true!*

The Duke's mouth fell open, his eyes became round and frightened at the sight of the human cabbage hurtling his way.

"They're killing you!" Ondine yelled as she launched herself towards the Duke. Everyone in the room gasped as she became airborne. She whacked the pastry out of the Duke's hand and managed to knock over a waiter with a tray of food at the same time.

Oooof! She landed with a thud in a shower of hors d'oeuvres.

"What is the meaning of this?" The Duke looked ready to explode.

Before she could censor herself, Ondine cried, "Please, Your Grace, you mustn't eat the food. It's got toxic rhubarb leaves in it. It's the Duchess's fault, she told the chefs to do it."

"How dare you!" the Duke thundered.

Oh no! Ondine had completely forgotten about the Duke not wanting to hear anything bad about his wife. But this time it couldn't be helped. If the Duke wanted to survive, he had to listen. Which meant Ondine had to draw every last skerrick of courage and tell him what she knew.

"Please, Your Grace, rhubarb leaves are poisonous. That's why you've been so sick. That's why Old Col got sick too. The Duchess told the kitchen staff to use them in the food and she knew the pastries were your favourite!"

"But –" the Duke started.

"I did noshing of the short!" Duchess Kerala strode towards them, glass of red wine in hand. She'd come dressed as a soldier, like her son, and the scowl on her face really made her look the part.

By this time, Hamish and Old Col had caught up with Ondine.

"Yes, you did!" Ondine's voice trembled as she faced down the Duchess. The entire room went quiet and she felt sick with fear. "Hamish overheard you, didn't you, Hamish?"

Everyone looked at Hamish.

Out of the corner of her eye, Ondine saw the Infanta, dressed as a 1920s movie starlet. The Infanta looked at Ondine and slowly shook her head. As if to say, Now you will see. Hamish will let you down.[1]

The room was full of people, but it was so quiet Ondine could hear Hamish shifting his weight in his new shoes. All the while she kept hoping, *No, he won't let me down. I know it.*

Time stretched to the point of snapping.

Silently, Ondine prayed, *Oh Hamish, please say something.*

"Aye, that's right," Hamish said.

Relief washed over Ondine at those three words. She couldn't help smiling as he continued; every word from his lips strengthened her claim.

"I saw ye tear strips off the kitchen staff for wasting food," he said to the Duchess.

"You're lying," she answered, taking another sip of wine.

Palpable tension rippled through the room.

"Mebbe if ye didnae drink so much, ye might remember," Hamish said.

The crowd gasped at the massive breach of protocol.

Jupiter's moons, but things were getting ugly! Yet at that moment Ondine had never felt more proud of Hamish.

The Duchess looked angry enough to shoot darts out of her eyes. "You have no right."

A lesser person would have withered under the Duchess's glare. Everyone stared at Hamish, most of them probably wondering who he was and how he had the nerve to say such things to the Duchess.

"He has every right." The Infanta stepped forward, and if Ondine didn't know better, she could have sworn Anathea was smiling. "If your drunken behaviour has put the Duke's health at risk, then this man is doing the right thing."

"You would shay that," the Duchess said.

Ondine cast a quick look around the worried room. She caught Old Col's glance and noticed her great-aunt staring daggers at the Duchess. "You will speak the truth!" Old Col commanded.

The Duchess made a strange sound in the back of her throat and clamped her teeth together, refusing to speak. In the crowd behind Old

Col, Ondine saw a lot of the witchy women huddling together, discussing things in murmured tones. She suddenly wondered if they were not pretending to be witches, but were real witches in real life.

"I don't feel so well," the Duke said, turning pale. Everyone gasped. Ondine thought they were all being pathetic and cowardly.

"Well, don't just stand around," she cried. "Someone get a doctor!"

The Duke slumped into Ondine's arms. He was so heavy, she couldn't hold him up. They fell to the floor in a flumph of green cabbage skirts.

Luckily for the Duke, there were three doctors in attendance at the Harvest Ball, one dressed as a ballerina, one as a lizard monster and the third as another witch. They laid him on a chaise longue in one of the libraries.

"It's kidney stones," the doctor dressed as a witch said. She was the one who'd treated Old Col and the Duke earlier. She made the Duke swallow a tablet the size of his thumb. "If what you say is true, and he's been eating rhubarb leaves, then he's lucky to be alive."

Ondine breathed a sigh of relief.

"Oh, my dear darling," the Duchess said, smothering her husband's forehead with kisses.

The Duchess's words didn't ring true to Ondine. She looked at Hamish and he looked at her. While everyone else fussed over the Duke, Ondine and Hamish snuck out of the room.

"Where do you think you're going?" Ondine knew that voice. Oh, why did Vincent have to turn up now? He stood right in front of them, blocking their path.

Squee! "It's you!" cried another voice that Ondine knew.

Brilliant! It was Hetty, and she'd just walked around the corner in her shimmery moon costume.

"Sorry, Hetty, you have to take one for Brugel," Hamish said. Quick as a flash, he grabbed her and threw her in Vincent's path. There were grunts of frustration (from Vincent) and shrieks of glee (from Hetty) as she smothered her idol in kisses.

"Nice one!" Ondine said as she and Hamish charged the rest of the way to the Duchess's rooms.

Her cabbage costume was so wide she knocked things over. They had to stop for a moment as Hamish helped pull the material over her head. She felt stupid standing there in a green polo neck and tights, but it was agility she required, not the latest fashion. Together they negotiated all the polished breakables.

In the bedroom freshly arranged ginger lilies filled the air with such a cloying smell Ondine sneezed.

The ledger was still there in its hiding place. The hand-written balance sheet too.

"We need them both, otherwise the Duke won't believe us," Ondine said.

"I know." Hamish unscrewed a bottle of white wine. "We have tae sell this right. We have tae stand absolutely firm."

"What are you doing?" Ondine asked.

"Drinking some courage." Hamish necked the bottle and took a good swig. A strange expression came over his face.

"Bad vintage?" Ondine thought the wine had turned.

Hamish stared at the bottle. "It's . . . it's nawt wine at all. It's apple juice!"

## 28

"Apple juice? That makes no sense." Ondine reached for the bottle and took a deep sniff. The sweet tang of apples filled her nostrils. She took a swig anyway and tasted the truth. Hamish had already moved on to a bottle of red wine. The label may have boasted a harvest from the previous decade, but, judging by his face, it might have been bottled last week.

"Grape juice," he said, offering it to Ondine.

She sniffed and tasted this one too. Although there was no alcohol content, her head started spinning. "But . . . if the Duchess is always a bit soaked, why are these bottles full of juice instead of wine?"

Hamish shook his head, then picked up another bottle and twisted the cap. "Hear that?"

"No."

"Exactly. No crinkly sound, no seal breaking. These bottles have all been emptied and refilled."

"By who?" In her head, Ondine heard her mother say, *By whom, darling.*

"By the Duchess. She's not a sad old drunk at all. She's as sober as the day is lawng. She just wants everyone tae think she's wasted so that nobody suspects anything."

Ondine felt her eyes grow wider at the thought. "No wonder she could put so much away, it was all an act."

"Exactly." Hamish grabbed two bottles and put them under his arm, then he picked up the ledger. "Ever notice how uncomfortable everyone is when she's wobbling around, getting all shouty? Ye look the other way. Ye don't want her tae target you, because she's a raving drunk. Except in this case, we're all looking away so that we won't notice what she's up tae."

"That's so clever!" Ondine blurted.

"Ondi, me love, she was trying tae kill her husband!" Hamish said, leading them back to the hallway.

"She did it right in front of us. You were there in the kitchen and you watched her yelling at the staff, but you didn't realise."

Hamish's voice dripped with sarcasm: "Thanks fer yer vote of confidence."

They jogged back to the room where the doctors had taken the Duke.

"Oh, Hamish, I've just realised," Ondine gasped. "You said the Duchess told Vincent, 'One day all this will be yours.' She really wasn't just saying that as a figure of speech."

"Aye: I only hope we're not too late fer the Duke."

Laid out on the chaise longue, the Duke looked stricken. Perspiration ran in rivulets down his face. His hair stuck to his scalp in wet dregs.

The Duchess sat weeping by his side while the three doctors discussed the situation amongst themselves in the corner. In a nearby chair sat the First Minister, and next to her, the Infanta.

"I think we'll need more than doctors," Ondine said.

The Duchess turned around and looked daggers at them. "Get these intruders out of here," she commanded.

"It's over, Kerala," Hamish said, holding up the two bottles of not-wine. "We know yer dirty wee secret."

"I have no secrets!" the Duchess said.

"I think you do." Ondine's mouth turned completely dry. "My Lord Duke, I am so very sorry you have to hear this, but your beloved wife has not only been poisoning you, she's been stealing from you, too."

The Duke whimpered but said nothing.

The Duchess screamed at them, "Are you trying to kill him?"

"No, but you are," Ondine said, her heart hammering behind her ribs. "We know the wine is just for show. It's only fruit juice. We have the ledger, and we have your secret bank account details."

"How dare you!" the Duchess said between clenched teeth.

The Duke whimpered some more, from the pain in his kidneys and probably the pain in his heart.

Old Col stared at the Duchess as she muttered a dark spell under her breath, ending with the hideous threat, "Speak truth not lies or the next Duke dies."

Ondine noted that she cursed the next duke, not the current one. The Duchess didn't care if the current duke died, but she cared very much about Vincent. No Vincent, no chance to rule on his behalf.

The Duchess grunted and tried to clamp her mouth shut, but Old Col's stare worked like a drill, digging through layers of obfuscation. The Duchess's words came out as a strangled snarl: "I did it for Brugel." Exhausted, she collapsed on the floor in defeat and said nothing more.

From his sickbed, Duke Pavla whimpered again.

The First Minister spoke up: "I shall convene an urgent sitting of the Dentate first thing on Monday."[1]

---

"DOES this mean Lord Vincent will still be the new Duke?" Ondine said as she and Hamish returned to the ballroom. They'd grabbed some warm trousers and a coat so Ondine no longer looked like a green bean. In the ballroom, the party atmosphere had evaporated – as it should, considering the circumstances. People had stopped eating the food because of Ondine's warning.

However, the police wouldn't let anyone leave, so the band kept playing, even though nobody was dancing.

"I hope not." Hamish shuddered at the thought. "So who will be the next Duke?"

"I think the First Minister is checking the constitution right now."

Speaking of which, the woman herself walked into the ballroom. "Ah, there you are," she said, making a beeline for the Infanta.

Ondine and Hamish were close enough to overhear without having to strain their ears.

"Your Grace, I have checked the constitution for the line of succession. It states that while the Duke is incapacitated for reasons of physical or mental ill health, the closest relative over the age of twenty-one shall rule in his stead, until such time as the Duke makes a full recovery or dies."

The Infanta's jaw dropped in shock.

"Do not be alarmed, the doctors expect Lord Pavla to make a full recovery in time," the First Minister said.

Ondine leaned closer to Hamish, an act that made her brain a bit fuzzy. "Does that mean Anathea will become Duchess of Brugel?" she whispered.

"It seems so."

Everyone in the ballroom stood and watched as the First Minister, dressed as a witch, made the Infanta, dressed as a silent film star, place her palm on a bound copy of the constitution and recite the pledge of Brugel.

The Infanta recited the oath word perfect, with a steady voice.

The First Minister shook the new Duchess's hand, then made a deep curtsey. "Thank you, Your Grace."

A team of waiters appeared with flutes of champagne and began handing them out. Hamish grabbed two flutes and offered one to Ondine.

The First Minister held her glass aloft. "I propose a toast. To Her Lord-ship Duchess Anathea the First of Brugel."

"Anathea the First," everyone said. Ondine and Hamish raised their glasses and took a sip.

The bubbles tickled Ondine's nose. Would anybody notice if she plonked in a sugar cube to improve the taste?

"Your Grace," Ondine said, performing a quick curtsey as Anathea turned to her.

The room fell silent again.

Anathea gave a nod and the briefest of smiles in return. "My brother's health is paramount. He is being well cared for, thanks in part to you. If anything is needed by you, you have only to ask."

Ondine's heart leapt into her throat with gratitude. She seized her chance to repay a debt. "Actually, there is one thing. Could Draguta Matice have her job back, please? The previous duchess sacked her and . . ."

Murmurs rippled through the crowd as people said, "rude girl", "ungrateful" and "pushing her luck".

Another small smile and Anathea nodded. "It will be done." She stepped forward, the ruling Duchess of Brugel, and shook Ondine's hand to seal the deal. Then, in a low voice, she said to them, "You must be Hamish. When things calm down a bit, you must tell me exactly what kind of employment you performed for the Duke. Your skills will be in great demand in the coming months."

"Aye," Hamish said.

Ondine reached for his hand, silently hoping he wasn't about to accept another position to keep them in this strange place during the winter.

The whole time, the First Minister hadn't taken her eyes off Ondine, making her feel under suspicion for something. "You are a very clever girl. I am going to invite you to lunch at the Dentate very soon."

"I would be honoured," Ondine said hardly daring to believe it. The First Minister unnerved her, but maybe over lunch she might loosen up? Time would tell.

Displaying his knack for being in the right place at the right time once more, Pyotr approached and made a low bow. "My Lord Duchess, to you and your household, I offer my services."

"Oh yes," Anathea said, sounding guarded. "And what services would they be?"

"In whichever way you see fit, Your Grace. I served at Duke Pavla's pleasure. I now offer my services and loyalty to you."

Ondine couldn't help thinking how quickly Pavla had made his move. "I need some air," she whispered to Hamish.

"Aye, I could use a clear head meself," he said, leading her to the rear gardens. They put their barely touched champagne glasses on a side table.

"Where are you going?" A police officer approached. "We will need your statements."

"We're just going out to the bonfires," Ondine said.

"As long as you don't leave the grounds." This was said in a tone that made Ondine feel like they were in trouble.

"Aye, we'll not go anywhere," Hamish said, putting a warm hand on Ondine's back as they walked outside.

The cool air helped clear Ondine's head. She pulled her coat collar up to protect her neck. Hamish draped a protective arm over her shoulder as they approached the bonfire. The full moon had been two nights ago. They could have had a fat orb in the sky tonight if not for the cloud cover.

There were several fires instead of one large one, spread over a vast area. People milled about each blaze, basking in the warmth of the orange and red glow. Those wearing especially flammable costumes stood back a little more.

As is the custom, people were writing their regrets on slips of paper and casting them into the flames, as a way of saying goodbye to the past and cleansing the future.

Ondine shook her head and said, "I think I've had about enough excitement for one night."

"Aye, lass, me too." Hamish gave her a devastating smile that turned her legs to noodles.

"I haven't written a note." Ondine reached into her pockets for a scrap of paper and came up empty.

Hamish looked about and saw some more witches. Steam rose from their warm drinks. "Could I trouble ye fer a pen and paper?"

He must have given them one of his trademark smiles, because the three witches giggled and gave him a pen and a whole notepad.

"Thanks," he said, then turned to Ondine.

They found a quiet part of the garden, near one of the smaller fires, and sat down on the damp ground. Ondine pulled her coat around her tightly. The piece of paper she held felt too small to fit all her regrets and bad habits.

She wrote, "I don't like telling lies." Below that she wrote, "I don't like spying on people," and, "I don't like getting other people into trouble." No sooner had she written that than she had another regret: "I wish I'd stayed at home."

When she read her note back, she squished her mouth up in thought. She and Hamish had just saved the Duke's life and prevented Kerala from poisoning her way into power. If they'd stayed at home, the Duke might be dead by now.

She crossed the last line out.

"Ye writing an essay, lass?" Hamish said, resting his chin on her shoulder to see what she'd written.

The cold wind kissed Ondine's cheeks and she angled her body so that Hamish became a windbreak.

"What did you write, Hamish?"

"Not much." He showed her the paper. On it he'd written, "I wish I'd spent more time with Ondine."

"Oh!" She choked back a sob, then grabbed her paper, turned it over and quickly wrote, "I wish I'd spent more time with Hamish."

Hamish pulled Ondine into an embrace and kissed her. It warmed her body from the inside, while the cold air settled around them and prickled her skin.

Ondine pulled away and breathed through her nose. "I think I can smell snow," she said.

Hamish's eyebrows shot up in surprise. "Ye can smell the weather? Ye sure yer not psychic?"

"I'm sure." Ondine grinned and said, "Close your eyes, breathe through your nose. Smell that clean, cold, ozone-y kind of smell."

"But it's only the last of October."

"You don't believe me?"

Hamish grinned, then shut his eyes and followed Ondine's example. His nostrils flared. He ducked his head and sneezed.

Ondine laughed and hugged Hamish again. "Come on, let's warm up."

Hand in hand, they walked towards the edges of a fire. The cold air clung to their backs, the bonfire thawed out their faces. Ondine scrunched up her paper and threw it on to the burning heap. It dissolved in the flames, sending a plume of tiny sparks into the night sky.

Hamish fashioned his paper into a dart and threw it lower down. It turned black, held its shape for half a second then dissolved into flaming vapour.

It felt so lovely standing near the bonfire, Ondine didn't want to leave. They stood together for a good ten minutes, balanced between the cold air and the blasting furnace. A step closer and they'd burn, a step back and they'd catch a chill. Hamish put his arms across her shoulders. She snuggled into him, feeling protected.

"Well, I'll be a –" Hamish nudged Ondine to look at the sky. "Look, Ondi, it really is snowing."

Ondine blinked. Flurries of snow flitted through the sky, evaporating as they touched the bonfire. She looked back towards the palechia, to see soft flakes landing on windowsills and the tops of perfectly manicured hedges, dusting every surface like icing sugar.

Ondine smiled and said, "Told you I could smell snow."

Hamish pulled Ondine into an embrace and kissed the tip of her cold nose. "I'm deeply sorry fer the trouble I put ye through. I should hae thought of a better way tae help ye than cheating at yer school tests."

Tears blurred her vision. "Oh, Hamish, I'm sorry for the way I reacted. I know you were only trying to find a way to help me stay here with you."

He hugged her a little bit tighter. "Ye broke me heart every time I thought ye might be leaving."

"I didn't like fighting with you. I'm not cut out for it," Ondine said. "Everyone here is so messed up it's contagious."

"Aye. Mebbe we should go back tae yer parents' pub."

Lightness filled her. He wanted to go home? She wiped her eyes. "You'd do that for me?"

"In a heartbeat." He gave her one of those grins she'd come to love. The ones that made her feel all warm and melty inside. And a bit giddy in the head.

She kissed him with all her heart. The kind of kiss that told him how much she wanted to put all this craziness behind them. He returned her ardour tenfold, making her wonder how she'd ever doubted his love in the first place.

When they pulled apart, he brushed away a fresh tear from her cheek.

"Then why are ye still crying?"

"Because I feel so guilty for doubting you. The Infanta . . . I mean, I guess she's the Duchess now. Anyway, she filled my head with doubts and I was silly and tired and stressed enough to believe her. She said you'd let me down. Her words were like poison and –" He silenced her with a kiss that sent firecrackers off in her head. When he eventually broke away, he looked short of breath. Snowflakes fell on their hair and shoulders, but Ondine felt warm right through. "I wish we could stay like this," she said.

"Aye, me too."

The sounds of the orchestra inside the banquet hall drifted outside. Hamish took Ondine's hand, bowed over it and said, "May I have this dance?"

Ondine giggled and put her hand on his shoulder, ready for a Brugelish three-step. They took a few steps this way and that, before the snow and cold wind made her hands freeze. She pressed her arms around him, under his coat.

"What kind of dance is this?" he asked.

"It's called a snow-shuffle."

Hamish chuckled. "Aye, I like this dance."

They shuffled and snuggled, in that thin zone between the bonfire and the cold air, as snow swirled around them, heralding the onset of winter.

"I love ye, Ondine."

She held herself against his warm chest and said, "And I love you right back."

–THE END–

# THE WINTER OF MAGIC

# 1

December is a fun month, wherever you are in the world. If you're in the southern hemisphere, you have long summer days at the beach ahead of you. If you're in the northern hemisphere, winter snow dusts everything with soft magic. All over the globe there are festivals galore and New Year celebrations. December is also way more interesting than March, which everyone agrees can be a bit of a dud. If December happens to be the month of your name day, it's also cause for a fair bit of excitement. Ondine de Groot, the star of this story – and the two that came before it – has her name day in December. [1]

Two days after her name day, Ondine's eldest sister Marguerite will marry her fiancé, Thomas Berger under the ceremonial elm tree in the botanical gardens. But before the wedding – and Ondine's name day – the de Groot family has customers to serve at their family pub, *The Duke and Ferret*, in downtown Venzelemma. [2]

On this particular Saturday in December, the day was short and wet, the night dark and cold. It rained and sleeted something miserable, but the weather didn't stop people from going out in the evening. Saturday nights were always busy in the pub, but in December they were frantic. This is because in Brugel you simply must "catch up" with all your friends before the end of the year, or you'll have hideously bad luck in the New Year. This entrenched tradition has necessitated the creation of "second dinner", a meal service that slips between the first evening meal and supper.

Even the new East Asian restaurant across the road, *On The Fang*, was booked out – for both dinners – every night. Ondine suspected they had somehow created a third dinner, but she was so busy she had no chance to check the truth of it for herself. [3]

Meal times – all of them – were so busy Ondine felt run off her feet. Or more precisely, run off her *hands*, which were permanently submerged in hot soapy water as she cleaned dishes day and night. [4]

Henrik the chef and Cybelle, Ondine's middle sister, worked together like an old married couple at the stoves, knowing exactly what the other needed at just the right time. Henrik had a pudding bowl of a tummy, which was a generally accepted work hazard in the cheffing world. He did have hair, and Ondine tried to remember what colour it was. It was hard to know, because he always wore a tall white chef's hat firmly on his head. Da, Ondine's father, p, Ondine's oured drinks in the public bar. He still had shocking white hair and the dark hairy caterpillar of a mono-brow, which made Ondine and her sisters simply itch to pluck it.

Da had a television on the wall to keep himself and the patrons enter-tained. The monitor was a 16:9 rectangle, but nobody knew how to set it properly so everyone on screen looked fat and blurry. Tonight the channel was set to the news, with a miraculous story of a plane crash at an airport in neighbouring Craviç, in which everybody walked out the wreck completely unharmed. (Some were suggesting magic had to be involved.)

And Hamish? The handsome lad with eyes full of mischief and a mop of dark hair that fell tantalisingly over his forehead had the easiest job of all. Ma had him waiting tables. With his Scottish accent, cheeky smile and boundless energy, Hamish had a knack for charming the guests. His sparkly green eyes only added to the package. In return, the tips had never been more generous. And these days he hardly ever turned into a ferret, which made Ondine all kinds of happy.

A defeated-looking Marguerite, her long wavy hair hanging lankly over her shoulders, walked into the kitchen with a tray of dirty beer mugs from the bar. Automatically Ondine pulled up her gloves and re-filled the sink with detergent and scalding hot water.

Ma intercepted Margi. "Darling, you're wrecked. Take a break or you'll have bags under your eyes for the wedding." Ma took the tray of dirty glasses and added them to Ondine's workload.

"Can I have a break too?" Ondine asked.

Ma shot her a sly grin. "When a fish dances on the table." [5]

Marguerite's soft chin wobbled as she touched her fingers to her cheeks. As the eldest daughter, Marguerite had worked for her parents from the moment she could carry a bowl of soup without spilling it. Tonight she looked far older than her twenty-one years. Long nights and hard work had a way of doing that to a person. Ondine felt exhausted too, but nobody urged her to put her feet up on the off-chance she'd look tired for her name day.

"Get some rest." Ma kissed Margi on the forehead. "I'll help Thomas and Josef at the bar. It's winding down now anyway."

At which point Thomas came in with another tray of dirty glasses. "Have you seen the news? The Dentate is changing the laws of succession." [6]

No, Ondine hadn't seen the news because they didn't have a telly in the kitchen. Ondine has been too busy to have the luxury of catching up on Brugelish politics. Nobody had brought a newspaper into the house ever since that food writer Dee Gustation gave them that excoriating review way back in summer.

"Really?" Ma said with extra-high raised brows. "Who's it to go to after Duchess Anathea then?"

"The daughters I guess," Thomas said with a shrug

Ma said, "That will put Vincent's nose out of joint."

At the mention of the young lord's name, Ondine rolled her eyes. [7]

Ma shot her a look. "They can change the laws all they like, won't make any difference to us. Because we won't have anything more to do with that lot, will we Ondi?"

"No, course not," she said.

Talk of Brugel's royal family reminded Ondine that she was still grounded for sneaking off with Hamish so she could work for Duke

Pavla at his Autumn Palace. This had been expressly against her parents' wishes. The punishment Ma and Da meted out on her return was both swift and hideous. No friends over. No parties. No extra-curricular school excursions and she couldn't visit anyone either. Just working at home and studying at school and that was it.

All things considered, she accepted the punishment and got on with it. Because being grounded wasn't that different from normal life in a busy pub. Plus, Hamish was here in the pub all the time, so why would she want to be anywhere else?

The dishes kept piling up, so Ondine kept on with her routine. In her peripheral vision, she watched Ma walk back towards the dining room and then suddenly gasp in shock.

Her first thought was, *Uh-oh, what's Hamish done?* [8] The next moment she chastised herself. She should have more faith in him – just because Ma got a shock didn't mean Hamish was the cause of it.

Silence enveloped the kitchen as everyone stopped what they were doing and looked at Ma. The family matriarch was rooted to the spot, staring at someone in the dining room.

A stranger's voice cut through the air. Female and demanding, she summoned the will of a field marshal and brought everything to a stop. "If I may have your attention please. Nobody is to leave."

"What?" Ondine shlucked off her gloves and raced to her mother's side to see what was going on. Her jaw dropped. There in the dining room stood five official-looking people in dark blue suits, (three women and two men), each holding aloft shiny official-looking badges for everyone to see.

Two suited men moved into the taproom, effectively blocking the remaining exits. They were serious; nobody was leaving.

Their leader, the woman who'd brought the evening to a screaming silence, had a voice that could shatter glass. "We are from the Department of Immigration and Employment. Pursuant to legislation passed this week in the Dentate, we are here to check everyone's identity documents, to make sure nobody is working illegally."

Cold dread filled Ondine as her gaze homed in on Hamish, who at that moment turned towards the kitchen with arms full of empty plates.

Ordinarily you might say 'dirty plates' but the hungry customers had used their complimentary soft bread to scoop up the last of the sauce. It must be the cold weather making people extra hungry, because lately the diners were sending their plates back, licked clean.[9]

Hamish winked at Ondine as he walked toward her. He was still in the dining room, she still in the kitchen, but he closed the distance between them. Happy harp music played in her head as she looked upon her wonderful, gorgeous, charming – and a teensy bit naughty – boyfriend. Uh-oh. The invisible harps clanged as reality intruded. The moment Hamish opened his mouth, the immigration inspectors would know he wasn't from around here. The lead inspector spotted Hamish moving closer to the kitchen.

"You there, do you have your work card?"

Fear for her beloved kept Ondine glued to the spot. Mentally she sent her thoughts to him, as if by sheer will she could keep him safe. *Just keep walking. Don't say a word.* Not that she had any psychic powers to speak of, but the will was there.

Behind her, she heard someone pick up the phone, dial out and then murmur down the receiver. It was Henrik the chef, saying things like, "warning", "immigration" and "get out". The compressed voice at the other end said, "too late".

"What's all this about then?" Ma walked into the dining room to create interference. Hope soared. Ma had magical powers of timing and could usually interfere just at the right moment. Alas, her hopes sagged as the leading inspector paid Ma no mind, charged forward and clapped her hand on Hamish's shoulder.

Hamish's eyes turned round like golf balls. Ondine's mouth dried up with fear.

"Show me your work card," the woman said.

Every single guest looked at Hamish and held their breath. You could have heard a knife and fork drop – which is exactly what happened. The plates wobbled in Hamish's hands and cutlery slid onto the floor with a clatter. Movement caught Ondine's peripheral vision and she looked to the pub's front windows. There, across the street, were people running out of *Fang's*. Some of them looked like diners. Two of them were wearing aprons, which meant members of staff were fleeing too.

"Tell me your name and where you're from. You look Slaegalese to me," the inspector said.

Silently, Ondine begged, *I know you don't like authority, but Hamish please keep quiet and –*

"I'm Scottish ye toerag."

*– Jupiter's moons! Why did you open your mouth?*

The inspector said, "Close enough. You're coming with us."

"No!" Ondine charged into the dining room without a thought as to what she should do or say when she got there. No way would she and Hamish be parted again, not after everything they'd gone through. Hamish dropped the rest of his plates in a series of sharp clangs and crashes. In the next half-second, he fell away into nothing, leaving only a pile of second-hand clothes on the floor. The inspector's palm clutched at nothing but air, her eyes astonishment-wide. As one, every guest in the restaurant gasped and looked at where Hamish used to be.

Ondine took advantage of the confusion and screamed at the inspector. "What did you do to him?" She bent down to scoop up the fabric, hoping against hope he would be in there somewhere. Also hoping she didn't stab him with the broken crockery lying about.

A ruckus broke out as everyone talked at once.

"– gone."

"– was just there."

"– what's in this plütz?" [10]

"– will they let us out?"

" – told you we should have come for first dinner."

Ma stepped forward and said, "Please, Ondine, you're making a scene. Tidy this mess up and get back to work." To everyone else she sounded like a peeved mother. But to Ondine, Ma provided life-saving interference.

"Yes Ma," she said, carefully carrying away the bundle. The clothes felt warm and smelled of hot dinners and Hamish. Something scratched at her wrist. It might be a chunk of broken plate but she didn't dare look. She kept walking, every moment wondering if one of the inspectors would grab her and drag her back to the dining room. Heart thumping, she tore through the kitchen and jogged up the stairs to the room she now shared with Cybelle – they'd set up Ondine's room for Thomas's parents so they had somewhere to rest after the wedding reception.

She kicked the door shut behind her and dared to breathe again. Heart crashing against her ribs, she put the bundle of clothes on her bed. There in the middle of it all, a lump began moving. Then the lump poked out from the neck of a shirt to reveal the face of a whiskery, black ferret.

The ferret looked up and grinned. "Didye miss me?"

**2**

---

The shock was *not* that Ondine's beloved Hamish had turned into a ferret – she'd had two whole books to get used to that – but that he'd transformed so quickly. He'd been in agony when he transitioned at the Duke's palace a couple of months ago, so the super-fast version tonight must have been super-painful.

"Are you hurt?"

Shambles – for that is how he was known in his ferret-form – winced and said, "Naw. Weil. A wee bit."

"Oh my poor darling." Ondine scooped him into her arms and gave a gentle hug, followed by a kiss on the top of his furry head. An ache took hold at seeing him like this. Just when she'd become used to him being human – complacent even, if she were honest with herself – he'd changed. He'd had to. Otherwise the inspectors may well have hauled him away in handcuffs. And seeing him hauled away simply wouldn't do.

Ondine knew she could put up with anything so long as she and Hamish were together. Yet she may as well be cursed too if they couldn't *properly* be together. And here they were, alone in her bedroom and everything.

"Oh would ye look at that," he said. "Get tae the window hen, there's something afoot."

"The inspectors have raided *Fang's* as well. I heard Henrik on the phone trying to warn them," Ondine said.

Shambles pressed his soft nose to the window and made a foggy pattern with his breath. From their vantage point, what with being upstairs rather than ground level, they could see the restaurant's outdoor decorations shining brightly in the dark night. Ondine loved their neon dragons with loaded kebab skewers for fangs. Shiny things like that really lifted the neighbourhood. The lights flickered on and off in a chase pattern, then suddenly they didn't come back on again. A trio of dark-suited inspectors escorted the last of *Fang*'s staff into the back of a white van, which was parked on the street.

"There but for the grace of Old Col, go I," Shambles said. [1]

Ondine rubbed at her head. "Are you telling me you don't have a work card?"

"I didnae think I needed one, what with being a ferret for so long. And then, weil, I was with you."

Yes he was. He hadn't been human in decades, thanks to Old Col cursing him a good one at her debutante ball. [2]

He hadn't rediscovered his handsomely human form until he'd met Ondine all those months ago. Even then he couldn't always be relied upon to stay human. But when he was, Hamish and Ondine had spent so much time busily falling in love; they hadn't spent any time contemplating the mundane practicalities of everyday life. Why did those realities have to intrude now?

"We'll have to get you a work permit," she said.

"Or I could stay like this for a while until things cool over?"

"No you can't." Ondine wanted Hamish to be human all the time, because her relationship with Shambles the ferret was nothing compared to her relationship with Hamish the lad.

"Och . . . we'll think of something." Shambles said, shifting his weight from side to side. "Oh dear. I just thought of something."

Ondine looked at him, too scared to speak.

"I just realised . . . I'm a lot older than I look."

"What?"

"Weil, on account of the fact I was like *this* fer so many decades, the real me didn't age. Remember yer auntie put that staying spell on me. If I had've aged, I'd be nearer Auntie Col's age."

Originally Ondine had been very glad of the staying spell and considered it a blessing. Now his advanced-age-yet-youthful-demeanour created only fresh problems because he didn't look as old as his birth certificate would say he was. That's if he could find his birth certificate.

And she'd so hoped after the awful time they'd spent at the autumn palace their problems might be over.

"So ye see lass, even if I had me work card, with me right date of birth and all, nobody would believe it was true."

"Oh dear." A washing machine churned inside Ondine's tummy.

Ma arrived at the doorway and bustled in. "Oh dear is right. You OK love?"

"Oh yeas, all ticketyboo." Shambles crawled into his trousers and began transforming into his lovely Hamish self.

Ondine rolled her eyes. She was fairly sure her mother was talking to her, not Hamish. All the same, pride surged in her heart at his bravery. He must have felt the worst pain in his life during that lightning-fast transformation, yet he hadn't complained one jot. Now he was back as his good self without a whimper. What a man!

Ma nodded. "Can't have you zapping down to ferret size every time the inspectors come –"

"Aye."

"– They had a lot of questions about how you vanished. I told them you were a hologram. Can't say they bought it, but as they couldn't find you, I took advantage of their confusion and said they must have imagined the whole thing."

Ondine's forehead creased. "And they believed you?"

"Not for a minute. But then they were called over to *Fang's* so they let us off with a warning. Hamish, we need you back on your feet. Promise me if they turn up again, you'll disappear, do you hear me? We can't afford to lose you."

"Aw, yer all heart Missers G."

"No I'm not. We can't *afford* to lose you because you bring in the most tips." [3]

Trust Ma to think of the business first. Ondine gave Hamish a hug. She then helped him into his shirt, but only because her mother was right there and it was the good and proper thing to do.

"Ondine, un-Velcro yourself from Hamish. He can't be seen in public again tonight, so I need you to finish up in front-of-house."

"Ma, we're in huge trouble. Hamish doesn't have a work card."

"I'm aware of that. You'll have to pick up the slack until we can get him one," Ma said.

Oh dear, her mother had completely missed the point. Ondine curved her hand in a 'come here' motion. "Have a look out the window."

The three of them watched the last staff member of *Fang's* stagger into the van. The inspector had his hand on the top of the woman's head so she didn't injure herself on the door frame on the way in. [4] The van zoomed off, leaving nothing but a dark, closed restaurant.

"That's not good," Ma said.

"Exactly. And they'll do the same to Hamish if he doesn't have a work card," Ondine said.

"Stop catastrophising everything, love. Hamish will simply have to fill out some forms at the nearest British embassy."

Hamish turned to Ondine and then Ma. "I'm afraid it won't do any good, Missers G. Me birth certificate would say I'm old enough to be retired. Unless my name is Dorian Grey, they'll not believe me." [5]

"Oh dear," Ma said. Time stretched as she pursed her lips, deep in thought. "Then we may have to appeal to the Duke."

"You mean the Duchess," Ondine corrected.

Ma shook her head. "Sorry. Force of habit."

It had taken a bit of getting used to, having a duchess as head of state instead of a duke.

Duchess Anathea was only the third ruling duchess in Brugel's history, so the entire country had a fair bit of adjusting to make. She wasn't even the proper duchess as such, she was merely standing in because Duke Pavla was too sick to rule and Lord Vincent too young to take over.

Something scratched Ondine's memory. The Duke knew Hamish could transform into a ferret, but did the Duchess? The last person Ondine wanted to deal with was the batty Duchess Anathea. They'd become sort-of-friends towards the end of their stay with Duke Pavla, but all the same Ondine wanted to steer well clear of the lot of them. Every member of the royal family made Ondine uneasy in the same way having a heaving mass of spiders on one's shoulder made a person uneasy.

Ondine, Ma and Hamish looked at each other, and as they kept looking, they kept saying nothing, which meant none of them came up with any alternative ideas.

Up and down went Hamish's Adam's apple as he swallowed hard. "Go to the top, eh lass?"

Ondine said, "Back to Bellreeve? I feel sick just thinking about it." [6] [16]

Hamish grimaced. "Mebbe we send her a letter explaining the situation?"

"Good!" Ma said, "That's sorted. Now, Hamish, you stay in the kitchen, out of sight. Ondi, you're with me. We have to clear up second dinner and reset the tables for breakfast."

And to think, before tonight, Ondine's worries had been all about her name day and what excitement lay ahead for her. This pushed all those lovely, excited, buzzy feelings aside and replaced them with niggly, naggly worries. Hardly a fair trade. Although she was only going downstairs to work, Ondine wrapped her arms around Hamish as if fare welling him for an eternity. "Please be careful," she said.

"Aye," he kissed the top of her head, "nothing will keep us apart lass. I'll make sure of it."

When they reached the kitchen, Ondine rolled up her sleeves to get back to the washing, only to find a towel, mid-air, drying a plate, also mid air.

"Wh –" She started to say. The towel dropped the plate, which smashed on the ground, the towel fluttered over the broken pieces.

"You're overtired," Ma said as she walked in. "Look at all these gleaming plates. I was crossing my fingers they'd be done quickly. Thank you Ondi, you've done a wonderful job."

Puzzled, Ondine looked at what her mother was gabbling about. That's when she noticed the neat stacks of clean, dry plates and bowls on the drying bench, next to the sparkling glassware and tubs full of glistening cutlery. So much work done in such a short time had to be the result of magic, but Ondine couldn't fathom where the magic had come from.

3

---

Two mornings later, Ondine woke to the lads and ladies on the radio discussing the magical qualities of the day. This appealed to Ondine no end, because it was her name day, so it was indeed already special.

Snuggling further under the covers, she listened to them blather.

*"Green lights all the way to work,"* the host said, before adding, *"That never happens."*

The other said, *"My toast fell off the plate and it landed butter side up, which I think breaks all the laws of physics!"*

*"We've banished Monday-itis. Today is officially Magic Day here in Venzelemma."*

*"Small amounts of magic. Give us a call and share your moment of magic with us."*

That suited Ondine just fine as she listened to the shared stories of good fortune. Being a Monday, she should be getting ready for school. What a shame the magic they were talking about on the radio couldn't chase Monday and the cold weather away.

Judging by the heavy grey skies and the tree branches scraping against the window, a properly cold arctic north wind was dancing through the streets. [1]

A rumble set off in her tummy and a ping of excitement went off in her head. What sort of name day breakfast might Ma and Da have in store for her? After all, it was still two days before the wedding, so she could get a little Ondine attention before everything turned Margi-wards. Thrills zapped through her and she lifted the end of the duvet off her bed to have a sneaky look underneath. Perhaps her parents had snuck a pressie under there during the night? Disappointment weighed her down. The only thing under her bed was a warren of dust bunnies.

No matter, there would be presents downstairs, she was sure of it.

The moving lump in the bed beside her showed Cybelle still asleep, so Ondine dressed quietly. This took some doing, because there wasn't much room and she kept fumbling and losing her balance, what with it being so cold her fingers could barely move. At this time of year she needed thermal underwear, t-shirt, polo neck and cardigan. She also wore leggings under her denim jeans and two pairs of socks. Then she remembered she had to shower and relieve herself, so it all had to come off again.

Being a school day, she put her summer uniform dress over the top of it all. You may be wondering why she didn't wear her winter uniform. That's because they were twice handed down from her sisters and therefore threadbare and revolting. So the summer uniform stayed. Not that you saw much of it because when she went outside she wore an ankle-length life-preserver coat and fur-lined hat with *Orschlappen*. [2]

Thoroughly trussed up, Ondine walked bulky-legged down the stairs to find her mother stacking folding chairs into their private room behind the kitchen. It used to be a family room, with a table long enough to fit everyone around it. Now it had one small round table where only three could sit, at a squeeze. This was particularly unfair considering how much her family had grown to include three new beaux.

The rest of the space was taken up with boxes of kitchen supplies including doilies and extra thick plastic food wrap. In fact, loads and loads and loads of boxes of extra thick plastic food wrap. Not forgetting the teetering towers of boxes of things for Margi's wedding. Boxes of *bonbonniere*, ribbons, linen chair covers, linen tablecloths and napkins, silk flowers and dried rice and carrot seeds for throwing on the bride and groom. [3]

Sneakily, Ondine shifted the boxes and peeked around them, wondering which one was her present. It was the perfect place to hide a box of something, in amongst all these other boxes. Huh? None of them looked remotely like a name day present for Ondine.

Her mother walked in with her arms full.

Ondine said, "More boxes, Ma?" Maybe one of them had her present in it?

"Yes, dear. Give us a hand, will you love?"

"Um . . ." She wondered if her mother was pretending to forget the importance of the day, or if she had forgotten it for real. "Where's Margi, by the way?"

"Getting her nails done, she'll be back soon." Ma wiped her brow as she gave an inventory of where the rest of the family was. "Thomas is picking up his suit, Da is having a haircut and Chef is at the markets. I assume Belle is still asleep. And you, my dear, are helping me before you head off to school. Come on, there's more in the van."

"I didn't think anything was open this early?"

"It's December, dear," her mother said, as if that explained everything. [4]

The north wind took bites out of Ondine's neck as she walked outside. The glums gripped harder than the cold weather as she wondered whether her parents really had forgotten what day it was. True to Ma's words, the delivery van had many more folding chairs that needed to come inside the pub.

"Can't we stack them in the garden instead?" Ondine hefted a chair in each arm and walked back inside.

"No, Ondi, they'll get wet."

"Can I at least have some breakfast first before doing more? Hang on a minute, Where's Hamish? He's good at carrying things."

"Right here." Hamish walked into the room, which was becoming more crowded by the minute.

Ondine's heart soared and sweet harp music played inside her head.

Hamish beamed. "Happy name day, Ondi love." He held out a decorative bag.

"Aw, thank you!" Ondine threw her arms around his neck, whacking her knuckles against cardboard boxes in the process. "You remembered!" Thank goodness someone had! Ondine gave him a rather too saucy kiss, which made her feel warm all over.

Behind them, Ma cleared her throat.

Ondine unclasped herself from Hamish and checked out the bag's contents. She pulled out the first present and unwrapped the tissue paper.

"That's from all of us," Ma said.

Ondine looked to Hamish for verification. Surprise filled his face. Ondine rolled her eyes at her mother's attempt to be inclusive and ripped the tissue paper away. It was a book, *All For Love: The Life and Times of Elmaree, the First Grand Duchess of Brugel.*

"Oh wow, thank you so much."

"Ye like it?"

"Yes. Can't wait to read it."

Hamish beamed again. "There's something else in the bag too."

Ma cleared her throat again. "That's from all of us as well."

Ondine took hold of the small square box and showed it to her mother. "Nice try." Then she turned back to Hamish, unable to stop grinning. Light beamed from inside as she lifted the lid and saw the sweetheart ring within.

"Oh Hamish." She held the silver ring up to the light – what little light could get in considering the boxes covering half of the window – and gazed upon the tiny writing on the inside.

" '*Mo ghaol ort*'. What does that mean?"

Hamish's warm breath tickled her sensitive skin as he leaned in close and whispered, "It means, 'My love with you'."

Happy tears blurred Ondine's vision. "It's beautiful! How could you ever afford it?"

He grinned. "The tips have been very good."

"Yes, we have been rather busy," Ma interrupted the moment. "Give us a hand with wedding things. There's a van outside."

"Of course I'll help," Hamish said, giving Ondine a sweet kiss that warmed her all the way to her toes. "Get yerself some breakfast, I'll help yer Ma with the boxes."

"Thank you." Ondine gave him a quick hug and snuck in one more kiss, then headed to the kitchen.

The light was much better in here as she slipped the ring onto her third finger, left hand. It spun loosely, so she slipped it onto the index finger, where it felt snug. [5] A thrill shot through her, because it felt just right.

FOR THE FIRST time since Ondine could remember, they did not have a breakfast crowd to feed that morning. The hotel was closed now, just to get them through the next couple of days so they could prepare for – perhaps even enjoy – the wedding. Which would probably go on for a fair while as half the wedding guests were staying on at their hotel afterwards. Ondine stood in the kitchen in the unfamiliar silence, a silence broken by her loud tummy rumble. A hearty warm breakfast for herself and Hamish would be just the thing.

Knowing her family, they'd all want some, so she made double-double measures and set about creating a pan full of scrambled eggs. With bacon chunks and chives.

"Oh it's you. I thought it might be Chef," Marguerite said as she trotted into the kitchen, following the smells. She held her fingers out, trying hard not to touch anything so she didn't mess up her manicure. "That looks fantastic. I'm starving." With care not to scratch her nails, she picked up the tongs and piled food high on a plate, then added extra cheese, black olives, roquette leaves, sundried tomatoes and potato crisps over the top of her plate, before heaping another spoon full of eggs. [6]

"Jupiter's moons, are you all right?" Ondine asked.

"Yes!"

"You're going to eat all that?" There would be plenty for everyone, but not if Margi kept shovelling at her current rate.

Marguerite looked at her like she had two heads. "I wouldn't put it on my plate if I wasn't."

Hamish sauntered in and delivered a beaming smile. "Yer a wonderful lass, making all that. And on yer name day too."

"Oh! Happy name day Ondi." Marguerite gulped down a wobbly fork full of eggs. "I've got your present on order but it hasn't come in yet."

This time it was Hamish's turn to roll his eyes, making Ondine giggle. At least Hamish hadn't forgotten her special day. Butterflies took hold in her tummy as she looked at the ring on her finger. How was she going to concentrate at school when every time she looked at her hand – and she'd be looking at it a fair bit – she thought of Hamish?

A twinge of hope – or maybe it was desperation – lodged in her heart.

Maybe her family was teasing her and she'd get her presents at the end of the day.

Or had they completely forgotten about her in the lead up to Margi's wedding?

**4**

___________

A heavy schoolbag slung over her shoulders, Ondine bounced through the back door with a cheery, "Hello family!" and headed straight upstairs to make a dent in her homework. It wasn't that she loved homework, but heading upstairs to study would give her family time to organise the surprise.

There *would* be a surprise, wouldn't there?

Somebody was bound to come to her room and say there was a job for her in the kitchen. And she'd head down there and they'd surprise her when she walked in. At which point she would act surprised and touched that they'd gone to so much trouble.

Hamish came up with a plate of biscuits and lidded-mug of hot chocolate. "I'm not interrupting ye, just making sure yer all right."

How she loved to see him in his human form, not least because when he was himself, he could carry treats like these to her room. "Thank you," she said with a knowing smile. She was positive he was simply making sure she wasn't aware of what they were up to downstairs.

"I'm nearly done. I'll be down for dinner later."

"When yer finished, can I get ye tae look over something for me? I'm writing tae Duchess Anathea for a pardon. Or whatever it is I need tae ask her for tae get the goon squad off my back."

Worries niggled. This sounded real. Not some made up problem to get her to stay in her room. Ondine felt sure their country's newest Duchess would remember how Hamish had played an integral part in her rapid change in fortunes. Memories of the Harvest Ball at the Autumn Palace played in her mind. The Duke had been sick, poisoned by his own wife. Hamish had spoken up when it would have been far easier to stay quiet. And they'd discovered the former Duchess's secret bank account. Surely Anathea would reward his good deeds with some kind of special consideration?

"Absolutely," she said. "You know I'll do whatever I can to help." The admiration in his smile made Ondine feel lovely and warm inside. Until fresh doubt deflated her. "I just realised. I don't think Duchess Anathea ever knew you could be a ferret. We'll have a lot of explaining to do."

"Aye. That's par for the course for us." He kissed her sweetly on the lips and gave her the smile she loved so much.

"Hamish?" Fear shot through her system. She grabbed his hand as if it might be for the last time. "Promise me if the inspectors come back you'll get straight out of the dining room, right away?"

"Of course, hen." His trademark confident smile stayed in place, which only made her worry more.

"This is serious. If anything happened to you . . . well it doesn't bear thinking about."

"Och, dry yer eyes lass." He leaned forward and kissed her forehead. It was a little patronising and not at all the sort of kiss she expected from him. "Nothing's going to happen to us."

"Promise?"

"I promise. I'll stick to ye like a limpet to a ship's belly."

"Not such a great image there."

"Sorry sweetheart." He kissed her properly, making her tummy flip at the loveliness of it. When he broke away, his face showed fresh mischief. "Never was much of a one for words."

He placed the letter to the Duchess into Ondine's hands, kissed her again and left her to it.

The room felt colder without him. The sooner she finished her home-work, the sooner she could traipse downstairs and be with him again.

Working at whiplash speed, Ondine powered through her media studies chapter, plotted an essay for Brugelish literature and made ten pages of notes for legal studies. By the time she finished, she felt her brain might leak out her ear, but at least her homework was done for the night. Time for Hamish's letter to Anathea. She took a deep breath to cleanse her brain.

My Lord Duchess Anathea, *(Nice start.)* [1]

My name is Hamish McPhee and I am a resident of Venzelemma. Until recently I worked at the Bellreeve Palechia for the former Duke, and was present at the evening of the Harvest Ball. You may recall I came forward at a particularly stressful time for all concerned, and helped discover the former Duchess Kerala's transgressions. *(Skirting around the issue a bit. I'm sure I can make this more to the point).*

Recent law changes have resulted in demands being made to produce work papers. As I have none of this I am writing to you to ask for an exemption to this rule. You see, I have none identification at all and don't want to be deported also. *(It's getting messy. And the grammar's all over the place. Mercury's wings I'm sounding like my mother.)*

Chewing the end of her pen, Ondine jotted down the main points of Hamish's situation on a notepad; finding the right way to say , "you owe us a favour because we were there for you when it mattered". Much like plotting an essay – except she had to be very, very careful in the wording of the letter. If she failed, it wouldn't mean low marks, it would mean Hamish's deportation.

No way had they survived the trauma at the palechia to be split up again later.

Not.

Going.

To.

Happen.

Happy with the re-writes, she found a stamp and an envelope, addressed it to the Duchess and had it ready for Hamish to read over, sign, and pop in the post.

Her parents had closed the restaurant on Monday evening – for both first and second dinner. Cybelle and Henrik prepared a grand meal for the family to have in the dining room. Well, the extended family which now included Thomas's parents and Thomas, along with Ma, Da, Margi, Cybelle, Henrik, Hamish and Ondine.

It felt strangely quiet, being such a large room but having so many empty tables and chairs nearby. Ma piled more logs and coal into the open fire to keep them warm. By this time, Ondine was in full funk as it became patently obvious her parents had overlooked her name day. She was ready to blow her lid.

"I propose a toast," Da said. "To Margi and Thomas."

Steam could have poured out Ondine's ears.

"Margi and Thomas," everyone said. Everyone except Margi and Thomas, because you don't toast yourself.

Not feeling hungry – high dudgeon will do that to you – Ondine cleared her throat to let rip. "Thank you for my lovely *name day* dinner, Henrik." She pushed her chair back and dropped her napkin on her plate.

Henrik looked horrified. "Oh! I'm sorry! I didn't know. Belle, why didn't you say something?"

Cybelle came over all defensive. "I've been flat out like a banker in a hammock with bridesmaid duties. I haven't had a chance to think! Ma, why didn't you organise something?"

"What are you all looking at me for?" Ma said. "I've been doing more than the lot of you combined! Anyway . . . Ondine, you're still grounded . . . so it's hardly punishment if we throw a party for you while we're trying to teach you a lesson. And I'm terribly sorry that Mr and Mrs Berger should witness such poor behaviour."

Should Ondine do the dignified thing and pretend everything was fine? No way! "Hamish, thank you so much for remembering how important today is for me. The rest of you can all . . . you can all go to Slaegal!" Then she burst into tears and ran out.

"Ondi wait!" Hamish gave chase.

Tears poured down her face. It took four drags of her sleeve to dry her cheeks. Even then it only lasted a moment before more tears splashed down. Mercury's wings, her nose started running too.

Hamish caught up with her at the first floor landing. "Hen, stop." He rubbed her shoulders, then guided her into his chest and wrapped his arms around her, holding on tight.

"You've every right tae cry. They should have done more for yer name day."

Footsteps sounded on the stairs. "Come on Ondi, stop making a scene." Ma said, "We can have your name day in a few weeks when all this is over."

"You're just saying that because you're feeling guilty that you didn't do anything for me. You didn't even make a cake!"

Ma pulled up short. "Did you have a bad day at school and now you're taking it out on us?"

Petrol? Meet the lit match: "School has nothing to do with this! And you know what? *I've* got nothing to do with this! It's all Margi, Margi, Margi. I'm not even a bridesmaid!"

"Of course it's all about Margi, she's getting *married*! You can have a name day every year but you only have one marriage in your life." [2]

"They should have set a different date!"

"Now you're being stubborn. There's only one more Wednesday after this one until Christmas. You know they have to get married before the New Year or it's bad luck." [3]

Somewhere in her subconscious, Ondine knew about the end of year marriage rush. But still . . .

"She could have set it for November."

"Without you? We didn't know when you would be coming back from the palechia. Or even if you'd *be* back. Which is why you're grounded in the first place! Having a wedding without all the family present? Your Da was beside himself with worry though he did his best not to show it. At one point I pressed Margi to go ahead without you but she wouldn't hear of it. To see the way you're carrying on now . . . well it's breaking her heart."

Really? Off kilter emotions gave her a wobble. She wiped her face and took a step back from Hamish. "But, she barely even notices I'm back."

"She's a *bride*, Ondi, her head's spinning faster than a hamster wheel. Now look, I am sorry for how this has turned out. I will make it up to you, I promise." Ma held her arms out for a hug of reconciliation.

"All things considered, your ma's had a lot tae take in," Hamish said, giving Ondine a gentle nudge in her mother's direction. Well, he would say that. He needed to stay in her parents' good books because he relied on their grace and favour.

Ondine threw herself into Ma's hug. "I'm sorry."

"There, there." Ma wrapped her warm arms around her. "I'm sorry too. I think we're all a bit strung out with so much going on. Things will settle down soon I promise."

With a huge sniff, Ondine pulled away to see tears in Ma's eyes.

"Ye should be savin' yer tears fer the weddin'," Hamish said. "I'm bringing industrial-size hankies."

---

LATER THAT NIGHT, as Ondine chased sleep, a soft tapping sounded at the door. Thinking it might be Hamish, she jumped up and opened it. "Oh." How disappointing to see her father standing there.

"Don't look so pleased to see me," he said.

"Sorry Da."

"It's all right." Da glanced up and down the hallway to make sure nobody was looking. In his hands he held a cupcake on a bread plate. "Chef's been making double dozens. He won't notice one missing."

"Oh yum!"

"Shhhh!"

Ondine whispered, "Sorry!" then snaffled a bite. The cake was soft and perfectly moist. The frosting buttery-smooth, tasting of chocolate and something else she couldn't quite put her finger on.

"He swished a little plütz in the mix," Da said. Next, he pulled a small box out of his pocket. "Don't tell your mother, because you're still grounded and you're not supposed to be having parties or presents."

She put the cupcake on the plate and reached for the package. What a thoughtful father she had. "Thank you. I knew you couldn't have forgotten."

"This is just between us. The punishment was your mother's idea and . . . I went along with it because we have to put up a united front."

Tears sprang free as she opened the box and found a silver necklace with an oval locket. The kind you can open up and put photographs in. No prizes for guessing whose photo she would put in there. "Thank you, Da," she managed as her throat closed over with emotion.

"Now get some sleep. You're still grounded."

Looping the chain around her neck, Ondine leaned into Da for a hug. With his free hand (the other held the plate) he stroked her hair and said, "My little girl, you're growing up too fast."

"You'll be saying that when I'm twenty, won't you?" she said, giving him a kiss on the cheek.

"I still say it to Margi," Da said, and then he winked and snuck out the room.

The pendant warmed against her skin as she snuggled down into bed. All things considered, she felt happier than anyone grounded for life had a right to. Well, not grounded for life, but probably until the Christmas and New Year rush was over. Her mother had never actually put an end date to it all. She'd simply said, "You're grounded until a fish dances on the table," and there was no knowing when that would be.

The door squeaked open. Could it be Hamish this time?

The footsteps sounded shorter and heavier than Hamish's. When she looked up, she found her mother creeping in. Quick as a flash, she hid the cake plate under her pillow, just as her mother sat on the end of the bed. Thank goodness it was dark and she couldn't see the crumbs on her face.

"Ondi darling, can we talk?"

"Yeah, Ma," she said as she wiped her mouth.

"I am sorry about today," Ma began. "It was your father's idea and I didn't want to undermine him. I didn't forget your name day, but we had to follow through."

Despite her mother's serious tone, Ondine felt a giggle threaten to break free. She stuffed the bed sheet into her mouth to hold back the laughter. All she could do was nod and steady her breathing so she didn't give herself away.

"I brought you this," Ma held out a cupcake on a plate.

Tears spritzed from her eyes as she fought off laughter. "I'm so sorry," Ondine managed to say through the sheets stuffed in her mouth.

Ma misread the emotion and moved in for a hug. She stroked Ondine's back in lazy circles, making soothing noises. All the while Ondine's body shook in silent laughter, which her mother read as tears and only hugged her tighter.

The only way to break free from this giggle trap was to think of horrible thoughts. Things that put her in a bad mood.

*Stop laughing. Think of something horrible.* The way her parents had swiftly hugged her then proceeded to punish her within minutes of arriving home from the palace with Hamish.

That had been miserable.

Hamish stuck as a ferret. That always made her tummy swirl with worry.

Hamish being taken away from her. Where had that thought come from? She didn't know, but the more she thought of it, the clearer the image became. Faceless people in uniforms grabbing him and tearing him from her arms.

It felt *awful*. It felt so terribly *real*, as if she were finally developing some kind of magical skill. It also did the trick, because she stopped laughing and felt utterly despondent.

"Don't tell Da, this is just between us." Ma gave her the cupcake. "And you're still grounded."

Ondine nodded, all traces of happiness gone as that hideous image of people tearing Hamish away from her replayed in her head.

*I'm not going to let that happen*, she promised herself. *Never, ever, ever.*

**5**

———————

The morning of the wedding dawned crisp and cold. Each breath Ondine exhaled created plumes of steam. She put on two dressing gowns and her thickest socks and stepped over to the window. Opening the drapes, the fog was so thick she couldn't even see *On The Fang* across the street.

"Don't worry, it's a good sign," Cybelle said on her return from the bathroom. "Fog in the morning means it will be sunny later."

Cries of anguish carried up the staircase.

"That will be Margi, getting it out of her system," Cybelle said as she reached for the hair dryer.

Judging from the noises, Marguerite sounded borderline hysterical. Curiosity – and a need for breakfast – took Ondine downstairs toward the source.

"It doesn't fit!" Marguerite wailed. "You took the seams in too far!"

Definitely hysterical. Ondine had never seen this side of her eldest sister. The stress of the wedding must have got to her.

"Calm down, love. Take it off, I'll fix it right now," Ma said with a calm tone. Considering the circumstances, the early hour and the importance of the day, Ma sounded heroically calm. *Suspiciously* calm.

Ondine found Margi standing on a box, wearing a pale slip. On the floor next to her lay a mountain of rich blue satin and fake white fur. Ma was burrowed underneath all that fabric. Her muffled voice came through the layers. "Morning Ondi, make us some breakfast would you love? Bit busy with a needle and thread right now."

"This is a disaster!" Margi stifled a sob. "The dress doesn't fit!"

Considering how much food Margi had been putting away lately, Ondine wasn't surprised. The filter kicked in and she decided now wasn't the time to mention that fact. [1]

"Now, now, mustn't worry. It will be all right," Ma said.

Margi burst into fresh sobs. Ondine had heard brides could become stressed, but she'd never seen her sister like this.

"There, all fixed, try this now," Ma said as she crawled out from underneath the rustling fabric and slipped the dress over Margi's head.

*Wow, that was quick.*

"Wow, that was quick," Margi said out loud.

"Yes, it was rather," Ma said. "It's amazing what you can get done when you set your mind to it. Let's see, oh yes, you look stunning. Josef, come and look at your radiant daughter.

Margi looked beyond amazing. She must be using some kind of magic because Ondine had never seen her sister look so gorgeous.

"In a minute!" Josef called back from somewhere near the kitchen. "I need to set the hot rocks."

Ondine beamed with pride as she made her way to the kitchen and set about making breakfast. The hot rocks were Hamish's idea. He'd told her about the tradition of placing smooth stones of granite in the oven to warm them. When wrapped in a sturdy blanket, they would keep the bridal party warm as they stood at the foot of the elm tree on a cold winter's day. [2]

"Nothing for me!" Margi yelled out. "I'm too nervous to eat and knowing my luck I'd spill something on my dress."

Ondine could hear Ma's voice carry all the way to the kitchen. "We'll wrap a towel around you. You must have something. How about a boiled egg?" Then she yelled out a bit louder, enabling her to carry on two conversations in two rooms. "Ondi, put a few boiled eggs on for us, love!"

A 'few' became sixteen, because Ondine had a feeling it was going to be one of those days where everyone would need to keep their strength up. Shame she didn't take her own advice – Hamish walked in wearing his wedding usher suit and she turned wibbly at the knees. He'd become freshly handsome all over again. The cheeky rascal had been holding something in reserve all this time! The suit fitted him perfectly, creating a tapered waist and broad shoulders and . . . somehow making him taller.

"What do ye think, lass?"

Did any words come out? Ondine didn't have a clue; she just stood there next to the bubbling pot of eggs, grinning away. Steam billowed over her line of sight, making it seem as if Hamish were walking through mist.

"I take it ye approve, lass?"

"Very approve." What a man, and he was all hers! "That reminds me, have you posted the letter to Duchess Anathea yet?"

"Oh yeas, did it yesterday."

Good. Now she could begin the mental count-down for how long it would take for the Duchess to reply to their appeal for clemency regarding the paperwork for Hamish's identity. She didn't want to think about what would happen if Hamish were deported over such a trifling bit of bureaucracy. Ondine's thoughts drifted all over the place, from thinking herself the luckiest girl in the world because Hamish was here, to wondering where the sound of harps had come from.

Seriously, *harps*?

"We need to relax," Ma said, walking through the kitchen with a portable stereo. A symphony of strings strummed through the pub as Ma turned up the volume. "That should do it. Ondi, thanks for the eggs but you'd better get dressed. We need to stay on schedule."

"Oh!" The steaming pot beside her bubbled with enthusiasm. She grabbed a spoon and pulled the eggs from the water. More steam poured through her vision. A moment later, everyone descended on the kitchen and grabbed one.

Cybelle, wearing an enormous tea towel bib to protect her brides-maid's dress, ate her egg – shell and all!

"Urgh!" Ondine said, "What are you doing?"

"The shell's the best part," she said, giving Ondine one of those 'you're bonkers' looks she did so well.

"She knows it's not an apple, right?" Ondine looked to Henrik, hoping he'd talk sense into Cybelle. The chef only shrugged and followed Cybelle's example, biting into the egg without removing the shell.

Hamish stood there and made a circling 'cuckoo' motion with his finger to his temple.

Ma walked in, "Ondi, get dressed, the hairdresser will be here in ten minutes."

"Right." Ondine picked up her egg, still warm to the touch. Curiosity got the better of her and she took a bite through the shell.  Jupiter's moons but it was revolting! All sharp angles and chalky. "Ptah!" She spat the shell into the closest sink and had to rinse her mouth three times to remove the grit from between her teeth. In the doorway stood Cybelle and Henrik, doubled over with laughter.

They'd set her up! For a fraction of a second she felt stupid and angry, then Henrik made a grimace and scraped shell out from between his teeth.

For his part, Hamish looked from Cybelle and Henrik to Ondine, in open-mouthed shock. Cybelle and Henrik high-fived each other and ran off, laughing at their successful prank. The laughter spread to Marguerite – "You made her eat the *shell*?" – who stopped crying hysterically for a moment to join in the fun.

Sure, they'd cheered up the bride, but it was at Ondine's expense, which only added one more item to the growing list of things that irritated Ondine about her family.

---

AS THE MORNING ROLLED ON, everyone calmed down and got on with their roles for the day. Ondine changed into her usher outfit; a long blue satin skirt – she could wear two pairs of leggings underneath and nobody would see – white ankle boots, white cashmere cardigan and white faux-fur bolero jacket with a thick collar she could turn up if the wind turned on them. Judging from the immovable fog out the window, it didn't look like they'd get the slightest breeze.

The hairdresser arrived in a floor-length pleather jacket and made a bee-line for Ondine. [3] She primped and teased and pulled Ondine's dark wavy hair into intricate curls and twists, slotting blue satin flowers here and there. She wrapped a tablecloth around Ondine's jacket and started on the makeup, dusting her face with powder, then moved at lightning speed to do her eyes, and (ouch!) pluck a few stray brow hairs away.

Ondine checked herself in the mirror. Wow! The blended eye shadow really brought out the colour in her dark eyes, the mascara looked sweet without going over the top. The first hints of an ache tugged at her forehead from her hair being tied up too tightly. But the tightening effect on her face was incredible. When she smiled, the corners of her eyes barely made a crease. She looked so much older, almost regal. She couldn't wait to show herself off to Hamish.

The reaction she wanted came soon enough, as she took to the stairs and found him standing at the bottom. His eyes locked with hers and her tummy flipped over. A look of adoration crossed his face as he put his hand over his heart. If she didn't hang on to the banister, she'd miss a step and land with a splat. Hamish said nothing, imperceptibly shaking his head, mouth falling open before slowly transforming into a broad smile.

"Well?" She stood on the last step so they could be at eye level. "What do you think?" She liked this newfound feeling of power over him. He looked speechless, which sent flurries of wonder through her body.

"I . . ." Hamish started, but couldn't finish.

Henrik walked past. "Ondi, you don't look half bad when you make the effort!"

If she could, she would have rolled her eyes, but her forehead was stretched too tightly to move a muscle. Instead she looked to Hamish to see what he'd say.

With a scratchy voice he said, "I hope you have more lipstick."

"Pardon?"

" 'Cos I'll be kissing it *awff* all day." He closed the distance between them and kissed her with such tenderness she nearly came undone.

Warmth spread through her and lovely fuzzies tickled her skin. It may have been Margi's big day, but Ondine felt like the beaming bride. For the first time since she'd found out she wouldn't be a bridesmaid – Thomas's sister and Cybelle had those roles – Ondine felt grateful for her reduced status. It meant spending the day working with Hamish. Sneaking in more kisses when everyone's attention was focused on the bride and groom. Truly, what more could a girl want?

"I hope that's not an example of your work ethic?"

Reluctantly, Ondine pulled away from Hamish to find Thomas smiling at them. He looked dashing in his groom suit, complete with a blue satin flower in his lapel. Not as handsome as Hamish, though.

"Is my bride ready?" Thomas asked. "The photographer wants her."

"Just upstairs getting her hair done with Cybelle. She'll be down in a minute," Ondine said.

"Good. If we can all gather in the front bar, he's setting up some lights to take group shots."

Suddenly, crashing metal rang through the air. Car horns blared. Tyres skidded on the cold road outside. *Crash! Crash! Screech-Bang!*

"What the?" Ondine grabbed Hamish's hand and ran to the window to see a seven-car pile-up at the intersection.

"The world's gone whirlypits," Hamish said. "Would ye look at the lights, they're all on green."

"Oh dear. Should we go out and help?" Ondine asked as she surveyed the damage in the street. Crumpled cars, steam escaping from radiators, broken glass all over the road.

"Aye, let's call for an ambulance first."

"Already on it," Henrik called out from the kitchen. "You two grab aprons and head on out."

Aprons? Good idea; it would protect their wedding clothes.

As Ondine and Hamish stepped outside, they found loads of people standing around shouting at each other. They had various cuts and bruises on their faces, from biffing them against the steering wheel or the inside of the car doors. [4]

"We've called for an ambulance," she said to nobody in particular.

"And I've called for my lawyer," one of the drivers said, his face red from anger rather than injury.

"And I told you the light was green! You were the one going through a red light!" That came from an hysterical teenager on the other side.

"I have never driven through a red light in my life!" another woman said.

"We might stay back here a bit, lass." Hamish took her arm to keep Ondine on the footpath. "They're fair affronted."

Nobody looked too badly hurt, so Ondine tried not to feel too relieved when Ma called out they were needed inside.

Inside, Ma said, "Best we don't tell Margi about the crash, she'll stress about getting to the elm tree on time."

The radio blared out a traffic report. There were pile-ups all over Venzelemma! Desperate to hear more, Ondine turned up the volume. Worries twisted inside her as she thought about the strange coincidence of so many weird things going on.

Henrik switched the radio off just as Margi walked through.

"What?" Margi asked.

"Nothing!" they all said at once.

Nothing was going to ruin Margi's big day.

**6**
———

The photographs at the pub took up the next hour and a half.

The bride and groom exchanging gifts. *Click.*

The respective parents (Ondine thought Thomas's mother's hair looked a bit too *foomphy* but that's what mothers tended to do). *Click.*

The bridal party. *Click.*

Just the bridesmaids pretending to straighten Margi's skirts. *Click.*

Now the groomsmen handing Thomas his tie (he took it off so he could pretend to put it on again). *Click.*

Ondine and Hamish stayed back, nibbling their cold boiled eggs – without the shell this time – and sitting together patiently. Every now and then they were needed for the 'everyone' photo, but most of the time they could take it easy and enjoy one another's company. Ondine nestled against Hamish, reading the book he'd given her for her name day about Grand Duchess Elmaree.

*Elmaree*
*Born under a tree.*
*Sits on the throne*
*Where a boy should be.*

She was up to the third chapter and it was getting really good. "Did you know she was born at the bottom of an elm tree straight after Grand Duke Savo and Flora Venzelemma said their wedding vows? Oh wow, I've just realised who our city was named after. That's so sweet!"

Hamish gave her a smile and hugged her again. "An elm, huh? Is that why Bruglers get married at the tree?"

"Must be. I wonder if it's the same elm?"

They snacked on triangle sandwiches that didn't drip (roast beef or cheese with no condiments) then the horse-drawn carriages arrived to take them to the botanical gardens. Henrik had been monitoring the news and thankfully the traffic snarls had cleared.

Ondine travelled with Hamish, Henrik and Cybelle in the first carriage, which was excellent because Henrik carried a vast picnic basket full of nibbly food and flasks of hot chocolate. They put the hot rocks at their feet and had extra blankets over their knees.

<hr>

As MUCH AS Ondine enjoyed sneaking kisses with Hamish in the gardens, they did have a job to do, so she peeled herself away from him and welcomed guests as they arrived.

"Hamish look, Mrs. Howser plus one is on the list."

"So she is."

"How did she score an invite?" Ondine asked. It wouldn't be Auntie Col inviting her; they had been friends many decades ago, but lately they were barely on speaking terms.

A thoughtful look filled Hamish's face. "It's only fair she should come. If ye invite someone to an engagement party, ye should invite them to the wedding as weil."

True, Mrs. Howser had been at Margi and Thomas's engagement party back in summer, but only because her parents had made a contra deal with the witchy Psychic Summercamp principal to make up for their outstanding fees.

Seeing the old witch's name on the list made Ondine uneasy, and she had a hard time explaining exactly why. "I didn't think she was that interested in my sister," she said. "She didn't stay long at the party."

"Aye, she disappeared pretty fast that night. Mebbe she won't turn up today?"

"Ah Hamish, you don't understand. Weddings are old-lady-magnets. She'll be here. I wonder who she'll bring as her plus one?"

They greeted more guests and took them to their seats. Soon enough, Mrs. Howser did appear, with an imperious look on her grey, wrinkled face. She was dressed in formal travelling witch attire: A heavy brown cloak, sturdy boots and multi-pocketed skirt. On her head she wore not the clichéd pointed black hat but a far more sensible deep brown fur-lined hat with earflaps.

And her plus one was –

"Melody! How are you?" Ondine beamed as she embraced her friend, who wore clothing that matched Mrs Howser.

But oh dear, there was so much less of Melody than Ondine remembered from their days together at Psychic Summercamp. Mrs. Howser must not be feeding her. Guilt pricked her conscience at their lack of contact in nearly six months. They last time they'd seen each other was just after Duke Pavla visited the pub and offered Hamish and Old Col a job.

"I'm good," Melody said, her cheeks pink and bright in the winter chill. Then she added in a whisper, "my stars, Ondi, Hamish is even more gorgeous now."

"Oh . . . you!" Heated embarrassment rushed up her neck as she stepped out of the embrace. "It's good to see you. Come on, I'll show you to your seats."

"So . . ." Melody leaned in closer to Ondine's ears. "What's going on with you two? Are you planning a walk to the elm yourselves?"

Behind them, she heard Hamish chatting to Mrs. Howser. Ondine figured if she could hear Hamish, he must be able to hear them. She chose her words with care. "I'm the happiest girl in the world, Melody, but this is Margi's special day and that's all I can think about. Look, here's your seat."

When Ondine turned around, she got the strangest look from Mrs.

Howser. Almost as if she were trying to smile and trying not to smile all at the same time. Ondine's belly did a strange twisty thing. Thankfully, none of this interior concern could express itself on her face, because of all the pins in her hair pulling her skin so tightly.

Just as Cybelle predicted, the fog dissolved to reveal a sunny day. Not exactly balmy, but the wind held off. Clouds of steam rose as their guests sipped hot drinks to stay warm.

The gardens looked beautiful, with garlands of blue satin flowers on the chairs. The wedding elm took centre stage, its huge bare branches fanning out above them. It was such a shame it couldn't have been a summer wedding, when the tree would be covered in lush green leaves. Or even autumn, when the changing leaves would fall gently around them like confetti.

*Ahhh, but if it had been an autumn wedding, Hamish and I would have missed it.*

Great-Aunt Col turned up with a beaming smile and formal witchy attire, similar to Mrs Howser's, complete with the heavy travelling cloak and boots. Altogether a sensible option for a snowy outdoor wedding. "Ondine my love, you're glowing," she said, giving her a kiss on each cheek. "Hamish you're far too handsome for your own good." She kissed him on each cheek as well.

This had to be a good sign, because Ondine couldn't help remembering that it was her great-aunt who, in a fit of pique, had turned Hamish the handsome lad into a ferret in the first place.

"This way Auntie Col." Ondine led her towards her seat in the front row.

"Aw nae," Hamish said as he turned away.

"Wha –" The words died on Ondine's lips as she saw three people in suits step out of a van. They looked exactly like the ones who had raided their restaurant the other night, and had then rounded up all the staff at *Fangs*.

Just as the thought, *They can't seriously raid a wedding for illegal immi-grants, can they?* passed from one side of Ondine's brain to the other, the man who had become so impossibly handsome from the mere act of suiting up, dropped to the ground.

"*Boak.*" [1] With a grimace of pain he vanished into a pile of clothes on the snow.

The snow on the ground wasn't nearly as cold as the ice roaring through Ondine's veins as she looked on her hapless boyfriend who'd had to ferret-ise himself to avoid deportation.

With a soft nudge of her foot, she scooted him and his clothes under the nearest row of seats and tried to act as if nothing was going on. Inside, she wanted to cry. Would life with Hamish ever be normal?

Oh, why had he only *posted* the letter? They should have delivered it to Duchess Anathea personally, then they could have had an answer straight away. Mentally Ondine counted the days until she could expect a response. Two days for it to be delivered, possibly another few days before she looked at it. Then a few more days and . . . oh it was so frustrating.

The string quartet started playing. The celebrant, a woman wearing a high-collared, navy blue woollen cloak to ward off the cold, walked to the base of the elm. She had a calm but happy expression, as if she were excited for the couple about to marry, but perfectly in control of her emotions and nerves.

The three men in suits walked towards their party. Fear pumped Ondine's pulse as they came closer. They weren't going to stop the ceremony, were they? Mercury's Wings, they *were*!

With a quick dash, Ondine intercepted them. "Can I help you?" Her panting breath made great gusts of steam as she spoke.

"We need to check the credentials of the bride and groom."

"Oh them!" Relief crashed over Ondine. "They're up the back, this way."

"What's going on?" Ma said as she and Great-Aunt Col came over.

The suited man held out his identification badge. "We need to check that the bride and groom are Brugelish nationals."

The quartet slowed down, so Ma turned and made some hand gestures at them to keep playing. Then she turned back to face the interlopers. "Why are you targeting us?" Ma put her hands on her hips.

He said, "Far too many marriages at this time of year: people desperate to become citizens and duck the paper, that sort of thing." [2]

"Come with me then," Ma said to the officials, then she looked at Ondine and said, "back to your post, you have a job to do."

"Yes Ma," Ondine said, doing her best to look chastened in front of the suit-squad, while dancing with relief on the inside. Thomas and Margi would be fine.

Back at her post, more worries added to the party of woe in Ondine's heart. Hamish was nowhere to be seen. His clothes lay in a pile on the snow where she'd kicked them, so she picked them up, shook them out to keep them dry, then shoved them under her faux-fur jacket. Wherever Hamish would be as Shambles, he'd at least have a real fur jacket.

She looked about for that familiar dark streak of fur. How hard could it be to find him in the snow?

"Over here, hen."

Following his voice, she saw Shambles the ferret, poking his furry face out from under the snow-laden branch of a weeping Slaegalpine. [3]

Quick as she could, but also not too quick in case people saw her running and wondered what the fuss might be about, Ondine made her way over.

"Throw me thae clothes will ye, I'm freezen mah tights off."

Using her body as a shield, Ondine faced the wedding crowd and made sure nobody was paying her any attention. No, they were all watching the immigration inspectors and seeing them off.

Phew, that was too close for comfort. And also, the need for Hamish to become a ferret at the slightest provocation was starting to do her head in.

She slipped Hamish's thermal underclothes through the branches. Behind her, she heard him wincing. "Och, these pine needles are sharp."

"Are you all right?" Ondine jammed his trousers and shirt through the branches again and tried not to spill too much snow on her sleeve, otherwise she'd end up with soaking wet arms.

"Didye bring me shoes and socks?"

"Sorry, forgot. They're right under a chair. I'll grab them."

Every nerve screamed to run back and get his shoes, but again that would draw people's attention so she had to walk and act normally, retrieve his shoes and socks as if it was all part of her usher duties, and get back to the tree before Hamish's feet snapped off in the cold.

The immigration team were over at the gazebo, where the next wedding party waited their turn for the wedding elm.

"They've moved on to the next group now," Ondine said as she slipped the shoes (with the socks rolled into them) through the branches. "Talk about ruin your big day."

In a fresh shower of snow, Hamish pushed the branches aside and made his way out. "Ouch, got a splinter," he said.

"Let me look at it."

"No hen, let's get back to the weddin'."

Back in position and with the inspectors busy with some other unfortunate bride and groom, Hamish slipped his arm around Ondine for some shared warmth as their ceremony began.

The celebrant stood front and centre, a smile fixed in place. Her voice created steam as she spoke. "Welcome everyone on this magical day to the marriage of Marguerite and Thomas."

As is the Brugel custom, the parents walked in from the left and the right, meeting in the middle. The symbolic joining of families. They exchanged small gifts and kissed each other on the cheeks, then separated and took their seats.

Then it was time for the groomsmen and bridesmaids to do the same, exchanging gifts and kisses. The celebrant smiled again and looked out to the crowd. There was a touch of pantomime involved as she raised her hand to her forehead as if gazing into the sun. "Do we have the bride and groom?"

"We are here," Thomas and Margi said together, half laughing.

Everyone stood to attention and turned to see them.

"Then come forth!" the celebrant said, beckoning them with an exaggerated hand gesture.

The quartet played a stirring wedding march. Thomas and Margi walked together, arm in arm to stand before the celebrant.

Hamish stood beside Ondine and placed a comforting palm in the middle of her back. Warmth spread through her.

As Margi and Thomas reached the base of the elm, a flock of birds twittered in the air above them and landed on the branches. Then, to Ondine's amazement, the tree's bare and skeletal branches burst into bud. The crowd gasped in surprise and awe as branch after branch, going higher and higher, became covered in pink and white buds. Those buds then unfurled into flower.

Everybody applauded, scaring the birds off temporarily, but as they stopped clapping the birds returned to the branches and chirped happily.

"That's a nice touch so it is." Hamish kissed Ondine on the top of her head.

"It's amazing!" Ondine wiped away a tear. "How nice of Old Col to do that."

"Ye think it was her?"

"She's the nicest witch here," she said.

The crowd broke into more applause as doves descended onto the branches and began to coo. Ondine rested her head against Hamish's shoulder and felt completely at peace with the world.

Old Col turned and looked at Ondine and Hamish, a puzzled expression on her face. It didn't look like the kind of face that had just made some crowd-pleasing magic. Then her eyes grew large and her mouth dropped open, as if she'd worked something out. Before Ondine could work out what it was Old Col had worked out, her great-aunt quickly shut her mouth and turned back to face the elm.

Hamish said, "Aye, nice to see Auntie Col using magic for good instead of spite."

The tree in full bloom completely changed the snowy scenery. Soon, some of the small pink and white petals dropped from the tree and fluttered down onto the crowd below like confetti.

The ceremony got underway. There were some loving words, they swapped rings, exchanged vows and held hands. Ondine and Hamish were so far down the back they didn't hear much, but they saw Thomas wipe his eye and Margi smile at him so sweetly it set everyone off in floods of happy tears. As one, the women clutched at handkerchiefs and dabbed their eyes. The men cleared their throats and coughed. The celebrant declared them joined forever. Margi and Thomas kissed and the string quartet started up. As ushers, Ondine and Hamish would need to move everyone on fairly soon. Being December, and being the wedding elm gardens, there were more brides and grooms with families and friends waiting nearby for their turn. So long as the immigration inspectors let them through.

Being so busy with her duties, Ondine barely registered Old Col approaching them.

"Making the tree burst into leaf is a charming touch," Col said.

Strings figuratively snapped in Ondine's head and she became even more confused than usual. "You didn't make the elm bloom?"

Old Col shook her head. "No."

Ondine felt sure Col's magic had made the tree bud. Was it Mrs. Howser? It seemed too nice a gesture to be from her. Perhaps Margi had extra talents she hadn't told anyone about? "If you didn't do it, Col, who did?"

Her great-aunt folded her arms across her chest and gave Ondine a searching look. "I would have thought that was obvious. You did!"

7

"Me?" Ondine drew in a staggered breath from the shock of it all. "But I don't have magic!"

They still had to move everybody on – issuing thank-you cards with a map on the reverse side directing them to the family pub, *The Duke and Ferret*, for the reception dinner. A van pulled up and a small team of workers appeared, collecting all the folding chairs and gathering up the decorations. They were so efficient they virtually swiped the chairs while people were still sitting on them.

"It has to be you, Ondi, who else could it be?" Old Col sounded annoyed.

"But I didn't do it."

"Aye, go easy," Hamish chimed in to defend her.

"Of course," Old Col took a breath. "I'm sorry if I sound cross. I'm so cold I'm trying to stop my teeth from chattering. But Ondi, I'm serious. Whether you realise it or not, this is your doing. Yours and Hamish's."

In mute shock, Ondine and Hamish looked at each other.

Col kept on. "Why is this a surprise? Surely you've noticed all the strange things going on? It started when we arrived in Bellreeve a few months ago. I thought it was the palace, but then the weirdness followed us back to Venzelemma. More to the point, it followed *you* back to Venzelemma."

"I'm nawt magic," Hamish protested.

"You can change into a ferret at will," Col said.

"Aye, but that was yer doing, nae mine."

Cogs turned in Ondine's head and a few twigs began to snap. A strange feeling grew in her tummy at the thought she might be capable of magic. It would be nice to be able to do some things, but what if she got cross and turned someone into a toad in a moment of anger and couldn't turn them back?

Then again, if she had magic, might that make life easier? A sprout of confusion and hope unfurled. Maybe magic could help Hamish get a work card? Questions swirled like snow flurries. If Col was right and she did have magic, why didn't she know it? Why didn't she *feel* it? Aside from feeling wonderful whenever she and Hamish were together, which was a kind of magic all of its own.

But on the serious side, if she did have magic, how was she supposed to use it to her advantage if she didn't even know when she was using it?

The last guest departed. The hired help did a lightning-fast job of clearing away any signs of Margi and Thomas's ceremony, so that the next group could set up.

Col took Ondine by the arm. "We'll talk about it on the way back. Our ride awaits."

Henrik held the carriage door open for Cybelle and helped her in, then he stepped in after her and they sat together, holding hands. Hamish followed and held his hand out for Ondine. She was so busy smiling at his gallantry she didn't register Old Col jumping in ahead of her.

Col winked at Hamish and said, "What lovely manners you have."

If her forehead weren't pulled back so tightly, Ondine would have frowned at her great-aunt's pushiness. Col sat herself in the middle of the bench seat, so Ondi and Hamish had to sit either side of her.

The hot rocks they had earlier placed in the carriage to keep them warm had gone cold but the flask still held hot chocolate, so that was a plus. Cybelle carefully poured steaming half-full cups to avoid sloshing it over their pristine clothes.

Ondine turned her collar up against the cold as the driver clicked his tongue and the horse clip-clopped down the cobblestone street.

Being a Wednesday, Ondine could see people bringing their drying clothes in from their window lines, in time for laundry curfew. [1]

Old Col made an exaggerated 'aaaaah' sound as she sipped her drink. "So, Henrik and Cybelle, have you noticed anything strange or out of the ordinary since Ondine and Hamish returned from their adventures with the Duke?"

"We're booked out every night," Cybelle said. "Not that there's anything wrong with that, but we've never been so busy. Christmas is going to be a nightmare."

"And they're eating more," Henrik said.

Ondine had noticed that too. "Everyone eats more in winter. Don't they?"

With a raised eyebrow Cybelle said, "Licking the plates clean?"

Baffled looks passed between everyone. Uneasiness spread through Ondine.

Col pursed her lips in thought, then said, "Let's talk about the bison on the sofa shall we?" [2]

All eyes fell on Ondine. "What have I done?"

"The elm, my dear. You made that happen," Col said. "Believe me, I'd take the credit for it if I'd thought of it, but all praise to you. It was a lovely touch."

Rolling her eyes – ouch, darned pins pulling her skin so tightly – Ondine tried to control her frustration. "But it wasn't me! Maybe some of Margi's friends are witches – or maybe someone from Thomas's family?"

Col shook her head. "I was sitting close to the Bergers; the magic didn't radiate from them. It came from behind me. The moment the ceremony concluded and everyone moved forward to congratulate the bride and groom, I started walking towards the origin of the magic. I was looking for a witch. Instead, I found you. I might also add Birgit Howser looked around as well, wondering who'd done it."

Hearing Mrs Howser's name made things move uneasily in Ondine's stomach. She also wished Col wasn't sitting between her and Hamish, because she could really use more of his support right now. "I was only looking at the elm and thinking about how much nicer it would be if they'd had a summer or an autumn wedding, but that's because I was cold. Everyone's cold! I'm sure everyone was thinking the same thing.

"In fact, if it *was* me doing the magic, why didn't I feel anything? And while we're at it, why can't I make this small carriage warm up a few degrees?"

At which point Col stood up and squished herself beside Cybelle. The movement left Ondine sitting alone with cold air swirling around. Hamish scooted over and wrapped his arm over her shoulder. She closed her eyes into the embrace and felt instantly warmer.

"Nice one!" Henrik said.

Ondine's eyes flashed open to see Henrik, Cybelle and Old Col buried under an enormous fleecy blanket. Henrik tucked it neatly around them and he and Cybelle cuddled closer. First eggshells, now blankets. Henrik and Cybelle were excellent pranksters. "Stop winding me up!" Ondine said. Honestly, it was as if Henrik and Cybelle had nothing better to do than tease her! "I can't believe you'd get Col involved in one of your jokes."

"Ondi love, I dinnae think it was them," Hamish said, swallowing so hard his Adam's apple bobbed up and down.

"Oh not you too?" Ondine couldn't bear the thought of Hamish being on Cybelle's side.

"Nay lassie. I think they're being serious this time."

"But I didn't wish for a blanket," she said. Hamish's warm body was no match against the cold fear nibbling inside her.

"I sure did," Cybelle said.

A look of remorse crossed Henrik's face. "I'm sorry for the joke this morning with the eggs. Because now you don't want to believe us."

Cybelle snickered behind her hand and turned to Henrik. "It was good though."

"The best." They bumped their fists together.

Why didn't Ondine and Hamish have a blanket as well then? What's the point of having magic if you can't make your own life more comfortable? A heavy feeling of dread grew in the area of Ondine's liver, then moved at a leisurely pace to her lower intestine. Ondine wished to heavens the feeling would go away, but it showed no intention of leaving any time soon. If anything, the hideous feeling invited its nasty friends over. A veritable party of sickness rocked and rolled inside her.

At least she had Hamish looking after her. He cuddled her into his body, sharing his warmth. "If I really do have magic, then why am I so cold?"

It was Cybelle's turn to roll her eyes. "You need to use it properly. Didn't you pick up anything useful at Summercamp? Apart from Hamish, that is."

A miserable, "why now?" startled Ondine with its whininess.

"Aye, I was wondering that meself. Why now, Col? Ye didnae raise this at Bellreeve and we were there fer weeks."

A look of resignation came over Col's greying face. "Because of the weird magic. Because of every light turning green and causing the worst traffic snarls we've ever seen. Because of what happened today at the elm. Because of what it signifies. I thought – mistakenly as it turns out – that things were strange at the palace because Bellreeve is an incredibly strange place and so many weird things have happened there over the years. But lately, every time something unexplained happens, you're there, Ondi."

Ondine swallowed her nausea. "You were there too! You were at the palace. The minute you crossed the threshold into the palace grounds, there was a tornado. It rained fish! And then today, you were standing by the elm tree with everyone else. Surely it's your magic, not mine?"

Col's words sounded so patronising. "My dear, when I use magic, I absolutely feel it. Today at the elm, I felt nothing."

"Well . . ." Ondine mentally scratched for answers. "You're old! Maybe you forgot what it feels like?"

Indignation radiated from Great-Aunt Col as she sat up straighter. "I will forgive you your outburst because of the stress of the situation."

"*Whoa Geta!*" So absorbed in their bizarre conversation, Ondine hadn't noticed they'd reached the pub and the horse's clip clopping came to a stop. A shingle proclaiming *The Duke & Ferret* hung proudly from the building's corner. They'd renamed the pub partly in honour of the Duke of Brugel.

"If I have magic, why couldn't I save The Duke?" Ondine turned to look at Old Col, the woman who seemed to know everything but never gave Ondine a proper answer to anything.

"But you *did*, dear girl. We were witness to what took place at the palace. You and Hamish saved the Duke from his crazy wife Kerala. A woman who is now safely removed from society and her children, by the way."

Normally Ondine loved it when Hamish held her hand, but as he helped her out of the carriage, insecurity wriggled into her brain. "Is Duke Pavla getting better?" On one hand, yes, they'd saved him from eating more toxic pastries, but by the time she and Hamish had worked it all out, Pavla had become so sick he didn't seem capable of recovering.

"He is . . . stable." Col had that look about her, as if she knew more than she was letting on. "We may have to get used to having Duchess Anathea at the helm for a while. At least until Lord Vincent comes of age."

The mention of Duke Pavla's son made things burn in Ondine's chest. Her mind raced back to all the mean things he'd done to her, and her family, over the last two seasons.

Honestly, today was supposed to be a day of celebration and love. Couldn't her great-aunt save all this for another time?

"Oooh, listen to them talk politics," Cybelle said.

"It's no laughing matter," Col snapped.

Henrik wrapped the blanket around Cybelle's shoulders. "Let's go inside. I'm looking forward to enjoying a meal I haven't had to cook myself."

The moment they were out of earshot Col looked to Ondine, pain evident on her face. "When I said stable, I meant to say he's not getting any better. Nor is there much chance of it. But I didn't want to be the bearer of bad news, not on such a happy day as your sister's wedding."

"Oh," Ondine said, failing to think of something wise and sympathetic to say.

"Ye cannae blame yerself Ondi, ye did the best ye could."

Col guided them in. "Come on child, let's enjoy the party."

That at least was something to look forward to. Ondine's parents, in a rare display of splashing out, had hired caterers for the day so that everyone would be able to relax.

Everyone except Ondine, who couldn't switch her brain off.

Old Col declared, "I want the two of you to stay together. For at least an hour."

"Aw that's a terrible hardship." Hamish gave Ondine a smile and a wink.

Usually when he did that she felt safe and warm and loved. But now she felt wibbly inside.

Meanwhile, the rest of her family and Thomas's were over by the windows having more photographs taken. Actually, Margi and Thomas were having more photographs. Cybelle and Henrik were chatting with Thomas's sister and their parents, who were sitting at a nearby table helping themselves to cups of tea and finger sandwiches. [3]

The tables were set out in a horseshoe shape, with several tables joined together along the top of the room for the bridal party and family. People hovered about the tables, looking for their decorative name cards to find where they should be sitting.

Col continued with her instructions to Ondine. "Remain close at hand. In fact, hold hands if you're able." Then she went off on a bit of a tangent. "Is it dark in here or am I having trouble adjusting to the light?"

There were candles on the tables, to provide a romantic mood, but they didn't provide much in the way of light.

"Now that you mention it, it is a little dark," Ma said.

Ignoring their concerns about lighting, Hamish clasped Ondine's hands in his and pressed them to his chest. His heart beat a steady rhythm under her palms. His easy smile and charm broke through the shroud of worry. Sunshine filled her soul.

"Beautiful light," the photographer said as he took more shots of Margi and Thomas.

Ondine, Hamish and Old Col turned to see a shaft of golden sunlight pierce the windows, creating a stunning, ethereal backlight to the bride and groom.

It looked magical.

Col crowed in triumph, "Now do you believe me?"

Ondine wanted to believe the sunshine was coincidence. But the multiple signs of weirdness were getting hard to ignore.

"Aye but it's lovely wee magic." Hamish kissed Ondine's forehead, the tip of her nose, and then her lips. Her palms, still pressed to Hamish's chest, could feel his pulse quickening.

"More than a little magic," Col said. "Take a look."

They stopped kissing and gazed around the room. "I cannae believe it." Hamish had trouble closing his jaw.

Roses and ivy grew all over the walls and ceiling beams. Vases overflowing with blooms appeared near the doorway. A look of wonder spread over Margi's face as she watched each new arrangement burst forth out of thin air.

"Thank you Auntie Col!" she said in a high-pitched squeal of bridal euphoria.

As one, everyone turned to Col, their eyes wide with stunned appreciation.

"Oh, don't thank me Margi – thank your little sister."

Margi charged forward and embraced Ondine, kissing her repeatedly on the cheeks. "It's just like I dreamed it! Ma said we didn't have the budget because we spent it on catering. Thank you so much!" Fresh kisses of gratitude rained down on each cheek, depositing lip-gloss over her skin. Then Margi let her go and charged back to Thomas to smother him in kisses.

Ondine stood there, feeling as if she were about to topple over.

"Have you worked it out yet?" Col asked her with a look somewhere between 'smug' and 'conspiratorial' on the spectrum.

Ondine asked, "Are we . . . making *other people's* wishes come true?"

"You bet you are!" Margi said, taking a napkin and wiping Ondine's face, but then she kissed her again and smudged her afresh. "Better get back to my husband. Squee! Husband!"

Margi ran back to Thomas's waiting arms. The photographer seized the opportunity and took rapid-fire shots to capture the action.

"Aye lass, making other people's wishes come true is a beautiful gift."

Hamish gave her a hug and moved to kiss her cheek. "And just so ye know, ye've made my all wishes come true too."

Warm things blossomed in Ondine as she and Hamish snuck in one more kiss, not caring if anyone was looking.

The caterers arrived with fresh trays of food and made their way through to the kitchen.

"No looking!" Cybelle's voice carried across the room as she held Henrik back from following them.

"Professional curiosity," he said.

"Come on, we're not working today," Cybelle said. "Ondi, can you fill his boots with lead so he can't sneak off?"

"I'm not a performing seal," Ondine said.

"I just want a peek." Henrik inched closer to the kitchen.

Cybelle hauled him back. "You are having the day off and you are going to like it."

Ma put down her teacup and walked over to Ondine, a broad smile on her face. "I knew it would only be a matter of time before your gifts manifested. I'm so proud of you, darling." Another set of kisses rained over her face. Surely there was no room left on her cheeks for any more lipstick?

"Ma stop, please. It's hurting my head. Aunt Col, you said before that you can feel when you're doing magic. Well . . . if you're saying all this other stuff –" she waved her hand around the room filled with more bouquets than a florist shop, "– is because of me . . . then why can't *I* feel it?"

Ma's palms were up in one of those 'calm down' gestures. "We'll work that out later. It's Margi's big day –"

"And mine!" Thomas yelled out.

Ma raised her voice, "– And Thomas's. Thank you, my newly-minted son-in-law!" Then she turned to her aunt. "Please, Auntie Col, I know you've always had a soft spot for Ondine. But let's have this day for Margi and Thomas."

Which was fine by Ondine, because she didn't want to be the centre of attention if it meant people expected her to do magic she had no real control over. It didn't sit right and she wasn't sure why. The thought of having magic had always appealed – it's why she'd gone to Psychic Summercamp in the first place. Unfortunately, her experiences there had shown her she didn't have an atom of magic in her. But now she had the gift to make other people's wishes come true. That had to be a good thing, right?

On a purely selfish level, she'd rather make her *own* wishes come true. Then, as Hamish wrapped a gentle arm around her shoulders and made her feel protected and loved, she realised she already had everything she'd wished for.

So maybe it was magic?

At which point Melody walked in and made a bee-line for the food, while Mrs. Howser walked in and made a bee-line for Ondine.

The woman pulled away her fur-lined hat, revealing masses of grey curls, skin like a wrinkled bed sheet and a glare that could cut an apple at thirty paces.

"My dear student, forgive the pun, but you're blossoming." Mrs. Howser said with a beaming smile. A smile that didn't sit right on her face somehow. As if it had been such a long time since she'd had a genuine smile, her muscles were out of practice. "And Hamish, how good to see you again," she said, the smile losing its way but refusing to ask for directions as she looked him up and down.

"Aye."

"Come now, let's not be so formal with each other" She flashed a set of pearly whites and kissed Hamish on one cheek, then the other. "My, but you're more handsome than I remember."

Did she have to squeeze his cheek?

Old Col cleared her throat with far too much gusto. "Something you wanted, Birgit?"

The last time Ondine had seen these two together, they were none too friendly. Were they about to trade insults? At a wedding?

"I think," Mrs. Howser linked her arm into Ondine's and steered her away from Old Col, "you could do with some proper instruction. You have incredible talent my dear – talent that can't be wasted here. You simply must come to CovenCon."

" – Ah –"

"No prevaricating. You are coming, and that's it. A talent like yours, my dear – oh the things you could do . . . As you well remember, Melody was on the verge of failing astral projection, but with my excellent tutelage, look at her now – she's flourishing. Oh Melody dear? A moment please?"

Any moment now Ondine's knees would turn to dough and she'd fall down from the shock. There was something very wrong about Mrs Howser being so interested in her, especially coming so soon after Old Col's bombshell about making other people's wishes come true.

At the buffet table, Melody stopped piling finger sandwiches on her plate and turned to them. Her cheeks were stuffed with food like a chipmunk preparing for winter.

Flourishing? The girl was reed thin.

Old Col took Ondine by the other elbow to steer her away. "All is well in hand here, Birgit. Ondine is under my tutelage." The words may have been sweet as syrup, but Old Col's lips were pressed into a determined line.

"Oh you sweet old thing," Mrs. Howser said, showing those shiny teeth of hers. "Of course you want to help, but Ondine here needs the very *best* instruction, and . . . no offence, but with all the goodwill in the world, she's hardly likely to get it here, is she?" [4]

"You always had a way with words." Old Col's attitude dripped with sarcasm.

Worries wormed their way through Ondine as the atmosphere turned so frosty their words were snapping as they came out.

"Don't let personal jealousies intrude, my dear," Mrs. Howser said. "You've had years to guide Ondine. It's time to let a professional take over from here."

"And you had decades with Hamish, and achieved exactly what?" Old Col shot back.

They still held Ondine by one elbow each and their grips increased as they tried ever so hard to remain polite.

"Come now, Colette, we're not still fighting over Hamish are we? That pot's boiled dry." [5]

They weren't fighting over Hamish, they were fighting over Ondine. She'd have bruises tomorrow to show for it.

Mrs. Howser's nails dug in as she spoke. The words were silk and kindness, the tone crafted from steel. "I think we can both agree Ondine here has tremendous potential. You would not deny her a place at CovenCon merely from spite, would you? Surely even you are not that cruel?"

"Of course I wouldn't deny her that."

Hamish interrupted with a tray of canapés. "Oh quick, ye need tae hold this, I'm gointae sneeze." His face contorted into the most bizarre shape.

Mrs. Howser let go of Ondine and grabbed the tray. He made the loudest, fakest sneeze Ondine had ever witnessed, but she loved him all the more for breaking the witchy standoff.

***

As wedding receptions go, Margi and Thomas's was a good one. The food and plütz flowed and everyone kept their speeches mercifully short. Da's was even funny, making Ondine wonder if she might be exerting even more magic than she imagined. When the string quartet played, they cheered as Margi and Thomas performed a Bruglish three-step. [6] Guests paired up and joined them on the floor. Hamish reached for Ondine's hand and asked, "May I have this dance?"

"Forsooth, My Lord." Ondine giggled as she made a curtsey to him.

"Eh?"

"Sorry, can't help it. It's the book you gave me; they're so formal and say, 'forsooth!' all the time and 'My Lord' and 'My Lady'. It's so cute."

"Ye know," he twirled her into his body as they moved among the guests, "I just remembered. I'm a lord."

Laughter bubbled in her heart, but Ondine played along and pretended she didn't know. "Oh *really*?"

"Aye, back in Scotland we say *laird*, but it's the same thing."

Batting her eyelashes for maximum effect, she asked, "And do you have a castle, my laird?"

He chuckled. "It's probably an old pile of stones by now. I havenae been back tae check."

"Then we must go one day."

"Aye. But ye wouldnae want tae go this time of year. Ye think it's cold here!"

A waiter walked past with a tray of sparkling wine. [7] Ondine reached for it just as her Ma turned to see her.

"Ondi!"

"Just a sip?"

"You're still grounded."

"Still?"

"Yes. Until a fish –"

" – dances on a table, I know." Mercury's wings but her mother loved that saying.

Hamish took a sip of his drink. When Ma's back was turned, he offered his glass to Ondine. The bubbles felt like mousse on her tongue but the taste reminded her of that awful night at the Autumn Palace when Duke Pavla nearly died.

"You're too young." Ma swiped the glass away from her.

Ah well, she had Hamish instead. He made her feel lightheaded at the best of times.

**8**

---

The shortest day of the year arrived with hideous news blaring out the radio as Ondine woke up.

*"Tributes are flowing in from across Europe at the news that Duke Pavla has passed.*
*He died in his sleep, attended by close family, however his estranged wife Kerala was not present.*
*Brugel will observe full mourning until Christmas Eve."*

Guilt set up base camp in Ondine's stomach. She wanted to throw up. The words, "I should have done more. I could have done more," played in her head as she dragged on her clothes and headed down to the kitchen.

"It's nae yer fault, hen," Hamish said, giving her a comforting hug as they stood in the kitchen, waiting for the kettle to boil. "We tried tae warn him aboot Kerala and he wouldnae listen."

"I can't switch my brain off. I didn't do enough, and now Vincent's going to take over, isn't he? We should have made Pavla listen." Hindsight dumped a trailer load of "would haves" and "should haves" at her feet. With a side dumping of "if onlys".

"Hindsight is always right, hen. But ye cannae let it eat ye up. He didnae want tae listen because in his heart, he knew the truth would kill him."

"But . . . Old Col says we've got magic, so why couldn't we save him?"

Hamish rubbed her back in a comforting way. Then he too sighed and his accent came out even thicker with emotion and regret. "Mebbe he didnae want tae go on. There's not much ye can do fer someone who's lawst thae will tae live."

"You suck at being a counsellor," Ondine said with a pathetic sniff.

"Do ye want me tae stop cuddling ye?"

"No, keep doing that. You're really good at that."

"Well that's a plus. And another plus, we have tae close for the day because we're all in mourning. So ye don't havetae goe tae school."

A huge sigh escaped. "School's closed for winter, sweetheart. But thanks for trying to cheer me up."

"Aye, and at least we goat the wedding over with, so that's a plus."

Yes, at least they'd had that magical day. Thomas and Margi were on their honeymoon by the Black Sea and nothing had happened to spoil that.

---

ONDINE HAD NEVER SEEN SO many people wearing black, which stood out starkly against a fresh overnight dumping of snow. [1]

Everyone wore armbands with the hexagonal flag of Brugel sewn on. Duchess Anathea called for three days of mourning, which meant all non-essential services had to close as a mark of respect. Ma claimed she was deeply upset by Duke Pavla's death, but Ondine knew her mother's bad mood stemmed from their having to close until Christmas Eve. It was normally their busiest time of year. When they re-opened, not even a fourth dinner would be able to fit everyone in again before the New Year.

On the bright side, Ondine was on winter break from school, which meant more delightful time with Hamish. This in turn made her feel guilty about enjoying herself during the official mourning period for

Duke Pavla, and the whole blaming-herself-for-his-death started over again. This did nothing for her state of mental health, although every time Hamish saw her looking sad – which was a great deal of the time – he gave her a warm embrace, lovely rubs on the back and beautiful kisses. Which in turn spiralled her into a fresh wave of guilt for enjoying his kisses when she should be miserable.

Because his kisses were so magical.

Both commercial networks televised Duke Pavla's funeral, which allowed people to watch from home in the warmth of their living rooms.

2

On the fourth day, which happened to be Christmas Eve, the mourning period was over and the customers returned to *The Duke and Ferret*. Ondine was back in armpit-deep soapy water washing the dishes from lunch.

Before her hands had a chance to dry, she then raced around the dining room with the vacuum cleaner before the "second lunch" service began. It was up to Ondine to carry the extra load, as Margi and Thomas were still on their honeymoon by the Black Sea.

"Can I help ye lass?" Hamish came up behind her.

Startled by his voice, she spun around, the vacuum nozzle slurping the end of Hamish's scarf. Before she could grab it, the machine sucked the fabric all the way in.

"Whoa!" Quick as a flash she tapped the machine off with her foot. "You shouldn't sneak up on me like that!"

"I wasnae, but ye couldnae hear me so I had tae get closer."

They then spent the next five minutes unravelling the scarf from the machine's dust bag, then had to turn the machine back on and suck the dust off the scarf, so Hamish could wear it again.

"Can you re-set the tables?" Ondine asked as she pulled the chairs out with one hand and pushed the vacuum cleaner nozzle with the other.

"Course I can." He grabbed a lace tablecloth and flicked it open, then laid it over the top of a table. Then he put the salt and pepper grinders in the central position, but just as he said "ta-da" he knocked the pepper over, spilling black and grey corns all over the tabletop.

"I'll get it." Ondine aimed the nozzle at the runaway corns, which clattered and scattered through the tube and into the bag.

"Need any help?" Old Col came sauntering in.

Flicking the machine off with her foot, Ondine looked at her great-auntie and said, "Yes, as a matter of fact. Could you magic this place clean and set the tables for me?"

Old Col gave Ondine a wink. "What's in it for me?"

Hamish answered with, "Free second lunch and as much plütz as the Old Man has left in the bar."

"Done!" The witch waved her arms in the air and flicked her wrists and may have even snapped her fingers. At least, Ondine hoped the noise was from snapping her fingers, rather than breaking a bone or something.

In a blink, the room was ready to receive new customers.

"Thank you Auntie Col."

"Good, now we can talk." With a flourish, she withdrew a card from a deep pocket, with the Royal House of Brugel stamped on it. "I have a royal summons from Duchess Anathea, and it's for all three of us. She wants to meet at the mid-winter fairground in Savo Plaza." [3] Old Col said. "It's early evening, around four o'clock, so you'll be back in time to work for second dinner."

Ondine nibbled the inside of her cheek, then looked to her great-aunt. "What does she want with us?"

"We'll find out soon enough," Old Col said.

---

It snowed something fierce as they walked to the train station on their way to Savo Plaza. If it wasn't snowing, or sleeting, or so cold their breath froze on their lips, they could have walked the distance. But winter in Venzelemma is not a sensible time to be walking anywhere outdoors.

Catching the train meant they were warm and dry for brief periods of time, as long as they didn't sit down on the wooden seats, which were dripping with mud and melted snow from everyone's snowcoats.

A blast of arctic air gripped Ondine's neck as they reached the station at Savo Plaza.

Her muscles cramped with the effort to keep warm and she felt like she was wearing her shoulders as earrings.

Once in the plaza, it wasn't nearly as cold, because the tall buildings formed three quarters of a circle, protecting those inside from the worst of the winter gales.

The sheer number of people packed into the plaza also defrosted the environment.

"There she is," Old Col said apropos of nothing. Her hand flew up to wave at Duchess Anathea who was standing on a gold coloured carpet, in front of a crowd at the Ferris wheel.

Nearby, a woman with a vacuum cleaner strapped on her back worked quickly to keep the carpet dry and free of snow.

A pang of jealousy hit Ondine as she wished she had someone to walk in front of her and suck up snow and slush all day.

The duchess was still in mourning for her brother, while also being dressed comfortably for the cold. A lush black coat with fur-lined collar and cuffs and matching fur trim at the hem, which came to just below her knees.

The length emphasised her fabulous mahogany-coloured boots with intricate buttons dotted up the side.

On her head she wore a fur-lined box-style hat, which sat so neatly upon her head it didn't damage her perfectly coiffed hair.

Her gloves matched her boots, but would have been made with much softer leather.

*Has she had more 'work' done?* Ondine wondered, as she took in the Duchess's unlined face.

Bud lighting shone from the bare trees. Decorative bunting in the Brugel colours of red, white and blue flapped in the breeze.

Paper lanterns hung in the shop windows. After all, it was Christmas Eve and people should be celebrating.

Especially after the drudgery of the past few days. [4]

Tight security kept Anathea safely protected from the crowds. This could be tricky. They couldn't very well walk up to the Duchess of Brugel and . . . OK, apparently they could.

"Colette Romano, my very good friend," Duchess Anathea said loud enough for everyone to hear. They embraced and kissed each other on the left cheek, then the right, then back to the left again. If Ondine's eyes widened any more she'd turn into a goldfish. Since when had Anathea and Old Col been such firm friends?

"Go *aloang* with it," Hamish murmured in her ear.

She'd go along with whatever Hamish said, that was a no-brainer. Before she even questioned what they were doing next, various officials herded them into a cabin on the brightly lit Ferris wheel. It had lights in a chasing sequence, radiating from the core, in Christmassy golds and reds and greens. Double bonus, they didn't have to queue up in the cold to get a ticket.

Anathea remained outside for a moment, as she wielded a pantomime-huge pair of scissors and cut a ribbon. "Let Christmas begin!"

The crowd roared and threw cheese balls into the air.[5]

The next thing Ondine knew, Duchess Anathea plonked herself into the cabin with them. Biscuit the dog charged in and leapt upon his master's lap. The dog still didn't have his teeth back to full size. Poor thing. [6]

"Now then," Anathea said to Ondine, Old Col and Hamish, "there will be smiles for the cameras."

Cameras clicked and flashes flashed. No point asking, 'What's going on?' because Anathea was too busy being fabulous for the media. A stray thought flicked through her head. Where was Vincent? Surely he'd want to be in front of a camera at this point?

The door finally closed and the heating came on beneath their feet. How clever to have heating inside the cabins! It warmed them up and fogged the windows, which only served to confuse Ondine. Surely the point of the ride was for the amazing view?

"Now the door has been closed," Anathea said, "we shall not be overheard."

"My Lord Duchess, you are truly marvellous to see us," Old Col said, "and on such an important day as Christmas Eve."

Anathea waved her hand to dismiss her. "No time for that. What is planned?"

"Whoops!" The cabin lurched, sending an alarmed Biscuit scuttling onto the floor and Ondine into Hamish's arms. She snuck in another kiss while she was this close. When she turned around, everyone was blanketed.

"Where did they –?"

"Thanks Ondi," Old Col tucked herself in.

The Duchess cast a quizzing glance Ondine's way. Ondine was about to ask, "Where did they come from?" meaning the blankets. But then she remembered the carriage ride home from the wedding. She and Hamish must have made the blankets appear, simply from having a quick smooch or being close to each other, at the same time that somebody else had made a wish.

The Ferris wheel started again. Biscuit poked his head out from under the blanket.

They weren't too high yet, but Ondine wiped her sleeve over the foggy window to gaze out at the pretty lights surrounding Savo Plaza, which had turned the scene into a snowy fairyland.

Anathea adjusted the blanket across her knees. "Tell me what is planned?"

"Planned, Your Grace?" Ondine asked back.

"Yes, planned. There are already rumblings about bringing forward Vincent's coronation. It must be stopped."

"But um . . . I'm not sure we're the right people you should be asking about that." Ondine tried very hard to keep her tone polite, but all the same she felt she was being terribly rude in refusing Anathea. Not that she really knew what she was refusing at this point.

"You are exactly the right people to be talking to," Anathea said. "You make people's wishes come true."

How did she know this? Ondine's eyes shot to her great-auntie, who looked guilty.

Col cleared her throat and gave everyone a huge grin, as if she'd worked out something very clever. "It's all falling into place. Just as I knew it would." Then she coughed, as if to hide her real thoughts. Because Ondine suspected Col was making this up as she went along. "As we know, children, it's Anathea's deepest wish to be the fairest and best leader Brugel has ever had. This will bring certainty and stability to the country. Your magic, when you become amorous, makes other people's wishes come true. May I suggest you –"

"Huahhhtzu!" Ondine sneezed into her elbow. "Ugh, sorry." She held her arm across her face to keep the germs in. "Does anyone have a tissue?"

Hamish shrugged and showed his empty hands. "Sorry, Ondi, I didnae think tae bring any."

"Don't look at me," Anathea said as all eyes fell on her. "I'm only given this purse to match the shoes. I have no idea what they've put in here." She opened her clutch purse to find it stuffed with butcher's paper. "Would you look at that. It's so new there wasn't time for the stuffing to be taken out."

Old Col rummaged around in her bag and produced a crumpled handkerchief.

"Danks," Ondine grabbed it in time for another volcanic sneeze. Then three more for good measure. By the time the sneezing stopped and they'd all said, 'Bless you,' Ondine felt her brains turn to goulash. "I'm sorry Your Grace, I must have picked up a bug on the train ride here."

"The train? Why were you not brought here by a taxi?"

"Couldn't get one for love, money or magic," Old Col said. "The traffic pile-ups we've been having must be contributing to the shortage."

Which made Ondine cringe in shame. The traffic situation had been getting worse, according to reports on the radio every morning. Like the multi-car collision the morning of Margi's wedding. Had that been a result of this newfound magic answering everyone's wishes at once? Every driver always wished for green lights at intersections, but if they were approaching from different directions and their wish was granted, they'd all crash into each other.

Cold air tickled Ondine's nose and she sneezed again.

"I take this to mean there will be no kissing?" Anathea asked.

"Weil," Hamish shifted in his seat as he moved away from her germs.

"Would you look at that?" Old Col wiped the fog from the window so they could see. Immediately next to Savo Plaza, in all directions, the city was pitch black. Like a doughnut of darkness spreading into the immediate neighbourhood. The only lights they could see were from car headlights as they tried getting through intersections without crashing into each other.

"Glad I'm not old enough to drive," Ondine said.

"The continuing power supply problems are being wished by Vincent, I'm sure of it," Anathea said. "Don't you think it's suspicious he's not here? Wouldn't he just love to be associated with something wonderful like Christmas Eve? Unless he's hoping things go badly wrong and people associate that calamity with me."

That got Ondine's attention. And Hamish's. Even Biscuit looked up to his master in surprise. They all looked at her and waited until she finished her dramatic pause.

"There are rumblings and rumours that Vincent should inherit early," Anathea said. "No doubt he is spreading them. There are those who say a woman at the helm is bad luck. There are those that might hasten Vincent's ascension."

"Yer saying the city is full of troublemakers," Hamish said.

"You catch on quickly," Anathea said. "What we're up against can clearly be seen. The darkness must be Vincent's work, but he's not doing it on his own. He must be getting help, and he must also be stopped. Brugel needs certainty and security. I can provide that. But the people don't yet trust me or love me. It must be remedied."

The thought, *we're in serious trouble*, plagued Ondine.

Old Col looked royally miffed. "Much like this ride, we're going round and round in circles and getting nowhere."

Anathea sat up to her full haughty height. "The answer to our problems can be easily grasped. I must be the most popular leader Brugel has ever had."

Even with magic on their side – and Ondine still wasn't all that comfortable with her magic – the Duchess was asking for the impossible!

"Is that all?" Old Col said.

"You're saying you're not up to it?" Anathea shot back. "I know you need something from me. I'm merely suggesting we help each other in our times of need."

"Er," Hamish spoke up. "Ye mean my work papers, on account of not being Brugel born."

"That has not been forgotten," Anathea said as their cabin slowed. "You'll be wanting this." She retrieved a folded paper from her pocket. It had the hexagonal Brugelish flag watermarked through it. "This will be signed and handed over once my succession is secured."

Their cabin came to a stop at the bottom of the Ferris wheel. Icy worries dug into Ondine. This felt a little too close to blackmail for comfort. But what choice did they have?

"Happy to help." Hamish made the decision for them and gave Ondine the sweetest kiss. It caught her off balance. Her nose was still blocked from her earlier bout of sneezing. Ordinarily she'd luxuriate in his kiss but breathing carried a higher priority. She pulled back and panted for breath.

"Wonderful!" Anathea said, clapping her hands. Then she stepped out of their cabin to face a phalanx of flashing cameras. "A wonderful time was had by all. Merry Christmas everybody!"

"Awff we go then," Hamish said, taking Ondine by the hand as the media pack followed Anathea's every step. "Let's get some cheese balls."

"Do you think the kiss made her wish work?" Ondine asked.

"I doubt one kiss will do it all, lass, but mebbe it's a start?"

A stray thought crept in. If their magic didn't work, maybe Old Col wasn't as good at guiding magic as she'd let on? In which case – the second stray thought said – perhaps she might need Mrs. Howser's help after all?

---

IF YOU'VE NEVER EATEN fried cheese balls, you haven't lived. Hot and crunchy and a bit saltier than is good for you on the outside, gooey and warm in the middle – they're perfect for cold months. [7] Ondine and

Hamish shared some as they sat on a bench in the midst of the Christmas market, racking their brains for ways to make Anathea popular.

Cinnamon and gingerbread mixed with diesel generator smells as they set about having a big think. Everyone around them carried on being festive. Adults sipped mulled wine and the children drank hot chocolate. Piped music and puppet shows kept the party flowing. Everybody was enjoying the sights, sounds and smells of the winter fair, carefree and happy. In stark contrast to Ondine, who felt matters of state pressing down on her shoulders.

"How will we know if the magic will work?" She asked as she chomped down on a cheese ball. "And another thing. If she wants to be popular, why can't she pay some PR company to do it? They'd at least know what they were doing."

"Aye. I'm thinkin' along the same lines as you, hen. But she must think we can do it if she's asked us."

"Yes but what if while she's wishing to be loved, everyone else wishes for something horrid to happen to her. And they don't even know they're wishing because they're just thinking it." It truly hurt her brain to think of the ramifications of their canoodling. "I mean, how far does the magic extend? Just the people around us or the whole city?"

"Aye. I heard on the radio this morning there were blackouts as far away as Craviç. Mebbe we should be careful about how kissy we get?"

Would they have to ration their kisses? Oh it hurt to think about that. Much better to keep her brain busy with practical matters. "She's holding a work card over your head."

"She'd call it leverage," Old Col said, bringing them a fresh basket of piping hot cheese balls. "You help her, she helps you."

"By the way," Ondine poured on the sarcasm, "thanks for telling the Duchess all about the magic. Way to blab it to everyone before I've even had a chance to get used to it."

"Because it works," Old Col said, "and it will work for Anathea."

"Yeah but, you should have told me you were going to tell her."

"There wasn't time, dear."

Muttering disdain to herself, Ondine fell upon a fresh cheeseball and bit into it. It was so hot she couldn't talk or swallow, but it was so gooey she couldn't spit it out.

"Ye right, lass?"

"Here you are," Col handed her a napkin.

Ondine dabbed at her lips and madly waved her hand in front of her mouth, as if that would cool things down.

"Hold on a minute." Hamish reached for another napkin and held it up so everyone could see the printing. *Fried Cheese Balls. Brugel's National Treasure.*

Then he grabbed a marker pen, crossed out the first three words and wrote "Duchess Anathea".

Ondine nodded. Anathea making private wishes was one thing, but maybe they could help her popularity in other ways too? If people thought of their Duchess as a National Treasure, they'd be on the way to loving her to bits.

"You're brilliant!" Ondine smothered Hamish in far too many cheesy kisses than was socially acceptable in public.

"Careful kids, you don't know what people might be wishing while you do that."

"Of course." Ondine pulled herself away from Hamish and scoffed another cheese ball.

"We have another problem." Old Col said. "How are we to pay for this advertising?"

"Anathea will. Won't she?" Ondine asked.

"She's broke," Old Col said.

That stopped Ondine in her tracks.

"I should clarify." Old Col split open a cheese ball in her fingers and blew on it to cool it down. "It's not quite at the 'selling off the family silver' stage yet, but it's getting there. That's why she can't afford to hire a public relations company."

Ondine bit into another cheeseball, but the fun of it grew cold. The task ahead of them felt insurmountable.

$$9$$

Heading home, Ondine replayed Old Col's words in her head as they trudged through the snow-lined streets. The train took them back to the station across the road from *The Duke & Ferret*, their family pub. But the lights weren't on, not for them, nor for *On The Fang*.

Every single streetlight was out. Through the foggy restaurant windows, she could see candles burning for light on the dining tables. The donut of darkness she'd seen from the top of the Ferris wheel was now all around them.

Hamish – clever, thoughtful Hamish – had a torch in his satchel to guide them across the street.

Inside, they found Ma and Da re-using the wedding dinner candles to help customers complete their meals in comfort. It added a warm glow to the room, complimented by the roaring fire. She waved to Thomas as he fed two more logs to it.

It took an effort to remove all their layers of hats and coats and scarves in the dark, in the private room behind the kitchen. Ondine lost her balance taking her boot off and fell backwards into a box of extra thick plastic food wrap. The cardboard split open and the contents rolled out.

Hamish shone his torch on the roll and Ondine had a closer look. There was something printed on the plastic. Which was odd, because food wrap was usually clear, because you're meant to see the food beneath it. This was opaque and as she unrolled it, and Hamish shone the torch to help them see better, she found herself looking at a keyboard layout.

"That's nae clingfilm," Hamish said.

"Cybelle!" Old Col said, her voice full of purpose. "I'll bet Brugel to a brick this is one of her schemes."

Schemes? What schemes did Old Col know about that Ondine didn't? Mind ticking over with possibilities, Ondine immediately wondered if these 'schemes' meant extra money coming in.

Being Christmas Eve, they found Cybelle and Henrik in the kitchen, frantically cooking and serving meals. Except they had the added problem of no electricity. Henrik and Cybelle were adapting to the situation, using every single gas burner to keep things cooking along. The ovens weren't working, as they were electric, but they could still boil and fry their way out of trouble.

The overhead fan wasn't working, so a fair amount of smoke billowed from the frying steaks. Ondine opened a window and a gust of snowy wind came in and blew the smoke clear.

There was still some hot water left, but it grew tepid so it would require even more detergent to break down the grease from the dirty plates in the sink. All the while she couldn't stop thinking about how on earth she and Hamish could help Duchess Anathea.

How would they pay for the advertising campaign to increase the Duchess's popularity? If it had been a normal year, her family might have been flush from the pre-Christmas trade. [1] But this year, thanks to Pavla's untimely demise, they'd had to close during the busiest, most profitable time of the year.

"We could re-name the pub after her, couldn't we?" Ondine wondered out loud.

"What's that dear?" Ma asked.

It would take too long to explain so she shrugged and said, "Don't worry."

Old Col came over with a hot saucepan full of steaming water to top up the sudsy sink. "I know we're desperate for ideas, but we're not *that* desperate," Col said. Then she tested the water with her fingers and decided it was far too cold. She wafted her hands over the water and muttered incantations. The water grew hot and steamy, then it boiled. The extra sudsiness bubbled over and dripped onto the floor.

"You've overdone it," Ondine said, not daring to put her bare hands anywhere near the boiling water.

"Sorry, must have had a senior moment. You know how it is. Or you will one day, at any rate."

"Don't worry about the water, I can always add some cold. How about you focus on zapping the power back on?" Ondine asked.

"You think I didn't think of that?" Old Col shot back, but judging by the guilty look on her face, she most likely hadn't.

Oh dear, maybe she really was having a senior moment.

Old Col held her hands towards the window and flickered her fingers, chanting under her breath.

"The window?" Ondine wondered why she aimed her magic that way.

"I'm gunning for the power supply on the corner pole," she said, wiggling her fingers afresh. She sang words under her breath and the lights came on in the kitchen.

"Yay!" Ondine said. The lights flickered on and off, then crackled and snapped out. The smell of burnt elements filled the room. "Oh dear," Ondine said, feeling terrible for her great-auntie.

"This isn't one of our regular winter blackouts," Col said. "There's magic behind this loss of power, I guarantee it. Only the witch that made a curse can break it." [2]

"I bet Lord Vincent's behind this," Ondine said.

"Don't be so content to pick the low-hanging fruit," Old Col arched her brow.

"Who else could it be?"

"Oh, I agree, Ondi, it most likely is Vincent, but he's not magic, so someone else is doing his magic for him."

With a sigh, Ondine guessed, "Mrs Howser?"

"There you go again."

Ondine grew frustrated. "Yeah, but I bet it is her."

Old Col creased her mouth in thought, then said, "Low-hanging fruit or not, I think you might be right."

A sheen of perspiration glistened on Ma's brow as she carried a stack of dirty plates from the dining room towards Ondine's sink.

"After we're done here, tell me everything the Duchess said. And Aunt Col? Josef needs a hand at the bar."

At that point, the lights in the restaurant suddenly came on again. Instead of popping out like they had in the kitchen – which was still dark – these stayed on. A cheer floated in from the dining room.

"Better late than never," Ma said as she wiped her hands on a tea towel. "How many more meals do you have to go, Chef?"

Henrik looked up. "This is the last one."

"Typical!" Ma threw her hands up and let out a frustrated sigh.

---

EXHAUSTED from the enormous night before, Ondine didn't wake until nearly ten o'clock on Christmas Day. In normal circumstances she'd be mad keen to open her presents. Instead, she luxuriated in the warmth of her bed and the serenity of Cybelle not being in the bed next to her, snoring up a storm.

Every few years the family closed the pub for Christmas Day so they could have a slodgy-slow day as a family. Considering they'd closed for Margi's wedding, then been forced to close in respect to Pavla, Ma was grabbing any opportunity to get customers. Unfortunately, they were still short-staffed because Margi and Thomas hadn't returned from their honeymoon.

"There's a pile of dishes with your name on it," Cybelle said as Ondine made her way to the kitchen by eleven.

*Blurble* went her tummy.

"Just kidding!" Cybelle said, "Have some sausages and marmalade. That'll perk you up."

"Thanks." Ondine inhaled the food on her plate. Only after she licked her fingers did she spare a thought for anyone else. "How many are out there?"

"Only twelve for brunch. Practically doing it in our sleep," Henrik said, looking so tired he might still be asleep.

"Merry Christmas Ondi," Hamish said as he came back in with empty water jugs to refill. She beamed at him and returned the greeting. Then they had a little smooch and didn't care that there were other people around.

Ma filled her arms with plates of food to take out. "Hamish, could you grab the dessert menus for me?"

"Dessert? For brunch?" Ondine boggled.

"It's Christmas!" Ma said.

Desserts were the most profitable items on the menu. Small serves, high prices.

"I'll tempt them Missers G," Hamish said with a wink.

"Be careful," Ondine said.

"Of what, lass?"

"The work inspectors," she said.

"Ye really think they'd be working on Christmas Day?"

"We are." Ondine couldn't help grumbling.

---

SURE IT WAS CHRISTMAS, but for the de Groot family, it was another workday to get through. Nothing remotely interesting happened until they'd seen off the last of the lunch crowd and were taking a breather in the private room before first dinner began. [3]

Da walked in with his arms full of take-away food. "Merry Christmas all!" he said, handing out hot boxes with sauce dripping out the sides.

"What's this?"

"Noodles from *Fang's.*"

"I thought they'd closed." Ondine remembered the night when their staff had been hauled away.

"They're only making it look like that, so the inspectors don't come back. Dig in, smells delicious."

"Merry Christmas Ondi," Hamish said, handing her a book-shaped present.

She tore the wrapper off and grinned. The second book in the series about Elmaree.

Oooh, the sequel. I'm going to love it. Here, this is for you." She handed him the little box wrapped with a flat bow. Not a frilly bow, because that would be too girly and she didn't want to embarrass him. Her breath stalled as she watched him open it. The little voice in her head said, *I hope he likes it, I hope he likes it.*

"It's brilliant," Hamish said as he took the broad silver ring from the box and held it. For a second Ondine wondered if he noticed the inscription she'd agonised over. Did it say too little? Did it say too much? Would he wear it?

In silent answer, Hamish slipped the ring on the last finger on his right hand, then he whispered the same words she'd inscribed on the ring. "You have my heart."

"What does it say?" Ma asked with a complete lack of tact.

"Something that means the world to me," Hamish said giving Ondine one of his heart-meltingly lopsided smiles.

They tucked into their food, a happy mood settling over them. Ondine saw how relaxed Cybelle looked and figured this might be the best chance they had to raise the issue that had been niggling at her.

"Belle, how are the keyboard covers going?" Because her mother heard everything, Ondine deliberately kept her voice as light and innocent as she could manage. It came out far too light, far too innocent and all too completely needy.

Cybelle froze, mid mouthful. "What do you mean?"

*Gulp.* "I accidentally knocked a box over and one of the rolls rolled out. It's a very clever side business. You've always been very clever."

Cybelle's eyes slitted with suspicion. "It's nothing."

"Oh, I'd never say anything to anyone else about it." Ondine backtracked as fast as she could.

"We're not making any money, if that's what you're after," Cybelle said.

Mercury's wings, that's *exactly* what Ondine was after. "I'm sorry it sounds like I'm fishing . . . but I was just saying I think it's really clever and I wish you and Henrik all the best with it. Sheesh, no need to get defensive," Ondine said, sounding mightily defensive.

Hamish chimed in, "We were hoping to get extra funds together, on account of the fact we need to do a job for Anathea and it's goin' tae cost us. And the tips are down on account of being closed for so long and –"

"We don't have any money." Cybelle's expression froze.

Henrik looked at the ground and kept his hands clasped together. A little too tightly, judging by the whiteness of his knuckles.

Ondine looked to Hamish. He squished her hand in support.

Ma let out an exaggerated sigh behind them.

Ondine tried again. "Belle, what you and Henrik have done is nothing short of incredible." Too flowery? Too verbose? To bluffy? Thinking she'd said too much but not enough, Ondine ploughed on. "I know I should help you more than I do, and I will after this, I absolutely promise."

"You help out plenty," Henrik said, his eyes still downcast.

Cybelle elbowed him in the ribs.

"What's all this?" Da said.

Henrik, Cybelle, Ondine and Hamish all said, "Nothing!"

Da crossed his arms over his chest. "Oh really?"

Henrik spoke in a soft voice. "This goes no further than this room."

As one, they nodded.

With a sigh of defeat, Henrik revealed all. "Back in November, just after Anathea took over, they made a new law about buying Brugel-made computers, which have to have the Dvorak keyboard on them. But everyone knows where the letters are on a QWERTY keyboard. Nobody wants to swap over. But they want to *look* as if they're complying with the laws. So we started making slipcovers with Dvorak layout on them. Put them over your existing keyboard and away you go."

Da's eyebrows shot upwards.

Ma dabbed at her eyes with a handkerchief. "My little entrepreneurs."

"OK. Here's our problem." Ondine brought it back to the big issue at hand. "Once Anathea is popular, she'll give Hamish his papers and he'll be free to work for us without fear of inspectors."

Ma sat up a bit straighter at that. They needed Hamish's free labour.

Ondine had everyone's attention. "We tried using magic yesterday in Savo Plaza. We're not sure if it worked. And in the meantime, we have some more ideas. Well, Hamish has a really good idea. But we need money to get it started and we're a bit broke except I was hoping Cybelle, that you and Henrik might lend me some of your money *and I'll pay you back.*"

She had to take a deep breath to recover from such a big explanation.

Henrik sighed and looked to Cybelle.

A pleading tone stole into Ondine's voice. "We don't need much. Just enough to get started."

Hamish gave her hand a squish of support.

Henrik cracked. "How much are we talking about?"

Cybelle groaned.

"I'm sorry love," Henrik said to Cybelle. "You've seen how poor the tips are when Hamish isn't out front."

Cybelle groaned again. "But it's our future fund!"

"I know." Henrik gave her a hug. "But . . . our future does kind of rely on Hamish being out the front."

Ondine beamed at the vote of confidence.

"Fine then!" Cybelle threw her hands up in defeat. "But if we're handing over money, I want a say in how it's used."

"Aw yeas!" Hamish cheered. He quickly explained his idea about putting Anathea's face on napkins.

"That's stupid," Cybelle said.

An invisible hammer whacked Ondine in the head at Cybelle's slapdown.

"It is?" She and Hamish said together.

The corner of Cybelle's lip curled. "You want people wiping their dirty faces on the Duchess? It sends the totally wrong message."

"Oh," Ondine and Hamish said together.

"Sorry, I didn't mean to sound so harsh. But if you think about it, napkins are only one step up from toilet paper."

Ondine instantly wished she could get the visual of Anathea on that kind of product out of her head.

Cybelle again. "Here's what we do. We make a stencil of Anathea's face and stamp it on the keyboard covers."

Ondine's forehead scrunched in confusion.

"As an inside joke," Cybelle said. "The covers are how people get around the new laws, which *she* made. Every time people see her face on the cover, they'll smile because they'll be happily using their old keyboard, yet they'll be complying with the law."

"It . . . sort of makes sense." Ondine said, wishing they could go back to the napkins idea.

Cybelle was ignoring Ondine's look of pain because she kept right on talking. "Think about all the things that make you smile."

Too easy. Hamish made her smile.

Cybelle groaned. "A *product*!"

Whoa, she could read her mind? Ondine guessed her love for Hamish must be writ large on her face anyway.

"Chocolate?" Ma suggested.

"Aye, that's good," Hamish said. "How about a warm open fire?"

Henrik grabbed a notepad and wrote the ideas down as they kept brainstorming.

Everyone began talking at once.

"Flowers?"

"Ginger biscuits."

"Hot soup."

"Tea."

"Fluffy kittens?"

"Hats with ear flaps?"

"Now we're getting somewhere," Cybelle said. She too grabbed a piece of paper and began scribbling. Before long she had some sketches of the Duchess's face and the hexagonal flag. "What we do is make some small posters, maybe half a page size. Small enough to fit on the curve of a lamppost, without getting distorted. We paste them up near where people buy things that make them happy. There's a florist down the street, we put these on the lampposts or the walls or street signs near that. [4]

"But, will anybody notice them?" Hamish asked.

"Possibly not, at first," Cybelle said. "That's the beauty of it. It's in people's peripheral vision. They won't make a direct connection, so they won't think it's propaganda. If we put an ad in the paper saying how much everyone loves Anathea, it will turn people off because they'll see it as a blatant add. This way is heaps better."

Henrik gave Cybelle two thumbs up.

TWO DAYS AFTER CHRISTMAS, the de Groot household became a flurry of non-food-related activity as Ondine, Hamish and Cybelle woke extra early to gather their half-page posters to slap all over town. They divided up the bundles of papers and everyone grabbed a pot of glue and a thick brush, then headed out to the shopping districts. Being Sunday, many shops were closed for the morning and the cold kept the crowds away. All the same, they had to work quickly. Not because they'd be spotted, but because the glue kept freezing in the pots.

One of the best spots Ondine found was the side of a hot soup caravan. She slapped a poster near the "Hot Soup For You!" logo.

Feet entirely frozen, she, Hamish and Cybelle scarpered home for a hot second-breakfast. Then she spent the rest of the day washing dishes, as was her lot. Between meal services she and Cybelle collated posters and marked out maps of where they'd slap up posters the next morning. Hamish worked upstairs with a vintage photocopier to make enough posters for them to paste onto walls and lampposts.

The printing left chemicals on his hands and sometimes the results came out a little blurry. But it gave the images a retro-look, which was so on-trend.

They stopped their subversive advertising program to deal with the New Year's Eve dinner crowds and then they gave themselves a rest on New Year's Day because they deserved it.

When January came around, Ondine had to go back to school, which meant getting up even earlier to get some copying and pasting done and keep the campaign rolling out.

It was cold, miserable work, especially when she had to trudge through snow. But it was also great fun to be doing something a little subversive and – in Ondine's mind – for a good cause. A good, secret cause.

# 10

In the middle of January, more snow came to Venzelemma, followed soon after by the arrival of hundreds of witches attending CovenCon. CovenCon garnered the largest gathering of witches and pre-witches in Eastern Europe. [1] This annual conference was to have been held in Norange, but Old Col had been instrumental in getting the location switched to Brugel.

The organisers were lured to the atmospherics of the Brugel's not-quite-world-heritage-listed Massa-Kuche, on the coastal side of Venzelemma. The direct translation of Massa-Kuche is 'Bulky lump on the hill'. Part castle, part ruin, Massa-Kuche has magnificent views over the Black Sea and is serviced by a funicular tourist railway and four-star hotel. [2]

Stepping from the funicular railway that brought them to the top of the hill, Ondine's nose tingled as she breathed the cool wintery air. Ahead of her was the castle, built on a ledge that she could see – now she was up this high – was part way up a larger mountain range.

The castle had a classic medieval-style drawbridge over a running river. To one side of the river was a tumbling waterfall that churned into white froth, which then charged under the drawbridge and fell dramatically down another waterfall which took a huge plunge down the sheer side of the mountain. As they walked over the drawbridge, the timber creaked and shuddered. Several staff members stopped more people from walking on it at the same time, lest it collapse under the weight. From the groaning drawbridge they walked into a hallway already heaving with people.

Many people have a traditional idea of what witches look like, but true Brugelish witches wear warm hats with orschlappen, and wouldn't be seen anywhere without their multi-pocketed travelling cloak and knapsack. They all wear strong boots and sturdy pants, even the gentlemen.

Here was where Ondine, Hamish and Old Col figured they'd be able to help Anathea become popular. *Properly* popular. If Anathea could behave herself – big if – and not irritate the tripe out of people – bigger if – their newly-minted Duchess just might endear herself to the crowds here. Because if Anathea charmed the witches, she'd be well on her way to winning over the rest of the country.

"I was always going to bring you to CovenCon," Old Col said to Ondine as they picked up their registration kits at the reception desk. "Ignore everything Birgit Howser told you."

Being told to ignore something is like being told not to think of pink motorbikes. The moment Old Col said not to, all Ondine could think about was Mrs. Howser and her persuasive words about how she could instruct magic far more effectively than Old Col could.

She rubbed her elbow at the memory of the tug of love.

Taking in the atmospherics of this centuries-old castle helped distract Ondine from less pleasant things. The solid stone walls – now sealed and polished and not at all dusty – were a lasting testament to the way Brugelers used to build their castles. 'Build' is probably not the right verb. 'Excavate' is more accurate; as they used to begin on the top of a mountain, then dig away until the castle emerged. [3]

"No matter what she says, child, you are far better off with me," Old Col said, interrupting Ondine's deliberate 'not thinking about Mrs Howser' thoughts. "Now stay close. I don't want her getting – heavens above, I can see her across the room. And she looks like she's looking for you."

Mrs Howser had come dressed for the occasion, in her 'look at me' luxurious purple hooded cloak with gold trim over a royal blue dress. Compared to the humble brown travelling cloaks the rest of the witches wore, nobody could miss her.

Before they could get a better look at Howser, Old Col pushed them sideways and dragged them through a nearby doorway, where they found themselves in an auditorium.

An empty auditorium, but one with the power to intimidate its hundreds of guests. Heavy velvet curtains draped behind the podium, while the walls were decorated with richly detailed tapestries.

"Quick, get under the lectern." Old Col shoved Ondine in the back and pushed them towards the stage.

"But the curtains?" Ondine started. They'd be a much more comfortable place to hide.

"Too obvious," Old Col said, shoving them closer to where she wanted them.

"We'll nae fit in that unless ye turn our bones tae rubber," Hamish said. "Ye nae gontae turn our bones tae rubber are ye?"

"Not in it, under it," Old Col said. Another push in the back, a push down this time where they could see the crawl-space under the stage. Plenty of room. For a ferret maybe. But a grown lad and girl?

The complaint was on her lips, then Ondine shut right up. It was the *perfect* place for squishy canoodling. So she didn't dare ask another question, such as why they had to hide from Mrs Howser when it had been Mrs Howser who had wanted to bring her to CovenCon in the first place.

"Now stay there and don't make a sound. Birgit's giving the keynote address and she cannot know you're there."

Ondine and Hamish wedged themselves into the small space. The only light came through the gaps in the floorboards above. Lying on dusty boards would have been uncomfortable enough, but they also had a spaghetti pile of cables and extension cords to contend with.

Gradually the auditorium filled with people who brought extra noise in with them.

"This is just like old times, eh lass?" Hamish kept his voice low as they crouched together under the stage. Ondine pressed her finger to her lips to indicate they should keep quiet. In return Hamish grinned at her. She couldn't help grinning back, especially when he bussed the tip of his nose against hers. Her insides turned mooshy.

Footsteps clomped above them. The timber boards creaked. Conversation in the auditorium lowered to a murmur as people noticed Old Col reach the dais and tap her finger to the microphone. An echo rang out, then the whiney pitch of feedback as she said, "Dobra." [4]

Not everybody hushed. Some were so caught up in themselves they forgot they'd paid good money to be here and kept gabbing on, their murmured words sounding like 'watermelon and cantaloupe' to Ondine's ears.

Old Col cleared her throat. "Her Lordship Duchess Anathea, Madam First Minister Cebotari, Lord Vincent, distinguished guests, ladies . . . and I see we have some gentlemen. Dobra and welcome to the twentieth annual CovenCon!"

Frustration knotted Ondine's tummy. Lord Vincent was out there too. Who gave him an invite? Desperate to find out, she found a gap in the boards and peeked through, looking for her nemesis. She didn't have to look hard. There he was, sitting in the front row next to the First Minister. He was dressed in his usually elegant city clothing with a touch of witchy-ness about him, like a travelling cloak instead of his suit jacket, so that he would fit right in. [5]

Bad boy charm oozed from his every pore as he flicked his dark blonde hair off his forehead.

*Tosser.*

As much as Ondine tried to listen to her great aunt's introduction while keeping an eye on Vincent, she found it hard to concentrate because nestling into Hamish proved so distracting.

It was silly to waste what precious time she'd have with Hamish by spying on Vincent. He wouldn't be going anywhere.

She and Hamish snuck in a few kisses. Warm kisses that made things flip in her belly.

Kisses that turned her head and made her forget about everything else. Kisses that made her bones sigh. Kisses that made a wet *shmack* noise as their lips came apart.

Pure magic.

Above them, Col cleared her throat and clonked her substantial heel on the floorboard, reminding them they had an audience.

*Oops, better behave then.*

On the other hand, if they became loved-up, it would make Old Col's wishes come true, which meant she'd be wishing thoughts along the lines of making Anathea as popular as possible.

They were kissing for Brugel!

Oh those kisses. Ondine could never get enough of them. Maybe it was the cramped space, maybe it was the rare moment of privacy, but she needed Hamish's kisses more than she needed her next breath. Despite trying desperately to have a normal life with him (after all the mayhem they'd been through in the late Duke's Palechia) they never had time to truly enjoy themselves and wallow in their love for each other. Deep down she knew this suited her parents just fine, but it only served to frustrate her all the more. One metaphorical foot was pressed hard on the accelerator while circumstances kept an anvil on the brake.

Emboldened, Ondine pressed herself into his strong body, her fingers playing with the short hairs at his neck. Their lips were made for each other, they fitted so perfectly. When he coaxed her lips open – not that she needed much coaxing – the touch of his tongue against hers sent fire-crackers off in her belly. He felt so, so right. His hand moved in lazy strokes over her back and rounded the curve of her hip. New and wonderful sensations took hold. The smell of him, a mix of soap and his earthy skin felt glorious as her heart staggered behind her ribs and her breath came in soft gasps. Her senses were in a tailspin. What freedom! A naughty thought flitted through her head – no wonder Margi and Thomas got married!

Above them, Old Col coughed again and stomped the floor. The muffled sound of applause burrowed through the floorboards. Was that Col's way of letting them know the magic was working? Should they keep kissing, just in case?

It took all her willpower to pull back from the kiss. She pressed her ear to Hamish's chest in an effort to slow down. His erratic pulse thumped against her skin, proving he was just as intoxicated as she.

She made the universal 'shush' motion in sign language, then pointed to the boards above them. Heavy boots clomped over their heads, the long skirt of her cloak swished about.

"Thank you Miss Romano for that excellent and *lengthy* introduction." The voice belonged to Birgit Howser at her sarcastic best.

*Oh dear*, Ondine thought. They should stop the lovefest while Mrs. Howser was so close. Who knew what she might be wishing at this moment?

"Dobra and welcome," Mrs. Howser said with a wavering alto that reverberated through the speakers. "I'm so impressed to see so many people here after the last-minute change from Slaegal to Brugel. Our motto this year is *Feel The Magic*, and I'm sure you will." [6]

Polite applause spread through the auditorium.

Ondine mentally tuned out. She returned her attentions to Hamish, lying beneath her. How sweet of him to rub her back. She closed her eyes and let his warm strokes soothe her. But not so much that she'd become distracted and start kissing him again. Oh all right, just one more kiss.

He delivered another of those devastating smiles, which filled her with more mooshy feelings. Slowly his warm hand stopped rubbing her back and he pointed to his eye, pointed to his heart then pointed to her. The gesture made her feel so loved she could have melted into him. With her free hand, she returned the sign language, then buried her head into his chest, content to lie with him in a cocoon of love, listening to his heart beating.

Through a crack in the timbers above them, Ondine could see Mrs. Howser standing at the podium, bobbing her right heel up and down. Her heel didn't make contact with the floor so it didn't make a sound. It looked like a classic case of nerves. But then something blurred behind the woman. A strange, shadowy shape moved out of her, then back into her.

Blinking, Ondine turned to Hamish and his eyes the colour of mischief. Had he seen it? Were people playing with the lighting and making shadows appear behind Mrs. Howser's back?

But, hang on. Shadows appeared on the ground, not in the air directly behind a person. This shadow was like a dark entity moving in and out of Mrs. Howser's body.

When it happened again, Ondine felt sure it was no trick. Mrs. Howser had an independent shadow moving in and out of her. A moment more staring and the shadow moved to stand directly behind its master.

". . . We call it many things, but the most common is 'Dark Magic'," Mrs. Howser told the crowd. "A name that has the power to frighten and make us wary. But if we look at it another way, with compassion and understanding, education and a fair amount of common sense, you'll see there truly is nothing to worry about. I call it 'Deep Magic' as its origins are from deep within our history. Deep Magic is a part of us; it is part of who we are."

She paused to take advantage of everyone's attention.

"Deep Magic is the shadow to sunlight. It is part of our everyday lives." [7]

Every time Mrs. Howser said the word 'magic' the shadowy shape ebbed and flowed from her body. Hamish held her tightly, indicating he'd seen it as well.

With the lights directed at the stage, and Mrs. Howser standing behind a lectern, the shadow was something only Ondine and Hamish could see.

The shadow that turned and twisted, then changed direction and came straight for the spot where Ondine and Hamish were hiding.

**11**

———————

Fear turned Ondine's belly to lead. While Mrs. Howser extolled the virtues of 'Deep Magic', the oily shadow stretched and flowed out from her in an egg-whites-from-the-yolk kind of way. Then it folded and twisted into something low and menacing, making no sound as it sank to the floor. Ears straining, Ondine heard no gasps from the crowd; the audience could not see what was going on.

The shadow had to be using the lectern as a shield.

Ondine and Hamish froze together, hardly daring to breathe. Like a sniffer-dog picking up a scent, the dark shape moved as if seeking them out. It found a gap in the timber and oozed through, pouring itself into their cramped space.

Moments earlier, lust had made Ondine's heart race. Now she felt the organ catapult against her ribs in terror as the shadow pulsed and leeched through the timber crack. At first a worm shape to get through the tiny space, the head of it spread out into something not quite human but entirely grotesque. It was featureless but it had rounded pits where its eyes might be. Coldness spread through Ondine as those pits turned directly at her. Hamish's body rippled with tension as he held her tightly. Neither of them dared breathe. She couldn't move a muscle from fear. The transparent oil-slick of darkness swayed hypnotically left and right.

Tendrils moved outwards from the bulbous end, creating a Medusa head of tentacles only a hand-span from Ondine's face.

The one thing that stopped her from screaming was the way Hamish held her. No sooner had that thought filtered through her brain than – *boomph* – he was gone and she rolled into the space where he used to be. Plumes of dust flew up her nose, but she didn't dare cough for fear of being found out.

Wait, what? Where was Hamish?

He'd turned into a ferret!

Fine then, he could run off for help. Good man!

The black . . . *thing* . . . didn't flinch. Its faceless head with dents where eyes should be and writhing tentacles for hair stayed focused on Ondine.

Just as she thought she couldn't be any more grossed out, the tentacles grew like pea-sprouts, curling and wrapping around the floorboards and beams for support as the rest of its octopus-body poured through the crack. Through another gap in the boards, she caught a glimpse of Mrs. Howser. The shadow was still connected to her, leeching out of her, stretching like elastic but not breaking.

All the while Mrs. Howser kept on with her speech, her voice reassuring, calm, and considerate. "We cannot have day without night, light without shade or a summer without winter. This Deep Magic is not to be shunned or feared, it is to be embraced. It makes us whole."

So believable.

So hypnotic.

Fresh panic shot through Ondine. Was Mrs. Howser mesmerising the entire gathering of witches?

Shambles. Where *was* Shambles? Had he run to get help? Run to warn everyone? Her ears strained for the sound of scurrying claws on timber. Instead, she heard something that sounded suspiciously like . . . eating?

*What?*

Turning her head, she saw Shambles chewing on wires.

*Buzz-bzzt!* Lights flickered. Sparks flew. Every hair on Shambles's body bushed out in shock. He chomped down.

An ear-cracking "Bang!" rang out.

"Aaaarrrrggghhh!" screamed Shambles in shock. He shot through the air, twisting and writhing, his furry body twice its normal size.

A new fear took hold of Ondine at the sight of the electrocuted, airborne ferret. One more twist, his body transformed back into Hamish in mid-air.

Landing squarely on Ondine, knocking the wind out of her.

The black shadow slurped out of sight, like liquid up a straw.

The lights went out. Ondine couldn't see a thing.

"Have I hurt ye, lass?" Hamish asked.

Ondine shook her head. But in the dark, Hamish couldn't see her, so she wheezed out a, "No".

Screams and panic broke out in the auditorium.

"Just a power cut," Mrs. Howser said, her voice no longer soothing and hypnotic. If anything, there was an edge of panic.

"Everyone relax," they heard Auntie Col say. "Let's make our way out in an orderly fashion. Try not to bump into anyone. Let your eyes adjust. Follow the green glow of the exit signs, that's the way."

Hamish rolled off Ondine in the darkness. She knew he didn't have a scrap of clothing on. Any other time she might blush furiously, but she was too terrified of Mrs. Howser above them to think straight. A booted foot stomped down hard on the boards, showering them with dust and the odd spider. Torchlight shone through the cracks.

"You!" Mrs. Howser's angry voice cut through. "I knew it!"

The auditorium lights came back on. Heat stole over Ondine's face as she tried desperately not to ogle Hamish in his birthday suit. Grabbing his clothes, they snake-crawled out of their hiding spot and crouched down behind the back of the stage. As much as she wanted to gaze upon Hamish, she averted her eyes while he dressed.

"What do you think you were doing?" Mrs. Howser said, hands fisted on hips.

"Um . . ." Ondine's mind turned blank. They were well and truly sprung. Also, the old witch must have seen him naked.

"We were checking the electrics," Hamish said as he pulled his shirt over his head.

*Brilliant!* Ondine thought, then immediately wished she'd soaked up more of Hamish without his shirt on.

"We didnae realise the time. The place filled up so quickly, as it did. We didnae want to disrupt things so we just figured it was best to stay there until you were finished, so we did."

"Sure you did." Mrs. Howser didn't sound like she believed them.

*Oh would you look at that.* Hamish had his shirt on inside out, so he had to take it off and put it back on the right way.

*Take your time, no rush.*

"There you are!" Old Col said too loudly as she approached. "You're not still checking the wiring are you?"

"Give it up, Colette." Mrs. Howser turned her full attention to Ondine. "This is what she has you doing? How is any of this helping develop your magic? You could be achieving so much with your life but she's got you crawling under floorboards. Spying on me? I could have you arrested! [1]

Old Col brushed past Birgit. "You'll have to bully them later. I came to let Ondine know Her Lordship Anathea requires an audience." [2]

"She does not," Mrs. Howser shot back. "You're bluffing."

"I assure you, she does. I'm sure Her Grace wouldn't mind if you tagged along, Birgit, just to see what it's like to be in the presence of greatness," Old Col said.

"Melody!" Mrs. Howser turned her attention to the front row of seats. "Wake up!"

There Melody sat, her eyes more glazed than a doughnut.

"I said, 'wake up'," Mrs. Howser shouted.

In the snap of a finger, Melody came out of whatever trance she'd been in.

Had she been sitting there the whole time and they hadn't noticed?

"Stop lazing about. Our Lord Duchess needs us."

Mrs. Howser was going to gatecrash their meeting with Anathea? That couldn't be good.

Col's stricken look proceeded some hasty backtracking. "After lunch."

"What?" Hamish said out loud, verbalising Ondine's thought.

"Beg yours?" Mrs. Howser said.

"After lunch. If we meet before lunch, we'll get all the wafty smells from the kitchens . . . er . . . wafting through, and driving us to distraction. Best we meet after lunch, when we're all fighting fit and ready to face the afternoon."

"I don't believe it. You *were* bluffing!" Victory shone on Mrs. Howser's face.

"Not in the slightest. I'm merely looking out for your protégée. Poor Melody here looks like she'll fall over the next time she sneezes."

"She's perfectly hearty," Mrs. Howser said.

Old Col wrapped her fingers and thumb all the way around Melody's upper arm. "She's *starving*! You dare accuse me of not looking after Ondine's magical interests. In turn, you're not looking after Melody's health and welfare. If you'd studied under me, dear girl, I could guarantee you four meals a day. First *and* second dinner."

"It always did come down to food with you," Mrs. Howser said. She clicked her fingers. "Melody, we're leaving."

There could be no stronger indication of the hold Mrs. Howser had on Melody than the way her fingers wrapped tightly around the girl's upper arm to draw her away.

If they didn't break the hold soon, Ondine knew by the tightness in her belly that Melody would grow physically weaker and Mrs. Howser would grow magically stronger.

Which added up to things going very, very badly for Duchess Anathea and Brugel.

**12**

———

With no idea what to do next, other than follow her great-auntie's lead, Ondine joined the queues at morning tea. Standing in line, she and Hamish piled sweet biscuits on their plates and waited for their turn at the urns brimming with tea, coffee, hot chocolate and an overly optimistic pot of chicory. [1]

"What d'ye mean we're not meeting with Anathea?"

"Hush, Hamish," Old Col hissed between her teeth.

"I can't believe you were bluffing," Ondine said.

Old Col glared at her.

Ondine didn't like being glared at.

"Keep your voices down," Col said, "The walls have ears." [2]

"Just asking," Ondine said, looking over to the wall to make sure there were no body parts stuck to them.

"Don't worry, everything is well in hand," Old Col said.

The queue moved slowly. Eventually it was Ondine and Hamish's turn. The tea and coffee urns were empty by this point, so they drained the last of the hot chocolate into their cups.

A collective groan sounded behind them.

"Sorry." Ondine looked at the untouched pot of chicory and then to her three-quarter-cup of hot chocolate. "Here." She gave her cup to the witch in line behind her.

"Yer a good lass," Hamish said, offering her a sip from his cup.

"They should just make two pots of coffee, then everyone would be happy," she said as they took a seat. [3]

Everyone else at CovenCon was taking a mental break at morning tea, catching up with friends or furiously networking. No such luck for Ondine and Hamish, as they spotted Mrs. Howser walking off somewhere, with Melody in tow.

This small event would not have been so noticeable if not for the fact that at the exact same moment, a waiter wheeled out a trolley with two fresh urns of coffee.

Witches swarmed for the caffeine hit. Except for Mrs. Howser.

It could be entirely possible for Mrs. Howser not to like coffee. But that didn't sit right with Ondine. The woman was strange, but she wasn't *that* strange.

"Where do you think she's off to?" Ondine asked Hamish.

"I have a feeling we're aboot tae find oot!" he answered back with a cheeky grin.

As they stood up, they saw Lord Vincent walking off in the same direction. A flash of blue caught Ondine's attention and she saw Lord Vincent still had that blue stain on his hand. The one she and Hamish had given him the night he'd tried to burgle their restaurant.

"Ye dinnae think they're in cahoots?"

"I have no idea," Ondine said, not knowing what cahoots meant, but knowing it couldn't be good.

Following at a safe distance, they came to a set of glass doors leading to the outside swimming pool.

Unless both Mrs. Howser and Lord Vincent were certifiably bonkers, it was a safe bet they weren't taking a dip at this time of year.

Through the glass, they made out the shape of Mrs. Howser standing near the potted palms that had withered and grown manky in the cold weather. Melody was close by, her witch's cloak wrapped tightly around her as she leaned against a lamppost.

They also saw the shape of Lord Vincent. Three sets of footsteps in the snow. Even if they found a place to hide out there by the pool, their foot-steps would give them away.

Time for plan 'D'. [4] "Let's try approaching the pool from the other end," Ondine said.

They wouldn't have to walk through those doors and they wouldn't be seen. On the other hand, they would have to go outside, and it was freezing.

"Aye, we'll need our coats."

"Good thinking."

---

IN NICER WEATHER, they might snuggle together for fun, but as they crouched under the shrubbery next to the terraced wall beside the swimming pool, Ondine and Hamish huddled together out of a desperate need to stay warm. Which only strengthened Ondine's belief that Mrs. Howser was truly horrid. At this time of year, a sensible woman – a *nice* woman – would have held her secret meetings indoors. It took every effort to not shiver and remain as quiet as possible to hear what Mrs. Howser was saying.

" . . . considered, I might not need your help after all." Which was Lord Vincent talking, not Mrs. Howser. It sounded to Ondine's ears as if he were rejecting whatever she'd offered him.

Then Mrs. Howser spoke, dripping with such sarcasm it figuratively ran down the walls. "Sweet, yet stupid. Your grandfather tried that tactic as well. It didn't do him a lick of good."

"I assure you Birgit, it's no tactic. What's two years' waiting in the long run?"

"Deluded as well. You think you can sit back and wait and it will simply come to you? That never got anyone anywhere. It won't get you anything either, not while Anathea's growing more popular by the day. If you want it, you have to grab it with both hands."

Vincent didn't sound convinced. "You're empire building and you're using me to do it."

"I'm getting things done. You might like to try it some day."

A pause in hostilities made Ondine wonder if one of them had walked off, but just as she thought about taking a peek through the shrubbery, she heard Vincent again. "You enjoy sharpening your teeth on the hand that feeds you, don't you."

"It gives me no pleasure. But I'll give you this for free: Promises ring hollow if there is no follow through."

"Promises? More like blackmail."

"Oh dear. Now we've resorted to name-calling. Listen to me, you jumped up bludger, you owe me –"

"– I don't owe you *anything*," Vincent said, his voice stronger, angrier. "Whatever deal you had with my grandfather is long gone. Don't think you can use *me* to collect."

Listening to them reminded Ondine of two dogs fighting over the same bone. They were circling and bristling their fur. Any minute now the snarling and biting would begin. It made Ondine fret for Melody, who must still be somewhere near Mrs. Howser, but had added nothing to the conversation.

Perhaps she'd been smart enough to go back inside?

"You are so lazy. You really think you can sit back and . . . and . . . *wait* for someone to *hand you the keys*?" Mrs. Howser said. "You do that while Anathea gets the laws changed to favour her daughters over you. Do you honestly think by the time you're twenty-one she'll step aside and just . . . give it to you?"

A nasty pause took hold. Ondine furiously held in a sneeze.

It may have been freezing, but Vincent's words carried plenty of heat. "Don't speak to me like I'm naive."

"Hah! Somebody needs to. Anathea's got what she's always wanted. No way will she let go of it. Have you seen how close she is to everyone that matters? Not just the First Minister but also half the Dentate? Give it six more months and she'll have charmed the other half. That's why you have to move now, while things are unstable."

"And in return, I'll be utterly beholden to you. I'm nobody's puppet, *witch*."

Ondine could have sworn she heard Mrs. Howser growling before she spoke. "Do you think magic grows on trees? This is a lifetime's work and I've yet to see a scrap of compensation. You *owe* me!"

"What?!"

"You heard me. If I hadn't used my . . . *talents*, your father would never have been born, which means *you* wouldn't be here either."

That shocked Vincent into silence. Ondine and Hamish were shocked into silence too as they huddled together in mute worry. It sounded awful. It also reminded Ondine of the conversations she'd had with Anathea back at the Autumn Palace. About the age Anathea had reached by the time her baby brother, Duke Pavla was born. Anathea was Duchess Presumptive until Pavla came along. But . . . how did Mrs. Howser have anything to do with *that*?

After what felt like the longest pause, Vincent said, "What . . . did you . . . do?"

Mrs. Howser made a scoffing noise and her hands gripped the railings with a rasp of dry skin on cold metal. It sent a flurry of snow falling below.

Ondine and Hamish smushed themselves further into the shrubbery to stay out of sight.

"I made sure your grandfather got what he wanted," Mrs. Howser said. "He wanted a son more than he wanted his next breath."

"Please tell me we're not –"

"– Related? Don't look so pale, boy. Trust me, I'm *not* your grandmother." Mrs. Howser made a shuddering noise and said, "Perish the thought! Although your grandfather was rather charming in his day . . ."

Hamish's eyebrows sat up so high they might fly away. Ondine felt her eyes grow wide. Her mouth dropped open, as if that would help her to hear better. [5]

Mrs. Howser said, "It wasn't like that. It was the most difficult thing I'd ever done. I had to call on every power I possessed to make sure it worked. It wore me out, but I did it for Brugel. I did it for your grandfather and your father. And for all that work, he didn't give me so much as the lint from his pockets. So whether you like it or not, you owe me, and I'm going to collect."

A beat of silence.

The wind howled.

Vincent broke the tension. "Or you'll stir up trouble I suppose?"

Mrs. Howser scoffed again. "I am giving you an incentive to help me."

Vincent said, "It's called blackmail and I don't want anything more to do with you."

At which point Mrs. Howser's voice softened. Ondine missed the next bit of dialogue so she dropped her jaw all the way down to open her ears properly.

" . . . It's called showing your true nature. You will soon show yours, so let's not mince words. You need me. I can help, for a fee."

"Don't touch me!"

Hello, Mrs. Howser must have gotten too close, Ondine figured.

"Get your hands off me. I don't need *anything* from you." Vincent sounded royally annoyed.

There were some footsteps, and a spray of snow flew over the terraces and landed on Ondine's legs. Were they having a scuffle?

A door opened. One of them must have gone inside to the hotel. A chill spread through Ondine, and it wasn't merely from the snow. The chill froze into fear as she and Hamish looked up to see that oleaginous, black shape ooze across the swimming pool, freezing the surface as it swayed and travelled over the water. Frozen thick enough for Mrs Howser to walk across, her heels cracking the ice but not breaking through.

Howser looked directly to where they were hiding. "You two are so predictable! Well? Don't just sit there. Run along and tell Colette everything you heard. That's what you're meant to do, right?"

In mute shock, Ondine and Hamish looked at each other for a second, then scarpered off in a flurry of snow.

**13**

———

Their long spell outside had left them shell-shocked, numb from the cold and starving. They had the dual task of trying to find Old Col to tell her what they'd heard while also avoiding Mrs. Howser. As they walked inside, the delegates were moving into the banqueting hall for lunch. Lunchtime already? They *had* been outside a long time.

This part of the castle looked recently built, but decorated to look as old as the rest of the place. The textured plaster panelling almost looked real, if you squinted, and you ignored the repeating block pattern.

As rotten luck would have it, Old Col and Mrs. Howser were standing side-by-side in the lunch queue. No chance to talk to one, no chance to avoid the other.

Hunger ruled the moment, so Ondine and Hamish joined the line for hot food.

Mrs. Howser was in fine voice. "Dear me, moving CovenCon from Norange to here . . . You had to make it all about you, Letty."

"We moved it because this is where the magic is. And if you call me Letty again I'll call you Limpy," Old Col said.

"I don't walk with a limp!"

"Not yet."

Hamish gave Ondine a worried look. The two old witches clearly had a lot of bad memories to hash out.

"Ondine!" On hearing her name, she turned to find Melody standing there. Or rather, leaning against the edge of a table. Somebody bumped her and she nearly went flying. Despite the food nearby, Melody didn't have a plate in her hand. She barely looked strong enough to hold a plate, let alone pile it with food.

Ondine forgot her appetite for a moment. "Melody, it's so good to see you." The lie flowed too easily, considering how pallid her friend looked. Cracked lips, strings for muscles and sticks for bones. Hugging her felt like embracing a lamppost. "Come and sit down with us and have some lunch."

"Oh, no, I'm fine," Melody said. "Can we . . . have a chat?"

Hamish gave a nod, indicating he'd get their food for them rather than lose their place in the line.

"Sure." Ondine looked around for a quiet place to sit. They spied a table way over in the corner. From the look of Melody, she might not have the strength to walk that far. The chairs by the wall would have to do. It was so noisy nobody would overhear them at any rate.

Scratch that. Ondine could barely hear Melody either, her voice was so soft. "I'm worried about you," Melody said.

Double-take time. Clasping her friend's papery hand in hers, Ondine said, "I should be the one worrying about you. You're fading away!"

At which time, Hamish presented Melody with a plate groaning with carbs. Pasta salad, potato salad and hot chips on the side. With a lemon wedge and pepper sachet.

Melody fell upon the plate. Mouth stuffed with chips, she said, "Mrs. Howser is taking an unnatural interest in you. *Mmmph*, this is delicious. She talks about you all the time. I don't know what you've done to get her attention but she's fixated. Thanks, more please." She handed her empty plate to Hamish but kept talking. "She's got me using magic night and day. So much of it is about finding out where you are, what you're doing, who you're with, and where you go afterwards."

Panic froze Ondine's limbs.

"Is she not feeding you?" Hamish presented Melody with a second plate, which she ate with the same speed as the first.

"Oh yes, you should see the food bills. But it's exhausting; she's working me so hard I have nothing left in the tank." Fat tears sploshed down Melody's cheeks as she shovelled the food away. Her words came out in a rush. "I'm so sorry sometimes I wish I never had this gift. I just want to sleep."

Ondine moved the second empty plate away and hugged her friend again. When they broke apart, Melody looked to the buffet. Some guests were piling their plates high; others were keeping to the salads and grilled chicken. "You can always tell the ones who really have magic. They have to eat like walruses because it takes so much out of you."

"Aye, like in the pub, eh Ondi?" Hamish said, "Licking the plates clean, so they are."

"Oh dear, then it really is spreading," Melody said.

"Or folks got tapeworm," Hamish said.

Lucky Melody had nothing in her mouth, otherwise she would have spurted all over Hamish as she laughed. Ondine didn't feel like laughing. She wanted to cry at the sight of her friend looking so poorly. And shiver at the thought of Mrs. Howser being so interested in her. And what was spreading? Magic? But everything she knew about magic said you were either born with it or not. You didn't catch it.

"I don't get it. Aunt Col says I have magic, but I'm not that hungry. Well, no more than usual in the middle of winter." Meanwhile, others nearby ate like there was no tomorrow. "Jupiter's moons, I just realised what this means!" Relief poured through Ondine like a geyser. "I can't have magic if I'm not hungry all the time."

Melody's tired eyes lit up. "Oh but you do. You have loads of it. But you're different because you're a carrier, not a subject."

"A what!?"

Melody kept her voice low, leaned in close and said, "Mrs. Howser put the spell on Hamish when he was living with her as Shambles, back at Psychic Summercamp. It was designed to start spreading as soon as he bonded with someone and became human again."

Ondine and Hamish shot each other looks.

"You lived with Howser?" Ondine asked.

"I had tae," Hamish said, getting defensive. "She took me in sharpish after the big dance when Old Col lost her temper."

"Oh yes, of course," Ondine shook her head with confusion. "I knew that. It's just that it happened such a long time ago, I'd forgotten that I knew it."

Melody rushed in, "Anyway, it's not your fault, Ondi. It could have been anyone. You're spreading magic, but you don't have any signs of it yourself. Just like Black Sonja." [1]

Ondine reeled in horror. "But she killed people!"

"OK, bad comparison. It's a bit like that. You're . . . oh, what did Mrs. Howser call you? A symptom . . . an *asymptomatic* carrier. You've got magic oozing out the yin-yang but you don't feel a thing. In the meantime, everyone's catching it from you."

Ondine gulped and said, "But that's horrible!" The word 'oozing' reminded Ondine of the gelatinous black shape they'd seen coming out of Mrs. Howser. Could she too have something similar to Mrs Howser's shadow?

"Is there any more pasta salad?" Melody eyed the buffet.

"Mel, you need a break from Mrs. Howser."

"But she is helping me get better at magic."

"Yes but, look at you. You're fading away to nothing. Come and stay with us and rest up." Her offer was two-fold. Chef's food would return Melody to health and the break would get her away from Mrs. Howser and her oozy black shadow.

Melody sighed. "That's a really sweet offer, but I can't."

Hamish returned with a plate of Singapore noodles. "Get some meat on ye bones. Ye turn sideways and ye disappear!"

The noodles looked delicious. Ondine's tummy rumbled, but she wasn't as ravenous as someone burning their energy with magic all day. "Why don't you ask your parents if you can –"

" – It's very kind of you, but no," Melody said.

"Why not?" Ondine fidgeted with worry. Had Melody's parents seen how ill she looked? She didn't need magic lessons; she needed to get to a fat farm. [2]

"She must know you're talking to me," Melody said while she shovelled in more food. A chunk of noodle flew out and hit Ondine on the cheek. Melody had that panicked look about her, as if she were in trouble. "She knows everything."

Ondine's words brimmed with sarcasm. "Kind of like, she's psychic then?"

Deadpan from Melody. "There is that."

Ondine stood up and made sure Hamish stayed with her friend while she headed to the buffet. Witches, pre-witches, seers and pre-seers crowded around the tables, piling their plates high, then getting sidetracked with talking to people and standing about, blocking the food Ondine wanted. [3]

"Excuse me," she said. "Sorry." She budged the person in front of her. "Can I get to the beetroot salad please?"

The chatty coven moved a few centimetres over, allowing Ondine access. So much to choose from. Sandwich points, pickled squid, pasta salads, slices of rare beef with horseradish cream, stir-fries, fruit and cheeses. At the allergy table they had sandwich fillings on rice cakes, leafy salads, fruit and more fruit and steamed vegetables with sweet chilli dressing. The vegetarian and vegan tables looked so colourful Ondine's mouth began watering afresh.

"Bingo!" someone said.

"Eggplant stack!" another said, at which point they burst into giggles. Ondine didn't get it. [4]

Armed with a good spread of lunch, she made her way back to Hamish, where Melody was mopping the last smear of dressing from her plate with a wedge of bread.

With several mouthfuls of food in her belly, Ondine didn't feel so hopeless. Another thought soon chased that away. Was she hungry from natural causes or witching ones?

Hamish helped himself to some of Ondine's rare beef.

Feeling full, Ondine put the plate to one side.

"Are you going to eat that?" Melody said.

"Give it laldy." Hamish handed it over.

"He means you can have at it," Ondine translated for her friend's benefit,

"There you are." Old Col and Mrs. Howser stood in front of them. Standing together. Like old friends.

Ondine gulped past the boulder in her throat.

"Time for our audience with the Duchess," Mrs. Howser said.

"Ye mean, all of us?" Hamish asked.

"Yes, of course," Mrs. Howser said. "Come along Melody."

**14**

———

Standing in the state receiving room, Ondine gulped hard as she and everyone else waited for Duchess Anathea to grace them with her presence. Guilt and fear swirled in her tummy, making her light-headed and lead-bellied. Guilt that they hadn't done enough to make Anathea popular. Fear that Hamish might never get his work papers and be arrested and deported.

Or be forced to spend the rest of his years as a ferret.

Every corner of the room dripped elegance. From the art deco light fittings to the towering vases of flowers on the side tables, this was a properly decorated room. Right down – or more accurately, up – to the glass dome above that flooded the room with natural light.

Not an ordinary urn of coffee on a table for this room. No. It had a proper coffee-making machine. One that warmed the cups, ground the beans, percolated the coffee at exactly the right temperature and steamed the milk. [1]

If it had been only her, Hamish and Old Col meeting the Duchess, she would have been nervous. But Ondine had even more worries because Mrs. Howser was in the room. Based on what she and Hamish had overheard by the pool, Mrs. Howser wanted to work for Vincent. She was also dead against Anathea becoming more popular.

Why had Col allowed her nemesis to come to the meeting?

So many questions swirled in Ondine's head she felt a thumping ache coming on. It started at the back of her neck and grew up the left side.

*Howser-shouldn't-be-here-thump-thump.*

*How-do-we-let-Anathea-know-this?-thump-thump.*

*Why-isn't-this-meeting-more-secret?-thump-thump.*

*Maybe-Aunt-Col-is-losing-her-mind?-thump-thump.*

*Speaking-of-Aunt-Col-I-don't-seem-to-be-learning-very-much-magic-Bong!*

The clock struck one as Duchess Anathea walked into the meeting room with her fluffy white dog, Biscuit-of-the-half-grown-teeth, trailing after her. Something had changed about Anathea since they'd last met at the Ferris wheel. Her face shone with more gloss than usual. She looked haughty, more commanding. Her blonde hair glowed with vibrant health. Being the head of state clearly agreed with her.

Hamish slipped his hand in Ondine's, partially dissolving her worries and head thumps. As one, everyone bowed their heads to show their respect. In the corner of her vision, Ondine couldn't help notice Mrs. Howser didn't bow as deeply as everyone else.

As Anathea sat, Biscuit leapt into her lap and made himself comfortable. The lapdog yawned to reveal a curved row of pointy teeth buds.

"Told you his teeth would grow back," Old Col said.

The Duchess craned the dog's jaw around to have a look. "Getting there."

"That would be Ondine's doing," Old Col said. "She's developing the most agreeable talents."

Locking gazes with Ondine, the Duchess said, "That is appreciated."

"Thank you," Ondine said, then silently thought, *I think.*

A flute of sparkling wine sat on the table in front of Anathea. She dipped a finger in the bubbles and held it out as Biscuit licked it off. Then she dipped her finger back in and did it again, before she had a sip.

Ondine's gorge rose.

"That's mockit." Hamish said.

Ondine squeezed his hand to silently plead for his . . . well, his silence, really.

"How goes the task that was set for you?" Anathea asked.

"Very well thanks," Ondine said, being careful not to mention the type of task Anathea had set, because if Mrs. Howser found out she'd –

"If I may be so rude as to interrupt," Mrs. Howser said, taking a step forward. "You need some special magic, and you need it rather quickly. I believe I and my protégée, Melody – stand up Melody, don't be shy – will be only too happy to help in any way you see fit."

A broad smile – one might almost call it warm – spread across Anathea's face.

"Naw, ye dinnae want that," Hamish blurted.

"Don't," Ondine said under her breath.

"Oh really?" Anathea said. "And why would I not want to use any help that might be made available?"

"Because it could dilute the magic, of course," Old Col chimed in. "Your Lordship, I'm not one to blow my own trumpet, but you'll get your very best results from Ondine and Hamish, I assure you. Mixing the magic with other spells could end up . . . ah . . . well, it could make something of a mess, you see."

"If I may speak freely?" Mrs. Howser said.

Anathea nodded.

"The original magic between Hamish and Ondine was *my* creation. As well-meaning as she might be, Colette Romano is misleading you if she thinks she can control it."

"I beg your pardon?" Auntie Col's hands landed hard on her hips.

Mrs. Howser continued as if everything was fine and dandy, when in reality Ondine was stomach-churningly nervous. "I mean no disrespect," Mrs Howser said. "But if you want results – real results – then allow me to humbly offer my services."

"Uh," Ondine started, but didn't know how to go on.

"There is an objection?" Anathea asked, her gaze locking with Ondine's. "Is Birgit Howser the originator of your magic or not?"

Ondine squeaked out, "Well, yes, she probably is." Then she cleared her throat and tried to explain. "At least, she put the spell on Hamish and then when he bonded with me it set off a chain reaction thingy, but please, Your Grace, let us keep working for you. It's working so well. The people love you more than ever." That last bit was a desperate attempt by Ondine to remind Anathea that they were doing their best to make her popular. Because if Anathea started thinking she didn't need them, what incentive would she have for granting Hamish his citizenship?

Anathea looked directly to Mrs. Howser. "You mean to say it's the spell made by you that makes people's wishes come true?"

Mrs. Howser made a bow to affirm this.

"Excuse me! I was the one that turned him into a ferret in the first place!" Old Col snapped.

It brought the room to a sudden and horribly uncomfortable silence. This could only get messier. Old Col looked weak and watery while Mrs. Howser looked more confident by the second. Mercury's wings, why did Col agree to let Howser join the meeting?

"It was one of *my* spells, Your Grace," Mrs. Howser said. "Of course, Colette here added her . . . *contribution*. But it's no idle boast when I assure you the mutating magic is all of my making."

"A ferret?" Anathea said, her eyes growing wider as she looked from Hamish to Old Col and back again.

Ondine wanted to bury her face in her hands. The cat – or ferret in this case – was well out of the bag. Now that Anathea knew of his other skills, Ondine would bet her life on Anathea wanting him to stay that way and spy for her. Just as the late Duke had done.

"Aye," Hamish said.

Biscuit the dog pricked up his ears.

Anathea looked from Old Col to Hamish again. "The night you made Biscuit's teeth fall out. You had a ferret spying under the dining table, didn't you?"

"Please, Your Grace, do not upset yourself with trifling matters," Mrs. Howser said, sounding as slippery as her greasy shadow. "It is enough to say that Colette Romano has been trying to impress you with another witch's magic. But as I am here now, and I forgive Colette for her trans-gressions, please consider me a convenient replacement for your magical requirements?"

"I have not been claiming credit for your work," Old Col said, her voice wobbling and her expression frail and senior. "That's not what's been happening at all."

Anathea raised her palm to shush them all. "A ferret you say? This is something to be seen."

Ondine and Hamish gulped in unison.

"Go on." Old Col sounded defeated. "You may as well show her."

"Aye." Hamish kissed Ondine on the forehead and let go of her hand.

The grimace on his face made Ondine ache for the pain he had to endure. This transition was slower than his flash-change under the stage, but no less shocking for Ondine to see her true love reduced in such a way. At first his face turned dark, then fur sprang out all over the place, even from his ears. His nose turned pointy as long whiskers sprouted from his cheeks. His ears shrank away into furry triangles. A moment later he vanished under a pile of lifeless clothes.

"What an interesting thing to be seen," Anathea said.

Shambles the ferret poked his pointy, furry face out from under a shirt. The ring she'd bought him for Christmas slipped free and rolled on the floor. An ache started up in Ondine's heart from the pain of seeing him like this.

"How very interesting. And how very, very useful," Anathea said.

"I was like this for dozens of years, until I met Ondine," Shambles said. "And when I finally came round, I was still fit-like, on account of the spell Col made. So ye see, she is a great witch, sure she is."

"How loyal he is," Mrs. Howser said. "He would have found it hard to expose Miss Romano's lack of usable magic, probably based on some kind of gratitude towards her. I'm sure they meant no harm in deceiving you, Your Grace."

Ondine protested, "It's not like that!"

Biscuit the dog shot out of Anathea's arms and charged at Shambles.

"Not again!" Ondine cried. In a flash, she scooped Shambles into her arms, away from the marauding dog. His teeth might be tiny buds, but she wasn't taking any risks. [2]

*Ru-ru-ru-ru.* Biscuit leapt at Ondine, then dug his claws into her pants. *Riiiip!* Those same claws tore an ugly gash in the fabric on the way down.

Defying gravity and lack of fitness, Biscuit leapt even higher. Chomp! His teeth closed around Shambles's middle.

"Arrrrrghghghghghghg!" Shambles cried out.

"Stop it! You're killing him!" Ondine screamed.

## 15

"Naw, naw, ahahahahahahah!" Shambles garbled.

It sounded like he was . . . *laughing?*

"Awwww, his teeth are so wee! Best tickle fer ages!" At which point Shambles burst into a fresh bout of ferrety giggles.

With a quick tug, Ondine pulled Shambles away. Biscuit slipped off him and fell to the floor in a puddle of fur. Shambles was covered in slobber, but at least it wasn't blood. Silently, she chanted, 'Don't kick the dog, don't kick the dog'. No amount of grovelling could make up for that. [1]

"I can see now why my departed brother wanted to have you around permanently." Anathea said. "I would like you to perform the same kind of services for me as you did for the late Duke."

Shambles said, "Ye honour me, Yer Grace, but I cannae leave Ondi. She's me life."

Such sentiment would ordinarily make Ondine grin with happiness, but not in this kind of atmosphere.

Anathea shrugged. "I hardly see what difference this makes. You are already supposed to be working for me. I propose it becomes more of a formal arrangement. Where you stay of an evening is entirely your business."

"So ye mean, ye want me to work for ye, here in Venzelemma?"

*No, Hamish, you're supposed to stay with me. We're never going to be apart again*, Ondine wished.

Anathea's brows made the slightest crease. "I'm not going back to Bellreeve, if that's what you're thinking."

Biscuit barked freshly at Shambles, desperate to gnaw his belly again. Ondine didn't trust that dog for a second. "Your Grace, it's not safe for Hamish and Biscuit to be under the same roof. Things will only get worse when his teeth grow back."

"Your Grace, thank you for this audience," Old Col said in a tone that told Ondine it was time they ended this meeting.

A commotion by the main doors distracted them. As one, everyone turned to see the cause of it. Ondine's stomach did that hideous dropping away thing as Lord Vincent sauntered in, blue hand and all.

Did he never wash?

Shambles crawled up her back to settle on her shoulder. "He doesnae look so good."

Understatement of the year. Lord Vincent looked like he'd been turned inside out and shaken a few times, then shoved back together in a rush.

"Dearest nephew," Anathea said with an imperial tone. "To what do I owe this interruption to my busy schedule?"

His said in a growly rush, "You are in grave danger." Perspiration gathered on his forehead, as if it took every ounce of strength for him to be here.

Like watching a tennis match, Ondine's eyes shot back and forth between Vincent and Anathea.

"Really? From whom?" the Duchess gave her return volley.

"From me!"

Terrible didn't even come close to describing how Vincent looked. He staggered forward and drew breath. His face turned grey. Had someone poisoned his food?

In his next breath he fell to his knees, his eyes rolling back into his head.

Morbid curiosity took hold. Ondine stepped closer, to get a better look. Vincent's head snapped forward. He jumped to his feet and thundered at full strength, "You! This is all your doing!"

Ondine leapt backwards.

Shambles whispered, "Ondi I think we should –"

"Die!" Vincent pushed his palm out. Time and space rippled before Ondine's eyes. A rolling shockwave knocked her to the floor.

"No!" It was Aunt Col's voice this time. Dizzy and half-concussed, Ondine saw her witchy great-aunt rebuffing the advancing shockwave. In the next heartbeat Duchess Anathea scooped Biscuit into her arms and hid behind Col, using her as a human shield.

Where had Mrs. Howser gone? What was she doing all this time? Saving the Duchess? No. She stood there, arms crossed, watching it unfold.

Melody crouched against the wall, her hands over her ears.

Thick, heavy pounding reverberated inside Ondine's head, as if she'd put her ear to a speaker at a rock concert. Shambles flailed about on the floor, moaning and groaning like he was about to revert to human form. He had the worst habit of changing at the exact wrong time. It would be an absolute disaster if he . . . Mercury's wings, he started changing.

"No Hamish!"

Vincent heard her. He stopped duelling with Old Col.

"Perfect!" In two steps he reached Shambles, drew back his foot and kicked.

Hard.

His boot made contact with Shambles, sending him soaring across the room.

"No!" Ondine screamed.

Shambles's body wobbled and twisted through the air until he hit the wall with a sickening crack, then slid lifelessly to the floor.

Ondine scrambled to his side, but something tripped her and she hit the ground again, smacking her chin on the tiles. Pain shot through her. She shut her eyes hard to ride it out. Tears sprouted anyway. Jupiter's moons, it hurt!

"Vincent! This madness must be stopped!" Anathea said, cowering behind Old Col.

Ondine tried to get up again, but she slipped on something wet and smelly. Biscuit piddle. She nearly threw up in her effort to move away.

*Hamish, I must get to Hamish,* she thought. But when she turned to where he'd fallen, he wasn't there. Had he crawled off. Had someone taken him away?

"He's possessed," Old Col said of Vincent, to nobody in particular.

"Help me!" Vincent called out, even as the magical assault continued.

Col yelled out, "Who's pulling the strings?"

Vincent made garbled sounds.

"Where's Hamish?" Panic constricted Ondine's chest. "What have you done with him?"

"The boy's mad," Anathea said. With a burst of panic, she ran for the door and pulled it open. "Security! Security!"

Meanwhile, Old Col and Vincent were still holding each other steady with equal measures of magic and bluster. Sound waves reverberated around the room turning everything hazy and blue. Noises crashed inside Ondine's head, giving her the biggest thumper of a migraine she'd ever experienced.

Mrs. Howser stood there with a satisfied look on her face.

Col's voice came out strong and sure. "Give up!"

"Help me!" Vincent yelled.

Anathea slipped out the door to safety.

"Where is Hamish?" Ondine pressed her hands to the sides of her head and staggered around the room.

"What?" Vincent lost his concentration for a split second.

Old Col seized her chance. "Stop!" The boom of a jet engine breaking the sound barrier pounded through the room. Light fittings exploded. The large dome above them shattered, showering everyone with broken glass and sending magic into the snowy sky like fireworks.

The thumping inside Ondine's head fell away. A piercing ringing took its place. Maybe, just maybe, if this had been an ordinary day without the spying and plotting and scheming, she might have the strength to make sense of it. Instead she felt twenty-seven kinds of wrong. Confusion held her in its grip. Vincent lay slumped on the floor. It looked like Old Col was saying something. Her lips were moving but nothing came out.

Gradually the piercing noise faded away, replaced by the buzzing of wasps. Through the buzzing, Anathea came back into the room, flanked by security.

"He's gone crazy. He's possessed," the Duchess said.

Old Col agreed. "He was fighting something, but he wasn't strong enough to hold it back."

Ondine leaned against the wall, waiting until the room stopped spinning. Turning, she saw Melody curled in foetal position.

Looking completely at ease, Mrs Howser turned to the security people and said, "Something is very wrong with that boy."

Anathea gulped as she looked at the slumped form of Lord Vincent. "He's always given me the creeps, that child. I truly fear for Brugel when he inherits."

Mrs. Howser stepped forward to help the Duchess. "There's plenty of time to declare him insane before then. Now, careful where you walk, there's broken glass everywhere."

Col's top lip curled in contempt as she looked at the security people. "Your Duchess could have used you a few minutes ago."

"Apologies, My Lord Duchess." The security guard dropped to one knee. His eyes sprang open as a glass shard punctured his skin.

For the next few minutes, Ondine regained her balance and ignored the confused talk and apologies. She only had one thing on her mind. "Auntie Col, did you see where Hamish went?"

His dishevelled face appeared around the doorway, along with a naked shoulder and bony knee. "Ondi, would ye mind grabbin' ma clothes, I'm fair freezing."

Relief surged through her. "Uh-huh." Ondine nodded and grabbed the bundle of clothes she'd dropped at some point. Unfortunately, she'd dropped them too close to the lake of Biscuit piddle so they had that unforgiving acrid smell. It would have to do until they got home and could wash this horrible day down the drain.

# 16

Back at the family pub, Chef approached Ondine, Hamish and Old Col with a cheerful smile. He caught one whiff of the dog-wee smell, scrunched his face up and ushered them towards the back room. "Get cleaned up, I'll get you some to-faux-fu soup." [1]

After they'd showered and changed and properly cleaned themselves up, Ondine and Hamish met up with Ma and Old Col in their private room behind the kitchen. The soup arrived and they slurped it down while they debriefed after an insane day.

But why did Ma need to be in here? "Aren't you busy?" Ondine asked.

"Have you ever known Tuesday nights to be busy?" Ma shot back.

"Good point."

Ma pressed on, keen to find out everything. "Will you tell me what's wrong? Was it the run-in you had with Lord Vincent?"

At which point Hamish began rubbing her back in a sign of support and love.

"Auntie Col told me," Ma said. "She filled me in on everything that happened."

"That would be everything except what we heard by the pool, eh lass?"

"You went swimming?" Great Aunt Col shivered at the thought.

"That's the bit we haven't had time to tell you about. We came back inside to find you but by that point Mrs. Howser was with you and we couldn't say anything."

Old Col huffed. "That woman! No wonder she stuck so close. She knew the more she stuck by me, the less you could say."

That may have been the case at CovenCon, but now they were home, they had plenty of time to relay everything, so that's exactly what they did. Everything they overheard and saw from their morning of spying on Mrs. Howser, including the black oozy shadowy thing.

A shiver spread through the room.

"No wonder you two didn't say much during our meeting with Anathea." Col said, shaking her head. "I knew Birgit was up to something. I thought an audience with the Duchess would expose that. Which, of course, it did. It's all falling in to place now. She met with Vincent and transferred some kind of controlling spell onto him. To do that she would've had to be close enough to touch him. Did you see whether she touched him? Shook his hand? Patted his head? You see, the higher up the body, the more powerful the spell."

Hamish piped up. "Weil, we didnae see anything, but we heard him say 'don't touch me,' so we did."

"He sounded really annoyed about it," Ondine added.

"Oh dear." Old Col sucked in her cheek in thought. "If she patted him on the head, it explains his lack of control."

"Maybe that's why he sounded so annoyed. Maybe he thought she was being patronising or something, when instead she was getting close enough to cast a spell," Ondine said.

Ma drummed her fingers on the table. "Couldn't have happened to a nicer person. He's caused you no end of grief. I would have thought you'd be glad to see him suffer."

"No Ma, not even Vincent deserved that. He was completely possessed. He was crying out for help. I felt . . . sorry for him."

Ma crinkled her brow. "Sorry?"

"Yeah. A bit."

"Must have been *really* bad," Ma said.

"I wonder, hmm," Old Col said. "When he said we should die, I thought it was rather extreme. But perhaps he was directing that to Howser and not Anathea?"

"That's kind of painting a nicer picture," Ondine said. "I don't want to think nicely about Vincent. He doesn't deserve my sympathies."

"True lass," Hamish said.

"But what I don't get," Ondine said, completely not getting it. "One moment Howser is trying to sweet-talk Vincent into joining her, the next she's sending him insane. What's all that about?"

"Motivation, dear child," Old Col said. "It's her way of showing Vincent 'you're either with me or against me.' There is no middle ground with Birgit."

It was Hamish's turn to crease his brow. "So she throws a witchy tantrum if she disnae get her own way?"

"That's about the sum of it. Today she's shown Vincent what a powerful enemy she can be. He can continue to defy her and pay the consequences, or join her and reap the rewards. It's a surprisingly persuasive argument," Col said. "And another thing, she's lying about not getting paid. She was paid, and handsomely. How do you think she got the money to start that psychic school of hers?"

That made Ondine blink with surprise. "You knew about her helping the previous Duke have a son?"

"I was there," Old Col said in a huff.

"Eww!" Ondine said.

"Not in that way! Honestly!" Old Col huffed.

Ondine stifled an inappropriate giggle. When she unscrambled her thoughts, she turned to Old Col again. "Why would Mrs. Howser lie to Vincent? About the money and all that?"

"Keep up, child." Old Col rolled her eyes. "Because she's greedy, that's why. Mind you, she wouldn't have considered it a lie. Knowing her as I do, she merely thinks she wasn't compensated *enough*."

All eyes turned on Col, waiting for the rest of it.

"Oh all right. You wouldn't think it, but we used to be close friends. We both worked for the late Duke. Or the later one, I guess. Pavla's father. Anyway, Birgit came into plenty of money but she never told me where it came from. I was too polite to ask at the time. Don't look at me like that; I can be polite when the mood takes me. Anyway, I thought maybe she had a wealthy lo – . . . uh . . . patron or something. I kept thinking she'd tell me who'd stumped up the money, but she never did.

"Things really fell apart after the Debutante Ball, and the rest, as they say, is lies and conjecture. [2] A few days later, when I'd calmed down, obviously, I searched for Hamish to reverse the ferret spell I'd put on you dear, but I couldn't find you. Or Birgit for that matter. I didn't know she had you, you see. And years later, when our paths would cross at CovenCon or at Halloween, she never let on. That must be why I've never been able to reverse the ferret spell for good, because she put another layer on top. Only the witch that placed the last spell can remove it."

Silence cloaked them for a while, until Old Col spoke again. "By the way. There's something you're all overlooking about today. I'm not bragging or anything, but it was *my* magic that held Vincent back. Birgit spent the whole meeting bringing me down, but when it came to it, I was the one that sorted things out."

"Thank you, Auntie Col," Ondine said. "You really came through." Which was as close as Ondine would admit to nearly being swayed by Mrs. Howser. Because Mrs. Howser had very nearly made Ondine wonder if her great aunt had started to lose her grip . . . on magic and other things.

She had to acknowledge a certain amount of jealousy over how far Melody had come in six months' tuition with Mrs. Howser. Compared to how little Ondine felt her great aunt had been able to teach her. On the plus side, Ondine could make other people's wishes come true; that was pretty amazing!

If only she knew how to control it. Then she'd *really* have magic.

Sadness swamped Ondine, because she had to acknowledge the magic had come about because of Hamish being under Mrs. Howser's extra spell, not the original spell from Auntie Col.

Which had Ondine's conscience juggling all kinds of disloyalty.

On top of those worries, Duchess Anathea now knew Hamish could be a Shambles-ferret-spy. To a paranoid Duchess, her beloved Hamish made the perfect package.

"Ondine, pay attention!" Ma snapped her fingers in front of her face.

"Oh yes, sorry." They were all looking at her.

"Ye must be tired, lass." Hamish rubbed her back again.

"Yeah."

"We're talking about where we go from here. Auntie Col and I were saying you and Hamish will need to work even harder to make Anathea popular."

"Uh-huh." Ondine nodded. "Um. No. Hang on. Why would we do that? The more we work for her, the more she'll want Hamish working with her all the time as a ferret. How does that help anyone?"

By 'anyone' she meant 'me'.

"Yes, but if you don't, she'll be unlikely to grant Hamish his papers." Old Col said. "*Quid pro quo*, and all that." [3]

Ondine thought out loud. "If we stop helping Anathea, we're going to lose Hamish, aren't we?"

"If you need to repeat things to help the world make sense, by all means carry on," Old Col said.

Frustration bloomed in her heart. "Yeah, but, don't you see? If we do keep helping her, I could still lose Hamish because he'll be ferreting around for Anathea. She said as much herself."

"You mean 'we' could lose Hamish," Ma corrected.

"Isn't that what I said?" Ondine mentally swatted away a whiny little 'why me?' buzzing about her head. No way. She would *not* give in to a fit of the sulks.


HAMISH RUBBED HER BACK AGAIN. "I'm nawt going anywhere, I promise."

"I'm not sure we have any other options," Old Col said.

Ondine thought of plenty more options, all of which involved running away with Hamish and leaving Anathea and the rest of Brugel to sort itself out. But in the end, she knew there was only one path she could take.

"We have to help Anathea to save Hamish," Ondine said, determined to not sniffle despite her vision blurring. "We're going to uphold our end of the bargain, come what may."

That familiar twinkle shone in Hamish's beautiful green eyes. "Aye, weil keep snuggling and making magic, fer the good of Brugel."

Well, there was *that*.

**17**

---

Considering the mayhem and trauma of the previous day, Ondine didn't particularly feel like going back to CovenCon the next morning.

Old Col told her in no uncertain terms they had to. "Life is full of things we don't particularly feel like doing, but we do them and we get on with it."

*Thanks for the support and understanding.*

When they arrived at the convention, security had been beefed up since the day before. There were extra people standing by the doors and checking nametags.

No sign of Mrs. Howser. What was the old witch up to now?

After the early plenary session and motivating speeches, it was time to split off into the various workshops on offer. [1]

Ondine and Hamish's job for the day was to stay close to Anathea, so that they could keep canoodling, so that Anathea could keep wishing she were more popular than fried cheese balls.

Their magic had to be working because so many people were looking at Anathea with admiration. Every session the Duchess visited became congested as so many wanted to be exactly where she was.

"Perhaps our work here is done," Ondine said as they grabbed a spare seat in the back row of *Harvesting Magical Ingredients*. Duchess Anathea was in attendance, so it was packed. *Oh, what a shame*, Ondine thought with a smile; there was only one seat left so she had to sit on Hamish's lap.

"Doin' it fer Brugel," Hamish whispered as he wrapped his arms around her.

The workshop itself provided nothing of interest for Ondine, not that she could hear much from way up the back. The guest witch invited the Duchess to take a quickly-vacated seat right up the front.

That earned Anathea a round of applause, merely for taking a seat.

Relief cascaded through Ondine. She whispered to Hamish, "I think it's working?"

It would have been disrespectful to the presenter to sneak out mid-workshop. Not that they could get out with the crowd pressed in so closely around them. So they sat quietly together playing 'handies'. This involved tickling each other's palms until the other person couldn't stand it any longer and had to pull away. All the while they had to be utterly silent. If you made a noise, you lost a point. If you pulled your hand away with the first tickle, you lost three points. If you squirmed, minus four points. And so on.

After five minutes, Ondine was losing far too many points and having a fantastic time. A woman in the next row turned around and shushed them. The woman beside the other woman murmured something about being catty.

Ondine had to bite the inside of her cheek to stay quiet, because Hamish kept moving his hands towards hers – but not touching. Merely the threat of a tickle had her silently shaking in fits of giggles.

Gasp! The woman in front of them grew a tail that grew out the back of her. Then the woman next to her grew a tail too. It was tan with orange stripes and altogether quite becoming. Down the row, every single person grew a tail. Thick furry ones, spotted ones, thin ones and even a ratty looking one with a kink in it.

Ondine looked to Hamish and whispered, "Did we do that?"

"I don –"

He never finished the word, let alone the sentence. Pandemonium broke out. People screamed and wailed as they suddenly noticed their new appendages.

"Ouch, you stepped on my tail!"

"Watch it!"

"Mind your own tail, this one's mine!"

"It's horrible!"

"Get it off!"

In the *mêlée*, Ondine grabbed Hamish's hand and scarpered, caught between laughing her head off and crying in panic.

In the hall, Hamish gave her a calming hug. "I've seen some weird things since coming tae Brugel, but ye *goat* to admit, tails on folks isnae something ye see every day."

Their tummies rumbled in unison as the conference staff set the buffet for morning tea. Any minute now people would swarm the tables, tails and all. Ondine grabbed a plate to beat the rush. Behind them, the noise from the workshop became too loud to ignore. Worried convention staff and volunteers pulled the doors open to see what was amiss.

People ran out, screaming and wailing and . . . *miaowing*? Yes, definitely cat noises coming from the crowd.  Ondine piled the chocolate slices on her plate, feeling perplexed and fearful. Would she and Hamish grow tails as well?

Old Col's crepe-paper-thin fingers clamped around Ondine's wrist. "Did you and Hamish do that?"

"I didn't do anything. We were just sitting in the back row, minding our own business." A pile of bricks called 'guilt' filled her tummy that she and Hamish might have caused it. They were merely being loved up so that people's nice wishes about the Duchess could come true.

So many thoughts assaulted her. Mrs. Howser. Magic virus. Spells. Conspiracies. Lord Vincent. Chaos.

The fire alarm blared. Staff ordered people to evacuate. Sirens wailed and emergency lights flashed.

Reluctantly, Ondine put her plate of morning tea aside.

They followed the crowd to the assembly area outside, with many standing well clear of everything over by the funicular station. To one side was the waterfall, which flowed into the river running underneath the drawbridge. It would have been a lovely place to stop and take photographs, if not for the incessant sirens and bumps and shoves from running, panicky people.

To judge from the ominous creaking sound beneath Ondine, they should get off the drawbridge. Emergency vehicles pulled up at an alarming rate. Police, Ambulance, Fire Brigade. Even a mobile coffee shop pulled over near the funicular, on the off-chance they might make a quick schlip. [2]

"What did you do?" Old Col demanded as she stared at Ondine.

They were still standing on the drawbridge. Safely out of the evacuated castle, but not out on the snow-covered lawn where the delegates were assembling. Ondine gulped. The timber whined and whimpered in protest beneath them.

Hamish defended Ondine. "We did what we were supposed tae!"

With a groan of frustration, Old Col glared at them.

"We were . . ." Ondine's mind went blank with the stress.

Hamish slipped his hand in hers for reassurance. "We were only holding hands, Col. I swear on my life we didnae do anything."

"Holding hands?" Old Col creased her forehead at them.

"Aye, it's nae crime," he said, at which point he caressed his thumb against Ondine's hand. They may have been standing outside in the depths of winter but his touch made her feel warm and loved.

Adding one more level of craziness, Ma arrived, her breath steaming in huge puffs as she tried to steady herself. "Please don't tell me the Duchess has a tail?"

What in the name of all the planets was her mother doing here?

"Where was the Duchess in all of this?" Old Col's stare drilled holes in Ondine.

"We were all together," Ondine said.

"The whole time?" Old Col asked.

"Yes! We stuck close to her like burned cheese on a casserole dish. We were doing our job!"

"And you were close to her the whole time?" Old Col's interrogation technique was seriously impressive.

"Of course we were – ooooh!" Ondine gasped and clapped her spare hand over her mouth as she realised. "Until she went up the front."

Ma's eyes widened. "You were separated?"

"Why are you here Ma? Don't you have a pub to run?"

"Cybelle and Henrik have it under control," Ma said. "Now don't change the topic, this is serious. How close were you to the Duchess?"

"Now, Messers G, don't take it out on Ondi. It wasnae her fault. The room was packed tighter than movie night cheap seats. We had tae share a seat and there were people standing all around us so we were hemmed in, so we were. And everyone was treating Anathea like royalty and they offered her a seat up the front, like."

"She is royalty," Ondine corrected him.

"Och, yes."

"Then you should have gone with her!" Old Col said.

Ma covered her face with her hands and muttered, "I knew this would happen."

"But we couldn't move it was so crowded," Ondine said. Honestly, why did her mother have to show up now? It's like the woman had some kind of magic to appear right when things got complicated.

Old Col crossed her arms over her chest. "Then you should have stopped!"

At which point a passing mailman dropped his trolley and began barking like a dog.

Fresh hell broke loose.

"There's your proof," Ma said as they scooted away from the fresh outbreak of screaming.

"Oh naw, that's too cruel." Hamish looked from Old Col to Ma to Ondine and back again. "Ye cannae blame us, it's naw our fault!"

"Ondine dear," Old Col began. She hardly ever called her 'dear', which meant things couldn't be good. "I wish, just this once, you could think beyond your feelings for Hamish and look at the bigger picture."

"And how exactly do I do that?" Ondine could have sworn angry steam poured out of her ears, to match the steam from her mouth as she spoke. "I don't know what the big picture is. This magic is all new to me.

I can't even feel when I'm using it. I don't know how far it reaches or how to control it or who's wishing what, when!"

Hamish tightened his grip on Ondine. "Dinnae take it out on Ondi, she's done naw wrong. So what if a few folks have tails? It's naw tha end of tha world, is it?"

"Ondine I'm so very sorry. You're going to hate me for this," Ma said.

Heavy sickness filled Ondine. Swallowing took so much effort she thought she might throw up.

Ma took a calming breath. "I thought perhaps you could control it –"

Old Col interrupted, "People are getting hurt. Innocent people."

Ondine opened and closed her mouth a few times. "It'll wear off . . . won't it?"

"It's naw as if we can control it," Hamish said.

"This is exactly my point. I thought you *could* control it, but you can't. Birgit Howser has truly excelled herself, creating a spell like this. Can't you see she's using you to create chaos? Sure, making people's wishes come true is wonderful, but that's only the good wishes. What of the bad ones? What if someone wishes something truly malicious? Someone near the two of you has wished someone else into a cat and look what it's done?"

Tears blurred Ondine's vision. "It's not my fault! I can't control what other people are wishing for!"

Ma stepped forward and embraced her. "I know that, love. That's why we have to do something about it."

The words sounded horribly ominous. It also gave Ondine an inkling of why her mother was here. Things were about to get horrible.

Ma continued. "You see now what Mrs. Howser is capable of. She's using the pair of you to create instability and fear. If it goes on, it will only destabilise Anathea and all of Brugel for that matter."

All breath left Ondine. The corners of her vision turned black and she clung to Hamish as if she were drowning. She sucked in a deep breath. "Use your magic to stop it then, Col!"

"I've been trying to dear, but your virus is spreading beyond anything I imagined. Just yesterday four of the Duchess's staff began sneezing in unison."

Hamish scoffed. "So they've *goat* colds. It's hardly chaos!"

"It is when they sneeze fire and burn down the connecting walls. The fire brigade arrived, blocking the streets. It was peak hour so that caused traffic snarls."

Ondine gasped in fright. She'd caused that? "Was anyone hurt?" Then she looked to Hamish for support. He looked even more worried than her, which didn't help one bit. One last attempt to blame someone else. "But it couldn't have been us. We weren't anywhere near Anathea's staff."

"It appears you don't have to be," Old Col said. "Other people are catching your mutating magic and infecting others." Her shoulders slumped, Ondine braced herself for more bad news. "I hate to admit it, but Birgit's spell is one of the best. The magic is making people's wishes come true all over the place. It's mayhem."

"Catching the virus like a second wave?" Ma asked.

"Exactly. Ondi and Hamish are 'patient zero'. They're passing it on to unsuspecting victims; in turn they're passing it on to more people. It's strongest at the source, at the epicentre."

Had Ondine heard right? "It's spreading?"

Sadness filled Old Col's weathered face. "I'm sorry Ondi, but yes, it's spreading. All the witches of Slaegal worth their salt are here, yet mutating magic is being reported in Norange."

Red mist clouded Ondine's eyes at the news her uncontrollable magic had reached Norange, the capital of neighbouring country Slaegal. "Then why did you drag us out here in public? Why did you let us spread it when you knew it was contagious?"

"I didn't know, I only suspected." Old Col looked defeated. "And I . . . thought I could contain it."

Tears blurred Ondine's vision. "Then Mrs. Howser was right all along. Your magic is rubbish!"

Ma grabbed Ondine in a bear hug. "Hush, darling, let's not say anything we might regret."

"But it's true," Ondine pulled away from her mother, stepped too close to the edge of the drawbridge and righted herself before she fell in the drink. "We all know who's got the real magic around here and it isn't any of us!"

Hamish squeezed her hand in support. "Ondi, love, I hate tae say it but . . . I think ye need tae hush."

"Don't tell me to be quiet!" The moment she said it, she felt sick to her stomach.

Nobody said anything for a long beat.

Hamish said in a low voice, "Mebbe we should be apart –"

" – What!" Ondine stared at Hamish.

"Just for a wee time. Until this settles down and we can get rid of tha spell."

Ondine stepped back in shock and again came perilously close to the edge of the timber. A large icicle dislodged from the drawbridge and splashed into the water below. "Stars! You've already talked about this behind my back, haven't you? Hamish, what are they making you do?"

The delay – just long enough to see his Adam's apple bob up and down on a swallow – gave him away. "Naw lass, it's nae conspiracy."

Ma grabbed Ondine away from Hamish, held her in a fierce hug and said. "We have to do this like ripping off a bandage. Get it over with quickly."

"No, Ma –" Stars and suns, that's why her mother was here. To take Hamish away from her.

Old Col latched on to Hamish's arm, to drag him off.

The drawbridge groaned as the boards warped beneath them.

"Wait!" Hamish stood his ground. "Ye said we'd be able tae say goodbye. Proper like."

Ondine fought free of her mother and threw herself into an embrace with Hamish. The drop to the river below was right at her feet. If they leapt to freedom, would they be all right? All the while she begged Hamish, "You're not leaving me. Tell me you're not leaving me."

"We have tae give it a try, for the greater good."

Head squished to his chest, she felt his heart thumping to break free. In an act of desperation, she locked her hands behind his back and refused to let go.

"I thought this might happen," Old Col said.

From out of nowhere, a new group of people appeared, blocking Ondine's escape. She looked for a way out, anywhere to run, but she was blocked in. The castle, Ma and Old Col behind her, the strangers advancing from the front of the drawbridge, and the steep drop into the water beside them. The advancing strangers wore those all-in-one hazardous material suits. They grabbed at Ondine's hands and peeled her thumbs apart, forcing her to release her grip.

"No! Ma! Make them stop!"

With a sickening wrench, they pulled Hamish away. Ondine kicked and flailed but somebody held her from behind.

"Nae like this!" Hamish yelled. "Ye lied to me, Col!"

Col's voice sounded thin and creaky. "I'm sorry. This is how it has to be."

"Sorry my ar- *armpit*!" With a burst of strength, Hamish broke free.

Hope surged through Ondine like a beam of sunshine as he ran back and held her. He may have forced his captors off him with the ferocity of a lion but he held her tenderly, as if she were made of glass. His chilled hands cupped her face, but when his lips touched hers she felt warm all the way through. If only Ma would let go of her arms she could embrace him properly.

That's when something seriously crazy happened. One of the haz-mat people grew octopus tentacles, wrapping them around Hamish like prey.

Hamish cried out, "You said it wouldn't be like this!"

Was he speaking about Old Col or Ma? It didn't matter. "Hamish, my love!" Ondine strained against her captors to press her lips back to him.

She met with nothing but air as the mob dragged Hamish away from her. The octopus tentacles gripped him. He couldn't move.

With a desperate shove Ondine broke free and hurled herself towards Hamish, the force breaking him free from his captors. The next moment, the man with the tentacle for an arm closed in on them. She grabbed Hamish and looked at the rushing water below.

Closing her eyes she jumped. Lurch! They both went sprawling over the edge and into the icy drink below.

Hamish's voice broke through the freezing water as he screamed in pain at the cold. He splashed and flailed and pushed Ondine further under. Daggers of ice stabbed Ondine as the water rose over her head. She screamed. Nothing but bubbles came out.

The current dragged them towards the next waterfall. She hadn't given a thought to how far it would drop. Desperate for air, she fought against Hamish to get to the surface. Wet clothes and shoes dragged her down. If she didn't get air she'd drown.

But if they went over the waterfall they'd die.

On a determined push, she broke through the surface and gasped for breath.

"I cannae swim!" Hamish cried out.

"Mercury's w –" Ondine almost said as he pushed her under again. He wasn't trying to drown her, not on purpose. He couldn't be. But in his panic he couldn't know what he was doing.

Churning water lay ahead of them. The edge of the waterfall, which landed who knew how far down. Strength failing her, she tried to push Hamish towards the bank. His clothes weighed him down. He flailed. She flailed and they both went under again.

The current took them over the rocks into freefall.

**18**

———————

Screaming, they slipped over the edge. No longer submerged in freezing water but in freefall. Any second now they'd crash onto the rocks below. Closing her eyes hard, Ondine clung to Hamish. She tried to say 'sorry', but the air stole her breath.

The wind blew furiously around them, turning her body to ice. She'd had her eyes closed for so long now, surely they'd hit the bottom soon? Daring to open one eye, she gasped in shock as their world turned blue and green and swirled with magic.

"Hamish, we're OK!" She cried out. They were in a bubble of enchantment holding them steady, floating above the waterfall and, most importantly, alive.

Not warm, though. But at least they weren't drowning any more, or tumbling down a waterfall. The magic bubble holding them wobbled through the air and brought them down towards the snowy lawns. Gasping and shivering, Ondine looked through the skin of the bubble to see Mrs Howser, her arm raised up, glowing magic dust streaming from her hand as she guided them in their bubble of safety to the icy ground, depositing them with a wet 'splud'.

"Thank you Birgit, we'll take it from here," Old Col said, her face grey like thunder as she and Ma bustled over.

Shivering, wet and miserable, Ondine tried to comfort Hamish. "I'm so sorry, darling, I just wanted to get us away."

All Hamish did was chatter his teeth.

"That's enough Ondine," Old Col said as she sat down beside her.

At which point, the hazmat people were back. They grabbed Hamish from under the armpits and hauled him to his feet. Mute and exhausted from shock and despair, she could only watch them drag Hamish away. Away from the convention. Away from her family.

Away from her arms.

Nothing worked in her body any more. Neither bones nor muscles held as a guttural cry rang from her. Pain consumed everything. They'd taken Hamish away, and all because of her love for him.

---

NUMB WITH HEARTACHE, Ondine shivered in front of the little fire in her bedroom hearth, feeding it bite-sized chunks of wood and watching said wood burn down over the hour to nothing but glowing coals.

It was dark outside; it could be dark forever for all she cared. No sunlight could pierce her miserable soul. Her ankle throbbed in pain. She must have sprained it as she tumbled off the drawbridge, but in the craziness she hadn't noticed at the time. The logs on the fire crackled, spitting sap from the wood. The flames, smoke and embers lulled her into nothingness as she sat there, knees tucked under her chin, arms wrapped around her legs.

The slow, hypnotic effect of the fire made her eyelids close. A second later, her body shuddered awake, gasping for air. Weird buzzing moved through her; mild electrical shocks that made her tremble and shake. Like the time Cybelle dared her to hold a light globe in one hand and press a nine-volt battery to her tongue.

Orange and yellow flames danced before her eyes. The next moment she fell asleep, her body fizzed all over, then jolted awake. Doze, fizzle, jolt, wake. The cycle kept going; Ondine had neither motivation to properly go to bed, nor willpower to keep her eyelids apart. Over and over again her body cycled through the weird sensations, sleep, buzz, jolt, wake up!

Saturn's rings, she was losing her mind.

Her warm bed waited for her only a few steps away, but as much as she wanted to crawl into it, her body stayed exactly where it was. At least she wasn't sharing a room with Cybelle. She could be properly miserable in private tonight.

More wood burned down to glowing coals. More time passed. All the while her heart ached to a familiar refrain.

*Oh Hamish! I miss you so much!*

Deep, wracking sobs broke through. All those platitudes she's heard over the years, about time healing wounds, did her no good at all. This pain was so fresh and raw.

And time took so darn long to come around.

She missed him so much, she imagined his hand on her back, rubbing slow circles and making everything all right.

"I'm sorry lass, I shoudnae come, but I hadtae see ye."

It had to be her mind playing tricks. Hardly daring to breathe lest she break the moment, she turned her head.

And felt her heart freshly breaking when she realised the only company she had was her overworked imagination and grief.

---

WHEN ONDINE WOKE, stark reality stabbed her heart. Cold ash sat in the hearth where the fire had burned last night. At some point she'd crawled into bed but she didn't remember. She still wore last night's clothes. Her bedroom door yawned open as everyday household noises carried up the stairs and down the hall. Regular noises from people going about their everyday normal routine.

As if this were any normal day.

As if the planets hadn't stopped spinning yesterday when they took Hamish away from her.

A twinge of soreness kicked her ears and throat. A vague headache caught her between the eyebrows. When she swallowed, it felt like sandpaper rubbing her throat. Her nose didn't work. Sure signs a cold had set in. Normally she'd chew on olive leaves to fight it off but today she didn't care. Let the virus do its best to make her miserable.

"Ondine, are you up yet?" Ma's voice carried down the hall.

"Nope."

Ma's head poked around the corner, a strained smile on her face. "I need your help in the kitchen, love, can you come down in a minute?"

"No."

"Right then. It's not really a request. I need you downstairs because we need a hand."

"I'm sick." She pulled the covers over her head.

Her mother's soothing tones disappeared as she switched to cold steel mode. "Stop moping and get up now."

Ondine barked from under the blankets, "No!"

*Rip!* Ma tore the covers away and exposed Ondine, "I know you're upset, but life goes on. Now get downstairs and get to work!"

This time she screamed, "I said no!" It killed her throat to do it too.

Ma's voice dropped low and deadly. "I gave you time off work last night because I felt sorry for you. And you repay that with rudeness? Now get downstairs and get to work!"

---

CRUMPLED CLOTHES, crumpled hair, crumpled heart. Ondine didn't bother with any kind of morning routine as she shlubbed down the stairs.

"If you fall and break your legs, I'll make you work in crutches," Ma said.

Did she have to be so brutal?

"Time's against us." Ma grabbed a napkin, dabbed it against her tongue and wiped the sleep from Ondine's eyes. "Take table four's order, there's a good girl."

"Don't we do buffet breakfasts?"

"Yes, love, we do. But it's lunchtime now. Table four, off you go, there's a good girl."

It was lunchtime already? Wow, she really had slept in. Ondine poked her head around the corner to see how many people were sitting at table four. Just the one. But it was the one person Ondine never wanted to see again in her life.

*Urgh, what's she doing here?* One look at Mrs. Howser seated in the dining room and Ondine wanted to run back upstairs and never come down again.

"Mrs. Howser is being an absolute delight and giving everyone a reading," Ma said in a too-bright tone.

Ondine kept her voice low. "But she's mental."

Ma shook her head and annoyed Ondine with a sage cliché. "While our friends watch out for us, we watch out for our enemies." [1]

*Everyone else is allowed to swan about and have a wonderful life. But not me, no, I get my heart ripped out because of what that witch did to Hamish and I have to keep working. And they expect me to carry on as normal!*

"Out you go, there's a girl."

Did her mother have to be so . . . annoying? Of all the people in Brugel, why had they let Mrs. Howser into their dining room?

"Can't we ban her or something?" Ondine asked.

"Only if she gets drunk or rowdy. And she did save your freezing soul yesterday. We should at least be grateful for that. But don't let Auntie Col hear me say that. Out of all the witches at the convention that could have saved you, it had to be Howser."

With a soft push in the back, Ondine felt her legs bringing her closer and closer to her nemesis. Old Col must have put her feet under some kind of spell, because no way would she voluntarily go anywhere near Mrs. Howser.

Before she could run back to the safety of the kitchen, she'd reached Howser's table. Pen and pad in hand, she poised, ready to take her order.

"Sit down, Ondine dear, we need to talk," Mrs. Howser said. "I see you've recovered since your slip in the river."

It wasn't a slip, she'd jumped.

"Uh . . . I can't really fraternise with the . . . I mean, we're really busy."

"Yes. I can see that. Not." Mrs. Howser waved her hand at all the empty tables nearby. With her foot, she pushed the opposite chair out. "Now sit down and let's talk like civilised people."

Ondine pulled the chair out a little further and sat.

Mrs Howser raised a brow. "You think I'm going to lay a curse on you?"

*Staying out of arm's reach, just in case.*

"You are a smart girl. Smart enough to work out who has the real power here. Smart enough to know you want more from this life than working non-stop for a family that doesn't appreciate you."

If Ondine had been the kind of girl to keep a diary, she could have accused Mrs. Howser of reading it.

"Oh Ondine, what are we going to do with you?" At which point, Mrs. Howser made one of those smiles that made her muscles crack.

"I'm fine, thanks," she lied. Conflicting emotions fought for dominance. The woman could not be trusted, yet she'd saved Ondine and Hamish from a watery grave.

"I am sorry about what's happening, dear," Mrs Howser said. "It doesn't need to be this way, of course. If only people would be more understanding, none of this need happen."

Why did she have to sound so *reasonable*?

"You are loyal to a fault," she continued when Ondine said nothing in reply. "As you should be. Family comes first, and all that. But at some point in your life, all the sacrifices you're making have to be worth something, don't they?"

"I'm . . ." *Rummage, rummage. Nope, still nothing.* "I'm fine, really."

"And yet, you're staying at the table. You're hearing me out. Is it so you can run back to your great-aunt and tell her everything I've said?"

"Course not." *Yes, actually.* "Ah, do you mind if I ask why you're here? Of all places?"

"I wanted to check on your welfare. And a woman has to eat. Your chef! He's magic, that one."

*Speaking of eating . . .*

"You're wondering where Melody is, aren't you?"

The witch was good!

"She's resting. Coven Con quite wore her out, the poor love."

"She looked exhausted," Ondine said.

"Looks can be deceiving, dear one. Magic is tiring, but I'm not making her do anything she doesn't already want to do. Nobody's magic is powerful enough to override free will."

"Then what happened to Vincent the day before last?" Because he sure seemed to be out of his mind and had no connection with free will.

Mrs. Howser didn't even blink. In her calming, sing-song voice, she explained, "He was merely giving his deepest wishes free reign. If he looked concerned, it was only because he surprised himself by how powerful his deepest wishes truly were."

It all sounded so . . . reasonable. That word again. It kept popping into Ondine's head. Had Mrs. Howser leaned forward and touched her hand or something? No. Had she put another spell on her? Not that either. Ondine shook her head, trying to make sense of it all. If she stayed here talking too long, she'd end up falling under this trance of complete *reasonableness.*

Disloyal thoughts set seed. Her great-aunt's magic wasn't really up to snuff, and her family had ripped Hamish away from her. Maybe Mrs. Howser could teach her some useful magic so that she and Hamish could be together again. "So um, now that you're here, um, what can we get you?" Ondine picked up her pen and paper.

"Why don't you surprise me? Bring me out a little of everything. I'm in a sampling kind of mood." It didn't seem possible, but the old witch's eyes tinkled with lightness and merriment. As if nothing untoward were going on at all.

"The soup is good," she managed.

"Yes, I'll have that, with the canapé floaters. And the prawn and avocado salad. And the filet mignon, rare as rare can be. That should make a good starter."

"Thanks, I'll get this back to Chef." Ondine rose from her seat.

Mrs. Howser leaned forward a little. "Is this really what you want to do with the rest of your life?"

For a morbidly curious moment, Ondine wondered if Mrs. Howser might make some kind of offer. Perhaps magic training. Real magic. Perhaps a way to bring her and Hamish together again. Because the only thought that filled her head and made any sense at all at the moment was Hamish.

Would it be disloyal to ask Mrs. Howser what she had in mind? It didn't mean she was taking sides, or turning her back on her family. Did it?

"I don't know," Ondine eventually answered with complete honesty. "All I want is Hamish." The moment his name left her lips, heat burned behind her eyes and she had to get back to the kitchen before she blubbered like a lost lamb.

In the kitchen the tears sprang free. Wordlessly, she handed Mrs. Howser's order to Chef before retreating to a corner to blow her nose. The radio was on, as it often was. Through the fog of her brain she registered that Venzelemma International Airport was closed because of too much snow. It made no sense to Ondine, because it snowed every winter and it didn't look or feel any worse than usual.

The news item finished with the words:

*"Authorities are refusing to confirm or deny the closure is related to the spread of a virus that has spread from Brugel to neighbouring Slaegal."*

A hand tapped on her shoulder, startling her. Chef's voice said, "I made your favourite pudding."

She turned to see him offering an espresso cup filled with chocolate mousse. "Donwannit," she sniffed. Silently, like an ungrateful child ready to strike with a serpent's sting, she started to think she didn't want anything to do with her family any more.

"I'm really sorry about everything," Cybelle said, moving in for a hug.

Ondine shrugged off her sister's advance. Her wrist caught on a nearby tray, sending it, and the tea set that had been on it, flying. A spectacular noise filled the kitchen.

"Look what you've made me do!" Ondine yelled. Tears spritzed all over the place and she couldn't hold them back.

"Calm down all." Da stuck his head in the kitchen. "They can hear you out front."

"Don't care." Ondine snivelled. Anyway, it was only Mrs. Howser out there, so what did it matter if she overheard?

"Fine. You've made your point." Ma's hands balled into fists and rested on her hips. "Ondine go back to your room and sulk. It's all you're good for."

It was the first sensible thing anyone had said all day.

**19**

———

Ondine couldn't get to her room soon enough. Resentment frothed and boiled inside her as she mentally listed the horrible things her family had done to her. Not just recently, but ever. In the past she'd never questioned working for her family, but she hated it now.

Her parents had grounded her the moment she'd got home from the late Duke's Autumn Palace.

Then they'd made a pantomime of forgetting her Name Day.

But the absolute worst punishment they'd exacted was in ripping Hamish away.

She could never forgive them for that.

Every bone ached as she flung herself on the mattress. To her continued dismay – and despite her most fervent wish – Hamish did not appear out of thin air. For the next half hour she failed spectacularly to go to sleep. The radio offered no company, it kept reminding people of poor traffic conditions, bad snow, closed airports and pleas for people to not visit overcrowded hospitals except for medical emergencies. Frustrated, she picked up the book on her bedside table. The one Hamish had given her on her name day.

*Everything* reminded her of Hamish.

As she read about the tribulations of Brugel's first Grand Duchess,

Elmaree, fat tears sploshed her cheeks. Just like Ondine, Elmaree's heart was set for the shredder.

When Ondine reached the part about Elmaree having to marry the war-mongering Prince Faddei of Slaegal, it became all too real and raw.

Poor Elmaree. Such huge responsibilities at such a young age. Trying to get elder statesmen to take her seriously, while they patted her on the head and told her to be a good girl. Ondine saw plenty of herself in the headstrong Grand Duchess, as Elmaree made her horrible choice: Give up her country or give up the man she loved.

*THEY STAND THERE, that wall of wickedness dressed in human flesh, watching me lift the quill to sign my life away. The oleaginous diplomats. The serpentine maids-in-waiting. Willing me to give my country and my lifeblood to them for the price of a line of ink on parchment.*

*Oh cruel fate that has cast me into such depths! What is this thing they call free will, when the only choice I have is whether to lose my heart or lose my country?*

*For I cannot have both.*

*Does it make me a terrible person to put my heart first? I am so afraid I do not think a true decision is possible. Why, if we have a heart, are we not free to bestow it to our person of choosing? Why did the maker give us such feelings if we were not meant to use them?*

*They are staring at me, waiting for me. I dip the quill deeply into the blue ink and lift it, watching the thick drops fall from the nib. The drops remind me of blood. Royal blood that will be spilled no matter how events from this moment unfold.*

*Follow my heart, I will lose Brugel.*

*Follow my head, I will lose the only man I will ever love.*

*I cannot give myself to Faddei. The suitor whose knuckles are caked in blood from dragging them on the cobblestones!*

*He terrifies me. He towers over me. He ignores me.*

*He could snap me like a twig.*

*The decision comes to me, like clear running water washing all away. Clarity of reason says Faddei will destroy Brugel whether we are married or not. If I refuse to sign, he will declare war. If we marry, he will dispose of me and consume my country.*

*They are holding their breaths, waiting for me to sign. My face gives nothing away as I lower the quill into the ink once again. My heart is racing as never before. I look to Faddei and execute the only weapon in my arsenal before all is surely lost.*

*That weapon is defiance.*

*I snap the quill. Dark blue ink spreads over my hand and blots the paper.*

*The room is in uproar. Everyone is shouting, questioning, crying, gasping.*

*All except Faddei, who looks at me with his face of stone. He must have known I would refuse. As if he were waiting for it. He will lasso the moon and use it to crush the house of Brugel, of that I am certain. But the act is done. I cannot take it back.*

*My actions may spell death for everyone in this room and yet it is the only choice I had.*

*We are all doomed.*

*And yet.*

*Somewhere, amongst this noise and mayhem, my heart sings.*

THE STORY ABSORBED and frustrated Ondine. She wanted to tell Elmaree to stop being so scared all the time, that things would work out. But then she had to admit maybe she was telling herself that. Every time she came to a scene where Elmaree and her secret lover stole time together, she couldn't help seeing the characters as herself and Hamish.

It made her ache for him all the more.

Another thing she noticed was Elmaree's ink-stained hand. It was only a coincidence that Vincent's hand bore a similar splash of colour. All the same, she couldn't help thinking they'd inadvertently done Vincent some kind of favour by linking him back to Elmaree.

Eight dirty tissues later, she had to stop reading. It was too upsetting and far too real.

SOME TIME in the night she woke up, her mind racing. As the fuzzy half-world of dreams evaporated, so did her hopes. Hamish was not coming back.

A fresh wave of resentment roared through her like a big roary thing that wouldn't stop roaring. [1] Somewhere inside, Ondine knew it was wrong to entertain ideas of ditching her family in favour of siding with Mrs. Howser. The trouble was, everything Mrs. Howser had told her made a strange kind of sense. Whereas her family made no sense at all. All they did was punish her.

What had Aunt Col said? Only the witch that laid a curse could remove it.

Therefore, Mrs. Howser had to be the one to remove the mutating magic from Hamish. But why would she want to remove it, when it was working so well for her? A little more instability in the country and both Anathea and Vincent would be begging her for help. Everything was playing perfectly into Mrs. Howser's hands.

A new idea shone through. Maybe if Ondine sided with Mrs. Howser, she might gain the old witch's trust. Then she would remove her spell from Hamish and they could be free.

Trouble was, Ondine couldn't think of a single reason why Mrs. Howser would want to do this.

Self-loathing settled in her heart. She shouldn't be thinking of abandoning her family, but if her family had been nicer to her, she wouldn't need to be thinking about joining Mrs. Howser, would she?

So really, it was their fault, not hers.

The pub, so busy from dawn to dusk, lay eerily silent at this time of . . . whoa, her bedside clock said two forty-three in the morning. No wind howled outside, the only noise she heard came from a goods train down the line.

And a weird squeak.

At first, she thought it might be a tree branch rubbing against her window. But with no wind, the branch wouldn't be moving itself.

Then a heavy thump and a creak of wood.

From above.

*This is the top floor. Why does it sound like someone is on the roof?*

Because someone *was* on the roof. There had to be. The more she listened, the more certain Ondine became that somebody – or maybe two somebodies – were on the roof.

Pushing the covers back as quietly as she dared, Ondine stepped out of bed. Her feet froze on the floor, which made her wonder how anyone could survive the arctic conditions outside. Grabbing a dressing gown, she ran to her sister's room. "Belle?" Ondine nudged her in the shoulder.

No response, just the steady snorfle of a heavy sleeper.

She walked out to the hall, towards the sound of a rattling tractor. She snuck her head in her parents' room. There was Da, squished right over to the side, while Ma lay like a starfish, hogging the whole bed. Snoring just like Cybelle.

"Ma, wake up." Ma snored even louder. Ondine nudged her shoulder again but got nothing. Her mother was out for the count.

She crept around to the other side and pulled out one of her dad's earplugs. "Da, wake up. Something's on the roof."

"Hmm," he said, sticking his finger into his ear to block his wife's snoring.

"No, seriously, you've got to have a look. Please."

Nothing. Not even holding his eyelid open could rouse him. No trace of alcohol on his breath either, so he couldn't have been at the plütz. Should she activate the smoke detectors? That would make too much noise and alert whoever was on the roof that they were on to them. In any case, they might have guests staying the night and they needed their sleep. Maybe Chef could help, but it didn't feel right waking him up because he worked such insane hours. She'd have to try Belle again.

It was a tough gig trying to run and stay deathly quiet so that she didn't alert the people on the roof, but she did a pretty good job and raced back to the room she shared with Cybelle.

By this stage, Belle had rolled on to her back and put her mother's snoring to shame. Cold aches tugged Ondine's heart. If only Hamish were here! He'd know what to do. At the very least, he'd be able to scarper up the drainpipe to see what was occurring on the roof.

Then a new thought struck. Maybe the noise *was* Hamish; maybe he'd come back to her after all. Maybe he couldn't find a way to sneak in? Yes, that had to be it. It had to be him.

It *must* be him.

She charged out to the garden, her feet becoming lumps of ice as she skidded to the shed to grab the ladder. The ladder was so heavy it nearly ripped the sockets out of her shoulders. But what did she care for discomfort when Hamish needed her?

"I'm coming Hamish," she said as she pulled the ladder back up the flights of stairs and dragged it through her parents' room to their small balcony.

If she'd been thinking straight, she would have wondered why the sound of someone dragging a ladder up the stairs and out to the balcony hadn't roused her parents. In fact, she hadn't roused *anyone*.

Alas, she was beyond thinking straight when it came to Hamish.

The old wooden ladder made a heavy clonk as she hooked the extension clips onto the top of the building. She couldn't feel her feet or her hands as she climbed the steps.

Her poor darling Hamish was up here, possibly freezing to death. A few more steps and she reached the last row of bricks that formed the parapet.

She peered over the top.

Instead of gazing into the eyes of her beloved, she found herself staring at Mrs. Howser.

"Looking for your boyfriend?" she said.

## 20

In her entire life, Ondine had never felt so cold as she held on to the ladder, staring at the old witch. Any thoughts of defecting to 'the other side' cracked like ice as the most horrible fear made her stomach churn. "W-what are you doing on our roof?" In the chill, she had to fight her jaw to get the words out properly.

"Taking back what's ours," Mrs. Howser said. She at least had come prepared for the cold night, wearing a fur-lined coat with matching hat. [1]

"Here it is!" Ondine heard another voice say. A male voice. She could have sworn it sounded just like –

Lord Vincent.

He'd come prepared for the elements, with heavy shoes and a thick fur-lined long-coat. Saturn's rings! Mrs. Howser must have got to him. He didn't look out-of-it like the last time she'd seen him.

The confident expression he wore told Ondine he knew exactly what he was doing, which was even more frightening. The two of them had to be hatching some kind of plan against Anathea. Although what it had to do with the pub roof was completely beyond her.

Lord Vincent climbed down from the top of the chimney with a large shoebox in his arms.

Their stares locked.

"It's all perfectly above board. My grandfather hid them here for safe-keeping. He used to frequent the pub in the old days."

"They're stolen." Ondine said.

"You can't prove that. Now, get out of my way!"

Mrs. Howser's claw-like hands dug into Ondine's shoulders to pull her up.

Desperate to get away. Ondine gripped the sides of the ladder and lifted her feet away from the rungs. She slid all the way down to the balcony below. Screaming non-stop.

Thump! She landed on the balcony in a smacking rush, knocking the wind out of her. Surely her caterwauling would wake everyone? Hobbling to a standing position, she looked up to see Mrs. Howser climbing down the ladder towards her.

Head first like a spider crawling down her web to her prey.

Sick with fear, Ondine ran into her parents' room, slammed the door and locked it. Her parents didn't budge.

"Wake up!" she screamed.

Nothing.

"Sorry Da." She pulled the covers back, rolled his flannel pyjama top to expose his rounded belly to the early morning air . . .

And stabbed her frozen left foot on his warm skin.

"Aaaarrrrggghhh!" Da screamed himself upright.

"Mrs. Howser's on the roof with Lord Vincent and they're stealing something." She looked through the glass door to the balcony. Bold as you like, Mrs. Howser stood there, one eyebrow raised.

Da rubbed his eyes. "She'll catch her death of cold out there." He rose from the bed to open the door and let her in.

"No Da!" Ondine pulled him back. "You have to call the police! She and Vincent were up there and they've taken something from inside the chimney."

Da tried to get up but lost his balance and fell back into bed.

He closed his eyes and drifted back to sleep.

"See you later." Mrs. Howser gave a finger wave from outside, then, with a swoosh of her hand, she created a slide made from ice which she and Vincent glided down.

"Fine, I'll call the plods." Ondine left her dazed father and snoring mother where they lay and ran to the kitchen.

When she picked up the phone, she heard Mrs. Howser on the other end. "Don't worry dear; your telephone will be working again soon. No need to make a fuss, we're merely taking back what's ours. Now go back to bed and forget everything you saw tonight. I do wish you'd had some tea, then I could have spared you the trouble."

Tea? A quick look at the drying racks by the sink showed a dozen washed teapots, all resting upside down. The witch must have read everyone's leaves and added something to the drink.

*Well I'll be! Throwing a fit of the sulks helped me dodge a bullet.*

If she could just work out what Mrs. Howser meant by 'Taking back what's ours,' she'd have the whole thing figured out. Taking back what? The small glance she'd had of Vincent only showed he had some kind of box. He'd said his grandfather had left it for safekeeping. Which didn't surprise Ondine, because they kept money in a safe under the kitchen floorboards, on account of Brugel's banking system being so unreliable.

But why had a Duke needed to use the roof of a pub to keep things safe?

Unless it was Vincent's *other* grandfather, on his crazy mother's side? That could make more sense.

*Think, girl, think!*

But all her selfish brain could come up with, as she stood there on the kitchen tiles, stomping her feet in a futile attempt to get the circulation going, was, *Why does all this craziness keep happening to me?*

Which was, by a circuitous route, exactly the kind of thought she needed to have. Because strange things *did* keep happening to her and she refused to believe they were the result of coincidence. It simply could not be coincidence that everything bad in her life had happened after she ran away to home, from Psychic Summercamp, all those months ago.

She made a hot chocolate to warm her from the inside and help her think. Chocolate made everything better. She also filled a soup pot with warm water and placed it on the floor, then stood in it. The heat flayed her skin and prickled her nerves. Slowly – painfully slowly – she wiggled her toes. The next sip of chocolate reminded her of Draguta Matice, the rail-thin laundry master from the Autumn Palace. Which reminded her of Draguta's teddy bear stuffed with trinkets. Then her mind tripped her back to the box of jewels they'd found under the dining room floorboards way back in summer. The same box Lord Vincent had tried to steal.

Mrs. Howser had said she was taking back what was hers. No, not hers, 'ours'.

Thoughts churned like cream into butter, until, to Ondine's utter surprise, one thought became more solid.

Mrs. Howser.

She was helping Vincent. Or using him. It didn't matter which; it only mattered that every event kept coming back to her. Mrs. Howser had to be in on everything.

Even the times when it seemed like Vincent was acting on his own, he had to have had help, and that help had to have come from Mrs. Howser.

Nothing else made sense.

The more Ondine thought about it, the more she became convinced Mrs. Howser and Vincent had been (or maybe still were) using the deGroot family pub as a personal bank. That had to be why they kept coming here.

Every visit one of them had made would have coincided with some kind of jewellery or cash deposit, secreted somewhere about their pub.

The private banking details she and Hamish had found in Duchess Kerala's private rooms in the Autumn Palace immediately came to mind. But now that Ondine thought about it, the banking couldn't have been for Kerala's future; but for Vincent's.

Meanwhile, the present Duchess, Anathea, had to save her pennies and use Ondine and Hamish as her private – and unpaid – public relations company because the royal family was broke. Well, they weren't really broke, it was simply that Kerala, Vincent and Mrs. Howser had siphoned so much away, there was nothing left.

Mrs. Howser had come to Margi and Thomas's engagement party, back in summer, but she'd retired early. At the time Ondine hadn't paid much attention to that fact, but she'd bet her next hot meal Mrs. Howser must have been snooping around for jewellery and other goodies while everyone else was distracted.

*Great Pluto's Ghost, I have to tell everyone, right now!*

Slap, slap, slide. Her wet feet splashed on the floorboards as she raced down the hall, all the while wondering what Mrs. Howser had been looking for – more jewels? Probably. Cash? It must have been in the chimney for decades because her parents had never mentioned it. They probably never knew anything about it.

She took the stairs two at a time and charged back to her parents' room, where they were both snoring.

"Get up! Mrs. Howser's drugged you!"

Nothing.

"The money!" she yelled, ripping the covers off their bed and exposing them to the cold night air. Ma and Da flinched and wailed and, yes, yes! Eventually they came round! "Mrs. Howser and Vincent have the money. It's why Anathea is broke, and it's why they kept coming here, why things kept happening to us. Because they used this building for all their stolen jewels and cash!"

"Coffee," Da groaned.

Ma reached for the duvet to pull it back over her, but Ondine ripped it away.

"The old coot drugged the tea so she could burgle us. She and Vincent were on the roof."

---

THREE BLISTERING cups of wake-up-juice later, Ondine's parents were finally catching on to the enormity of the situation as they sat in the kitchen.

"It all makes sense," Ma said. "Ondine I'm so sorry. We should have seen this coming. Howser must have planned it for so long. I was ever so grateful that she had a spot for you at Summercamp. But it seems . . ."

They all took a sip from their respective cups. Now was not the time for Ondine to admit she'd entertained thoughts of joining Mrs. Howser. Thank goodness she hadn't!

" . . . She set us up from the start." Ondine rubbed her temple. "On the plus side, maybe now you'll believe me when I say I'm not psychic?"

"There is that," Ma said.

A quiet 'hooray' sounded in the back of her mind, but she'd celebrate this personal victory later, when things weren't so crazy. At this point, her parents believed her. That would have to be enough for now. "Mrs. Howser and Vincent must be panicking that Anathea is becoming too popular. We need Aunt Col. And we'll have to tell Duchess Anathea because she needs to know what's going on."

"You sound like a field marshal," Ma said.

Ondine beamed at the compliment, and then acknowledged that the coffee had made her more talkative than usual.

"I'm calling the police," Da said.

"If the phone's working." Ondine remembered what happened earlier.

"Hooray for small mercies, I have a dial tone." Da put the receiver to his ear.

"Ma? Once we get through all this, maybe we can find a way to help Hamish?"

A patronising smile crossed Ma's face and she patted Ondine on the head. "Dear girl. I know you miss him, but in time you will move on."

Ondine slapped her mother's hand away. "Don't say that!" Heartache burned afresh. "I love Hamish with all my heart."

"But you're so young."

"You're one to talk! You were already married by my age!"

Tense silence filled the room as they stared at each other in mute shock. She could hear her father's voice as he spoke to the police, reporting the thieves on the roof who stole a deposit box from the chimney.

Finally Ma said, "I'm sorry love. I was about to say, 'Things were different then,' but that would have set you right off."

Ondine muttered, "Got that right."

Ma moved in for a hug and Ondine gladly accepted it. It was a warm, squishy, rocking-back-and-forth hug offering comfort and a big dollop of nostalgia. How many times had her mother cuddled and rocked her as a baby, as a little girl, as a big girl? Even now she still needed hugs to make everything right again.

"Thanks Ma. Your hugs are better than magic."

Ma sniffed and kissed the top of her head. "Thank you, love."

The hug chased away just about everything bad that had ever happened, if only for a moment. "Magic's stupid. Hugs are better."

Ma kissed the top of her head again as Da finished his phone call.

"The police will be here in a few hours, so we can make our statements. It might save time if we write them down beforehand." He looked at his watch. "Maybe we should try and get some sleep before breakfast?"

"I'm wide awake," Ondine said.

A few minutes later, Chef and Cybelle walked in with drag-along shopping trolleys in preparation for heading to the markets.

Cybelle said, "You're up early. What's going on?"

"We had a break-in during the night," Da said. He relayed the events of the past hours.

"You can't let the cops in!" Cybelle looked to Henrik with panic in her eyes. "They'll find the keyboard covers."

"Then you'd better shove them somewhere the police won't see them," Da said.

Ondine buried her face in her hands. This was going to be the longest day ever.

## 21

I t would have been much easier on everyone if the police had come the next morning. Or even the day after that. To Ondine's continuing frustration, they took three days to arrive, turning up in the midst of lunch service, which threw the family into panic.

Not Ondine, of course, who in her misery of missing Hamish, nothing much panicked her. Nothing cheered her up either, but as she had to pull herself together and get on with it, she did just that.

Henrik and Cybelle had moved the rolls of cling film into the kitchen, hidden in plain sight. Ondine and Da took the police to the surprisingly-spacious-now-the-wedding-was-over private room out the back for the statements.

"You saw what they stole?" one of the officers asked.

The answers had to be to the point. No "I'm not sures" or "I think sos" allowed.

"Correct," she said. "I saw Vincent taking a box from inside the chimney. A small chest, a bit bigger than the size of a shoe box. I'm positive it's full of money from his mother Kerala's secret stash. She was hiding money from the Late Duke, you know. How's the investigation going into that by the way?"

"Er, we're not involved in that," the officer said as he looked to his partner for backup.

More note taking from the officers before one of them asked, "This box was a shoe box?"

"About that size, yes."

"For sandals or boots?"

Boggling, Ondine tried not to show contempt for the question. "Probably a box big enough for boots, because it took Vincent two hands to carry it."

"So you're telling me Lord Vincent, the heir to the Duchy of Brugel, is stealing boots?"

Her eyes rolled all on their own. "No. He stole something that could fit in a box that would be large enough for boots."

"So you don't actually know what was in the box in the first place?"

Deflated. "I don't have x-ray vision. But why else would you go to all that trouble to steal a box from a chimney, in the middle of the night, in the middle of winter?"

The police officer looked at her and shrugged. "Unless you can tell us what was in the box, we don't really have much to go on."

There was no point learning the officers' names because Ondine had the sinking feeling she would never see them again. Their attitude didn't match the importance of the crime. Squashing down her frustration, she said, "Officer, I saw two people: Mrs. Birgit Howser and Lord Vincent. They also saw me. So even if I'm not sure what they stole at the very least they should be charged with trespassing."

"Duly noted. Thank you for your statements. Unfortunately, we can't prioritise this case."

"Why not?" Ondine bristled.

"If you've been paying attention to the news, it's a really bad 'flu season. All units have been called in to assist in hospital waiting rooms, what with people making threats to staff. That takes a higher priority to trespassing on a roof. We'll be in touch if we have anything further."

They would so not 'be in touch', Ondine thought. Then another horrible thought landed. Police needed at hospitals? She hadn't heard anything about the 'flu ... unless it was . . . "Do you mean the mutating magic?"

"Do you know something about that?" The other officer asked.

Ondine clamped her mouth shut and shook her head.

***

As the afternoon wore on, things went badly wrong. Customers sent their meals back, barely touched. As the week wore on, things became dire. And not just because Ondine missed Hamish as if her heart had stopped working.

"Is everything all right?" Ondine asked as she took a diner's plate. They had shifted the food around but barely eaten a mouthful.

"Yes, it was fine, I just couldn't get through it," he said.

"I can get you something else if you'd rather?"

"No, truly, it was delicious. The serving was too big."

The rest of the customers on the table nodded.

"OK," Ondine said, taking his word for it.

Inside her head, a small light began to beam. If the customers weren't licking their plates clean, they weren't starving from using magic they might or might not know they had. This could mean the mutating magic was wearing off. Which lead her to the next step in this logic ladder – that she and Hamish could be together again.

She took the uneaten meals back to the kitchen. "They're saying they're not hungry enough."

Chef and Cybelle exchanged worried looks.

Ma bustled over and tasted an untouched portion of the food herself. "It's perfectly good."

"We know that." Hope lit a match inside Ondine. "It's a good sign, isn't it? The magic must be wearing off."

Ignoring her discovery, Cybelle picked up a fork and had a taste, also from an untouched section. Because eating something with somebody else's saliva? Eww! "It's a crying shame to send back food this good. What's wrong with them?"

Ma tasted the trout from another quarter-eaten plate. Her eyebrows clamped together and she made a soft groan. "That. Is. Divine." She had another mouthful and made little noises of pleasure.

"Of course it is. Was in the tank only an hour ago," Chef said.

Ma finished another mouthful. "Belle darling would you pop that in the fridge so I can have the rest later? At least we know there's nothing wrong with the food. Should we cut back on the bread rolls on the table? Have smaller servings?"

Cybelle and Henrik set the next order onto plates. Steam rose from the vegetables as Cybelle handed them over. "Table five is ready."

Da came in with the takings from another table. "They paid at the bar. Said they had to leave early. Didn't even leave a tip."

That really crushed the mood. Magic wearing off was one thing, but people not leaving a tip? It was downright miserable.

Ondine said, "If Hamish were here, we'd have better tips."

"Don't make me roll my eyes, dear," Ma said.

"I said table five is ready," Cybelle said.

"Oh! Sorry!" Ondine picked up a tea towel and grabbed one hot plate, balanced the second on her forearm and picked up the third in her free hand. As she walked towards table five, her heart sank.

They'd gone.

Confusion made knots in her tummy. Back in the kitchen she double-checked the order with Ma and Cybelle.

"Definitely table five. Four adults and two teenagers," Ma said.

"Not any more. They left," Ondine said. "Has anyone else ordered the same meals Belle? I could take these out to them."

"Pop them in the *bain marie* while I check."

Henrik rubbed his temple. "This is seriously weird. Did they see the police and run off or something?"

"Ma? Can I talk to you for a minute?" Ondine thought of a plausible reason and it always came back to her one true love. "This never used to happen when Hamish was here."

"Oh Ondi, we all miss him. But I doubt even Hamish could help if people don't want to eat at all."

*It was worth a try.* "Something is *really* wrong though. People don't leave three quarters of their lunch. And they don't leave before it even gets to the table. There's something else going on, there must be."

"We're having a bad day, that's all."

"Ma, come on. This is *beyond* bad. This is . . ." a light bulb went off in her head, "Mrs. Howser must have put a spell on us!"

Ma's shoulders slumped. "I wouldn't put it past her."

Ondine jumped in with, "Then we must get Hamish back."

"That's all you can think about, isn't it?" It was Ma's turn to roll her eyes. "Sweetheart, I know you miss him, but I think you're clutching at —"

"Ma please! We never used to have half-eaten plates when Hamish was here. And if Mrs. Howser has put a spell on us, then surely when Hamish comes back, he can help fix it."

With less to do than usual, Henrik took a moment to turn up the volume on the TV. More traffic snarls and jammed intersections, and now the trains weren't running because of too much snow.

*"We get snow every winter, why is this year different to any other?"* a frustrated commuter complained to the camera.

*"Woot! I can't get to work, so it's a day off for me!"* another said, looking really happy.

*"No school tomorrow."* A student beamed. *"Snow day, yeah!"*

*"I blame the Duchess. Too busy throwing parties to get the trains running on time."*

Ondine put it all together. "Ma, people have been wishing for snow so they don't have to go to work?"

"That's a no-brainer darling," Ma said.

"Yes, but think about it? Hamish and I are nowhere near them, and their wishes are still coming true."

"Ye-es, I thought we'd gone over this?" Ma's brow creased.

"Yes but," Ondine had to slow her brain down so that she didn't trip over herself, "bad traffic, no trains? The magic is out there anyway and we can't stop it. Meanwhile, people don't realise they're wishing for bad things that stuff the place up. Everyone's going to blame Anathea and it's not her fault. She's going to become even less popular! Unless Hamish and I can fix it,

Anathea's polls will nosedive and Vincent will take over! And he'll probably have Mrs. Howser as his closest advisor. But if Hamish and I are together, we can use Mrs. Howser's magic against her and make everything better in Brugel." Great Pluto's Ghost, she'd never felt so clever for working it all out.

"Heavens girl, I know you want to be with him but we can't have people growing tails and causing even more craziness."

"Whoa!" Chef yelped as he pulled a trout from the tank. "We've got a live one!" The fish put up a fight, slipping from his hands and flip-flopping on the kitchen bench. For a bizarre moment, the fish flexed so high it was practically standing on its tail fin.

"Well I'll be. There's a fish dancing on the table," Ma said.

Ondine cried out, "Woo hoo! Does that mean I'm not grounded anymore!"

"Don't try to take advantage of me when I'm confused," Ma said, her eyes round as she watched the flipping fish.

"But Ma! You said!" Ondine felt desperate.

"Maybe."

A "maybe" was better than a "no", but not as solid as a "yes". It gave Ondine hope.

Down the end of the kitchen, Da rolled his sleeves up and began washing dishes.

"Why aren't you at the bar, love?" Ma asked.

"They've all gone home."

Meanwhile, from the TV, everyday people complained to the reporters about how hard life was. Everyone kept shooting the blame home to Duchess Anathea.

Ondine and Ma looked at each other, then Ma said, "I think you're right, Ondi. We might need Hamish back."

Mercury's wings! She was glad to hear those words. How hard did she squeeze Ma in delight and relief? No idea, but when she let go Ma almost passed out.

"Sorry. Got a bit carried away."

Everyone turned as two new arrivals walked into the kitchen. They were tanned and glowing and happy. Everything Ondine wasn't.

"Darlings!" Ma called out at the sight of Marguerite and Thomas. She embraced them in a three-way squish.

"It's so quiet out there, I've never seen the like," Marguerite said when Ma eventually let go of her.

"You both look wonderful!" Ma gushed. "I told you the Sun Bubble Resort would agree with you." [1]

"Mrs. Howser's put a spell on us." Ondine said.

Marguerite's eyebrows disappeared under her fringe as she turned on her mother. "You still haven't paid the Psychic Summercamp fees?"

"I'll fill you in later. It's lovely to see you." Ma gave them another hug. "I'm glad it's quiet out there, you can tell me all about your travels. I love your outfits, I love the colours on your poncho!"

"It's the latest in Sleag-Mex," Margi said.

Da walked up and embraced Margi, then gave Thomas a handshake before pulling him into a hug as well. "Welcome home, kids."

A snort escaped Ondine. Margi and Thomas were married adults, but Da would always see them as children. They should consider themselves lucky because at least they weren't the "baby".

Her parents, sister and brother-in-law vanished into the sitting room in a blur of hugs and giggles and luggage, leaving Ondine feeling empty and left out.

And irritated that she'd lost yet one more chance to ask Ma about when Hamish could come back.

# 22

The next morning, still no sign of Hamish. Where was he? Surely if her mother had said he could come back, she'd have passed on the message to wherever he was and he'd be here like a shot.

At least he should be!

He'd better *want* to be!

The rest of the family was huddled around the table in their private room behind the kitchen, passing around honeymoon photographs from the Black Sea. In each photo either Marguerite or Thomas smiled out at them. Sometimes it was both of them at a strange angle, as they'd put the camera on the edge of a banister or tree branch to get a couple-shot.[1]

The photos were so sweet. Smiling faces in every one of them. A spike of jealousy caught Ondine. Her sister had the freedom to be with the man of her choice. And she'd taken a holiday with him. Jupiter's moons! When was the last time she'd had a break? Never!

So absorbed in holding her emotions in check and making the right kind of happy noises as she looked at each photo, Ondine didn't hear Great-Aunt Col walk in.

"Margi, you're positively glowing. Marriage suits you. Oh goodie, I do so love photos; let me have a look," Old Col said.

Joy flooded Ondine's system. If Old Col was here, surely that meant . . . ?

"Hello Ondine dear, Colette's filled me in on everything."

Nodding, Ondine tried to smile at her great-aunt, but she was far too interested in who could be behind her.

"You're distracted by something." Old Col giggled as stepped closer to Ondine. "Give me a kiss dear."

Huh? Mechanically, Ondine kissed her great-auntie's cheek, but her gaze stayed locked on the door she'd walked through, her heart kicking against her ribs in anticipation.

The man of her dreams walked in, lugging an old suitcase behind him.

"Hamish!" She nudged Old Col aside to throw herself at him.

Hamish dropped the case and wrapped his arms around Ondine, holding her close. It felt beyond wonderful to be with him again. A gulping sob racked her body as she clung to him.

"Ach, dry yer eyes," he said.

Pulling back, she wiped her face with her sleeve and said, "Where have you been? I think your hair's grown. Has Col been feeding you? Are you OK? Where did Col keep you?"

"Col was doin' her best tae help with tha curse, lass. Dry yer eyes, I want tae see yer smiling face."

"Nope."

"Awww. Then cry all ye want, but ye'll have tae give me a proper kiss sooner or later."

"Gladly!" Ondine wiped her face with her sleeve again and planted a kiss on him. Within the bounds of propriety with her entire family watching.

Immediately the phone rang. Ma raced to pick it up.

"Thank you, Ondine." Margi suddenly wrapped them in a three-way hug. "I needed an album to put all these beautiful photos in!"

Confused, Ondine turned to see that the pile of photos that used to be all over the table were now lovingly arranged in display books. She scratched her head and said, "You're scrapbooking?"

"It's a legitimate craft!" Margi shot back.

Ma came bouncing back in, clapping her hands. "Twelve more for dinner tonight. Thank heavens you're back, Hamish!"

That's when Ondine noticed the clock on the wall sporting thirteen numbers. "Did anyone wish for more time in the day?"

Henrik raised his hand.

"Best we wish that one back I think," Ma said. "No knowing how far that wish might go."

Good point. Ah well, if it meant kissing Hamish again, Ondine would do it.

For Brugel!

"Get a room you two!" Belle said.

"Leave the door open," Ma said.

"Wide open!" Da said.

Henrik snorted with laughter as heat raced up Ondine's neck. Da glared at Henrik so the chef pretended it was a sneeze.

———

How wonderful to be back in Hamish's arms. A pile of homework beckoned once they reached Ondine's room. She'd get to it, eventually, but first she recharged her emotional batteries with a warm cuddle with Hamish by the window.

He rubbed her back as she gazed out across the street. The Asian restaurant, *On the Fang,* must have recovered from their immigration raid because people were queuing up on the footpath to get in. They had to be serving seriously good food to warrant such a wait in the snow. Not that Henrik was any slouch, his meals were incredible.

Phone ringing sounds echoed up the stairs. That had to be the result of Ma wishing they were booked out every night. This respite from frantic work might be their last in a while.

Ondine kissed Hamish and could have sworn her heart grew to twice its size. How she'd missed his warm lips, they way they melded with hers so perfectly, as if they were made for each other. The way they parted and made her sigh with pleasure. The way his tongue teased hers and made things explode in her head.

Utter, utter bliss.

Such beautiful kisses. The more she took, the more she wanted.

The more she thought about them, the more her head turned to mush and weird sensations took over. The way her head felt lighter but her body felt heavier. The excitement in the way he responded to her, safe in the knowledge they couldn't go very far with the door open.

Hamish pulled back from the kisses, making them shorter, just like his breathing. They were both smiling so much it was difficult to kiss properly. It didn't matter as Hamish held Ondine close and caressed her cheek.

"Aye, this is magic."

Placing her palm to his chest, Ondine felt his heart thumping and had to agree this moment was the most magical of her life. Plus he kept smiling at her, which turned her brain to mush and made her heart race. The soft touches against her cheek, the way he tucked a stray tendril of hair behind her ear.

"Were you all right, all this time? I was so worried about you," Ondine asked.

"Och, I havetae admit, when those folks turned up wearing radiation suits, I thought I was off tae a laboratory or such like."

His accent sounded so thick, on account of not hearing it for a so long.

"But I was at yer auntie's all this time. She was making me take potions and lotions, all so she could work out what other spells I could be under."

"Oh you poor darling!" Ondine kissed him afresh.

"What rot!" Auntie Col said as she passed the open doorway, "You slept most of the time."

Hamish pulled away and defended himself against the witch's accusation. "Aye, because ye made me intae a ferret most of the time." He resumed kissing Ondine, making up for lost time.

A warping, buzzing noise filled Ondine's body like electricity shorting out.

No, not her body. The electricity really *had* gone off.

Across the street, *Fang's* neon dragon blinked out. On the corner, the traffic lights blinked amber. A train departing from the station stopped before it reached the crossing. In the distance they heard a car screech.

"Ondi!" Ma's voice carried up the stairs. "Down here please, and bring candles."

Candles wouldn't make any difference in the middle of the day. Ondine rolled her eyes, knowing her mother was using the power outage as an excuse to call her back to work.

Old Col made a tisking noise, then said, "Just heading downstairs for a cup of tea. Can I get you anything?"

"No thanks." Less talking, more kissing. So much kissing.

"I'll ask your mother to fill me in on everything that's been going on, you carry on dear."

A little more kissing, a few more sighs. Eventually, Hamish pulled away and said, "Come awn lass, there's always work to do."

"Just a few more minutes. The lights will be back in a sec anyway."

Hamish's chuckle rippled through her as they savoured their last cuddle.

Before they had to return downstairs.

Before they had to be respectable again.

***

"I'm surprised the power's not back on yet," Ondine said as they took the stairs.

"There you are," Ma said. "Hamish? Put more logs on the fire. Ondi? The dishes are stacking up. Your father's off finding batteries for the radio so I've put Thomas in the bar."

To hear her mother's frantic tones you'd think it was a national emergency, instead of a regular Brugel blackout, which they'd worked through plenty of times before. "We're fine, Ma. If the power doesn't come back on we'll put the food outside in the snow. That's just as good as a refrigerator."

"It's all across Venzelemma." Da walked into the kitchen holding a small blue toy monster with a radio in its tummy. It had been one of Margi's favourite playthings and later handed down to Ondine. She remembered how she used to fall asleep listening to it, then waking in the night to a soft hiss of failed reception as the batteries died.

Ma raced over to him. "Any word on how long it will last?"

"Nothing yet."

"How are they able to broadcast if there's no power?" Ondine asked.

"Diesel generators love," Da said, turning the volume up. It made strange squeaks and crackles as he tried to fine-tune to the station's call-sign using the monster's red nose.

*… EXPECTED TO LAST SEVERAL HOURS, possibly into the next day. Authorities are asking people to check on their neighbours and make sure they're all right. Temperatures are set to drop to minus twenty tonight. Hospitals and essential services are still open but residents are urged to cut back on electricity usage where possible.*

"How can we cut back on electricity, we don't have any?" Cybelle asked.

Sick guilt swirled in Ondine's tummy as she felt responsible for making this happen. She'd been canoodling with Hamish so much their magic must have spread out to the street. Somebody nearby must have wished for a total blackout across the city.

"It's a better reception over here." Da walked a few steps closer to the door, "Right. They're saying there was a fire at the power plant and output is down to twenty per cent. This could go on for days. Shops are closing," he relayed.

"Shouldnae told us how long it would go fer. They'll be looting next," Hamish said. "No security. Tha police will have their hands full."

Ondine's eyes peeled wide at the thought. "It's chaos."

Old Col walked in with her empty teacup and saucer. She must have been having a quiet cuppa in the family room. The teacup was upended, from reading the leaves. "I was planning on heading home later, but I think I'll sit by the fire instead if it's all the same."

"Of course. Can't have you out in this weather," Ma said.

Not that Old Col left the kitchen. Instead she rummaged around for something to eat.

Hamish hugged Ondine. "We'll be fine. Plenty of food and wood fer the fire."

"Speaking of which," Ma interrupted and pointed her thumb to the dining room, "We have customers and there's a job for you out there."

"Aye ma'am."

Niggly, naggly worries kept Ondine standing still. They'd had plenty of power shortages before. Three or four every winter from cold snaps and ice storms. But they only ever lasted an hour or two. Never for days. This had to be deliberate. Coming so soon on top of everything else that had happened. It was too much to be a coincidence.

"It has to be Vincent!" Ondine blurted out to nobody in particular. "I bet any money he and Mrs. Howser are doing this." Mentally she prepared a whole heap of arguments to push her case.

"I think you're right," Ma said with no equivocation.

"Me too," Da said.

"Aye," Hamish said.

As one, her sisters and Henrik nodded their heads and agreed. Considering Ondine had spent the better part of her childhood not being believed or taken seriously, it was a huge moment.

Everyone stood, boggling at each other, until Hamish said, "So then, what are we gointae do about it?"

"Anybody want this last biscuit?" Old Col asked as she held the tin in her hands.

"Call the police," Ma said.

"What?" Old Col looked aghast.

The muscles in Ondine's head prepared to roll her eyes, but Da beat her to it! Her own Da rolling his eyes!

"I mean about the blackouts," Ma said, "not the biscuits. Eat as many as you like auntie."

Old Col shrugged. "Do we have any more, this tin's empty?"

"Colette love, normally I'd say 'That's a good idea' to call the police, but how do you think they're going to solve this when they can't even follow through on a basic break and enter?"

"Oh." Ma's face fell. "Do you think maybe Mrs. Howser has put a spell on the police as well?"

"Aye, filled their heads with treacle," Hamish said.

"I just had a horrible thought," Ondine said, "People are going to say the power shortages are the Duchess's fault. They already blame her for the trains not running on time."

Cybelle chimed in, "Maybe we should let the Duchess sort out her own problems. We have enough of our own."

Ma gave her middle daughter a hug. "Cybelle, under any other circumstances I'd agree with you. As much as I'd love nothing more to do with that family, we are in lock-step with them."

Cybelle didn't sound convinced. "I think you're needlessly getting yourselves involved in things that aren't our concern. If we hadn't gotten involved in the first place, none of this would have happened."

"Belle." Ondine rolled her eyes faster than her father could. "You forget that *they* came here in the first place. They started it. We were just minding our own business when Vincent came snooping around looking for that stash of jewels."

"And why was the jewellery hidden here in the first place?"

"They were using it as their private bank," Ondine explained. "That way they never had to declare anything or put it on record. And where better to hide something than in a public pub where there are always lots of people around, coming and going at all hours."

"I never knew anything about it," Ma said. "And I'm certain my parents never did either."

The pub had been in Ma's family for decades. Her parents had run it until they'd finally succumbed to the lure of the caravan and joined the greying throngs clogging up the roads around the Black Sea. [2] They'd spent many good years of retirement doing this until they had to respond to the call of the nursing home. [3]

Things stayed quiet for a while, until Ma spoke up, "If we are to have any hope of dealing with this, we're going to have to fight magic with magic. Aren't we Ondi? Now, stop slacking about everyone, we have hungry customers to feed."

Yes, of course, *get back to work everyone*, that was Ma's default position.

That's when Ondine gave herself a mental slap. They were missing a vital ingredient in their 'fight back against Mrs. Howser' plan. "Hang on everyone! We're going to need Melody."

For a moment everyone stopped and gave their best 'I'm so confused' face, before Old Col declared. "Ondine is absolutely right."

It's always a nice feeling to earn a compliment, especially when it really mattered. With all eyes on her, Ondine pressed home her advantage. "You said only the witch who put the spell can remove it; they need to be her words, yeah? Well, there's no way Mrs. Howser will fix the spell she put on Hamish, not when it's all working so well for her. But Melody, she can do it for us. She's a whizz at astral projection; she can go into people's memories when they're asleep, without them even knowing and —"

"— Get her to reverse the spell in her dreams, and she won't even know she's done it!" Old Col grabbed Ondine in a hug. "My girl, you're brilliant!"

All of a sudden, things were turning in Ondine's favour.

Why did that thought scare her all the way down to her boots?

## 23

Ondine was having an awesome dream where she met Melody in Savo Plaza and talked her around to joining their side. The dream felt so real, especially as Ondine and Melody were in their pyjamas and it was snowing something massive in the plaza. Also, Melody pleading with Ondine to, "Save me from this barking mad woman" had an air of authenticity to it.

When Ondine woke up with cold, wet hair, she knew it had been no ordinary dream and that she had in fact been outside in the snow. Melody has gone the full-astral and projected Ondine into her dreams. Or vice versa. Whichever the case, Ondine felt certain her friend needed their help.

Today, they'd get Melody back.

It was one thing to declare a plan of action and feel positive and upbeat about it. It was another matter entirely to put that plan *into* action. Especially when it involved meeting people outdoors, in the depths of winter. Ondine, Hamish and Old Col headed out, mid-afternoon (there was no way Ma would let them leave before the lunch service was over). Being winter, it was already growing dark and it wasn't yet four in the afternoon. They hoped to find Melody at Savo Plaza, if Ondine had correctly interpreted her dream last night.

One of Ondine's gloved hands held Hamish's, the other gripped a vacuum flask filled with Chef's best soup. It was their first plan of persuasion – lure the girl away with food.

"Don't take it personally if she says 'no'," Old Col said. "Or if she's not even there."

"Ye of little faith," Hamish said.

"Faith is something I have by the bucket load," Col said, "the fact is, we don't know what kind of hold Birgit has over that poor girl. We have to tread very carefully."

With each step, Ondine's confidence shrank. "What if she's not there? What if I only dreamed I'd talked to her last night?"

"I'm confident if she can be there, she will be," Col said. "Trouble is, I'm sure Birgit Howser won't be far behind."

Arctic winds chomped at Ondine's neck as she, Hamish and Old Col shuffle-walked through snow-laden footpaths towards Savo Plaza. The low sun cast long shadows, but the streetlights were not on. It was hard to know if this was part of the blackout, or if it simply felt really dark because it was so darn cold.

"What's that?" Hamish grabbed Ondine and pulled him close.

Ondine heard something as well. Peering around the corner, they saw people furtively sticking to the shadows. Their arms were full.

Full of what?

It was hard to see clearly, what with so much snow falling, road workers had shunted the snow towards the kerb, creating snow walls that now reached shoulder height. It turned pedestrians into mice, negotiating a snowy maze. [1] It also provided looters with something to hide behind.

Several people wearing scarves across their faces huddled near the windows of a technology store. Some unseen command had them placing their hands on the window. Were they going to push it in? The glass wobbled and . . . melted onto the path at their feet. Glowing red, then cooling and cracking in the cold air. The looters climbed in over the windowsill and took whatever they wanted. Arms and shoulder bags bulging with stuff, they walked out the store, calm as you like.

"Mercury's wings, did you see that?" Ondine asked.

"Aye, some folks have no respect for law," Hamish said.

"I mean the way they got in. The window just melted off."

"Now you see why I had to split you up for a while. Too many people making bad wishes come true," Old Col said.

Speaking of bad wishes, they heard a whining engine and felt the ground rumble.

"Uh-oh!" leapt out of Ondine as a tank came rolling around the corner. Not a current model Brugelian Army tank either. Something tricked-out and crazy from a graphic novel.

An eruption ripped the sky apart as the tank fired a missile that sailed over their heads and broke the doors of a bank.

From the sidelines, people rushed into the now-broken bank to loot the contents.

"Some folks' wishes are way out of hand!" Hamish grabbed hers and they ran towards Savo Plaza.

They were three blocks from the fairground when a deep rumbling sound greeted them.

"Not again!" Ondine feared another tank would make an appearance.

"Relax, dear, they're power generators." Old Col said. "Back in my day, every block of flats had them."

The acrid aroma of burning diesel assaulted them as they walked closer. Luckily, this was soon overpowered by the delicious smells of melted cheese from a food van. It was using its own generator to keep the kitchens firing and the hot food coming.

Ondine shrugged and said, "If things go badly, we can console ourselves with deep fried cheeseballs."

The cheeseballs were a highlight of Martisor, a festival that kicked off in late January. The locals called it 'Fat week'. It lasted for ten days and people ate so much they could explode. [2]

Turning the corner, Savo Plaza opened out before them, but instead of glittery prettiness, they found a few stallholders trying to make a go of it and the rest of the plaza in darkness. The generators were loud and obnoxious, casting a pall over the area as they tried to keep the festival limping along. If felt damp, empty and unsafe.

No sign of Melody yet; on the plus side, no sign of Mrs. Howser either.

At least there were still some food booths operating, selling hot food dripping with cheese. [3]

Oh bliss, there was a candy silk van selling bags for a schlip each. [4] Ondine was in heaven.

A few of the same rides were here from the last time they'd visited, defying the cold weather and black-outs affecting the rest of Venzelemma.

"The key is to have a good time and act normally," Old Col said as they walked through the fairground.

Ondine nearly laughed at the suggestion. Could she remember what normal was?

"Sit yourselves down; I'll get us some cheesy chips," Old Col said.

A pang of guilt shot through Ondine at how wonderful her great aunt could be at times. Not long ago, Ondine had entertained the idea of defecting to Team Howser. They'd only been thoughts though; it wasn't like she'd acted on them or anything.

Hamish sat shoulder to hip with her on the bench seat to share body warmth. The moment Col returned with the steaming chips, they dived in. After two bites, Ondine could feel her arteries complaining and her stomach rejoicing. Warmth won out over good health and she had another handful, the melted cheese forming string bridges between the bowl and her mouth.

"Ondi!" Two wiry arms latched around her and hugged hard.

Ondine yelped in shock.

"Got ya!" Melody said, taking a seat beside her.

"Melody!" Ondine threw her arms around her friend, careful not to rub her cheese-oiled hands on Melody's thick woolly coat.

Considering how furry and dense the fabric was, it was a wonder Ondine could feel Melody through it at all. Part way through the hug, fear settled in. If Melody were here, could Mrs. Howser be far behind?

"I'm so glad you're here," Ondine said. "Here, I brought you some soup." She unscrewed the wide lid of the vacuum flask, which doubled as a mug, and poured out the soup. Steam rose in great clouds. "Careful, it's hot!"

Of course Melody ignored her. She was starving and freezing, and the soup was her salvation. Half her face was obscured by her enormous brown fur hat with the requisite ear flaps for this time of year.

"You'll burn your tongue!" Ondine watched her friend gulp it down.

"It's divine!" Melody held the mug out for a refill.

*OK then*, Ondine refilled it and took her chance. "Loads more where that came from, it's one of Chef's specials. Why don't we go back to the pub and warm up?"

Melody shook her head, downed the soup and held the cup out for thirds.

"You poor thing, you're so hungry." They'd been counting on her state of famished-ness to persuade her over to their side. "Come and have dinner with us, you can have as much as you want." Ondine attempted to place the emotional wedge. "I'm surprised Mrs. Howser didn't bring you along when she came over to our pub the other day."

"Mmmmm. Wait. What?"

"Oh, I'm sorry, I feel like I've really stepped in it," Ondine said, watching for Melody's reaction. "Weren't you invited?"

"She visited you, and she didn't take me?"

"Er, yes," Ondine said, acting crestfallen on the surface, while privately rejoicing at how well this was going. "Chef's food is always fabulous. She ate a bit of everything, especially the soup with canapé floaters."

"When was this?"

Doing her best to look like she'd put her foot in her mouth, Ondine named the date. "It was after CovenCon. Maybe you had some magic to catch up with?"

Looking deflated, Melody pushed the empty mug back to Ondine. "It's no use. I can't come with you."

Jupiter's moons, the girl was three steps ahead of them. Ondine kept trying. "But you work so hard for her, don't you want a bit of time off? When was the last time you hung out with your friends?"

"Or your parents," Old Col said.

*Oh yes, parents, good point.*

"She knows." Melody closed her eyes tightly and tapped the side of her head. "She sees and hears everything."

Old Col produced a super-sized bowl of cheesy chips. Melody's eyes sprang open and she grabbed four chips and shoved them in.

"Still *goat* yer appetite then?" Hamish said.

Ondine elbowed him in the ribs. Then she leaned in to Melody. "Are you here by yourself?"

Melody shook her head. "Even when I think I'm alone." Again she tapped the side of her head.

Ondine scrunched her forehead.

Reluctantly, Melody stopped shovelling food in her gob and looked about, as if Mrs. Howser was about to leap out from behind a tree. Then she grabbed the tassels of her fur-lined hood and tied the ends together, pulling them tightly.

Worry burrowed through Ondine. Melody was choosing her words carefully, trying to give them a message that she couldn't say out loud. Could Mrs. Howser hear everything they were saying? In which case, *they'd* have to choose their words with utmost care –

"Ye need tae leave the crazy witch," Hamish said.

Ondine slapped her palm to her forehead.

Melody looked at Hamish, blushed furiously and lapsed into giggles.

Did she have to react like such a girly girl just because Hamish looked at her? Hang on . . . Ondine watched as Melody reached for a napkin and began to write.

Which would ordinarily be pretty *ordinary*, except for the fact Melody didn't have a pen in her hand. Plus, she had her eyes closed the whole time and kept right on giggling as if they were having such tremendous fun.

On the napkin she wrote: *She hears everything I hear.*

Jupiter's moons!

Catching on, Ondine joined in the giggling to disguise her fear that Mrs. Howser was listening to their every word.

Then Melody wrote:

*And see.*

They were absolutely stumped. If they couldn't talk to Melody without Mrs. Howser knowing everything, the old witch may as well show herself now.

They needed Melody in so many ways. Breaking the bond between Melody and Mrs. Howser was the only way to weaken the witch, and therefore weaken her grip on Vincent. And it would help break the curse Hamish was living under. Oh yes, and they also had to make Anathea the fairest of them all.

It was so hard to think of the big picture when her thoughts were so full of Hamish.

"Have another chip," Hamish said.

Melody giggled, this time there was no matching expression of embarrassment on her face. Instead, she looked at Ondine and mouthed the words, "Help me."

Ondine plastered on a smile. "Of course I'll get more chips."

Mercenary thoughts crept in. Maybe they should simply kidnap Melody and wait for Mrs. Howser to try and get her back? In the meantime . . . no, Mrs. Howser would know what they were doing . . . so it wouldn't work. Also, something else tinkered at the edges of Ondine's thoughts. It would be getting really dark across the rest of Venzelemma, which meant more looters with more bad wishes could be about. They needed to get Melody home with them, and soon.

Frustration took hold. "We need to break the link between you and Mrs. H. Can you hear me you old witch? That's right. This ends now. Let Melody go –"

"– Are you out of your mind?" Old Col cried out.

"I'm sick of waiting. Melody, do you want your freedom back?"

Melody's face crumpled as if she were about to cry. Instead of speaking, she closed her eyes and nodded.

Frustration had Ondine feeling messier than the sick people staggering out of the rides.

Wait a minute. *The rides!*

"Auntie Col, if Mrs. Howser can see and hear everything Melody does, let's use the fairground rides to shake her loose."

"So much for subtle," Col threw her hands in the air.

They were in a fairground, which fairly reeked of happiness – and diesel fumes – while the rest of the city descended into chaos. This could work. "Let's go on that one," Ondine said, pointing to The Pretzel. It spun up and down and twisted back and forth. The most sickening ride in the plaza.

Hamish baulked. "*Noat* that one."

Old Col paled. "Count me out."

"You get a free pass," Ondine said to her great-auntie. Sure, her elderly relative was looking a lot healthier these days than she had been at the palechia, but there was no way she'd subject the dear old thing to The Pretzel. "Come on Melody, I dare you."

"I'll be sick!" Melody protested.

"And so will Howser." Ondine looked directly into Melody's eyes, as if they were a window to Mrs. Howser. "Do you hear me you old witch? Break it now or we'll pretzel your brain."

"Are ye sure, hen?" Hamish's complexion dropped a few shades too.

Ondine shot back, "Don't tell me you're scared?"

"Course I'm nae scared of a wee ride."

Perfect. "Stay here, Col, we'll be back soon," Ondine said, dragging them towards the ride.

To get to the pretzel ride, they had to walk past a group of patrons who'd just got off it. They looked like vomit zombies, which only made Ondine all the more determined to make her plan work. If Mrs. Howser could see and hear everything via a link with Melody, a psychic link with someone spinning round a fairground should mess her right up. This ride had pods on the end of long arms, which went up and down, side to side and could also flip back and forth. A squeeze from Hamish's hand gave Ondine reassurance.

She'd been so caught up in severing the connection between Melody and Mrs. Howser, she'd overlooked a huge flaw in her plan.

She hated spinny-sicky rides.

Because they made her so spinny and sick.

Too late to back out, the woman with the 'Carnie Crew' baseball cap ushered them into their cabin with its scratched paint in lurid colours and showed them how to fasten the five-point harness.

Five points?

Mercury's Wings, how did she ever think this was a good idea?

All the while, she plastered on a smile as the flashing lights flashed around them and the tinny music played, to show the others how fake-excited she was instead of for-real-petrified.

Just as Melody clicked her shoulder strap in, an old woman's hand reached into the cabin. "Not so fast."

Mrs Howser!

Of course the old witch would show up right now.

"You're not going on this ride," Howser yelled at Melody. Then she turned her fury on the Carnie. "Get her out of this, now."

Showing no fear of hysterical old ladies, the Carnie turned to Melody and asked, "Do you want to get out sweetheart?"

For a second Ondine feared Melody would back out and leave her and Hamish twisting like . . . pretzels.

"Er . . . no. I'm fine thanks."

"You are not!" Mrs. Howser yelled.

Luckily for Ondine, the people in the queue were getting grumpy and moaning about how much time they were wasting.

"You are coming with me!" Mrs. Howser climbed into the cabin and sat beside Melody, clawing at the harness to get it off.

Hamish wound his free hand into Ondine's and brought it to his lips. "Isn't it *loavely* that we ken make other people's wishes come true?"

A bell went off in her head. "You're so smart, have I told you that?" She knew if they shared a hug or a kiss, magic would happen – for other people. And right now, Ondine bet her next hot meal Melody would be wishing Mrs. Howser would get out of here.

Ondine leaned forward, but her harness held her back from Hamish's lips.

Mrs. Howser kept tugging at Melody's harness to get it off. "You are not doing this to me, not after all the work I've put in!"

Hamish leaned forward as far as he could. Their lips were millimetres apart.

"Got it!" Mrs. Howser cried out in victory as one of Melody's shoulder straps came free.

The ride started up. "That's against health and safety!" the carnie cried out, as she pulled the emergency shutdown lever. It sparked and smoked, but failed to stop the ride.

Mrs Howser was probably the one making it run. If Ondine could kiss Hamish, she could make the carnie's wish come true. The wish she should be having about stopping the ride. Unless the carnie was having worse wishes that Ondine didn't want to think about.

Pressing forward, Ondine tried to reach Hamish. Their lips remained frustratingly apart.

"I have tae change," Hamish said, pulling back.

The pain would be hideous, but if Hamish changed into a Shambles ferret, he could slip out of his harness. But that would mean he'd be a ferret and Ondine had become so used to him not being one. Plus, if he changed back into human and didn't do it exactly the right way inside his clothes, the ride would lose its PG-12 rating.

"Wait!" Ondine cried out as Hamish's face turned fuzzy and black.

"No!" Mrs. Howser screamed as she noticed what Hamish was up to. In a flash of light and noise, she struck Hamish with a burst of magic to stop him transforming.

"Right, out you get!" Mrs. Howser crowed with victory as she pulled Melody from her seat.

Defiantly, Melody screamed, "I will not!"

Ondine lunged; the momentum caused the harness to slip off her shoulder. Her face smacked into Hamish's almost-fuzzy chin in the least elegant, least romantic kiss on the planet.

Hamish cradled her face with his palms; fuzzy palms that were not-properly-Hamish-like. His face too was gnarled and hairy.

Not the tiniest bit lovely, the way she loved her loveable Hamish.

"It's me, Ondi, and I'll love ye till the day I die."

She looked into his face, a face dark around the edges but not completely transformed into his other persona. Hair sprouted from his eyebrows, ears and nose. She needed to love him with all her heart yet all she could think of was how ferret-like he'd become.

Perhaps, perhaps if she truly kissed him with a pure heart, he might change back? "I love you Hamish." She breathed in, then planted the most beautiful, the most tender, the most emotional kiss she had in her arsenal.

Fireworks went off inside her head.

Mrs. Howser screamed like a kicked dog.

The cabin door slammed shut.

Ondine and Hamish broke away from their most beautiful kiss in the universe and looked at the two seats opposite. Melody was strapped in again, nice and tightly.

And so was Mrs. Howser.

Melody must have wished it!

The ride whirred into action.

"Arrrrrghghghghghghghgh!" Mrs. Howser screamed.

Hang on. Melody was supposed to wish the old witch out of here. Not keep her with them. Unless . . .

"Suck it up!" Melody said, sounding very un-Melody-like as she peeled her eyes wide open. "Set me free or you get a double dose!"

Because of Mrs. Howser's connection with Melody, she would get twice the ride and twice the sickness.

"Melody you're brilliant," Ondine said.

Hamish screamed as they spun and tumbled and fell and rose and lurched in every which way. Much to Ondine's disappointment, their incredible kiss had not cured his face-fur.

Nausea kicked in. Nasty, lurchy, hot-and-coldy nausea that grabbed Ondine in the guts and twisted. Hard.

She clamped her mouth shut.

"Nooooooo!" Mrs. Howser cried.

Ondine felt so proud of Melody – what a fantastic wish under pressure. Having Mrs. Howser with them was the perfect punishment. Her grimacing gave Ondine something to focus on while they dropped and soared and dived and twisted and churned and rolled and rolled again.

It felt like the ride would never end. Just as it slowed it sped up again, sending them through all those hideous motions once more.

Thank goodness they'd left Old Col out of this. She wouldn't have survived.

"Break the link!" Melody yelled.

"Never!" Mrs. Howser's voice cracked but her expression remained defiant.

Melody clung to her shoulder straps in the same way her hair clung to her perspiring face. "The ride won't stop until you break the link. I wished it that way."

Beside Ondine, Hamish moaned. She didn't dare look in case he disgraced himself. Lurch. Shudder. Drop. Rise. Tilt. Tumble. Wobble. Hot sick burned the back of her throat. If this ride didn't stop soon she'd make such a mess. The lurching and twisting plastered her hair over her damp face, but the g-forces pinned her arms back making her unable to clear her vision.

"You are in so much trouble!" Mrs. Howser cried out.

It couldn't be true. Melody was enjoying herself? "That goes double for you!" She yelled back.

Spin. Drop. Twist. Spin. Pike. That was just for Ondine. Mrs. Howser was getting it in stereo.

"Make it stop!" the witch cried.

Melody pressed her advantage and said exactly what Ondine was thinking, "It stops when you break the link!"

An anguished howl erupted from Mrs. Howser. "Nooooooo."

"Do it!"

"Never!"

"Then we stay here forever."

"You can't!"

Determination filled Melody's face. "I can and I will. I'm having a great time, wheeeeeee!"

## 24

———

The ride, would it never end?

Mrs. Howser made a pathetic mewling noise and began to cry.

Ondine's stomach leapt into her throat.

Over and over they tumbled and spun in space, held firmly in harness. No way out for any of them until Mrs. Howser gave in.

The interminable ride rode on. For the rest of Ondine's life if she never saw a fairground again it would be too soon. She resorted to silent begging, as if she had some kind of psychic link to Mrs. Howser to beg her to stop.

Lurch, spin, twist, drop, spin, drop, lurch, lurch.

With a weak admission of defeat, Mrs. Howser said, "Make it stop." A sob escaped and she crimped her eyes shut. "You win."

Suddenly, the ride stopped.

Ondine's stomach crashed back into position.

The Carnie lady opened the cabin door with a huge smile. "All done? Who needs help with their –" Her jaw dropped for a second. Then she called out to someone they couldn't see. "Marko? We're gonna need the hose again."

If the world would stop spinning, Ondine could give Melody a hug for being so very brave and clever.

Mrs. Howser was the last to leave the ride. She staggered out, all crumpled of spirit and damp of face. "You'll pay for this."

As if her brains were still spinning (and lurching and dropping and tilting and rising, then tilting and dropping at the same time) Mrs. Howser's words dropped in to Ondine's brain and flew straight out again. Let the woman say or do what she liked. Nothing Mrs. Howser could magic could possibly make Ondine feel any worse right now.

"Oh you poor thing!" they heard a man call out.

Through the blur of moving buildings and spinning lights, Ondine's stomach clenched harder.

Turns out it was possible to feel worse because Lord Vincent came into view.

He looked . . . he looked concerned and almost, *kind*. How he managed that Ondine had no idea.

"You poor dear, let me help you," Vincent said as he approached Mrs. Howser and held her steady. That blue hand looked bluer than ever. Had he turned it into a tattoo? "Everything is all right now. Here, have some cold water, it will make you feel better."

By this point in Ondine's life, she should have known the expression, "Things can't get any worse," was a total lie. Because right now, Vincent's act of chivalry in offering Mrs. Howser a cool drink in her moment of distress made everything a whole lot worse.

"What a nice man," someone in the crowd said.

"I think that's Lord Vincent," another said.

"Isn't he lovely?"

"So sweet."

"He makes me swoon."

And so on *ad nauseam*.

Hamish's clammy hand held Ondine's. "As if the ride wasnae sickening enough."

Ondine looked into Hamish's handsome face and jumped in shock. His features were still fixed in the starting-to-turn-into-a-ferret phase.

"What's wrong, hen?" Hamish's hands flew to his face, where he must have felt the fur for himself. "Aw naw! I'm ugly!"

Ondine gulped and tried not to admit anything. She felt sick enough from the ride, let alone his messed-up face. "We'll fix it, I promise."

"Let's scram," Melody said as she reached Ondine.

Ondine barely dared hope. "Is the link . . .?"

"Broken? Yes," she confirmed.

"Then let's get oot of here," Hamish said.

Old Col ambled up with extra napkins so they could wipe their faces.

"Don't suppose you've got any water?" Ondine asked.

Old Col tisked. "That was too clever of Vincent. Turning up at the right moment, helping a lady in distress. You can bet it will be all over the news inside an hour. Meanwhile, where's Anathea? What's she doing to make people like her? Hmm? What's she doing to get the crowd on her side? And . . . Hamish dear, what's happened to your face?"

"Can we work that out tomorrow? I need to lie down," Ondine said. No sooner were the words out of her mouth than she fell upon a bank of snow as if it were a bed. "Oh. This is so good."

"That's enough, child," Old Col said. "We need to get home quickly. The rest of the city is probably in lockdown because of the blackout and the looting."

As far as Ondine was concerned, those were real-life problems affecting other people. She had to ice the nausea away before she could even think about walking home. That gave her a new thought. "Old Col, if there's no electricity, how do we get the train home?"

"They'll most likely switch to diesel engines," she said.

<hr>

THE NEXT DAY they still didn't have reliable power, so they burned candles for light, boiled water in an old gas-top kettle and bought the newspaper instead of listening to the radio or watching television.

The main story in the newspaper featured the "gallant" Lord Vincent coming to a distressed woman's aid in Savo Plaza.

The rest of the pagers were filled with stories of looting and the hospitals being overrun with patients presenting with a viral strain of magic they were calling Ant Flu Hn26. Named not because it was spread by ants, but because it was marching all over Europe like ants on a discarded box of cheeseballs, across Brugel, Craviç, Slaegal and even Wallachia.

Ondine, Old Col, Hamish and Melody were down one end of the kitchen, reading the newspaper and talking over the events of the night before.

Henrik and Cybelle were at the stoves, cooking breakfast, making extra for Melody so she could get back to full strength.

"I think it's safe to say Vincent has magic *and* a PR company helping out," Old Col said. "There's no way this happened by chance."

"The Ant Flu?" Ondine asked?

"Not that, the bit with Lord Vincent being in the right place at the right time."

"Aye," Hamish agreed as he took a plate of food from Henrik. "Vincent and Howser have tae be in this together."

Ondine's appetite was back as she guzzled her scrambled eggs on toast. "How do we compete? We try and make her popular by putting up posters, which costs us money; he gets in the papers for free."

"Why are you helping Anathea?" Melody's brows crinkled.

"She's goat me papers," Hamish said, scratching at his beardy half-ferret face. "We help her hold on to the throne, she helps me stay here and not get deported."

"Oh," Melody said.

"Yeah, Oh," Ondine said. "And it's getting us exactly nowhere." It was hard to look at her lovely Hamish, what with him being stuck mid-transformation. Old Col should be helping more on that front. In fact, Hamish should be doing his best to transform back and forth and fix himself.

Unless he couldn't? A thought which made food stick in her throat.

"Forgive me for asking, but," Melody's voice took on a placating tone. "why *do* you want to help Anathea? Aside from making sure Hamish doesn't get deported."

"Because she should have been duchess all along!" Ondine said, unable to stop the whine in her voice. "And if you got to know her, you'd know she's really nice and she's concerned about people, and she's a darn site better than Vincent."

"Are we done with politics?" Cybelle asked.

"For now yes," Ondine said, feeling incredibly glum about the mess they were in and their lack of progress.

"Aren't you forgetting something?" Melody said as she accepted another plate of food from Cybelle.

Everyone looked at her.

"You've got *me!*" she said with a huge grin. Then she grabbed the last two sausages from the serving dish nearby and ate them straight off her fork without putting them on her plate first. "And thank you so much for breaking the link. I can't tell you how good it feels to be free."

"You're looking better already," Ondine said, "and – and I don't want to put a dampener on our celebrations, but how are we going to help Anathea win hearts and minds when Howser and Vincent have all the resources and magic and loads of money?"

"Too easy." Melody beamed with confidence as she accepted a plate of scrambled eggs from Henrik. "Howser's been linked to me; I've been linked straight back to her. I know all her secrets."

Hamish hugged Melody with glee.

A stab of jealousy caught Ondine by surprise. "What sort of secrets?"

"All of them," she replied. "Her spells, and her stratagems for Vincent. It's all in here," she said, tapping the forked sausage to the side of her head.

Hamish must have seen Ondine's face because he backed away from Melody a little. Which only made Ondine feel more awful.

She shovelled in food to block out these new, nasty feelings. Hamish still looked too ferrety from his half-transformation last night.

Would he be stuck like that forever?

The lights flickered on again, and they had electricity. It was good news for the restaurant, but bad news as the fluorescent lights did nothing for Hamish's hairy complexion.

"Can ye find Howser's spell so I can be meself again?" Hamish asked.

"Too easy," Melody winked, "we'll have you back to handsome in no time."

It had to be battle fatigue. That was the only way to explain Ondine's sour mood when they should be celebrating Melody's rescue. Ondine had read about war weariness in the book about Grand Duchess Elmaree. Elmaree and her supporters had fought for so long, they never had a chance to simply enjoy a normal day and be themselves.

Like Elmaree, Ondine had a to-do list that stretched to the horizon. Make Anathea popular; get Hamish his work papers; get Hamish back to his gorgeous self; and then defeat Vincent and Mrs. Howser.

"We should have done this last night, but I was too sick and wonky," Melody said. She dropped her dirty plate in the sink and reached for Ondine's hand with her left and Hamish's with her right. "I know you never got the hang of astral projection, Ondi, but I love it. Join up and we'll go travelling."

Ondine gave over her hand and reached for Hamish with her other. Before she could, Old Col wedged herself beside her and took it.

"What are we doing?" Ondine asked.

"We're beating Birgit at her own game. You're coming with me into her memories."

Ondine creased her brow. "You sure you know what you're doing?"

"Of course," Melody said. "Done it heaps."

Not entirely convinced, Ondine asked, "But won't she be up and about already?"

"Doesn't matter." Melody winked. "It works just as well if the person's awake or asleep. They don't feel a thing."

"Are ye sure, hen?" Hamish asked.

Jealousy twisted Ondine's stomach again. "Hen" was his special name for her, not other girls.

"Uh, yep. Quite sure." Melody blushed furiously, making Ondine instantly suspicious about whose memories she'd been visiting. Before she could ask any more questions, Melody said, "Ready? Close your eyes, let's go."

Everyone closed their eyes and squeezed hands. Ondine had to stay with them or she'd break the chain. Or be left out. And there was no way she wanted to be left out of this.

When she closed her eyes, Ondine saw only darkness and heard only background noise from the pub. Slowly the everyday noises and darkness faded away. Small sparkles of light danced behind her eyelids. Her body grew lighter, until she was little more than a –

"Imagine you're a jellyfish, floating with the tide," Melody said.

– jellyfish. Yes, That's exactly how she felt. Hope unfurled that this experiment might work. She certainly felt lighter and . . . *driftier.*

"The floatier you feel, the better," Melody said. "We're all connected so we'll keep each other floating along. I'm guiding us towards Birgit Howser and we're going to access her memories."

Coldness danced around the edges of Ondine's perception.

Melody said, "Don't worry about the chill. It means we're getting close. She's always been a cold stone, that one. I can't thank you guys enough for breaking the hold she had on me. I thought I was going to freeze to death."

Interesting, Melody seemed to be –

"Reading your thoughts. Yes. First things first, let's fix Hamish's beautiful face, yeah?"

*Oh yeah.*

In a flash of noise and lights and spinning, Ondine was back in The Pretzel car and everything was going haywire. Memories and nausea from last night came rushing back. Ondine's eyes were already shut, so she couldn't shut them any more. Could they hurry up and –

"Get this over with?' Melody said. "Right, we can see her, and we can see us, but *she* can't see us. We're going to rewind to the point where she . . . ahhh, here we are."

"Is this what you went through last night?" Old Col asked. "I'm so glad I sat it out."

The real life scene flicker-jumped back and forth, as if someone were zapping through the adverts in the story of their lives. Melody reached the exact point where Mrs. Howser cursed Hamish to freeze, mid-transition.

"Gotcha," Melody crowed in triumph. She captured the words in the air between them, then took them to the other side of the picture.

The words hung in mid-air, written backwards.

Instead of saying 'Freeze!' Melody said, "Ezeerf!" She turned to

Hamish to reverse the spell. Not the Hamish strapped into his seat in the Pretzel Ride, but the Hamish floating above her.

Melody's hand was still holding Hamish's as she waved it in the air. "Ezeerf!"

Ondine saw the dark bristles over Hamish's face retreating. His whiskery nose smooshed back to his Scottishly handsome one. His eyes morphed from black to sparkly green.

Gratitude overwhelmed Ondine and she nearly threw herself at Hamish.

"Don't break the link," Melody said, giving her hand a reminder-squeeze.

As desperate as she was to throw her arms around her beloved, Ondine held back. As soon as this session was over though, she'd cling to him like an orangutan.

"One more thing," Melody said. The five of them drifted high above the Martisor fairground and bobbed along on the wind. Soon the city fell away and they followed the train lines into the countryside.

It may have been night when they were at the fairground, but by the time they reached the forested hillsides, silver pink dawn dusted the horizon. Behind them, heavy clouds built into ominous anvil shapes.

It looked surprisingly familiar to Ondine.

"We're in Bellreeve," Melody said.

"Aye, I thought I recognised the place," Hamish said. "It looks different too."

"I know when this is," Old Col said. "We've gone back a few years, haven't we Melody?"

Melody giggled and said, "Told you I was good."

"That's enough showing off from you," Old Col said.

As if to punctuate her speech, a flash of lightning rippled through the sky, followed by rolling thunder.

They floated on, above the path Ondine, Hamish and Old Col had taken when they first approached the Autumn Palace. On the rise of the hill they saw the gatehouse. At first Ondine thought the guard on duty was asleep. Then she noticed he was under a spell.

Splattered spots of rain fell.

There, standing by the flagstones near the gatehouse, stood Birgit Howser. She looked much, much younger. In her arms she held a ferret.

Shambles!

Mentally, Ondine worked out the time frame. It had to have been soon after the debutante ball, if Hamish was already a ferret.

"I dinnae remember her doing that. Mebbe I'm asleep. Och, hen, do I look that bad when I'm like that?"

"You have your moments," Ondine said.

Old Col said, "Bit of shush, please."

"It's quite all right. Remember, we can see her but she can't see us," Melody reminded them.

They floated above Birgit as she made ready to cast a spell over the flagstones. Those same stones Ondine, Hamish and Old Col had walked over when they'd arrived at the palace, setting off a chain of crazy events and huge helpings of weird magic.[1]

Hamish said, "Ye know lass, I never did see a Mister Howser."

"Shush!" everyone said.

"Dinnae shush me, she cannae hear us."

"No, but we need to hear *her*," Melody said. "She's about to say the spell."

*When first love and ferret pass this way,*

*The warning signs will fly and fray*

*The end will come for Brugel's head*

*My payment, now, or he'll be dead."*

Brugel's head? Ondine wondered. "She means Duke Pavla, right?"

Old Col huffed. "At least she didn't rhyme Duke with puke."

The five of them floated towards the ground so they could stand on the reverse side of the spell and catch every word.

Ondine creased her lips in thought, then said, "Howser set this trap, like some kind of remote alarm system. But why? I mean if you set up magic, wouldn't you want to be around to see it happening?"

"Not necessarily," Old Col answered. "Having strange magic happen when you're not around does give you a certain amount of deniability."

Ondine screwed up the rest of her face in puzzlement.

"It means, dear, that she can have the perfect alibi for when things go wrong. She sets things up to go wrong in the first place, then swans in offering help and nobody suspects her. Very clever, really."

Birgit Howser looked up, her unlined, years-younger face looking no less evil than her old wrinkly one had last night.

Her eyes turned hard as stone and she glared at Ondine. Time froze as the old witch's eyes bored holes through Ondine's soul. Lead filled her belly and she had to swallow a few times before she could whisper, "Are you sure she can't –"

Mrs. Howser pointed her finger and screamed. "Get out! Get out of my memories!"

Ondine screamed.

They all did.

She pulled her hands back to cover her mouth. Too late, she'd broken the link.

Flashes filled her eyes. Ondine opened them to find herself back with everyone in the kitchen, gasping in shock.

"I'm nae sure that was supposed to happen, lass."

Old Col sniffed. "I fear we've really upset her now."

"Yeah," Melody said, chewing on her thumbnail. "How did she do that?"

While Melody and Old Col conferred with each other, Ondine found she only had eyes for Hamish. Because he was back to being so handsomely Hamish again.

"Ondine, snap out of it," Old Col said. "Help us think of ways we can fix this."

Huffing and feeling tired, frustrated, emotionally wrought and – despite the enormous breakfast – still a bit hungry, Ondine crossed her arms over her chest. "I don't know how any of this magic works."

Muttering just enough for everyone to hear, Old Col said, "If we can't fix this, Howser will keep making chaos across the country."

Added to that, Mrs. Howser now hated their livers. [2]

It was an absolute certainty that the moment Ondine thought, "things can't get worse" they absolutely would. "Yes but . . . Hamish and I can still make nice things happen." Did anyone notice how desperate she sounded?

"Ondi's right," Hamish said. "I'm glad I'm me again, and we've freed Melody, but we havnae made Anathea the best and fairest, so mebbe it's a good thing we havnae broken Howser's wishing spell, so we can still use it." Then he flashed a smile Ondine's way and made her tummy flip. In a nice way, not in a stuck-in-The-Pretzel-ride way.

"You're right, of course," Old Col said. "We'd best use the magic while we still have it. Let's get close to Anathea and make her wishes come true."

Which sounded remarkably like their earlier plans. Before Old Col and Ma had split up her and Hamish.

Melody put her hands up. "I have an idea. The Snow Maze Festival comes straight after Martisor. Big crowds. The Duke always cut the ribbon and gets to go through first.

Obviously it will be Anathea this year. Loads of people turn up. They should have the power properly back on by then."

"She's a clever one, isn't she Ondi?" Hamish said. "Lots of people there to boost Anathea's popularity ratings."

"If Vincent and Birgit show up, as they're bound to," Old Col added, "we can have it out with them, once and for all."

The lights flickered above them, as if applauding the ideas Melody and Old Col were creating. In the midst of everyone congratulating each other for being so clever, Ondine sighed and thought, *Why didn't I think of that?*

## 25

Like an unwelcome guest, winter made itself completely at home and messed the place right up. Where light snow had covered the world with pretty magic at Christmas, the deep freeze of proper-winter slathered everything with a thick layer of hard ice.

Every day, just before lunch and then in between first and second dinner, Hamish, Josef, Henrik and Thomas took a shovel each and headed out to clear a trench through the snow so their customers could get to the front door. They threw the snow into the kerb, adding height to the walls of snow and ice. In the middle of the night, the street sweepers also cleared the streets like some kind of snow-eating alien with a lightning-fast metabolism. Gorging itself at one end, squirting it out the other. The snowspray slathered the walls of icy debris at the kerb, making them higher and wider than before. Snow buried lampposts, rubbish bins and bicycles, if they happened to be chained to the post at the time.

Walking the streets felt exactly like walking in an enormous maze of snow. Which conveniently put people in the right mood for the next festival. Between Martisor and Easter, Savo Plaza held the annual Snow Maze Festival. Some people complained about so many festivals arriving one after the other, but they were quickly hushed up with a well-aimed snowball. After all, there was no point in having an empty plaza. [1]

And at this time of year, they had plenty of snow with which to build the maze, which cannot be said for summer.

The sun kept its distance and the heavy white stuff kept on falling as Ondine, Hamish, Melody and Old Col walked the cobbled streets to the Plaza. Banners hung from buildings, groaning and creaking with the weight of snow piled over them.

Despite the cold, it was a much nicer walk than the last time they'd come here, because the power was back on, alarm systems were working and so were the traffic lights.

"Here's how it's going to play out," Old Col said as they shook the snow off their umbrellas. Steam poured from her mouth as she spoke. "When we get near Anathea, Ondine and Hamish will get loved up. That way, Anathea's wishes will come true. It's going to work. I can feel it in my bones."

It would work. It had to. Ondine worried her bottom lip in thought. "Aunt Col? I don't want to be a downer but, are we sure Anathea is going to make the right kind of wish?"

"What is wrong with you? I'm telling you to get sucky face with Hamish, and you're asking questions?"

Trust her great aunt to get to the meat of the matter. "I dunno." She made tracks in the snow with the toe of her boot. Something was missing, but she couldn't name it. As if they hadn't quite resolved all the outstanding issues that had arisen. "I guess . . . I'm worried about what everyone else is going to be wishing for when we do it." Because last time they'd been loved-up in public, people grew tails. Chaos broke out. Worse still, she and Hamish had to break up.

"I'll make sure that doesn't happen." Melody said. "I'll be sending out astrals that put everyone in a good mood and make them think positively."

"Aye, that's Barry," Hamish said, giving Melody a grin. [2]

Jealousy pricked Ondine each time Hamish complimented Melody-With-All-The-Answers. Meanwhile, she slipped further into the sulks and became Stressed-Out-Ondi-With-No-Answers. And that niggling, nagging feeling of having forgotten something pretty huge kept . . . niggling and nagging at her.

Old Col grabbed her by the elbow. "Come along. There's the Duchess. Let's get in close so we can make an impact. Ready child?"

"Not really."

"Love conquers all, my dear, just you remember that," Col said.

Dread filled Ondine as she looked upon the golden carpet near the entrance to the snow maze. The maze was a huge thing; taller than an average person so you couldn't see were you were, and made entirely out of snow.

Light snow drifted and fell on the carpet, but not for long as a worker with a vacuum backpack worked away quietly to keep it clean.

It wasn't the maze filling Ondine with thoughts of failure, but the people standing on that carpet near the front. The First Minister Cebotari stood proudly beside Duchess Anathea, both of them resplendent in heavy brown coats, solid outdoorsy boots and hats with earflaps. Even little Biscuit the dog had a brown coat on and booties on his feet. Standing beside Anathea was the last person in the world they expected to see, Lord Vincent.

Hamish asked, "What's that balloon doing here?" [3]

"He *is* next in line," Melody piped up.

Col shot back, "Not if they change the laws of succession."

Hamish suggested, "Mebbe she had no alternative? She has to be fair and let him tag *aloang*?"

"Of course he'd turn up," Ondine said, her eyes almost rolling in frustration, "He's trying to out-popular Anathea."

Judging by the number of screaming, squealing teenage girls in the crowd, he had that competition easily won. Yes, he was handsome, but only at face-value. Ondine knew the real Vincent, she knew he was ugly on the inside.

But he was young and looked like a pop idol. How could Anathea compete?

"Melody, you have to do something," Ondine said. "We can't make Vincent's wishes come true, because we know what he'll be wishing for and it won't do any of us a lick of good."

"Already on it," Melody said with a look of concentration on her face.

"I'm sending blockers. But um, there are a lot of people here and I can't do all of them."

So many *squees* erupted from the crowd; it hurt Ondine's ears. How could an old crone like Anathea compete against a rock star like Vincent?

Old Col coughed into her closed hand. "Do your best Melody. As long as you block *him* and keep Anathea positive, we should set everything to rights."

A voice boomed over the crowd. "My Lord Duchess, Lord Vincent, Her Honour the First Minister, distinguished guests, ladies and gentlemen . . ."

Ondine followed the sound upwards and noticed loudspeakers cabled through the high branches in the trees.

"Better get smooching," Old Col said.

"Not here," Ondine said. They were drowning in a sea of overhyped fangirls who were mentally writing themselves into Lord Vincent fan fiction. "If this lot get their wish, they'll rip Vincent to shreds."

Old Col turned and raised an eyebrow. "You say that like it's a bad thing."

Hamish gave her hand a squeeze. "Yer a good lass for lookin' out for him, even if he doesnae deserve it."

The compliment boosted her spirits and she squeezed his hand in return.

"Over tae the side, weil be closer tae Anathea and away from the squealies."

They pushed and squeezed through the crowd until they reached the very edge of the audience section. At which point Anathea noticed them and gave a curt nod, as if she'd been expecting them.

Ondine was expecting a lot from Anathea as well. They weren't doing this out of the kindness of their own hearts or for the good of Brugel. They were doing it for purely selfish reasons. Ondine wanted Hamish forever, but if he didn't have his work papers allowing him to stay in Brugel, he'd either have to live the rest of his public life as a ferret or be shunted home to Scotland.

No matter how angry and used and tired she felt, she had to push every negative thought aside and kiss Hamish with all her heart. She didn't want to think about the consequences of failing. Of him being deported. Of Anathea getting booed off stage. Vincent triumphant and becoming Brugel's next Duke. Mrs. Howser's shadow casting a pall over everything.

Panic caught in her throat, making her feel even less loved-up and smoochy. Thinking about Mrs. Howser had a way of draining every nice thought from her head.

Hamish's steady hands cupped her face and he winked, but the lovely swirly whotsits that normally swirled in her tummy did not leap into life.

"We havetae kiss, it's fer Brugel," he said, lowering his lips onto hers.

Nothing.

No fireworks. Not even a sparkler or a small candle.

"Mercury's Wings, Mrs. Howser must be here somewhere, sucking all the fun out of me." That was the only way Ondine could explain her lack of gushiness. Hamish's kisses always made her feel loopy and silly and fabulous. They'd never made her feel *nothing* before.

"But we freed Melody from her." Hamish scrunched up his forehead.

"Maybe she's put a spell on me or something and . . . I can't love you any more?"

"Nae possible. Sure'n she's evil, but lass, ye heart's so big, no mangey *spell* can stop our love."

A bony hand clamped hard on her shoulder and dug down hard. "No you don't!"

Everything happened in slow-time. Noises stretched and warped, vision blurred. Hamish fell away from her. Or did she fall from him? Whiplash emotions bombarded her system as Mrs. Howser's face loomed.

"You're not doing anything," she said, calm as you like.

To add bizarre on top of the strange, Mrs. Howser's voice and movements were perfectly normal, while everything else around them moved with the speed of cooling toffee. They were in some kind of time bubble. Ondine couldn't speak or move or even think clearly. Everything in her system started shutting down. Great Pluto's ghost, this was the niggly naggy thing she'd forgotten.

They hadn't dealt with Mrs. Howser directly; they'd merely tried to get around her. Look what good it had done them. They'd chipped away at the edges of their problems but the big one, the bad magic maker, would make their life hell if they didn't deal with her directly, once and for all.

These thoughts surprised Ondine in their clarity. Up until this point, she'd only been able to think of herself and Hamish. Suddenly – and with a fair amount of deep personal guilt – she realised there were some things in this life that were bigger than her.

Every instinct told her to shut down, to collapse under the weight of the negative magic Mrs. Howser bore down on her. But that would be giving up. That would be letting the baddies win.

It wasn't going to happen.

It *couldn't.*

Outside this magic time-bubble, Hamish reached for her, his body moving in slow motion. Inside the bubble, she had to move fast. Mrs. Howser's hand was still clamped on her shoulder, and she was pushing down, making her blend into the footpath.

Ondine said, "No." A single thought, but a powerful one.

"You can't win." Mrs. Howser's words felt heavy and cold, dissolving Ondine's willpower like acid. Drip, drip, drip, they ate away at her resolve. Why did her eyelids weigh so much all of a sudden?

"That's right, you're going to have a nice big sleep," Mrs. Howser said. The worst of it was how sweet and reasonable the woman sounded.

Sleep. Oh sleep, that would be so good right now . . . but there was something she had to do first. Something about . . . oh that's right. Mrs. Howser was going down!

It took a breath. Then it took a mental image of steel filling her marrow. Then it took every ounce of strength she had.

"NO!" Ondine yelled.

"You're a feisty one."

A tiny victory, but enough to begin the re-group for the next attack. "No," Ondine said again, her voice sounding firm and satisfying to her ears. One little word, a world of strength behind it. "No."

The hazy skin of the magic bubble stretched and strained around them, but did not break.

"You think one simple word can stop me? Can stop this?" Mrs. Howser flicked her hand and the bubble wall grew thicker, stronger, the people on the other side blurred into vague shapes. New fears tugged at Ondine. She was no match for this kind of magic.

"No," the word came out as a whisper, more an expression of shock and surprise than intent.

"You've got to expand your vocabulary child. And your magic. I can teach you how to do this. You have so much potential. Let me help you shine."

Honeyed milk, that's how the words played over Ondine. All smooth and lovely and sweet and special. Like an extra treat after a long day of working so hard she could sleep forever. *Sleepity sleep sleep*. Now there's a thought. Sleep would be so good. If only there were some place nearby where she could lie down and sleep and . . . Outside the bubble, Hamish had stopped moving. His blurred face came into focus through the skin of magic between them.

Hamish. She felt all kinds of magic when he was around. They'd been doing something here, something she couldn't quite remember but . . . it had seemed important at the time.

A giggle formed. Ondine felt so light and carefree she could have sworn she was floating. Looking down to her feet, she saw a gap between her boots and the snowy ground. Yes, definitely floating.

Oh what a marvellous feeling. She could get used to this.

"I wonder if Hamish can see me floating?"

"Let's float away from here," a soothing voice said. Such a calming voice. Such a persuasive voice.

Belonging to Mrs. Howser.

Why did Ondine not like her? She seemed so nice. And yet the rest of her family had it in for her. Silly, really. Maybe it was her great aunt being jealous? That must be why they hated each other with such venom. How strange, now that she thought about it. It took so much energy to hate someone, when liking them was so easy.

So very easy.

Like Hamish. She'd fallen in like with him from the start and it hadn't taken long for it to turn into full-blown love.

A cold seed of doubt sprouted in her belly as she floated inside her bubble. Had she and Hamish fallen in love because they wanted to, or had they fallen under some kind of spell?

Turning her head, she saw Mrs. Howser smiling so sweetly.

"You made the spell," Ondine said.

"What spell, my dear?"

"The spell that made Hamish fall in love with me."

"You're welcome," Mrs. Howser tilted her head to accept the praise.

Only Ondine wasn't praising her. She was accusing her. Accusing her of exploiting her feelings and yearnings. Hamish was in love with her, but was it real or only magic?

"What if it's only the spell that's making him love me?" Ondine asked.

"You have nothing to worry about, child. He truly loves you. No spell is so great it can circumvent free will."

"Is that so?" Ondine asked in her dreamy state. The confirmation gave her a boost. She landed on the ground on steady feet. Then she looked Mrs. Howser straight in the eye and said, "Then I can stop you, and I can stop this."

Panic flickered across the witch's face before she composed herself. "What I meant to say was –"

"– No. You're going to shut up now." Ondine waved her hand towards the bubble's edge and poked it. The skin pressed outwards under the pressure, then shredded like a popped balloon. "You are going down," Ondine said.

Instantly Mrs. Howser waved her hands and a new bubble sealed around them. Ondine poked it again – same shredding effect.

"How are you doing that?" Mrs. Howser rapidly erected a third bubble.

This was getting tiresome. Ondine said, "Stop meddling in everyone's lives and leave us alone!"

"So you can be with your beautiful Hamish, I suppose?"

Oh, she had her there.

Time to be honest. That was pretty much the hardest thing to do, but it always achieved the best results. "That too. You'd love it if all I could think about was Hamish, but I've worked it out. Sure it took me a while, but even I can see truth. I'm not selfish all the time."

Mrs Howser creased her forehead. "There's nothing wrong with being selfish. It's how we get things done."

"You're right. I was so selfish I couldn't see past my own little bubble with Hamish. But I can see past that now," she said, glaring at Mrs. Howser.

Mrs Howser shot back, "Don't you look at me like that!"

The way out of this shone clear in Ondine's mind. "You don't have magic."

"Excuse me, I have more magic in my little finger than you'll ever have –"

"Magic's not in your hands. It's in here," Ondine said, pressing her hand slightly to the left of Mrs. Howser's bony sternum, where her heart would be. "And up here." With her free hand, she tapped the side of the old woman's head. Then Ondine turned and for the last time looked at the bubble surrounding them. She blew a puff towards the skin of the bubble, turning it into smoke. Another puff and the smoke wafted away like a snuffed candle.

"If you were really psychic, you should have seen this coming," Ondine said, pouring lemon juice on the old woman's wounds.

"Ondi, get back!" a girl behind her yelled. Suddenly Melody was grabbing at her, pulling her away.

"It's OK, I'm fine," Ondine said.

"Your hands!" Melody yelled.

"What about my –" Turning her palms over, she watched the tips of her fingers dissolve into smoke and drift off in the breeze. A scream filled her ears. Then more screams as the people around them saw what was happening.

Jupiter's moons. The smoke had dissolved down to the first knuckle already. Panic took over. All Ondine could do was stand there and scream and scream until she thought she'd black out.

## 26

Like four fat incense sticks plus a stubby one on the side, Ondine's fingers and thumbs ended not in bitten-down nails but curlicues of smoke and ash.

"They're burning!" she cried out. Mrs. Howser would pay for this.

In a flash, Hamish scooped snow off the ground and sandwiched her hands between his. Drip, slurry, slop. The melty-ice dribbled to the ground. When Ondine looked at her hands again –

"They're still burning!"

"They look a bit red," Hamish said as he slapped another pack of slurry onto her skin.

Red? They were on *fire*!

"She's getting away!" Melody and Old Col called out at the same time.

So many things happened at once it was hard to put them in order. Ondine's fingers were trailing smoke and freaking her right out. Mrs. Howser dashed off towards Lord Vincent on the stage. Melody took off after her.

But the strangest thing – Hamish was not panicking anywhere near as much as he should.

"Mebbe yer too cold; ye need yer gloves on."

"They're burning!"

"Aye, my hands are so cold they feel hot at the ends too."

"No!" It wasn't nice to yell at her beloved, but he clearly wasn't listening to her. Shoving her hands directly in front of his face, she said. "They're smoking! Like Chimneys!" Any more exclamation marks and her head would explode.

Clasping her hands in his again, Hamish kissed the tips. The smouldering, ash-lined tips. "Ondi lass, they feel colder than a glare from ye Da, but they're nae on fire. I promise ye, they're only so cold they're hot, but they're nae on fire. Howser's messing with yer heid, so she is."

"But they're . . ." Confused and frightened, she pulled her hands out from Hamish's warm embrace to see they were perfectly normal. Incredibly cold and yes, the tips felt hot, possibly an early sign of frostbite because she wasn't wearing gloves. But they were normal, all the way to her completely normal fingertips. "Oh thank goodness, they're back to normal. Thank you Hamish."

"She touched ye, didn't she?"

Actually, Ondine had made the mistake of touching Birgit Howser.

"She *goat* ye in the head," Hamish said, his eyes filled with kindness as he turned her palm over and kissed the centre.

Oh lush.

Whoa, no time for that. "Jupiter's moons, she's going for Vincent!" But why would she do this, in such a public setting, would ruin everything for her. Had she completely lost her mind? They turned to see Mrs. Howser take a flying leap onto the stage. Lord Vincent flinched at her approach. Security guards leapt on her.

It looked like it was all over.

Melody and Old Col raced to the security pile-on. A puff of grey smoke swirled through the bodies and into the sky. The security crew untangled themselves and looked about, confused as all get-out.

Everyone looked like they were thinking the same thing. *Where did she go?*

"She's got Vincent," Melody yelled as she stood up on the stage.

The security guards leapt on Melody and Old Col instead and buried them under a hill of people.

"You've got the wrong witch!" Old Col shouted, pointing to Vincent and the smoky shape of Mrs Howser standing behind him, on the stage. "Get *her*."

The squeeing tone from the crowd changed to all-out screaming, and not in a good way.

Eerily calm, Vincent remained standing, confident the security would do its job. The guards were utterly useless against a whiff of smoke swirling around them. Invisible hands clonked the guards' heads together and they fell like rag dolls.

Another puff of smoke appeared behind Lord Vincent, swirling around his body, then his head, like a translucent scarf. He turned to see where it had gone. Then it zipped over to the other side of him, before slamming into his body.

He jolted forward as if he'd stuck a nine-volt battery on his tongue. [1]

Ondine was having such a hard time keeping up she didn't know how to properly describe it, but from the looks of things Mrs. Howser had turned herself into a shadow and jumped inside Lord Vincent.

"Silence!" Lord Vincent yelled out.

No megaphone could carry his voice half so well. The audience of screaming fan-girls were stunned into quiet. Even the security guards looked gobsmacked.

The pastiness of Vincent's face reminded Ondine of the time at Coven Con. They'd had an audience with Duchess Anathea and Vincent had turned bonkers.

"She's got into him!" Ondine gasped. Because as sure as winter brings on blackouts across Brugel, Mrs Howser's smoky form was in Vincent, infiltrating his brain and body. She was going to overtake him completely and make him her puppet.

Beneath the hill of women and men in uniform, a crumpled and half-broken Melody tried to crawl out. They slammed her down again, convinced they were doing Vincent a favour. Meanwhile the man they should be protecting was already possessed.

On the other hand, if the security detail were busy flattening Melody, they wouldn't be able to stop Ondine. She leapt onto the stage, heading for Mrs. Howser-as-a-smoke-form-residing-in-Lord-Vincent.

Without a clue what to do when she got there.

In Brugel, there is a word for this kind of chaotic mayhem, but it doesn't translate very well into English. But the most chaotic type of chaos ever seen broke out as Ondine neared Lord Vincent.

Everybody screamed and shouted. Except Vincent, who stood there looking utterly lost.

Ondine stared at Vincent and yelled, "Get out of him!"

Security detail from goodness knows where launched at Ondine, knocking her sideways. Through a gap in the arms and legs restraining her, she saw Great Aunt Col had gotten away from her captors and was standing in front of Vincent.

"Time's up, Birgit, you've lost," she said to the woman inside him.

Vincent clamped his mouth shut. He wobbled and shuddered, his face paled some more until it turned the colour of curdled milk. Then he collapsed.

Was it over? Ondine hoped so.

"Man down!" Great Aunt Col cried out.

The audience by now were screaming, the noise of it piercing Ondine's eardrums. But her arms were pinned by security so she couldn't block the noise drilling in. Way off at the other end of the stage, she saw Duchess Anathea and the First Minister clamping their palms over their ears.

Anathea cried out, "Make it stop".

Suddenly Hamish was on the stage, peeling back the layers of people smothering Ondine.

The security in suits were about to pounce all over Ondine again when Old Col threw her hands out and cried, "Freeze!"

The men and women froze in place. Hamish held out his hand to help Ondine back to her feet. Then his warm hands held her face steady, her gaze captive to his. His green eyes sparkled with mischief. "Have ye forgotten what we came here for?"

A strand of candy-silk-loveliness spun inside her tummy. Oh yes. They were supposed to get loved up and make people's wishes come true. When her gaze locked with Hamish's, the commotion and chaos died away, leaving the two of them in a magical world of their own making.

"D'ye remember the first time I turned into me. We were gettin' ready for yer sister's engagement party and I pulled the table cloth down ontae meself . . . and ye were there."

Heat stole over her face at the memory. He'd transformed from his Shambles-ferretness into his gorgeous Hamish self, with only a tablecloth for modesty. A girl didn't forget a moment like that! The memories set more flurries free until the flurries were joining hands and dancing along her veins.

He made a lopsided smile and began to blush. "So ye do remember?" His eyes shone with mischief. If Ondine didn't know better, she'd swear he was using some kind of wonderful magic on her. He lowered his forehead onto hers; their temples warm despite the deep winter chill. "I love ye Ondi. Ours is a love for the ages. No magic can hold us back."

And then he kissed her. The sweetest brush against her lips. A tender buss of his nose against hers. Another kiss, frustratingly light again and yet so perfect an angel might have put it there. Needing more, her face tilted upwards, her lips at the ready.

"I love ye Ondi, yer my heart and soul. I want to grow old with ye. Will ye marry me?"

Oh!

Time stopped. Her heart as well. Then it kicked against her ribs and a husky, "yes" tripped from her. The rest of the world could have fallen into a snowdrift as Hamish's lips descended on hers. Warmth and love and the sweetest caress blocked out the cold winter's day. Her eyelids fluttered shut as sunshine filled her body.

"OK you two," Old Col said. "You'd better start k–. Oh, I see you're already at it. Carry on."

Buried under an avalanche of sensation, Ondine had no idea what was happening around her in Savo Plaza. All she wanted was for these magical kisses to continue. They sent her mind into a spin, her belly into a flip-flop and her heart into a canter.

Hamish wanted to marry her.

Old Col's bony hand pressed down on her shoulder and pulled her away. "That's enough."

Ondine's lips detached from Hamish's with a schmack of lost suction. Dizzy with love, she turned to see why her aunt had called a halt to it.

Savo Plaza had become a sea of flowers.

The ribbon over the entrance to the snow maze was still uncut as Anathea tossed bouquet after bouquet to the cheering crowd. Yes, cheering now, not screaming. Thank heavens for that.

"It worked?" Ondine could hardly believe it. Maybe they should kiss a bit more, just to make sure it wasn't a fluke.

Nearby, they heard a reporter make a speech to a camera, in which she described Anathea as the fairest of them all.

The clouds parted, filling the square with bright winter sun.

A light so bright it exposed a dark shadow behind Vincent. A shadow that looked suspiciously like Mrs. Howser holding strings that tied themselves in knots around Vincent.

The crowd gasped.

Mrs. Howser jumped back. Fully exposed, she had nowhere to go. The security guards flattened Mrs. Howser in the fastest ever game of Stacks-On.

They had her!

Oh dear. They only had her body. Her smoky shadow slipped away from them and headed straight for Anathea.

"No!" Ondine and Hamish yelled in unison as they leapt at the shadow.

Hamish threw himself on the dark shape, but it slipped out from beneath him. Ondine tried to grab at it – anywhere would do – but each time she clamped her fingers around a section, it morphed and squeezed away.

They were fighting a shadow. And losing.

The wind flurried snow around them, swirling the oleaginous shape into the air.

Jumping, Ondine tried to grab at it, but it was out of reach. The smoke shadow was zigging and zagging around the stage. Biscuit the dog barked like he'd been electrocuted as the smoke headed for the Duchess and First Minister. It wound around Anathea's body, then rolled itself around her neck and head like a long smokey scarf with a mind of its own.

Behind them, doing her job as she should, was a janitor vacuuming the golden carpet.

"Anathea! Use the vacuum cleaner!" Ondine screamed and pointed at the same time.

Several miracles happened at once. Anathea heard her, she saw where Ondine was pointing and she took action, grabbing the vacuum hose out of the janitor's hands. The rest of the machine was stripped to the cleaner's back.

"Everyone get down!" Anathea shouted.

Everyone did just that.

Anathea held the nozzle into the air. Mrs Howser's elusive shadow that could withstand choking and flattening had no defences against the fabulous sucking motion. Floating in the air, it had nothing to cling to, and with a howl of wind it slurped into the hose.

Anathea handed the vacuum hose back to the puzzled cleaner. "The contents should be incarcerated. And in a separate facility to Mrs Howser's body."

"Yes, Your Lordship." The cleaner did a quick curtsey and scarpered off, looping the incredibly long extension cord over her shoulder as she went.

"Anathea is amazing!" Ondine said.

"Brilliant!" Hamish said.

The crowd roared with applause.

The two of them embraced Duchess Anathea like the saviour that she was. Busy rejoicing, they missed something, but the crowd was gasping. Ooops, had they overstepped the mark by touching the royal person? Embarrassed, Ondine pulled back, only to see that the crowd's reaction wasn't for them. It was for Vincent, who lay slumped on the ground like a dropped marionette.

"Darling!" Melody cried out as she sprang towards him.

"What's she up tae?" Hamish said.

Instead of tackling Melody, one of the guards guided her towards

Vincent. There, she tenderly held the lord's hand and caressed a lock of hair from his face.

Old Col made her way to Ondine, Hamish and Anathea. "Well done, all of you. Your Lordship, that was some fast thinking."

Duchess Anathea beamed. "It was, rather, wasn't it? It couldn't have been done without Ondine."

Beaming at the compliment, Ondine looked again towards Melody and Vincent. Near them, the security detail dragged away a deflated and weak Birgit Howser, empty and soulless without her dark shadow.

"She is to be placed in the city asylum," Duchess Anathea called out. The hefty security people nodded and dragged her away.

Ondine pursed her lips in thought. "Does this mean Lord Vincent is free of Howser's influence?"

"That is to be hoped," Duchess Anathea said. "Perhaps he can be reasoned with now?"

"Er, he looks a bit busy," Hamish said.

Ondine, Old Col, Hamish and Duchess Anathea, in fact the entire crowd for that matter, watched as Melody helped Vincent to his feet, caressing and calming him all the time. His eyes were locked with hers. As he righted himself, he gave her a tender kiss of thanks on her cheek.

The crowd went insane with cheering.

"It would seem that in all things, everyone has an agenda," Old Col said. "That includes Melody."

Ondine could scarcely believe it. "Melody has a thing for Vincent?"

Hamish squeezed her hand. "Aye, every girl in the crowd has a *thing* for Vincent."

Ondine bristled. "Except me."

"Weil, yeas, but ye have excellent taste." He touched his nose to hers again, making her warm all over.

Vincent must have been wearing a microphone, because they could hear Melody's reassuring voice on the loudspeakers nearby. "You're free now. She can't ever harm you again."

Ondine couldn't work out if Melody put Vincent's arm across her shoulder or angled herself in such a way that he had to. Either way, they were leaning closely together.

"I did *noat* see that coming," Hamish said.

"She's a dark horse that one," Col said.

"Saturn's rings!" Ondine said. "We were so caught up in making Anathea's wish come true, we didn't pay attention to what Melody was wishing."

"Let's not get sidetracked," Col said. "The two of you did your job and did it well. Ondine, by giving Anathea a method of defeating Birgit, you made her the hero of the day in the public's eyes. Well done."

"Thank you, Ondine, I'd say you've more than earned Hamish's freedom," Anathea said, as her eyes wandered over towards Vincent.

Ondine beamed, "Do you have the papers?"

But the Duchess wasn't listening anymore as her attention found a new focus. "Now, if I may be excused, Vincent needs a good talking to."

They watched as she walked over to her nephew, the lad who wanted to kick her off the throne. Melody was smiling as the Duchess approached. So was Vincent.

"There has been so much enmity between us," they heard the Duchess say.

Yes, he definitely had a microphone on, and everyone could hear their conversation. What a clever woman that Anathea was, Ondine thought, to make sure they had a crowd full of witnesses to this event.

Vincent nodded. "Your Lordship, thank you for your fast actions today. You have not only saved my life, but my soul."

"We are family. Family is the most important thing in the world," the Duchess said.

How uncharacteristic of her to speak in active voice all of a sudden, Ondine thought. Perhaps the old dear was changing for the better as well?

"Peace?" Vincent held out his hand.

The Duchess shook it. "Peace."

The crowd roared its approval.

When the crowd calmed down and the security team made sure they wouldn't be interrupted again, Anathea took hold of an over-sized pair of scissors to cut the ribbon at the entrance to the snow maze. The crowd roared with the kind of noise you'd hear at a football match after a winning goal. Anathea beamed. Even little Biscuit looked happy to be there.

In years past, Duke Pavla (may he rest in peace) would have been the first to explore the maze with a guide. The same was about to happen for Duchess Anathea. But instead of going straight in, she held her hand out towards Vincent, in front of thousands of witnesses, inviting him to explore the maze with her.

"I'd be honoured," he said.

Melody stayed by his side, ready to support him should he wobble.

The media turned their cameras on Anathea and Vincent as they held hands and walked together through the ice-bricked entrance.

Keeping two paces behind, Melody followed them into the maze. Colours bloomed inside the icy walls, as if lit from within. The crowd cheered and applauded like crazy.

"Looks like our work here is done," Col said with satisfaction.

Ondine turned to her. "You never told me what you wished for."

Old Col rubbed her hands together against the cold. "I do believe I wished to knock some common sense into Vincent and Anathea."

A laugh escaped Ondine. "That was a really smart wish."

"It was rather!" Old Col giggled.

The crowd milled and chatted and became a bit noisy, as crowds do. The winter sun shone weakly, bands began to play and the smell of fried cheeseballs permeated the air.

After a short while Anathea and Lord Vincent emerged from the snow maze entrance into the open. [2]

Arms looped at the elbow, like old friends.

They were even . . . Ondine had to blink a few times to make sure . . . yes, they were laughing!

"When you wish, Auntie Col, you wish good!" Ondine said.

Everything was absolutely, wonderfully, perfectly perfect.

"Uh-oh," Hamish said when another development developed right before their eyes.

*Saturn's rings.* "Lord Vincent and Melody are kissing."

"Just when you think you've seen everything, eh lass?"

A wave of relief spread over Ondine. They had defeated Mrs. Howser and set Duchess Anathea on the road to becoming the most popular and loved ruler in Brugel's history. [3]

Everything had been put to rights.

And yet, as they walked home to the family pub, Ondine couldn't help feeling deflated, despite their success. Would Anathea come through with Hamish's work papers, allowing him to stay in Brugel? More importantly, would they ever break the mutating magic spell they were under?

**27**

———————

Such expensive clothes!

Even at her sister's wedding, Ondine hadn't worn the like. The tag itched the side of her ribs, but she was under desperate instructions not to remove it. Or leave any stain or smell on the fabric. Ma warned her, "You can't take clothes back for a refund with sweat stains on them, can you?"

If it was cold as the snow outside, perspiration wouldn't be a problem. But inside? Someone had turned the heating way up to keep everyone toasty warm, which meant Ondine couldn't help feeling hot under the armpits.

The air felt supercharged with electricity as Ondine, Hamish, Old Col and Ma sat in the balcony of the Dentate's public gallery to watch the vote officially recognising Anathea as Duchess of Brugel. The long bench seats were made from thickly padded leather, with pull-down timber desks for people to take notes, should they want to. Around the walls hung paintings from Brugel's history, from the early days of labour-intensive wheat production right through to the development of the plough.

Looking down on Brugel's elected representatives dressed in their finery, Ondine couldn't help feeling as if she too were present during a great moment in Brugelish history. Every time a politician mentioned

Duchess Anathea, a cheer went up in the gallery. The speaker of the house acknowledged their excitement but had to call order so they could actually take the vote before they broke for a celebratory lunch.

Provided they had something to celebrate.

"They should call the vote sharpish," Hamish said. "Me stomach's about tae eat itself."

That put a fresh smile on Ondine's face.

"Don't forget the reason you're here. Your work is not over yet." Old Col said.

Which wiped the smile straight off Ondine's face. It was ridiculous that she should fear the outcome of this vote. Their make-other-people's-wishes-come-true magic had helped Anathea become Brugel's most popular leader of all time, but the Dentate members still had to vote and make it a reality.

Hamish curled his fingers into Ondine's and caressed her palm with his thumb as the speaker called for the members to cast their votes. He nuzzled into her ear and kissed the tender spot just below her ear lobe.

Everything turned fuzzy and a wee bit lovely for a moment.

"You're in public, keep it nice," Ma said.

"It's for Brugel, Ma," Ondine said, surprised with how coherent she sounded as Hamish playfully nipped her ear and turned her brain to syrup.

They lost track of time and completely forgot there were people around them, as couples are wont to do when they are so deliciously loved-up.

"You can stop now, they've all voted," Ma said with an elbow to Ondine.

Heart almost stopping with anticipation, Ondine waited for the numbers to play out, with the counting of 'igens' to pass the law and the 'nincs' to shoot it down. [1] At the end of the tallying, the vote cleared with one hundred and eighteen in favour of the bill, eighty-three against.

"Ye did it!" Hamish nudged her shoulder and gave her his wickedest grin.

"We did it," she said with a massive sigh of relief.

Looking across the gallery, they saw Anathea in the royal box. She was on her feet, waving to the politicians below and blowing kisses to the public gallery. The new law secured Anathea's tenure as the Duchess for life. In time, it could even be possible for her daughters to inherit ahead of Vincent, but that would be another vote for another time.

"Vincent will be spitting cheeseballs," Hamish said.

"He promised he'd make peace. We all saw it," Ondine said. "Anyway, I'm sure he's distracted with Melody right now."

"Just as we shall soon be distracted with a free meal," Old Col said with a gleam in her eyes. "The Duchess invited us to a celebratory luncheon. Come along."

Ondine, Hamish and Ma followed Great-Auntie Col to the Dentate dining room. Ondine gave Hamish's hand a squeeze as a waiter showed them to their table. How lovely to be dining out somewhere other than her family's pub. Not that the food would be up to Henrik's standards, but she felt so much more relaxed knowing she didn't have to clean up afterwards.

She didn't even have to pay the bill!

Talk about posh! The tables were covered in cream-coloured linen with matching napkins. Each centrepiece had sprigs of budding willow surrounded by lush red tree peonies. As they sat down (the waiter held her seat back for her) Ondine couldn't resist turning over the cutlery. A surge of national pride came over her as she saw the silver maker's hallmarks and the hexagonal stamp of Brugel.

Somebody else filled their glasses with chilled water and asked if they'd like anything from the wine list.

"I'm not sure I should," Ondine said, feeling heat roar up her face. What would her mother say?

She didn't have to think long about that. Sitting at the adjacent table, her mother leaned over and said, "I'll give you a taste of mine."

That seemed like a fair compromise, so she ordered a pineapple juice in the meantime.

A hush stole over the room and everyone stood to attention. Ondine looked to where everyone else was looking. The doorman announced the arrival of "The Honourable First Minister of Brugel, Natalya Cebotari."

After the applause softened for her, he announced, "Her Lordship, the Duchess of Brugel."

Rousing applause greeted Anathea as she made her way to the centre of a long table, raised on a dais so everyone could see her.

Under their table, situated towards the back of the room, Hamish rubbed his foot against the side of Ondine's. "Look at us, eh lass."

"I know!" giggled Ondine. She could hardly believe they were here. Having lunch in the most exclusive, invitation-only restaurant in all of Brugel – The Dentate Dining Room.

"Ye deserve it, for all ye've done." Hamish held up his glass of water. Ondine responded by clinking her glass against his.

Mercury's Wings, this was the life.

The courses – and they were numerous – were each more delicious than the last. For a moment Ondine wondered if Henrik had a doppelganger working in the Dentate kitchens, the food was *that* good. After the waiters took the main meal plates away, Duchess Anathea rose from her seat.

Everyone in the restaurant stopped what they were doing and rose from their seats in respect.

"Thank you," Anathea said. "This luncheon has been beautifully prepared. The chef is to be congratulated."

The guests applauded in agreement. Ondine nearly called out "hear-hear" but held back in case it was a breach of protocol.

As Anathea looked out across her audience, her eyes rested on Hamish and Ondine. She smiled and made the slightest nod in recognition. That's when Ondine noticed Biscuit the dog was not around. Wow, that had to mean this was a seriously formal occasion if she didn't have the dog with her.

"Ladies and Gentlemen, thank you from the bottom of my heart for taking time out of your busy schedules to attend today's historic vote in the Dentate and dine with me."

Polite applause. For Ondine, her busy schedule included washing dishes. Hmmm, menial housework or go to lunch? What a no-brainer.

Anathea smiled as much as her barely-moving face could smile. "In these changing times, we seek certainty in all things. Brugel has experienced times of uncertainty, but the late Duke Pavla's legacy will be carried on now that the tenure of the Duchy is secure."

Despite the goodwill in the room, Ondine felt she couldn't relax. Not until Hamish had his papers so he could stay in Brugel instead of facing deportation.

"We'll all be jogging home to work this off," Ma said as she patted her stomach.

"Enjoy it," Old Col said as a waiter came and refilled their wine glasses. "Oh, no more for me please, I'll fall off my broomstick."

"Yes ma-am," the waiter said without a blink. "May I suggest a stroll through the gardens after your meals? Don't worry about being cold, the conservatory is virtually tropical this time of year."

"Thank you," Ma said. "That's a lovely idea."

After their lunch was over, they took the waiter's advice and visited the orangery, where the outdoors came indoors. Trees and shrubs grew in proper dirt and flowers bloomed in well-tended beds, all under the protection of huge sheets of glass overhead.

"Ru-ru-ru-ru," they heard a dog yap.

Hamish turned to Ondine. "That sounds like . . ."

"Biscuit?" Ondine said. They turned to see a familiar white fluffy dog barrelling towards them.

"Not the clothes!" Ma held up her foot to ward the dog away.

"Biscuit, heel!" Duchess Anathea said as she came into view. She'd changed into a cream-coloured suit that swished with each step she took. "Ondine, Hamish, thank you once again for all your help. I would never have thought about using the vacuum cleaner without your prompting."

"You're welcome," Ondine and Hamish said together.

"And now, there is a debt to be repaid." She turned to Hamish and reached into the inside of her jacket for a sheaf of folded paper. "Thank you again, for everything you've done for Brugel. This document, signed by myself and First Minister Cebotari, grants you Brugelish citizenship and gives you the freedom of the city."

Tears of happiness blurred Ondine's vision as Hamish took the papers from Anathea and made a low bow. When he finished, he said, "Och, come here," and gave the Duchess a massive squeeze.

"Steady!" Anathea said. "This suit can't be returned if it's wrinkled!"

"Aye." Hamish un-squeezed himself from Anathea. Then he unfolded the document so he and Ondine could gaze upon it. She couldn't read it through her happy tears.

"Thank you," Ondine said, as she wiped her cheeks. No crying onto the paper, it would leave splotches. And she dare not cry onto her clothes either because tear stains left salt-rings.

"Now, we need to talk about Birgit," the Duchess said.

"Must we?" Hamish and Ondine said together.

"Is she still . . . ?" Old Col asked.

"In a secure facility? Yes," Anathea said. "In two of them, in fact. Her person is in the asylum and her soul is in the vacuum cleaner bag, in a safe. As long as we keep the two pieces apart, she can do no further damage."

Old Col made a sniffing sound. "That's the best we could hope for I suppose."

Tucking the certificate inside his coat pocket, Hamish turned to Ondine and reached for her hand. "I think we did good, lass."

Ondine beamed and nestled into him, feeling that at last, all was right with the world.

"Don't crease your clothes," Ma said. "Or we won't get the refunds."

"Yes, Ma," Ondine said with a giggle.

"Come on kids, let's go home." Old Col said.

# EPILOGUE

Weak afternoon sunshine greeted them as they walked to the railway station. The banks of snow on the streets were melting into brown slurry. It sloshed down the steps to the platform, spraying Ondine's boots. She raised her hem to avoid staining her skirt, but the act only exposed her legs to cold splashes of mud.

"Allow me," Hamish scooped her up and carried her in his arms.

Ondine snuggled into him, feeling warm and protected. She heard Old Col tisk behind them.

They caught the train home, but dared not sit on the wet wooden bench seats in case they left stains on their fabric. Throughout the day other passengers had brought slurry on the train with their boots and bags, coating every flat surface with slop. Possibly because passengers had been standing on the bench seats to avoid the river of slush sliding and slopping up and down the aisle.

At last they reached their station. The late afternoon sun tried desperately to wring out the last little bit of shine on the neighbourhood. The streetlights were already on and the neon dragon out the front of *On The Fang* flickered into life.

"Oh how sweet!" Ondine squeezed Hamish's hand as she saw an early sign of spring. The raised garden beds near the station still had plenty of snow, but a clutch of bright yellow crocus flowers had broken through.

"Aye, I'll be glad to see the back of winter."

"On that, I agree," Old Col said.

LATER, after they'd swept the last of the customers out into the cold, slushy February night, Ondine banked the open fire and locked the screen in place. Her back ached from leaning over the sink all evening washing dishes and she was about ready to collapse into bed.

"Yer mother works ye too hard, lass."

She turned to find Hamish grinning at her, holding something behind his back. With a self-conscious flourish, he produced a bouquet of golden crocus.

"They're beautiful," she held them to her chest, "thank you."

"Ye've been on yer feet all night; ye need to sit down fer a while."

Good idea. Ondine plonked her crocuses into one of the table vases, then reached for a dining chair and pulled it out to face the fire. Hamish did the same and sat beside her. It felt so natural to rest her head on his shoulder and, oh how lovely, he put his arm around her and held her close.

In the background, the radio news invaded their idyll with stories of strange magic spreading to the United States, Japan and even as far away as Australia.

With a heavy sigh, Ondine said, "I can't help wondering if that's all my fault."

"Dinnae fash yerself," [1] Hamish said as he played with her hair.

"I can't help it," she said with an even louder sigh. "I mean, we've won this battle and helped Anathea, but I can't help thinking there's a bigger war that's only just beginning."

The last coals of the fire glowed dimly, giving out scant heat. Ondine shivered as the cold air and even colder thoughts took place.

Hamish produced a blanket and tucked it over her, keeping her warm. She snuggled in further, sharing the warmth. He'd thought of everything, hadn't he?

"This is going to sound strange," she said, "but I think I like being magic. I like making other people's wishes come true. And if there is more of this weirdness going around, I'd much rather have some magic in me to tackle it, than no magic at all."

"Aye, that's because ye've got a heart as big as Brugel," he said, touching the tip of his nose to hers.

She luxuriated in his attention, then pulled back for a moment. "You have put your papers somewhere safe, haven't you?"

"In the strong box under the floor in the kitchen." He pressed his forehead lightly against hers. "Now dry yer eyes, all is right with the world."

"No Hamish, don't say that out loud. The minute you do, the universe conspires to make something awful happen."

Hamish chuckled and held her closer. "OK, I'll nae say it again. I'll just think it."

"Don't even think it." She gave him a poke in the ribs.

He tickled her in retaliation and they became silly and giddy for a moment. When they eventually stopped, and Ondine caught her breath back, she said, "I don't think I've ever been as happy in my life as I am right now."

"Och, lass, it's just the beginning."

He kissed her so sweetly she thought she'd float away. There was no heat left in the fire, yet her body radiated warmth.

"I love you, Hamish."

"And I love you, Ondi."

They shared more sweet kisses and snuggled under the blanket, feeling yummy and lush. They stayed there, wrapped in each other, until the sun peeked over the hills heralding the beginning of a new day.


–THE END–

# THE SPRING REVOLUTION

# PART I

**1**

___

Astral projection. Some people are great at it; others are famous for sleeping right through it.

Take the almost-sixteen-year-old Ondine, for example. By all accounts she's a healthy teen, eats well, has her regular share of bad and good hair days. (Long, wispy and brown. What can you do?) Being our brave and clever heroine, Ondine is blessed with 'resting curious face', which means she often looks like she knows what's going on. Even if she doesn't.

At the end of a long day of working for her family in their pub, *The Duke and Ferret* in downtown Venzelemma, the capital city of Brugel, Ondine is also blessed with the ability to fall asleep three minutes and twenty-two seconds after climbing into bed. She has neither the energy nor the inclination to develop her astral projection abilities. It would involve meditating, then separating her spiritual body from the physical to then journey – along what is known in psychic circles as the astral plane – from her mind and project herself into the mind of another.

Or travel to various psychic destinations.

On the other hand, witch-in-training Melody, who is getting the colour back into her cheeks after the strain of working with the 'bad witch' Mrs Howser, is an absolute natural at astral projection. Melody and Ondine first met at Psychic Summercamp, three seasons (and three books) ago. Melody proved to be so good at astral projection, she can now travel by day or night and visit people who are either asleep or awake – sometimes without the recipient even knowing. Plus, Melody can take people with her on these journeys, visiting places or people anywhere in the city, or indeed any part of Brugel (a country in eastern Europe that has still not won the Eurovision Song Contest).

So it came as no surprise to Ondine, as she was asleep in her bedroom above the family pub, to see and hear Melody appear at the end of her bed one rainy spring evening, sitting as comfortably as you like. Even though it was the middle of the night, and, as previously stated, it was raining. Pouring down, it was. Hitting the windowpanes at a fierce angle and diluting the last of the winter snow into slurry. Exactly the kind of weather you don't want to be out in, even if you do have seriously important news you simply can't wait until morning to tell your friend. Which is again why astral is so useful, as travel along the psychic plane is not weather-dependant.

Melody looked dry and warm as she folded her travelling witch cloak over her knees and smiled her brightest smile for Ondine.

"You're totally owning astral," Ondine said.

Melody beamed with confidence. "Yeah, I am. You're still asleep, by the way."

"Am I?" Ondine made to rub her eyes, like she normally did upon waking, but found that her arm had turned rubbery and she only mooshed her head into the pillow instead. The pillow felt as soft and squishy as pizza dough. So doughy. So drowsy.

"I have something you need to see," Melody said, holding out her hand. "Come with me."

"Do I have to wake up?" Ondine nibbled at the corner of her pizza dough pillow. Mmmm, yeasty.

"No, it's best if you stay asleep for this," Melody took her limp palm. "This is really important, so hold my hand the whole time and don't fall asleep on me, OK?"

"I thought you said I *was* asleep?"

"You know what I mean."

As Ondine's hand slipped into Melody's, she saw a third person appear in the room.

"Hey there sleepy head," Hamish said, giving her a cheeky wink.

Suddenly Ondine hoped she wasn't having one of *those* dreams where she turned up to school naked. She checked herself and noted, with a relieved sigh, she was completely decent. If you could count her nattiest flannel pyjamas with holes in the armpits decent.

For his part, Hamish was dressed in a dinner suit straight out of a classic 1920s movie. High white collar, black bow tie, tight-fitting dark grey suit and black lapels. Not to mention the creased pants and shiny black shoes. Despite his fancy appearance, Hamish's black hair refused to sit right, with a disarming lock blocking the vision from his cheeky green eyes. ('Cheeky' is so a colour.) He tugged at his neck and complained in his endearing Scottish accent, "I couldnae dream about being at a toga party, could I? That would be far too comfortable."

Curiosity ate her up as Ondine took in the lush sight of him. "What were you dreaming about?"

"My worst nightmare. Ballroom dancing."

For many, ballroom dancing would be the subject of an exciting dream, but considering Hamish's back story, where he was first cursed by Ondine's great-aunt Col to be a ferret when attending her debutante ball, that kind of setting was a source of constant upset.

"Was I in it?" Ondine asked.

Melody made an exaggerated harrumph. "Can you two stop gushing and pay attention? This is serious."

"Yes ma'am," Hamish said.

Ondine nodded.

"Good," Melody said. "Now, prepare yourselves this won't be pretty. Lord Vincent is visiting his mother at the asylum, and we need to make sure he doesn't do anything stupid." [1]

"What sort of stupid?" Ondine wondered.

"Seriously stupid," Melody said. "You know Mrs Howser is being kept at the same facility, don't you?"

"No," Ondine and Hamish said together at the mention of their nemesis and Ondine's former Psychic Summercamp teacher.

"And you know that the vacuum bag with Mrs Howser's soul in it has gone missing, don't you?" [2]

Did they have to be talking about Birgit Howser? The woman had gone from being a batty old pest to becoming Ondine's mortal enemy. Sickened by the revelation that the bag was missing, Ondine looked first to Hamish then to Melody. "I didn't know that."

Melody's eyebrows shot up. "It's been all over the news! What have you two been doing?"

Something on the floor became incredibly interesting as Ondine studied the carpet at her feet.

"Fine!" Melody tisked loudly and tightened her grip on Ondine's hand. "I'll catch you up to speed on the way there."

"Eh lass? I can't go out like this."

Ondine looked up to see Hamish's spiffy suit had vanished, replaced by the more comfortable toga he'd requested. He even had a laurel wreath on his head, his dark locks brushed forward to fan his temples.

"It doesn't matter what you're wearing, they won't see us anyway, we're astraling," Melody said. "Now stop yammering and pay attention. The future of Brugel is at stake!"

"It sounds so dramatic when she says it like that," Hamish said as he gave Ondine a wink.

The bedroom melted away and they floated out into the dark sky above. It rained all around them, yet they didn't get wet. It wasn't even cold, for which Ondine was incredibly grateful.

"Are we spying on Mrs Howser?" Ondine asked.

"Only a little," Melody said, then quickly added, "I know last time didn't end well, but this will be different."

The 'last time' of which Melody referred, had ended very badly. Mrs Howser had seen straight through Melody's magic and had screamed at them for invading her memories. It was the kind of unpleasant encounter that put Ondine right off wanting any repeats. Now Melody was dragging her straight back to the old witch.

"Is it too late to go back home instead?" Ondine asked.

Melody wore a determined look. "That would be a 'yes'. We're here already."

Looking around, Ondine took in what Melody meant by 'here'. They were in a hallway with fake wood panelling to mid-height; the rest of the walls were painted in custard-yellow, while the ceiling was half a tone lighter. Prints of cottages in impossibly pretty country settings were set along the walls. Beige linoleum covered the floors and curved the first few centimetres up the walls.

The acrid smell of cold chicken soup hung in the air.

Hamish wrinkled his face. "Are we in hell?"

"No, we're in the Duchess Yelena Memorial Asylum," [3] Melody said, "If I've done this right . . ." she leaned sharply towards a door, nearly clonking her head on the knocker. Instead of being hurt, the top half of the young witch's body vanished right though the wood, like a ghost. Just as Ondine was about to yelp with the shock of it all and loosen her grip, Melody pulled herself back into the hallway. She gave a smile of triumph and finished the sentence she'd started so much earlier, "... Vincent and his mother are behind that door."

"And they didnae see you, lass?"

A wary look came over Melody. "Course not."

Ondine murmured, "You said that last time."

Ignoring their scepticism, Melody said, "We're going to be very quiet and float in like dust motes. Then we're going to listen in. No talking, OK?"

The instructions had Ondine wrinkling her forehead. "I thought you said they couldn't hear us?"

"They can't, but if you're nattering on I won't be able to hear *them*, got it?" Melody said.

"How about I wait out here?" Ondine asked.

Hamish gave her a lopsided smile and said, "You're not worried it's going to all end badly are ye?"

*Zhoop*, before Ondine could answer, they dissolved through the door and into the room. Here was Vincent sitting beside his mother, the Dowager Duchess Kerala.

At first Ondine didn't recognise the frail woman in the room, her hair thin and balding under a cotton cap. She was missing her shiny dark helmet of hair and ubiquitous glass of wine (which had turned out to be apple juice, just to throw people off the scent of her nefarious activities). The room was a far cry from the splendour of the Autumn Palace at Bell-reeve. The linoleum from the hallway continued in here, as did the enforced cheer of the yellow colour scheme.

"If ye weren't crazy already, you soon would be, eh?" Hamish whispered.

Ondine nodded and murmured back, "It's giving me a headache."

Melody glared at Ondine. "Be quiet."

"How come you told me off and not him?"

"Because he's charming and you're not, now hush."

Moving closer, yet also keeping their distance (Ondine still wasn't convinced they'd be unnoticed), the trio floated towards Kerala's bed, where they found the former duchess sitting up, dressed in a mauve, velour tracksuit.

As they were floating above their targets, Hamish tilted his head to indicate a small patch on the top of Vincent's golden head with less hair than the rest. What with Vincent's glossy dark shoes, neat suit, perfect gold tie and golden cufflinks, he looked like a young man with the world at his feet. If only people didn't look too close to the scalp. Ondine snorted at the sight of the lord's future bald patch, which earned her another glare from Melody. With a waft of her hand, Melody sent a trail of glimmering dust through the air towards Vincent, repairing his tresses to their youthful lustre. Ondine threw up in her mouth a little at the sight of Melody's blatant adoration of Vincent. Honestly, the girl really needed to get out more.

When Ondine turned back to Hamish, her breath hitched. Amongst his lustrous dark locks were three glaringly silver strands of hair. Silver! Alas, they weren't here to worry about Hamish's hair – or Vincent's – they were here to eavesdrop on a conversation. Ondine stopped her noisy internal thoughts and listened in.

"You're doing so well, I knew you would," Kerala said, softly touching Vincent's cheek in a loving gesture.

The former duchess and husband-knocker-offer had certainly changed in strength and tone from the last time Ondine had seen her. Much calmer now. Not ranting and weeping like she had over Duke

Pavla's frail body, pretending to care even though she'd been the one slowly poisoning him all that time.

Vincent's voice was calm and low as he spoke. "You're being good here, aren't you? Taking your medicine?"

"I'm a good girl." Kerala became infantile and needy as she spoke. "I've always been good."

Is this it? Is this what they'd come to hear? In that case Melody could have come on her own. "Is this relevant?" Ondine asked.

With a tilt of her head, Melody indicated Vincent's satchel, which he'd left slumped on the floor. Something moved inside it, like a rolling lump of . . . something lumpy.

"I brought you a present," Vincent said, reaching into that very satchel. He withdrew a bulky present, wrapped badly with too much paper and sticky tape. He must have done it himself, in a hurry.

"Is it my birthday?" Kerala asked, her face wobbling in fright. "Did I forget it was my birthday?"

"No, course not," he said. Kerala's smile returned as Vincent pressed the gift into her hands and said, "Can't I give you a present just because?"

"Of course you can. I love presents." Her fingers dug into the paper and battled with the tape to reveal an over-stuffed teddy bear. "Oh I love it!" She squeezed it to her chest, making dust blow out.

Looking to Hamish, Ondine mouthed, "Dust?"

"I have to go now, dear Mother," Vincent said, giving her a dutiful kiss on the forehead. "Be good now and keep taking your medicine."

Kerala hugged the teddy, sending more dust into the room. The teddy's stomach bulged under the pressure.

Vincent turned, lifted his now-empty satchel from the floor and tucked it over his shoulder as he walked out. Melody began to waft after him, tugging Ondine's hand towards the door. "Was that an heirloom or something?" Ondine asked.

"Aye, I was wondering that meself, although it looked new," Hamish added.

"It is new. You haven't worked out what's inside it, have you?" Melody said as she drew them after Vincent.

"A bag of dust . . ." Ondine thought out loud. She would have slapped her forehead in realisation had she not been gripping Hamish and Melody's hands so tightly. "It's the dust bag from the vacuum cleaner. The one with Mrs Howser's soul in it."

"That's why we're such good friends, because you're so smart," Melody said, giving Ondine a wink of encouragement.

"But why would Vincent give Howser's soul to his mother? Are they going to merge or something so Kerala can use Howser's magic to escape the asylum?"

"I doubt it," Melody brought them through another closed door, where they found Vincent crouching down to speak to a woman who was kneeling in the corner of the room. She was curled up, her arms tucked tightly over her knees, rocking slowly back and forth. Her hands were covered in mittens, which were securely fastened to a solid jacket she wore.

Vincent touched the woman's shoulder, but she didn't react to him. With a tug of her hand, Melody pulled Ondine and Hamish around to get a better view, which resulted in them emerging through a connecting wall.

The woman was Mrs Howser. Her face was gaunt and grey, the lines deeper after rapid weight loss and perhaps a nervous breakdown. The shocks kept coming when Mrs Howser opened her eyes to reveal opaque irises and pupils; like dirty windowpanes in need of a good clean.

Cold fear prickled Ondine's spine. They thought they'd been safe from Mrs Howser, after her body and soul separation last month in Savo Plaza. But now only a child-woman and her teddy bear separated the most powerful witch's body from her evil essence.

Thank goodness for the mittens, so she couldn't touch anyone and transfer magic, Ondine thought.

"Now you see why I brought you here," Melody said, pulling them upwards, away from Vincent.

"He won't stop till he's Duke, will he?" Ondine asked, although she already knew the answer, so it was more like a statement.

"Exactly." Melody said. "Which is why I already have a plan. I'm going to work with Vincent and keep an eye on him. Meanwhile, you have to help Anathea any way you can. We'll meet up and share what we know, to make sure Brugel stays on the straight and narrow."

Of course Melody would volunteer to work with Vincent.

"Ma's going to kill me," Ondine said. "She doesn't want any of us having anything more to do with the royal family ever again."

"Then don't tell her," Melody said. "What she doesn't know won't hurt her."

"Aye. It'll be like old times eh lass?" Hamish gave her a wink.

Ondine's lips twisted in thought. Could she really do this? "I thought we'd have a little more time for normal things before everything turned bonkers again."

"Come on." Melody gave her hand an encouraging squeeze. "As if you could ever stay away from the crazy."

**2**

---

A few evenings after their frightening astral projection excursion with Melody, Ondine was doing her level best to act as if nothing had happened.

She and her family were in their pub, *The Duke and Ferret*, tapping their feet to music. It was the end of a long night, and Ondine's clever and talented, and, more importantly, *in-tune* sisters Marguerite and Cybelle were performing a classic four-chord pop song for the customers.

Despite finishing their meals, desserts, coffees and nightcaps, the customers showed no signs of wanting to leave. They did, however, show many signs of still being infected by magic every time Ondine and Hamish showed public displays of affection. Things like fresh flowers appearing at the tables, people's hair-styles looking amazing all night and matronly customers seeming to grow younger as the hours wore on. It was probably the reason why the restaurant was so popular, along with the incredible food and just mentioned entertainment. Extra money manifested in people's coat pockets as they said yes to a second dessert. Ma didn't seem to be too worried about so much wayward magic, so Ondine decided not to let it worry her either. [1]

Ondine leaned into her beloved Hamish as they watched the singing from the kitchen doorway. They'd had so many adventures and near-heartaches and real heartaches to last a lifetime, which was why moments like these were so precious. Not that Ondine could focus on the negative when her sisters sang so beautifully and her darling Hamish held her close, as he did right now.

"This is pure magic, eh lass?" Hamish murmured into her ear. Then he kissed her earlobe and her knees turned to pâté. "And yer all magic to me."

He said the sweetest things.

Margi and Cybelle finished their song to rapturous applause. In the middle of the room, Margi's husband Thomas set a camera onto a tripod to record their next performance. Since the wedding, Margi's face had taken on an almost angelic glow. Her Cupid's bow lips didn't *fix* the way they used to, as she was nearly always smiling and laughing. Cybelle was as cool and composed as ever, having radically trimmed her perfect bob of hair on one side, giving it a stylish and sharp angle.

"Thank you." Margi beamed as the applause died down. "We'd like to sing something original that we hope you'll like just as much. It's called *You Are My Star*."

Thomas blew her a kiss and pointed to the camera. "It's going straight to BrugelTube." [2]

The footage would also end up in Ondine's media studies portfolio for high school. Media studies had become her favourite subject, although she very nearly hadn't enrolled, thanks to her parents wanting to dole out suitable punishment after a particularly awful family altercation back in summer. But since then Ondine had proved she could be good, and the increase in the pub's income meant they could afford the camcorder fees. Now that she had a camera, everyone else loved using it too.

Cybelle nodded to Margi and launched into a power ballad, filled with soaring chords that could make you fly. Ondine, battling to focus on her sisters because Hamish was nibbling at the place where her neck met her shoulders, thought the song was amazing. The chorus lifted the room as Margi sang, *"You are my star, and I'm the one who's shining in your light."*

The room, so raucous only moments earlier, was utterly still as Margi performed. She hit every note and finished the song with tears in her eyes. The restaurant erupted into applause. Margi beamed, her gaze fixed on Thomas, who stepped forward and wrapped his wife in a loving embrace.

Behind her, Ondine heard Hamish sniff. She turned to him, tears pooling in her own eyes. "It's beautiful, isn't it?"

"Aye, the best. I wish I could write a song like that for you."

Ondine wiped his cheek with the pad of her thumb. Uh-oh, more silver strands appeared at his temples. She cupped his face in her hands and turned his face side-to-side, panic rising in her chest.

"What's wrong lass?"

"Hamish, you're turning grey!"

"I'm nawt. Am I?"

Grabbing his hand, she whisked him off to the bathroom to show him the truth.

"Aww no! I'm getting old!"

"There aren't that many. I can pull them out for you, here." Ondine grabbed a set of tweezers and set to work.

"Awww! Stop it." He batted her away. "I can do it meself."

Out of nowhere, Old Col appeared at the bathroom doorway. "There you are. Ma's looking for you, saying you need to clear plates. What are you doing in here?"

"Getting rid of Hamish's grey hairs," Ondine said.

"Goodness, if I did that, I'd be bald," Old Col patted her head. "Wait a minute, Hamish, how old are you?"

"You tell me?" Hamish pushed the tweezers away. "You're the one that put the staying spell on me."

Old Col's face lost a shade of colour at that, her skin taking on a grey tone.

"What's wrong?" Ondine didn't like where this could be going.

The original spell that Old Col had cast on Hamish to turn him into a ferret had included the phrase, 'and you can stay like that', which was why he hadn't aged since he'd been ferretised. "Is your spell wearing off Col?"

"Maybe it is," she said, with a heavy swallow that made the wattle at her neck wobble. "Anyway, let's not dwell on that, Ma is calling for you. Come along."

As Hamish and Ondine set to clearing the plates in the dining room – Ondine's thoughts swirling over her worries about Hamish ageing – a woman approached Margi and Cybelle and gave them her business card. Ma stepped forward and hugged her daughters, then kissed them multiple times on the cheeks. Josef, their father who usually tended bar, approached with a bottle of *Busuioacă de Bohotinand* and a tray of glasses. [3]

Her father, being friendly? *Giving away wine?* Ondine felt sure something momentous had just happened.

"Oh, by the way Hamish," Old Col said as they returned to the kitchen with arms filled with plates. "Would you do me the honour of partnering me at my abnormal formal?"

"Your what?" Ondine and Hamish said together.

"My do-over debutante ball. We didn't get it right the first time around, so let's try again for old time's sake. It's not until May. Plenty of time to rehearse."

The old dear had such a hopeful look; Ondine didn't want to let her down.

Considering how much her great-aunt had done to help the two of them this past year, it would be a good way to return the favour. Then something zinged in her brain at how fortuitous this could be. It would give Ondine and Hamish the perfect excuse to be out of the house, which meant she could dart off and meet with Duchess Anathea and keep her informed of Vincent's nefarious endeavours. "Of course he'll do it, won't you Hamish?"

"Aye," he agreed with a nod. "It's the least I can do for ye."

"Lovely!" Old Col clapped her papery hands together. "This will be such fun. Oh, and you might want to dye your hair for the big night if the grey keeps sprouting out like that."

HAVING SPENT a significant part of the past three seasons slagging off The Democratic Republic of Slaegal, it is important to note that Brugel's eastern neighbour has a great many good points. [4]

It has more beach frontage of The Black Sea than Brugel, and therefore more holiday resorts and a larger tourism industry. However, their claim to have more sunny days per year than Brugel is completely false. [5]

They have the ordinariness of a rectangular flag, although their unique selling point is that theirs is the only completely blue and red flag in the world, being mostly blue with a horizontal slash of red at the top. Their national motto, "Proudly Not Brugel", resonates with the country's longstanding animosity with their neighbour. This sets Slaegal apart from nearby Craviç, whose motto is, "We are so different to Moldova."

Slaegal has more wine production than Brugel and also produces a national car, the Slabi, which doubles in value when filled with petrol. Being further north than Brugel, Slaegal takes longer to wake up from winter. Snow is still thick on the ground in March, when only the bravest yellow crocus and snowdrops dare show their heads. [6]

On this particular not-really-spring afternoon, Lord Vincent of Brugel stood in a Norange street. Standing beside him, the young witch Melody puffed a cloudy breath onto her gloved hands.

"Thank you, for your help with this." Steam poured from his mouth as he spoke.

"Happy to," she said with a nod and another puff of steam.

It had been winter when Melody came into his life; she'd brought sunshine and possibilities with her wherever she went. When she'd offered to assist him just a few days ago, he'd accepted.

The house before them was a big sloppy lump of a thing, which tapered like a badly built sand castle. Behind the windowpanes were hinged timber panels, closed against the cold of winter. Heavy columns stood guard near the front door, with lavish baroque cherubs smiling down upon visitors. On closer inspection, the cherubs weren't smiling but were cracked across the face from centuries of weathering.

"Are you ready?" He asked.

"Let's do this." She answered.

Straightening his shoulders, Vincent rapped on the heavy wooden door. Footsteps echoed, somebody opened the door with a shudder and a pained creak. A butler in faded clothes greeted them, his greasy hair dragged back into a ponytail.

"Please wait here," the butler said, as they stepped into a vestibule. The umbrella stand in the corner lay empty. A panel of wood nailed to the wall would have held their coats, had there been any brass hooks on them.

The butler kept walking.

Vincent shot Melody a confused look. In turn she volleyed him an equally confused one straight back. Were they supposed to stand around or walk after the Butler? Maybe it was a Slaegal thing, where "wait here," really meant, "follow me".

They followed the butler until they came to an atrium in the centre of the house. He then nodded and walked off, leaving them there.

Right in the middle of that atrium grew an impressively huge tree with a trunk so wide it would take four people to hug it. The bark was deeply furrowed like a grandfather's forehead. Its roots twisted in and out of the soil, creating crevices and rolling hills for moss and mushrooms.

Its branches reached outwards in all directions, resting on the balustrades and balconies of the upper floors. Some branches cut straight through the floors of the upper rooms, or, more correctly, the upper floors had been built to allow the branches to keep growing.

"That's some tree," Melody said as she gazed at the snow-covered glass ceiling. More accurately, a cracked and groaning snow-covered glass ceiling, as the top of the tree pressed hard against its bonds in an effort to break through.

On a soft breath, Vincent said, "I'm sure you're just bursting to tell me about it." Chatting about something innocuous would stop his terrible fear from taking over. The fear that reminded him that every day spent outside Brugel was another day out of the public's sight. Every day allowed his aunt, Anathea, to become entrenched as Duchess. Which was why he was here, doing everything he could to gain support for his claim. His *rightful* claim. Even if it meant going to Slaegal.

"It's a gorgeous custom," Melody beamed. "The oldest families in

Norange plant the Slaegalpine trees first, then they build their houses around them. As the tree grows, they add further storeys to the houses. But never taller than the top of the tree." [7]

Vincent looked up and caught a subzero snowflake in his eye. The pine was not simply pressing against the ceiling; it had broken through in places, allowing rain and snow to fall through.

"The tree is hundreds of years old," Melody continued. "So is the house. You would have noticed the different architectural eras on the facade? I mean, of course you did. Because you're so clever."

He didn't want to dampen her enthusiasm, but there had to be a way to deal with this annoying crush of hers in a non-traumatic way. He just hadn't worked out how yet.

He puffed a warm breath into his chilled hands. If they had to wait any longer, the Zendgraf and Zendgravine would find their visitors turned into frozen ornaments. [8]

Hardly conducive to having top-level meetings if Vincent's mouth froze shut.

Changing his weight from left to right, gently stamping his feet to keep the blood flowing, Vincent exhaled with relief when the butler emerged through a set of double doors with an elderly couple behind him.

"My dear cousin." Vincent held his arms wide to embrace Nikolai, the Zendgraf of Norange. "How good it is to see you again." When they embraced, as family is wont to do, Vincent was gentle so as not to damage his frail-looking relative, who was of the same vintage as his aunt Anathea.

"And I you, cousin-mine." The Zendgraf said. [9]

Being closer gave a better view of the *gin blossoms* on his cousin's aged face, no doubt the result of the cold climate breaking his capillaries. [10]

The matronly Zendgravine Bohdanna extended her liver-spotted hand, indicating Vincent should bow over it and kiss it. A year ago she would have curtseyed to him. Not that he'd show signs of discomfort here. If cousin Bohdanna wanted her status, she'd get it. He didn't want her respect. Just her money.

"This is Melody, my witch," Vincent said, indicating the young woman at his side.

"I'm honoured," Melody said, making the most courteous of curtseys.

*Good girl.* He'd thank her later for picking up on the vibe.

"A real witch?" Bohdanna raised one eyebrow. "Or a personal assistant?"

"A little of both," Vincent said, keen to hurry them on to business matters.

"An *asswitchant*," Nikolai said.

Melody nodded but Vincent was pleased to see her keeping her opinions to herself. He opted for, "I like it." *I hate it.*

"Let us honour the tree," Nikolai said, his hand wafting towards the pine. His fingers did not straighten. The long winters must be agony on his arthritis.

Bohdanna linked her arm with her husband.

*Must we?* "Of course," Vincent said, having no clue what Niko was on about. "When in Norange." [11]

"Be my guest," Nikolai motioned his bent fingers to a wooden pail that sat near the edge of the tree trunk.

What was Vincent meant to do with it? If he asked, he'd be exposing his ignorance of Slaegalese customs. Doing the wrong thing would insult his hosts; a terribly bad way of beginning negotiations.

The water in the half-full wooden bucket had iced over from the cold. Leaning against it was a long-handled wooden spoon. [12]

Silently moving beside him, Melody touched her un-gloved (and cold!) fingers to his wrist. Enough to transfer magic, so he'd know what to do. With a nod to his hosts, he took the spoon by the handle, cracked through the ice and ladled a splash against the base of the tree. Then he turned and offered the spoon to Melody, who did the same. Melody passed the spoon to Bohdanna who gave a gracious nod, as if everything were in order and she was pleased. Not that she smiled, but at least she wasn't grimacing. When it was Nikolai's turn, his hands shook in the effort to hold the wooden spoon, but he managed to water the tree all the same. Then he leaned the long wooden ladle against the bucket.

No, not quite, the spoon slipped. Nikolai grabbed it and straightened it again. It slipped, so he straightened it again. Vincent didn't know where to look. The longer Nikolai took, the more Vincent wondered if he should step in and help. The water's skin began freezing over. Cold drafts clawed at Vincent's sleeves and crept inside his coat. He couldn't feel his feet. Flakes of snow fell between his neck and his collar.

At last Nikolai was satisfied the spoon wasn't going to slip away. The butler directed them to a room off to the side.

In comparison to the atrium, it was a tropical paradise in here.

"You honour us with your adherence to our customs," Bohdanna said as she patted the cushion beside her, inviting Vincent to sit. "I feared there was too much Brugel in you."

"I'm adaptable," Vincent said as a wave of relief fell over him. "Would you care to honour one of our customs?"

"I know the one," Nikolai said. "How I miss the taste of plütz."

Melody delved into her witchy satchel and produced a cloth-covered bottle. Then she retrieved a set of shot glasses, also wrapped in cloth to prevent breakage. With a deft flick of the wrist and a metallic crack, Melody opened the plütz and poured four shots; filling the glasses so high they spilled onto the tray below.

They each took a glass, Vincent saluted their continued good health, then they crashed their glasses together so a little of everyone's drinks slopped into the others'. [13]

They downed their drinks in one swallow. When the burn left his throat, Vincent said, "Who needs a roaring fire when you have plütz?"

Nikolai and Bohdanna exchanged glances, then Bohdanna said, "You should have mentioned you were cold. Living so much further north than you, we are quite acclimatised."

Did she have to come right out and say how soft he was? "I am very comfortable," Vincent lied so smoothly he surprised himself. "How are the children, by the way?" Not that he should call them children, when they were all older than he.

A smile plumped Bandanna's cheeks and crinkled her eyes. "They are doing well and send their regards. It is a pity they cannot be here to receive you. Boris is at a manufactory and Kolja is giving a speech at the university."

"Given the choice, I'd much rather be busy than idle," Vincent said.

"Oh yes, we're all terribly busy," Nikolai chimed in.

"In which case." May as well push on. "Now that the formalities are out of the way, perhaps we shall get down to business?"

"Of course," Nikolai sat on the opposite sofa. In doing so, his sleeve caught the doily on the armrest, revealing threadbare stitching beneath. He laughed it off. "That's the trouble with antiques, not built for today's bodies."

"I shall not take up much more of your time," Vincent said. "I'm sure you have been following our family's fortunes, and how my dear Aunt Anathea has taken my birthright from me."

Bohdanna accepted another shot of plütz. "But she is older than you, she has more experience."

"This is true," Vincent agreed. "But she never had the training, nor the *expectation*, of leadership. And now my cousins, Ausra and Viktorija . . . and the other one . . ."

Silence hung over them.

"Electra," Melody prompted.

" . . . That's right, Electra. The three of them are getting way above their station," he said, with what he hoped sounded like concern, not distaste.

"Perhaps," Nikolai looked to Bohdanna. "They are merely showing support for their mother?"

"You are being far too kind," Vincent said, as he too had another shot of plütz.

Finally he was starting to feel warm, although his feet remained stubbornly numb.

"Let's be honest. Anathea's not up to it. We know I am; yet I lack the finances to change things back to the natural order. To draw this to its obvious conclusion, I need money."

3

Vincent's blunt words hung in the air like a poison gas nobody dared breathe.

"I see." Nikolai said at last, taking another shot of plütz.

Vincent waited. Nobody said anything further. Nikolai and Bohdanna didn't make eye contact. Another shot of plütz ought to do it. No, he still couldn't feel his feet.

Enough of this waiting. "It is the truth. I need money from you," he said, hating that he had to state the bleeding obvious.

"Ahh," Nikolai said as he put his glass down. "That could be problematic."

"We cannot be seen to interfere with another sovereign state," Bohdanna said. "Not only would it be unconstitutional, it would be unseemly."

"I understand my request has come at short notice," Vincent said, idly playing with the doily over his armrest. Something caught his eye; the label on the reverse side came from a discount supermarket chain.

"Perhaps we should leave the Zendgraf and Zendgravine to consider your request?" Melody said as she screwed the lid on the plütz bottle and wrapped everything back into her satchel. Either Melody had seen the signs of thrift or she was very, very good at reading his mind. Maybe she'd cast some kind of exposure spell, so Vincent would see for himself why his cousins were so reluctant to help?

"That might be for the best," Nikolai said, rising from his seat.

The handshakes may have been friendly, but the atmosphere was colder than the atrium as Vincent and Melody said their goodbyes.

As they walked through the snow-slurried streets back to their rental car, a late model Slabi, Melody put on her chauffeur's cap and took the wheel.

"Thank you," he said. "For the spell."

"It's as old as dirt. Drink as much as you want and not get drunk. Helps tremendously when you're negotiating. Of course, it has the effect of making the other people drunker, but that's no bad thing."

Vincent scratched his head. "I meant the revealing spell, so I'd see the truth. They can't afford to replace the glass roof, let alone help my cause."

"I didn't cast that kind of spell. But I will at the next one, if you want me to?"

What a mess. What a miserable, cold, waste-of-time mess they were in. "Please do."

Melody negotiated the streets of Norange like a local. Vincent tapped his feet to get the circulation moving. "I guess you didn't need a spell to see how broke they were."

"The Sletto clothing was a dead giveaway." [1]

"And the lack of heating," he said, leaning forward and flicking the car's thermostat up so his toes didn't snap off. "I bet Boris isn't visiting a *'manufactory'* or whatever they want to call it. He's probably working in one."

"Manufacturing is very important," Melody said as she negotiated a three-lane roundabout.

Vincent let out some pent-up expletives. Melody held up her palm to stop him. "Your fine words butter no parsnips!" [2]

Vincent dragged his fingers through his hair and looked out at the sleet-filled sky. "Any idea what the hell we're going to do?"

"Oh yes," Melody beamed as she wove their car into another round about streaming with traffic, "I know just the right person, I set up a meeting with him, just in case the Old Money didn't pay out."

"Not another relative without a bean to fry?"

Melody pulled out of the traffic like a rally driver. "You're going to love the next one. He's Babak Balakhan. New money. Emphasis on *money*."

"Good," Vincent felt his body warming, his circulation *circulating* again. "Should I ask where he gets his money from. Because I've never heard of his family."

"It's not *family* money, it's oil money. That's what his wiki says. [3] He also bankrolled Slaegal's last three PopEuroTube entries." [4]

"No taste in music then?"

With a rueful smile, Melody turned off the side road and onto timber-lined track that slipped and slopped in the mud. In front of them lay a field of icy brown slush. In the midst of it loomed a three-storey concrete extravaganza, shrouded in scaffolding and tradies. [5] They parked on more mud-set slabs of timber that substituted for a car park. Melody exited first and unfurled a double-width umbrella, then opened Vincent's door. More planks of wood lay in a haphazard pathway towards the door. Every step squelched as the wood sucked and slopped in the thick wet clay. By the time they reached the doorway – there wasn't a door in place yet – Vincent's hair was streaked with damp.

Babak Balakhan himself stood there, a huge smile on his cold-blotched face. "Ah! Beloved guests. Welcome, welcome!"

The man wore a black three-piece suit that only just buttoned up over his ample stomach. His hair was shaved low to disguise how fast it marched backwards. A thick twist of gold sat around his neck, while the fingers on both hands were studded with chunky jewellery. He looked more like the head of security than the head of a household.

Extending his hand in greeting, Vincent said, "Gaspado Balakhan, I am so pleased to meet you." [6]

"So formal, My Lord!" He grabbed Vincent in a bear hug, "Call me Babak. All my friends do. Come, come, let's be out of this miserable weather."

"I tell you, never build in a Slaegal winter. Build during the other three weeks of the year. Ha!"

Vincent grinned but he refused to guffaw. That would be unseemly. As if to ram home his wealth, Babak's silk tie flipped over in the wind to reveal the logo of a Paris fashion house. No discount Sletto clothing for him.

"Babak, may I introduce my personal witch, Melody?"

"Oh but you are beautiful!" Taking her free hand, Babak kissed it on both the back and the palm.

It pleased Vincent to see Melody blush. If Babak charmed her enough, maybe she'd shift her romantic attentions to him instead.

"Thank you." Melody took her hand back, then fumbled as she closed the umbrella.

"I have never met a witch before," Babak said, "We don't have so many in Slaegal, Brugel is hogging them all."

Inside the construction-zone mansion, they found an atrium. It was completely open to the sky, with no tree. Good, Vincent thought, they wouldn't have to make nice around the trunk while their toes snapped off. Unlike his cousin's crumbling pile, Babak's halls and promenades were dotted with portable oil heaters, throwing a deep red heat out to anyone nearby.

"It's freezing here, you'll catch your deaths," Babak said. "Come into the . . . sitting room, I think they call it. My office is not yet finished. Ah, and we have something for your umbrella. Here, here," he gestured to a series of ornate galvanized hooks.

"But it will drip on the floor." Melody hesitated.

"And the rain won't? Ha! There is such mud and rain, with an open sky and the trucks outside. The cleaners do their best, but eh, what can you do?" He shrugged, as if damaged timber flooring was of no concern. "Come in here, out of the cold."

A servant stepped out of nowhere and opened the triple-glazed doors that led to an airlock. The next set of doors were triple-glazed as well, and once they were closed behind them, they were warm and draft free.

"Ah! The tree!" Babak said as he looked out the window.

A heavy tray-truck backed into the yard, its fat tyres sinking into the gloop.

"So," Babak said as Melody unpacked her satchel and prepared three shot glasses of plütz. "You are here for money, yes?"

Vincent tried – and failed – to keep his expression neutral as he turned to face his host.

"Ha! I am direct. But then, being direct is a good thing." Babak held his arms wide as if to show off his luxurious house and all that it entailed. His success. From being direct.

"I guess now you've said it, I have to say you're right." Vincent felt the tension ease out of his shoulders. Being direct would save them a lot of messing about.

"Everyone wants money from me." Babak said. "How much, and what will I get in return?"

A quick glance to Melody's contrite face revealed her interference. She must have used some kind of revealing spell in here, to reveal what Babak really wanted. Laid it on a little thick, though.

Swallowing past a rock in his throat, Vincent's mind fast-forwarded through the polite chitchat and shadow boxing he'd prepared, so he could move to the end game. "I honestly don't know. Because it could take a while to –"

"Stop now. The rain may drip here with no end, but my money is no endless winter. You want to be Duke again, yes?"

The man's brain moved fast. Vincent had to adapt. "I have not yet been Duke, so I cannot be Duke *again*. But I will regain my birthright."

There was a steely gleam in Babak's eyes as took his shot glass and held it up. "I shall meet you under the table." [7] Babak downed his drink, so Vincent grabbed his and downed it too. It wouldn't do to let the man drink alone when they were supposed to be . . . what, friends?

Melody refilled their glasses, but did not serve herself.

"You. Drink too," Babak's gaze homed in on Melody. "I don't trust people who don't drink. There is no truth in them."

Melody poured a shot and drank hers, then turned her shot glass upside down for no more refills. "I love the stuff, but I'm also driving. The conditions out there are woeful and I need a clear head."

Babak laughed. "Slaegal weather. What's not to love? More booze."

This was some kind of game where Vincent didn't know the rules. Babak had said he'd give him money, which was a plus. It didn't stop a lump of dread growing in his belly. Not even the plütz could dissolve that.

Babak tilted his hand to the window, to see the tree being unloaded from the truck. "Look at my beautiful pine! Is it not the very best money can buy?"

It surely had to be. The workers wrapped thick hessian strips around the tree base, then fastened a set of hooks on the end of a crane. Slowly, securely, the crane lifted the hundred-or-so-year-old pine into an upright position. It swayed in the wind and the crane driver slowed progress to make sure it didn't crash into the building.

"This is a good meeting," Babak slammed his glass down and motioned with his hand for a top up. "I have plenty of money and no respect. You, Vincent, have the name and respect, but no money."

He'd summed it up perfectly.

"So, what's standing in the way of you becoming Duke, eh? Your aunt? Your cousins? That's a lot of people to push aside."

Panic burned the back of Vincent's throat. "No! Not like that." He steadied his hands on his thighs to stop them shaking. "My cousins cannot be harmed. That's not how we're going to play this."

"Play what?" Babak looked offended and pointed to his empty glass as he eyed Melody. "More booze."

Dammit, Vincent felt five times heavier now he'd insulted his host. Scrambling to get things back to where they should be, he said, "The issue is, yes, I do want to be Duke. I'm here because I'm broke. What's in my favour is my people want me to be Duke." Oh dear, was that the plütz talking? Had Melody cast a spell on him too? He was saying far more than he should.

"Good. We are near the truth. You should be in politics, not waiting for relatives to die. More booze." Babak clinked his glass to Vincent's and nodded.

The alcohol wrapped Vincent in a fuzzy blanket. How lucky he was already sitting, because his knees no longer worked.

"What is wrong with your cousins?" Babak asked, while also encouraging Melody to pour more shots.

In the edge of his vision, Vincent could see the pine flying higher outside. Yikes, the plütz had gone straight to his head. But wait, hadn't Melody put that spell on him to stop the effects of alcohol? There was no food in here to space out the drinks. No water to dilute it. He and Babak were sure to meet under the table very soon at this rate. Wait a minute, his brain said, the tree wasn't flying, it was on the end of the crane, and the crane was lifting it up so it could lower it into the middle of the house and into the atrium.

A sigh of resignation seeped from Vincent. "There's nothing really wrong with them. They're just not . . . not suited, not trained, not sensible. Not anything."

"You should marry the oldest one," Babak said. "Then you'd be Duke."

"No I wouldn't. I'd be consort to an unsuitable Duchess. And they're all broke as well. That and the fact I'm not the cousin-marrying kind."

"I like your truth." Babak upturned his glass to show their drinking session was at an end. "Now here is mine. You have ambition and status, but no resources. I have all the resources in the world, but no respect. Let us make an alliance. My money, for your respect."

"What's the catch?"

Melody shot him a look, like he was forgetting himself. Because he was in the throes of "plütz truth", that terrible affliction that removed the social conventions of keeping your secrets.

"My daughter," Babak said. "She is very much a catch."

Vincent slumped, Melody sat up straighter. The man with all the money reached into his inside suit pocket and pulled out a phone. "Ruslana, come to the sitting room. There's someone here I'd like you to meet."

The room swayed. The woman who walked in took Vincent's breath away. In a really, *really* not-very-good-way at all. The girl had whiter than white blonde hair that sat up a good ten centimetres above her forehead, which then flicked and flailed its way down to mid torso. That wasn't the worst of her.

Despite the cold, she wore a cut-off tank top that came perilously close to showing underboob. But even that wasn't the worst of her.

The mini skirt the width of a seat belt and the platform lace-up boots did her no favours either, but they merely served to highlight the very, *very* worst of her.

Her skin. Her terribly *orange* skin.

The public would have a field day with this orange from Norange.

***

COULD that be the sun peeking through the clouds? Ondine peered through her bedroom window at the finger of light hitting the neon dragon that guarded the front door of *On The Fang*, the restaurant across the road from their pub in Venzelemma.

*Come on spring, where are you?*

Trudging downstairs, Ondine knew a good way to keep warm would be to submerge her arms into a sink of hot soapy water, filled with breakfast's greasy dishes. Which was exactly what her family needed her to do this morning, just as it was every other morning. Yawning her way into the kitchen, she nodded her family greetings. Sure, she was tired, but she couldn't complain. Everyone else had been up a few hours earlier to cook and serve breakfast to the customers.

"Happy birthday darling," Ma said as she landed a kiss on the top of her head.

Sunshine flowed through Ondine. Today was her sixteenth birthday, and her family had remembered. Not that birthdays were as important as name days in Brugel (her parents had botched that spectacularly a couple of months ago) but it was lovely that they were making the effort.

"Thanks Ma," she said with a grin as her mother handed her a card with sixteen cupcakes on the front. Opening it, a twenty-schlip note fell out and she caught it before it could land in the sink and get wet. Then she gave Ma a hug and sat the card up on the high shelf above her.

Da poked his head around the corner. "Has Ma given you our card?"

"Sure did. Thank you very much."

Da moved in for a hug, and excellent excuse for Ondine to put off doing the dishes for a few more minutes. "You're very generous, I'm feeling well-loved."

With a soft chuckle as the hug continued, Da said, "Wouldn't even pretend to forget, not after your name day dramas."

Trust Da to bring that up. "Already forgotten."

Da planted a kiss on her forehead. "When did my baby girl grow so mature?"

It rankled that he called her a baby girl, but she pushed it down. "Don't worry Da, if it makes you feel better, at least I'll never be as old as you."

"Cheeky." He tickled her chin. "Aww come here again, my big baby."

There was no escaping this hug as Da gave her an extra squishy squish.

"Happy birthday Ondi," Cybelle said, jamming a card between their bodies.

"That's from me as well," Margi called out.

It was the excuse Ondine needed to pull back from the suffocating love. Da headed back to the dining room. A five-schlipp note fell out of the card. Seriously, five? She pocketed it all the same and put their home-made card on the shelf, away from soapy, soggy-making water. Hamish sidled up to her. He too had a hand-decorated card, but coming from Hamish it held far more meaning. It proved he'd taken the time to make something for her. As opposed to her sisters, who'd simply been cheap. And he'd put a twenty-schlipp note in there.

"Yer ma said this was all I was allowed to do."

A smile broke over her face. "You're so thoughtful."

"Aye, that's me all over." His immodest words led to utterly immodest kissing, which Ondine took part in fully. They did things to her brain, his kisses. Melted reality and warped time. Made her feel like the most important person in the world.

"All right you two, back to work." That would be Ma, interrupting them as usual.

One more kiss, then she'd stop.

"Come on," Ma said.

Reluctantly (was there any other way to end a kiss?) Ondine pulled away and promised she'd kiss him for longer next time. Hamish left her side and she faced the dishes. Before plunging her hands in, she turned the radio on to bring in some music. She nearly dropped a plate when she heard Margi and Belle's voices, singing on the radio.

"Everyone, listen to this!" she grabbed at the volume up with her sud-soaked hand.

"Turn it up!" That was Cybelle.

"I'm trying."

"Give it here." Not normally pushy, Cybelle nudged Ondine aside and turned the noise to maximum. Margi's clear voice washed over them, but Ondine could tell by the look on Belle's face that she was listening to the music more than the lyrics.

Da stepped back in to the kitchen. "Is that yours?"

"Shush! Yes!" Belle said.

Margi's eyes were huge with delight as she ran to Belle and hugged her. They jumped up and down on the spot.

Pride soared through Ondine for her sisters' success. It was a great song. The kind that would be sung at weddings, or played in the background while loved-up couples had a really good snog. Josef stood there in silence, beaming at his daughters. Then Ma joined in the three-way hug. Henrik and Thomas gave each other high-fives.

When the song finished, Margi and Belle started giggling and jumping up and down again.

"You can turn it down now," Da said, rubbing his ear as the radio played something modern, which Ondine loved but knew her parents hated.

Great-Aunt Col sauntered in to the kitchen and dished herself a plate of scrambled eggs from the stovetop. "Good morning everyone, how are we?"

"Good thanks. Um, Auntie dear," Ma said, as she took the plate away from her and handed her a bowl of stewed fruit instead, "You are welcome to stay any time, as you know, but please don't take food from the mouths of paying guests."

"Yes Young Col," Old Col said as she reached for the tongs beside the hotplate of bacon, "But I need protein this morning. Hamish and I have dance rehearsals."

Dancing lessons would provide the perfect cover for Ondine to sneak off and visit Anathea, so she could warn her about Vincent.

Grabbing a piece of bacon she declared, "I'm coming too."

LORD VINCENT, Melody, Babak and his citrus-skinned daughter Ruslana stood in the freezing atrium of the Balakhan mansion while an army of landscapers rushed around shifting soil and securing ropes to stabilise the gargantuan pine tree into place. On the floors above, tradies worked in the swirling rain to tie the tree's multiple branches to the balconies. Each kiss of cold wind deepened Vincent's misery. If only Babak hadn't brought his daughter into the negotiations. He needed Brugelish people to like him, but with Ruslana on his arm, the predominant emotion he'd get would be ridicule.

Another worker rushed in and gave Babak a cardboard box.

"Ah! Excellent! Ruslana, you have long nails, help get this open for me."

In a moment they had it open, Babak held the bubble wrap and was popping the little bubbles, while Ruslana held a small wooden pail and matching spoon.

"What is it, Daddy?"

"New tradition. Ah! I have idea," Babak turned to Melody. "Young witch, pour the plütz in here."

"Is that good for pine trees?" Melody raised her brow.

"Eh, we'll mix it with Slaegal rainwater. Best in all of the Europe."

Somebody must have been paying attention, because yet another tradie approached with a metal bucket, filled with clear water. He poured some into the wooden pail, then stepped out of the way. Melody handed the plütz bottle to Babak.

"Excellent. New Slaegal and Brugel tradition. Wonderful combination," Babak said, pouring the plütz in. A peachy aroma floated on the swirling breeze. "Ruslana, Vincent, please do the first honours."

Sickness swirled through Vincent like sleet through the atrium. *Do I have to?* "Thank you, I'd be honoured." Together, he and Ruslana dipped the spoon in the plütz-water and splashed it on the base of the tree. Ruslana's perfume clogged his nostrils as she leaned to his ear. "You're the fourth boy he's tried to marry me off to."

This was beyond ridiculous. "Fourth time lucky then?"

"What's she saying? Eh?" Babak said as they returned the spoon to him.

"Nothing," Ruslana and Vincent said together.

"Ah!" Babak rubbed his hands with glee. "What a great match. Talking sweet nothings already." Then he grabbed Vincent in a strong hug. "Welcome to the family. You can call me Daddy. Now, what is this on your hand, eh?" The man gripped Vincent and turned his palm back and forth. "Why is it blue? It is not so cold?"

"It's stained. Won't wash off."

"A stain? From what?"

With a shrug of his shoulders and honesty-plütz still in his veins, Vincent said, "My inheritance was . . . scattered. I was retrieving some of it from a hotel in Venzelemma when I was captured and treated to this."

"Your inheritance? So you do have money after all?"

"Accessing it proved difficult."

Babak turned Vincent's hand over again before declaring, "Stain it again, darker now. It will be your symbol. Your rallying cry. Your signature, eh?"

Vincent curled the corners of his mouth down in thought, then found himself nodding in agreement. "Good idea. A blue hand for Brugel."

"It will link you to Elmaree," Melody offered.

All three looked at her like she'd spoken in Craviçian. Melody explained. "Your ancestor, Grand Duchess Elmaree. She had a blue hand, after she broke her writing quill and refused to sign her marriage contract with . . . oh I can't remember who it was. But I remember reading about her blue hand. They called it Elmaree's Stain."

Of course, Elmaree's Stain, Vincent thought back to his history lessons and remembered it now. The *someone* Elmaree had refused to marry was a Slaegalese prince. No point mentioning that while standing here in Slaegal, getting himself shackled to this neon-Slae-galese heiress.

"Ha! Excellent," Babak grabbed Melody in a fierce hug and kissed both her cheeks. "A blue hand, it is a sign from above that Vincent is the true Duke of Brugel. And Ruslana darling will be his Duchess."

## 4

Weak sunlight tried to warm the ground as Ondine, Hamish and Old Col walked several blocks towards the dance hall. The icy northern winds pinched their ears. Snow landed in Hamish's hair, making him look so much older than he should. Ondine chastised herself for being so superficial. Everyone looked older in winter, what with all the frowning at the dark clouds above.

Turning her collar up, Ondine shuddered. "Is it just me, or is spring not coming at all this year?"

"You're getting soft," Old Col said. "Plenty of winters that wouldn't let go back in my day."

On they trudged, the ballroom coming into view as they reached the next intersection. At first, Ondine thought its stately stonewalls and arched windows had been decorated in that modern 'distressed' look. On closer inspection, it really was a distressed building. Peeling paint curled along the walls and orange streaks ran from the rusty guttering above. The windowsills were no longer flat, having become lumpy and white from decades of bird droppings.

Inside offered no respite from neglect. It was a draughty place that had seen far better days. Leaky stains drizzled down the walls, bubbling the paintwork. The floorboards creaked and whined with age. As did the masses of people assembled for rehearsal.

With a shrug, Old Col said, "It will look better on the night, and you won't hear the floorboards over the music." [1]

Two young instructors wearing shiny black leggings and tank tops, with sheer, fluttery pink skirts tied around their hips swanned in. "Places everyone," one of them said. [2]

The men and women paired up. Slowly. Old Col looked like the spriteliest one there. Ondine giggled at the thought of the big night having defibrillating machines and ambulances on standby.

A tinny stereo filled the air with classical music. One of the instructors stepped forward. "Positions! *Gentlemens*, take your ladies for the Brugelish three-step. Ahhhhhhnnnd *One two three, one two three, one two three, rest! One two three, one two three, one two three*, rest! *Excellaimont!*" On the instructor went, counting and resting and exclaiming. The dancers, who previously moved at glacial slowness to get up from their chairs, glided around the room like youngsters. The music and movement did, as Col promised, drown most of the creaky floorboard noises out.

"*Excellaimont!*" The woman said again.

*No such word.* Ondine promised to look it up later.

"No, no, no!" The lady moved to Hamish and slapped her palms hard on his upper arms. "No touching your ears with your shoulders. Down. Down. That's better."

"With all due respect, it's *noat* like I'm interested in a career in dancing." Hamish shot back.

Where was the heating? Ondine wondered, because the snow from Hamish's hair hadn't thawed.

"That may be," the instructor said, "but your partner here needs her night to be special, and if you are not in the right position, arms held the right way, you will not guide her properly when she twirls."

"Oh," he said.

Watching from the sidelines, Ondine couldn't believe it when the instructor produced a twisted bar, which she slotted over Hamish's shoulders to force him in the shape of a warped scarecrow.

"Are you sure we need that?" Old Col voiced Ondine's thoughts.

The instructor tut-tutted. "He must hold himself like a gentlemans!"

From where Ondine sat, Hamish looked more like a yoked cow than a 'gentlemans'.

"The more you fight it, the deeper the bruises," the instructor said. "Now, off we go again, *one two three, one two three, one two three*, rest!"

All dancing came to a sudden stop as somebody important walked into the ballroom. Instantly everyone made a gracious bow or curtsey to acknowledge Duchess Anathea's entrance. Beside her stood a dashingly well-preserved man, his hair streaked with silver.

"Who's that?" Ondine whispered as Old Col and Hamish stood to the side of the assembly.

"I think it's an old beau," Old Col said, trying to get a better look. "Don't stare, it's rude."

Was he a former husband? Ondine recalled a conversation she'd had with Anathea many months ago, about an ex who had dumped her because they'd only produced girl children. "I thought he left her because he wanted boys?"

"Not that one," Old Col said. "This is the other one; the one her family didn't like. Don't they make a lovely couple?"

In that case, Ondine was happy for Anathea to rekindle an old flame.

"My Lordship, what an honour," the instructor said as she walked towards Brugel's ruling Duchess.

Anathea smiled to all assembled. "How are the rehearsals coming along?"

"Eh, we've jest started," Hamish said with a shrug.

Ondine winced as the bar across his back held him firmly in place.

"Carry on, pretend I am not here," Anathea said as she made her way towards Ondine.

Oh goody, now was her chance to let Anathea know about Vincent. "My Lordship, I have important news I must share with you."

Without turning her head, Duchess Anathea said, "What deeds are being done?"

Keeping her voice low, she said, "Vincent visited his mother in the asylum, giving her a teddy bear which had the bag of vacuum dust that was full of Mrs Howser's spirit. Then he went down the hall and saw the rest of Mrs Howser."

Anathea swallowed, but made no outward sign of distress. "Was the bag of dust checked by anyone first?"

"Probably not, it was inside the teddy bear."

"Oh dear me." Anathea said. "If Mrs Howser's body and soul are reunited, untold damage could be done to Brugel. How far apart are their rooms situated?"

"Not far enough," Ondine said.

From her clutch purse, Anathea produced silvery coins. "Where can the nearest payphone be found?" [3]

"This way, My Lord," Ondine said, a buzz flickering to life inside her. She had done good work today. The Duchess would order increased security at the asylum, somebody would confiscate the teddy filled with the vacuum dust bag and Mrs Howser's soul, and then life would go back to normal. [4]

When they reached the payphone, Anathea slipped her fingers into the coin return to check for loose change.

"Sorry, old habit." Then she picked up the handle, slipped the coins into the slot and dialled a number.

Silently, they waited by Anathea, the dull brrr-brrr of the ringing phone echoing from the receiver. It kept on ringing.

Finally someone picked it up. "Venzelemma Asylum, how may we help you?"

With a quick clear of her throat, Anathea spoke firmly down the line. "This is your Duchess Anathea. I would like to be told of the where-abouts of a Mrs Birgit Howser."

"Yes, of course it's the duchess, and I'm Catherine The Great. Pull the other one why don't you?"

"This is not the response due to me. I will be put through to the management."

Leaning close to Hamish, Ondine whispered, "They think it's a prank call."

"Give me the phone," Old Col interrupted. Then she muttered some incantation down the line about speaking the truth and the voice down the line completely changed.

So did Old Col's expression. And her pallor. "I see. Thank you."

She hung the phone up.

Anathea slipped her fingers in the coin return to see if any change would fall.

Old Col said, "Don't let anybody see how upset we are. We must absolutely behave as if nothing is wrong."

Which meant everything was completely and utterly wrong.

"Let's have it," Hamish said.

Old Col took a breath and squared her shoulders. "Mrs Howser has escaped the asylum."

*Gulp*, Ondine gulped.

"Oh dear," Anathea said. "Events have quickly been escalated."

---

"WHAT HAPPENED BACK THERE?" Vincent couldn't get enough air into his lungs as Melody drove them away from the Balakhan estate. How long had they been there? Was it late evening or early morning? He'd lost track of time and geography.

"You got engaged. That's what happened. To an Oompa loompa."

His breath fogged the side window as he leaned his head on the cool glass. "I think maybe you used too much magic and we all said things we should have kept to ourselves."

"I didn't use any." The car took a sharp turn.

Vincent reeled. "You must have."

"I read up on Babak. He is direct and blunt. Pouring honesty magic on that would be like tipping rocket fuel on a bonfire."

"Not buying it." Residual nausea from his sudden engagement grew into full-blown dry-heaves from Melody's driving. "You used too much magic and it backfired."

"I didn't use any."

"Why not?"

"Because . . . I needed to show you how life would be without me."

A filthy curse leapt from Vincent, followed by, "You put the entire negotiations at risk!"

She gave him a sarcastic look, which meant she wasn't watching the road and fresh panic surged inside him.

Clearly not noticing his discomfort, she kept on talking. "You're such a good negotiator, I knew you'd be all right."

Eyes back on the road, she overtook a slow car and accelerated away.

"Then tell me, oh clever witch, what am I paying you for if you're not using your magic?"

"You're not paying me, you're broke." They veered sharply as she overtook another car.

"Hey! Take it easy!"

She took the next bend sideways.

Vincent's heart crashed into his ribs. "Slow down, you'll kill us both."

In a screech of gravel and slurry, Melody pulled over. She slammed the gear lever into neutral, but kept the engine ticking over.

Grateful she'd stopped, Vincent waited for his panicked pulse to climb down from the roof. "What the hell has gotten into you?"

"You!" She started slapping at him with her palms.

"Ow! Ow!" It didn't hurt so much as annoy. Vincent trapped her hands in his to make her stop. The face looking back was wild. "What is wrong with you?"

"You can't work it out?" Melody cried. "I'm in love with you, you idiot!"

Damn. "Well," not letting go of her hands, he shrugged, "I knew that much. Obviously. Why else would you bother helping me?"

Her face displayed utter puzzlement.

Vincent let out a sigh. "What I don't get is why you are so upset now."

Her cheeks turned a shade of purple and her lips thinned. "Because you're going to marry that . . . that rich *nobody* you only just met."

"Yes. I am going to marry her. Because her father is loaded and I'm broke."

"But . . . you were supposed to get money, not get engaged."

"You didn't think a rich nobody with a weddable daughter would hand over a fortune with no strings?"

In a pathetic voice she said, "You were supposed to marry me!"

He could have sworn he heard something screeching to a halt. Perhaps it was his brain. "Was I? But what could you possibly bring to the marriage?"

A gasp from Melody, then a quick recovery. "I'd bring *me*, you insufferable turd!"

---

"HOW WAS REHEARSAL?" Ma asked the moment they stepped through the door of the family pub. "Ondi love, the sink is full of dishes, there's a good girl."

Best get the bad news out of the way early. Taking a dramatic breath, Ondine said, "Mrs Howser has escaped the asylum."

"Oh yes?"

"I know, it's terrible!" Ondine said. "Wait, what? Why aren't you worried?"

"Should I be?" Ma said as she handed Ondine a pair of washing gloves. "It's not like we're involved in any way, are we?"

Oh, about that –

"Exactly," Ma said, as if to answer her own question. "Back to work, now, there's a good girl."

Several stacks of dishes later, Old Col came sidling up to Ondine and waggled her fingers at the water to suds it up with magic. The finger waggling produced zero results, so Ondine handed her the bottle of detergent instead.

Keeping her voice low, Old Col said, "I've been making some calls. Mrs Howser has turned up at Fort Kluff."

"Why does that sound familiar?"

Handing Ondine another dirty plate, she whispered, "It's where the late Duke Pavla sent Vincent, to drum some sense into him."

Ondine dropped the plate into the water with a sudsy splash. "There's no knowing what damage she could do at a place like that."

"Tell me about it. Especially as the magic is still spreading."

"What magic?" Ondine asked.

That earned her a stern look.

"I mean, what magic in particular?"

Uh oh, Old Col's expression told Ondine she was in for a lecture. She might not have been psychic, but she always knew when she was in trouble.

"My dear girl, do you think your ability to make people's dreams come true has simply gone away?"

"Oh, that."

"Yes that. It doesn't just end when you're not with Hamish. The people who've caught it still have it, and they're still spreading it about as well."

That horrible, plummeting feeling came over Ondine. "But I thought we stopped it when we caught Howser at the snow maze festival, and Anathea trapped her soul in the vacuum bag."

"We did, but it was only temporary. And now her body and soul are back together, and so the spell is working its mad magic all over the place."

"What are you two conspiring about?" Ma said as she arrived with more dirty dishes.

"Nothing," Ondine and Old Col said together, making them both sound incredibly guilty.

It earned a suspicious look from Ma who said, "Nothing? As in 'I have nothing to do with any of that lot any more,' right?"

Mutely, Ondine nodded assent and wished she didn't have to lie to her mother, because it felt so incredibly wrong to be doing that. At the same time, the news that Mrs Howser's horrible magic was working again, and that she was at Fort Kluff, set light to the idea that she had to do something to make it stop.

If only she knew what that *something* should be.

Driving over the border from Slaegal to Brugel, the roads became bumpier and the potholes harder to avoid. After the seventh jarring thud, Vincent whined, "Someone should fix these miserable roads!"

"At least you're not giving me the silent treatment any more." Came the reply from the uptight young witch in the seat beside him. She'd spent the last forty kilometres fuming away. He could tell by the way her lips were so tightly pressed, and the huffing and the overdramatic sighs. Even her blinking was noisy.

"Take a right here."

"That's not the way to Venzelemma," Melody said.

"We're not going to Venzelemma," he said, then mentally counted down from ten, waiting for her interjection. Which never came. Instead, she kept driving, a tightly wound bundle of fuming upsettedness.

They took the curving road upwards and onwards, the dense pine trees dripping water as the last of the snow melted. The engine whined down into a lower gear as they reached a long hill, until eventually they came to a wide gravel driveway.

Still Melody said nothing. Perhaps she'd put a stewing spell on him or something, to make every tiny thing annoy the tripe out of him. Well, she'd know soon enough where they were, especially when they saw an enormous sign, fixed on a gate next to a security checkpoint.

Fort Kluff.

"What the hell are we doing here?" Melody hit the brake.

"Catching up with an old friend. Keep driving, there's a gatehouse coming up."

When they reached the gatehouse, he showed his old Fort Kluff Cadet identity card to the woman on guard, who welcomed him like an old friend. A *respected* friend. "Welcome home, Sir."

The gates opened, they drove through and Melody found a parking spot near the entrance.

"Right this way, sir," the guard surprised him by opening his door. She gestured towards a security gate near the administration entrance. Here they swiped Vincent's card through an electronic reader, which earned him smiles all round.

"Can you please sign in?" The woman said. At first Vincent thought they were referring to him, but then he noticed Melody behind him. Melody signed the book, showed her driver's licence and they allowed her through.

"She will be in the gymnasium," the guard said to Vincent, then checked her watch, "Although training won't be over for another half hour."

He nodded. "I'll get to see her in action then."

How his chest puffed at the sight of the gymnasium. Dozens of male and female cadets, their heads universally shaved short, snake crawling under a low net, running across obstacle courses, shimmying up ropes, huffing and puffing but otherwise making as little noise as possible.

In the centre of it all stood Mrs Birgit Howser, dressed in a heavy winter witch-cloak with military-style epaulettes on the shoulders. She was quietly directing the human traffic to go harder, faster, stronger. She didn't need to yell; she had them all completely under her control with hand gestures and a baton, conducting the students like an orchestra.

Melody sidled up closer to him. "Are they all . . . ?"

"Cadets, yes."

"But are they under some kind of spell?"

"No, this is normal. I'm sure we'll be treated to the cadets under a spell soon enough." If Vincent had harboured any doubts about Mrs Howser's usefulness, they evaporated as he took in the sight of her working the cadets into the fine fighting specimens he saw before him. And to think, all he'd had to do was remove Mrs Howser's ego from her soul trapped in the dust bag and she'd become so . . . what was the word he was looking for? Useful.

No, even better, she'd become *reliable*.

Mrs Howser spotted him near the doorway and made her way over. "It's an honour to see you, My Lord," She said with a Brugelish military salute. Her right hand came over her heart and formed a fist, while she nodded her head.

Outranking her, Vincent returned the right-fist-over-heart salute but without nodding his head. "You're settling in well here," he said.

"It's good to be using my talents."

Melody did not greet Mrs Howser, nor did the old witch acknowledge the younger.

Noticing they had an observer, the cadets worked harder. The room filled with the noise of their heavy breathing from lifting their knees higher and climbing faster. Vincent smiled and nodded to the class in appreciation. "I like your *talents*. When will they be ready?"

"They will be ready when you give the word, My Lord."

"And what will you be expecting in return?"

"Nothing, my lord. I live to serve."

A wry grin formed, but he fought it back as he watched one cadet fight off three others in hand-to-hand combat. "I recall a time where you demanded a great deal for your services."

"That was a lifetime ago. I find without ego to cloud judgement, one can achieve so much more." Mrs Howser turned to the battle scene playing out before them and said to the cadet under attack, "Finish them off."

The battle was quick and exacting. The cadet's defeated opponents writhed on the ground in various states of distress.

"Has she broken their bones?" Melody whispered to Vincent.

"So what if she has?" He shot back. If he wanted to be Duke, he needed warriors, not wimps.

"Very good," Mrs Howser said to the triumphant cadet. "Come here."

Puffed but steadying her breath, the cadet obeyed, doing her best to salute and show due deference to her betters, despite her exertions. Sweat trickled down the side of her face, which she wiped away with the back of her hand. This revealed her marked palm.

"What is that tattoo?" He asked Mrs Howser.

Mrs Howser smiled and turned to the cadet. "Introduce yourself and answer his Lordship."

"Raluca Pflüg, My Lord. The marks indicate I've reached level six."

She held her hand out, so Vincent could see what looked like a wheel with eight spokes. On closer inspection, he saw the spokes were not quite perfectly aligned, and some were more recently marked than others. She must have earned each stripe as she rose in the ranks.

"Very good," Mrs Howser nodded to Raluca to take her hand back. "You are ready to move to the advanced group."

"If you deem me worthy," she said.

What an obedient student, Vincent thought.

"If you will come this way, My Lord, Ms Pflüg and Melody," Mrs Howser said, indicating a door at the other end of the training hall, "We shall see how the enhanced students are developing."

*Enhanced* students? He already liked the ones from Raluca's group. All except the moaning trio on the ground, who were only now getting to their feet and saluting, the slackers. The enhanced students were down a hall, up a set of stairs and behind another security door, which Mrs Howser opened with a series of palm and retina scans. Vincent wasn't even aware Brugel had that kind of security.

"Bought it from the Broaku markets," Mrs Howser said, without prompting. [5]

Inside this training hall were twice as many cadets as the last one. This group carried the close-cropped hairstyles of the other cadets, but that was where the similarity ended. These cadets had weapons, built into their bodies. One man who looked barely Vincent's age, had an arm that turned into a whip, slashing at his assailants and tripping them down. The fallen cadets flicked their hands into long knives, slashing chunks off the end of the whip each time it neared them.

Screams filled the air, along with gunfire.

"Is that –?" Melody started.

" –Live ammunition? Yes," Mrs Howser said. "Which is why we need to remain behind this protective glass. Raluca, come here and get a closer look." The old witch took the young cadet by the hand and held it, palm upwards. "You are level seven now. Be careful what you wish for."

Vincent's ears pricked at that last phrase. He didn't want to say anything stupid such as 'what do you mean by that?' but at the same time he couldn't help wondering exactly what Mrs Howser did mean by that.

"The mutating magic is still going, isn't it?" Melody asked. She was standing on the edge of the group, the furthest away from Mrs Howser, yet her words were directed to her former mentor.

Ignoring that they were talking over him, Vincent listened in.

"Of course it is. My separation only placed the spell in hiatus. Now that I'm whole, the magic is fully operational once again."

"But it was just to cause chaos around Ondine and Hamish," Melody said. "Wasn't it?"

"What a waste if that's all it was going to be. Don't you see? Ondine was the stone in the pond, these cadets are the ripples." Mrs Howser waved her hand out in front of her, encompassing the group of mutated cadets. "What we have here is the third wave; the magic feeds their need for obedience and order."

Raluca saluted Mrs Howser. "I am ready." A second set of arms sprouted behind her back, giving her the appearance of Kali, the Hindu goddess of destruction. "I am the end. I am the beginning." Then she charged into the *melée* of cadets and fought all who came near her.

It was impressive viewing. Whips, shields, live bullets, a flamethrower too! Vincent was in heaven. Whoever survived this kind of training would be invincible. The exact kind of soldier he wanted on his team.

The noise of battle rattled the protective glass. Melody took a step back. "We're perfectly safe," Vincent assured her.

"What makes you so sure they're on our side?" Melody didn't have to keep her voice low, not with the cacophony around them. All the same, Vincent only just heard it.

"You make a good point." He turned to Mrs Howser and asked, "Birgit, how do we know the cadets will remain loyal to me?"

"They have sworn an oath, but even so, you shall know their loyalty through their actions." Looking over the crowd, Mrs Howser singled out Raluca, battling four assailants at once, cracking skulls together with her multiple arms. "Cadets, stop now!"

All fell silent. Mrs Howser's smile widened. "Cadet Pflüg, confirm your fidelity to Vincent."

At once, Raluca fell to one knee and spoke with the deepest sincerity. "Lord Vincent is the true born Duke of Brugel. He has my lifelong allegiance, in word and deed."

Another cadet sprang forth to attack Raluca while she knelt. Raluca rolled with the attacker's weight and quickly dispatched her with a resounding thud into the mats, her four arms pinning the other woman down. The other woman's legs turned into octopus tentacles, wrapping around Raluca, ripping and whipping her face and body. With magical speed, Raluca knotted the octopus legs into pretzels.

"Show me your loyalty," Mrs Howser said. "Finish her off."

Another cadet stepped forward. "Please, no! She could be useful."

"Raluca?" Mrs Howser raised her brows.

With a slash of something sharp through the air, Raluca grabbed a sabre from the shield of a nearby cadet and stabbed it through her octopus attacker's heart.

Melody gasped and ran from the room.

Stunned by the savagery, Vincent couldn't fault the effectiveness of Mrs Howser's training.

"Clean the training area, then you may take breakfast." Mrs Howser said. Then she turned to Vincent. "I hope you never have need to question my methods, or my cadets again. They are precious to me and I would hate to lose another one."

## 5

There were noises of family waking up and getting on with work in the pub, but Ondine refused to join them, pulling the covers over her head and chasing a few more minutes of sleep. She'd just had a particularly thrilling dream about spending private time with Hamish. Then Melody had to go and ruin it by astrally projecting into her space.

Wait, Melody was here. Or at least, astrally here. That meant something important must have happened.

"Ondine, I have to be quick," Melody said. "Something important has happened."

"Why isn't Hamish here?" Much to Ondine's embarrassment, this was her first thought. She quickly added. "Are you all right?"

"No, I'm not." Melody said, joining her cold hand to Ondine's warm sleepy one. "I'm at Fort Kluff. Mrs Howser is back in one piece and the mutating magic is worse than ever. I've just seen her training cadets. They're unstoppable. It's the same magic she put on you and Hamish. It didn't end when we took her soul away; it only took a rest. Now she's back and the magic is more powerful than ever."

Images of mutated army trainees filled Ondine's sleepy vision. One of them had four arms, taking on all comers and sending them flying. Then Vincent asked Mrs Howser something about loyalty and the scene played out in all its horrible detail, the four-armed cadet impaling the tentacle-legged one into the mat. "Someone's coming," Melody said. "Tell Hamish. Tell everyone. Anathea won't stand a chance against them!" The young witch pulled her hand away and blinked out of the room.

Sitting up with a jolt, sickness rocked Ondine. The cadets she'd just seen. Were they real or a figment of Melody's fevered imagination? No, they had to be real. Melody had never lied before. Sure, she might have a thing for Vincent, but she was keeping Ondine updated with events, just as she'd promised. And what horrible events they were.

Climbing out of bed and pulling on her dressing gown, Ondine headed to Hamish's room to pass on Melody's message. And to figure out what to do next. Warning Anathea would be high on the list.

"Hamish, wake up," she said, stepping into his room and closing the door behind her.

He did not wake up. The little light that seeped under the curtains made it hard to see, but the lump in the bed didn't move. Hamish must be fast asleep.

"Wake up, Melody just gave me terrible news." She pushed against the lump in the blankets and her hands felt no resistance. "What?" Pulling the covers back, she found Shambles the ferret curled up into a tight ball. Furious, she scooped the ferret up into her hand and dangled him in mid air. He still didn't wake, hanging there limp like a dead animal. Fear overtook her, was he dead? No, his little heart beat against her palm. And he was warm to the touch. And soft and floppy. He had to be alive. But why was he sleeping as a ferret? "Wake up!"

"Whoa! I am awake!" Shambles twisted and turned in her hand and flipped himself onto the bed. "I'm awake, where's the fire?"

A thousand questions fought for attention, but she kept calm and concentrated on the important things first. "Melody just appeared to me in an astral projection. Mrs Howser is training the cadets in Fort Kluff. They're all affected by mutating magic and they're unstoppable."

"I'm listening," Shambles said as he dived under the covers. The fabric bulged and stretched, he groaned a little from the pain, then a moment later, properly human Hamish poked his head out.

Ondine reached for the side lamp and had a good look at her charmingly dishevelled boyfriend. Here they were, alone in his room, and they couldn't take advantage because there was so much mayhem going on all around them.

One day, though. One day.

"Your hair," she said, running her fingers through it. "The grey is gone."

"Thank goodness for that," Hamish let out a huge breath of relief. "I wasnae sure it would work, but remember when I broke my jaw at the palace and when I changed intae meself it was all fixed? I was hoping that would be the same."

"We have bigger things to worry about than you going grey," Ondine said, remembering the bigger picture just in time.

"We must tell Auntie Col about the cadets and work out what to do."

"Between you and me, best let her sleep a little longer, she was into the lunatic soup last night." [1]

"I was not," a voice said from the doorway. They looked up to see Auntie Col, dressed and ready for a new day. "It was a drop of plütz with dessert to calm my nerves. Now, what's this about Mrs Howser's magic?"

They quickly relayed the news, Ondine remembering more details with the second telling.

"This can't be good," Old Col said after a moment of turning things over in her mind. "It sounds like Mrs Howser's magic is stronger than ever. If she's still using the two of you to set off the mutating magic, more and more people keep catching it. Perhaps it would be best if Hamish was a ferret as much as possible, to stop you kicking off a new wave of magic?"

"It's not that bad, is it?" Ondine said.

"We need to find a way to stop it," Hamish said.

Ondine and Col said together, "Exactly."

---

SLEEP-GLUE KEPT Vincent's eyes shut as he slump-rolled over in bed, wondering what vengeful deity he'd offended to feel so hideous this morning. It was the morning, right? Grey light filtered through his closed lids. There were morning-type noises funnelling down his ear, like a coffee machine and somebody stacking crockery. The chug and thrum of the traffic outside crept into the room. Somebody was walking around; their footsteps growing louder as they came closer.

A radio blasted out good cheer.

As long as he kept his eyes shut, he could pretend the world didn't exist. It wasn't that he had a hangover. He knew how to hold his plütz.

It wasn't bad food eating away the lining of his stomach either. It was that horrible, inner-nag of a conscience, kicking him from inside his head. He thought he'd stomped on that voice years ago, yet here it was, telling him how stupid he was.

Worthless.

He wasn't worthless, he reminded his brain. He was the rightful Duke of Brugel. Mrs Howser's cadets at Fort Kluff would provide the muscle; the Balakhans would provide the money.

"Good morning, *affiance*." A woman kissed him on the forehead.

His eyes snapped open. He was in a hotel room. It took a few shakes of his brain cells to remember the hotel was in Slaegal. He'd come back here after visiting Fort Kluff. He was awake now and looking around him in horror. The bed sheets were covered in orange smears, as if someone had washed half the bed in fruit juice. Memories flooded him. Last night, he'd met with the Balakhans in Norange again. Last night he'd drunk plütz again.

"Look at you!" The woman – it was Ruslana – said, "relax, you idiot, nothing happened. But you fell asleep before you could be a gentleman and offer to sleep on the sofa." She said the last thing with a shrug, which made Vincent look at the sofa and wince. Made of white leather, it would have been a vibrant citrus colour if she'd slept on that. He reached for his dressing gown and shrugged out of bed.

"I called for breakfast. It came a couple minutes ago," she said, lifting a silver lid off a plate.

Tentatively, Vincent walked to the table and sat opposite Ruslana Balakhan, his fake-tan fiancé.

"Relax." There was that word she liked to use. "You're not my type."

Spearing his bacon, he dared to ask, "What is your type?" He shoved it into his mouth and crunched down.

She cast a meaningful look at his groin and gave a conspiratorial grin. "You. Not my type."

Vincent couldn't help smiling. Relief, yes, that was the emotion coursing through him. He only had to sleep beside an Oompa loompa, not with one. "Then we're going to get along great."

"I know what you're thinking," she said. "Why bother with the marriage if it's of no use? Yes?"

He needed more vitamin bacon. "That did cross my mind."

"Because it will please Daddy. He wants the best for me. As far as he can tell, you are the best for me. And for him. And it will not be forever. I can spare a few years to make Daddy happy."

He topped up his coffee. "Does he know about your . . . *type?*"

"Of course. But he also thinks I . . ." she made quotation marks in the air with her fingers, "Haven't met the right man yet."

Fragments from the night before came back. He, Melody, Babak and Ruslana had signed papers and agreements and sealed the deal with plütz. There had been singing at some point. It was all a bit of a blur. Melody had been quieter than usual. He didn't blame her. The scenes at Fort Kluff had been unsettling but necessary.

"We need some ground rules," He said as the coffee kicked in.

"I like rules. Thank you for signing the pre-nuptial agreement."

That must have been one of the documents he'd put his name to during the evening, signing his family name for the promise of a future.

"Daddy says most of the money will flow when there are grandchildren. He thinks becoming a mother will be good for me."

That brought a chunk of bacon flying up Vincent's throat. He swallowed it down, hard. It was one thing to marry for mercenary reasons, but quite another to bring children into it.

"Good. You are listening," she said. "I am not having children. Not to you or anyone."

"We don't have to talk about that. I'm sure we'll find some way to work around it later."

"You are not listening!" She banged the table with her fist. "This," she pointed to her stomach, "is not for getting babies. Full stop!"

Vincent retreated into sarcasm. "Oh my sweet. Our first tiff. However will we go on?"

A knock came at the door. Ruslana crossed her arms over her chest and refused to get it. Vincent went to the door.

"Good morning My Lord." It was Melody, making nice with a forced smile. "I trust you slept well. Here are your newspapers and schedule for the day. If you need anything, I shall be in the car."

"Thank you Melody," he said. "I will be right down in a minute." [2]

"I like her," Ruslana said after Vincent closed the door. "When Daddy's money starts to flow, you'll be able to pay her."

When her father's money began to flow, he'd be able to do a whole lot of things.

"He really likes you," Ruslana said. "If you hadn't come along, he probably would have bought another football team. And I so detest all that . . . *testosterone*."

"Good morning beautiful children!" A voice boomed at the door.

Babak came strolling in, sucking all the oxygen from the room simply by being in it.

Melody came trotting along in his wake. "He borrowed my key card."

Interesting. Melody must have had that key card earlier, yet she'd knocked.

"You are going to love this," Babak said as he handed a sheaf of papers to Vincent. No sign of any embarrassment on his part of walking right in to his future-son-in-law's hotel room. "This, my son, is how you win your crown back. Now, very important. Make sure your hand stays blue. Paint it. Colour it. Get a tattoo if you have to, but keep it blue."

He'd submerge his whole body in printer's ink for the amount of money Babak was offering.

Bakak said, "I have found a way to get your Aunt Anathea out of the picture, in a way that everyone benefits."

"She won't get hurt?" Vincent's mind darted back to Mrs Howser's deadly cadets, equal parts impressed with their brilliance and terrified of their power.

Babak looked at Vincent as if he were something stuck on his shoe. "It will only hurt if she does the wrong thing." He rubbed his hands together. "Now, I hope you have terrible taste in music, it's time to put on a show."

---

ONDINE, Hamish and Old Col were in a constant state of worry about what Vincent and Mrs Howser were plotting, and doing their best not to let Ma and Da know they were worried about national affairs and royal intrigue. Because Ma had stated they were to have nothing more to do with Brugel's royal family, and Ondine didn't want her to know they'd ignored that edict.

Fortunately for Ondine, something else was happening in the pub to divert everyone's attentions. The music executive who had liked what she'd heard and seen in Cybelle and Margi several nights ago, was now encouraging them to enter BrugelMelody, which, if they won, would see them compete at PopEuroTube in May. [3]

All attention in the pub had since turned to music and performances and winning competitions, allowing Ondine, Old Col and Hamish to worry and fret about the nation's problems in private.

On this particular morning, they privately fretted while walking to the fresh produce market to buying food for their customers. For the next hour or so, Ondine and Hamish, along with Henrik and Cybelle, bought seasonal fruit and vegetables, hustling and haggling their way through the rows of traders. Spicy aromas assailed them at one market; stinking fish assaulted their senses in the next. At the end of one particularly stenchsome row, Ondine nudged Hamish out in to the fresh air, which just happened to be near a donut van. [4]

These were especially good donuts because they weren't always cooked right through, so the centre could be lush and gooey. For an extra schlip, you could have hot jam in the centre. Ondine always said yes because she was in love with the way they slammed the donuts onto the nose of a model dolphin to inject the jam in.

Hamish gave her a weird look. "Ye going tae eat that?"

"I bought plenty to share." She offered him one. "Watch out for the lava in the middle."

Screwing up his face, he took the tiniest bite then grimaced. "Pure carbs are nae good fer me."

"I know you can't eat sugar when you're . . ." she dropped her voice, "a ferret. But when you're you, you can, right?"

"Best not, just in case, eh?"

"Suit yourself," she shrugged then scoffed it. The heat burned her throat, pricking tears in her eyes. The heat moved to her tummy and radiated warmth as she licked her sugar-encrusted fingers, then wiped them on her coat. Bliss.

"Sign the petition?" A young woman about Ondine's age stepped in front of them with a clipboard and a pen. Behind her was a makeshift stall with more volunteers surrounded by signs and posters calling for the restoration of Lord Vincent's inheritance. Oh they were clever, standing near the donut van. A captive market or what?

Looking at the clipboard, Ondine saw pages and pages filled with signatures.

Hamish asked, "What's all this about?"

The volunteer brightened and said, "Lord Vincent should be Duke. We're collecting signatures to take to the Duchess and the Dentate, to show how much support Vincent has for his claim."

"But I thought everyone *loaved* Anathea?" Hamish said.

"Oh we do!" the woman said. "We think she's wonderful. But it should go to Vincent. We've collected three thousand signatures already. Sign here."

"Uh, I really don't get involved in politics," Ondine said.

"Yes you do." Somebody from the pro-Vincent team came over. "I saw you at the Snow Maze last year, you were there."

Then he noticed Hamish and said, "and he was there, you were both up on the stage in the end." [5]

"Mistaken identity," Hamish said, grabbing Ondine's hand and dragging her away.

When they were safely beyond reach of Team Vincent, Ondine said,

"They're so organised already. It's only been a couple months since Anathea was officially sworn in."

"Aye, but he's wanted this for years. Now he's stepping up the campaign. Can't let Anathea get too settled, people might start liking her too much."

# 6

Weeks of worry passed for Ondine. The spring equinox had come and gone, but winter refused to let go. Grey skies above only added to her gloomy mood. Hamish had taken to sleeping as a ferret in order to stay young, which meant even less time to sneak in cuddles and kisses with his human self.

Her older sister's songs were getting frequent airplay on the radio, which drew the crowds to the *Duke and Ferret* hotel, making Ondine work even harder and wash even more dishes than before.

Which meant she had no time to sneak off and warn Duchess Anathea about what Vincent was up to. Instead, she wrote letters. Old fashioned letters that required proper handwriting, an envelope and a stamp. [1]

Each letter sent earned Ondine no reply, which added to her already growing list of worries, which she had to squeeze in between her regular classes at school and her increasing workload at home.

Thankfully, they had a rare night off with nobody for dinner and no guests staying overnight. It was a Monday night, and for the first time in Ondine's memory, her entire family were out together. They were at VTV6 studios, located in the foothills of Mt Verka Serduchka, to the east of Venzelemma. [2]

The air hummed with nervous tension as the television crews moved cameras into positions and checked lighting and sound levels. All the production people wore headphones with microphones attached. Turning to the very back of the studio, Ondine could see a row of people sitting behind a glass wall, the lights of an enormous control panel reflected on their concentrating faces.

Sitting – but mostly fidgeting – along a row of flip-down seating sat Ma and Da, looking proud and incredibly nervous. Next to them sat Henrik and Thomas, along with Thomas' parents and his younger brother Alexei. Ondine and Hamish sat on the other end of the row. Old Col had warned Ondine not to flirt or canoodle outrageously with Hamish in public, lest their 'make other people's wishes come true' magic got out of hand.

She'd also put a dampening field around Hamish to make sure Ondine's emotions didn't run wild. Even though Ondine knew she loved Hamish with all her heart, she didn't have the slightest inclination to sneak off somewhere privately with him. Drat that witchy great auntie of hers for having such strong magic.

"To think we paid full price for these seats, when we're only using the edge of them," Da said.

Margi and Cybelle were somewhere backstage, waiting to perform, along with several other acts representing the length and breadth of Brugel's musical talent. Being a proud nation, the rules of BrugelMelody stipulated that the music, lyrics and performers all had to come from citizens of Brugel, or at least permanent residents, to compete. [3]

A woman with auburn hair so shiny you could see the audience reflected in it, took to the stage. "Good evening ladies and gentlemen, I am your warm-up host, Marta Pompeii. Tonight's search for Brugel's next PopEuroTube star will be recorded completely live, which in real terms means it will be broadcast later tonight after editing out the mistakes and slotting in the adverts. We would not be able to put on such a wonderful show without you, the audience. So can I have your very best round of applause when I say, "go", so that we can record it. Okay, go!"

Everyone clapped, cheered, whistled and stamped their feet, shaking the studio.

"Thank you thank you. One more time to make sure we get it, and go!"

It didn't seem possible but the audience was even louder.

Ondine's hands smarted from slapping them together.

"Better keep yer powder dry for yer sisters," Hamish said.

Marta raised her hands, "OK, everyone, great job. Now please get ready to welcome your host to this evening, Me! Yes, I'm so cheap I do my own warm-up act!"

Marta paused and the audience gave a smattering of laughter.

"Tonight is BrugelMelody, our judges and voters at home will be sending Brugel's next act to PopEuroTube in May!" Another pause for applause. Ondine wasn't sure how much longer her flayed palms could take this.

"In order to get there the fairest way possible tonight, we have three judges, all experts in the field of performance, composition and technique. They will score each act, and in the case of a tie we'll call on the services of a mystery judge!"

The studio lights shone on the three judges. One extra chair sat further along, with its back to the audience. From the side of the chair, a hand came out and waved.

Ondine gasped. The waving hand had a familiar blue stain to it. "Did you see that?" She nudged Hamish.

"Aye. D'ye think it's him?"

"I'd bet my last fried cheeseball on it." That Vincent, he was getting into everything. Burrowing his way into Brugel like a botfly. [4] Meanwhile, where was Anathea? She should be here, so the people could see her and love her.

The music contest, when it eventually started, was pretty awesome. Nerves writhed in Ondine's belly as the first act finished their song. Then the next.

Every performance sounded better than the last.

*Can we have one dud, just so Margi and Belle have a better shot at winning this?*

Ondine's wish was granted with the next group. Five lads in white boiler suits danced so hard they couldn't carry their notes properly. Plus their choreography looked five years out of date. [5]

*"Give me the code to your heart and I will give you mine.*

*Girl you're so fine,*

*You're always on my mind."*

"They're so bad they could win it," Hamish teased.

Ondine shuddered. Hamish lifted the armrest that formed a barrier between them and pulled her in for a snuggle. She used his shoulder to block sound in one ear, then snuck her hand under her long hair to block the other ear.

Much better. The crowd damned the boiler-suited boys with polite applause when the song finished.

The next group was a proper rock outfit with two massive drum kits, three violins, a cello, three guitars and a robust woman out the front on vocals. [6]

She didn't merely belt out a song, she gave them an *anthem*.

A flag-waving, chest-thumping, patriotic-as-Brugeldirt rallying cry.

The chorus was so memorable that when they came to it a second time, people stood up and joined in.

*If we go then we go.*

*If we fight, then we fight,*

*If it's the end of the world my friend, let it be tonight.*

Jupiter's Moons, Margi and Belle were sunk and they were up next. Ondine forgot to breathe as her sisters took their respective places behind the microphone and piano. They looked like superstars; their hair perfect, their makeup glamorous but not overdone, their outfits timeless.

"We've seen some incredible acts tonight," Marta Pompeii said as she walked out in front of Margi and Belle. "Remember, voting will open in ten minutes, and you can only vote once. Don't go away, we're going to take a quick word from our sponsors and be right back." [7]

Ondine wished she could dash home and make a phone call. Then she wished she could be sick. Did they have to drag things out so much?

"It's all right dear," Ma leaned over to reassure her. "Auntie Col is voting for us."

But as much as Ondine adored her great-aunt, who had been there for her through many adventures in the past year, how would one vote make a difference?

"She's made sure all her Coven buddies are watching and voting as well," Ma said, in answer to Ondine's thoughts. Relief rolled over Ondine. Then, a fresh burst of panic. "What about –"

"– The phone lines? If a witch can't get through, nobody can."

OK, her mother's reassurances would have to do for now. Hamish squeezed her hand for luck as Marta Pompeii started talking again.

"Welcome back to BrugelMelody. It's been an insanely great show tonight, but we have more to come. And now, ladies and gentlemen, the song you have all heard and fallen in love with already. It's Margibelle with *You Are My Star!*"

The applause was so intense it smacked Ondine inside her head. As one, the crowd was on its feet.

"Margibelle?" Ondine mouthed to her parents.

Ma shrugged and shouted back, "It's better than Cybguerite."

Ondine could hardly breathe as the audience fell silent. Cybelle caressed the keys to start the song.

How could her sisters look so relaxed when Ondine couldn't breathe for the knots in her belly?

But, oh what beautiful music her sisters made! Margi's voice wrapped the audience in a collective hug. The crowd swayed and moved as one, then started clapping and stamping their feet as the song reached the bridge. When Margi hit the first big note of the chorus, the crowd screamed with delight. They knew the words and sang along.

Tears verily *spritzed* from Ondine. Hamish wiped his cheek. An unspoken bond united the audience, Cybelle, Marguerite and the nation itself.

Magic. It had to be magic. How else to explain the overwhelming sense of love in the studio?

*Please win, please win, please win!*

Margi sang true. Her voice united everyone as they moved from the verse into the coda with its incredible endnote.

*Get the note, get the note.*

Not a flicker of worry on Margi's face, not a wobble in her voice as she belted it out.

A silent beat as the audience let the song finish, before they erupted in delight. The noise bounced inside Ondine's chest as she let out her long held-in breath. Had she breathed at all during the song?

"They did it!" Hamish grabbed Ondine in a massive hug and lifted her off the ground. Ma and Da hugged and kissed each other and grinned and cried. Both of them. Down the line, Thomas and Henrik chest-bumped and jumped up and down and waved to their beloveds on stage. Thomas stuck his fingers in his mouth for an ear-splitting whistle.

The next ten minutes were going to be the longest in Ondine's life as they waited for viewers at home to cast their votes. Marta came back on stage and held up her palms to calm the audience down. She was enjoying herself, as if the applause was for her.

"Remember. Viewers' votes will be worth fifty percent, and the jury votes will be worth the other fifty percent. You have nine minutes left to vote."

"'Scuse I." Henrik nudged past them, Thomas in close pursuit.

Ondine climbed on her seat to make room for them. They had their 'visitor' passes clearly visible. "Give them our love," Ma cried as they headed off towards the green rooms.

What now?

Ondine was on such a high she didn't know what she'd do if Margi and Cybelle – *Margibelle* – didn't win. Leaning into Hamish, she said, "I think I'm going to be sick."

"Ye need fresh air, lass."

"Tell you what," Da handed him a lanyard with a spare house key. "Why don't you both go home and relax. There's nothing more we can do now except wait. We won't know the outcome for hours."

Ondine shook her head. "Hours? But the voting ends soon."

Da gave her a wink. "Yes, but remember they said it would be delayed so they could put the ads in and all that. Proper voting might not start for another hour. This way, you have time to get home and get on the phone."

A thrill charged through Ondine at the thought she could actually do something productive to help her sisters.

"Aye, I'll keep the pub safe till ye get back." Hamish looped the key around his neck and ushered Ondine towards the exit.

The cool evening air slapped Ondine's cheeks. "I'm not cut out for this. It's too intense!" Keeping her breathing even, her pulse finally stabilised. The nausea that had earlier threatened to swamp her eased away. Chills moved in and she shivered involuntarily. "If I'm this nervous now, what will I be like if they actually make it to PopEuroTube?"

With a chuckle, Hamish squished her sideways and kissed her on the cheek. "Ye'll be a mess."

"Aww. Have I told you lately how wonderful you are?"

"Aye." He tilted her face and properly kissed her on the lips. "And I'll never get tired of hearing it."

Just as they were about to walk away from the studios to catch the next train home, Lord Vincent came around the corner.

All three stopped and stared at each other.

*Hurk*, went Ondine's stomach. Luckily nothing but air flew out, although in hindsight she wouldn't have minded throwing up on him. A moment's hesitation, then Vincent confidently smiled. "Ondine, Hamish, how lovely to see you both. How have you been?"

Nothing came to Ondine, as she looked around to make sure there were no cameras or other people nearby. It wouldn't do to have witnesses if this ended badly.

"Aye, Vincent, yer the secret judge then?"

He winked. Actually *winked*, as if they were old chums in some kind of prank together. "If I told you, it wouldn't be a secret, would it?"

"Shouldn't you be back in there, judging or something?" Ondine said, massively impressed with how sensible she sounded considering the emotions tumbling inside her. Vincent was a slimy toad of a person who had caused her nearly a year's worth of strife. This was as polite as she could possibly be.

Vincent kept his gaze locked with Ondine's. "The public voting will be close. Very close. It might come down to the wire. It *may* come down to my vote deciding who goes to PopEuroTube and who misses out."

"Why are ye talking tae us then, lad?"

He sighed. "Time was, I could order you to call me 'My Lord' and you'd have to. Now I must endure your Scottish insults. You might not believe it, but I have matured. I harbour no ill feeling towards either of you, or your family. Everything I do now is for the good of Brugel, not myself. It's ironic, don't you think, that I have lost my title and yet become a more responsible man?"

He really expected them to believe that? Ondine stilled her eyes so they wouldn't roll in contempt. She cast a look to Hamish to see if he believed any of this either.

"I deserve your derision," Vincent said. "And your pity, if you have any. There is no easy way to build up to this so I may as well straight-out ask. I need your help."

*Jolt!* Ondine had to take a step backwards to steady against the shock. "You –?" she started

"– Need our help?" Hamish finished.

"Yes," Vincent confirmed.

Stunned, Ondine shook her head. "Saturn's rings! Why would I help you?"

Palms forward in surrender, Vincent said, "For the good of Brugel."

"Fer the good of yerself ye mean," Hamish said.

"Let's not be churlish. Ondine, you and Hamish helped my Aunt Anathea become loved and popular. I saw what you did and despite having scant resources, you managed to make my batty auntie respectable to the majority of people. Now I find I'm in need of something similar."

The images of the cadets at Fort Kluff, which Melody had terrified her with via astral projection, chilled Ondine more than the cold evening air. Not that she could say anything right now, because Vincent would then know Melody had blabbed.

Hamish scoffed. "Ye want to bump yer auntie off and ye want everyone to love ye while ye do it?"

*Careful*, she wanted to say to her beloved.

"Nothing of the sort. I truly believe Anathea is good for Brugel. She's had a steadying influence on the nation, and the public has a fondness for her, which would have seemed unfathomable only a year ago. I have absolutely no intention of curtailing her reign either."

He had to be lying so she'd lie right back. "I've got news for you Vincent. We can't make people's dreams come true any more. Look, I'll prove it." She kissed Hamish squarely on the mouth and it felt . . . weird! Not exactly wrong, but the zings and rushes of blood she normally felt were curiously absent. Pulling away, she checked the traffic. No double sets of green lights. The weather didn't become warmer. The people walking on the other side of the street were not suddenly drinking hot chocolate. Vincent was still standing in front of them, and he didn't have the smug expression of someone who had everything he wanted.

No magic.

Wow, Auntie Col's dampening spell must be doing double-time.

"Told you," she said, needing to appear triumphant while her belly swooped with fear. Old Col's extra spell was working, but what if it kept on working and she and Hamish lost their love for each other? That would be terrible! "I don't want to get involved in political intrigues any more, I just want to be normal and boring."

"Your sisters don't," Vincent said.

His words were like an arrow to her heart. If Ondine didn't help him, would he vote Margibelle down? Just because he could?

"But how could I help you?" Ondine asked.

"Oh goodness," Vincent's face brightened, "you came around much faster than I thought."

"No!" Ondine spat the word out like bad food. "I didn't mean how *can* I help, I mean, *how*, exactly? Logistically and all that, because we don't have magic any more."

"The irony is, I don't actually need magic."

"No?"

"No. What I need is a miracle."

Morbid curiosity took hold. As much as Ondine didn't want to help Lord Vincent, she couldn't stop wondering exactly what he needed their help for. Plus, he held Margi and Belle's future in his palm. Competing in PopEuroTube was Margi and Cybelle's dream. Could Ondine really stand in their way because of her antagonism towards Vincent?

Against her better judgement, she found herself saying, "Show me what you need."

$$7$$

Ondine's muscles felt as weak as failed soufflé as Lord Vincent guided her and Hamish back into the studios. Knowing all she knew about Vincent, she must be insane or have some kind of death wish to be helping him. The second she thought about turning around and running out of there, an image of her sisters shone brightly in her mind. If she walked out on Vincent, she'd be walking out on Margibelle too.

Vincent led them through a rabbit warren of narrow corridors until they arrived at his private dressing room. "Brace yourselves. This is messy."

He opened the door. Ondine's jaw dropped as there, in front of a mirror sat the *orangest* looking woman she had ever seen. Who was this citrus creature? On the sofa, sitting behind her, sat Melody with her face in her hands, quietly weeping.

With a firm 'snick', Vincent closed the door on the five of them. "You see my problem now?"

Turmoil churned Ondine's stomach. She moved to the couch and gave Melody a hug. It was good to see her, and if there was any chance she could get Melody alone, she might be able to get her away from Vincent.

"I failed," Melody said.

Ondine hugged her friend and whispered low, "You're doing great. We'll get you out of here."

Vincent cleared his throat. "This is my fiancé Ruslana Balakhan."

Ondine looked at the woman whose skin bore a striking resemblance to a glass of breakfast juice.

Vincent nodded and made something of a grimace. "She needs to look the part of a proper Brugel bride-to-be."

"I see what ye mean," Hamish said, casting a worried grimace towards Vincent and then Ondine.

Ondine had heard the name Balakhan from somewhere. Melody murmured, "Her father owns a football club." A twig figuratively snapped in her head as Ondine made the connections; Lord Vincent with all those cadets, plus the Balakhan money, would be unstoppable.

With Melody here in the room, they already had a powerful witch. Yet she obviously hadn't been able to help transform Ruslana into something presentable. Vincent was right, they'd need more than mere magic to convince the people of Brugel to accept Ruslana as their next Duchess.

"I don't mean to be rude, but what have you done to your face?" Ondine asked. [1]

Ruslana looked up. "My face is my fortune."

The twig snapped again. Ondine – and Melody – knew magic could only work if the magic-ee willingly went along with it. Or deep down believed it to be true. Free will always won out against magic. How could they change Ruslana if she wasn't willing?

Hamish piped up. "At Margi's weddin' ye all looked like royalty, so ye did."

"My sisters!" Ondine suddenly remembered they would be in their dressing room. And they'd looked stunning on stage. Even better than on the day of Margi's wedding. They must have had help. "I'll be right back."

With that, she darted out of Vincent's dressing room and charged towards the performers' green rooms. Excellent! There was Margi and Belle, and Thomas and Henrik. She rushed forward and hugged them all. "You were perfect tonight. Beyond amazing!"

"I'm so nervous I could puke for Brugel," Cybelle said.

Seeing their faces, knowing how much they wanted this, galvanised Ondine's decision. She'd already agreed to help the hideous Vincent, if it meant her sisters' dreams came true. Yes, it was cheating, but if she didn't do it, Vincent could just as easily vote her sisters down out of spite. It didn't make it right, but she'd have to live with it. The sooner she put this incident behind her, the better. The make-up lady they'd hired for the wedding was in her sisters' change room, in her familiar pleather pants and jacket. Excellent. [2]

"You were great, but I need to borrow her for a bit. S'cuse me," Ondine grabbed the woman's pleather-clad arm and said, "Your country needs you."

Her sisters, brother-in-law and brother-in-law-to-be all shouted at once,

"What's going on?"

"Steady on."

"What?"

"Ondi, what's the –"

"Sorry everyone," Ondine said as she guided the confused make-up lady out of the dressing room. "State secret." With that, she bundled the woman down the corridor towards Lord Vincent's dressing room.

"Thank you for coming along. You can't tell anyone about this, OK?"

"Where are you taking me?"

"You'll see soon enough. It's all above board, nothing dangerous, but you'll need every skill you possess . . . and maybe even some you don't."

The woman pulled up. "Is this dangerous?"

"Oh, not in the least," Ondine grabbed her arm again and marched her down the corridor, then stopped and said to her, "Although you might end up traumatised."

Bursting in to Lord Vincent's room, Ondine found everyone where she'd left them. Melody, on the couch, hiding behind a curtain of hair. Vincent pacing the room. Hamish leaning against the wall. Ruslana sitting in front of the mirror, pressing on a set of false eyelashes.

"Everything is going to be OK," Ondine said, then turned to the make-up lady and lowered her voice. "I'm sorry, I've forgotten your name."

"Charlene," she said.

"OK." Ondine quickly made introductions, then guided Charlene towards Ruslana. The faster she did this, the less time she'd have to acknowledge how much she was helping her sworn enemy. "This er . . . lovely . . . young woman is engaged to Lord Vincent. Please do your very best to make her look like a future Duchess of Brugel."

With a sideways tilt of her head, Charlene took in Ruslana and said, "I'm not used to working with such a ... colourful canvas."

Ruslana ignored her, turned to the light-studded mirror and brushed a layer of glitter across her décolletage.

Charlene took a few steps towards Ruslana and narrowed her eyes, then lifted her hair in places and studied her features. "I'm going to need help. I don't suppose anyone in here is a witch?"

With a sigh, Melody raised her hand. "I've tried, but she's too wilful for the magic to work."

"Let's start with the face, shall we?" Charlene picked up a swab. "We'll get the layers off first and see what we have to work with."

"You're not touching my face!"

"Wait a minute," Ondine beamed at her own cleverness. "Ruslana might be fighting the magic, but Charlene's the one who needs it. Melody, if you cast a spell on Charlene, it won't matter how much Ruslana complains or tries to fight it, right?"

Hamish grabbed her in a hug and kissed her cheek. "Have I mentioned lately how clever ye are, lass?"

Ondine glowed from the compliment.

Sizing up the situation, Vincent rubbed his chin in thought. "Melody, can you do it?"

"Of course I can do it. Take a look?"

While they'd been asking Melody to perform, she was already on it. Buzzing vibrations and sprinkles of green light infused the room. Charlene worked at mega-magical speed, spinning Ruslana around in her chair, dabbing cotton pads into industrial strength make-up remover and scraping off layers of *slap* from Ruslana's face. As each stripe of bronzed orange came away, they caught a glimpse of Ruslana's pinked skin underneath.

"There's a real woman under there after all," Vincent said.

Then Charlene's hands flew through Ruslana's hair, denuding the mass of synthetic extensions from the real tresses.

"Stop it!" Ruslana slapped at Charlene's hands. "I look like I crawled out a crypt!"

"Don't stop now, whatever you do," Vincent said.

In mere seconds, the hair extensions were a skanky pile on the floor.

"Is it real hair?" Ondine leaned forward and massaged the fibres between her fingers. "It's so dry." Then she sniffed it and wished she hadn't. "Smells worse than you, Hamish, when you're a ferret."

He inhaled the piece Ondine offered. "Urgh! That's mockit!"

Meanwhile, Charlene kept up her pace. Ruslana's face turned clean and shiny pink, her hair stripped of extensions and back to its natural length.

Ondine held her breath as she watched Melody, still sitting on the couch, still hiding behind her curtain of hair, muttering incantations to bind Charlene to the swirls of magic so she could get the job done.

"Moisturiser," Charlene said, finding a tub of the stuff on the bench beneath the mirror. She slathered it all over Ruslana, turning her white. Then she wiped most of it off again and the last smears of mascara released their hold. "Let's go for a more natural look, eh?" Charlene dabbed foundation on Ruslana's jaw, then her hands vanished into a blur of activity as she applied fresh make-up.

Ruslana tried to climb out of the chair. Lord Vincent put his hands on her shoulders and pressed her down. "Sit."

More magic swirls and activity continued until a triumphant "Done!" from Charlene, as she stood back to admire her work.

"I'm invisible," Ruslana said.

Vincent looked at his fiancé in the mirror and shook his head, his words croaking with heartfelt emotion. "You look beautiful."

Melody slumped on the sofa.

Ondine gave her a hug. "You're doing great. I know you're exhausted, but please keep going. We're nearly there."

"Stage two, the hair." Charlene's hands worked her magic – or more precisely, Melody's Magic – styling Ruslana's 'do' into a regal helmet of coiffidly curled perfection.

"You turned me into my mother," she grumbled.

"Exactly," Vincent said. "Keep going my good woman. Melody, you have my deepest gratitude."

"I know," Melody said with a sigh.

Although fascinated with the Charlene's skills, Ondine noticed the lingering sadness in her friend. "Oh Melody!" Keeping her voice incredibly low so that nobody else would hear, Ondine said, "You love him, don't you?"

With a dramatic sniff, Melody nodded and then wiped at her face, tugging her hair away in the process. Her eyes were red and puffy. "I'm such an idiot."

"You poor, poor thing." Ondine gave her another hug. "And you're not an idiot. You're amazing."

Somebody rapped on the door. A stage assistant walked in before anyone could say, "Don't come in!" [3]

"Five minutes until you and Ruslana are needed on stage, Sir," he said to Vincent.

"We'll be right there in a minute," Vincent said, ushering the man out and closing the door behind them. Looking to Charlene and then to Melody, he said, "Hurry up."

"I'm using all the magic I have," Melody said.

"Then use more."

Hadn't he heard her? What did he want, the last breath in her lungs? Looking at her rapidly exhausting friend, Ondine wondered if Melody might end up giving him exactly that.

"Nearly there," Charlene's hands were utter blurs as she finished Ruslana's makeup. "Do you have any better clothes?"

"What's wrong with my clothes?" Ruslana could have broken the mirror with her daggered look.

Another quick double-knock and the stage assistant came straight back in. "Four minutes."

Vincent tisked and said, "Yes, yes, I said I'd be there."

"It's just that it takes two minutes to walk from here to the stage. Let's get the microphones hooked up." The assistant walked over to Vincent and put his hand up the back of his shirt to connect a tiny microphone at the front of his lapel.

"Done!" The make-up lady turned the chair around so everyone could see Ruslana.

The stage assistant clipped a transmitter block on the back of Vincent's belt. "Can you say 'testing one two three,' please?"

"You're beautiful!" Vincent said, ignoring the stage assistant.

Not that Ondine was in the habit of agreeing with Lord Vincent, but Ruslana did look stunning.

"I'll be in the car," Melody said as she hauled herself off the couch and walked out.

"We really have to go, Sir, it's –" the stage assistant caught sight of Ruslana and became stutteringly lost for words.

Vincent beamed. "Come, Ruslana, it's time for Brugelers to meet their future Duchess."

Ondine glanced at him, silently reminding them of their deal. He made a slow blink, as if to say "I know" as he left the room.

Would he stick to his word? Ondine didn't trust him as far as she could throw a cheese ball.

---

EERIE QUIET GREETED Ondine and Hamish as they returned to the empty pub. In the past, there was always some kind of "goings-on" going on. Guests in the hotel, Chef preparing food, and the general noise of noisy people, even in their sleep. They checked the premises to make sure everything was where it should be and that thieves hadn't taken advantage of their absence. But then, according to the television promotions, everyone would be watching BrugelMelody. That had to include thieves too? [4]

"Put the telly on and let's find out who wins, eh lass?"

"Good idea." It would provide noise so they wouldn't have to talk. Because talking would invariably lead to a discussion about Lord Vincent, and whether or not they should have helped him. It hadn't felt right at the time, and now Ondine felt nothing but remorse. She kept herself busy making hot chocolates, took a deep breath, fixed a smile in place and joined Hamish on the couch. [5]

They'd tuned in to find Marta Pompeii announcing the top five finalists. Battlefront's *Anthem* made it to the top five, as did the boy band in boiler suits that Ondine was sure would disappear without a trace.

"Vincent had better come good on his promise," she said. Oh dear, she'd said it out loud.

"Aye," was all Hamish said.

"I did the right thing, didn't I? I mean, I didn't really have a choice."

"Aye," he said, giving her a rub on the shoulder. But no bone-melting kisses. Did that mean Old Col's anti-magic magic was still working, or was Hamish upset with her?

A rock outfit made it to the top five. As did the krumpers on skateboards. One place left, Ondine forgot how to breathe. Nerves stretched tighter than a slingshot, Ondine held her breath until she nearly passed out. Watching this at home was killing her.

"Margibelle!" Marta finally announced. Ondine and Hamish cheered at the screen and hugged each other, spilling their drinks and not caring. They hugged and kissed and bounced in their seats. A top five finish! Amazing! Maybe they really could win this?

Marta, all white of teeth and bouffant of hair, stood in front of the five acts. There, on the telly, were her sisters known as Margibelle, standing amongst the winners, smiling and waving at the crowd.

"Ladies and gentlemen and special guests," the Marta said, "These are our top five finalists!" She paused to allow the audience to go crazy for a while. "This is truly an historical night. In the first time ever at BrugelMelody, we have a three-way tie for first place!"

Ondine choked. Hamish patted her on the back to help her recover.

"As much as we'd like, we cannot send our top three acts to PopEuroTube. Although the quality was so high this year, it would be a crime if Slaegal and Craviç didn't immediately grab the runners up to represent them. This of course means we'll need to call in our mystery judge to make the final decision of who will represent Brugel at the PopEuroTube Song Contest."

The crowd went wild. Ondine and Hamish held each other, afraid to let go. On the telly, the curtains to the side parted, to reveal Lord Vincent, waving his blue hand to the crowd, a stunning Ruslana by his side, every millimetre the future Duchess of Brugel.

The presenter beamed and asked Vincent if he'd made his decision.

"I have," he said, then smiled again.

"Then may we have the result please?"

Would Vincent stick to his side of the bargain?

Ondine couldn't breathe for nerves. Margibelle had to win. They simply had to.

**8**

———

Pain lanced Ondine's chest as she waited for the result of Lord Vincent's casting vote. He had to come good on his promise.

"We have a three-way tie." Marta said, hamming it up for the audience. "Would you like to know who our three winners are?"

The crowd went insane. Ondine's head was going to explode from the tension.

"Our three winning performers, in no particular order are, Margibelle! Battlefront and –"

Ondine didn't hear the third band. It didn't matter. She squealed and squished Hamish, who cried out with joy as well. They'd won. Well, they'd equally won. They were tied for first.

Making a great show of the results, Marta Pompeii on the television turned to Vincent, who handed over the envelope with his casting vote. Marta then opened it slowly, dragging the tension out so long it breached the Geneva Convention. "This year's winner, with Lord Vincent's casting vote, to represent Brugel at PopEuroTube is . . ." she paused and looked at the three final finalists. Margi and Belle were holding hands and turning blue from holding their breaths. Marta turned back to the camera and said, "Battlefront!"

Blood rushed through Ondine's ears. "What? What!" Her jaw

dropped, further opening her ears as the noise of the televised crowd poured into her brain.

"It's a mistake," Hamish said.

"But Vincent said –"

"– The toe rag –"

"– that they'd get in."

"– lying piece of scum."

She couldn't hear properly over her thundering pulse, but her eyes weren't lying. There on TV, the members of Battlefront, who'd sung *Anthem*, were leaping with joy. They would represent Brugel at PopEuro-Tube. Not Margibelle. Who were hugging and consoling each other and then being absolute troopers and congratulating the members of Battlefront.

Deflated and defeated, Ondine fell back on to the couch and kept shaking her head at Vincent's deception. "He said he'd help. Why did I trust him? He used us!"

"Can I turn it off now lass, it's nae gointae get any better."

"I want to flip tables and start a riot!" Tears of frustration blurred everything as the words, 'he lied to us!' rang in her ears.

"We have plenty of tables in the dining room if ye want tae make a start."

Molten lava-anger fried Ondine's brain as she kicked over the side table. Then she quickly righted it again because flipping tables didn't solve anything. Except make her feel marginally better for having done it.

But still.

What else could she kick?

Noise wafted in from outside. A group of people were singing *Anthem* out in the street, as if they'd deliberately burst into song just to drive her mad. The singing became louder as it reached the back door. They were carousing now, right outside her family home. Talk about rubbing menthol into her eyeballs! [1]

Hamish did what Hamish did best and wrapped Ondine in a hug. She howled out the unfairness of the world into his chest. Encased in Hamish's arms, his biceps should have smothered the sound of other people singing. But it became even louder. How was that possible? Then the noise came inside their room and she pulled away from Hamish to see her family walking in, twirling sparklers in the air and popping streamers!

They were singing *Anthem!* Had they fallen into a vat of plütz? Margi and Cybelle were hugging their men and singing. Ma was making strange ululations like a gypsy queen and Da was singing the low notes in some bizarre attempt to harmonise.

The Bergers joined in as well, as their son Alexei lit a fresh sparkler.

They looked . . . happy?

Eventually Ondine's family paused for breath, giving Hamish the chance to ask, "Have ye all lawst yer minds?"

"Watch the sparks on the carpet!" Ma said.

Margi broke away from Thomas and grabbed Ondine in an embrace. "Oh Ondi, it's wonderful!"

That would be yes.

"They haven't seen it yet," Thomas said. "Turn the box back on, you'll see what happened."

Mute with confusion, Ondine did Thomas's bidding and switched the set back on. But by now they'd finished the broadcast and were showing an old movie.

Margi's smile grew larger. "Ondi, we're going to PopEuroTube anyway. We'll be representing Slaegal! Isn't that wonderful?" At which point Margi squealed, grabbed Cybelle and the two of them bounced around and made giddy noises. They moved into the beer garden to continue the party. Alexei had a fresh box of small fireworks that he was keen to set on fire.

The world had officially stopped making sense.

"You'll never believe it, darling," Ma said, coming over to smother Ondine in a hug. "Lord Vincent cast the vote for Battlefront to sing for Brugel, and we were crushed let me tell you. But then he told us the good news."

Ondine came up for air. "But how does he have any say in what Slaegal does?"

"It wasn't him, it was his fiancé Ruslana. Her dad's the head of the Slaegal delegation and they want Margibelle to sing for them."

"But . . . *Slaegal?*" [2]

Eyes fever-bright, Cybelle said, "Don't you see? This means we've got an even better chance of winning. Brugelers can't vote for Brugel, but they *can* vote for us because we'll be Slaegal. Just for one night."

Whooshing weirdness filled Ondine's head. "I guess that's good then." All the while she couldn't shake the feeling Vincent had tricked her. Margibelle were supposed to represent Brugel, not their enemies across the border.

"Good?" Cybelle said. "It's *amazing.*"

Henrik kissed Cybelle on the cheek and spun her around.

Hamish whispered in Ondine's ear. "Ye done good, lass. Vincent came through after all."

"Yoo hoo!" Came a familiar voice. Old Col sauntered out to the garden, "I came as soon as I could to join in the party!"

Old Col's eyes lit on Alexei and his box of exploding tricks. "Oh yes, let's set them off!" The matriarch and the newcomer to Ondine's extended family then set about setting fire to things.

At least they weren't doing it inside!

The excitement in the garden broke through Ondine's glumness. As a firework launched into the sky, Col waved her hands casting a spell. Vibrant red and gold sparks exploded outward creating a picture of Margi and Cybelle's faces against the starry night.

Ondine's sisters screamed with delight at the impromptu pyrotechnics display. She'd never seen the family so happy. Their emotions proved contagious and Ondine found herself grinning and hugging her sisters for the sheer joy of it.

Nobody needed to know about her deal with Vincent.

*Bang*! Another magic firework illuminated the sky, this time with Ondine and Hamish's virtual visages beaming down at everyone below in brilliant blue and purple.

"Oh how lovely Col!" Ma exclaimed, clapping with delight.

As the real Ondine gazed up in wonder, her sparkly-likeness broke into a smile. Then Hamish's apparition winked, morphed into a ferret and then faded away into smoke.

A heat wave swept through the garden, as if the trees had caught fire.

"Be careful, Alex," Mrs Berger said.

"Now that was a hot flash!" Ma said.

No harm done, everyone laughed and kept partying.

"Whoops, must have given it a little too much!" Old Col said.

More family phantasms flew across the sky above the pub, bringing gasps of joy to all. Alexei stuck a pinwheel to the decorative lamppost and set it blazing. Flames and sparks flew out in all directions as it whizzed around.

*Creak*! The pinwheel's heat buckled the lamppost.

Mr Berger said, "You've done your dash boy, get inside."

"We'll pay for the damages," Mrs Berger said.

"Not Alexei's fault!" Old Col jumped in. "I gave it a little extra. Sometimes I don't know my own strength."

"Is everything all right auntie?" Ma asked.

"Perfectly fine!" Old Col sounded way too defensive. "Josef, why not break out the plütz? The good stuff this time."

***

Rehearsals for the abnormal formal continued apace, but the Duchess Anathea did not appear at them, making Ondine even more worried as they trudged back to the family pub after an afternoon of dancing. Hamish winced as he held the door open for Ondine.

"Are you all right, darling?"

"Jus' me shoulders hen, on account of gettin' me posture right."

Old Col swished past. "Posture is the most important part."

"Aye," he said with a dramatic sigh. "After a good sleep I'll get the blood flow back into my arms sharpish."

"You could be a little more appreciative, Col," Ondine said, then suddenly felt terrible about speaking so harshly.

"Considering he ruined my first debutante ball, yes, Ondine, I *appreciate* that Hamish is at last making amends for his appalling behaviour all those years ago." [3]

Twigs figuratively snapped inside Ondine's head. Her great aunt had never sounded so tetchy before. She'd always been playful and full of mischief. Even when things were crazy, Ondine had always been able to rely on Old Col to steer them right. Now she looked and sounded downright mean. It wasn't like her at all. "Auntie Col, are you, y'know, all right?"

"Course I'm all right," she snapped.

"No need to snap."

"I didn't snap," she snapped. Again.

*Ping*, went Ondine's brain. "It's the ball, isn't it? You're getting worked up about it."

"Nonsense."

"It's going to be all right, you know." Ondine hoped Old Col would calm down. She needed her great auntie to be her great self. Not this snappish . . . *snapper*. "Hamish is working his shoulders off so that he'll be ready on the night. He wants it to be a success just as much as you do." And Ondine wanted the Duchess Anathea to be there so she could warn her again of what Vincent was up to. Honestly, sometimes she felt like everyone else had become so caught up in their personal issues they'd forgotten about what was really important. Protecting Brugel from Vincent!

People began filling the streets, heading towards the city centre. Dread filled Ondine's belly as the crowds kept coming during the late afternoon, with dozens of people waving flags as they walked. On the flags were blue hands.

This was a rally *for* Vincent.

Jolted into action, Ondine raced upstairs and grabbed her camera, although what she'd be able to do with the footage was anyone's guess. [4] She had to at least document what was going on. Maybe, when she showed the footage to Anathea, the Duchess might start to do something.

Music played, the spring sun beamed from the sky and the air filled with delicious fragrances of fried cheese balls. Although they were tired from rehearsals, Ondine and Hamish slipped out the side gate and followed the tide of people. They soon found themselves in Savo Plaza, where music and fun filled the air. Cadets created a percussion of precision drumbeats, streamers caught on tree branches filling them with colour. It was the biggest street party Ondine had ever seen.

"Gotta hand it to the lord, he does throw a fine céilidh,' Hamish said. [5]

If Vincent kept up this charm offensive, there would soon be a tipping point, which would tip Duchess Anathea out of Brugel entirely.

---

IN ORDER TO avoid his palm fading back to whitish pink, Vincent plunged his hand into the toilet cistern, which had an old-style dark blue hygiene block in it. His skin came out a rich shade of blue.

This was his symbol, as Babak Balakhan had decreed. Having a blue hand linked him to his ancestor Elmaree. And it looked great on the banners. [6]

For the briefest moment he wondered if the chemicals might not be entirely good for him, but staining his hand wouldn't be forever, just until he had the Dukedom back.

"Ready? Let's go," his bride-to-be said as he walked back into the hotel suite.

Happy crowds gathered in the plaza below their window. So many were dressed in blue, or holding banners of blue hands. There had to be a few thousand people already. Impressive. Babak had paid for everything. The security guards, the traffic management, the stage, the public address system, the entertainment and the food vans giving away free cheeseballs.

A second-tier celebrity presenter introduced the acts. "And now, ladies and gentlemen, boys and girls of all ages . . ." A troop of Fort Kluff cadets beat out a drum roll to build excitement.

In the hotel suite, two security guards, a male and a female knocked and entered. They wore identical, dark blue suits, aviator sunglasses and little clear coils of audio equipment clipped into their ears.

"We're ready to escort you to the stage, My Lord," the woman said.

"Excellent," Vincent said, "I'll be right with –"

A rock crashed through the window, shattering glass over the carpet.

The woman pushed Vincent to the floor and shielded him with her body. "Stay down!" she yelled.

The noise and drama sent Vincent's pulse soaring.

"Breach in Lord Vincent's hotel room!" the man said, moving sideways to the window.

"Don't suppose anyone's going to jump on me?" Ruslana said with a petulant hand on her hip.

Squashed under the protective guard, Vincent tried to steady his breathing. He had to beat this panic, he couldn't let this spoil his day. He hissed out, "You're wrinkling my suit."

The woman let him up. "We need to get you somewhere safer."

"I don't think so," Vincent heard the wobble in his voice, so he played with his cuffs until his nerves calmed down. "The show must go on and all that."

Ruslana walked over and picked up the rock, which had a note secured with an elastic band. "Anathea forever," she read out. "Oh look, they've made all the letters from cut up newspapers. Bless."

Ruslana's sarcasm in the face of adversity gave Vincent the boost of confidence he needed. He held his arm out to her. "Shall we face the music?"

"We'll get this cleaned up right away," the woman said. "And replace the window."

With no glass in the window, the noise from the plaza came through clearly. The MC was whipping the crowd into a frenzy. Perhaps the crowd was so distracted, nobody had heard or seen the pro-Anathea rock?

The MC put on a strange voice and elongated every vowel " . . . Pleeeeease give a thumping great welcooooooooome to the band representing Brugel at this year's PopEuroTube, Baaaaaaattlefrooooooooont!"

The crowd cheered. The band members walked on, waving and blowing kisses to the crowd.

"Hello Venzelemma," the lead singer boomed out. "Are we ready for a good time?"

"Right," Vincent adjusted his tie in the mirror. Hmmm. Was this a tie type of occasion or not? Nah, too formal. He wrenched it off and popped open the top button on his shirt.

Melody piped up from behind the sofa, where she must have leapt when the rock came through. "If it's all right with you, I'll stay. I can see the stage from here if you need any magic."

Ruslana went to the phone and dialled.

"What are y –"

"– I'd like a basket of cheeseballs delivered to room two twenty please. Oh, and a bowl of potato wedges with three dipping sauces." Placing the receiver down, she turned to Melody. "Carbohydrates are on their way."

Of course. Ruslana was looking particularly attractive today. Her skin looked human, her hair shiny and healthy, her make up classic and understated. Melody must have been using a lot of magic to achieve that, and Ruslana must have been letting her.

"You are the luckiest son-of-a-duke in the world," Ruslana said as she took his hand and walked him into the hallway towards the lift. "You have me and you have Melody. The best of both worlds."

There was that.

"Looking at you now makes me appreciate Melody all the more," he said.

"When we break up, I'm keeping her," Ruslana said.

The lift made the universal 'ping' to let them know the car was at their floor.

"Shouldn't that be Melody's decision?" Vincent said as they stepped in. He hit the ground floor button with the knuckle of his non-blue index finger. It wasn't that he was particularly germ-phobic, but he'd seen stories about pathogens on everyday items such as lift buttons, mobile telephones and supermarket trolley handles. It turned his stomach. Sure, and he'd had his other hand in the toilet cistern only a few moments ago. All part of the sacrifice to get his inheritance back. [7]

Ruslana broke into his thoughts. "Don't tell me you actually care about Melody?"

It made him uncomfortable. "I care enough not to treat her like a commodity."

She gave him a single raised eyebrow.

He was saved from saying anything more by the 'ping' as the doors opened to the hotel's reception.

A barrage of media jumped into their way, lights on, cameras running, microphones at mouth height.

"Smile and wave dear," Ruslana said, giving his hand a squeeze, "I've got this."

As if born to the role of Duchess, Ruslana put them all at ease, her tone at just the right pitch to be heard, but not raucous.

The reporters, however, shouted over one another as they fired fresh questions at Vincent and Ruslana as they headed towards the stage outside in the plaza.

Outside, Battlefront's lead singer finishing another song to huge cheers. Then, as she looked back and acknowledged Vincent, she turned to the crowd and got them really excited.

"I know the song you want to hear. We can't wait to perform it for the rest of Europe!"

The crowd made piercing whistles, blasting Vincent's eardrums. The singer rocked out *Anthem*, the audience went berzerk in support. If Battlefront performed like this at PopEuroTube, they'd collect dozens of 'treize-points'. [8]

"Thank you Venzelemma! Thank you Brugel!" the singer cried out to the crowds. "See you at PopEuroTube!"

The MC revved the crowd into pure mania, gearing them up for Vincent's appearance. "And now, it's my absolute pleasure to introduce our next guest on the bill." The MC said. "He's the reason we're here today, to show our support. Ladies and Gentlemen, I bring you the next Duke of Brugel, Lord Vincent!"

The crowd went completely insane. Fried cheese balls flew through the air.

He turned to Ruslana and held out his hand. "You coming with me or staying here?"

"Oh sweetheart," she gave him a cold wink, "we're in this together."

He helped her take the stairs first, then followed. She waited for him on the side of the stage, before taking his hand again and holding it aloft, like a winner.

The crowd was delirious, taking five minutes to quieten down enough to listen to anything he had to say. The clouds parted. A brilliant shaft of sunlight played upon Savo Plaza. Wild and passionate applause broke out. He hadn't even said anything yet.

"Thank you," he said, waving with both hands to the crowd, who cheered again. Beside him, Ruslana took a respectful step backwards, demonstrating that he was the important one here.

"How fantastic is Battlefront, right?" It wasn't in the speech at all, but it matched the mood. Adoring whistles and cheers filled the plaza.

"I want to thank everyone for coming out today, your support is humbling and I'm incredibly grateful. As you know, I have dedicated my life to Brugel and will continue to do so for as long as the people of Brugel will have me." The goodwill from the crowd told him he was saying all the right things. Movement to the side caught his attention. He looked over and felt stones pour into his gut at the sight of Ondine and Hamish in the crowd. For the briefest second their eyes locked. They weren't here to support him; he knew that much. But he wasn't going to let them ruin his big moment. They were but two people in a sea of supporters. It was important to stay positive.

"I appreciate everyone being here today. Thank you Venzelemma. Thank you Brugel." He stepped back from the microphone and waved as the crowd made crazy noises. Groups of people were stamping their feet on the cobblestones to make a drum roll sound. The cadets from Fort Kluff, looking resplendent in their military uniforms, set up another precise drum roll that lead into the start of a classic marching beat. The MC rushed to the empty microphone "Let's hear it for Lord Vincent!" People cheered and whistled so loudly, Vincent could barely hear what the journalists were asking him as he stepped off the stage.

Oh, they weren't asking him anything. It was for his bride-to-be.

"Ruslana, what's it like being engaged to Brugel's next Duke?"

"It's wonderful," she said without missing a beat. "Because he is a wonderful, caring, considerate man."

Laughing out loud would expose them both. Vincent blushed and looked to the ground in an effort to compose himself. Who knew she'd be such a good blagger? [9]

"When we met I didn't know who he was," she added.

That was true.

"Where did you meet?" A woman asked.

"We meet at a charity function in Norange," she said.

That wasn't a lie either, really. If he had to describe how he was feeling about Ruslana right now, Vincent came perilously close to admiration.

"When is the wedding?"

"Late summer," they both said on top of each other.

Their audience laughed and Vincent found himself smiling at Ruslana. She was handling herself beautifully in front of the media. Without a trace of orange skin, she was lovely to look at. All Vincent had to do was stand beside her looking supportive. Just as it had been on stage, where he'd said very little. The voice in his head said, "I have a feeling this is all going to work out beautifully."

**9**

———

On the first Sunday in April, the clocks moved forward by two hours to herald the beginning of Brugel Summer Time, even though it was still spring, and only just if the weather outside was any guide. Ondine loved having hours of light in the evenings, but it came with a price of woefully dark mornings. And two hours' less sleep that first night.

"Up you get darling, it's already nine o'clock." Ma shook her shoulder to rouse her from her bed. "Even though it's really only seven."

Defensively Ondine slapped the pillow over her head. "Lemme sleep in."

"You say that every year. Come on lazybones, get up."

"Not lazy, sleep deprived."

"You say *that* every year as well. Come on. We have guests for breakfast."

Why did her parents take bookings for the first weekend in April? It was always chaos in the morning as everyone felt the effects of the time change. Bumping into the doorframe on her way out, Ondine staggered from her bedroom and turned down the hall, finding herself outside Hamish's bedroom. Huh? Her brain hadn't consciously decided that, she'd just found herself here. Oh well, now she was here, she may as well see if Hamish was up.

She rapped on the door, "Has Ma come and shouted at you yet?"

No reply.

Another rap and repeat question. Another bout of silence. Curiosity eating at her, Ondine half-covered her eyes with her hand and turned the handle. "I'm coming in, hope you're decent. No reply at all. She pulled her hand away and looked at the bed. At first it appeared empty, but then she saw the hint of movement. Pulling back the covers, she found Shambles the ferret curled into a knot of fur where Hamish the man should have been.

"How dare you!" The words flew out in a burst of disappointment.

The ferret didn't move. She picked him up by the middle, and he sagged at both ends like gloppy pizza dough. "I can't believe you're doing this to me!"

The ferret twisted and spun in her hand. "I'mawakeIpromise," he jumbled and then dived under the covers. As he transformed into his gorgeous Hamishness, Ondine grew more and more furious. "You don't need to sleep as a ferret. You're not sick, you're not injured. Why are you doing this?"

"Awww lass, it's too early."

He mustn't have adjusted his clock. She'd caught him before he'd had the chance to wake up and change himself back. "You slept all night as a ferret, didn't you?"

Being so tired, his accent sounded thicker and even less understandable than normal. "Mustae had a wee tummy ache in the night and turned in mah sleep, so I did."

"In your sleep? Then where are your pyjamas?" They should have been mushed up under the covers somewhere, but instead they sat there like the incriminating evidence they were, folded on the side chair.

Normally when Ondine was right, she felt victorious. Now she felt hollow. "Don't lie to me."

"I'm sorry lass, I didnae mean to. Honest. I just panicked a wee bit."

"So you *were* sleeping as a ferret?"

"Aye, I was. But I did it fer you! You've seen me grey hairs and all. I'm turning into an old man in front of yer eyes. Between you and me, I think Old Col's magic is warping out of control. I'm scared that if I don't sleep as a ferret every night, I may not wake up at all!"

WITH SO MANY stressful scenarios about her like spinning plates on bamboo canes, Ondine had to get at least one of the worst worries off her list. That afternoon she made a personal visit to Duchess Anathea. [1] After that, her conscience would be clear about state matters and she could get back to more important fretting about her great aunt losing her magic and her beloved Hamish turning into a wrinkly old prune.

"Ondine dear, how lovely to see you," Anathea said, as if they were old friends.

They were in a private room on the southern side of the building, to make the most of the light. At least, that's what Ondine assumed as there were no curtains at the windows. The room had a two-bar heater sitting in the hearth of an open fireplace, but only one bar was active.

The last time Ondine had been in the ducal estate in Venzelemma had been summer. She'd come with her father and Shambles – the ferret wrapped around her neck like a scarf – to warn Duke Pavla about a threat to his life. This time it was to warn the Duchess of something much worse. Vincent was about to overthrow her, of that Ondine was certain.

"Thank you ever so much for seeing me."

"I assume you're here because you have news?"

"Yes, and it's all about Vincent I'm sorry to say. I have been sending you regular reports but I'm not sure you're getting them?"

"Marvellous," Anathea said as she walked to her desk and began flicking through a diary. Not the reaction Ondine expected. Anathea carried on as if she'd simply been told the lunch menu for the day. "Has all your school work been finished for the term?"

"Err . . . My finals will be in a few weeks. I'm going to Business College, which starts in September. I want to run the family pub when my parents retire. But that's not important. You must know what Vincent's up to. You saw the rally, didn't you? And all the cadets?"

Flicking a page in her diary, Anathea looked up and said, "Summer will be a busy time for you."

It was like they were talking about completely different things. "You don't seem worried?"

Anathea nodded. "Walk with me, I am to be fitted for a dress in ten minutes."

They left that marginally-warmer-than-an-igloo office and stepped into a chilled hallway. As they walked, Anathea fired questions at her. "What sort of following does he *really* have?"

So she *had* been listening. Perhaps she was worried about somebody else listening to them?

"His popularity is getting bigger every day, and you know how Mrs Howser is free. She's training cadets at Fort Kluff and I've got to tell you they terrify me. They're totally mutated by magic."

Anathea grabbed a door handle to lead them into a new room. Strange that nobody opened the door for the Duchess of Brugel. Perhaps she'd had to cut back on staff? They walked in to find a dressmaker with a tape measure for a scarf, and a wardrobe on castors, with racks of clothes inside zippered bags. She wore a heavy fur-lined cloak and matching hat with the earflaps turned down, which she quickly turned up as Anathea neared. There was no heating in here at all.

"Ondine, you may keep talking as I have pins stuck in me by Luminita here. Be careful, Luminita, there is padding to be had, but it is not to be pricked at."

"So I guess you need a plan to counter Vincent's popularity?" Ondine offered.

"Do I? I can't do much about other people being popular with the mob, can I?"

A twig snapped in Ondine's brain. This was not the Anathea of old. "Yes you can. Making you popular is all we've been doing for the past few months. Why are you slacking off now?"

Anathea glared. "You forget your place. I will not be spoken to in that way."

Ondine shrank at the rebuke. The dressmaker ducked out of the way, pretending she wasn't there. Ondine wanted to say, "You're not nearly as worried as you should be and I'm starting to think there's some kind of magic spell on you. Vincent suddenly has loads of money and is incredibly popular and people are taking to the streets to show their support." Instead, all she could manage was, "I'm sorry, Your Lordship, but I'm worried about you, and I'm worried about Brugel."

A slow smile spread over Anathea's face. "So you *do* care."

Ondine blurted, "Of course I do."

"Good." Anathea's expression softened. "Then you will understand why I need to look my best at all times. I can tell by the way you're locking your hands together that you're cold. The circulation in my feet may never be felt again. But to the outside world, I look the part. Plus, the law is on my side."

"But he's loaded and you're broke!"

The dressmaker's mouth dropped open. Pins fell to the threadbare carpet.

"You will be paid," Anathea assured her.

"Cash," Luminita said.

"Of course." Anathea shook her head.

"Today," Luminita said.

"The bursar will be given your invoice on the way out."

Luminita asked, "Which one is the bursar?"

Anathea quietly cleared her throat. "The one behind the desk."

Luminita began packing her things. "You mean the one who drives your car and opens doors and answers phones and makes your tea as well?"

Anathea sighed. "Yes, that's the one."

"I will go now," Luminita said.

Anathea held her hand out. "The dress will be ready in time for the opera tonight?"

"When I get paid, I'll come back." With that, Luminita zipped the duchess's jacket into a protective clothing bag. "I'll see myself out."

"You're going to the opera?" Ondine gulped with worry.

"The premiere of *The Cholera Tourer*. An historical piece loosely based on the story of Black Sonja." [2]

"You will be safe, won't you?"

"I have my earplugs at the ready." A dreamy look clouded her features, "and I shall have Valentin at my side."

"Is he the handsome man you brought to dance rehearsals?"

Anathea's face glowed. "He's such a silver fox, don't you think?"

If she were into older men, Ondine would agree. She nodded anyway, just to be diplomatic. Strange thoughts drifted through Ondine's mind as she looked at the Duchess's expression and realised how very lonely Anathea must have been all these years. Then her gaze drifted to the peeling wallpaper, the dust-encrusted furniture and worn carpets. For a moment she wondered if being the Duchess of Brugel was more a burden than a blessing.

"You think this room is bad?" Anathea broke into her thoughts. "State dinners cannot be hosted because the floorboards in the dining room are beyond repair."

From a side door, Biscuit the dog barrelled in and ran for his mother. She cuddled him and buried her face in his fur.

Saving Anathea felt like such an impossible task, until a stray thought took root in Ondine's brain. "Vincent's got money now, if he's so determined to take all of this. Get him to start paying for repairs."

That made Anathea stop for a moment and look at Ondine. "Did Vincent send you?"

"I'm not working for Vincent." Ondine tensed. "As if that would ever happen."

Guilt swamped her and she looked at the floor.

"I won't be lied to," Anathea said.

*Gulp*. "I'm not lying. And I'm not working for him."

"But?"

Since when was Anathea so astute? With a sigh of defeat Ondine said, "I helped him. But only a bit. And I wasn't really helping him, I was helping Ruslana. All I did was grab our makeup and hair lady to make Ruslana look presentable. Because Vincent said if I helped him, he'd help my sisters get in to Pop Euro Tube." It felt so good to get that off her chest.

"People can be persuaded with the right motivation," Anathea said.

They walked back to Anathea's office. Somebody had turned off the little bar heater while they'd been out. It was the kind of cold Ondine felt right between her shoulders after she'd been sitting at her desk for an hour, doing homework.

"Rurururu," Biscuit barked. Anathea let him down and he trotted over to a little bed underneath her desk.

"Where are you daughters, by the way," Ondine asked.

"Why do you ask?"

"Because they should be here, working for you. That way they will save you money on hiring staff, and they'll learn what's involved in being Duchess. And you can do a media charm offensive yourself, so people will see your daughters here, putting in the hours, and they'll get used to them being around."

"Why should my daughters work?"

Ondine scrunched her brows in confusion. "Everyone needs to work. I've worked for my parents my whole life. It's normal."

"Ah but Ondine, your normal is very different to *my* normal. And my daughters will not be subjected to merchant-class expectations of normal."

"But . . ."

"Mm?" Anathea's eyebrow rose in smugness.

Ondine couldn't help staring at Anathea for longer than was strictly polite. Now they were back in her office, the duchess was back to being obscure and a little rude again. "Are you sure you're not under some kind of spell?"

"Positive."

Ondine's hope deflated like a day-old balloon. "That's a real shame."

"Why is that?"

"Because I don't think you're taking the threat from Vincent seriously enough. And . . . I don't know! You're not *you* any more." If this was Anathea's real nature, how had it taken Ondine so long to see the Venn diagram, where Anathea appeared in one circle and 'The real world' took up another, but they only crossed over in the middle for a millimetre?

"My dear Ondine," The Duchess said, her face tightening, "There is so little we agree about, I can't see why you're still here."

Chills buzzed her system. "I guess I should go then."

"See yourself out, there's a good girl."

Numb with shock and disillusionment, Ondine staggered towards the door. "Oh, before I go. Thank you for your time, My Lord Duchess."

"Keep the door closed, you're letting the heat out."

"What heat?" Ondine said as she shut the door with a snick.

The whole way home on the train, Ondine couldn't help wondering where it had all gone so horribly wrong. She may have backed the wrong horse in Anathea, but there was no possible way she'd transfer her allegiances to Vincent. If Anathea was batty, Vincent was positively poisonous.

Which left her exactly where?

THROUGH THE KEYHOLE in the wardrobe door, Lord Vincent watched as his aunt took her position behind her desk. The dog slept beneath, barely snuffling when Anathea placed her stockinged feet on him. "Nicely done." He stepped into the room and gave a slow clap. "I thought you'd never get rid of her."

"That poor girl's had her heart broken. I hope you're happy."

"Very. Now, where were we?"

"My daughters' educations, my clothing allowance and the restoration of this crumbling old pile."

Looking around, all he could see were the faded signs of a once proud room. "If we get started on the renovations, it should be ready by my twenty-first birthday."

She gave him one of those looks, it silently said, "I have so much to say I don't know where to begin."

He waited. Eventually she said, "Those renovations should have been done by your father."

"We both know he was broke. That's why he married my mother."

"Ah yes. We come from a long line of marrying into money. I see the tradition is being carried on."

"I'm nothing if not practical."

The dog under the desk stirred.

When he was sure she had nothing else to say, Vincent asked, "Speaking of daughters, where are my beautiful cousins?"

Another sigh from Anathea, making the dog wake up and grizzle. "My daughters are in school, as you know. Have the tuition fees been paid for the term?"

Vincent stroked his chin where a beard might one day be. Should he grow the split moustache like his father? "They have been enrolled for the past year, have they not?"

"They've been home for holidays and such. They have not completely lost touch with Brugel. What's your point?"

"My point is, you enrolled them before you had any known way of paying for it. What would you have done if I had not become engaged to a means of income?"

A shrug. "Their father would have been petitioned. In fact, I think *your* father was petitioned as well, and he didn't get back to me before . . . well, before he was poisoned by your mother. My, what a lovely family we have."

"My father's passing was to your benefit as much as mine." He couldn't help a little snort of contempt escape. He could have sworn he saw a plume of steam from his nose it was so cold in here. "Let's take a walk, dear aunt." He offered his arm. It wasn't so much that he thought a stroll in the gardens would change things, but standing around in this cold room did nothing for his circulation.

"Everyone can see what you're doing, you know." Anathea said as she walked through the doorway.

"I'm doing what's best for Brugel," Vincent said.

"You keep telling yourself that."

"Because it's true." Why couldn't she see that? "It's far better to have stability at the helm."

"Saying stability implies I am unstable. Anyone can see I am being actively undermined."

"All I propose is a smooth transition period and a respectful handover, which will be beneficial to everyone."

They reached the double doors that lead out to the parterre garden. It crimped his heart to see the overgrown edging of the flower beds where once had been laser-straight lines. He held his arm to the side in the hope she'd take it. She did, and he drew her closer as they stepped out into the weak spring sunshine. If there were any photographers around, they would capture them looking friendly and comfortable. The pictures would also capture the dilapidated garden, which would not hurt his cause one bit.

"How are my darling nephews?" Anathea asked.

"The nannies at Bellreeve tell me my brothers are doing well."

"Are they taken to see their mother?"

"Yes. I'm told they have supervised visits to the asylum on a regular basis."

"How often has Kerala been visited by you? I'm sure you're missed."

Something dried his throat, but he had to look calm and in control, just in case somebody in the public saw him. Because he had his public face on, the one that told the world that everything was all right. "As much as I miss her, it will do none of us any good to be seen with her."

"You're sounding very grown up about it."

"I don't have a choice."

"There are choices. You could retire from public life to grieve in private. To deal with the mess your mother left behind. To help your brothers. Instead you pursue attention as if the death of your father were a springboard to be taken into public life."

"It sounds so calculated, coming from you" he tucked his head down and caught sight of another overgrown garden bed. Green shoots of . . . something . . . fought through a tangled blanket of weeds. He tried to remember what was there last year. They were red and white flowers of some kind.

"The first thing you're going to do is hire a gardener. Or ten. Send me the bill."

"Dearest of nephews. The building is falling to bits, and you're worried about geraniums?"

"It's the first thing people see when they visit. That's another thing. You're going to open the gardens to the public."

"I don't think that should be done," she pulled up short and glared at him.

"Dearest of aunts," he shot back, "This garden is public, therefore it should always look its best."

"There are so many more pressing things that need to –"

"– There always are, but they are on the inside, and the public will not see it." He felt so proud of the way he didn't let any of the disappointment or upset show on his face. At least, he was fairly sure it wasn't showing on his face. Those muscle relaxants he'd borrowed from Ruslana were really messing with his head.

<hr>

IF ONDINE HAD a thesaurus with her for the train journey home from visiting the Duchess of Brugel, she would have found herself feeling flat, cheerless, dejected, despondent and all-over generally *blah*.

But she didn't have one with her, so she had a hard time knowing exactly what she should call the melancholy settling over her. It was the kind of thing that made her want to listen to sad songs.

Once she reached the warm embrace of the family pub, she followed her nose to the kitchen. It wasn't her eyes that told her something was wrong but her nose. There was nothing on the cooker. (Nor were there any people).

The only thing she could detect were remnants of cold scrambled eggs and toast scrapings. They carried the distinct scent of having been cooked some time ago and were now congealing.

Peeking into the dining room, she found her family helping Margi with some vague ideas of choreography that would allow her to move around while also singing and hitting her notes. [3] Cybelle, of course, was excused from any dancing because she would be on piano the whole time. No sign of Hamish anywhere, which added to her growing list of disappointments. Nor Old Col. Maybe they were at the dance hall.

"You look like you're at a loose end," Ma said as she came into the kitchen and turned the coffee maker on. "There are always dishes to do."

"I have a stack of homework." Which was absolutely true.

"Everything all right?" Ma gave her a funny look, as if she knew something was up but was waiting for Ondine to confess.

"Just tired I guess," she said with a shrug. The tremble in her jaw gave her away.

"Darling, what's wrong?" Ma put one arm around her and directed her to their private room behind the kitchen. Then she did the most bizarre thing. Ma closed the door to the kitchen, blocking out the sound of her sisters' music to give them real privacy.

"Everything." Ondine slumped into the nearest chair.

"Did the meeting with the Duchess go badly?"

"How did you know?" Of course her mother knew everything.

"You've had so much excitement this past year, it's not surprising you're feeling flat now. Best get your homework done while there's time. Thank goodness Every Pop Top will be over soon."

"PopEuroTube."

"That's the one. I never thought I'd say this but, hooray for Slaegal."

"Who are you and what have you done with my mother," Ondine said. Then she pulled herself together. "Seriously. The pub's closed; you're being wonderful and understanding and . . . really calm. Are we all under some kind of spell?"

Ma sighed and slumped her shoulders. "Not a spell, exactly."

Ondine forgot to breathe as she waited for Ma to tell the truth.

"Ruslana is being very supportive." Ma's palms went up in a defensive-yet-shushing motion to keep Ondine from jumping to conclusions. "Don't jump to conclusions. But she wants Margibelle to do well and for that to happen they need time to rehearse, which means turning customers away from time to time."

"You don't have to call them Margibelle when it's just us at home, you know."

Ma shrugged, "It's kind of catchy."

Ondine got up and said, "I have homework to do." As she reached the foot of the stairs she turned back. "Exactly how much support is Ruslana giving us?"

"Enough. She wants Slaegal to win. And you have exams soon so you'll benefit with more time to study."

Shaking her head, Ondine knew she should be grateful. All the while she felt a horrible sense of unease, as if the very ground had shifted under her feet.

# 10

The next few weeks of April passed in a blur of essays, assignments and exams for Ondine, rehearsals and costume fittings for Cybelle and Margi and a whirl of chiffon and feathers for Col and Hamish. Great-Auntie Col was the one in chiffon, obviously, and she paraded herself around the closed dining room showing the gown to its best advantage. The dress had fluffy white ostrich feathers at the neckline, collars and hem; many of which became ensnared in Hamish's hair as he held her hand and practised their 'walk' they had to do for the presentation. The peach-coloured dress draped and flowed over Old Col's body like water over boulders (being as old as Old Col was, there were a several boulders). When she twirled, the skirts fluttered outwards, delicate and shimmery like a hibiscus flower. It hurt for Ondine to look at Hamish in his impossibly gorgeous suit. It was the same suit he'd worn to Margi's wedding, except now he had a matching peachy cummerbund and a rose bud in his lapel. It wasn't a real rose, because it wouldn't last the distance between the rehearsals and the big night.

Having finished her second last assignment in Brugelish Literature, Ondine had time to watch Hamish and Old Col rehearse. It was still light outside, thanks to Brugel's two-hour jump in to daylight saving time.

This time of year they'd normally have customers in the dining room and the garden, if it were warm enough.

In the closed dining room, Margi and Cybelle had created something of an impromptu party. The girls were singing while Chef and Thomas clapped out a beat. Hamish and Old Col were performing a Brugelish three-step.

"Hey, Ondi!" Hamish said. At which point his footing slipped and took Col for a tumble.

Everyone gasped, all eyes turned to Old Col to see if she was hurt.

"Sorry Col," Hamish said, "I got distracted."

"Yes." Her voice was sharp enough to cut fabric. "Don't do that again."

"Aye-aye captain." He gave mocking salute, deflating some of the tension. Then he turned to Ondine and her heart melted a little more. He was under so much pressure to be the perfect partner for Old Col; the lady should be thanking him, not speaking daggers.

"Ondi, help me out of my dress," Old Col said as she approached her. "I can't let it get wrinkled before the big night."

"Of course. Auntie Col, when is the do-over deb?"

"Didn't I tell you? It's May twelve. Hamish you should have told her."

"The twelfth?" Hamish said, "I thought you said it was the Saturday afterwards?"

"No, they brought it forward."

Margi, Cybelle, Ondine and Hamish all looked back and forth to each other. Eventually Margi expositioned, "But that's the same night as PopEuroTube!"

"Is it?" Old Col gave a nonchalant shrug. "I guess you won't be able to come then. No matter, I know my debutante ball is hardly something you younger folk'd be interested in."

"I don't think that's what she means, Aunty Col," Ondine said. "I think we'd all like to be at both events."

Another shrug. "Be a dear and get my zippered apparel bag would you, we'll need to put the dress in it the moment I take it off, so that it doesn't get any dirt from the floor. Come along."

Ondine followed Old Col to the private room behind the kitchen.

"I have a bone to pick with you, child. What is going on with Hamish? The more we rehearse, the worse he gets."

"Nothing," Ondine said feeling terribly disappointed. Because they'd been doing a whole lot of *nothing* lately, and she'd been rather hoping that they could have at least been doing a little bit of *something*. "I'm sure he's trying his absolute best. And I think you should have told us earlier that your dance would clash with PopEuroTube. Is there any way you could hold over the deb until next year?"

The woman scowled and her cheeks turned red. "There won't be a next year!"

"Are they not having one?" Or was there something about her great aunt's health she wasn't telling them?

"Stop pestering me," Old Col said.

Old Col had always been a fixture in the family. If she was sick, if something was wrong, she should tell them. Ondine's hands shook with worry as she helped her great-aunt out of the dress. Ostrich feathers came loose as she breathed in, causing her to splutter.

"Mind the dress!"

"Yes Col."

"Stop spitting on it!"

"I have feathers stuck in my mouth." It was a wonder Ondine didn't yell back. In fact, she could have sworn she was using up her very, *very* last reserves of *nice*. Right, the dress was safe. She handed it to Col and tried to keep her voice calm. "Something is wrong. You're being mean, and that's not like you. And I didn't want to worry you but your magic isn't as strong as it used to be so Hamish has been sleeping as a ferret."

"I am fine."

"No, you're not." They stared at each other, the tension in Ondine's chest growing by the second.

With a deep sigh, Old Col said, "I'm cross because there's so much to do. Hamish hasn't been getting any better and the dance is in two weeks!"

"Come and talk to me when you're out of denial." All the aggravation did Ondine no good, so she left Old Col to stew in her bad mood and followed the music back to the dining room. They'd pushed the tables and chairs into the corners to create a dance floor in the middle of the room, and the radio was on. Ma danced with Da, Cybelle danced with Chef and Margi danced with Thomas. Hamish was sitting it out, but he had a huge smile as he clapped along to the beat.

"Lassie, would ye do me the honour of this dance?" The power of seeing him in that formal suit turned her emotions to mush.

Nestled close in his arms, she saw sprigs of silver through his hair. More of those silvery strands grew along his temples. When he smiled at her, his eyes crinkled and twinkled, but then when he stopped smiling, the crinkles stayed exactly where they were.

Her heart flailed at the sight of his weary face. He'd be sleeping as s ferret again tonight.

---

THE DAY MA re-opened the pub doors, everyone in Venzelemma wanted a table. They'd ask, "Is this the Margibelle Restaurant?" and her mother would beam and say, "It sure is!"

Lord Vincent, curse him, publicly said their pub was one of his favourite places to visit. The demographics in the dining room changed to a much younger, more demanding crowd. Customers didn't order as much, preferring an entree as their main. Then they'd stay in their seats when they were done, listening to Margibelle perform.

Ma carried a set of empty plates into the kitchen and turned to Ondine. "Can you head out to table three and get their dessert orders for me?"

Taking a peek at the table – a group of teens perhaps a year older than her – Ondine doubted she'd have any luck. "How much do you want to bet they get an ice cream on the way home instead."

"Recommend the *crème brûlée*. Nobody can resist that."

"We're out of *crème brûlée*," Henrik the chef said from down the end of the kitchen.

"We have lemon tarts, we can burn the top of them," Cybelle called back.

Ma took a breath and pushed the menus into Ondine's hands. "Improvise."

As luck would have it, right at that moment Lord Vincent, Ruslana, Melody and an older man came walking in to the restaurant. Ma dashed past Ondine in a blur and quickly cleared a table for them.

Ondine approached the table she'd been assigned, doing her best to ignore her nemesis in the room.

One of the diners on her table said, "He'll make a great duke."

"Hello," Ondine interrupted brightly. "Would you like something for dessert or do you want the bill?" The unspoken part being, "so you can clear off."

They all said variations of "Oh yes, dessert," as they looked towards Vincent and decided to stay.

"What takes the longest to make?" One of them asked.

"The lemon-lime sorbet. We make it from scratch." Ondine said. Not a lie. They had made it from scratch. Four days ago. The diner should have asked, 'which dessert takes the longest to bring out to the customers?'

"Sorbets all round then."

Taking the menus back, Ondine headed to the kitchen to find everyone in their regular blur of activity. Hamish, bless his peach-coloured cummerbund, stepped in to the kitchen, having just returned from another rehearsal.

"Excellent," Ma said as she clapped eyes on him, "you can look after Vincent's table. He's just arrived for second dinner."

"Aye," he gave her a tap-to-the-head salute and peeked around the doorway into the dining room. "Who's that lummox with them?"

Being unable to look away from her beloved, Ondine only had eyes for Hamish. And the thick bands of silver hair at his temples that were not there this morning.

"Hush now," Ma said, "He's Ruslana's father, and with any luck, one of our new patrons. Whatever they order is on the house, by the way."

"Sorbets for table three," Cybelle dinged the service bell from the other end of the kitchen.

Ondine grinned as she settled each fluted bowl on her serving tray and made her way out to the table. The customers barely noticed her as she set their desserts down. Too busy gawping at Vincent. "I took the liberty of bringing out the bill at the same time," she said.

No response.

Fine then.

Back in the kitchen, she sought out Hamish. "How are you feeling?"

"Not well. I found even more grey this afternoon."

She examined his temples, streaked with salt and pepper. "I can see that."

"I wasnae talking about me head."

Heat roared up her neck and she snarfled behind one hand. If she made too much noise, Ma would want to know why. [1]

"It was on me chest, lass. Where d'ye think I meant?"

She playfully swatted him on the arm. "Come on, let's see if table three has paid the bill." She lead him towards the wall partition, where they could look out onto the dining room without the diners feeling as if they were being monitored.

"For someone about to get married, she doesnae look so happy," Hamish said.

Ruslana sat there, all slumped of shoulders and pouted of lips. "And you say she only wants a salad?"

"Aye, and nothing to drink."

If Ondine could see the woman's dour expression from this far away, so must everyone else in the restaurant. "If she keeps cracking the sads, it will be bad for business," Ondine said. The moment her mother walked past, she pounced. "Ma, they're as miserable as a wet cardigan out there. I think Hamish should take them a complimentary bottle of plütz."

"A whole bottle? Best check with Da."

"Don't pick on Ruslana," Margi said as she joined the spying. "If it wasn't for her, Belle and I wouldn't be going to PopEuroTube."

"I helped," Ondine blurted, then wished she'd kept her mouth shut.

"Yes, your cheering in the audience made all the difference," Margi said with a roll of her eyes.

Hamish said, "You'd think they were planning a funeral, not a wedding."

"You're jumping at shadows." Margi took another peek at the table. "Is that your friend with her back to us?"

"That's Melody," Ondine said. "She's allowed to be miserable, because she's carrying a torch for Vincent."

"She likes the sauce," Margi said, indicating with a tilt of her head.

Oh dear, should Melody be having alcohol? Ondine thought they were the same age, which meant her friend shouldn't be touching the stuff for a couple of years yet.

"Any danger of the two of you getting any work done?" Ma asked as she stuck her head around the corner.

Ondine had never felt more hopeless. Melody was their insider in Vincent's camp, but she hadn't fed them anything useful for ages. "I'm not sitting by while Vincent swoops in and undoes all my hard work. I mean, *our* hard work."

"There's a fraudulent slip if ever I heard one," Hamish said. [2]

"We need Melody on our side. I'm going to get her." Ondine strolled out to the dining room, her pulse krump-dancing behind her ribs.

Melody sat semi-slumped in her chair, enveloped by glum-fog. Ondine opted for her brightest tone. "How are your meals tonight? Is everything to your liking?"

"Beautiful. Delicious," Babak said. The man ate like a farm harvester, ploughing through the food in a solid line across his plate.

Vincent's knife and fork were resting on the side of his plate as he chatted to Ruslana. "It's as good as I remembered," he said, giving Ondine a smile that in an earlier season could have melted her heart.

Her insides shrivelled but she kept her smile steady. "I'll pass that on to the chef. Can I get you anything else? Desserts? More plütz?"

"Yes, more plütz." That was Babak. "Tell me, where do you get your supply? It's so hard to find in Norange."

"I'll send Da over, he's our resident expert on the best places to buy just about anything. Uh, Melody?" turning to her friend and placing a kind hand on her shoulder. Melody jumped, as if she'd been in a trance. Or perhaps she'd been busy making spells all this time? That would explain her distraction. But not the lack of eating. Using magic was supposed to make a witch ravenous, yet her friend had barely touched her meal. "Is everything all right?"

"Oh yes, it's fine. You gave me a really large serve, that's all."

"Are you sure?" Leaning in closer, "He is looking after you, isn't he?"

She nodded. "Yes."

"Perhaps you should lie down," Vincent interjected. "This is a hotel, there's bound to be a spare room where you can rest."

"She can stay." Ruslana placed her hand on Melody's wrist, clearly meaning to keep her at the table.

"I don't want to cause any trouble," Melody said. She wasn't as twig-like and waifish as she had been with Mrs Howser, but there was no light in her eyes.

"No trouble at all, come and have a rest in our private lounge," Ondine said. Then they could be alone and have a good talk.

Vincent said, "It's absolutely fine with me. Take a break."

Chin puckering with emotion, Melody nodded and rose from her seat. All eyes fell upon them as Ondine lead her friend through the kitchen and out to the private lounge . "Have a slouch on the couch here and I'll build up the fire."

"I'm not cold," Melody said.

OK then. "I was going to ask if everything is all right, but I can see it's not." Ondine moved in for a hug and her friend's arms wrapped around her with the gusto of an orang-utan.

Eventually Melody pulled away. "Who's the psychic one now?"

Ondine shook her head. "I thought it would be like old times. A bit of spying here and there, feeding Anathea information and then somehow everything would fall into place and we'd save Brugel again."

Melody gave Ondine a strange look, crinkling her forehead into hori-zontal lines. "Save Brugel? From what?"

"From Vincent, obviously."

"But he's the best thing to ever happen to Brugel."

Something screeched in Ondine's brain. "No he's not. How can you say that?"

Silence stretched between them.

"Because it's true! Everyone loves him." Melody's eyes brightened. "He'll give Brugel stability."

Wait, what? "But he's *awful*. And he's done so many horrible things to my family –"

"Like make sure your sisters got a shot at fame and riches in PopEuroTube? Yeah, I can see how badly that's working out for you."

Ouch! "I don't mean that." This was going off the rails superfast. "I mean all the things before. He's a power hungry . . . *I don't know what*. But he'll do whatever it takes and use whoever he needs to use to get there. We have to stop him. For the good of Brugel!"

Shaking her head, Melody said, "He would have been duke if Anathea hadn't interfered."

Ondine rocked back in shock. "She did not interfere! It always should have been hers except Pavla came along."

"And we're lucky he did!" Melody dragged her sleeve across her tear-stained face. "I can't believe you're trying to drive a wedge between Vincent and me!"

"Melody, please, why can't you see reason?"

"I was going to ask you the same thing! Now get out of my way. The Duke of Brugel needs me." Melody lifted her head and walked serenely to the dining room.

"That went about as bad as can be expected," Hamish said from the doorway.

Anger and frustration burned Ondine's heart. Nothing would change her mind about Vincent being bad for Brugel. But how in heaven's name could she make Melody see that?

"Ondi?" Margi showed her divine head around the corner and then she stepped closer. "What did Melody mean?"

Panic turned her brain numb. "What bit?" How much had she heard?

"The bit about making sure we had a shot at PopEuroTube?"

All of it then. Ma appeared. So did Old Col.

"What is going on?" Cybelle asked.

How many more people were going to crowd in here? Ondine blew her fringe in frustration. Tiredness seeped through her bones and she let go of the horrible secret that had tied her stomach in knots. "I helped

Vincent that night at BrugelMelody. And in return, he made sure you went to PopEuroTube."

Silence chilled the air by several degrees.

Cybelle tilted her head. "Wow, you really do think it's all about you."

That was not the response she was expecting. She'd just bared Her Terrible Secret and they'd thrown it back in her face. "I'm not trying to take credit. He really did promise me he'd help you if I helped him."

"Aye, he put her right in it." Of course Hamish came to Ondine's defence. He was a champion like that. "Anyone else would have told him to sod off. Yer lucky to have a sister who cares so much about you."

Cybelle's hands curled into fists on her hips. "A sister who's so jealous she'll tell lies to make herself important."

"That's not what happened ye numpty eejit!" Hamish had never used bad words against any member of her family. Except perhaps for Old Col. "I was right there. And Vincent tightened the screws. Ye should be thanking Ondi fer helpin'."

Margi put her hand on Cybelle's arm to guide her away, but Cybelle shrugged her off. "You can't stand it that you're not in the spotlight! Don't you dare come to PopEuroTube, Ondine. I don't want you there. I don't want you pretending it has anything to do with you. This is *our* moment and you're not going to ruin it!"

They stormed off in high dudgeon. Hamish came over and gave Ondine a gentle hug.

"I'm an idiot," she said, her body crumpling into his. "I thought I was helping. I really did. It's only made things worse. My sisters hate me."

"And the country's charging headlong into Vincent's grip."

"Yeah, that too," she admitted. Up close, this late in the evening, Hamish's hair was more grey than black. His eyes that used to sparkle with mischief had a cloudy lining inside the lens. Cataracts? But only old people got them. As much as she wanted - needed - more hugs from her dearest love, she stepped out of the embrace. "You'd better get your sleep." The unspoken part being 'as a ferret'.

With everything falling apart around Ondine, she couldn't bear it if she lost Hamish.

## 11

_________

The day of PopEuroTube and the Abnormal Formal dawned. Ondine stretched as she woke, all languid and soft, and sleepy and at peace with the world. Then she woke up and reality flooded her with all its recent disappointments.

Her sisters had left for Craviç the week before so they could attend rehearsals and media events. Today, Ma, Da, Thomas and Henrik were heading off to Craviç in a rented campervan. This was the first time Ondine could remember her parents ever taking a holiday. It left Old Col, Hamish and Ondine in by themselves in Venzelemma.

In their private room behind the kitchen, the television was on, with the crew from *Good Morning Brugel* chatting about events. It was one of those shows people left turned on in case something interesting came up, a noisemaker in the background to fill the silence. Ondine's ears pricked at the sound of a familiar voice.

There on the screen was Lord Vincent, adding to the saturation coverage of PopEuroTube promotion.

*"The grand final will be so exciting. I encourage everyone in Venzelemma to come to Savo Plaza, it will be a huge party. We'll have a giant television screen to watch the whole event."*

*"Can I ask a question without notice My Lord? Will there be something extra special announced?"* The co-host asked with a cheeky smile.

For a question 'without notice' it sounded awfully well rehearsed to Ondine.

Vincent positively beamed down the camera. *"There's no sneaking anything past you Cristina. Yes, we will be doing a live cross from Savo Plaza to announce Brugel's voting results!"*

A heavy sigh deflated Ondine. With most of her family away, she could have had all sorts of shenanigans with Hamish today, if only she didn't have the bone-deep certainty that Vincent would be staging a *coup d'état* tonight.

Old Col's hand fell sharply on Ondine's shoulder. "Don't worry about him. Let's move tables and chairs out the way so Hamish and I can dance."

Mouth dropping open in shock, Hamish said, "Won't that make us too tired for the real thing?"

"Nonsense. It will keep us in peak condition."

Shaking his head, Hamish said, "It's a deb ball, Col, not The World Cup." [1]

Throwing her hands in the air, Col yelled, "I knew it! I knew you'd ruin it! Why did I let you talk me into being my partner when I knew you didn't have your heart in it?"

"Steady." Ondine placed her palm on her great-auntie's upper arm. It wasn't Hamish that had done the convincing anyway, it was Old Col's idea.

"Don't touch me!" Col shrieked.

Ondine gulped. She'd never seen her great-auntie like this before. They'd been through some pretty stressful situations in the past but she'd never been so tightly wound up. "Calm down Old Col."

"Old Col. *Old*! That's all I am to you, an old woman, an inconvenience, someone to be humoured while the rest of you have a wonderful life and forget about me!"

*"Cummoan."* Hamish crossed his arms over his chest. "Ondi's always been good to you and you're sponduletising." [2]

Ondine's forehead crinkled in confusion. So did Col's. But at least Col had stopped complaining for a moment, even if it was to wonder – as Ondine was – what in heaven's name Hamish was talking about.

"I'll get ye a wee nip of plütz. That will steady yer nerves."

"Nerves? I don't have nerves."

"Make it a bottle," Ondine said.

"I do not have nerves!"

"Oh, you've got nerves," Ondine said, "that's why you've been in a bad mood for weeks."

"I have not been in a –" Auntie Col stood to her full height and breathed hard. "It's true I have anticipated this night, but I do not have *nerves.*"

Not buying it. "You've been mean to Hamish ever since he said he'd be your partner, and the whole time he's been doing his best. And you've been tetchy with the rest of us.

There's no need for you to be like this when you could just magic up a spell so you look awesome on the dance floor."

The old woman glared at Ondine.

"Here, drink this, it'll make ye feel better," Hamish handed Old Col a nip of plütz in a brandy glass.

"I don't need it," she said, drinking it anyway.

Ondine tried again. "Chef's left us plenty to eat. You must be starving, why don't we sit down and relax?"

"Not hungry," Col said.

"Any sausages?" Hamish asked.

"It must be nerves then if you're not hungry," Ondine said as she raided the refrigerator.

"How many times do I have to say, 'I don't have nerves'?" Old Col said.

"But you must be starving. Magic uses up so much energy and –" Ondine stopped, then looked hard into her great-auntie's eyes. "If you're not hungry, maybe you haven't been using magic. Why haven't you been using magic, Auntie Col?" Invisible hooks pulled Ondine's stomach as she waited for the woman to answer.

Col creased her brow, then jutted her chin. "There's nothing wrong with doing something the old-fashioned way from time to time. I want to do this right, that's all."

"Why aren't you using magic?" Ondine put the dish of leftover sausages on the bench.

"I told you, I don't want to –"

"Liar!" Ondine flung a cold sausage at her great-auntie.

The woman turned but the meat splodged onto her sleeve before dropping onto the floor.

"Five second rule." Hamish picked it up and ate it.

Ondine had seen enough. "You could have magicked that away, but you didn't. What's going on Col?"

"I simply fail to see why you're resorting to violence –"

"– Ease up, hen –" Hamish reached for the dish of sausages to stop her flinging any more away.

"Why aren't you using Magic, Col?"

At first, Col's face held defiance. Were they in for more lies? Then a tightened top lip and chin tremble. "It's gone." Her eyes, surrounded by flaky-pastry skin, turned pink with the effort of holding back tears.

"Gone?" The truth bounced off Ondine's brain, refusing to go in.

Hamish stopped eating.

"Yes, gone," Col said with a whooshing sound as she let all her breath out and sagged before them. "I thought I was having a few senior moments, like at the wedding and, you know, afterwards a bit. But now it's . . . it comes and goes in flashes, I must be in wiccapause. It's only a matter of time before it's completely gone. I promised Anathea she'd be safe at the abnormal formal. That I'd look out for her. I can't stop thinking something terrible will happen tonight and I won't be able to do a thing to stop it."

"Col, I'm so sorry," Ondine stepped closer and wrapped her arms around her great auntie's shoulders. It helped to hide the stark terror freezing her inside. This was why Hamish was ageing so quickly each day, why he'd had to sleep as a ferret every night instead of sneaking in lovely cuddles and kisses with her. It was something Ondine had tried so very hard to ignore for so long. Sadly, denial could only last so long. More than half a century ago at her debutant ball, when Old Col placed the spell on Hamish that turned him into a ferret, he was just 17 year old. When Old Col died (hopefully not for a very long time) that staying spell would end and Hamish would revert to his original age.

If they didn't fix this magic issue, she could lose Hamish forever.

And the thing about Anathea's safety, that was important too.

"It's always been there in the back of my mind. That I could lose it one day," Col said.

Wetness slid along Ondine's arm. Was Auntie Col wiping her nose on her?

"When did this start?" Ondine asked.

"I think it started . . . or started to stop I suppose . . . at the autumn palace, back in September or October it must have been. It was coming and going, in fits and spurts. I guess I knew then it was only a matter of time." She looked around and found a chair, dragged it over and slumped into it. "Hand over the plütz."

Hamish asked, "Is that wise? It's still pretty early and we need to be on our feet all night?"

"Give her the plütz," Ondine said.

When Hamish gave Old Col an unsure look, the woman shrugged and said, "It's happy hour in Moldova." She took a few sips, coughed then cricked her neck from side to side. "OK kids, unless something radical happens tonight, we'll wake up to Vincent being Duke any day now. What in heaven's name are we going to do?"

---

ONDINE SLIPPED a lanyard with the hotel and house keys around her neck, then slung another lanyard over the first – this one had her video camera strapped to it. The spring day felt warm and inviting as they began their walk to the station. The perfect weather for street parties and kick-starting a coup. A short train ride later; the three of them were standing in the reception foyer at the Venzelemma *castlette*, asking for an audience with the Duchess.

Which is exactly when the wheels fell off their grand carriage of a plan.

"What do you mean she won't see us? Do you know who I am?" Old Col creaked and cracked as she stood to full height.

The assistant turned florid. "The err Duchess is . . . indisposed and can't be disturbed."

"She's not sick is she?" Ondine asked.

Giggles echoed from another room. The three of them turned as Duchess Anathea walked in, her hand set in the crook of Valentin's arm. So besotted with her middle-aged beau, the Duchess of Brugel kept right on giggling as she walked past Ondine and out to the balcony beyond.

"She completely ignored us," Ondine said.

"Aye. Terribly indisposed, so she is," Hamish said.

"That's not good," Old Col muttered. "Seriously not good."

The assistant bustled the trio out a servant's exit so they were once again out on the streets.

"He sure did pick a fine time to show up, don't you think?" Ondine asked. "It's like she doesn't care about Brugel any more."

"She's thoroughly distracted lass."

It made no sense to Ondine. "Being the Duchess is all she ever wanted. And she was so desperate to hang on to the position and . . . and be popular. How can she walk away from that? Oh!" She slapped herself on the forehead. "Maybe Vincent's asked Melody to put a spell on Anathea so that she doesn't care?"

Old Col tilted of her head. "I'd say it's Valentin who's put the spell on Anathea."

"He's a witch?" Ondine asked.

"No. But he's a charmingly attractive man, and they have a history."

Every one of Ondine's plans and ideas to help Anathea and thwart Vincent had fallen to bits. This was not how things were supposed to have happened! Depression weighed upon her. "This is doing my head in. Every time I've tried to help, it's either gone badly or gone nowhere."

"You can't save the world every time, lass," Hamish said. "Ye've done so much for Anathea, told her everything you learned about what Vincent's up to. Ye cannae do any more for her."

"But I have to try!" She said.

"And that's why I love you." Hamish tucked a tendril of hair behind her ear. "And I know ye won't stop trying to help, even if she won't listen. Tell ye what, we'll see Anathea again, at the debutante ball. We'll make her listen to reason."

"It will be too late by then," Ondine said. "There'll be thousands of people in Savo Plaza watching PopEuroTube on the big screen. I bet my next hot meal Vincent will be there, absorbing all that goodwill. We're sunk!"

"Nothing more to be done here. Let's get to the dance hall," Old Col said.

Deflated, they walked towards the nearest station. Which was exactly when their luck changed for the better as a well-dressed man stepped across the road a little way ahead of them.

Ondine whispered, "That's Valentin."

"Aye, where's he off tae?"

It looked like he was catching a train, just as they were. Ondine reached into her pocket, getting her camera ready to capture anything, should anything present itself as being capture-worthy.

"Wonder where he's off to?" Old Col asked. "The way he was making eyes at Anathea just before, you'd think he couldn't bear to part from her."

Keeping a respectable and not-at-all-stalkerish distance from Valentin, they followed him down a flight of steps and ended up on the same platform. Once again luck stepped in and saved them from having him notice they were there, as a crowd of teenagers in the middle of the platform talked in high-pitched squeals about how exciting everything was going to be tonight.

"Is he catching the same train?" Ondine whispered to Hamish.

Being a head taller, he could see more clearly. "Aye, I think so."

"The three of us together are too obvious," Ondine said. "Let's split up."

The train pulled in. It had seven carriages. Ondine slipped in with the noisy teens. Away from the protective reach of Old Col and Hamish she felt disconnected. Like her skin didn't fit properly and she couldn't get comfortable. Also, she couldn't see Valentin, and suddenly she wished she hadn't come up with the idea to separate. What if Valentin got off at another station?

The rowdy mob didn't take seats, preferring to stand and chat and giggle all the way. Ondine squished her way through the crowd to the connecting section to the front carriage, where she found Hamish and Old Col walking towards her. A smile burst free, so she stayed where she was and waited for the two of them to get to her.

"He's not in this carriage, is he lass?"

"No, so he must be further back," Ondine said.

He wasn't in the next one, or the one after that. How many more carriages were there again? Sneaking glances through the connector to the next carriage, Ondine searched for Valentin.

Another station came and went.

"Did he get off?" Ondine asked.

"I couldn't tell," Hamish said.

"He didn't." That was Col. "There are more people in the last carriage now, we could go in and nobody would notice three more."

They took the risk and walked through the remaining connectors until they were in the final carriage, trying desperately not to look like they were looking for someone. "That's him down by the doors," Ondine said as she turned her back to face Hamish. "I saw him just before I sat down."

"I think I can see him," Hamish said as he craned his neck. "Now he's checking his watch."

"And you know why he's doing that?" Ondine said.

"Tae tell the time?"

Rolling her eyes, "Because he's obviously meeting with someone."

"You're making it sound nefarious," Old Col said. "I like it. Who needs magic when you've got a brain like yours, eh?"

Hamish nudged her. "Course she's got a good brain, she chose me, dinshe?"

"Where is Valentin?" Old Col asked.

Ondine looked further down the carriage. "He's getting up. Bother, he's heading out."

"Owf we get then," Hamish said.

Heart thwacking against her ribs in the effort to execute her espionage, Ondine walked as casually as she could manage to the train door.

They stepped on to the platform and Col looked around. "He's not there?"

"Are you sure?" Hamish asked.

Old Col tisked. "I've lost my magic, not my eyesight."

"Oh no," sickness flipped Ondine's belly. The doors behind them closed with a swish-thud. "He didn't get off." They turned to see Valentin standing on the other side of the train door, waving to them.

Ondine said, "Saturn's rings!"

Old Col said, "Hogs and hazels."

Hamish said something that defied translation.

**12**

---

Disappointment curdled Ondine's emotions as she struck 'espionage agent' off her imaginary list of future career opportunities. Dejected, they walked the rest of the way to Savo Plaza. The crowd soaked up the pre-PopEuroTube entertainment before the main even beamed in live from Craviç on the big screen. Hamish spotted two empty cafe chairs around a table. Old Col ordered the second cheapest thing on the menu, a tea and biscuit combination. [1]

If Ondine were being honest with herself, she had to admit things were looking more than hopeless for them. The thought of giving up made her all kinds of cross, but the way forward was more confusing than ever.

And yet they'd come so far, they couldn't give up now.

Which meant the only course of action was to keep on going, hoping for a miracle.

As they sat there, taking sips from the one teacup and sharing the two biscuits between three, Ondine sitting on Hamish's lap because of the chair shortage, a man in a suit darted out of a laneway towards the Plaza Hotel entrance.

"Psst," Ondine said to Hamish and Col. "Look over there at your nine o'clock."

They both looked in different directions.

"Over there," she said, pointing. "It's Valentin. He went into that hotel."

Patting the camera around Ondine's neck, Old Col smiled. "Get to it then."

Ondine made sure her camera was ready. Steadying her breathing, she walked to the hotel, even though her body screamed for her to sprint.

In the hotel lobby, there wasn't anyone around who looked like Valentin. *Jupiter's Moons, I've lost him!* Needing to un-panic, she strode to the ladies' bathroom and locked herself into a cubicle. A moment later, two women came in and chose the cubicles either side of Ondine, both chatting all the way through relieving themselves. There was no option but to overhear all of it.

*"I think you're being mean by not helping."* One of them said. Her accent didn't sound entirely Brugelish, but it was hard to tell with their voices bouncing off the tiles.

*"I hardly need to help, he's getting everything he wants."* The other woman said. A woman who sounded exactly like Melody.

The video camera weighed heavily in her hands. Ondine really needed to get out of here. She also wanted to record the conversation but the machine made a little 'beep' sound when it came on, which would alert the ladies. She flushed to make enough white noise to drown out everything, then pressed the 'record' button. Which made her feel all kinds of sick in the head at the fact she was recording a conversation in a women's toilets.

Time to get out of here and leave the others to talk in private, so she could get it all on tape.

"Oh, hello!" Melody said far too loudly.

*Quick, act surprised it's her.* "Oh wow, what are you doing here?" *Real smooth, brain, thanks a lot.* "Hello, it's Ruslana, isn't it?" They went to shake hands, then Ondine remembered she's been in a bathroom. "I'd best wash them first." Mercury's wings, if she used the taps, the rushing water could drown all sound completely. Instead she wiped them on the tops of her skirt in slap-dash fashion. "Are you staying here at the hotel?"

Ruslana tilted her head. "Yes. Why don't you come up and take tea with us?"

"Sure? I just . . ." *I can't tell them I have a camera sitting on top of the toilet. Oh great, now they're washing their hands and leaving. So much for spying. Time to get back in the stall.* "Ah, I think I've eaten too many fried cheeseballs, I'll be another couple of minutes. Oh this is so embarrassing. S'cuse me."

"We'll wait for you out in the lounge then," Melody called out as they left.

"Thanks." Quickly Ondine locked herself behind the cubicle door and retrieved the camera. OK, the first attempt was a bust, but if she slipped the camera into her coat pocket – as bulky as it was – she could record whatever future conversation came along without alerting anyone to the giveaway 'bleep – you're being recorded' noise.

Not that she could see Ruslana or Melody when she walked out to the foyer. Where had they gone? There were plenty of people milling about, but none of them were who she wanted them to be. First she'd lost Valentin, now she'd lost Melody and Ruslana. Frustration twisted her lips as she headed to an area that looked more like a greenhouse than a lounge. Potted plants taller than the average person screened the guests, while golden spring sunlight poured in from the floor-to-ceiling windows.

There, relaxing on a lounge chairs with a glass of tea-coloured liquid (which obviously wasn't tea) was Anathea's second-ex and current beau, Valentin. Sitting across the low table from him was Lord Vincent. Sitting beside him was Ruslana's father, Babak Balakhan.

The body language was far too relaxed for people who had only just met. Heart threatening to leap out of her throat, Ondine breathed into her coat lapels to muffle her noisy breaths. With trembling hands, she checked the camera to make sure the little red light was still on. It was! Hooray, she'd done something right at last. As quietly as she could manage, she placed the camera into the coconut fibres at the base of the plant and checked the view. It captured all three men, Valentin front-on and Vincent and Babak from the back.

Time to retreat to the foyer.

"There you are!" Melody said, out of nowhere. Ruslana was standing beside her.

Ondine jumped, her pulse beating a tattoo in her brain. "I didn't hear you," and she patted her chest and laughed to show how silly she was. That should be enough to disguise how guilty she *really* was.

Melody embraced Ondine. "Are you all right?"

"Err, just feeling off colour, because of the, um, you know, the cheese-balls." Best lie ever.

"Why don't you stay with us for the night?" Melody asked. "We'll have a lovely time catching up. It's been so long since we've done that."

This was a completely different Melody from the love-struck misery she'd argued with back at the family pub. "Oh, you don't want me cluttering up the place. I'm too tense about tonight, I'll be a mess when Margibelle come on." Not a lie.

Ruslana quirked the corner of her mouth upwards. "Is that the only reason why you're tense?"

"Well . . . " Ondine looked at her feet. *Come on brain.*

Nothing.

"Stay with us," Ruslana said, "we're going to watch the show from the hotel balcony. We have the best view of the big screen."

"Maybe um," she started again, fighting a sickening sense of panic that they would tie her up for the rest of the evening. Then a really, really good idea came to her. "Actually, perhaps we can catch up another time. Hamish is in the plaza and um," she felt herself blushing deeply, which reflected how she really felt, but also gave her enormous relief that her lie held a massive dollop of truth, "this is kind of the only privacy we've had for the longest time."

Ruslana and Melody made an 'O' with their mouths and blushed right along with her, before smirking behind their hands.

"Be good. Be safe," Melody said with a wink.

"Of course," Ondine replied, blushing even more furiously.

"Wait a minute," Melody looked her up and down. "You're not feeling funny in the tummy because you're –"

"– No way!" Ondine cut her off, then dropped her voice. "No, it's not that. Definitely not that."

"OK, well, be good, you hear?" Melody said.

"Yes ma'am," Ondine gave Melody and Ruslana a quick salute and headed back to the bathroom to:

a) breathe

b) laugh

c) buy time and work out how to get the camera out of the hotel's planter pots without anyone seeing her.

Sickly heat threatened to leap out of her mouth as Ondine waited for as long as she could in the bathroom. Hands slippery with fear-sweat, she stepped as quietly as she could towards the greenery. The seats were empty. At last! Something had gone her way! She wiped the coconut fibres off the camera. It was switched off. Had someone seen it and messed with it? Had it reached the end of the tape and switched itself off?

Desperate to review the footage, but doubly-desperate not to be sprung sneaking about with a camera, she slotted it into her coat pocket. *Please let there be something on this.* Just as she turned around the plants, Hamish appeared.

"Ah! You scared me!" Like she wasn't tightly wound enough!

"Sorry hen, but I was worried about ye. Ye've been gone so long and I lost sight of ye."

"You've been looking out for me?" Harp music played in her head and her heart soared.

"Of course I have," he kissed her for good measure. It was a really good measure. Then he tilted his forehead against hers and lowered his voice. "I saw Valentin leave, so I think we're safe. Col's gone to the dance hall already, she said she needed time to get dressed."

"Goody." They were unchaperoned. This earned a properly lovely kiss on the lips, which sent sweet shivers all the way through to her toes. She needed kisses like this, they were all-too-rare these days with Hamish spending a third of his life as a ferret.

Life was crazy, Brugel was crazy, her family was crazy. Ondine didn't even know what extra crazy tomorrow might bring. But one thing she did know for sure; in the midst of all the craziness, she and Hamish would still be together. They belonged together, and she'd do whatever it took to make sure they'd stay together. If their attempts to disrupt Vincent from his claim to the throne failed, and she was starting to suspect that they would, no matter what happened, she'd have Hamish.

And he'd have her.

Which lead to another, not altogether welcoming thought. They'd come too far on this crazy journey to go back to the way things used to be. Then a truth-bomb hit. They couldn't 'go back' to the way things were, even if they tried. Only now did. Ondine realise she and Hamish had to keep going. They'd do their best to stop Vincent, even if it meant going down in a big screaming heap. Because even if they failed, and that was looking like the most probable outcome, at least Ondine would know that she and Hamish had tried their hardest to stop him.

Together they walked further down the street to find another cafe – they'd lost their spots from before, as the crowds grew even more crowded in Savo Plaza – to grab a seat and check through the camera's little rectangular screen for anything usable.

"If you want to sit here, you have to buy something," the samovari said. [2] He had that tired look of someone who had to repeat himself all the time.

"Two teas, no sugar." Hamish said.

"Sugar's on the table anyway," the samovari said.

Ondine begged the heavens she'd captured something useful.

"You can clearly see it's Valentin," Hamish said. "You're amazing."

"Your teas," the samovari turned up with a tray loaded with hot cups of deep brown liquid with floating slices of lemon.

Thanks," she said absently as she kept looking at the small picture, wondering how it could help them at all. "Saturn's rings!" She nearly knocked her tea over in excitement. "Look, they've giving him something in an envelope."

"It's *goat* to be loaded with cash, hen. Ye've got him."

"It's not enough." She worried her bottom lip against her teeth as she kept playing the footage. "We can't see who's giving him the envelope of money."

"Mebbe they get up in a wee bit and we'll see their faces?" As he said it, the three men in the image did indeed rise from their seats, their business transaction over. As they rose, they stood out of frame, so their heads weren't visible any more.

"I'm going to have to swear," Ondine said. "Really, properly scream and swear." But to make a liar out of herself, she buried her head in her hands, clamped her eyes shut and clenched her lips together.

"We havnae failed, yet," Hamish said as he rubbed her back in gentle circles. "Let's have another look and see if there's anything we've missed."

"And then I can swear?" Ondine said behind her hands.

"Aye, I'll teach ye a whole new set."

Sniffing, Ondine dragged her sleeve over her face, then set to making her tea sweet enough. She fished out the slice of lemon and added in two teaspoons of sugar. In her frazzled state, it wasn't enough. Two more teaspoons swiftly followed. Perfect.

If only a cup of tea could fix the sick feeling of failure coating her like a damp blanket. Deep in her bones she knew Lord Vincent was going to take over the country tonight. This tiny bit of footage was her only weapon against him.

"Let's have another look. Here's Valentin," Hamish said, replaying the footage. "And then we see Vincent give him the money."

"That's not Vincent, that's Babak," Ondine said. "He was sitting closer to the wall."

"Aye, so his hand is the one covered in bling."

A true observation, the man had chunky gold rings on every finger.

"That's Vincent now, shaking Valentin's hand," Ondine said with a heavy sigh.

"Wait a minute, is there a zoom on this? Aye, here it is. Let's get a closer look."

Each press of the zoom button made the centre of the picture larger, showing a familiar hand. "It's blue!" Ondine squealed.

"Way hey!"

Pure joy spun like a tornado through Ondine as she bounced up and down on her seat. Hamish threw his arms around her and kissed her all over.

"Ye did it lass, ye *goat* him!"

"Are you going to order more tea or what?" The samovari asked.

"Later," Hamish said as he pushed his chair back and drew Ondine to her feet. He kissed her solidly on the lips and said, "You're amazing."

When they eventually stopped kissing, reality snapped back into focus. It was dark and Savo Plaza was packed with people, many of them had blue hands and carried the Brugelish hexagonal flag. Some wore the flag like a cape, tied at the neck, which pushed patriotism over the line towards ranty-nationalism.

A column of drummers and Fort Kluff cadets marched past. In the distance, a clock 'bonged' five times.

"Let's get to Old Col," Ondine said, grabbing Hamish's hand and leading them down a side street towards the direction of the ballroom. "We can't be late for the abnormal formal."

Running nearly the whole way, they reached the ballroom with lungs fit to burst. Fire and cramps greeted every breath Ondine dragged into her throat. "Haveto (gasp) find Anath (gulp) ea and show her (wheeze) the tape of Valentin."

"Aw naw hen," Hamish pulled up sharply. "She's already dancing with him in the ballroom."

How did he get back here so quickly? Ondine wondered. He must have had a car.

"I'd best get changed, sharpish," Hamish said, then disappeared into the gentlemen's rooms.

Like magic, he reappeared moments later in his formal clothes.

Old Col spotted them and came over. "I thought you'd never get here," she said to Hamish, while giving only the briefest nod to acknowledge Ondine. "I've waited a long time for this, I'm going to have my dance with Hamish."

It would be beyond rude to take this moment from Collette Romano, who had waited decades to right this old wrong.

Hamish, looking resplendent, guided her to the dance floor and they twirled and danced with charm and grace.

Last time they'd been here, the dance hall defined 'shabby chic'.

Now, filled with people dressed in their finery, it came to life.

Flower vases on pedestals added glamour and life.

A chandelier twinkled and sparkled, casting bubbles of light around the room.

The walls were festooned with streamers and rosettes, adding colour and vibrancy.

Couples danced, their skirts and suit tails swishing and swaying with fairytale elegance.

*I'll give you two minutes*, Ondine thought. *Then we'd better get on with our mission.*

As if psychic – and there was every chance the elder witch had that ability – Old Col and Hamish approached Ondine about one minute and fifty seconds later.

Old Col said, "Thank you, Ondine and Hamish, for allowing me this lovely dream."

Tears welled up in Old Col's eyes, as she turned to her dance partner. "Hamish, you've made an old woman very happy. I forgave you a long time ago, but now you've truly redeemed yourself at last."

"Aye. This is how it should have been all those years ago. But if you hadn't cursed me and turned me into a ferret, I wouldn't have found my true love Ondi."

Old Col smiled with serenity, as if everything was right with the world. Then her faced snapped back and it was all business. "Right, moment's over, what's next?"

Hamish said, "Ondi's captured brilliant evidence of Vincent on tape. We need to show it to Anathea."

"Well then, we'd better show her." Col said. "I suggest we dance close to her, then swap partners so I'll dance with Valentin and you dance with Anathea. Guide her down here to the kitchen so Ondine can show her the tape."

Her great auntie had snapped into commander-in-chief-mode. Ondine liked it. "Sounds like a plan!"

Hamish and Old Col twirled closer and closer to Anathea and Valentin. They took light steps, making it look effortless as they homed in. Then the switch! Old Col stepped to the side, then she and Hamish bowed to Anathea and Valentin.

Shame Hamish had his back to Ondine, she couldn't see what he was saying, nor his expression. After a painful heartbeat of time, Anathea accepted the offer and swayed into Hamish's arms. Auntie Col smiled, tilted her head then turned to Valentin to await his offer. [3]

Gliding across the floor, Hamish steered Anathea neatly through the guests, moving her surreptitiously towards Ondine. Meanwhile, Valentin hadn't offered for Auntie Col's hand. She stood in the middle of the dance floor, waiting. The expression on her face somewhere between expectant and mortified.

*Ask her you clod*, Ondine silently begged. A heavy ball of doubt rose in Ondine's throat. If Old Col waited any longer, she'd turn into a statue. People were looking, craning their necks this way and that.

Then, horribly, Auntie Col made a bow to Valentin, even though he had no rank over her. Jupiter's moons, Valentin turned his back and returned to his table. In a cloud of peach chiffon and ostrich feathers, Old Col glided towards the powder rooms. At that moment, Hamish guided Anathea into the kitchen. *Oh, the camera!*

"What is so important that it must be seen right away?" Anathea asked.

"It's this, My Lord Duchess." Ondine held the viewing screen out so she could see what they had. "I recorded it today. I'm so sorry to be the bearer of bad news, but your Valentin is taking payoffs from Babak and Vincent."

As Anathea watched the footage her breathing became more rapid, then her face froze. For a second Ondine thought their beloved leader would flip a table and storm out.

"Valentin has been properly identified?" She asked. "It looks like him, but without my glasses I cannot be sure."

"You wear glasses?" Ondine and Hamish asked together.

"There's nothing wrong with wearing glasses," Anathea said. "Although I am on the young side."

"Yeas," Hamish agreed with her. "Far too young to need glasses."

"And how will people know that this is Vincent giving him the money?"

"It's not Vincent, it's Babak, you can tell because of all the rings on his fingers. Vincent's the one who is shaking his hand just . . . now. See that."

Anathea shook her head. "It's just a hand. It cannot be proved that it's Vincent."

"When it zooms in, you can tell it's him, because the hand is blue."

The Duchess of Brugel frowned enough to make a tiny crease in her forehead. Then she took a step backwards and held the edge of the table. *Grrrrk!* The table skidded on the floor under Anathea's weight. Ondine stepped in to steady her.

"It's a horrible shock, I'm so sorry My Lordship," Ondine said. "But we had to show it to you. You needed to know the truth."

Steadying herself, Anathea removed some invisible lint from her sleeve and took a deep breath. Then she made a pathetic sigh and her voice came out so softly Ondine had to strain to hear her. "That lying bucket of wee. He was supposed to be helping."

"Eh, which one, Valentin or Vincent, Me Lordship?" Hamish asked.

Anathea made a dismissive sniff. "Both of them. I should have twigged Valentin's timing was too perfect. Same with Vincent, offering to pay for renovations, all the while he was paying for Valentin to romance the throne away from me."

"Aye. But aside from the obvious heartbreak, it's amazing news, wouldn't ye say?" Hamish asked, his face full of hope. "This exposes Vincent. Once we show this to the world, nobody will trust him ever again."

Anathea's chin wobbled.

"We have tae find a way to play it on the big screen in the plaza tonight, then everyone will see what Vincent's been up to, so they will," Hamish said.

"No!" Anathea stood straight up, knocking the table backwards again. "It cannot be played."

"What?" Hamish and Ondine said as one.

"It is humiliating." Anathea said. "Dear heavens, I will be laughed at. I will be derided. I will be seen to have no judgement. No, it cannot be played. You are expressly forbidden."

The figurative plates Ondine had been spinning on bendy poles came crashing around her. "But if people don't see it, Vincent will win."

"I won't be held to ridicule," Anathea protested.

Old Col joined in, having clearly heard a fair bit of the conversation. "Then say the footage is yours, My Lordship. Tell Brugel *you* managed to catch Vincent doing these horrible things."

Anathea's chin wobbled again. "Because horrible things *are* being done to me! I am being taken for a fool!"

"Naw hen, not like that. You'll be the messenger, and if ye sell it right, folks'll think you were on to Valentin the whole time." Hamish said.

*Had he just called The Duchess of Brugel 'hen'?*

Silence passed between them, before Anathea finally said, "You want me to get on stage, in front of everyone, and say my suspicions were confirmed and Vincent cannot be trusted?"

"Yes," Ondine nodded.

"That will not do," Anathea said. "Vincent needs to be spoken to. I will go to him at once."

"He wilnae listen," Hamish said with a headshake.

"What about the rest of the debutante ball?" Old Col asked.

Ondine said, "We can tell the orchestra to play faster."

Colour draining from her face, Anathea said, "Would it be terribly unducal of me to have a quick puke?"

---

IF THE ONLY WORRIES ONDINE HAD THAT night were making sure Hamish danced beautifully for the entire evening, she would have been nervous. But the situation with Valentin taking bribes to fall back in love with Anathea chewed her confidence to shreds. Then there was the extra matter of stopping Vincent from taking over the country. That thought poured a fresh cup of acid into the churning washing machine of her stomach.

But most of all she had no idea how her sisters were doing at PopEuroTube because the ballroom's kitchen, where she spent most of her time, did not have a television. She made her way to the women's changing rooms and discovered several ladies crowded around a portable television set. Oooooh! They could catch glimpses of the acts between dance sets.

"There you are," Old Col said to Ondine, "Call me when Margibelle comes on."

"Shush!" Somebody shushed.

Anathea walked in and everyone sprang away from each other and pretended they weren't doing anything wrong, even though they looked incredibly guilty.

"When are Margibelle on?" Anathea asked the room. "The suspense is killing me."

"Another quarter hour, My Lordship," one of the debutantes said.

"I'm so tense!" Anathea said, then put a broad grin to her strained face. The Duchess looked tense all right, but it surely had more to do with her ex-husband accepting bribes to woo, and her nephew planning a coup, than anything happening in the world of music.

The debutantes exited but left the television on. Their partners, no doubt, were huddled over a radio or television in the men's room.

"I had no idea the room could be cleared so quickly," Anathea said as she moved towards the basin and played cold running water over her wrists.

"Have you burned yourself?"

"No dear, stemming the nausea. I'd make a cold compress, but that could trickle water onto the dress and a stained dress can't be returned."

Ondine's nerves hitched and she checked the door to make sure nobody else was coming in, then she took up position at the basin next to Anathea. "Valentin doesn't suspect anything, does he?"

"No. He's being charming tonight. Just as he was when we first met." Anathea righted herself and tucked a stray hair behind a pin. "On with the show, eh?"

In the ballroom, the duchess was a picture of a serene, regal woman, smiling and enjoying the company of the elegant man seated next to her. She looked so comfortable and at ease, the polar opposite to the nauseated wreck Ondine had witnessed in the restrooms.

From the side of the room, a couple of men in tuxedos guided in a television set on a trolley and plugged it in. People looked confused and glanced from it to their partners and then to the duchess.

The dance set finished with a swirl of strings from the orchestra.

Anathea rose and walked to the podium. "Ladies and Gentlemen, it has been my delight and honour to receive you this evening. It's a special night for everyone here, but it is also a very special night for Brugel. I too am guilty of stealing away to keep track of events concerning PopEuroTube."

Nervous laughter washed through the crowd.

"Rather than keep you exiled from our marvellous performers, let formalities be suspended for a short while so we may enjoy Brugel's moment."

A huge cheer rang through the ballroom as people crowd-rushed the television set. It was on, it was in colour and someone had turned the sound up so high it distorted.

Wait a minute. They were supposed to be speeding things up so they could get out of here early, not delaying proceedings. Did this mean Anathea had lost her nerve about confronting Vincent?

Nevertheless, she squished in to watch the performers from Craviç sing their boppy melody. The Craviçians were dressed in long frilly peas-ant-skirts and overblown blousy tops. Absolutely ripe for a sudden costume change mid-song. A cheer erupted as the Craviç singers hit the chorus, spun around and revealed their sparkly under-costumes of mini skirts and tube tops. It didn't take long for Craviç's song to be over. [4] The next group, from the Kingdom of Radzvilla, were interminable with their wheezing piano accordions and spiky hats that looked like giant red pine cones.

"Radzvilla's a real place?" Hamish asked.

"I'll check an atlas," Ondine said.

Oh joy, at last it was time for Slaegal's entry to come on. Normally Ondine zoned out when the neighbouring country appeared, but this was different.

"I'm sorry we cannae be there for real," Hamish said, rubbing circles on her back.

"Ah well." Ondine tried to forget the blow-out argument she'd had with her sisters. "At least I'm with you."

He kissed the top of her ear and gave her a squishy hug as the lights dimmed. Margibelle took their places. The auditorium at PopEuroTube was silent. Watching on television, the ballroom for the abnormal formal was silent too. Ondine felt her ribs cramp as she forgot how to breathe.

*Be amazing. Just. Be. Amazing.*

"Shhhh!" Someone said. As if they needed reminding. It might be their neighbour on screen, but everyone knew Margibelle were home-grown Brugelers.

The note. Oh the glorious note Margi hit to launch into the song. It was sublime. It was soaring. It was heartbreaking. It hit true and strong and set everything in motion.

Someone turned the volume down to stop the distortion, so they could enjoy it for the magical music it was. Nobody in the ballroom spoke. Nobody even moved. Ladies held their taffeta gowns in their fists to stop them rustling.  The musical bridge built the song and took it soaring into the chorus. The chorus had the PopEuroTube auditorium on their feet, waving flags and singing along.

Tears sprang from Ondine. She didn't dare sniff as the noise would disrupt the transcendent music. Music her sisters had made. There was no fear on Margi's face. She was one with the music, and the music united everyone in this little patch of Eastern Europe. The last note came on sure and strong. The crowd went crazy. Margi came out of her musical-dream-state to acknowledge the crowd. Now her voice broke, now her eyes shone with unshed tears. *"Thank you, I love you!"* She cried out.

The ballroom, filled with everyone in their finest and on their very best behaviour erupted with howls of joy and sheer relief for Margibelle's amazing performance. Ondine grabbed Hamish in a bear hug and knocked him sideways with a mash-pash. They kissed and laughed with relief and kissed some more.

The commentator on the television said, *"And they've done it, the fire-crackers representing Slaegal have brought the house down with that wonderful ballad."*

*"Just when I was losing the will to live, we get a reminder of what PopEuro-Tube is all about,"* his partner in the commentary box said.

*"Yes. Poaching acts from other countries."* They both chuckled at how clever they were.

*"Now here comes something we've all been waiting for. If you ever need a theme for stealing a tank and liberating a city, this is it."*

*"It's the band from Brugel, with a song that will get people marching in the streets. It's Battlefront with* Anthem.*"*

On screen, people of all nations waved flags, whistled and cheered. As the first chord blared out, noise dropped to a hush. In the dance hall, they were silent as well, swaying in time with the stirring music. Grudgingly, Ondine had to respect Battlefront. It was an amazing song. It made you want to cheer, carouse, smile and weep. The chorus boomed through the speakers. Everyone around Ondine and Hamish joined in. Any other year, Ondine would have sung along, but she couldn't stop the knives of jealousy stabbing her heart. Her sisters should have been singing for Brugel instead of Slaegal.

Somebody turned the volume up even louder. The drumbeats came in so strong and heavy Ondine could felt it all the way from her feet.

*Boom-boom, boom-boom-boom. Thump-thump, thump-thump, thump-thump.*

Wait a minute. The thumping wasn't from the television. It was the floor rattling. The walls too. Looking up, the chandelier shuddered and shook, the lights flickered. The doors burst open. A group of cadets marched in. Armed cadets. With serious looking weapons.

Everyone screamed.

Hamish grabbed Ondine and made a run for the rear door, just as more cadets burst through this entrance too. Standing before all was Birgit Howser, dressed in a traditional Brugelish travelling witch cloak, the shoulders trimmed with epaulettes. Her eyes lit upon Ondine and she gave a slow shake of her head. "Run along now, silly girl."

"I'm not going anywhere," Ondine shot back, her heart rate doubling, her breathing coming hard and scared. Because despite the brave words, she was terrified of what Mrs Howser might do. What the cadets might do. "Why can't you leave us alone?"

"Oh bless, she's still talking," Mrs Howser said. The witch turned to a cadet and said, "Shut her up for me."

The cadet, a lad who looked younger than Ondine, nodded, then thrust his hand out.

Ondine tried to scream, but nothing came out. Hamish said a horrible swear word.

Mrs Howser smiled. "Well done." Then her gaze roved the crowd until it rested on Duchess Anathea with a bone-freezing smile of victory.

"Protect the Duchess," Old Col said to anyone who would listen.

All heads turned to Anathea, standing completely still beside Valentin. "Something must be done," she squeaked out.

"Of course," Valentin said. He took Anathea's hand and kissed it. Then he spun her around so fast he pinned her arm behind her back.

Ondine screamed, "Let her go!" Except nothing came out.

"Nobody move!" Valentin said, pinning Anathea's arm even tighter and making her yelp.

Mrs Howser scoffed, "That's *my* line!"

Valentin nudged Anathea towards the cadets and Mrs Howser.

"Good," Mrs Howser said. "If everyone behaves, nobody will get hurt."

"Really Birgit," Old Col marched towards her witchy foe. "You could have at least waited until we'd finished the ball and been presented. And to think we used to be friends!"

Mrs Howser rolled her eyes. "Of course. It's *always* about you."

"You have to take your spell off Hamish as well" Old Col acted as if she and Mrs Howser were alone, having a friendly old spat, instead of being surrounded by armed cadets.

"As if I'd ever do that!" Mrs Howser said. "Now get out of my way, I have so much to do, and so little time!"

"You know the spell!" Old Col was shouting now.

Everyone was looking at Col as if she were a few nuts short of a trail mix. The twig snapped for Ondine. "Oh! *That* spell!" She would have said it out loud, if she'd had a voice. Instead, she said it in her head. But, at least she knew what to do now. She grabbed Hamish, placed her palms on either side of his face and drew him down for a kiss. The spell, which Old Col had been referring, was the one that made other people's wishes come true whenever she and Hamish became amorous. The magically contagious spell that had caused so much mayhem in Brugel in the first place.

Many times in the past, Ondine had kissed Hamish good and proper. Tonight, she kissed him with the hope of a happy future for the two of them, and for Brugel. Which had her quietly thinking how clever and selfless she was. For his part, Hamish kissed her back with all the passion she'd come to love. What a kiss. Behind her closed eyes, searing bright lights flashed around the room.

Something slumped to the floor. It sounded like a sack of potatoes. Ondine broke away from the kiss to see Great-Auntie Col on the ground in a crumpled heap.

"No!" Ondine silently cried.

"This is too good," Mrs Howser said, leaning over Old Col, lifting her arm and letting it flop back onto the ground with a soft *thud*.

Fear jarred Ondine's joints. Old Col didn't move. Didn't make a sound. Her once proud expression fell sideways under the weight of gravity. Her closed lips didn't move, her nostrils didn't flare.

In her mind Ondine cried out, "What have you done?!" Wailing grief poured through her. "No, no no no! Col! Aunty Col! Wake up . . . the dance isn't over yet."

"Trying to use my magic against me. *Honestly*!" Mrs Howser shrugged. "Once a witch is past wiccapause, you're better off dead anyway."

Furious, Ondine sprang at the witch. The cadets leapt to defend their leader. Things got messy quickly. Behind her, Hamish shouted. Something solid and heavy bashed Ondine's shoulder, the pain sharp and hot. Something else equally heavy smacked the back of her knees, sending her to the ground in a screaming heap. Pain immobilised her. Looking up, she saw Hamish leaping at Mrs Howser's throat. Mid-air, he transformed into a ferret, his claws and teeth bared for maximum damage.

A cadet swiped him with a rifle butt, sending him flailing.

Ondine scrambled to her feet despite the searing pain in her shoulder. With a desperate lunge, she slid along the parquet floor, catching him millimetres from impact. Momentum kept her sliding. Ferret in hand, she could not stop the wall coming closer. She hit it. Hard. If the world had turned black it would have been a relief. Instead she felt every twisted tendon, every bruised bone and every bleeding muscle. Concussion wouldn't take her out, all she could do was curl into the pain, close her eyes and groan pathetically.

Mrs Howser shouted, "Everybody out!"

At which point, Ondine prised one eye open to see the cadets marching Duchess Anathea, Valentin and the rest of the guests into the street.

"Her too," Mrs Howser pointed to the prone form of Old Col on the ground. "Bring her, she could still be useful."

A cadet who looked like nothing more than string and gristle in a uniform, crouched down to Old Col and lifted her into his arms.

Was it the flickering lighting? The stress? The pain? Ondine wasn't sure, but she could have sworn she saw Old Col wink at her.

**13**

———————

The view from the hotel suite filled Vincent with a palpable sense of something ominously good waiting for him. Everything was coming together. On the television behind him in the hotel suite, and on the enormous screen down in Savo Plaza, the PopEuroTube presenters talked in rhyming couplets.

The man said, *"That is the end of the music and art."*

The woman said, *"Now it is time to play your part."*

*"The voting will open in just a minute."*

*"Phone us now to see who will win it!"*

Shudder.

"We go now?" Babak said, slapping a meaty hand onto Vincent's shoulder.

Ruslana remained on the couch, nibbling pistachios. *Crick, tink* they went, as she cracked each green nut, then tossed the hard shells into a stainless steel bin by her feet. Melody sat by the window, sending glimmering waves of green and silver sparkles wafting into the crowd gathered in the plaza.

The PopEuroTube co-hosts recapped the performances from the night.

*"It's been such a night, we don't want to stop."*

*"Here are the songs again, right from the top!"*

"Rhyming ham and cheese. We'll be lucky not to get a riot," Babak said.

Melody turned to Vincent. "They're ready now." She looked sweaty and grey, like she'd been locked in a sauna and force-fed green bananas.

"All right, everyone," Vincent clapped his hands, revving himself up. "Let's meet the people."

Babak took his daughter's manicured hand, wiped the pistachio salt from it, then guide-yanked her out of the chair until she was on her feet. "The people are ready for their new Duchess."

"She needs her wig," Melody said no louder than a breath.

"Good catch," Vincent said.

Unsteady as she may be, Melody picked up the exquisite helmet of hair from where it rested on a polystyrene head on the sideboard.

"Coming." Ruslana stood before the mirror to make the hair sit the right way.

If they timed this correctly, when Battlefront's song recap came on with *Anthem*, Vincent would step out in front of the big screen and take the microphone. Not that he liked to brag in clichés, but he'd have the mob eating out of the palm of his hand.

---

WAKING up in the abandoned ballroom, Ondine fought through multiple layers of soreness to get on her feet. Everyone was gone, which angered Ondine all the more as it denied her a long-awaited showdown with Howser. Damn that witch! Her voice came out as a croak, but at least it was back. "Hamish, where are you?"

"In here, lass," he said from a darkened cloakroom.

Her eyes adjusted quickly to the darkness and she made out his human shape as he rifled through a pile of clothing.

"We'll need warmth if we're tae venture out." He returned to her with an overcoat and slipped it over her shoulders.

"Whose is this?" She asked as she creaked her bruised arms into the sleeves.

He shrugged. "Somebody else's. They left in a hurry."

Heavy rumbling shook the floor again. Grabbing her hand, Hamish dragged her to the doorway. "I never knew ye got earthquakes in Brugel."

"We don't," Ondine's whole body shook. The windows rattled and paint flaked off the walls. It hurt to talk, but the more she did the easier her voice came back. "Let's see what it is."

It didn't take long. Shrinking themselves into the darkened doorway, they watched a tank roll through the cobblestone street. Its caterpillar tracks rattled and shuddered past, the main gun pointed ominously forward.

The question, 'where is it going?' formed, but the moment she'd thought it, Ondine knew. "The plaza," she said, running out onto the street as soon as the tank was gone.

Realisation smacked Ondine upside the head. "Jupiter's moons! Half of Brugel is in the plaza tonight! This was Vincent's plan all along. Everyone is penned in! It's a trap!"

"Aye, ye worked it out faster than me."

"This way, I know a shortcut."

The pair jogged at a heavy-breathing pace towards Savo Plaza, taking alleyways too narrow for a tank to pass through. The cool air of the spring evening, and the mission to save her country invigorated Ondine. But they could only keep going so far before they had to stop. They turned to find a wall of people blocking the road. People waving banners with blue hands printed on them.

"Wait a minute," Hamish pulled her into the shadows of a doorway. "There's a bloke with a megaphone instructing them."

These were no PopEuroTube revellers, they were an organised gang. A gang supporting Lord Vincent and heading straight for the plaza. Skirting around the blue hand mob, Ondine and Hamish took a side alleyway heaving with people. "Excuse me, sorry, please let me through? Can I just . . ." Ondine said on a repeating pattern as she budged and nudged her way closer to the big screen to see what was going on. The further they pushed, the thicker the crowd, until it became impossible to breathe for the crush of people.

On the big screen, countries took it in turns to deliver their scores.

Someone just gave the ultimate thirteen votes for Slaegal. Zings of happiness zipped through Ondine on behalf of her sisters.

Hamish squished her around the middle. "Margibelle are in front lass!"

The crowd roared enough to shatter the roof. Luckily they were outdoors and there was no roof to shatter.

The next set of votes came in, and the voice giving those votes sounded hideously familiar.

"Good evening Europe, this is Venzelemma calling!"

The crowd's enthusiasm flew off the scale.

There on the screen was Lord Vincent's face, five times larger than life. He had his back to the rapturous audience in Savo Plaza, delivering his long-winded time-wasting piece about how wonderful the night had been and what a brilliant show everyone had put on.

Ondine's eyes moved from the big screen, to see Vincent in the flesh on the stage below. He was speaking into a camera, a chunky cable trailed from the back of it. That cable had to lead somewhere, and it had to be plugged into *something* in order for Vincent to get his live messages across to the millions of people watching PopEuroTube all over Europe.

"I've got a plan," she said, grabbing Hamish by the hand. "Let's unplug him!"

Pulling the plug wouldn't stop the show, but it would stop Vincent's grandstanding by killing his live feed.

The crowd hushed as Lord Vincent delivered the lowest five scores. Ondine hoped he'd drag it out so they'd have time to get to whichever power socket that cable was connected to.

*Keep talking, wind bag.*

Then Vincent announced, with a long drawn out pause, that Brugel was giving nine points to Craviç.

A small part of Ondine wanted to know the rest of the results, but they had to pull the plug on Vincent and get people out of the plaza before the Fort Kluff cadets and Mrs Howser arrived.

There it was! The cable fed straight into an outside broadcast van.

*Bang bang bang* Ondine smacked the van's door with her palm. A frazzled woman wearing a headset opened the door and glared at them. "What do you want?"

"Who are *you*?" Ondine said, fuelled with bluster and adrenaline. "Where are Yovanna and Berol?" There was no Yovanna and Berol, she'd made those names up, but she hoped the tone of her voice would confuse the staff inside.

Vincent dragged the points out, delivering "Ten points to the outstandingly wonderful performance from Haute Montagne."

"Never mind who I am, who are *you*?" The woman said. "And what do you think you're doing banging on the door during a live broadcast?"

Not falling for it, then.

"Ondi lass, will ye hold me?" Hamish said, one eyebrow raised as he held the door wide so the woman inside couldn't slam it closed.

"Yes darling. Of course." Ondine wrapped her arms around his waist, threading her thumbs through his belt loops as she did so. The man she loved made a howl of pain and crumpled into her chest. His clothes fluttered in the cold air and she quickly rolled them into a ball in her hands.

"On guaaaard!" Hamish cried out, leaping his Shambles-ferrety self up the steps and into the van.

The woman's screams pierced the sky. Madness filled the van. Shambles leapt from shelf to shelf, down to the floor, spun in the air, leapt onto his feet, twisted and tumbled, scarpered up a wall and somersaulted down again. A mesmerising display of agility and insanity.

Outside, Vincent delivered Brugel's eleven points to Moldova. A small part of her wanted to know who Brugel would give thirteen points to, but there was an army on the way and she had to act now.

The frazzled woman screamed again and charged after the furry intruder.

Ondine slipped inside the van and looked for the 'live' video feed amongst the technology and the wizz-bangery. There! She saw a label stating "LIVE CROSS UPLINK." That had to be it.

*Flick!*

People outside in the plaza hollered and booed.

She must have done something right.

The van rocked. With a crunching thud Ondine landed on her tailbone. The van door slammed shut as the mob outside rocked them back and forth.

"What have you done?" The woman held on to the walls for balance as she rounded on Ondine. "You've cut the live cross. Get everything back the way it was or we'll have a riot on our hands!" The woman, who should now be called The Furious Woman, turned to Ondine and yelled, "Get out!"

Shambles leapt onto the (furious) woman's lap. She yelped and jumped into the air, all arms and legs and pointy angles. "Get it off!"

"I've called security," a man said. He must have been in the van all along. His cardigan was so dirty and worn only the stains held it together. "I don't know what your game is love, but we've got no money. No point robbing us at ferret-point."

Ondine took a desperate look at the array of buttons and knobs and things that slid up and down, and little windows with needles that wobbled from side to side.  Why could there not be a simple master switch? It was one thing to silence Lord Vincent, but if the big screen kept on playing the rest of PopEuroTube, people would stay in the plaza and be trapped by the tanks.

Great Pluto's Ghost. There it was! A fuse box with a master lever.
*Flick*!

Everything switched off. The world turned black. Ondine groped for the door and shoved it open. Light spilled from outside as she scrambled to collect Hamish's abandoned clothes. A blur whisked beside her; Shambles leapt clear out of the van and scarpered up a nearby pole. In the plaza, the great screen stood like a monolithic art installation. Impressive but useless. The crowd grew restless, throwing empty cheeseball cups and drink cans at the screen.

Hope bloomed. She'd stopped it. The party in the plaza and the big screen showing PopEuroTube. All of it came to a shuddering stop. Surely everyone would go home now, right?

STANDING on the blacked-out stage confirmed Vincent's deep-seated fears that he wasn't allowed to have nice things. "Melody! Fix this now!"

"On it!" she called out from somewhere. It was so dark he couldn't tell where that somewhere was. With a flash and a *bzzt*, the lights came back on, along with the rest of PopEuroTube on the big screen. The crowd behind him cheered and whistled. He kept looking down the barrel of the camera, waiting for the red light to come on.

The operator behind the camera pulled his headphones off his ear and said, "After the live cross cut out, the show's hosts in Craviç read out Brugel's final votes going to Slaegal. So they're not crossing back unless the vote is close at the end of the night."

Damn.

The live feed restored, the big screen showed the delegate from Trajikstan announcing her votes. Thirteen points to Brugel.

The crowd in Savo Plaza, so distracted by the power cut, were now firmly back on board, cheering and hollering Brugel's top vote.

The leader board had Druvitzia first, Slaegal second and Brugel third, then a huge gap of thirty votes to fourth place, Craviç.

The broadcast went to a quick replay of all the acts during the night. On stage in front of the big screen Vincent grabbed a spare microphone from his jacket, flicked it on and spoke to the crowd.

"Ladies and Gentlemen, no matter the result, Battlefront has made Brugel proud tonight."

The crowd roared its approval.

Adrenaline charged through Vincent. "Straight after the results, we will have a special announcement, but for now, try not to bite your nails off while we wait to see who wins!"

It should be Brugel, but to Vincent's disdain, the last two countries' votes – and they took their sweet time delivering them – did not go their way.

Then the PopEuroTube masters of ceremonies were back on screen with their rhyming couplets.

*"It's the end of the night,*
*we've had so much fun.*
*It's our pleasure to say*

*Druvitzia won!"*

Savo Plaza erupted with howls of disapproval and deep rumbling booing noises. Looking out at the crowd, Vincent knew he had to keep things upbeat. It would have played out so much better had Brugel won, but things were already set in motion, so it didn't matter in the grand scheme of things.

That's when he looked out at the broadcast van and saw Ondine and Hamish standing nearby. Right then he knew they must have been responsible for the blackout a few minutes ago.

He didn't think he could hate them any more than he could right now.

* * *

Staring Lord Vincent right in the face, Ondine crossed her arms and willed herself not to leap on stage and strangle him with the microphone cord. Then she remembered she was a nice person who didn't go in for public displays of aggression. Even though she was sorely provoked. Yet there he was, standing in front of the big screen, hogging the limelight and all the goodwill.

"Ladies and gentlemen, Battlefront was amazing tonight!" Vincent said.

Behind him, the big screen changed from showing images of the winners at PopEuroTube to something very different. The interior of a public building.

Huh?

Ondine tried to work out where she'd seen this building before. It was cavernous, with dozens of well-cushioned chairs arranged in a u-shape around a long central table. That's when it hit her. The inside of Brugel's dentate building. At the centre of the room, near a long table, stood Brugel's First Minister Natalia Cebotari. Beside her Duchess Anathea stood trembling, a sheet of paper in her hand.

Ondine's bile rose.

The crowd hushed as they listened to the quavering voice of their Duchess.

. . .

*"To the people of Brugel. Congratulations on an outstanding performance at tonight's PopEuroTube. You have done your country and yourselves proud. Brugel's future on the world stage stands strong and assured.*

*"Tonight, it is with an eye on such a future that I announce my abdication as Duchess of Brugel, effective immediately, handing over rule to my nephew, Lord Vincent, who will from this moment on be known as Duke Vincent the third.*

*"I have also resolved to disband the dentate and open the government to free and fair elections at a time of Lord Vincent's choosing.*

*"I must stress that I arrived at this decision myself. The decision was mine alone to make.*

*Thank you for being the best people in the world, from the best country in the world. I will as ever, be your humble servant, Anathea."*

A pretty speech that hushed the crowd watching it in Savo Plaza.

Ondine knew the duchess had not written it herself. For a start, it wasn't written in that passive style of *things being done by someone else* that Anathea favoured. But mostly it didn't ring true because of the way Valentin and Mrs Howser had treated Anathea at the ballroom earlier tonight.

On stage Vincent spoke into the microphone again.

"Ladies and gentlemen, people of Brugel. I accept this honour. I must now travel to the Dentate and sign the necessary paperwork. Thank you for making history tonight!"

Ondine wanted to throw up, cry and tear her hair out all at the same time. The very worst thing had happened and she hadn't been able to stop it.

The mood in the plaza changed from friendly to confused in the snap of a twig.

A metallic rattling noise came closer. But from which direction? Craning their necks, Ondine and Hamish looked around.

"It's over that way lass," Hamish said, pointing to the right as a tank pushed its way down a street.

"No, it's this way," Ondine said, pointing to the left as another tank creaked into the edges of the plaza. Cadets flanked both the tanks, blocking the exits.

More tanks and cadets arrived and clotted access to the remaining streets. Riding on the top of one, came an all too familiar old witch. Mrs Howser, her cape flowing behind, looking like the queen of the world.

"Mercury's wings! We're trapped like rats in a cage!"

Wasting no time, Mrs Howser stood at the front of her tank and waved her arms. Sparks of dark magic flew through the air and landed like snow on people's heads, melting into their clothes and hair.

Any confusion evaporated as the crowd's mood switched firmly into full-on support for Vincent. Cadet's moved through the crowd, giving out blue banners and noisemakers. People chanted for Vincent in not-quite-unison (like they would properly chant at a football match). The original supporters held placards on sticks in favour of Vincent, yet covered their mouths with bandanas or surgical masks. Some of them wore those rictus-grinning face-masks from an inexplicably popular movie.

The giant screen showed the buoyant mood, as the cameras captured the pro-Vincent crowd and broadcast it to the rest of Brugel.

For a moment, Ondine lost her mind as euphoria for a new leader took hold. But wait, this couldn't be right. Mentally shaking herself, she dug deep, all the way to her boots, to remember why she and Hamish were here in the first place. They were here to stop Vincent, not support him.

No magic spell could counter-act such strongly held free will, and when it came to battling Lord Vincent, Ondine had an over-supply of free will.

Uh-oh, Hamish's face had already glazed over as he fell under Mrs Howser's spell.

"Snap out of it!" she yelled to her beloved.

He did not snap, nor did he come round when Ondine gave him a shake.

"Hamish, remember why we're here! We can do this, this spell can't stop us!"

But he looked so far gone, as if he'd become another person. "Come back to me, Hamish!"

With every fibre of her love, Ondine kissed Hamish, hoping it would knock some sense into him. If things weren't so desperate, it could have been a timeless kiss that developed into a lovely snog session. But Ondine didn't have that luxury.

When they eventually pulled away, Hamish smiled, then winked at her. "I needed that. Right, let's see what's to do?"

"Howser's put a spell on everyone, taking the goodwill in the crowd and turning it into a pro-Vincent rally. Our kiss hasn't affected anyone else. I can't very well go around kissing everyone in the entire crowd to break the spell!"

Looking about them, Hamish nodded. "We're in the thick of it now, lass."

The tanks cranked up again and began reversing down the streets. The cadets marching along side them. The mesmerised crowd stayed behind, watching events unfold on the giant screen.

A chant broke out in the plaza as someone started shouting on a loud-speaker, "Blue hand group. Blue hand group."

"I wish I had one of them," Ondine wailed.

"Like this?" Hamish produced a megaphone from behind his back.

"Oh my stars I love you so much!" Ondine threw her arms around his neck and kissed him all over the face, including, obviously, the lips. Her lips stayed on his for a while longer, because she loved him *that* much. It was Hamish who pulled back, and handed Ondine the megaphone.

Climbing onto the top of a stone plinth, Ondine cried out, "People! People, listen to me!"

They weren't listening.

"Helps if ye turn it on," Hamish said.

"Oh." Feedback whine. Take two. "People, listen to me!"

Great volume!

The people stopped. Actually stopped. Whoa, power! Ondine's nerves jangled as the crowd turned to her.

"It doesn't have to be like this! You're all under a spell, but it won't last! It was obvious that Vincent forced Anathea to make that speech. She's still our Duchess!"

Hundreds of revellers looked at Ondine. Waiting for her . . . to do what? To know the right thing to say? To give them answers?

"This is not the Brugel way. I love our country and I know everyone here loves our country too. Brugel . . . is what makes Brugel great."

Not the best start, because her brain hadn't caught up to the situation yet. "I'm sorry Vincent and Anathea are fighting. But we can sort this out. Life will go on tomorrow. Because we are a thoughtful people, and we look after each other. We have so much love to give. That's what our country needs now. We don't need to kick out the Duchess, we need love!"

Voice cracking with emotion, she flicked the button off so that she wouldn't amplify her aside to Hamish: "D'ye think it's working?"

"Keep giving it laldy," Which was Hamish's way of saying, 'give it all you've got.'

She flicked the loudspeaker back on again. "I love my country, I love our Duchess Anathea, she is a national treasure. She needs us and we need her."

People lowered their blue fists and banners. Having their attention made Ondine bolder. "Go home to your families and loved ones. Show the people closest to you how much they mean to you. That's the spirit of Brugel. That's *love*."

One by one, people turned to each other, as if waking from Mrs Howser's spell. They were shaking their heads, confused about what was going on.

"It's worked," Ondine turned to Hamish.

The crowd dropped their banners and signs.

"Love is the answer!" Ondine cried out.

She'd done it!

As one, the crowd suddenly let out an almighty roar and charged towards Ondine and Hamish, turning on them. Panicked, Ondine dropped the loudspeaker. Hamish grabbed her free hand, hauling her away from the angry mob bearing down on them.

"Up," Hamish said as they reached a tree. He linked his palms together to make a step. Ondine slotted her foot in and he *hoiked* her up. She hauled herself into higher branches, the crowd forming a sea of people below.

"Hamish?" She glanced at the base of the tree. Panic shot through her. He was nowhere. "Hamish!"

"Right here lass," he said, as his ferret form shot out of his clothes and scarpered up the trunk. "They're raging now."

People began pushing each other up the tree. The branch Ondine clung to, now with a Shambles ferret on her shoulder, leaned over the awnings of a shop. She crawled along the branch, her weight bending the arm low. Splinters bit her hand. There wasn't time to check for injuries as she scrambled from the branch onto the makeshift balcony. With a satisfying twang, the branch sprang back, throwing the other climber into the crowd below.

"That went about as well as could be expected," Shambles said.

Now they were higher up, they had a better view of the rioters. More people climbed the tree to get closer to Ondine. Someone else shimmied up a nearby flagpole.

Claws digging into Ondine's shoulder, Shambles yelled, "Run!"

*Clang, clang,* her feet crashed over the metal awnings as Ondine ran away. Then she came to a halt. The next awning was made of canvas, with huge mould and moss patches. No way would it take her weight. *Clang, clang,* someone else's feet closed in on them. Holding on to whatever parts of the wall she could, Ondine shuffled and hauled herself along, using window sills as footholds and –

*Riiiip!*

The person following had tried running across the awning, only to tear straight through it and land on the ground.

"The drainpipe!" Shambles yelled in her ear.

"Easy for you!" Ondine yelled straight back.

The claws left her shoulder and the ferret scarpered up the drain, all scritches and scratches as he found footholds in the rust. The rioters below were screaming and hollering now. She'd become the fox and they were a pack of slavering dogs.

"Hurry!" Shambles again.

"What do you think I'm doing? Taking a leisurely stroll?" Desperate for something to grab on to, Ondine reached up and clutched the lip of the guttering with one hand. Then she wedged her foot between the downpipe and the bracket holding it to the wall, pushing herself up. Her other hand grabbed more guttering.

"Gotcha!" Someone grabbed Ondine by the other foot and pulled on her.

Desperately she clung to the guttering, her arms burning in pain.

The crowd erupted in screams.

Claws raced down her arms. It had to be Shambles. Ondine felt but couldn't see Shambles scarpering down her body towards her attacker. The other person suddenly screamed in agony and let got. Shambles must have bitten him good and proper.

"Get up lass," Shambles yelled.

Muscles burned as she clung to the guttering and scrambled to the roof. "That's it, nearly –"

*Whoosh!*

The guttering buckled, sending freezing dirty water and last autumn's slimy leaves over them. Rivers of sludge poured into Ondine's armpits, then drizzled down her torso. Somehow – probably adrenaline coursing through her from the fear –instinct had her hanging on. With a few more shuffles and shimmies, she found a new section of guttering that held her weight. Her legs found the top of a window for purchase and she pushed with all her might.

A hand grabbed her by the wrist. "I've got ye."

She looked up into Hamish's smiling face. Hamish back in his human form, with both his hands around hers, hauling her up onto the roof.

She fell against him, breathing hard with relief. He spluttered as her wet hair fell across his face. Her wet, stinky, slimy hair.

The crowd below them hollered. People were climbing trees to get onto the shop awnings – avoiding the ripped canvas – and clawing their way up the side of the buildings. No way did Ondine want to hang around to see if they reached the roof.

The solid body of Hamish vanished out from under her and his ferret form scarpered to the roof ridge. "This way. Come on."

All things considered, it made a frustrating kind of sense to Ondine that he'd reverted straight back into a ferret. The sight of a naked man crawling over the roof wouldn't exactly be a calming influence on the mob, would it?

Spreading her weight out to minimise the chances of falling through, Ondine crawled on all fours, following Shambles. On the other side of the roof ridge, several shops opened out to a courtyard below. At the back of the buildings they found a narrow ladder, but the rungs were too far apart for Shambles to climb down safely, so he scrambled onto Ondine's shoulder and took the easy way down.

"Don't take this the wrong way, lass, but ye stink."

"You're hardly a rose garden yourself," she shot back.

He rewarded her with a ferrety kiss on the cheek. Shame it wasn't a human one. She could really do with one of them right about now.

**14**

———

The irritatingly slow drive to the Dentate had Vincent chewing at the nubby bits of skin on the side of his nails. If they went any slower they'd go backwards, but the crowds made it impossible to get momentum. Despite Babak's security detail, supporters leapt too close to the car, slapping the panels and windows in support.

"I'm getting out to walk," he said.

"No," Babak's hand slapped hard on his shoulder, welding him to the seat. "You are in no rush. You are patient and wise beyond your years. Yes?"

"Yes, you're right."

"You're going to be wonderful," Ruslana said.

"Where's Melody?" He hadn't seen her since the lights had gone out during the glitch.

"She said she was going back to the hotel for a rest."

Had she abandoned him at his moment of triumph? "What if I need her?"

"All good," Babak said. "It's all done now, you're the Duke. Relax and enjoy it."

Finally (had it only been ten minutes?) they reached the Dentate. A row of cadets stood guard by the side of the road, with a tank behind them. Floodlights lit the neo-classical facade with its fluted columns and stone steps.

The driver pulled up. Babak, Ruslana and Vincent slid along the leather seat and climbed out the car, to a phalanx of flashing lights as the media throng jostled for the best shot. Vincent took his time, smiling and waving, as if greeting an invisible friend just on the other side of the photographers.

He took the steps at a regal pace as reporters fired a barrage of questions at him:

"Did you convince the Duchess to resign?"

"Have you been planning this?"

"What about democracy?"

*Keep looking relaxed and unhurried. Keep looking in control. Because you are in control.*

The reporters kept firing questions, he kept right on walking and waving.

"What will happen to Anathea now?"

"Is this against the constitution?"

"How do you feel, now that you're Duke?"

The media crush managed to move aside enough for Vincent to make his way to the Dentate floor. Anathea and the First Minister would be waiting there for him. He'd sign the papers and dismiss them. Then he really would be Duke.

One foot in front of the other. It was a miracle he could see at all thanks to the flash burns in his vision. Gradually the black rectangles faded to reddish blotches. Anathea came towards him, hand out to shake his. "Be good for Brugel," she said.

Before he could respond, she stepped away. The camera-flash blotches in his vision cleared enough to see Mrs Howser in the gallery, along with a few cadets. They'd been brilliant tonight, turning up and lending support at just the right moment.

Melody may have bunked off earlier tonight, but maybe he didn't need her any more as long as he had Birgit Howser in his corner?

Natalia Cebotari, the first minister, guided him towards a table, where a series of papers waited for his signature. The fact the first minister had said nothing in protest only proved how powerful Mrs Howser's magic could be. He'd reward the witch accordingly.

Vincent took his seat and picked up a pen. Cameras clicked and flashed. Reporters kept firing questions but he ignored them. The only thing people needed was to see him signing papers. One by one he set his name to the space on each page, confirming his ascension.

Quietly, Ruslana appeared at his side, her manicured hand lightly touching his shoulder in a show of support.

KEEPING to the shadows and away from the rioting mob, a dejected and defeated Ondine trudged home with the ferret on her shoulder. The mob had heard her message of love and utterly rejected it. Everything they'd done to help Anathea had failed.

"We'll be all right lass," Shambles said with forced cheeriness. He'd taken up position on her shoulder. "As soon as we get home, I'm running ye a nice hot bath with lots of bubbles."

Soaking in something clean and hot would be heavenly.

"Aye, and I'll wash yer hair for ye."

How lush. "Thanks."

"Although I cannae promise I'll be able to stay out of the bath meself."

Despite the chill, heat bloomed on her cheeks. When he was Shambles, he could be so delightfully inappropriate. On they trudged, the cloudless sky sucking any remaining city warmth into the stars. Trembles and chills filled her body.

"Only a few kilometres to go, hen. We'll be there soon."

Shame having no clothes meant he couldn't become his Hamish-self and give her a piggyback instead. She turned her collar up against the cold, only to find it wet and slimy from the gutter splash.

"Mebbe if ye jog it will warm ye from the inside."

Lights twinkled up ahead from a mobile food van. The enticing smell of fried cheese balls carried on the wind. "Lend me a fiver will you?"

"Err . . . I dinnae have any."

Now she really would cry. From the cold, from her wet clothes, from her sore feet and her all-over misery. "But you had money –"

"– In meh pocket, when I had meh pants on, so I did."

The pocket of his pants, which were now lying somewhere at the bottom of a tree in central Venzelemma.

"I could go back for them. If ye want me to?"

"No point," she said with a huge sigh. Honestly, she could sigh for Brugel at this rate. She couldn't face walking all the way back to the base of the tree they'd climbed, in the forlorn hope of finding the pants Hamish had abandoned, let alone finding any money left in the pockets. The mob could still be there. They might recognise her. And she did *not* have the energy to go though all that again.

"I'm just glad I have the keys." Reaching inside her soggy clothes, she pulled out the lanyard. Where the keys had been were now the tattered edges of torn polyester. They must have ripped off during the tree climb. Or the roof climb. Or scrambling over the guttering.

"I give up," she slumped to the kerb. Any second now sobs would rack through her body and she'd be a blubbering mess on the cobblestones.

"Whoa!" Shambles nearly fell off her shoulder. "Lass, dinnae give up. We've had a setback, that's all. When we get to yer pub, I ken still scarper in and unlock the door from the inside."

Trudge home they did. Being an old city, many of Venzelemma's streets were made from cobblestones. Beautiful for postcards but hell on the ankles. They came across cadets on street corners, moving people on.

"Where are you going?" One of them asked Ondine.

Dread filled her stomach. "Home," she snuffled.

"You go straight home then, and stay out of trouble," the cadet said.

She wasn't going to argue with them. Finally they made it to the family pub. "I'll be right back," Shambles said as he scurried over the gate at the back of the family pub.

*Snick* went the lock and the gate opened with a satisfyingly old creak. Good. At least they were in the beer garden. But still outside. Oh, hello, Hamish was his Hamishness. He'd pulled a tablecloth from the clothes-line and draped it around himself, for modestly. What a shame. "Right, now, where do ye parents leave the spare key?" Hamish looked about the potted plants and checked under the back doormat.

She drew the tattered ends of lanyard from her pocket. "They used to keep it on this."

"Right." Hamish chewed on the inside of his cheek. Lost in thought. Then a look of determination came over his face and he stepped in and gave her a kiss. "I'm gointae get ye that bath I promised. Hold this for me."

He gave her the edge of the tablecloth. Just as she thought she might see something saucy, he flashed back into a ferret. A few minutes later, she heard footsteps from inside the hotel and a partially dressed Hamish opened the door. In his other hand – oh bliss – was an enormous bath towel.

"I've *goat* the bath running already, so up ye get. I'll get yer pyjamas for ye."

In the bathroom she shucked her slimy cold clothes off and climbed in. It was cold.

Of course it was cold. It would be generous to even call the temperature tepid. The lack of steam should have given that away, but she hadn't noticed. At least the water wasn't freezing, because then she would have screamed. She turned the cold water tap off completely and stuck her head directly under the hot – but really tepid – water to get the slime out of her hair.

It was her fault the water was cold. Because the rest of her family were away and it was just herself and Hamish, she'd turned the hot water service to mornings only, because they didn't have guests and for once, she wouldn't spend evenings up to her armpits in hot soapy water, washing dishes. She'd give anything for some hot water now. But the system was in the laundry, and that was in the room next door. That would mean getting out of the bath and getting *really* cold. Instead, she stayed under the hot tap until it got so cold she couldn't stand it, then she turned it off and grabbed a fresh towel and rubbed her skin raw to help warm it up.

There was a radio in here, against the wall. It crackled as she turned it on, which wasn't surprising considering the years of condensation turning its belly to rust.

"*. . . reeling from the sudden abdication of Anathea, Duchess of Brugel in favour of her nephew Lord Vincent.*" A man's dulcet tones said.

Ondine's feet were so cold they'd started burning, which only served to boggle her all the more. How could a body part be so cold it felt like it was on fire? Wrapped in towels, she opened the door to find Hamish with a pile of nightwear in his arms. "I wasnae sure what ye wanted, so I brought a selection."

"You're so sweet," she gave him a kiss. "Put them on the chair over here."

On the radio, the reporter gave a description of what was happening in the streets of Venzelemma. "*There's a carnival atmosphere down here, as if people know they're part of something momentous. It could be the excitement of the night, or it could be the need for youth to express their individuality.*"

"Howser's spell sure did a number on everyone in the plaza, even the reporters," Ondine said.

"Aye. No mention of the tanks, or the confusion. The world has gone whirlypits." [1]

The report mentioned only the excitement of the night, and Vincent's triumph.

Ondine slipped an oversized nightshirt over her head, then modestly wriggled her towel out from beneath it. "Let's get a fire going."

An hour or so later, they sat together, staring into the flickering light of the small fire. So much upheaval in one day meant neither of them would get much sleep.

"Sometimes I feel so selfish," Ondine said in a scared voice. Admitting the truth did that. "I want us to run away from all this . . . this mess. Just so I can be with you and to hell with the world. The trouble is, the next minute I want to storm the streets and liberate Brugel in a tank."

He rubbed her back but didn't interrupt. That's how wonderful he was.

"What kind of person am I Hamish? Am I a coward or a fighter? I'm so scared this is it. That I'm not going to survive whatever crazy thing happens next."

He kissed her softly on the lips. "I'm so glad you said that, lass. I've been thinking the same, and thinking meself a scaredy cat for having thunk it."

He understood. Of course he did. He was her soul mate. With a shaky sigh, she admitted another truth. "Then there's the devil on my shoulder not wanting to die a virgin."

He made a soft (but never condescending) chuckle. "Aye. I have one of them too saying the same thing."

As difficult as it was admitting her fears, she loved Hamish even more for accepting them and sharing his. That's why they would always be together. They understood each other.

They kissed with a mixture of passion and sorrow, until reality crept back in, thanks to a sudden rapping at the pub door.

"Stay here, lass I'll sort it." Hamish's footsteps disappeared down the hall.

Ignoring his instructions, Ondine padded after him, just in time to see Hamish untying the rope from a lumpy hessian sack on the doorstep. Old Col climbed out!

She spluttered and complained. "Birgit Howser better sleep with one eye open from now on. Look at my beautiful dress, it's ruined!"

Overcome with relief and delight, Ondine flew at her great-auntie and wrapped her in a solid hug.

"Don't blubber on the bodice!" But there was no venom in Col's words as she folded her arms around Ondine, her frail body shuddering with sobs.

"It's good tae see ye Old Col, ye must be fair puckled."

Wiping her eyes, Old Col looked at Hamish. "If you mean exhausted, you're right. I could sleep for a week."

"We've lost, haven't we?" Ondine said as they drew Old Col towards the fire so she could warm up too. She spoke the words she never thought possible, her voice cracking with exhaustion and disbelief. "It's all over. Vincent's won."

"Weil get through this lass." Hamish gave her hand a squeeze. "It might be rubbish for a while, but we've still *goat* each other."

Such kind words did little to balm her ragged nerves.

"Anybody home?" A shaky voice said.

"Melody?" Ondine and Hamish said together.

There she was, slumping against the doorframe.

Hamish went to her, offering his arm for support. "Ye look done-in."

"I'm so sorry. For everything. I thought I could make him better. I thought maybe if I loved him enough he'd change. But he didn't, and I had to leave or I would have lost my mind."

Ondine wasn't entirely sure Melody hadn't lost her mind already. Why had she arrived now, of all times? Was she here under Vincent's orders or had she really left him?

Hamish grabbed an extra chair while Ondine piled more logs on the fire to keep the warmth coming.

"I'm so sorry for behaving so badly," Melody said without prompting. "I lost sight of what was important. And I know I let you down."

It sounded genuine to Ondine, what with the contrite look on Melody's face and the complete absence of 'ifs'. "What if Vincent asks you to come back and work for him again?"

She shook her head. "He won't. Well, he'd better not, because I'll send him off with a flea in his ear."

"A what?" Ondine asked.

"I'll tell him to shove it," Melody said. "Anyway, he doesn't know where I am. I left a note saying I'd gone to my grandparents in Craviç."

Old Col said nothing as she looked into the flames, but her worn face told Ondine all she needed to know. They were well and truly defeated. Vincent had won and nothing would ever be the same in Brugel again.

# PART II

---

EIGHT MONTHS LATER

## 15

If life could be measured in suckage, Ondine's life easily out-sucked the most powerful vacuums in the world. Every day of Vincent's reign brought fresh bad news.

The morning after Lord Vincent had become Duke of Brugel, a palpable sense of dread descended as they waited to see what would happen to their country. At first it was the little things. The newspapers Da loved to read each morning suddenly weren't available at the shop. In the afternoon, when they'd tuned the radio to their favourite music channel, they'd heard nothing but static.

Then things became much more blatant. Cadets turned up at intersections all across the city. They weren't doing anything, as far as Ondine could tell, but seeing them in such public positions, in such great numbers, made her uneasy. As if she couldn't simply go for a walk down the street without someone watching over her.

Reporting on her.

The seasons passed in a blur of misery. Summer had been brief and hot, giving everyone sunburn and sleepless nights. Not that people enjoyed walking in the late afternoons as the streets were full of mean-looking cadets. Autumn had been pretty with all its changing leaves, but

Ondine's mood was too sour to enjoy it. Her mood didn't improve in winter either. Instead of glorious snow dusting the world with magic, it had rained something rotten, making everything soggy. The winter festivals and the snow maze didn't happen, on account of the lack of snow. Christmas had come and gone with few customers in the pub and scant tips.

And now it was heading into spring again, but Ondine didn't dare hope for anything good happening any time soon. Life was too crapulent for that. They weren't living. They were existing.

"It's called 'outrage fatigue' dear," Ma had said one morning over breakfast. "One unrelentingly ghastly thing after another tends to wear you down."

Eight months of 'unrelentingly ghastly' things had worn Ondine down, that was for sure.

The worst of 'the ghastlies' had to be the curfew at sundown. All citizens had to be off the streets by five at night and they couldn't emerge until seven the next morning. Which made evening travel and socializing near impossible! This had devastated the DeGroot's earnings immediately, as most of their business came from the dinner crowd and overnight guests. Although everyone had been equally affected by the massive changes to Brugel daily life, Ondine couldn't help thinking Vincent had targeted her family in particular.

Education had gone by the wayside, too. Ondine had planned to enrol in a business degree in the autumn, so she could learn even more about running a business and one day take over the family pub. Alas, the college she'd chosen had tripled its fees and closed half its courses. This necessitated taking a gap year to defer her studies. Officially she was working in her parents' hotel. Unofficially she was just as broke and unemployed as everyone else.

The private family room behind the kitchen was often overcrowded. They could eat in the dining room, where there were plenty of tables and chairs, but they had to keep the restaurant clean and tidy on the off chance a paying customer might come in. So they huddled together in their little private room, taking breakfast in shifts.

On this particularly miserable spring morning, Ondine and Hamish took first shift with Melody, Margi and her husband Thomas Berger. Adding to the squeeze was Thomas's younger brother, Alexei. Alexei was a brash young thing, full of grand ideas about where Brugel had gone wrong, and how to fix it. He loved regaling them with historical facts about revolutions, which he'd learned about in school the previous year. He'd make a wonderful lecturer in politics, when things returned to normal.

Whenever that was.

Fortunately for Alexei, he had terribly sensitive skin, so he was unable to submerge his hands into hot soapy water. Alexei and his parents had moved in with Ondine's family during the miserable winter just past. The Bergers had worked at the Brugel Science Institute all their careers. A month after taking office, Lord Vincent declared a budget emergency and cut all science funding. With months of no income, the Bergers put their house up for sale and moved in with Ondine's family. After all, the pub had plenty of vacant bedrooms.

Ordinarily, having a crowd of people in the pub was no big deal. But these were not paying guests, they were extended family, and that meant Ondine had to spend extra time finding useful things for people to do. This in turn gave her less time with Hamish. Much to her continued frustrations, Hamish had even less time for Ondine. His 'staying spell' that Old Col had put him under from the very beginning was losing its potency. Hamish aged far too quickly during the day and had to recuperate as a ferret all night.

Melody, who'd also come to stay, was earning her keep by creating health spells for Hamish.

Ma and Da had taken in family on Ma's side – GrannyMa and GrandDa had come home from their retirement travels, because their pensions had been cut off. They'd parked their caravan in the beer garden. Old Col had also come to live with them full-time, which was excellent as it meant they could keep an eye on her health, both magical and physical. And her mental health, truth be told.

Old Col and the grandparents were in the second breakfast shift with Ma, Da, Cybelle and Henrik. Col had always been batty, but since her horrible night with Mrs Howser, which she still refused to talk about in any detail, she'd been even battier.

At least she was still with them, which was more than they could say for Anathea. Ever since her abdication, there had been no sight of Brugel's former duchess. Rumours swirled about her fate, from living in exile with her ex-husband in the mountainous kingdom of Haute Montagne (the kindest outcome) to not being amongst the living at all (an awful outcome) to being kept prisoner in a rat infested cellar (the awfullest).

The only nice thing to happen was when Margi and Thomas announced they were having a baby. That had at least shone some light into their dim world. They'd announced the news soon after Christmas, and all the oldies had immediately burst into tears of joy and love and they kept hugging all afternoon. This conveniently overshadowed how miserly their Christmas had been.

Now, each time Da walked past Margi, he stopped her, kissed her on the head and then said, "see you soon my little Berger," directly to her belly. [1]

A creaking door and chiming bell told them someone had walked into the dining room.

A customer?

Wiping the breakfast egg from her mouth (the family had brought in chickens and were raising them in the laundry, where it was warm and the hens could produce all year round), Ondine headed out to see who had walked in.

It was Ms Cebotari! "First Minister, how wonderful to see you!"

"Just Natalia these days," she said with forced smile. Her dark hair had grown longer, revealing a wide parting of grey roots. Without makeup, her skin looked spottier, with little red blotches along her jawline. She slipped on a pair of glasses and looked closer. "Ondine? It is you. I'm so glad you're still here."

With a mirthless laugh, Ondine said, "Where else would I be?"

"I've come to see how you are faring."

" 'Badly' pretty much sums it up." Then Ondine remembered her customer service training. "Would you like breakfast? Coffee? We still have real coffee if you'd like."

Natalia creased her mascara-free eyes in seriousness. "You're not cutting it with chicory are you?"

"No ma'am. We'd sooner close for good than do that."

"I always knew you were a good sort," Natalia embraced Ondine in a hug. Then she dropped her voice into conspiracy territory.

"Is Vincent still your patron?"

"No way." Ondine kept her voice low as well. "We haven't seen him for months and I hope we never see him again."

Natalia sighed and smiled. "I'm so glad you said that." Then she released Ondine, dashed for the front door, opened it again and said to somebody waiting outside, "The coast is clear."

In the next minute a dozen people walking in singles and pairs entered the dining room. Natalia made the introductions. "Everybody, this is Ondine DeGroot, a true friend of Brugel. Ondine, it's my pleasure to introduce you to the Brugelish Resistance."

As the Brugelish resistance ambled in, Ma entered the dining room and clapped her hands with delight, instantly mistaking them for people with money. "New customers, how wonderful!"

---

VINCENT COULD NOT REMEMBER EVER BEING SO happy. Which was saying a lot considering how well things had been ticking over this past year. He'd refinanced his life thanks to the generous Balakhans, removed his annoying aunt and become the Duke of Brugel. All before his twenty-first birthday.

He sat behind a Brugel Oak desk, admiring the grain and the glossy finish. This was the desk his father Pavla had inherited from his father and his father before him. It wasn't in such great shape when Vincent found it, covered in dust. Dented. Stained. That's why he'd had the surface replaced, and the drawers remade and all the neglect sanded out and varnished. Some of the original Brugel Oak was still in the desk, and really, that's all that mattered. The connection to history. Thankfully, he hadn't had to keep dying his hand blue every couple of days, so that connection didn't have to remain.

Like many over-achievers, Vincent didn't want to rest after his early victories. What would be the point? Resting meant stopping, and he wasn't for stopping. Stopping would mean he'd peaked too early. The door to his office creaked open. Babak Balakhan and Birgit Howser walked silently across the thick carpet, folios tucked under their arms ready for their weekly meeting. From another door came a quick rapping sound, then a waiter walked in with a tiered tray of fruit, cheese and crackers. Unlike Vincent's desk, the meeting table in the middle of the room was not made of Brugel Oak. That sacred timber was getting harder to obtain. Apparently the dust from Brugel Oak sawmills played havoc with people's allergies.

Vincent took a seat at the head of the meeting table. Once he sat down, Birgit and Babak took their seats. He nodded to both of them and said, "How goes our fair Brugel this week?"

"More petitions to end the curfew, or at least drive it back by a few hours," Babak said. "There are claims it's bad for business to have to close so early."

"Most businesses close at five o'clock, don't they?"

"Yes, Your Lordship, they do, but the petitioners are saying their staff need to be home well before curfew, so many are closing as early as three. I have to say I can see it from their point of view."

Vincent shrugged. "What's our next item?"

"I'm proceeding with the database of all witches, as per your request," Mrs Howser said. "And the *normals* who caught mutating magic. It's enabling us to keep track of citizens with useful magic, now and in many years to come, when I am not here."

It was the first time she'd hinted at an inability to carry out her tasks. "You're planning on leaving?"

"I serve at the Your Lordship's pleasure. But age catches up with us all, and there are some things not even magic can cure."

For a moment he'd thought she was planning on leaving. Now he understood it was more about her mortality, he wasn't so concerned.

"Let's not get melodramatic about it." He turned to Babak. "How are the negotiations proceeding with Slaegal?"

"We're on target for the merge in the next six months. We should work out a timetable for releasing information to the public. Advance warning runs the risk of stirring outrage."

"So? We closed all the media outlets critical to us."

"That is true," Babak said with a satisfied smile. "My concern is any lingering doubters."

"I'm fixing that," Mrs Howser jumped in. "The dampening field will be ready ahead of schedule, so we won't have to worry about assemblies via astral projection."

Vincent loved the way Babak and Howser competed with each other to be the favourite. "We shan't have to worry at all if we sell the merger right. Bringing Brugel and Slaegal together will make us stronger. What about Craviç, any feelers out there to see how that will be received?"

"Their ramshackle protest movement is voicing concerns about us," Babak said. "They're putting the blue-flowered flags on their homes and cars." [2]

Vincent shrugged, "Blue flowers go well with blue hands." Then he thought some more and came up with something better. "Let's make new flags. We'll put the blue hand holding the blue flower as a sign of our friendship."

"I like where you're going with this," Babak said.

"What shall we do about the elections?" Mrs Howser asked.

Vincent frowned. "Who's banging on about timetabling them now?" [3]

"Nobody. Or at least, nobody publicly. My thoughts are that we set a date in late summer –"

"– That will give them far too much time to prepare." Babak interrupted.

"Not if we don't tell them until August." Mrs Howser said. "Say, four weeks' notice?"

"I've always liked the way you do business, Birgit," Babak said. "Four weeks sounds perfect."

Nobody had touched the platter, fruit or otherwise. It was a game Vincent liked to play, knowing Babak and Birgit wouldn't dare eat before he did. He made himself wait longer and longer without eating, to the point where his tummy cramped as the smell of the softly warming cheese teased his nose. "Do you have anything for me to sign?"

Mrs Howser produced several pieces of legislation. "These are from your edicts last week."

"Good." A government of three people was so efficient.

**16**

———

It didn't look in any way suspicious to have members of the newly formed Brugelish Resistance taking afternoon tea at Ondine's family pub, *The Duke and Ferret*. This is because nobody, aside from the members themselves, knew of the existence of the Brugelish Resistance. To people on the street, walking past the pub, it simply looked as if *The Duke and Ferret* had customers in the dining room.

"It's so lovely to have guests here for afternoon tea," Ma gushed as she wheeled the samovar over to Natalia Cebotari's table.

Ma lit the candle beneath the pot and spooned tealeaves into the water. "Chef's making puppy boxes for take-home dining. First Minister, may I show you the menu?" [1]

"It's just Natalia," then she quirked a brow. "Puppy boxes?"

"Our version of a doggy bag," Ma said with a chuckle.

Although Ondine constantly felt the resistance's cover could be blown at any moment, it was also a massive relief to have customers again. When the restaurant was empty, people walked past, noted the empty dining room, then kept walking. Thanks to Natalia and her buddies, the people outside walked past, saw that others were enjoying themselves and came in. A classic case of success creating more success.

"Give me a hand with this out to the footpath will you love?" Ma said as she tottered over with an A-frame chalkboard. On one side she'd writ-ten, "Curfew special: A warm meal and a warm bed!" on the other side she'd added, "Come for dinner, stay for the duvet!" The two of them huffed as they lifted the heavy frame. "We have to try something for the evening crowd, the curfew is killing us! I can't believe it's still set at five o'clock when it's light now until six. And when daylight saving comes in, it will be light until eight."

"Careful," Ondine said as they shuffled the frame into position on the street outside. If someone overheard them, they might think her 'careful' was in the context of, 'be careful with the board, you might hurt your back,' but in fact she was hoping her mother would realise she really meant 'careful' in the, *'Be careful what you say, someone could easily report you to Lord Vincent for being unhappy'* kind of way.

Safely back in the dining room, Ondine noticed one of their patrons (not a member of the Brugelish Resistance as far as she could tell) sipping tea while working on a laptop.

"Plugged into our wall and using our electricity!" Ma said under her breath.

She had a point. Why would a person need to be working on a portable computer in a restaurant? Sure, electricity supplies were unpre-dictable at the best of times, so that might explain it. Or the customer could be writing a novel (she'd heard that sometimes happened). But the really scary thought, which pushed all other thoughts aside, was that the woman with the laptop, drinking only tea and sucking their power out of the wall, might actually be a spy. Which meant she had to suspect there was something worth spying on, here at *The Duke and Ferret*.

Ma refused to confine herself to the kitchen and bustled about the tables, offering tempting samples of their most profitable items and pushing the puppy boxes. It was 'adapt or die' time, with a higher focus on take away items to counteract the lack of dinner crowds after curfew.

It must be how *On the Fang*, across the street, had survived the past year as well.

If Ondine's family didn't find new ways of bringing in customers earlier in the day, they'd go broke. It was getting close to that point, which was why Ma 'over bustled' in the dining room. You could smell the desperation on her.

Making herself useful, Melody now donned Ondine's old gloves and did the washing up. It had been a thankless task when Ondine did it, but 'the glasses had never been shinier' according to Ma. Ondine could do without the implied criticism, but she was nonetheless grateful that Melody was paying her way. It freed Ondine to wrap her arms around Hamish whenever she had the chance.

Which wasn't anywhere near as often as she'd hoped.

Taking a new tray of dirty teacups towards Melody, Ondine whispered, "I think we have a spy in the dining room. Is there any way you can find out?"

"Oh yes." Melody shifted her shoulders and clicked out the kinks. Then she held onto the edge of the sink, closed her eyes and breathed deeply. A hard line formed between her brows and her mouth tightened.

"Saturn's rings, she is a spy," Ondine gasped.

"It's not that," Melody said, her chin puckering with concentration.

"It's something else?"

"It's bad," Melody opened her eyes and shook her head. "I can't get through."

"She's blocking you then?" Only people with magic and something to hide would block astral projection.

Therefore she was a spy!

Melody kept her voice low, but the worry on her face spoke volumes. "Not just her, I can't get through to anyone. I can't astral at all."

"You haven't . . . lost your magic as well have you?"

"I hope not," she waggled her fingers over the hot water, it bubbled and frothed, the dirty teacups plonked themselves in and came out sparkling. "Nope. Still got magic! That's a relief. What do you mean 'as well'? Has someone else lost their magic?"

*Quick, don't let on about Old Col,* Ondine thought. "So why can't you astral?"

"It's like there's a blanket over me when I try to reach out astrally. It feels like it's made of lead and I can't lift it and I can't see through it."

"Has Mrs Howser put something on you?"

Melody rubbed her forehead, resulting in suds in her hairline. "I should have known they wouldn't let me go so easily."

"Ondine, out front please lovvie, we have more customers," Ma said, producing a new tray of dirty teacups and side plates for Melody.

A new couple had come in to the dining room.

Ma tended them while Ondine waited on/spied on their customer with the laptop.

Honestly, coming in with something that flashy was bound to make her stand out. [2] With what she hoped sounded like chirpy tone, Ondine asked, "Working on a book?"

The woman stayed focused on the screen and said. "I come here for the solitude."

Point taken.

Ma fussed over the new customers, whom she'd seated at the table by the window. [3] They were two women dressed in dark suits, which reminded Ondine of the night last year when immigration inspectors had come into the pub and tried to deport Hamish. Shudder.

At Natalia's table, Ondine poured more tea and gave them two jam tarts to share between the four of them.

Over the next ten or so minutes, the suited 'window couple' spent the whole time looking at the menus. Ondine watched them from the safety of the kitchen doorway, wondering why someone should take so long to decide what kind of tea to have. Especially when they only had four types. Peppermint, Regular Black, Green and Brugelish Blend. [4] They needed to hurry up and get some food on the table so more people walking past could be lured in. It was already past three in the afternoon. By four, everyone would need to leave so they'd be home in time for five o'clock curfew.

"I can't seem to get them to order anything, they're saying everything looks so delicious they can't make up their minds," Ma said as she came back into the kitchen.

Ondine grabbed an empty plate and turned to Henrik. "Put a scone and a slice on it and we'll call it a sampler."

"Just one scone," Ma added.

"I'll cut it in half," Henrik said.

The result was a half-scone with a scraping of jam and a delicate drop of cream on top, next to a wafer thin slice of apricot delight. It had been apricot cake yesterday, but they'd had so much left over, Henrik had repurposed it into something closer to a brownie. Except it was apricot.

Ondine took the plate, added a red nasturtium flower as garnish and headed out to the dining room. With a warm smile, she approached the table and slid the platter between the two suited women. "Ma said you were having trouble deciding, so I brought you our house specials. Please enjoy."

The woman on the left asked, "Is this complimentary?"

Mercury's wings, cheapskates in suits? Maybe they *were* spies. Or maybe they were just city workers who'd ended up with too much month at the end of the money. "It's a sample platter, they're a schlipp each." Ondine beamed at how quickly she'd made that up.

The woman on the right said, "There weren't any sample platters on the menu."

"This is true," Ondine stalled for time, then inspiration struck. "There's a backlog with the printers and we have to wait." Of course there would be a backlog at the printers. They, like every other business, had to close early because of the curfew.

"Can I bring you some tea?"

Instead of answering, the woman on the left asked, "Why is that woman using a computer?"

Definitely a spy-like question. Best get them out of here as soon as possible. "Because the library doesn't let you eat at your desk. I'll be back in just a moment with the samovar."

Back in the kitchen, Ondine refilled the samovar with fresh boiling water and set the tea light candle underneath. The candle was an affectation really, keeping the water warm but hardly boiling. It wasn't even a proper samovar, just an enormous teapot with a faucet near the base, but that didn't matter either. With everything loaded on the trolley, including all four kinds of leaf tea ready to get spooned in, Ondine wheeled it towards the suited women. "Have you decided which blend? You only need pay for the first cup, refills are free." Ondine said.

"Then we'll share one cup of Brugelish Blend," the woman on the right said.

Ma bustled in with a plate of hot delicacies. They smelled divine; mushrooms and cheese wrapped in something bake-able. "I heard you couldn't decide, so I brought you our delicious mini savoury parcels. Resistance is futile!"

*Resistance?* Really bad word choice, Ma! Ondine felt like her heart would stop as she made her way back to the kitchen as fast as she could without looking like she was running. Stupid Vincent and his stupid curfew, ruining everyone's lives. If it wasn't for his mandatory home-time, the resistance would be able to meet anywhere they liked under cover of darkness.

Which, now that she thought about it, was obviously why he'd brought a curfew in.

"Eh lass, whatja gawpin' at?" Hamish said as he sidled up beside her.

Hamish was here. Everything would be all right now, wouldn't it? "The women on the window table. I think they're spies."

"Weil, they'll be gone soon, it's nearly curfew."

Ma walked past and noticed Hamish. "Be an angel and dash over to *Fang's* for me. See if they have any potatoes? There's a good lad. We'll pay them back later."

"Hurry," Ondine said, giving him a quick kiss. "And be careful. There are cadets on every corner."

"Och, lass. I'm always careful," he said with a wink.

Staying busy so she wouldn't fret about Hamish, Ondine headed over to Natalia's table. As she stepped closer, the two suited women by the window took an increasing interest in everything going on. If they were spies, they sucked at it.

Keeping her voice bright, Ondine said, "More scones ma'am?"

"Thank you, yes, and tea," Natalia said, then she dropped her voice into conspiratorial range. "If those women on the other table think they're going to follow me home, they've got another thing coming."

"I'll freshen the samovar," Ondine said.

The light outside dimmed. Time marched on. Clearly Natalia wasn't leaving before the suited women left, but the suits were so slow they could have doubled as buskers dressed as statues.

Another ten minutes passed. Hamish came back from *Fang's* with a small bag of potatoes and presented them to Ma, who gave them straight to Henrik. "Soup for dinner again Henrik. Let's see how far we can stretch it."

The entire situation did Ondine's head in. The women in suits had to leave, right now, if Natalia had any hope of making it home before legal lights-out. "What are they doing?" She asked Hamish, "Playing curfew chicken?"

"I've given the suits by the window the bill," Ondine said. "But they're not moving. I think they're spying on us."

"Why would we have spies in here? Honestly!" Ma said with a roll of her eyes. "Stop being a drama llama. Maybe they want to stay for dinner and a room?" Ma said.

That got Ondine's attention. "They'd be our first dinner guests in months."

Ma said, "It's about time we started having hotel guests again. We'll need to offer them a full Brugelish Continental breakfast in the morning." She rubbed her hands together in anticipation and headed over towards the women in suits, to suggest they stay the night.

Clearly, her mother didn't have a clue how serious this was. They had the leader of the Brugelish Resistance in their dining room, and two spies spying on her. Outside, there were cadets on street corners, watching everything. Natalia and her friends had to leave soon or they'd have to stay the night as well. Did they have enough food to feed everyone?

And another thing, where was everyone going to fit? They had plenty of rooms for family, of course, even the extended family plus Melody. But they only had one or two spare rooms and . . . uh oh, Ma returned with a gleam in her eye.

"Ondi love, you and Hamish get rooms ready. We're going to have overnighters again! Right, hand me the menu. Chef, Cybelle, tell me what we can offer them for dinner."

"Er, soup?" Cybelle said. "And their body weight in scones."

"Soup and scones?" Ma shrugged. "Eh, where are they gonna go at short notice anyway?"

"Weil, there is *Fangs* across the street," Hamish said.

Ondine gave him a nudge.

"Ahhhh, but they're only a restaurant, not a pub. If people stay too long at dinner, they'll have to sleep at the tables," Ma said, heading back out to the dining room. Her voice sounded two notches too loud, as if there were far more people than the measly handful. "My lovely guests, can I get anyone more tea? Apricot slice?"

The front door tinkled and three new people came in. Watching from the kitchen, Ondine could see them look directly to Natalia. A flicker of recognition flashed across their faces. The women on the other table cricked their necks back and forth to observe the exchange.

More people? Nobody would get home in time for curfew at this rate. Which meant things were going to be very crowded in the hotel tonight.

"Three more for the dinner special," Ma said as she came back into the kitchen. "Time for FHB."

Cybelle gave Ma a confused look.

"Family Hold Back. Paying guests first, us second."

"We don't have enough food?" Ondine didn't want to believe it.

"Not at the moment, but after they pay their bills, we'll re-stock," Ma said.

In protest, Ondine's stomach made the loudest gurgle heard this side of the Caucasus Mountains.

Da came in with extra fire-wood to keep the dining room warm. "If they're staying the night, how about we take their money up front? Then I can dash down to the market and restock now. I don't know about you Ondi, but I can't think straight on an empty stomach."

"But it's nearly curfew," Ma said.

"I'll be fine." Da headed into the dining room and built up the fire.

Ma said, "Hamish, you're good at getting people to part with money. Be a champ and collect deposits for the board and breakfast."

"Aye," he said.

Flustered, Ma shook her head. "We've never taken money from people up front before."

"We're doing lots of things we haven't done before," Ondine said.

A few minutes later, Hamish handed the deposit cash to Da.

"I'll be back before anyone has a chance to miss me," Da promised. He walked past Margi and kissed her on the head. She grabbed his hand and pressed it to her rotund belly.

"It kicked!" Da's face split with a smile. "Keep cooking little Berger. We'll see you when you're done!"

Ondine and Hamish followed Da towards the back door, Hamish asking the very question at the top of Ondine's list of worries: "I didnae think thae market was still open."

"It's not," Da said. "But I know a place."

"The cadets will see you, they're right out the front," Ondine said. Nerves pumped her heart, trembled her fingers and shortened her breath. Da was acting as if this were nothing more than a shopping trip, but if he was caught out after curfew he could be arrested. Or worse.

"I'll create a diversion, lass," Hamish said with a wink. "I like the look of their trousers!"

"Be –" Hamish vanished into his clothes, and Shambles the ferret crawled out of the crumpled sleeve on the ground. "– careful."

"Right, I'll head out the front door sharpish, Da can sneak out the back."

"Thank you Hamish," Da said.

"Awff we go then," Hamish as the Shambles ferret darted towards the door adjoining their private room behind the kitchen, only to pull up short. "Er, lass, I didnae think this through. Would ye mind opening the door for me? I cannae reach."

Reluctantly, Ondine turned the handle and opened the door enough to let the ferret out into the cool evening air. Through the gap, she saw the cadets sipping something from a hip flask.

While Shambles bounded out to the street, the door to the beer garden creaked open and Da slipped away.

Please be safe, both of you, she silently begged.

SLEEPING as a ferret at night in his safe, warm bed was one thing, but being a ferret out in the open, on the road, as the light faded for the day had Hamish feeling twenty kinds of nervous. Being so low to the ground made him vulnerable to the kind of heavy boots the Fort Kluff cadets liked to wear.

As a ferret, his adorably fuzzy little ears gave him excellent hearing. Da's footsteps faded off down the road, now was the time to act. Wailing like a banshee, Hamish leapt into the air and spun around on the spot, landing with a wet thud into a gutter puddle. Cold and wet, he wailed some more. A totally natural wail as it turned out.

"What?" One of the cadets noticed Shambles' efforts and walked across the street to get a closer look. "Hey Gregor, look at this funny cat!"

"I'm nae cat!" Shambles yelled. Standing on his hind legs brought him eye level with their kneecaps. Their tasty, vulnerable kneecaps.

The one called Gregor yelled and took a step back. "It talks!"

Diversion well and truly made, Shambles tapped his foot on the kerb. This was going so well he could barely believe his luck. "I can dance too, if ye want."

The other cadet said, "What's it saying?"

Gregor ran back to his post.

"Come back and play with me," Shambles called after him. As the cadet checked left and right to cross the street, he did a double take in the direction of the beer garden. Da should be long gone by now. Shouldn't he?

"Rav, get backup," Gregor said. "We've got an 'out after curfew'."

Desperate, Shambles leapt after Gregor, locking his claws into the cuffs of his cadet pants.

Gregor violently shook his leg. "Get off me!"

Dizzy and shaken, he clung on for his life, the fabric ripping where his claws dug through.

"What is that?" The other one said.

Shambles was in no position to tell who said what, as he clung on for his life. Being flung around like a rag doll, he focussed on survival.

"Don't worry about me, call it in!"

"But it's ripping your trousers!"

"Hurry up, he's getting away!"

The shaking stopped. Dazed and dizzy, Shambles clung on, took a second to get his breath back, then scarpered up Gregor's leg and on to his back. The cadet's arms flailed and whipped backwards, trying to grab him.

"Get this thing off me."

A hand clamped around his tail and pulled. Shambles let out a whelp of pain and dug his claws in to Gregor's uniform.

"He won't budge."

Shambles clamped his teeth down on something and locked his jaw. He was going nowhere.

"Unit three-seven-three reporting in, we have a citizen out after curfew. Has decamped in direction of unit three-seven-seven. Please advise."

A scratchy voice came in from a speaker somewhere. *"Advising unit three-seven-seven to apprehend."*

Shambles's hopes fell faster than a ferret dropping from a man's back. He scarpered to a safe distance and looked back. The cadets were checking the damage on Gregor's uniform and not chasing Da down the street. Which was a good thing. But no, it was bad, because the cadets stationed further down the street could already be in pursuit.

How could he be so stupid to think distracting the cadets on their corner would make a difference, when there were so many cadets stationed on street corners all over the city?

Dejected, he crept back to the pub and hoped that by some miracle, Da would be all right.

Naturally, Ondine was waiting for him. "How did it go?" She asked.

"Weil, ye Da got away at least," Shambles muttered, heading to his room to change back into human form and proper clothes.

"He'll be all right though, won't he?"

How could he answer that without crushing her spirits?

**17**

———————

I t was the first time they'd had overnight guests in months. Ondine, Hamish, Thomas and Alexei madly tidied five guest bedrooms, taking their own belongings out and shoving them into other rooms for the mean time. Alexei would share with his parents, Ondine, Melody and Cybelle were with Old Col, and GrannyMa and GrandDa were with with Ma and Da. That left Thomas and Margi with a room of their own (seriously unfair as far as Ondine was concerned) and Hamish would share with Henrik.

Rooms sorted, Ondine hoped the two women in suits would be happy to share a twin room. It was the darkest room, with west-facing windows so the early morning light from the east wouldn't wake the guests too early. Ondine loved this room because it guaranteed a sleep-in, especially in summer. With any luck, the two suited women would sleep long into morning.

At the opposite end of the hotel, the early morning sun ripped through the south-east facing windows. Natalia and her resistance friends could stay in this room, wake early and head out before the two suited spies had even opened their eyes.

A most excellent plan.

An hour dragged by. It was past curfew and growing dark outside. In the dining room, everybody stayed in their seats, sipping tea and dabbing at the crumbs of their afternoon tea. In the kitchen, things were getting crowded as GrannyMa, GrandDa and Old Col arrived for their dinner. Not that there was much to eat. The miserly soup would have to do. Where was Da with the food? Ondine looked out the back door again, willing her father to walk back in, arms aching with all the food he'd said he'd bring back.

"Looking isn't going to make Da come home any faster," Ma said.

"I'm getting worried." Ondine confessed.

"We all are, love."

The radio news came on in the kitchen.

*"Duke Vincent has announced there will be no Brugel Daylight Saving Time. This means the clocks do not need to spring forward and nobody needs to be sleep deprived."*

Everyone groaned amidst a chorus of "oh what?'s" and "come on's".

*"Duke Vincent also announced there would be no need for the public holiday on the Monday the clocks used to go forward, which will be excellent news for productivity."*

Henrik said the rudest word Ondine had ever heard.

"Can this night get any worse?" Ondine muttered to Old Col.

"You should know by now not to say things like that," Old Col said as she collected her soup and dinner roll.

Another hour dragged by. The oldies retired to the family room behind the kitchen and the rest of the DeGroots and Bergers prepared a thin dinner for the paying customers.

Margi, her pregnant belly bumping into everyone and everything, was relegated to the back corner of the kitchen where she sat at the bench and made dinner rolls out of flour and water (no yeast). She'd grown so large she had to sit side-on to the bench, but at least she was productive and contributing.

Where was Da? Ondine fretted. He had to come back soon.

Melody was up to her elbows in hot soapy water. Every few minutes she'd magic up more hot water and bubbles, saving the family money in heating and detergent costs. Unfortunately, using magic only made the girl hungrier, so she ate the raw dough from Margi's tray.

"Ooooh!" Margi sucked in her breath.

Everyone froze for a second, until Margi composed herself. "Kick in the kidneys, nothing to worry about."

Everyone sighed with relief. Margi's baby wasn't allowed to arrive early, not without Da home yet. Where *was* he?

As the minutes turned into hours and the evening wound down, Ma showed their assorted guests to their respective rooms for the night. Ondine dared open the gate to the beer garden to sneak a look down the alley.

"Where are ye awff tae?" Hamish gave Ondine a cuddle from behind.

"I wish I knew where Da was," she snuggled into Hamish. "He should have been back ages ago."

In the distance, sirens wailed and tyres screeched.

"I bet he's being extra careful coming home, that's all lass," Hamish said. "He's probably spotted trouble and is laying low until it all blows over."

"I know you're trying to make me feel better, but I won't stop worrying until Da's home."

"Then I'll go find him meself."

"But then I'll have two people to worry about."

Ma came to the back door. "If you want something to do Ondi, I've got a list."

"I'm so worried about Da."

"We all are lovvie," Ma stepped forward and embraced Ondine.

"I'll find him," Hamish said.

"Don't you –" The word 'dare' hadn't even reached her mouth before Hamish shrank himself into ferret form.

He stood up on his furry hind legs. "It might be illegal for folks tae be oot in thae street, but nae ferrets."

"Please be careful," Ondine said.

"Aye, I'll be right back, and I'll bring Da with me."

Just like that, he was out the gate and down the street. Ondine's gaze fixed on his furry tail until it and the rest of him dissolved into the dark night.

Something crept into her side vision. A pair of urban foxes slinked around the corner. With a metallic clunk, they tipped over a rubbish bin and helped themselves to the contents. In the absence of people, animals now owned the night. Animals that wouldn't think twice about snapping a ferret in their jaws. The animals turned towards Shambles, their ears pricking, senses on alert as they detected his scent.

Fear charging through her body, Ondine ran out onto the street. "Shoo! Shoo!"

The foxes stopped but didn't back away.

Two cadets came around the corner. "Get back inside Miss, it's long past curfew," one of them said. She looked familiar. Ondine rummaged around in her brain until she remembered where she'd seen the girl before. It had been via Melody's astral projection. This was the cadet whose powers had mutated so much under Mrs Howser's tutelage that she was capable of anything.

Fear tied knots in her lungs as she struggled to breathe.

"Everything all right?" The cadet asked.

Silently, Ondine nodded.

The other cadet picked up some debris from the ground and hurled it at the foxes. "Go-on, get!"

The foxes took a few steps back. The cadet hurled something else and it shattered into pieces on the ground. The foxes slunk back into the shadows.

"Miss, you need to be back inside," that first cadet said.

The other said, "We'll take care of the foxes."

"You'd better," Ondine said, full of bluster to hide her terror. "They're sniffing around our chickens. They've scared them so much they've stopped laying."

They looked like they were trying not to laugh. Good, at least they weren't angry with Ondine or suspicious. "We'll do that Miss," the first one said. "And you get back inside."

---

AT BREAKFAST THE NEXT MORNING, food was scarce. Sleep had completely eluded the over-worried Ondine, who was none-too-gentle as she ruffled each hen's feathers in the laundry, looking for eggs. Four eggs, five eggs, six. Her elbow biffed the wall and she dropped one, tears spritzing her eyes as the gloop oozed out over the floor.

Back to five eggs. She used Henrik's swear word from the night before. It sounded good and purposeful, so she said it again. Cursing herself, her tiredness, the mess she'd made and the reduced food they'd have. For good measure she cursed Vincent a few times too. Even though he was Duke, refusing to call him by his new title made her feel better.

Taking extra care, she took the eggs to the kitchen, saying nothing of the broken one because that would only make everyone upset, and they didn't need any more upset.

Ma said, "Only five eggs? We'll need to add a fair slosh of milk to make the scramble go further."

"I'll add bread crusts," Cybelle said.

"Curfew will be lifted in half an hour, we can send them across to Fang's if they're still hungry." Ma said.

Ondine peeked into the dining room, where the suited spies sat at their same table by the window. No sign of the novelist leeching their electricity out of the wall. That was a plus.

"Did Natalia leave early then?" She asked.

"No love, I don't think she's up yet."

What? Ondine wanted Natalia to get away early. Keeping her breathing steady, Ondine said, "I'd better wake her."

"You'll do nothing of the sort. I gave them the north room." Ma beamed. "The former First Minister deserves a dark room and a restful sleep."

Great. Not that she could tell Ma anything about the Brugelish Resistance and why Natalia should get away quickly. Best to change the subject. "Speaking of people sleeping in, what time did Da and Hamish get back last night?"

With a sigh and a chin wobble, Ma said, "They didn't."

"They're still out there?"

"Keep your voice down. Yes, they're still out there."

"We have to find them! What if . . ." Ondine couldn't comprehend the horrible possibilities facing the most important man in her life. And her dad.

"Go watch some telly. You're no good to me distracted."

Stomach rumbling with hunger, Ondine poured a cup of tea (not to the brim, because her nerves would slosh it out) and flicked on the set in their private lounge.

Huh? Brugel six had a static picture. "What's wrong with it?"

GrannyMa, sitting in the corner with her crochet and wool, looked up. "It's a test pattern, Belle. I mean, Margi."

"I'm Ondine."

"Course you are."

"What's a test pattern?" Ondine flicked channels, only to find all the regular stations had similar static pictures. "Why are they all on test patterns?" At last she found a station that was working.

"That will be the government broadcaster," GrannyMa said. "Takes me back to the old days, it does. One channel, one message. Isn't that right Col?"

Old Col had walked in and seated herself beside her sister, kissing her papery thin cheek. "Have they pulled the plug on the media?"

"It's Stalin one-oh-one all over again," Granny Ma said.

"Nothing if not predictable," Col said.

The two spoke in sister-speak, laughing about the old days. It wasn't a laughing matter as far as Ondine was concerned.

The only channel working was the government broadcaster, which had an exercise program.

"I knew they'd run that!" GrannyMa said. "Come on Col, up we get."

The two of them rose from their seats and imitated the action on screen. Young men and women in exercise gear bent and stretched and marched on the spot. "Gets the blood flowing, does the heart good," Col laughed as she spoke. "Oooh, eye candy. That's an improvement."

Grannyma and Great-Auntie acted like they were under hypnosis, moving their arms about and lifting their knees (not lifting them by much, but lifting them nonetheless). The world had officially gone mad. Twitchy with nerves and bored with only one channel to watch, Ondine went back to the kitchen and grabbed Melody by the arm. "Let's go to the market." The subtext being, "and find Hamish."

"I have to wash these dishes," Melody said, loudly enough for Ma to hear.

"The dishes can wait."

Just as they headed out of the kitchen, they came face to face with Natalia Cebotari.

"Quick, out the back," Ondine said, shoving them towards the rear door.

"Ahoy-hoy, going somewhere interesting?"

Uh oh. It was the two suited women.

"We're going to market," Natalia said to them, bright and cheery and as un-guilty as can be. "Would you like to come?"

Was she mad? They were supposed to be getting away from these spies, not entertaining them!

"What a splendid idea," and "lovely," the spies said.

Natalia, Ondine, Melody and the two spies headed for the back door. Natalia's friends were nowhere to be found. Which was when the twig snapped. If Natalia kept the spies pre-occupied, her friends could get home without being followed.

"Can I come too?" Alexei popped his head around the corner. "This place is so boring." Then he quickly added, "No offence."

---

THE WINDS HOWLED over Mount Verka Seduchka, sending petals and spring pollen through the air. Rugged up against the elements, Duke Vincent stood beside Birgit Howser, observing the team of Fort Kluff cadets dismantling the commercial broadcast towers.

"Don't bend it!" Birgit yelled. "You break, you pay!"

Such admirable people skills, Vincent thought.

"Once we move these towers to the old castle, they'll provide a huge boost to the dampening field," Mrs Howser said.

"Which will block Melody." It irked him how much he'd felt the young witch's absence. For one thing, it necessitated spending more time with Birgit Howser. Melody had been so easy to work with. He'd taken advantage of her desire to be near him. She'd been happy to do his bidding. At least, he'd thought she was. Mrs Howser on the other hand was a slippery fish. She'd become malleable since her time in the asylum, but would it last?

"It will block all witches, not just Melody," Mrs Howser said. "Can't have the resistance using astral projection to bypass curfew."

"There's a resistance group?" Vincent asked. "Already?"

"There's *always* a resistance group. Melody's in it, you know."

"She can't be." The moment the words left his lips, he knew it had to be true.

"You should have given her hope. Or at least the impression of it. A woman can only pine for so long before she eventually wakes up and smells the chicory." [1]

"Who else is in the resistance?" Vincent asked.

"A couple of former politicians, of course. I've had my best witches keeping an eye on them. Melody tried to use astral projection to determine if they were spies. Oh don't worry, she failed. The short-range dampening field around *The Duke and Ferret* is holding, the cadets I've stationed on their corner are making sure of that. This tower will spread the net far wider. Once we get it running, it will cover half of Brugel."

**18**

---

Tension stretched to snapping point, Ondine followed Natalia for a walk to the morning market. The two women in suits – she still didn't know their names, which in ordinary circumstances would be considered extremely rude – followed a few steps behind. They wanted to visit the markets, which they'd 'heard so much about'. Melody had her arm linked with Alexei's; a sweet development for her friend and brother-in-law. Alas, it served to remind Ondine that she had nobody to link arms with because her beloved Hamish had not come home.

"We won't be too long, will we Natalia?" Ondine asked.

The former first minister muttered, "Just long enough to lose these two."

Ondine didn't feel right leaving the pub. "Because, I was thinking maybe you could stick with Alexei and Melody and . . . you know, I'm probably not needed."

"You want to be home in case your boyfriend returns and you're not there?" Natalia said.

"If it's OK with you?"

"It's not. Stay with me, I'll need your help to make a distraction."

Perhaps the trip to the market would distract Ondine from her stomach-churning worries of Hamish's and Da's welfare. No, nothing could make her stop worrying. Instead, she carried her tight tummy and pained heart with her as they walked on.

They neared the markets, the smells and noises hitting them from across the street. Considering how much life had changed since Lord Vincent became Duke of Brugel, it was good to visit something comfortingly familiar. The same rows and rows of fresh produce, crowds of people, colourful banners, music, hot donut vans and yet more noise as people called out their special deals, fast and jarring.

*"Apples, apples, apples! Get your bananas here."*

It was the kind of call that dug into Ondine's brain, making her pay even more attention to the fruit on display. Especially the bananas. Tummies rumbling from a scant breakfast, Ondine and Natalia bought a banana each and walked amongst the teeming crowds.

Gee that Natalia was clever, Ondine realised. The market was heaving with people. Because of the curfew, the markets opened later and closed earlier. There was less time to shop, so people bought and traded with determination tinged with panic. In all the mayhem, it was seriously easy to lose sight of one another. The first to vanish from Ondine's notice were Melody and Alexei. One moment she could have sworn the two were haggling over the price of potatoes and the next they weren't. The two women in suits had halved, in that Ondine could only see one. The trouble was, they both looked so alike, she couldn't tell if she kept seeing the same one, or both of them at different times. But perhaps the suits had split up, one of them following Melody and Alexei, the other sticking close to Natalia.

*"Apples, apples, apples. Get your bananas here."*

A freshly crushed apple juice would go down nicely. Pushing against the flow of the crowds, Ondine guided Natalia towards a market stall selling juices and apple blinchikis. [1] Thankfully Natalia had a few schlips in her purse because Ondine's pockets were empty.

"Melody should be safely away by now," Natalia said, her neck craning back and forth as she checked for their none-too-subtle watcher.

Ondine looked around, "Has she gone back to the pub?"

"No, she's headed out of town to see how far the dampening field reaches."

The what?

"She hasn't been able to astral, has she?" Natalia said.

Ondine's eyes widened and things began to fall into place. "The spies weren't spying on you at all, were they? They were tracking Melody."

"They're not completely disinterested in me," Natalia said.

"Of course. No offense."

"None taken. Well, a little." Natalia leaned in low and conspiratorial-like. "We've been building the resistance, using astral projection to meet with people, but a week or so ago, astral stopped working. I knew Melody so some of us came to your pub. But then we couldn't even reach Melody in the next room and we knew there had to be some kind of dampening field."

Ondine was seriously impressed. "You can do astral projection?"

"Course I can," Natalia said with a grin. "How do you think I lasted so long in politics?" Then she looked over her shoulder and spotted one of their suited women. "She can follow us back to the pub, then I'll head home. It doesn't matter if she follows me, we've got our answers, and we've got Melody on the case."

"But what about the other one in a suit?"

"If she is following Melody, good luck to her. Once they reach the edge of the dampening field, our suited friend won't stand a chance against Melody's skills. Come on, let's see if your father and Hamish are back."

Ondine sipped the last of her apple juice. "Can we get some blinchikis to go?"

---

THE MOMENT ONDINE opened the back door, a streak of dirty wet fur charged past her. "Hamish! I've been worried sick. Wait a minute, where's Da? Where are you going?"

"I need tae get dressed lass. I'll not come home t'ye lookin' like this!"

The ferret bolted upstairs, his wee claws skittering on the floor.

Ma rushed in. "I heard Hamish. Where's Josef?"

Several minutes of confusion followed. "Da?" Ondine called out, walking to the back door again and checking the beer garden, on the off chance she'd walked in ahead of him and shut the door in his face.

GrannyMa and GranDa stuck their heads out of the caravan. "What's that love?"

"Did Da come through here?"

"No," they said in unison.

"I found him lass," Hamish said, catching up to them.

Relief flooded Ondine as she wrapped her arms around him. Proper Hamish, in his proper human form. Jupiter's moons she'd been so worried.

"I'm not following any of this," Natalia said.

"Neither am I," the woman in the suit said as she walked into the beer garden.

So she *had* followed them back to the pub. How predictable.

"Have you come to check out or will you be staying another night?" Ma asked.

Seriously, how did her mother stay so civil with a customer – and a poorly paying one at that – while Da was still missing? How admirably the rest of the family were keeping it together at a time when they wanted to run around screaming and wailing. If she ever went missing, she hoped the rest of her family would put on more of a show.

A hand wrapped around Ondine's elbow and pulled her inside the hallway. "Ye have tae keep it quiet lass, but I found ye Da."

Bells and clangs went off in her head, but she steadied her breath and asked, "Where?"

Clever Hamish disguised their conversation as a cuddle, so he could keep his voice low next to her ear. "He's in the lockup, *goat* arrested. They've charged him with being out after curfew."

"Arrested!" Her mind screamed but she said nothing out loud in response to the awful news. Instead, she hugged Hamish as tightly as she could, turning her fears and worries into muffled sobs.

"He's safe, lass, but it's no place for ye Da. I'm sure we can pay a fine or something and he'll be home in no time."

"WE DO NOT ACCEPT BRIBES," the constable said.

Ondine, Hamish and Ma had gone to the lockup. After Ma had (politely) cleared their guests out of the pub. The lockup wasn't a horrible building by modern standards, or even Brugelish ones, but it lacked anything resembling what Brugelers liked to call *bonhomie*. Built and decorated perhaps forty years earlier, the walls were covered in yellowing remnants of decades-old sticky tape. New posters declaring, "If you see something, say something," stood out for their bright colours against fading posters of missing people and road safety messages. The front door creaked and groaned each time somebody opened it, while the internal door behind the main desk had completely lost its hydraulics and banged like a gun every time a police officer came or went.

Ma drew in shocked breath. "Oh no! It's not a bribe. Not in the slightest. Oh goodness, what a terrible misunderstanding. We're here to pay his fine."

Ondine's hand curled tightly into Hamish's.

"Let me see," the officer checked a list of prisoners in the lockup. "Josef de Groot, no, his charge is too serious, he has to go to court."

Court? For being out after curfew? Ondine would have screamed at the officer in rage, but he'd probably arrest her on the spot.

"Can we at least see him? Bring him some food?" Ma lifted the lid on her basket and produced a wrapped tea towel.

With a sniff, the officer lifted the wrapping away, then grabbed a metal ruler from the side of his bench and slapped it through the crust. Chunks of pastry crashed and crumpled, the pie completely lost integrity, mashed into chunks of chicken and vegetables on the tea towel. Then the officer wiped the ruler on the towel and nodded. "That's fine, you may take it in. I'll get you an escort."

He walked through the internal door, which crashed shut, making Ondine jump.

With trembling hands, Ma wrapped the desecrated pie into something resembling its original shape and made for the connecting door to visit Da in the holding cells. Everyone lined up behind her.

The internal door opened and banged shut again as the officer came back to the desk. Then a second later, a woman followed him, opening the door and letting it bang shut. Could the first one not have held the door open for the second, thus reducing the bangage?

"Only one visitor per day, that's the rules." The officer said.

It was impossible not to roll her eyes, so Ondine hid them under her eyelids.

"Come on lass, let's go home," Hamish said as he wrapped his arm around her. He was a good man, that Hamish, leading her out of the police station before she completely lost her temper and ended up sharing a cell with Da instead of visiting. If only one of them was allowed to visit Da, it should be Ma.

For the entirety of the walk home, Ondine didn't have one single idea of what she could do next. Nothing came from Hamish either, which made her feel even more despondent. Hamish was brilliant at encouragement and ideas, but now their collective mood was so heavy, not even he could lift it.

Melody could, though. She was full of smiles as she met them at the door, with Alexei by her side. Ordinarily this would be an interesting romantic development in the private lives of the ever-growing number of folks living under the pub's roof, but now wasn't the time.

"We found out what's causing the dampening field," Melody said. "There's a new tower that's gone up, at the castle where we had Coven-Con. It's blocking all our astral projection signals." She sure knew how to deliver bad news with a smile. "And they're monitoring the phone lines, when they're working that is."

Alexei had drunk from the same 'happiness well' too. "Now we know what's causing it, all we have to do is pull it down."

"That's nice," Ondine said. *Outrage fatigue,* as her mother had called it, had left her completely fatigued.

"You could be a little more pleased," Melody said.

Ondine could only sigh pathetically.

"We've had a wee bit of bad news," Hamish said. "Da's in the lockup. They arrested him for being out after curfew."

"Do you need money to pay his fine?" Alexei asked. "I'm sure my parents have a little saved."

If only. Ondine sniffed, "We tried to pay his fine but they accused us of trying to bribe them. And they'd only let Ma go in and see him."

"And not for long either," Ma said, walking into the house and collapsing into a nearby chair. "They've set his trial for a week from today. They let me in long enough to give him the pureed pie, then they pushed me out. He said to give you all his love. They've told him he can ask Vincent for a pardon, but to get that he has to first plead guilty to treason."

"Treason!" Everyone yelled at once.

"Thank you, I didn't need that eardrum," Ma rubbed the side of her head. "Lord V– I mean, Duke Vincent can only give a pardon to a charge of treason, so Da has to plead guilty to that charge in order to qualify for a pardon."

"But he hasnae done it!" Hamish said.

"We know that, but you can't get a pardon for a crime unless you admit to it first."

Ondine threw her hands in the air. "The world has gone whirlypits!"

"That's my line!" Hamish said.

"I've had enough," Ondine said. "Ma, Hamish, get everyone together, we're having a family meeting. We need a proper plan and we need it fast."

A YEAR AGO, if someone had told Ondine she'd be plotting to overthrow the government of Brugel, she would have laughed. A good derisory laugh too. Despite this, Ondine found herself sitting at the table in the family's private room, surrounded by family and friends, plotting to oust Duke Vincent.

He had it coming, really. If he hadn't made life so difficult, Ondine and her friends would have been up to their necks in college work and assignments. Instead, they had enough time on hands to gather plenty of supporters to plan a really good revolution. [2]

"Alexei, I need you to –" Ondine was about to say 'stay here and help Ma and Thomas' but Melody jumped in with:

"– Get the bicycles."

All heads turned Melody's way at whiplash speed.

"Thae what?" Hamish asked.

"Bicycles," Melody confirmed. "They're quiet and we'll cover more ground than walking or running. Plus, if anyone does spot us, we can bike away faster than they can run after us."

"What if they're in a car?" Hamish asked.

"Then we'll improvise."

Ondine smiled and embraced Melody in a hug. Then she pulled away and said to Alexei, "You heard her, get the bikes."

With a quick salute, Alexei headed toward the gate.

"I'll help," Melody said, taking off after him.

"Aww, so nice, they're in *loave*," Hamish said, giving Ondine a squishy squeeze.

Ondine couldn't help smiling. Melody deserved some 'nice' after everything she'd been through.

---

"MAY I ENQUIRE, where is *my* bike?" Old Col said as Alexei produced the fourth bicycle that afternoon.

"You're not serious?" Ondine looked at her great aunt, who, it had to be said, was looking frail these days. And the woman had dodgy magic; she'd admitted as much. What could she offer their young group, aside from a handbrake to slow them down?

Hamish, Melody and Alexei suddenly made themselves busy, dusting off cobwebs, oiling the chains and pumping up the tyres.

Old Col cleared her throat. "Birgit Howser's been the biggest thorn in my side since I can remember. I want to be there for her downfall."

"But Col . . ." Ondine searched her brain for an excuse, then found it. "The more of us there are, the more chance we'll be seen."

"I know her weaknesses," Old Col said.

"And she knows yours," Ondine shot back. "Please stay home. I don't want to be worrying about you, OK?"

Grumbling and muttering about 'missing out on all the fun,' Old Col turned back to the house. Only after she closed the door did Ondine sigh and get her thoughts back to tonight's task.

"Help me remove the reflectors," Alexei said. "Less chance of being seen."

"Good idea. But we'll also have to be extra careful of cars because they won't see us." Ondine said.

With a shrug, Alexei said, "The only cars out after curfew are police vans anyway."

"Backpacks everyone," Hamish said as he handed them out. "Careful with yours Alexei, it's full of explodey things."

"Melody's got the matches in her pack. Safe as houses."

"We travel in pairs," Ondine said, "no bunching up, otherwise we'll look like a mob. Alexei, Melody, you two go on ahead, we'll be right behind you."

"Yes sir," Alexei said, giving Ondine a salute.

---

IT WAS WAY past curfew as the four of them cycled at a steady pace under cover of darkness. Stealth underpinned the success of this mission. If they were caught out, they'd share Da's predicament. The weather gave them no assistance. It may have been spring, but the chill rain coming in from the north spat in their eyes as they rode. Squinting made it harder for the rain to pelt her eyeballs, but didn't stop the icy drops from biting into Ondine's cheeks and neck, slipping down her clothes and chilling her body.

This had to be done tonight, weather be damned. If they waited until summer to assault the mountain, Da's fate would be sealed.

Up ahead, Melody and Alexei vanished around a corner. The side of the road hit an incline. Ondine had to pedal harder to keep moving. The bikes rattled as they hit cobblestone alleys, jangling Ondine's nerves. Putting her palm directly over the bell on the handlebar silenced the metallic dinging.

The night grew thick with darkness and rain as they pushed away from the last of the street lamps. They were heading out of the city towards the castle on the hill. Memories of last year's CovenCon came back to Ondine as she pedalled into the night. The crowds, the natty little funicular railway to get to the top, the way Mrs Howser had utterly creeped Ondine and Hamish out that time by the pool. And the other time with that oily shadow thing growing out of her. Plus all the other times Mrs Howser had made her skin crawl.

Beside her, Hamish too worked his bike faster. They couldn't see Melody at all now. A 'whoosh' sound came from behind. Ondine turned to Hamish to see if he was breathing hard or something.

'Woosh.' there it was again.

Then Old Col flew beside her. On a broomstick.

"Darn site quieter going over cobblestones let me tell you. And more comfortable." Old Col said.

Ondine nearly crashed her bike. "I thought you'd lost your magic?"

"I'm having a hot flash, dear. Might as well put it to good use."

**19**

―――――――

As they neared their target, Ondine, Hamish, Alexei, Melody and Old Col stopped for a quick regroup. The castle was at the top of a nearby mountain, hidden aloft in the murky darkness. They'd have to go the rest of the way on foot, which meant leaving the bikes behind.

The five of them huddled together behind some bushes. Old Col calmed everyone by conjuring hot chocolates out of thin air. The hot drink gave Ondine a glimmer of hope that Old Col's magic might stabilise enough to help them in this mission.

After their drinks, they crept down a quiet path that was little more than a goat track. It followed the side of a stream that splashed over rocks, masking any noise they might be making but also splashing the track and turning it into mud. Shivers spread through Ondine. Were they doomed to perish in the elements before they'd even reached their target?

The river slipped into a culvert that went under a road. The culvert was too small and tight to allow people through. The road looked promising, as was the paved driveway leading up the mountain.

Taking the driveway would make their mission so much easier, but of course there was a blockage – a security gatehouse. Floodlights around the outpost reached into the night, skirting the road and making a full circle of the area. Alexei drew a stopwatch from his backpack and timed the rotations.

"They're on a set loop," he said, "Once they go past us, we have thirty-four seconds to get over to that ledge over there," he pointed to the other side of the rain-slicked road. "There's another track on the other side, it goes past the pond and the waterfall. We can take the funicular railroad. Once we get over, we stay low."

In the darkness, everyone nodded. Well, Ondine nodded. She assumed the others did as well.

"I'll go first," Alexei said.

Ondine heard Melody say, "Be careful," and then heard something that sounded like a kiss.

A grin crept over her face as she needled Hamish in the side with her elbow. Hamish needled her back again. The blinding searchlight swung over their heads and moved on, giving Alexei his cue. With admirable stealth, he darted out and padded across the road, barely making a sound. He made it with time in reserve as the light swung over them again and they all ducked down.

"Me next," Melody said. Darting out, she tore across the road, her feet padding just like Alexei's. In the darkness, Ondine squinted to see how she did it.

Melody was safe with Alexei, thank goodness. Even if they stuffed up now, at least two of them were across the road and closer to their target.

Old Col touched Ondine's shoulder. "Run on your toes. Makes less noise."

The light swung over them again and Ondine whispered, "Go!"

"Nah, I'll wait for the next one," Col said, sounding incredibly calm. "Let's give Melody a moment with her beau."

Hamish quietly snorted.

"We're on a mission here," Ondine said as a fresh shiver rippled through her body.

The light swung over their heads again. This time Col darted out immediately after it cleared, her feet making no sound at all. At which point Ondine realised Col had used her broomstick again and could have flown above the searchlight anyway.

"You next, lass," Hamish said, then gave her a quick but thrilling kiss. "All this excitement is making me jumpy."

Waiting was killing her, but she had to time it perfectly or she'd miss her chance. The light moved over, Ondine shot out. Staying on her toes, she stepped lightly but quickly over the road. Every nerve on heightened alert as she raced to the other side. Lungs burning from exertion, face freezing from the rain, she pushed hard while being as silent as she dared.

Safe!

It felt like forever for her breath to settle down. Making noisy gasps for breath could alert the people in the gatehouse. Would she doom them all because of her noisy breathing? Oh why had they not trained for this? When Ondine finally felt able to look back towards Hamish, her heart thumped even harder and her whole body fizzed with nerves. The light swooped, Hamish crept out, sneaking over the road with his body low. Just as a car came hurtling around the corner.

Ondine opened her mouth to scream. Old Col slapped her hand over her to keep her silent. The car headed straight for Hamish. The driver of said car opened his mouth in shock, then lifted his arm to cover his eyes.

Hamish stood there in the middle of the road, until suddenly he wasn't. His clothes, previously filled out by a human, crumpled away, folding in on themselves. The car motored right over him, catching Hamish's shirt onto the radiator, carrying it off for several metres before it fluttered away.

But no Hamish. No hideous thump and crunch of bone and muscle on the bonnet. Hamish simply slipped under the car as it kept right on going.

The car stopped in a screech of brakes. Ondine, Melody, Col and Alexei squished themselves as low as they could, all while saying nothing and keeping their breaths as quiet as possible. Desperate to see what had happened, and desperately worried about her beloved Hamish, Ondine parted a bush limb aside and dared to peek.

The driver got out, torch in hand, searching the road looking for whatever he'd hit. Or missed. Had Hamish ferretised in time or not? If so, was he becoming human again and reclaiming his clothes, or was he out cold or . . . no, don't even think of the worse thing. The spotlight from the security gate rolled over the road on its regular sweep, blinding the driver and exposing his car.

"State your business!" a voice said over a megaphone.

Was that for Ondine or for the driver?

"It's all right, I'm just doing a milk run. I have papers allowing me to be out after curfew," the man shouted back. "I think I ran over something."

"Approach the checkpoint." Megaphone said.

"Fine." The man sounded disappointed.

This could be their chance to get away. At the sound of his car starting and reversing towards the checkpoint, Ondine felt a tap on her shoulder. It was Alexei, showing that he, Melody and Col were heading towards the funicular tracks.

They couldn't leave Hamish behind, could they?

"If we stay here, we'll be seen," Alexei said in a low murmur.

"I'm waiting for Hamish," Ondine said.

"But we have to go," Alexei said.

"Would you leave Melody behind?" The defeated look on Alexei's face proved Ondine right, so she added, "You go on, I'll catch up."

Which he did. The rotter! Not that she could blame him. They had to get the dampening transmitter down so Melody could get the astral word out. Or the *thought* out.

Sitting alone, Ondine shivered with fear as she looked for signs of Hamish on the road. The car was now up near the checkpoint, but too far away to hear what they were talking about. When the searchlight crossed the road again, her heart could have stopped. No sign of anything at all. No clothes and no ferret. On the up side, no wiped out boyfriend splattered on the bitumen either.

A whoosh of air blew hair across her eyes. In a rush of breath, Hamish landed on the ground beside her. Disregarding their need for stealth, Ondine threw herself onto him. "Oh my darling! I was so worried."

"Not half as worried as me, lass. Hush now, let's get to the others, sharpish."

He had far too much bare skin where there should be fabric. Which ordinarily would be a lovely thing, but not when they were in the middle of a dangerous mission on a cold spring night. "Where's your shirt?"

"In me hands, along with me pants. I had tae leave me shoes behind. Give me a second to get dressed."

No shoes? "You'll get frostbite," Ondine said.

"I'll worry about that when it happens."

The moment he donned his clothes, they scarpered towards the beginning of the funicular track, ready to climb the sleepers up the side of the mountain so they could reach the castle and the transmitter at the top. Silently, everyone gave Hamish hugs of support and relief, but these were soon over because they had a climb to make.

At least, they'd *planned* to climb up the sleepers. Because the funicular railway, one of the steepest in all Europe, and certainly steeper than anything Slaegal had to offer, was not switched off as they'd assumed. If it had been switched off, with the two carriages stored safely in their homes at the top and bottom of the mountain respectively, they could have made the cold, slippery climb unencumbered. Now they would be massively encumbered as the carriage descended towards the bottom station, leaving them no climbing room or time.

"We need plan B," Alexei said to Ondine.

Luckily they were from Eastern Europe, where the old alphabets were still in use. If plan B failed, they had another 34 letters to go.

"If the train is switched on, we use it," Ondine said, with more confidence than she felt. "Climb on as the carriage goes past."

Hamish grabbed Ondine by the shoulder. "Get back!" he whispered, at the same time dragging Melody down with him. Old Col and Alexei followed suit. A group of guards were sitting inside the descending carriage. Another group heading into the lower station, ready to switch over with them for the next shift. How would they make it to the top unseen now?

Utterly trapped, they waited until the groups changed over. The only good thing coming from this very near disaster was that the guards' heavy boots drowned out the noise of Ondine's panicked breathing. "OK, here's what we do now," Ondine said. "As it goes past, we climb on the back of the carriage and hold on."

"Not all of us will be strong enough to do that, dear." Old Col said.

"We'll all hold on to each other," Ondine said.

"I have an idea," Alexei said. "Melody and Old Col go up first, the rest of us get the next one."

"You and me go first Alexei," Melody said. "We can –"

"Don't argue, the carriage is right here and you two need to be at the top first." Alexei grabbed Melody by one hand, Old Col with the other and darted to the carriage. With a solid grunt he lifted Old Col onto the back, where a narrow fender gave her a foothold, and the rear light mount provided a welcome seat. Next he pushed Melody into position and saluted her.

The whole time Ondine's heart was virtually in her throat as Alexei managed the impossible. Now all she and Hamish had to do was wait for the corresponding returning carriage to come past them and they'd get their ride. Worst luck, when the return carriage reached the bottom and Melody and Old Col's carriage reached the top, the guards climbed out and the entire railway shut down.

Alexei, Hamish and Ondine looked at each other, sighed at the job ahead of them and started the arduous climb to the top. For the next twenty minutes they did nothing but put one foot ahead of the other on the next sleeper, one arm reaching ahead of the other, scaling the steep incline. Naturally the rain became heavier, because nothing in life was allowed to be easy.

Every few minutes a searchlight would swing over the tracks, making them flatten down between the rails. Ondine didn't dare move until it was completely dark again, but she'd only have a few minutes until the next sweep of lights.

Wet, cold and sore, they finally reached the top and sat there, gathering their breaths and their bearings for the next stage of the plan.

"OK, where are Melody and Old Col?"

"Psst!" they heard from behind some huge rocks.

Good. They were all together. Sure, Ondine was aching from the exertion and shivering uncontrollably from cold and adrenaline, but the plan was still holding.

"Let's get to the tower," Ondine said. "Col, we're going to put roman candles all over the tower legs. I don't suppose you have a some magic to make them burn hotter?"

"Once they're in position, I'll see what I can do." Old Col said. "You lot take on the tower, I'll keep a lookout. If anyone comes, I'll hoot like an owl."

"There are no owls up here," Ondine said.

"Exactly, so you'll know it's me." Auntie Col said.

From his backpack, Alexei took out a grappling hook and cables, then handed them to Hamish. The rest of his pack held what could only be described as a firebug's dream arsenal. Pinwheels, Roman candles, small rockets and crackers. The noise was going to be intense. They'd have to get this done in one shot or it would all be over for them.

"Wish me luck, lass." Hamish gave Ondine a quick kiss before turning into a ferret again.

Hook in mouth, Shambles scrambled up the transmitter tower, Ondine and Alexei fed the cable after him. Melody rolled her shoulders and made herself ready with whatever she needed so she could astrally project their revolutionary message.

The cable in Ondine's hand tugged three times. All set. Shambles shimmied down the struts and landed at Ondine's feet. Then it was time to take Alexei's fireworks up there. Being a ferret, he could scarper up and down quickly, but being so small and lacking opposable thumbs meant he had to repeat the climb and descent so many times.

Then it was time to take the last of the big bangers up the tower. Old Col came over, twirled her hands above the giant cracker and showered it with sparkly white magic. The air felt hot, Ondine took a step back.

"No need to fret," Old Col said, "It won't blow up in our faces."

"Nor mine, eh?" Shambles said as he grabbed the firework carefully between his teeth and scrambled up the metal once more.

This firework had a particularly long fuse, which dangled all the way to the ground. Shambles scurried down for the last time.

"One more thing," Old Col said, stepping up to the tower leg. She pressed her hands against the metal. Light beamed from her palms and the rivets on one side popped free. "Now!" She yelled.

Alexei struck a match and lit the fuse. The tiny flame raced up the tower leg. For the tiniest of semi-seconds nothing happened, then the most thunderous racket broke out as the fireworks exploded in a brilliant chain reaction. Had this been any normal celebratory night, it would have been gorgeous to gaze upon the sparkles in the sky. Red, green, orange and yellow clusters burst out from the tower, looking impossibly pretty. The structure began to sag and bend a little.

"Heave now!" Hamish cried out in his Shambles form. (He hadn't yet changed back.)

Ondine, and Alexei pulled together on the cables. As they hauled and strained, Ondine was stricken with panic that the noise and sight of the incandescent colours in the sky would bring all the guards down on their heads. Suddenly Hamish was beside them, dressed again, pulling on the cables as well. Everything shuddered and groaned, until, like a statue of a deposed tyrant, the tower came down in a sudden rush of creaking, twisted metal. It tumbled over the edge of the platform and dropped down the side of the cliff. It came to rest in a mangled heap at the foot of the mountain, next to the base of the waterfall.

"Now Melody!" Old Col said.

"On it!" Melody said, standing tall and holding her hands wide as she looked over Venzelemma.

The rest of them stood in frightened silence while Melody projected her message. Inside her head, Ondine could hear Melody pleading with all good people of Brugel to take to the streets and gather in Savo Plaza. "Turn the lights on in your homes to show you heard the message. Join the revolution!"

*Please let this work, please let this work, and hurry up and work because we made so much noise people will be here any second.*

Slowly – so slowly Ondine thought she was imagining it – lights came on across the city. Neighbourhoods brightened as homes lit from within, chasing away the gloom. Venzelemma shone brightly.

"It's done," Melody said, her hands falling to her sides. "I gave the message. Savo Plaza, nine tonight."

"Nine?" Everyone else said.

"Doesn't give us much time to get there ourselves," Old Col said. "Can't have a revolution if there's no-one to lead it."

Filled with excitement and adrenaline, the five of them made for the railway to scramble back down and get away.

A familiar, haughty voice said from the darkness, "You won't be going anywhere."

Ondine should have known things had gone far too well for them, as she turned to face her nemesis, Mrs Howser. "You've lost!" She said. "You're too late! We got the message out!"

"I don't think so." Mrs Howser raised her hands and shot a bolt of cold light straight into Ondine.

The magic lifted Ondine off the ground, spinning her in the air. Ondine screamed as she tumbled and tipped. Hamish leapt at Mrs Howser. Mid leap, she blasted him sideways. Ondine kept spinning, tumbling and turning and flipping and flopping, nausea threatening to spill out at any moment.

A bolt of green magic shone in the sky. It hit Howser hard on her side; she screamed and fell on the ground. Ondine dropped with a sickening lurch, falling not on rocky ground but into Hamish's waiting arms. "I've got you lass."

"Get out of here, kids!" Old Col shouted, her stance ready for battle.

Old Col? Firing bolts of witchcraft? What a brilliant time to have a magical hot flash!

"I'm going to enjoy this," Mrs Howser said as she righted herself, seemingly unharmed. "The young ones should stay." Howser summoned purple orbs of magic, growing them in her palm. "They can watch me destroy you!"

Hamish grabbed Ondine and pulled her towards the funicular. Melody and Alexei were right behind them. Troops marched into position near the top of the railway, blocking their exit.

"Jupiter's moons, now what?" Panic raced through Ondine.

"This way," Melody yelled.

Melody darted off. Old Col kept trading magic blasts with Howser. One incendiary flash after another.

"Get out of here!" Old Col yelled at them.

On the four ran, slipping and tripping over the wet and rocky ground.

"Where are we going?" Ondine asked, then saw the answer. The waterfall, straight ahead.

"There's a path behind it, over this way," Melody yelled back.

*Boom!* A blue flash from Mrs Howser transformed the waterfall into solid ice, blocking their escape. The freeze extended to everything damp, spreading like an ice-fire, freezing grass, mud and Ondine's feet. Stamping hard on the ground, chunks of ice fell off her shoes, but she couldn't feel her frozen toes.

They were trapped. They had troops behind them, a wall of ice in front, a steep hill to one side and a vertiginous drop to the other. Panicking, Ondine looked to Old Col, still trading magic blasts with Howser. In a crackle of light and boom of thunder, Col split a green ball of magic in two. One headed to Howser, the other straight to Ondine.

Ondine threw herself down. What a time for Col's magic to wonk out! But no, the wayward ball of light was deliberate. It flew over her head and hit the waterfall, carving a slalom-style slide across the face of the vertical drop. Melody and Alexei ran for it. Hamish hauled Ondine up and ran towards their icy escape route.

*Ratttatatatatata!* Bullets fired over their heads.

Melody and Alexei leapt onto the slide. In a swoosh, they vanished down the slope, twisting and flailing around a hairpin bends Col had magically carved out of the ice.

"Col! Hurry!" Ondine yelled as Hamish dragged her to the slide.

"Get going!" Col yelled back.

It was all the distraction Howser needed. The evil witch threw an enormous bolt of deepest purple straight into Old Col's chest, sending her sprawling.

"No!" Ondine cried out, clawing at Hamish to let her go.

"We havetae go!" Hamish yelled back, pulling her onto the slide and away from the mayhem.

Down they went, sliding and twisting out of control. Ondine could see the mountain, the purple glowing sparks from Howser as she aimed both hands towards Old Col and blasted her. Col screamed. Ondine screamed; her skin froze as she slipped further away from Col.

"Get up, Col! Get up!" Ondine begged as they dropped away from the battle. Twisting around, she fought to get a clear view, but Hamish was barrelling after her, his body in the way. Another bend, other sickening lurch and she twisted around again. No more green sparks flew on the mountain. Only that horrible purple, all raining down on her great aunt, who wasn't moving any more.

A guttural sob came from Ondine at the thought Old Col was dead. That Mrs Howser had killed her. By staying behind, Col had saved Ondine and her friends, but not herself. Then a sickening crash smacked into her as the slide ended and the road came up to meet them.

Hamish dragged her to her feet. "Come on, Ondi, we havetae get away."

A bolt of cold light slammed the ground, sending dirt and ice exploding into the air. Another soon followed, shattering the ice slide. At least Mrs Howser wouldn't be able to follow them down that way.

Dodging magic, live bullets and icy debris, the four of them ran off to the shrubbery, to the place where they'd parked their bicycles.

Melody was the one with a clear head, she found the bikes first.

Crying while riding, Ondine gulped for air and sobbed every breath. On she rode, with blurry vision and runny nose. Grief had her in its grip and she couldn't stop it. Great Auntie Col was dead.

Ahead of her, Alexei and Melody kept up a punishing pace. A shirtless Hamish pedalled alongside, urging her to keep going. The next long while passed in a blur of narrow bike paths and alleys, Alexei choosing the routes where cars couldn't follow. Ondine lost all track of time and purpose as a single thought beat the drum of her heart.

Old Col is dead.

Old Col is dead.

Who knew how much time passed as they rode into the city outskirts?

"Let's split up, we'll go on ahead." It was Melody's voice inside Ondine's mind. Good, if Melody could still astrally project into Ondine's head, it meant Mrs Howser hadn't switched the dampening field back on.

But for how much longer?

"Howser's trying to get into my head, but it's my turn to block her now." Was the next message Melody sent through.

Good. Give the old witch a taste of her own medicine, Ondine thought. At which point her legs finally ran out of puff and she had to pull up beside a closed convenience store and slump to the ground.

"Eh lass, we have tae keep going," Hamish said, shivering.

They should have brought extra clothes.

They should have had a better plan.

"I can't. I just can't go one more block. Col's up on that mountain and we just left her there and I just can't . . ." Breaths came in big ugly gulps.

Warm arms wrapped around her. She pressed into Hamish's chest, seeking the security he offered. "Dinnae cry lass, or I'll come undone meself."

Which only set Ondine crying even more. "She shouldn't have come. I should have made her stay home."

"Aye, and then we might all four be dead on that hill instead of safely on our way to the city."

A howling noise came from somewhere deep inside as she gave into her grief.

"Please, please, Ondi love," Hamish begged, tucking her lank hair behind an ear. "I don't mean tae be callous, but we must keep going. Col stood up to Howser so that we could get away. It will all come tae naught if we don't get tae the plaza in time."

"I know, I know." He was right, of course. But her emotions were out of control and her brain couldn't see reason. She dragged her sleeve over her face. "I can't stop bawling my eyes out."

"I'll give ye a backie. Up ye get on thae handlebars." [1]

The cobblestone streets were so jarring Ondine felt each bump and jolt. But she held on and endured, taking the punishment for wasting time indulging in an emotional meltdown. At least the physical pain took her mind off her emotions. Maybe, just maybe, Old Col had somehow eluded Mrs Howser and they'd all meet up at the family pub, regaling each other with stories of daring and skill.

On Hamish pedalled, his breaths louder with the effort of carrying an extra person.

"I should never have helped Vincent," Ondine said. "That night at the BrugelMelody competition. We should have gone straight home and had nothing to do with him. Then he would have had to present Ruslana as his orange from Norange and people would have laughed him out of town."

"Aye, it's been playing on me mind as well," Hamish said through several grunts. His voice sounded scratchy, as if he were coming down with laryngitis. "I should have spoken up."

"I should have kicked him in the shins," Ondine said.

"I should have held him while ye did so."

If felt good to share their regrets, neither blaming the other, just wishing they'd done things differently.

The puffing and straining from Hamish became too much for Ondine. "I can walk from here, let me off." As she set down from the handlebars, she looked back to Hamish.

A gasp leapt out of her throat. "Saturn's ring! You're white!"

"Eh?" he said, with a phlegmatic rattle usually reserved for nursing homes.

"Your hair, your face, oh Hamish, what happened?" Ondine took in his face, the tissue-paper-thin skin, the deep lines, the gravity-sag. His neck displayed the ravages of encroaching jowls, his eyes drooped with age. And his hair, his rich, dark hair had turned completely white, gathered in a horseshoe of tufts around his scalp.

Putting a hand to his head, Hamish cried out, "I'm bald!"

Ondine held him close, pressing her ear to his chest, hearing the crackle in his breaths. "You're ageing so fast, you have to change into a ferret, right now."

"Aye, I'll do that sharpish," Hamish said, bracing himself for the pain.

Which didn't come.

"We're running out of time," Ondine said, wiping frustration-tears away.

Hamish stood there, slack-jawed and unchanging. "I cannae do it. It's nae happening."

"Why not?" Ondine sounded so whiny. Tired, cold and aching all over, she petulantly stamped her foot on the cobblestones, sending jarring pain up her leg. "Just do it, will you?"

"I want tae, lass, I honestly do, but the spell's gone and I dinnae ken how tae get it back."

The abyss of despair pulled Ondine onto the cold ground. "Then she's really gone," it came out as barely a squeak. "Old Col. The curse she put on you was, 'you can stay like that for all I care'. So if she really is d–, if she's not with us, then she's not here to *care* any more and keep the curse alive."

"Oh dear," Hamish said, reaching for Ondine and noticing the liver spots on the back of his hand. "Ondi love, I'm so sorry. About everything."

Choking back a fresh bout of crying, Ondine stood up.  "Hamish, don't get me wrong, but we have a job to do and I can cry later. We need to get to Melody."

"Aye?"

"Yes. You're in no shape to start a revolution. The first bump and you'll break a hip. We'll get Melody you get your youth back and when all this is over I can fall to bits at my leisure."

"I loave you so much," he said, leaning in for a kiss.

She ducked her head and turned it into a hug instead, not wanting to offend him. "We're going to fix you," she said, the unspoken part of that being, "I'm not losing two people I love in the one day."

On they walked, past the shops and houses, Hamish making quiet little grunts and complaints about his knee giving him trouble.

Thanks to the message Melody had sent out on the mountain, every single streetlight was on. Behind every window, lights glowed with golden warmth.

"You know what I really should have done?" Ondine asked as Hamish brought them to the edge of the plaza. "I should have realised Vincent was hell bent on becoming Duke. Whether we helped him or not, nothing would have changed the outcome."

"I love ye Ondi," Hamish said. "I've been laid low with guilt for so long about all this. Wishing I'd done more, wishing things were different. Wishing I hadnae been so selfish. But ye just hit the nail on the head, so ye did. Nothing we could have done would have stopped Vincent from becoming Duke."

Hands on hips, Ondine took a deep breath. "And now, we are going to make sure he's not Duke for much longer."

Melody and Alexei appeared from a shadowed doorway. Alexei examined his feet, looking bashful. Melody stepped forward. "Oh, there you are!" Her lips looked chaffed, her hair mussed. Her mouth dropped as she saw Hamish. "Oh dear! You won't last a minute in the plaza."

"So it seems. Ye wouldn't happen to have an elixir of youth on ye perchance?"

Melody chewed her bottom lip in thought. "I have an idea. Hold hands."

The four of them stood in a circle, holding hands. Slowly, a warm energy began to radiate from their hearts, spread through their hands and moved from Melody, Alexei and Ondine into Hamish. Glowing, Hamish's hair grew back and turned a youthful black, the skin on his neck tightened and the curve in his back straightened.

"I feel *wonderful*." Hamish said. "What are ye doing?"

"I'm transferring some of our energy to you," Melody said.

"How much energy?" Ondine asked.

"Enough to get us through tonight," Melody said.

"And then what?" Ondine asked. "One night isn't much help."

Melody let out a sigh. "If we get through tonight, I'll work on a more permanent solution."

"Don't you mean *when* we get through tonight?" Ondine asked.

Melody nodded her head. "Let's stop internalising this and face the music."

Still holding hands, the four of them walked the final few metres into Savo Plaza, ready to meet their fate.

**20**

---

So many lights shone in Savo Plaza Ondine virtually needed sunglasses. The best kind of festival vibe filled the air. Such an enormous crowd had gathered it was hard to see much of the plaza itself, and getting through it involved a lot of squishing and 'Excuse me's.

Hamish jumped to get a better view and then smiled to Ondine. "Lass, you're gonna *loave* this." He lowered his cupped hands to help her step up and lean on his shoulder.

There, on a makeshift stage, stood Cybelle and Margi. Singing and dancing and encouraging the crowd. Cybelle swayed her arm above her head to the beat of the music. The crowd followed her lead. Margi, her belly protruding like a second floor balcony, merely swayed a little from side to side. Thomas drummed wooden spatulas onto an upturned catering bucket. Henrik played metal spoons on his knee. A palpable sense of goodwill filled the plaza. They had safety in numbers. After all, the government couldn't arrest everyone for being out after curfew, could they? The numbers would show how many people disapproved of Vincent. How much they wanted change. Vincent would have to listen to them now.

"People Power!" Cybelle called out.

The crowd threw cheeseballs into the air and cheered.

"Come on," Melody grabbed Ondine by the hand and hauled her through the crush towards the stage.

Cybelle told the gathering, "Thank you everybody for hearing and answering the call. Tonight, we take Brugel back! Brugel for the people!"

The crowds went crazy. It had been a year since the coup in this same plaza, but the mood tonight was completely different. Melody pulled Ondine onto the stage, blinking like a stunned deer. Cybelle thrust the microphone into Melody's hands.

"Thank you, everybody, for coming out tonight," Melody said. "No doubt all of you have suffered terribly this past year as Vincent has done whatever he liked with Brugel. We're here to say 'Time's up' for Vincent. He has to give Brugel back!"

The crowd went insane with joy and began chanting, "Give back Brugel! Give back Brugel!"

"Ondine," Melody pushed the microphone into her hand, "Tell them what your family has been through."

Dry of mouth and trembling of knees, Ondine tried to swallow past the boulder in her throat. "Hello, everyone. This is an amazing turn out," she said.

The crowd murmured and gave a little clap, but not much.

"My name is Ondine, and my family, just like yours has been hit hard. My family runs a hotel, but we've gone broke because of the curfew. Vincent has made our lives impossible. As he's made yours."

The crowd clapped a little more, warming to her subject.

"We've taken in all our relatives, and some friends, because everyone's doing it hard. But then we ran out of food, so Da, I mean, my father, he set out to get us some food, but it was past curfew and they arrested him. Just because he was trying to get us some food! Now he's being told he has to plead guilty to treason by next week. We don't know if we're ever going to see him again! Since when was it treason to try and feed your family?"

More sympathetic clapping.

"My sister," Ondine looked behind her, to see Margi standing nearby. She and Cybelle had clearly been entertaining the crowds with their music. Despite the cold, performance-sweat shone on Margi's face. "My sister is having a baby any day now, and our Da won't even be there to see his first grandchild!"

The heavy sound of 'boo' and disappointment rippled like a wave through the crowd.

"But the worst thing is my great aunt –" a sob caught in Ondine's throat and she couldn't go on. It didn't stop her from trying though. "Her name was Colette Romano, and she was batty and funny and cranky and wonderful, and she was up on the mountain with us and –" Instead of words, sobs fell out. Ondine had to hand the microphone over to Melody.

Melody wrapped Ondine in a warm embrace. "I'll tell them," she said, assuring Ondine.

Margi and Cybelle both moved closer to Ondine, worry writ large on their faces.

"What happened to Old Col?" Cybelle asked.

"It's too horrible," Ondine cried.

Stepping away from the tearsome huddle, Melody faced the thousands-strong crowd and said, "We lost a great woman tonight, and a brilliant witch. She battled Mrs Birgit Howser, Vincent's right-hand-witch. Colette Romano sacrificed herself so that we could escape and get here to the plaza, to tell you what's going on. And we're here to tell you that tonight, Vincent's reign ends. Tonight, we take back Brugel!"

The crowd went insane, cheering and whooping.

"We don't need some pushy little lord telling us what we're allowed to say and when, what time to go to bed, when we're allowed to get up."

Wow, she really had fallen out of love with Vincent. And hard!

"And you definitely don't need one precious little prince doing all this when we used to have an elected government."

The crowd brayed and cheered so loudly they could have lifted the cobbles from the street. Ondine's heart grew so big her ribs might crack.

"We want our country back!" Melody shouted.

The girl was born to control a crowd. A genius behind the microphone, she knew just what to say to get the people on side. Perhaps Melody was using a little extra witchcraft to help her along?

This time Melody waited for the crowd to settle down.  Then she lowered her voice and spoke clearly, making sure her words were under-stood. "What we need is a massive show of people power. Good people, using good power. And here's what we're going to do. We are going to take back Savo Plaza as a place *for* the people." Now her voice rose, along with her passion. "We are going to show that love and hope can over-come. We will show Lord Vincent the door. He has no power over us."

The crowd went insane with joy and threw even more cheeseballs high in the air.

Melody turned quickly to face Ondine and Hamish, "Hurry up and smooch, will ya!"

Huh?

"Kiss already!" Melody twirled her finger in the air and sparks flew, twining Ondine and Hamish into a squishy embrace.

Of course! The magic curse! They had a plaza full of people making good wishes for Brugel, and here's where it could all come true. Because Mrs Howser had never lifted the curse on them, so when they kissed, Ondine could make other people's wishes come true. A whole plaza full of people who wished to get rid of Lord Vincent and Mrs Howser.

Wrapped in her love for Hamish and her country, she pressed her lips to his for a beautiful kiss for the ages. Her hands fastening to his bare chest, because he still hadn't managed to get another shirt in all this time.

And oh how they kissed.

For freedom.

For Brugel.

On they smooched, forgetting the outside world and luxuriating in this most wonderful moment of love. Ears ringing from the cacophonous crowds and stomping feet, she closed her eyes and immersed herself into her love for Hamish. The rumbling grew louder. The crowd wild with delight. No, wait, the noises didn't sound the same. Fear spiked Ondine and she pulled away in time to see tanks rumbling into Sava Plaza.

Heavy boots thumped on the cobbled streets. Grinding metal shrieked from the tanks' caterpillar wheels. With a burst of white, the invaders fired water canon on the crowd. People fled but couldn't get out. Screaming filled the skies as panic set in. The blast of water sent people slipping and smashing into each other. But instead of fleeing, the good people who'd come to protest against Vincent got to their feet and stood tall. United.

Melody sent magical sparks into the crowd to protect them against attack as the battle between good citizens and a dark army of cadets kicked off. If Ondine wasn't afraid for her life, she could have revelled in the epic nature of the battle.

People linked arms and shouted, "Hey no, we won't go!"

Blasts of magic crashed through the air. Weapons fired. Smoke and gas rained down from the skies. The screaming rose by 20 decibels as confusion gripped everyone in the plaza. Small bottles with burning rags jammed in the top hurled through the air, crashing and splattering flames and flares all around. These *Ribbentrop cocktails* didn't do much damage, but they burned everything they crashed into, including clothes. [1]

In all the chaos and open warfare, Ondine forgot about Margi. Where was her pregnant sister? This was no place for her; they had to get her out. But the battle had blocked every lane and road leading out of the plaza. From the corner of her vision, a bubble floated past.

A bubble?

Time to take cover, as Ondine raced to the back of the stage and found Margi and Cybelle, crouching behind some potted plants. Bangs, crashes and explosions filled the air. They were coming closer. Ondine poked her head out and saw a shiny, rainbow globule, wobbling and bobbling in the air. Then it exploded on the side of a statue of Lord Vincent.

Wait, what? *A statue?*

Since when had there ever been a statue of Lord Vincent in Savo Plaza? By all means, put a reminder of Savo himself, after whom the plaza was named, but Vincent?

Nope.

More bubbles popped against the statue, giving Ondine the best idea she'd had in minutes.

"Look after Margi," she said, putting her sister's hands into Thomas and Hamish's care. (They were also sheltering at the back of the stage) Then she ran to where the bubbles were coming from. Sure enough, there was a bubble machine at the side of the stage, always a welcome addition at a party, but a total distraction in a revolution. Sneaking between the fighting crowds and the closed vans of the hot cheeseball vendors, Ondine made her way to a Fort Kluff water canon. No time to second guess the craziness, she climbed on top and opened the hatch. Only to find a person inside it, but no water.

"Don't mind me," she called out, slamming the hatch shut.

Yikes. Where exactly was the hatch for the water to go in?

Ooops, wrong type of canon. This was just an every day tank. The water canon was several meters away, and guarded as well.

"Melody! Help me out here!" Ondine screamed.

"Hey, what are you doing?" A group of cadets turned on Ondine.

Her belly lurched. Time to sound important. "They sent me over to put an additive in the water. Purple dye so you can find people later to make arrests." *I'm so impressed with me, I can't wait to tell Hamish later.*

"You think we're stupid?"

Maybe not. Gears and cogs clicked in her brain. Something rumbled over the cobbles, coming closer. Hamish poked his head out the top hatch.

"You want to know what I have?" Ondine said. "I have a tank right behind me."

The cadets combined their dark magic to hold the tank at bay. The lid shut down hard on Hamish's head, muffling a yelp from inside.

Jupiter's moons, this wasn't supposed to happen.

To Ondine's relief, another group of protestors turned up, their focus not on the tank, but the cadets.

*"They've got your good magic,"* Melody said inside Ondine's head. *"We're going to win!"*

The display of good magic was simplicity itself. Every single rivet popped out of the tank behind the cadets. The machine fell apart like a rusty bucket. A puff of glittering yellow magic dust blew all the components into the air, leaving a shivering cadet sitting in the driver's seat, control knobs in his hand.

Another cloud of magic swept the cadets from their feet, sending them wafting through the air like a swirl of snow. The crowd of revolutionaries cheered and jeered at their defeated foes.

No time to rejoice, they still had a revolution to win and Mrs Howser would be here soon with her henchmen and women. Or hench-cadets. Hurrying, Ondine found the water canon's inlet cover and poured the bubble mix into the reservoir. Then she cranked the nozzle high into the sky and hunted for a switch. They all looked round and green. Nothing so simple as a big red lever.

Silently she reached out to Melody, hoping the clever witch was somehow keeping track of her, despite the chaotic battles surrounding them. *Please help me? I need superconcentrated good magic and I need it now.*

In three heartbeats, nothing at all happened, then suddenly a burst of magic entered Ondine's body, swirled in her brain and poured through her hands. She pressed a small green button and a water fountain charged into the sky, spreading bubbles through the air.

"Are ye right lass?" Hamish said as he came over and stood beside her.

Bubbles continued to spray into the sky, falling in snowy drifts all through the plaza. As each feather-light bubble landed on a cadet, it's popped and showered them with good magic, putting love back in their hearts instead of anger.

The fighting continued, but bubbles kept landing on the cadets, confusing them momentarily, before they dropped their weapons and started playing with the bubbles instead of fighting.

Good magic was winning against evil. People slipped and giggled and laughed as the ground became slick with detergent.

*Clomp, clomp, clomp.* A new threat marched into Savo Plaza.

Leading a platoon of cadets, Mrs Howser hovered on a broomstick. Just to pick over that fresh emotional scab, Ondine noticed that broomstick was Old Col's.

Everyone froze. The water canon switched off. People turned to Mrs Howser as she hovered above the melée and aimed her finger directly at Ondine. A blast of magic hurtled through the air. Ondine leapt behind the water canon as Howser's magic crashed against the machine, instantly freezing the metal. Being wet, Ondine stuck fast to the frigid surface. She ripped hard and tore her sleeves off, but at least she was free. A huge boom echoed around the plaza as the water canon exploded into icy powder.

*Run!* A voice yelled inside her head. It didn't matter whose, she heard it and she ran, ducking and zigzagging to get away from Mrs Howser and her magic bolts of frozen death. Running for her life, Ondine's face burned red with panic. Her heart hammered so hard it blocked the sound of her boots on the cobbled stones. A laneway came up, already blocked with fleeing protestors. Ondine shoved into the panic, carried along with the flow of people until she fell out into an open street.

Screams came from the plaza, from the innocent people she and Melody had summoned here. The people who'd risked being out after curfew to show their support – except Ondine had run like a coward and abandoned the very people she needed.

Stopping, she turned back to the plaza, but her feet wouldn't obey. Nerves had taken hold, she couldn't move. "Get back in there!" she yelled at herself. But her feet weren't listening. Stupid feet. And the flow of people squeezing out that one small laneway meant she couldn't get back in if she tried. The crowd were coming to her, pouring through the bottleneck of the lane and out towards the next major open area only a block away.

On she ran, ahead to the clear space, which just happened to be the steps of Brugel's Dentate.

In the old days these steps would be teeming with night markets and festivals, assemblies and general tourism. Tonight those steps were bare and glittery wet in the cold night air. Ondine's feet raced towards those steps, where an enormous, permanent screen featuring images of a beaming Lord Vincent mocked her approach. The urge to rip off her boot and hurl it at the screen had never been so strong. Unfortunately, her hands were so stiff with cold she couldn't manage the laces.

"Stop running, girl," Mrs Howser said from behind her.

Only her last reserves of courage held her up. It took a few breaths but eventually she turned to face her nemesis. Mrs Howser was sitting on that broomstick, floating in the air. No doubt she'd ridden over everyone through the lane to get here.

Meanwhile, people kept teeming out of the plaza, into the open streets.

The enormous screen flickered and crackled, making Ondine turn around. Lord Vincent's face was gone – hoorah! – but now it showed the back of Ondine's head. It took a few double-takes, but somewhere on the top of a car, or up high, somebody had a camera aimed at her. And Mrs Howser. Aha! There on the walls of a building were several cameras and projectors, capturing everything and beaming it onto the screen for all to see. Ondine's showdown with her arch enemy would be massively public.

And massively humiliating for one of them as well. Ondine hoped it wasn't her, but with the way her luck was going, she couldn't be sure. Clever words and speeches deserted her as she trembled on the steps.

Mrs Howser advanced on Ondine and growled, "This ends here, girl." Then the witch turned around to face the crowd now gathering at the base of the steps. The people should have fled. Nope, they were hanging around to see what happened next.

Clomping feet and rattling metal brought the rest of Mrs Howser's dark army to the edges of the crowd, creating a new barrier to escape. At the head of this dark army, Ondine recognised that powerful cadet, the one she'd seen in her street the night Da had been arrested. The same one from the shared visions with Melody, who had trained under Mrs Howser at Fort Kluff. Looking at her now, Ondine could see rips and tears in her uniform, where she'd engaged in direct combat. Her face had no bruises at all, showing just how one-sided the cadet's battles had been.

At that moment Lord Vincent himself stepped out – of where, Ondine couldn't tell – and quietly walked up the steps to the top, as if taking control of proceedings. But he wasn't in control. Neither was Ondine. Mrs Howser was the one in control as she raised her hand and sent a hideous dark shadow flying out from her fingers. The shadow arched in the air like a net over a school of fish.

"Kill them!" Mrs Howser cried out to her dark army. "Kill them all!"

"No!" Ondine leapt towards Mrs Howser.

"Arrrrrrggggggggghhhhh!" Hamish's familiar cry carried up the steps as he ran towards Ondine, making her heart soar.

Dripping with sarcasm, Mrs Howser shouted, "Oh come on!" She threw a fresh bolt of magic and caught Hamish straight in the chest.

He absorbed the impact but it didn't stop him taking those last steps to be closer to Ondine.

Mrs Howser glared at Ondine and Hamish as a fresh ball of darkest green magic built in the palm of her hand. "This ends. Now."

The ball rocketed towards Ondine. Hamish leapt out to take the blow. The sound of crunching gravel filled the air. Hamish's entire body froze in mid-leap.

"No!" Ondine screamed as she grabbed him, her hot skin pressed against his marble-cold form. Beneath her arms, his flesh turned to stone. She pressed herself against his chest, feeling the last thuds of his heart as his body fossilised in her arms. Blubbering now, she held on, as if her softness and warmth could transfer to his body through sheer force of will. "No, no, no. Hamish. Oh Hamish. It wasn't meant to happen like this."

Mrs Howser, her voice low and deadly, said, "Yes it was. It's exactly how it was meant to happen. This was how it was always going to end, right from the start."

"Not like this. Never like this. Even you can't be this cruel."

"Yes, I can. This is *my* magic. I designed it so everything would come to this point. And beyond." The witch stood closer, gloating her victory. "I made it so that once he bonded with someone, their affections would make other people's wishes come true. That's how the magic spread so beautifully in the first place. As each wish came true, people absorbed the magic and passed it on. Such a marvellous virus."

"Shut up!" Hot tears blurred Ondine's vision. They ran down her cheeks and fell with a splatter on Hamish's granite form. He was heavy in her arms. So heavy. So solid and cold. Too heavy to lift, she lay him along the step.

"It's my best spell ever, even if I do say so myself." Mrs Howser smirked. "Contagious magic that everyday normals can catch! Don't mean to brag. Well, actually I do, because it was so, so clever and you never even worked it out."

Hamish's body wasn't getting any warmer, or lighter. Ondine

couldn't move for the weight of him, or the sheer terror of being fixed in Mrs Howser's glare.

"I designed it so the first normals to catch it would be ever-so-sweet and lovely and *good*," Mrs Howser shuddered, "that you wouldn't be able to help yourself spreading even more. And then, and see, this is the bit I'm really proud of, then the good ones would keep spreading magic to even more people, like ripples in a pond, and then it would mutate and get darker, and so many more people would catch it. Enough to fill a whole army with dark magic."

Frustrated and sick with fear, Ondine yelled, "I don't believe you!" Even though in her heart, she knew it was true.

Mrs Howser cackled and wafted her arm out. "Look around you, gaze upon my magnificent dark army. They are here because of you, Ondine. In a way, this is all your fault."

The dark army filled the streets, standing to attention, waiting for their next directive.

"Don't you dare blame me!" Ondine said through gritted teeth. "This is your horrible magic, not mine!"

"Let me show you, my dear." Mrs Howser tapped her wrinkled hand on the top of Ondine's head and her vision filled with images and memories.

Disgusted with the images filling her head, Ondine turned away from Howser. Yet those same images now played on the big screen at the top of the steps, for everyone to see.

Pain lanced Ondine as she looked at her beloved and batty great auntie, dancing at a debuntante ball with Hamish. It wasn't recent Old Col, it was a much younger version. On the sidelines, a youthful Birgit Howser was glaring at Col and Hamish waltzing past. Ondine almost didn't recognise Howser, because she looked so wholesome. On the screen and inside her head, images bounced around.

Near the drinks table a furious Howser was now yelling at Col. "You knew I wanted to partner with Hamish. So you cast a spell on him so he'd choose you over me! I'll never forgive you for this Col!"

Later, after having too much alcohol to drink, Hamish slurred "You tricked me you witch!" He then accidentally stepped on Col's feet, falling over and ripping her dress. Looking embarrassed, Col waved her hands casting a spell on him, "You revolting little weasel. How dare you break my heart? You can stay like that for all I care. You're all the same, you lot."

Up on the screen, for all to see, Hamish the handsome lad screamed as he transformed into Shambles the ferret for the very first time.

Then the image flickered to a new scene, with Mrs Howser taking in Shambles after Col had spurned him. Time then flew forward again, to a moonlit night at the Psychic Summer Camp. As Shambles slept, a now middle-aged Howser stood over him. She chanted and waved her hands, casting another spell on Shambles.

*"A* GIRL *of whom you are fond,*
  *the two of you will form a bond.*
  *You'll make other's wishes come true,*
  *When she becomes closest to you.*
  *Those wishes will turn dark and loyal,*
  *To make an army for one who is royal.*
  *A new Brugelish ruler to be adored,*
  *And I shall finally get my reward."*

IN THE NEXT IMAGE, Mrs Howser was at the Autumn Palace, placing her curse over the stones at the gatehouse, which she knew Shambles would one day cross over, therefore setting all her twisted magic into motion.

Then a memory played out of Ondine, from nearly two years ago, at Psychic Summer Camp, where she found Shambles face-deep in her Brugelwürst sausage.

"And now we've come to the end of the memories. For you at any rate," Mrs Howser said.

Footsteps sounded. Melody charged up the stairs. "What have you done?" She was out of breath. "Tell me I'm not too late?"

"Oh dear," Mrs Howser said. "My protégée is here, and she is too late. He's already dead."

Vincent, who had said nothing all this time, interrupted. "Won't Hamish's death mean the end of your curse that made the dark army?"

Ondine inwardly swore. *Vincent's such a selfish basket.*

"You are especially thick tonight," Mrs Howser said. "His death means nothing. I made the curse, the curse lives on as long as I do."

Melody's eyes rounded like saucers. Ondine's breath staggered in her lungs. Mrs Howser's showboating had just given them the key to ending this. If the old witch died, the curse would die with her.

"Kiss him," Melody urgently whispered to Ondine. "One more make-a-wish kiss."

"No you don't!" Mrs Howser said, delivering a nasty blast of magic towards Hamish.

In Ondine's arms, Hamish the man shrivelled into a cold, stone ferret.

Tears poured from Ondine as she looked at Howser, standing over them. "Only you could be so cruel!"

"Kiss him anyway!" Melody said.

The deepest sorrow from losing her one true love welled inside Ondine. Her dry lips met his stone head, the only warmth came from the tears running from her face onto his icy body, begging him to come back to her. Then Melody's voice rang inside her head. She was sending out another message, to every magically-receptive mind in the crowd: "Wish that Ondine becomes more powerful than Howser."

Ondine held Shambles, willing his stone ferrety body to warm. "Come back to me. Please, please come back to me. Hamish I love you with all my heart and my being. You are mine, you hear me? Mine. Now come back to me. Please." Another soft kiss on his hard little head, then a sob of pain as she stroked his cold ears and felt as if she too would rather turn to stone than live without him. Nose pressed to the tip of his, she cried and sniffed and made a mess of his face. Reverently she wiped the slick with her sleeve and kissed him afresh.

He felt warmer this time. Probably a trick of her hot tears warming his stone skin. "I'm not done with you," she said, her voice choking with emotion. "You have to come back. I love you Hamish. Pure and simple. I love you and you love me."

Something magical stirred in her chest and her belly as she kissed him again. A tinge of golden mist came from her lips this time. Magic. Coming from *inside* Ondine.

The people in the streets were holding hands and wishing for stronger, kinder magic.

*Thank you Melody.* Hope surged within. "Come back to me, my love." Ondine caressed Shambles's stony forehead.

"Right well. Busy schedule," Mrs Howser said, turning her hand left and right, building a new ball of magic in her palm. "This has been fascinating to watch, but time's a'wasting."

"Stop!" Still holding Shambles's prone form, Ondine stared at Mrs Howser. "Stop now."

Wisps of gold traced through the air, from Ondine's lips towards Mrs Howser. The woman did indeed stop, her body slowly curved inwards, as if her entire being formed a scowl. "How are you doing this? You have no magic!"

"I do now, thanks to yours," Ondine said, putting the pieces together. "Hamish is alive. He's coming back to me right now. And I have your curse to thank for it."

"But . . . you can't!" Crumpling now, as if her body was imploding, Mrs Howser curled around her ball of magic, unable to fling it away.

"I can." Boldness filled Ondine. Something magical and calming settled inside her. Fear lost all meaning as Shambles's body warmed in her lap. In a few seconds, his ferrety head grew back into his lovely humanly Hamish face, gold sprites played about his head as his hair changing from a carved solid into the lush strands she loved playing with so much. All the while, Mrs Howser stood there, curling into herself.

"It's all your magic, Birgit. The people wished me to have it, and so I have. You shouldn't have bragged. Only the witch that created the curse can take it off. The curse doesn't die until the witch that made it dies. When you're dead, your curse will lift and life will return to normal."

"I'm not going anywhere," Mrs Howser said. With a gasp and a grunt, Mrs Howser threw her ball of magic towards Ondine.

"No!" Ondine held her palm out to protect Hamish from the blast. Mrs Howser's ball of power ricocheted off Ondine's hand and barrelled back towards its maker, crashing straight into her heart.

For a moment Mrs Howser sat there, looking stunned and shocked that events should have come to this. For a moment. In the next, her body shook as she desiccated on the steps of the Dentate. Howser's body capsized like a vacuum-sealed bag, sucking her ever inward as her cheeks hollowed, her eyes sank and her body shrivelled. Accelerated ageing turned her limbs into virtual sticks, clothes merely hanging in place, wafting in the breeze. Her lifeless body collapsed, her skeleton no longer supported with life-giving muscle. All that remained was a pile of powder and crumpled clothes.

A breeze picked up the bone dust, swirling it into the sky, leaving nothing but a few clothes and a smear of ash on the Dentate steps.

"And I love ye lass," Hamish said from where he lay on the steps, breathing hard and holding his hand out to her.

Melody quickly draped Mrs Howser's abandoned cloak over him for modesty.

Ondine and Hamish celebrated with lush kisses and more tears, but these were tears of happiness. The cheers from the crowd lifted their spirits as high as the stars.

When they stopped kissing – this took a few minutes – Ondine looked out at the crowds before them. People were hugging and kissing each other with victory, cheering and yelling and throwing cold cheeseballs into the air.

The cadets who had formed Mrs Howser's dark army were not as cheery. If anything, they looked confused and upset, as if they'd woken from a particularly hideous dream. Ondine's gaze alighted on a familiar female cadet. Previously she'd appeared battle-hardened and strong. Now she stood, leaning against the wall, her arms wrapped around her torso, weeping copiously. "I tried to resist, but it was so strong, I couldn't fight it!"

"Melody, I think she'll need your help," Ondine said.

"Aye," Hamish added, as he took in the scene of celebrating citizens and confused cadets. "We have a lot of people affected by magic who won't know what to do with it."

"Too right," Melody jogged down the stairs towards the upset cadets, holding her arms out for an embrace. To let them know they too had been under a curse, but there was a way back.

From the corner of her eye, Ondine saw Vincent stepping away from them. Quick as a flash she blocked him. "Where do you think you're going?"

**21**

———————

A hush fell over the crowd. Those in cadet uniforms sat down, exhausted. They took their helmets off and rubbed their heads or necks, trying to make sense of the world.

The dark army Mrs Howser had created stood (or more accurately, sat) defeated. Demoralised.

Vincent stood nearby on the Dentate steps, unmoving. "Thank you. Howser was becoming a liability."

Panic flooded Ondine. Would he make a run for it? Would he escape the punishment he so sorely needed? Wait, *what*? "I don't want you thanking me," Ondine said.

"We are not on your side!" Melody spun around, hands balling into fists.

"Of course you are." Vincent took a step closer, his palms up in what could look like surrender. *As if.* "You're my main witch. We're going to rule Brugel, we're going to form an alliance with Slaegal and become the most powerful nation in Eastern Europe.

"I'm not your *anything*," Melody said. "You used me. And against my better judgement I let you."

It all sounded far too personal to be discussed in such a public theatre, but Ondine was in no position to interfere. Yes, she wanted to smack

Vincent on the head, but Hamish needed her. He'd nearly died and although he'd come around, his skin had a grey marbled sheen to it instead of healthy pink.

"Oh lass, I'm so sorry. I wish things had turned out different."

She pulled her sleeve down over her wrist so she could wipe his perspiring brow. He needed to go home and rest, but she lacked the strength herself to get him feet-wards. Plus Melody had come back to face-off with Vincent. Ondine wanted to see how things would turn out between them.

"Without Howser, you're nothing," Melody said.

"I still have you," he said, getting close enough to gently tuck a stray lock of her hair over her ear.

"No, you don't." Melody pushed his hand away. "You're finished."

The image on the big screen flickered to life again. The video was from events that took place almost a year ago. There were three men in the picture. One was handed an envelope bulging with cash, then they all shook hands. One of them had a blue hand.

"My camera!" Ondine leapt to her feet in delight.

"Boak!" Hamish's head tumbled from her lap and he splayed out on the steps.

"Oh my darling, I'm so sorry!" She rushed to cradle him. "But look, look what's playing on the big screen. It's from when Vincent and Babak were bribing Valentin to distract Anathea into giving up the throne! Isn't that wonderful?"

"Yes hen."

Wait a second. "Who is doing that?" Ondine asked Melody.

"Alexei," Melody said with a too-wide grin.

"Aye, he's a good lad that one," Hamish muttered.

"I'll say," Melody beamed.

As the crowd watched the image play and replay, they began to boo and heckle.

"You've got a lot of grovelling to do Vincent," Melody said.

"I'm sorry. Is that what you want? An apology? OK then." Vincent said, "I'm sorry that I knew I was the only one who could give Brugel stability and was brave enough to step up."

"Oh come on!" Melody said.

Vincent's face puffed red. Bits of spittle flew from his mouth. "I'm sorry you got hurt along the way, but that's just how things turned out. Without me, Brugel is nothing."

"You really suck at apologies," Melody said, stirring up a ball of magic out of thin air, then flinging it at him. A strap of blue plaster slapped over his mouth, leaving a small breathing hole so he didn't suffocate.

Ondine couldn't believe her friend's restraint. "If I had your power, it would involve a hedgehog going somewhere tender. Sideways."

"That would be unkind to hedgehogs," Melody said, sending another blast of magic Vincent-wards.

He ducked and the ball of energy exploded, showering sparks over him and setting fire to his hair. Frantically he slapped at his scalp to put it out, but there was so much gel in there it only fanned the flames. He ripped the tape off his mouth. "Get it out!" He screamed in panic.

A flick of Melody's wrist and a bathload of icy water tipped over his head.

The crowd cheered and hooted their applause.

Shivering from cold and fury, Vincent rounded on Melody. "Seize her!" He yelled.

To whom?

Anyone, anyone?

Looking around, Ondine couldn't see a single person leaping to Vincent's rescue. There were a few cadets still hanging around. Sad, dejected cadets who had marched with Mrs Howser. Now that her spell over them was gone, they were creasing their foreheads and wondering what they were doing out in the streets at night.

"It's over Vincent," Melody stood toe to toe with him. "I don't know what I ever saw in you."

"Same here sista," Ondine said.

A shuddering sound came through on the wind. Staccato and rhythmic, like a ceiling fan cutting through the air. It grew louder and closer. A fresh spotlight fell on Vincent, from a helicopter, hovering into view. A rope ladder unfurled beside Vincent. He wrapped his arms around it and stepped up, climbing higher.

The crowd surged towards him, darting past Hamish and Ondine on the steps, pushing Melody aside in their efforts to grab Vincent. They were too late. The helicopter lifted Vincent above their grasping hands.

A woman with orange skin looked down at them through the open helicopter door. Her blonde wig flew off and fluttered to the ground.

The crowd burst into song, which involved a lot of 'na-na-nanas' and ended with 'goodbye.' Nobody was sad to see Vincent go.

"You didn't finish him awff?" Hamish groaned as he got to his feet.

"Oh, he's finished. Utterly," Melody said. "He's stuck with Babak and Ruslana in the heli. They'll probably take him to exile in Haute Montagne."

"Where's that?" Ondine scratched her head for a mental Atlas.

"In the mountains." Melody shrugged, but her smile betrayed a secret delight. "It snows a lot. When it's not snowing, it's raining."

The crowds were still here, staggering about, aimless. Like the born leader she was, Melody set off sparks into the sky like fireworks. Showering the air with goodwill and love. The revolutionaries had a new focus: celebrations.

"Lord Vincent and Mrs Howser are gone. Brugel is once again free." Natalia Cebotari appeared with a microphone. Ondine hadn't seen any speakers located anywhere, but the former First Minister's voice rang out anyway. "Good magic has prevailed. Brugel belongs to the Brugelese!"

Politicians eh? Ondine thought. So keen to step into the spotlight the moment they got a chance. Quietly she turned to Hamish. "If I never see another politician or duke or duchess again, it will be too soon."

"As of this moment," Natalia declared, "All political prisoners or those charged with being out after curfew will be set free!"

The crowd erupted with cheers and began to chant, "No more Vincent, no more Vincent!"

"And another thing. The curfew is rescinded!" Natalia yelled over the screaming.

People hooted, clapped, stamped their feet, whistled, yelled and hollered.

Alexei appeared, racing up the steps towards Melody. They locked together, Melody kissed him all over his face.

Hamish looked at Ondine and winked.

Ondine nodded her assent. "Melody deserves a happy ending."

"As do we lass. Now, what's a lad got tae do around here tae get a lift home?"

An impromptu party erupted around them. Sensing a profit, fried cheeseball traders pulled their vans into the street, along with people selling all sorts of drinks by the cup. Euphoria filled the streets and people burst into song, turning Battlefront's *Anthem* into a song for the people. Refuse bins were piled together to make a bonfire. Cadets, now free from their dark magic spell, emptied their weapons and threw them onto the flames.

None too steady on his feet, Hamish leaned against Ondine for support. "Thank ye lass."

"We'd best get home, yeah?" Ondine beamed. "A good meal and a solid sleep is just what you need. And maybe some of Melody's magic."

Melody and Alexei were so busy kissing they probably didn't even notice the chaos around them.

"Awww so nice," Hamish said.

"Yeah. Let's leave them to it. They'll come home when they're ready."

They shuffle-walked down a laneway into Savo Plaza, stopping from time to time for Hamish to get his breath back. "Naw lass, I'm fine, let's keep going."

"I can barely support you as it is. If we keep going and you pass out on me, neither of us will get home."

Home, where Ondine could deliver the good news tinged with bad.

"I'm nawt likely to pass out," Hamish said.

Oh really? Ondine moved towards a bench, then shifted her weight just enough to make Hamish support himself. His knees immediately buckled and he slipped into the seat.

"That was uncalled for, lass," Hamish said.

A current of people moved around them, spreading the festive spirit through the streets of Savo Plaza and the steps of the Dentate. Getting Hamish through them would be tricky at best.

"Rest right here, I'll get you cheeseballs and something to drink."

He obeyed her to the letter, his eyes fluttering shut as the rest of him slumped onto the bench. Any moment now he'd be snoring. Good. Checking the crowd, she found people towards the right side of the street were moving towards Savo Plaza, while on the left they were heading out to the Dentate. She stepped into the current and made her way into the Plaza, where she scanned the crowds, the shops and the stage for her sisters and their men. She'd last seen Margi and Belle just behind the stage.

People were pelting the statue of Vincent with eggs, while other more sensible folk had set up a first-aid station and a makeshift treatment area. *Jupiter's moons, please let them all be all right.*

Scanning the patients, Ondine staggered in shock. Four patients, all very familiar. Thomas, Henrik, Cybelle and Marguerite sat on a blanket. Racing to them, her heart beating faster than her ears could hear it, she screamed out, "Are you all right?" She reached them, relieved to find them unbloodied and otherwise healthy. "Why are you here in the –" the rest of Ondine's words vanished on the breeze as Margi sucked a fast breath through closed teeth.

"It's not coming now, is it?" Ondine felt sick with fear at the thought. Out here, in Savo plaza, on the cold cobblestones! That's no place to give birth!

Pale face, dark hair sticking to her forehead with perspiration, Margi looked up and nodded.

"No. You're not having it here," Ondine said. "I'll get help. Stay here."

"You just said she's not having it here," Belle said.

"Not *right* now. I'll be back in a minute with Melody, Alexei and Hamish."

Turning around, who should she run into but Hamish, one arm over Melody, the other over Alexei. "How did you kn –"

"You were screaming loud enough in your head." Melody grinned.

"Right." Ondine went into organising mode. There was a baby coming! "OK, Henrik and Alexei, you get Hamish back home. Melody, stay with me and put some magic on Margi so she doesn't deliver in the street. Belle, keep Margi calm. Thomas, you and I are going to cross arms and make a seat so we can carry Margi back home."

Melody yanked Ondine by the collar and pulled her in closely, then dropped her voice. "I don't have magic to stop a baby coming."

"That's OK," Ondine kept her voice doubly low. "She just needs to think you do."

"Gotcha." Melody suffused the air with gold and blue glitter and sparkles that smelled vaguely of oranges and vanilla. It had a calming effect as Cybelle helped Margi to her feet, then into the makeshift seat Ondine and Thomas created with their linked hands.

"Keep that magic coming, it's lovely," Margi said, leaning on to Thomas's shoulder. She sucked in another breath and curled into the pain. As much as she could curl into that enormous stomach of hers.

Ondine said, "You're going to be fine, Margi." The lie came so easily she nearly believed it. "I doubt an ambulance can get through this crowd. We'll be home in a minute and we'll call an ambulance from there. Tell you what, Belle, why don't you run on ahead and make the call?"

"On it," Cybelle gave Ondine a salute and raced on ahead.

"Keep that wonderful magic coming," Ondine urged Melody.

Curlicues of pink smoke filled her vision as something seeped into her brain. It made Ondine calmer, her heart rate steadied. Her arms, on the other hand, burned from the strain. "Hey Melody, have you got anything up your magic sleeves to make me stronger? Sister here is heavy!"

"Got an extra life-form on board." Margi protested.

"You're doing great and I love you to pieces," Thomas said, giving her a messy kiss on the forehead as they marched over the cobbled streets towards the family pub.

From Melody's twirling hands and wiggling fingers came a ribbon of gold, sparkling around everybody, infusing Ondine with a cool sense of recovery. Her muscles had turned to hot blocks of wood, but the magic flowed through and big Margi miraculously lightened in her arms.

"We're nearly there," Melody said, spritzing them with fresh magic. "Almost home."

The sight of *The Duke and Ferret* hotel was like a refreshing drink.

Arms and legs burning with the strain, Ondine couldn't wait to put her sister down.

A spasm clutched at Margi just as they reached the door to the pub.

Ma came charging out the front. "Oh my baby, my baby! You're having a baby!"

How clever, Ondine thought, for her mother to state the obvious. At least now they had extra people to help. In fact, there were people everywhere, holding the doors open, holding Margi's hand, making soothing noises and promising that an ambulance would arrive.

Arms aching from all the effort, Ondine stayed out on the footpath for a moment, rubbing her tired arms and catching her breath after all the excitement.  So much had happened tonight, so much adrenaline had coursed through her veins she was likely to fall down if she didn't lean against the wall for support.

Her stomach plummeted when a police car pulled up to the kerb and two Fort Kluff cadets got out of the car.

"Ondine de Groot?" The female cadet asked, walking closer.

Ondine was about to say "Now what?" When she suddenly recognised the cadet. The scary-fit woman who could destroy all she encountered. The one who, perhaps a half-hour ago, had looked so distraught after Mrs Howser's dark magic spell wore off.

"My name's Raluca Pflugg. I wanted to help. This is the only way I know how. And I want to say sorry," she said, extending a hand to Ondine.

Scared of potential reprisals, Ondine extended her hand. But then her attention moved to the other cadet, who opened the passenger door.

Da stepped out. He made a few grunts as he did so, but he was able to step out of the car unassisted.

"Da!" Ondine cried. She pushed Raluca aside and ran to her father, grabbing him in a firm hug.

"Ooof, gentle," Da said.

There wasn't as much of him as she remembered. Less padding around the middle, more gristle, but it was her wonderful Da in her arms nevertheless. In one piece. Otherwise healthy. Tears blurred her vision. "I'm so glad you're out. And you're safe."

"We came as soon as we could," Raluca said from somewhere behind Ondine. "When Ms Cebotari said all curfew prisoners were to be freed, I remembered your speech. About how your Dad had been charged and, um, we went and brought him home."

Stepping back to take in her father's face – grey whiskers had infiltrated his marvellous black eyebrows – Ondine smiled anew. "I missed you so much."

"Me too baby girl. And I missed Henrik's cooking as well. Don't suppose there's anything to eat?"

His attempt at nonchalance had Ondine cry-smiling. "We never gave up on you Da. We did everything we could. We kept fighting."

Da said, "I know you did. It's why I'm out. Raluca filled me in on everything you did tonight. My brave baby girl, I love you so much."

Ondine was happy to surrender to Da's suffocating hug.

"Let's leave them alone," Raluca said to the other cadet in the car.

Ondine stopped the hug and turned to face the cadets. "Thank you for bringing Da home so quickly."

"Let me know if I can ever be of help," Raluca said. "If it wasn't for you and the Brugelish Resistance, I'd still be under Birgit Howser's spell. I did some horrible things under that spell, things I'm not proud of. If it wasn't for you, I'd still be doing them. Or maybe I'd be doing even worse things. Thank you for setting me free."

They nodded, a simple gesture acknowledging so much. Then Ondine held Da firmly by the arm and took him into the family pub. A cheer went up as they walked in, nearly blowing out the windows. Suddenly everyone converged around them, all talking at once. Crying, kissing, hugging, laughing, crying some more, sniffing, laughing and sighing in general exhaustion, happiness and amazement.

"Hey! Having a baby over here!" Margi yelled.

"You got back just in time," Ma said, kissing Da all over his face. "Everyone's home safe."

Resting on a nearby sofa was Hamish, a bowl of soup and bread roll at the ready.

Da looked around the crowded room. "Where's Old Col?"

Concrete poured into Ondine's stomach. Memories flooded back and fresh tears flowed. "Auntie Col was so brave. She . . . took on Mrs Howser so we could get away and start the revolution."

Da opened his mouth to say something. He and Ma looked at each other in shock.

Cybelle bustled past with the phone stuck to the side of her face. "She's just here. Yes. Right. OK, she's sitting on the floor. No I don't think she can get up into a chair at the moment. Right, I'll do that." Then Cybelle shouted to the room, "We need towels and blankets."

Margi grimaced through another contraction. Melody stayed close by, summoning more of her glittery gold to swirl around the scene. Ondine didn't know what the magic Melody was using, but even if it was just some pretty sparkles, it was having a calming effect on Margi, so she may as well keep doing it.

"We need to time them?" Cybelle said to the phone. "OK, that one lasted for about ten seconds . . . oh, you mean the time *between* them? How long since the last one Margi?"

Margi growled like a demon and spoke several swears into one long string of agony.

"OK, Thomas, you need to time the cont –"

Margi cried out in pain.

"That was another one," Cybelle said.

Ma turned to Ondine, her expression torn between wanting to know about her aunt and wanting to help her labouring daughter.

GrannyMa stepped in to the fold. "What's my crazy sister gone and done now?"

"She was so brave," Ondine said. She couldn't say the words past the knot in her throat.

In the background, Margi's moans turned into a full scale roar of pain. Melody swirled the magic sparkles so thickly it was a wonder anyone could see Margi underneath them.

Ma stepped away from her eldest daughter and came to Ondine's side. "Tell us the quick version then."

Like ripping off a bandage, Ondine blurted out, "She and Mrs Howser had a magical battle on the mountain. She sacrificed herself so the rest of us could get away."

Ma pulled Ondine into a tight hug, then kissed her on the forehead. "We'll mourn her properly when we have time. You've been so brave tonight, all of you." Then she let go and raced back to Margi's side. "I'm here my darling. Yes, you're being very brave as well."

Henrik and Alexei brought towels. Thomas was by Margi's other side, letting her crush his hand with each contraction.

"Everything's going to be fine," Ma said. "The ambulance is coming lovvie. Oooh, I'm going to be a GrannyMa!" Then she looked around and barked orders. "Henrik, grab me a tablecloth for modesty please. Margi, pants off, get ready." Then she grabbed the phone off Cybelle and spoke to the ambulance dispatcher. "This is Margi's mother, tell me what to do and I'll do it. Yes. Uh-huh. Dilated? How much? I'll have a look. Let me have a look Margi. Oh for goodness sake, I changed your nappies, it's nothing I haven't seen before. Oh great heavens, she's crowning already!"

Unable to look away, but not wanting to pry, Ondine crept towards Hamish on the couch to check in on him. He too had that expression of mild nausea mixed with excited anticipation. A new baby was coming into the world. But they really didn't want to watch it because it was kind of disgusting. And noisy. Maybe if it was their baby it would be a different story.

For now, it was best to keep out of the way, rest up from an insanely crazy night and let her body come back from the extremes she'd put it under.

"We're going to be SuperMa and SuperDa," GrannyMa said, giving GrannyDa a gentle squeeze.

Da knelt beside his Margi, holding her free hand now that Ma was busy at the business end of things. Thomas kept making lovely reassuring noises, even though every bone in his hand must be crushed to powder by now.

Meanwhile, Ondine suddenly remembered something about washing hands and cleanliness, so she leapt up and grabbed a box of food handling gloves from the kitchen and started passing them around. When she came back out, Ma was under the tablecloth, Belle was reaching under it with one hand, holding the phone to Ma's ear. "Right, the cord's fine, it's not around the neck."

Margi cried out in agony. The wail of the ambulance matched the wailing of the purple (and pretty slimy) baby that rushed into the world with a ripe little cry.

"It's a strong little girl," Ma said, tears of happiness pouring down her cheeks.

"You did it!" Thomas cried in astonishment.

Da grabbed Thomas by the face kissed him.

"In through here," Alexei led the paramedics into the dining room, where they set about taking measurements and readings of both mother and baby.

"My little girl," Margi said as her baby daughter squawked like a bird. "Good set of lungs."

"Awwwww," everyone said.

"Have you thought of a name yet?" Ma asked?

Margi smiled up at Thomas, then back to their daughter and said, "She's our little Colette."

Da said, "That's beautiful. Hello little New Col!"

*New Col.* Ondine wiped tears away. She hugged Hamish and cried out her happiness and relief right along with everyone else.

"She can't be New Col. I'm to young to be an *Old Col!*" Ma said.

The paramedics safely lifted Margi and New Col into the trolley and loaded them into the back of the ambulance.

"We'll see you at the hospital soon," Thomas said, giving Margi and his new daughter a kiss.

"I think this calls for some plütz," Da said.

"None for me, thanks," Ondine said. She was feeling so weak now, one sniff of the stuff and she'd fall over.

"I meant me," Da said, giving her a wink.

"Come on lass, we've had a big day," Hamish said, drawing Ondine into a hug. "We've earned some time off."

# EPILOGUE

L ife had a way of falling into a happy pattern of regularity in the weeks that followed. Not normality of course, because nothing in Brugel is ever really normal.

Cybelle and Marguerite still treated Ondine as if she were a baby who told fibs to make herself important, but older sisters can be like that at times. Ma and Da had re-opened the restaurant, the public bar and hotel rooms again and the place was as busy as it usually was in spring. Week-ends were booked out, and with the curfew gone, people enjoyed their dinners late into the evening.

The sun shone that little bit warmer every day. Figuratively speaking, the cold north wind got the memo and calmed right down for a while, letting the gentle, early summer breezes come out and play.

The Duchess, Anathea had come back from her exile. The Duchess was broke, of course, so she urged the Dentate to give her more money so that the Venzelemma palace would be restored for posterity.

Ma made Ondine promise that she would never, ever, *ever* get involved in political intrigues again and Ondine readily promised. When a letter arrived offering Ondine and Hamish a commendation for their actions in restoring Brugel they ticked the "Please deliver my award in the post" box instead of the "I would be delighted to attend the ceremony" box.

The Dentate, led by Interim First Minister Natalia Cebotari, called for fresh elections. As the voting age in Brugel was eighteen, Ondine, being only seventeen, was too young to vote. The rest of her family, however, were excited by the prospect, and dinner times became fuelled with friendly political speculation and intrigue. The rest of the family were so engrossed in their politics, it gave Ondine and Hamish time to slip away unnoticed and have a lovely time together.

They were so busy being in love, they didn't give a second thought to intrigues. Ondine would never, ever, *ever* get involved with them again.

Or help them.

Not in the slightest.

She'd much rather spend her beautiful summer evenings working in the family pub with Hamish, even if it meant spending hours each day elbow-deep in sudsy water, washing dish after dish.

Every morning for the next month, Melody, Alexei and Ondine would help restore Hamish to a little more of his earlier Hamishness. Being unable to replenish himself by sleeping as a ferret was everything Ondine had ever wanted. Of course, rapidly aging into an old man was not, so they relied on Melody's extensive knowledge of magic and witchcraft to restore him back to full health.

Not that Melody stayed at *The Duke and Ferret* the whole time. She had a whole new career opening up before her, taking over the running of the late Birgit Howser's Psychic Summercamp.

In a classic example of, "It's not what you know but who you know," Ondine and Hamish scored the catering contract for Psychic Summercamp. There may have been more qualified caterers in Venzelemma, but there were certainly none more loyal.

One sunny morning in June, as Ondine and Hamish were unloading their latest delivery, a fresh group of witches arrived for registration.

"This food might only last two days," Alexei said, wheeling a trolley around to help them out. "We have so many witches arriving now, all times of the day and night. Word sure is getting around. Might have to increase our order to three days a week at this rate."

"Are you getting any more cadets?" Ondine asked. They were the ones who needed the most help, in her opinion. They'd been turned into fighting machines by Mrs Howser, they needed help finding their way back to being normal.

"Heaps of them," Alexei said. "They keep turning up asking for help, and here they are. We don't have the heart to turn them away. Like lost souls, really."

"Of course Melody wouldn't be able to turn them away," Ondine said. "She has the biggest heart in the world."

"Aye, Melody took you in, eh lad?" Hamish said, winking at Alexei.

Alexei playfully batted Hamish on the arm and pointed to more boxes of food that needed shifting.

Hefting a box of lettuce and cabbage, Ondine strode towards the communal kitchen. She was pretending not to listen, but she couldn't help overhearing Hamish say to Alexei, "Yer a canny one for securing yer privacy out here instead of staying at the pub."

Alexei furiously coughed in reply.

Melody came into the kitchen with a clipboard under her arm. When she and Ondine saw each other, they both dropped what was in their hands onto the nearest bench and seized each other for a hug.

Hamish laughed. "Ye havnae seen each other for three days, but ye act like it's three months."

"Hugs are important," Ondine said as she broke away from the embrace and started sorting through their crates of goodies. "And anyway, it's not like Melody holds your youth and longevity in her hands. Oh, wait, she *does*!"

"Come 'ere," Hamish said, grabbing Melody in a bear hug and making her squawk under the pressure of it. "How's my favourite witch today?"

"I'm good, and you're good. We've been working on a health treatment for you that you're going to love."

On they chatted, unloading groceries and checking them off, enjoying the splendour of the mundane activity.

"Can I come in?" A voice said at the door. Raluca Pflugg came in, eyes downcast, arms clasped firmly together as if she were sure to be expelled any moment.

"Ah, Raluca, we were just thinking about you," Melody said, taking the girl under her arm and bringing her into the centre of the kitchen. "Are you sure about this?"

"Yes, we all are, and you've already done so much," Raluca said.

Intrigued by the spy-speak, Ondine's brow rose. "What are you up to?"

"We've got something for Hamish, if that's all right. We think we've come up with a way to give his health a boost."

"Aye, and what's in it?" Hamish asked.

"If you'd come this way," Raluca said, her expression nervous and timid.

Curious, Ondine followed, pulling Hamish by the hand behind her. Melody and Alexei came along too, a little slower than Ondine. She suspected they were being deliberately slow to sneak in some kisses. Couldn't blame them really.

They followed Raluca outdoors, into a garden area filled with dappled light. Here, dozens of witches and former cadets were standing in a circle, holding hands, waiting for them.

"What's this?" Hamish asked.

"It's our way of helping," Raluca said. "You all did so much for us, it's the best way we could think of to return the favour. Please, won't you link hands with us?"

Hamish took Raluca's hand in his left, then Ondine's in his right. She in turn joined hands with a boy witch to her other side. Melody and Alexei joined in a little further along.

Raluca started humming. The rest of them followed. A warm sensation filled Ondine as an overwhelming sense of happiness and good health vibrated all around them. It was similar to the time Melody had helped them transfer a little of their youth into Hamish just before they headed into Savo Plaza, but this was on a much bigger scale. The world shimmered and glowed as positive energy flowed through everyone like a living, breathing thing.

When they stopped, her darling Hamish looked healthier than she'd ever seen him.

"Weil," he gave her a wink. "I'm all ticketyboo again."

"You've got that right." Ondine kissed him with all her heart. It was one of the best kisses they'd ever shared, and she never wanted it to end.

---

AND THAT, dear readers, is where we must leave Ondine and Hamish.

In the coming years they will have more adventures and tribulations as they grow even more in love with each other.

Eventually they will grow terribly old and wrinkled.

Some of Hamish's hair will fall out, but that won't matter to Ondine, because she'll consistently forget to wear her glasses and won't notice.

I think everyone can agree they've generously shared their personal lives with the world over the past four books.

But now they deserve a little privacy.

Probably a lot of privacy.

Yes, lots.

–THE END–

# ABOUT THE AUTHOR

Well hi there! You made it to the best part of the book, which is all about me!

I'm the author of the stories you just read.

I have lived all over Victoria, including Lorne, Maldon, Narre Warren and Ballarat. But not in that order.

Would you like to keep in touch? Visit my website here
www.ebonymckenna.com

and Join my newsletter to grab yourself a free read straight up, because that's awesome, and then stick around for pictures of my cat, cake fails (and a few wins) and other fun stuff.

author@ebonymckenna.com

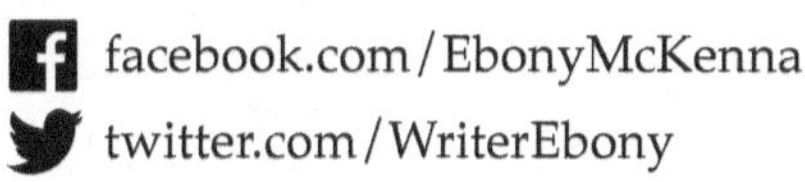

facebook.com/EbonyMcKenna
twitter.com/WriterEbony

# FOOTNOTES

## The Summer of Shambles

### Chapter 1

1. One of the dozens of former Eastern Bloc countries, Brugel is mostly famous for three things. It has the only hexagonal flag in the world. Its main export is plütz, which is a tasty yet highly volatile vodka made from peaches. It has also never won the Eurovision Song Contest.
2. From a strategic point of view, Brugel was so insignificant during World War Two that neither the Allies nor the Axis bothered to bomb it. This is why so many of its old buildings are still standing.
3. This was during the enormous gimgaw craze, so everyone had them. You won't find them now though.
4. She'd found him face-deep in her secret stash of Brugelwürst sausage, a local delicacy.
5. The flowers did their best to mask the smell of the ferret, but the ferret easily overpowered them.
6. Bampot is a silly person. A Daftie. Gets low grades at school and later in life rarely earns more than minimum wage.
7. Venzelemma is home to one of the oldest elektrichka train fleets in Europe. Their sparse interiors and spine-jarring wooden bench seats evoke equal amounts of old world nostalgia and sciatica. Most physiotherapists in Brugel are located within hobbling distance of train stations.
8. Pure denial. Shambles lost his social skills years ago.
9. An animal form of supernatural spirit, who aids a witch in performing magic. Sometimes they're helpful, but in most cases they're useless. Have you ever seen a cat fetch the morning newspaper? Vacuum the floor? Make breakfast? Exactly.
10. Neep. Short for turnip.
11. Plütz is Brugel's number one alcoholic export. It is made from fermented peaches, is 32 per cent proof and is the main ingredient in divorce proceedings.

### Chapter 2

1. In case you're wondering, Ondine's mother was very good at doing several things at once, so she talked like that too. On a good day she could get five or even seven subjects into a single sentence.
2. Although the elder Collette Romano's hair and 'dark' parted company decades ago.
3. If you have a head like a guiser's neep, you're an incredibly ugly person. With reference to the hollowed-out turnips with candles in them, used on Guy Fawkes Night. Imagine someone with a face like a turnip that's probably been smashed in a few times. And then run over.

# Chapter 3

1. It should be noted that you can't just rock up to the Duke of Brugel's city estate and say hello. He's a very busy man. He has a whole country to run. In this case, because of the seriousness of Ondine and Da's claims, the Duke decided to make an exception.
2. The Duke's city residence is so big it has its own postcode.
3. The philtrum is the cute little indent just below your nose. It is also the trickiest part to shave and requires a steady hand and very narrow razor.
4. Brugel uses the metric system, which can be terribly confusing to the three remaining countries in the world not using it. (Hello Burma, Liberia and USA) One metre is about three feet, ten kilometres is about six miles. However, newborn babies the world over are still weighed in pounds.
5. Every time this happened, she promised herself she'd use these great lines next time she and Da had a barney. But it never worked out like that.

# Chapter 4

1. Mockit – filthy and disgusting. Like armpits and road kill.
2. Cold stovies are leftovers from the stove. Builds up the immune system.
3. The average age for a first marriage in Brugel is one of the lowest in Europe. It's 22.4 for men and 21.1 for women, so Marguerite is bang on average. In nearby Poland it is 26.2 for men, 23 for women. In contrast, Sweden is 32.9 for men, 30.4 for women. The link between early age of first marriage and lack of anything decent on television is yet to be proved.
4. Stoat the ba' – when a man and a woman love each other very much and have a very special cuddle. Only in this case the woman is very young and isn't yet legally supposed to be having those sorts of cuddles. And the man is well aware of that fact.
5. Chefs work long and odd hours. They are awake at night and catch up on sleep during the day. It's rare for them to get out much, or to see the sun. Just as you should never trust a thin chef (because if they're not eating their food, neither should you), you should never trust a chef with a tan.
6. A fiddler's biddin' is a last-minute invitation.
7. To say this is flat-out rude. It means "you're talking pish"

# Chapter 5

1. Committed to the 'loony section' of the nearest asylum. Those in severe mental distress are sent to the writers' section.
2. Ferrets require a diet high in protein and fat, and low in carbohydrates. Sausages fit the bill nicely, provided they are not filled with breadcrumbs. Sausages can also become a bit tedious. It doesn't matter what you do with a sausage or how many herbs or semi-sundried tomatoes you add, after a while they all taste the same.

# Chapter 6

1. Always have a big breakfast. It gets the metabolism going for the day and helps you think straight. Skip breakfast and you lose ten IQ points.
2. It was for twelve people. Ouch!
3. In a parallel universe, Ondine remained at Psychic Summercamp and failed all her subjects, then returned home to find a pile of smouldering ash where the hotel and her home used to be. Josef had walked into the kitchen and discovered Cybelle and Chef in a passionate embrace. He'd lost his temper and thrown the nearest thing to hand – a jug of water – at the pair of them. The jug missed its target and landed in the roiling deep fryer, which exploded and set the kitchen on fire. They didn't know the health inspector was due to arrive the next morning, but in any case, his visit was a moot point.

   In yet another parallel universe, the health inspector decided to arrive two weeks early and was hit by the 7.05 express as he attempted to cross the train tracks. This was because the pedestrian walkway hadn't opened yet.
4. In Brugel banks are open Mondays from 10 a.m. to 3 p.m., Tuesdays from 4 p.m. to 7 p.m., Thursdays and Fridays from 11 a.m. to 6 p.m. Closed Wednesdays and weekends.

   As an interesting side note to history, Brugel's First Minister vetoed Euros in 2004 after he saw the first pressing of Brugel's 20-cent Euro coin featuring a banker in a hammock. The coins were withdrawn from circulation, but are available for bids over US$20 on BeBay, Brugel's answer to eBay.

# Chapter 7

1. Prior to decimal currency, Brugel had a brief period of cinquimal currency. Five Drops to the Schlip, five Schlips to the Pennig, five Pennigs to the Lipp. The closest equivalent of the Lipp is about two Euros. Or as people remember it fondly, many a drop is schlip between the pennig and the lipp.
2. A completely unnecessary yet strangely compelling device to attach sparkly plastic jewels to your clothes.
3. a) Something that looks good at first but turns out to be horrible, or just plain rubbish. b) Used to make sausages.
4. Before the Internet, there was the Dewey Decimal System, created by American Melville Dewey in 1876. It's still in library use across the world today. While an excellent organiser with the kind of OCD most pedants can only dream of, his spelling was atrocious. Leading by example, he changed his name to Melvil Dui to encourage 'Merikans to remoov redundt letrs.
5. Naphthalene is a magnificent compound for preventing moths and silverfish from eating your clothes. However, the smell is almost impossible to eradicate, which explains why your nana smells like that.
6. Ancient Brugler-Latin for 'born to rule'.
7. You may be wondering why Ondine didn't just get on the Internet and look this up. But remember, this story happened twelve years ago, and things were different then. Not that they've changed all that much. Truth be told, Brugel is the only country in

Europe without broadband. They also have high tariffs on imported computers, to encourage people to "Buy Brugel Made".

Their phone system is prone to outages as well, which is why they still have a voting panel for the Eurovision Song Contest instead of phone and SMS voting. Brugel always gives twelve points to Slovakia, which has led to accusations of vote-rigging. Especially the year when Slovakia wasn't even in the finals.


# Chapter 8

1. Oose – mighty big clumps of dust that gang up into fluffmonsters. The origin of this phrase is impossible to verify, much like a Freemason's secret handshake. For more information on Freemasonry, follow the adventures of Pierre in Tolstoy's *War and Peace*. Or check out *Freemasons for Dummies*.
2. Ferrets are famous salad dodgers, and are unable to process sugars or even vegetable protein. Don't feed them raisins, as ferrets are also known to hoard their food. The sugar rush from a raisin bender can put them in a coma. Likewise with alcohol, but that's just common sense.


# Chapter 9

1. Sit Nice. Instruction for children to behave, used sparingly if at all, because of its negligible value in teaching children anything. More often used as a precursor to a smack. As in, "I told ye tae sit nice and ye didnae. (Smack!) Now stop crying and go to your room."
2. Often spoken in comfort, but just as often not, depending on tone, e.g. "Oh, did ye drop yer wee bottle of ginger and it's all splished away? Ach, dry yer eyes."

   Compared to: "Ye fell out the windae and got a compound fracture? Ach, dry yer eyes." Closest modern equivalent is "Suck it up and get back to work."
3. It may seem short notice to be having the engagement party so soon after Josef discovered his eldest's intentions. However, just as Ma had kept a good secret from her husband about Margi and Thomas, she'd also kept the party secret, only telling Josef the day before that it was on. Her reasoning was that if she didn't tell him until the last minute, and everybody they'd invited was coming, it would be too late to cancel it.
4. Vomit. A lot. Usually after drinking. A lot.


# Chapter 10

1. They'd "shrunk" in the wash during Colette's first pregnancy with Marguerite. Men often gain weight when their wives or partners are pregnant. Some call it sympathetic eating, others claim it's Couvade's Syndrome, where a man experiences the same pregnancy symptoms as his partner because he's so "in touch" with her feelings. The most likely explanation is too many pies.
2. If you're the kind of person who likes steak "well done", consider this: Do you like it incinerated because you really do want to get cancer from eating burnt food, or is it

because you can't handle the sight of blood? If it's because you can't handle a bit of pink, then you're a wuss. Steak should be well-pink inside, and dripping beautiful bloody juices on to the plate. And another thing. If you order your steak "well done" you'll get the lousy piece of meat, because the chef thinks you don't know anything about how real food should taste.

3.  It's a known fact that parents do have these superpowers, but only in limited supply. Many possess glares that can root you to the spot. Mom's spit on a napkin is the most powerful grime solvent in the known universe. They also have unlimited resources to make you feel guilty for doing just about anything even remotely out of line. They are also good at getting lids off jars with seemingly little effort, and know just about everything about anything, so you will never win an argument. Children of the world rejoice, for kryptonite is at hand. Make them breakfast in bed and tell them you love them, often. For then they will be yours and they will do your bidding.

4.  It would be rude to suggest that she was doing that deliberately so she could get a look at his trim backside, which fitted rather snugly in Josef's old pants. But yeah, she looked, and it was good.

# Chapter 11

1.  Unpleasant business. The result of which seriously dented Charles Lamb's writing career. Shakespeare suffered no such problems.
2.  Beer goggles make everyone look much more attractive than they really are. Especially at closing time when there aren't many singles left in the bar.
3.  A popular form of entertainment, with dancing and music, pronounced "kay-lee". Not to be confused with "Kylie", who is a popular entertainer.
4.  Fancy French finger food. Pronounced "or-dervs" with a hint of garlic breath.
5.  Ferrets are incredibly handy at Ferreting. This involves finding a rabbit warren, blocking off all exits bar one, and sending a ferret or three into the burrow. All the trapper need do is wait at the exit with a large Hessian bag and an appetite for rabbit stew.
6.  In which further grocers claimed Ondine would send them to the poor house and that they'd have to come begging at the hotel for food, or sell their children on the black market. In Brugel, traders take drama classes so they can bring their A-game to haggling.

# Chapter 12

1.  You liar, I'm going to hit you.
2.  I'll put my fist where it's not welcome.
3.  I'll get my revenge.
4.  And don't even think about trying to silence me.
5.  Sorry to break it to you. Ach, dry yer eyes.
6.  How to judge parental mood by the name they call you. e.g. Ondi = Ma in a good mood.

    Ondine = Ma is busy.

    Ondine de Groot = Ma is really narked.

Ondine Benedicte Wilhelmina de Groot = Ma's just walked in and Ondine's standing over a dead body with a bloody knife in her hand
7. This had been her first Serious Kiss, so it required capitalisation. Considering Ondine is fifteen, it shows how protected her life had been up until that point.
8. What is it with parents always correcting your grammar? They'd never do it to their friends.

## Chapter 13

1. Brugel's government school system is nominally free, a legacy from the Soviet days. However, parents are required to make "voluntary" payments in exchange for copies of their children's term reports. There are also fees for subjects that incur extra costs for excursions or equipment. The most expensive electives are winter sports (ski fees) and media studies (camcorder fees). Both these subjects were high on Ondine's list of electives.

## Chapter 14

1. While it's true Colette Romano did not drink alcohol until she was nearly twenty-five, she made up for it pretty quickly after that.

## Chapter 15

1. Anyone whose parents run a restaurant will attest that these things do happen. Friends who come home with you after school think it's "fun" to iron tablecloths and do the dishes. That is, until they realise at the end of the night the parental units think it's all "fun" as well, and give lollies instead of cash payment for work done. Said "friends" will then never come back.
2. Seriously, what's with the scrunched-up napkin in the middle of a dirty plate? It looks revolting. Have you any idea how hard it is to get blueberry roulade stains out of linen napkins? Just line your knife and fork together across the centre of the plate, with the tip of the knife at twelve o'clock. If you've grown up with digital clocks, seek urgent deportment lessons.
3. All reekie - smelly. Not to be confused with Auld Reekie, otherwise known as Edinburgh.
4. Giving it laldy - to do something with great vigour, whether delivering a beating, using a credit card or playing the piano.

## Chapter 16

1. Pale or blanched. Like when the colour drains from your face when a gorgeous man suddenly appears under your bed.

2.  Sit down, shut up, hold your tongue and pay attention.

## Chapter 17

1.  The fact that "Brugel" is an anagram of "burgle" is a total coincidence.
2.  Brugel's top military school. Technically it's a reform school with nicer uniforms. And guns. Which is pretty disturbing when you think about it – they take the worst delinquents from the richest families, then teach them how to use weapons.

## Chapter 18

1.  "Scudded" is so a word. It means "thoughts that shoot through". Just like Scud missiles, sometimes they hit their target with devastating effect. More often than not,

    they go way off course.
2.  New Zealand is about the furthest away from Brugel you can get on the planet. If you try and get any further away, you'll start getting closer again.

# The Autumn Palace

## Chapter 1

1.  The Duke of Brugel is the hereditary head of state for the Constitutional Duchy of Brugel, a former Soviet bloc country in Eastern Europe that still hasn't won Eurovision. Venzelemma, where Ondine lives with her family, is Brugel's capital city. Some people might ask, if Brugel was a Soviet state, how did the Duchy survive? Good question. For answers, read *The Complete History of Brugel*, by Shaaron Melvedeir – 250 pages of folklore, facts, figures and the occasional photo. Another book, *Everything Shaaron Melvedeir Says is Rubbish*, by Isaak Drixen, 745 pages, is the subject of Brugel's longest-running defamation action.
2.  City Savers are very good value, but only for off-peak travel. All visitors to Venzelemma should buy a ten-pack to see the best the city has to offer. The central hospital with its neo-gothic exterior, flying buttresses and vaulted ceilings in the foyer are a must. The hospital is conveniently located within staggering distance of Brugel's largest fish market, so visitors overcome by the stench of rotting seafood can get prompt treatment.
3.  In Brugel, each dropped object carries a unique verb. For example, dropped cutlery clatters, dropped luggage cludders.
4.  This was no disparaging comment, merely the truth. Colette Romano was a witch. The fact that she needed less than an hour to be ready for travel – and levitate five packed cases across a street – proved it.
5.  Second is the logical yet slightly insulting term used by Bruglers (the residents of Brugel, who speak Brugelish) to describe any thing that is not first. It can mean as much as missing the 100-metre final by a gnat's wing, or losing three sets to love in the first round of the Venzelemma Grand Slam.
6.  "Palechia" is Brugelish for "palace". It is pronounced "pe-cha". Scholars insist the word was originally pronounced "PAL-e-CHEE-a" as recently as two hundred and fifty years ago. When Wiwyam The Gweat became Duke in 1799, his fondness for

removing people's heads from their shoulders made the rest of his advisors wewuc-
tant to cowwect his many speech impediments.

7. Numpty means unwise. If a witch has previously become very cross with you and
   turned you into a ferret, you'd be numpty to think you could ever trust her.
8. See *Ondine: The Summer of Shambles*.
9. When the Duke met Old Col, he took a shine to her. Naturally, he wanted someone
   with her witchery skills to be working for him. If not, she might end up working
   against him, and that was a chance the Duke wasn't willing to take.

# Chapter 2

1. "Barry" means "very nice", "great" even. Nice meal, great place, fabulous view, etc.
   Outside Edinburgh, "to Barry" means to be sick. It's really important not to confuse
   the two, otherwise you might end up insulting someone.
2. Usually backstory does not belong at the front of the book. Ondine was aware of this
   and kept her episode of reminiscing brief.
3. Darjeeling is expensive fancy-pants tea. It was introduced to Brugel when Marco Polo
   opened up the spice trade to Asia.

# Chapter 3

1. In the process of receiving World Heritage Listing. Knocks Argentina's Ischigualasto
   for six.
2. Not to be confused with Lake Omski, just outside Budapest, which has nude
   sunbathing (in summer only).
3. An old saying in Brugel, which means you have lots of money. It does not refer to
   actual pillows of gold, as they are uncomfortable to sleep on. The phrase originates
   from rich people hiding banknotes and valuables under their mattresses for safekeeping. This behaviour is a result of Brugel's archaic banking system and the protracted
   recessions of 1972 to March 1987, and September 1987 to early 1996. Then from 2008
   until the present day.
4. The palechia is one of the grandest estates in Eastern Europe and is sometimes called
   the Versailles of Brugel. A little-known fact: the palechia inspired the redesign of
   Polesden Lacey in Surrey, England, which is built on a far smaller and, dare we say,
   more affordable, scale.
5. "Goiven" is a word that means nothing, but can stand in the place of a great many
   swear words.
6. Bellreeve has had several name changes over the generations. At various points it has
   been known as Trelteman, St Basil and Glückentenk.
7. In some countries people might say, "the penny dropped", which means somebody
   has finally figured something out. In Brugel, the popular expression is "the twig
   snapped", a reference to the sound and effort of someone having to think really hard
   to arrive at the answer. Next time you ask your parents a really difficult question, like
   "Why do I have to go to school?" or "Where do babies really come from?" listen carefully. Hear that clicking, snapping sound? It's their brains hard at work.

8. When Old Col was young, Hamish had embarrassed her terribly in front of high society at a debutante ball, so she had turned him into a ferret. Her spell included the words, "You can stay like that for all I care," which explains why she is now old and wrinkly, but Hamish isn't.

# Chapter 4

1. "Seneschal" is a fancy name for "housemaster", which is a very important job. The seneschal answers directly to the Duke and therefore wields enormous influence over the rest of the staff. Pick a fight with the seneschal and you'd better start looking for a new job.
2. Which was remarkably similar to her old job. You may have noticed it was a Sunday afternoon and there were people working. Just like hotels, weekends are the busiest times at the palechia, so laundry workers take their weekends on Tuesdays and Wednesdays.
   Ondine's timetable looked like this:
   Monday School & Laundry
   Tuesday School
   Wednesday School
   Thursday School & Laundry
   Friday School & Laundry
   Saturday Laundry
   Sunday Laundry

# Chapter 6

1. This kind of thinking began after the Soviet days, during the time of new freedoms and transparency, when "everything not expressly forbidden is permitted". A marked change from the gruelling days of "anything not expressly permitted is forbidden".
2. Jacques Delille, 1738–1813. He had loads of friends in high places, but his own father refused to acknowledge him.
3. Or watching every episode of *Lie to Me* and applying it to your real life.
4. With a slice of lemon is how Bruglers traditionally take their tea. In some cultures the expression is "with a pinch of salt". This makes no sense at all because tea with salt tastes awful!

# Chapter 7

1. Invented by those gourmets the French. An aperitif is a pre-dinner alcoholic drink, designed to get the appetite going.
2. Studies the world over find that red and yellow increase the appetite, while blue and green can aid the subconscious to eat less. But don't go over the top and paint your kitchen green and blue, or you'll make people feel queasy.

3. Zucchini are called Courgettes, if you're to the west of Italy.
4. At the risk of turning this into a manual on Brugel's unusual grammar, "fenudging" is a common adverb describing the flickety fidgety movements of people who otherwise ought to be sitting still.
5. Quite frankly he deserved a medal. Next time you do something mild, like stub your toe or get a paper cut, see if you can remain completely silent.
6. Biscuit's real title is Cardrona King Ivanovich, five times Best Breed, twice Best in Show, Venzelemma Ducal Dog Show.
7. He snarled too, but the Brugelish spelling of dog snarls is too complicated to print here.
8. As this is the first time anyone had ever heard teeth falling onto the floor, a new word had to be invented for it.

# Chapter 8

1. Rabies is a particularly nasty virus transmitted via the saliva in bites from infected animals. The virus attacks the victim's central nervous system and sends them completely mad. In later stages of infection, the victim foams at the mouth as their body produces copious amounts of saliva. If not treated quickly, it is almost always fatal.

   In an attempt to placate nervous tourists, Brugel declared itself rabies free in 2005. However, neighbouring countries Slaegal and Craviç make no such claims. As everyone knows, wild dogs and bats (which are the main carriers) cannot read Brugelish, and frequently walk or fly straight past the signposts advising them to keep out.
2. Bet you wish you'd read the first book now, eh?
3. The capital of Slaegal is called Norange. It's the only known word that rhymes with orange. Some people dispute this and say "strange" is close enough, and, indeed, it is a strange place.
4. From former US Secretary of Defense, Donald Rumsfeld: "There are known knowns. These are things we know that we know. There are known unknowns. That is to say, there are things that we know we don't know. But there are also unknown unknowns. There are things we don't know we don't know." Feb. 12, 2002, Department of Defense news briefing. Mr Rumsfeld forgot to add that there are "unknown knowns". These are things that you do know, but have forgotten.
5. In Brugel, it is mandatory for all children to attend school until the age of sixteen. You can stay on longer, of course, and many people do. It's common to find senior-school students in their twenties. The rise in mature students became so alarming in the 1990s the education department had to allocate designated campuses for twenty-somethings. It also created the uniquely puzzling situation of some students being older than their teachers.
6. In some European countries, it is correct to address an infanta as "Your Highness", but only if she is the daughter of the ruling king or queen. As Brugel is ruled by Duke Pavla, and the Infanta is Duke Pavla's older sister, this is not the case. Brugel tradition requires her to be addressed as "My Lordship", even though she is a woman. Thereafter she is referred to as "ma'am". By calling her "Your Highness", Ondine had promoted the Infanta to a station above the Duke, and the Infanta had no intention of correcting her.

7. "To queef" is to mentally have a little puke, without producing anything. You might also press your lips tightly together and blow your cheeks out like a bubble-headed goldfish.

8. This happened in Ondine's previous adventure, and, luckily for her family, Hamish gave everyone ample warning that the health inspector was on his way.


# Chapter 9

1. Brugel had not yet turned the clocks back and was still in Summer Time. In spring, Bruglers turn their clocks forward two hours on the first Sunday in April, then have the Monday and Tuesday as public holidays, to help them get over the shock. In the autumn, they wind the clocks back one hour on the first Sunday of October, and another hour on the first Sunday of November, so they get two sleep-ins.

2. Quickly discuss things, so that everyone knows what everyone else is up to. But not talk for so long that people get bored and fidgety.

3. A scimitar is a nifty and terribly dangerous curved sword from the mystical east.

4. Over the centuries Brugel has had several national anthems. During Soviet occupation they sang (through gritted teeth) *Sing to the Motherland, Home of the Free*. These days people sing *Oh, Brugel, My Heart* with gusto and pride. Except at the Olympics, because they have yet to win a gold medal in any event. They do have a chance if lift jumping ever becomes a recognised sport. Lift jumping involves cramming people into a lift. Everyone jumps just as the lift moves up or down. Last person standing wins.

5. A great many national anthems contain confusingly "poetic" phrases that make little sense to the modern citizen. As Brugel is almost land-locked, it has at least been spared the ridiculous lyric "girt by sea".

6. The way Brugel celebrates Halloween is different to the rest of the world. There is no "trick or treat, give me lollies" palaver, and there are no pumpkins – because Brugel's Halloween pre-dates the arrival of pumpkins from the Americas by several hundred years.

    Bruglers hang wreaths of wheat in their windows and place apples on the sills for good luck. They eat copious amounts of turnips and cabbage, (fried, in soups, roasted, etc.) then venture outside in the full moon and gather around the village square for Bonfire Night. Bruglers write down their bad habits or regrets on notes, and cast them into the fire, as a way of saying goodbye to the past and cleansing their futures.

    It's considered tremendous bad luck to remain inside on Bonfire Night. Because of the mountain of turnip and cabbage consumed, and the lower-body explosions that ensue, staying outside is not just tradition, it's vital for good health.

7. The Brugelish word for cabbage is slang for "fart".

8. Ondine is not wrong per se, but the general area Brugel occupies on the map of Europe has been around in some form for centuries. The specific date to which Ondine refers is the signing of the Treaty of Venzelemma, the site of Brugel's capital city.

9. Just about every culture has a backstory involving a flood. Floods are handy devices. You can pretty much make up any story of life "before the flood" because there's very little evidence around to prove you wrong. Geologists, palaeontologists and archaeologists would disagree, but that's their job.

10. You could argue that a sample size of two women versus two hundred men is hardly a comparison at all, and leaves a very wide margin for error. The current Duke of Brugel would argue that this interpretation of history is completely sound, and that having a Duchess at the helm is proven bad luck for Brugel.

# Chapter 11

1. Swimming is not a major sport in Brugel, so most women maintain the narrow shoulders they were born with. In "big swimming" countries like Australia you can spot the serious swimmers, they're the ones who have to turn sideways to fit through doorways. One Olympic champion's shoulders were so wide she became stuck inside a marquee tent on her wedding day.
2. Don't even think of googling this or there'll be a SWAT team at your door faster than you can say, "I need a lawyer."
3. A Brugeloak tree is quite remarkable. It matures in six years, producing large edible white berries that taste like a cross between apples and peaches. The large seeds inside taste like hazelnuts and can be ground to make paste. However, close to ninety per cent of people develop an allergic reaction to the paste and therefore sales of Brugeloak butter are low.

    For more information about Brugel's unique flora, grab a copy of the bestselling *What Caused This Rash?* by noted botanist Kerk von Dennegelden.
4. This is very true. Just as every generation gets taller, every generation gets heavier. Take out a mortgage, then sit in a chair from Brugel's renaissance and see how easily it breaks under your weight.

# Chapter 12

1. In most cases dirty objects are placed in baskets or rubbish bins. On the odd occasion you throw them towards the bin and they miss their target, they make this noise on landing.
2. Brugel is often used as a unit of measurement amongst the eastern states of Europe. For example, "Every day, an area of rainforest the size of Brugel is bulldozed in the Amazon."

    It is true that a dog's mouth is a total bac-fest, but the exact number of bacteria is anyone's guess. If the dog's had a good clean-up at the vet, the numbers will be lower. If the dog has snaffled week-old road-kill, it's time to get out the hazmat suits.
3. Attending the opera should be a beautiful night out. In Brugel, however, their opera is monumentally bad. Noted Slaegalese critic Zarah Bragiç likened it to wailing cats. In a cement mixer. Which is why it was far too dangerous to allow Duke Pavla to attend – the shock to his system might kill him. There is a silver lining: where Bruglers fail in the singing department, they more than make up for in earplug manufacture.
4. A traditional Brugel cold remedy involves equal measures of fresh milk, plütz, tomato juice and gunpowder. Mix and drink immediately. After that, a sniffly cold is the least of your problems. It's also expensive, as fresh milk can sometimes be hard to obtain.

# Chapter 13

1. Another problem with parabolas is pronunciation. Is it PA-ra- BOWL-a or pa-RA-bo-LA? You can waste a good five minutes in class arguing that one.
2. Another term for parabolas.
3. This is Old Brugelish, which has origins in German and Latin. The language is so frustrating and illogical that studying Old Brugelish is the leading cause of nervous breakdowns in modern scholars.

# Chapter 13-A

1. Compared to Ondine's schooling and laundry work, Old Col and Hamish have scored the much better deal so far. Sampling food, opening mail, eavesdropping, partaking in a little gossip. All far too easy. However, they do have the burden of the Duke's welfare on their shoulders, and they need to find out who is plotting his downfall. And they might want to hurry up with that, because things are about to get a lot worse.
2. Brugel is famous for its lace-iron work. Lace-iron is a process of super-heating iron until it bends, giving it a stretch so it becomes thin, but not so thin that it breaks, and lacing it together to create a decorative flat surface. Many unwary customers are fooled into buying shoddy knock-offs made from a flat circle of iron with a lace pattern stamped into it.
3. If you need to keep your voice low while giving a message to someone, murmuring is far more effective than whispering. Whispering involves far too many "esses' and people will overhear you and want to know what all the fuss is about.
4. If it was expected, it wouldn't be a surprise. The Infanta's arrival at meal times was one of those "known unknowns'. You know she'll turn up at some point, you just don't know when.
5. In other words, the Infanta thinks the Duchess is a drunken lush. If you want to talk about anything sensible with her, you'd best do so early in the day before she's had too much to drink.
6. A type of inexpensive processed 'meat' with huge portions of fat. Each slice is so full of fatty chunks it resembles crazy paving.
7. Brugel's answer to e-Bay, where the auctions work in reverse. The seller nominates a high beginning price, then reduces it by increments. The first bidder to put their (electronic) hand up "wins' the bid. Many Brugel estate agents try the same technique, with mixed results.

# Chapter 14

1. Female butlers are common in Brugel and also in neighbouring Slaegal, but Craviç is having none of it.
2. Brugel coinage, of very little value.

3. A beloved expression of Bruglers. It means someone thinks they have everything sorted out, but they've forgotten the basics. For example, if you want to cook roast beef, you must first get the cow.

# Chapter 15

1. Over the centuries, the Autumn Palechia had had many modern conveniences added. Ducted heating and air conditioning have made life more comfortable for the modern resident (although not for the staff, who wear two pairs of fingerless gloves in the cold mornings). But none of the dukes in the history of Brugel had seen fit to install lifts. Or a dumb waiter.
2. Little knick-knack figurines that look like Trotsky.
3. It's a little-known fact that the term 'squee' began in Brugel.
4. Not a bad little science experiment in itself. If you wish to tear paper silently, make sure it's wet. The same goes for opening scrunched paper – if it's wet it barely makes a sound. If it's really wet, however, you may find it impossible to read the contents.
5. In the weeks leading up to the Harvest Festival, the Duke of Brugel gives a pardon to a chicken – or several chickens, depending on his mood – in order to spare them from ending up on the dinner tables.

# Chapter 16

1. In Brugel, an employee accrues eight weeks' long-service leave at full pay (or sixteen weeks at half pay) after six years' continuous employment with the one employer or company. This seems overly generous on the face of it, but in reality two out of three businesses in Brugel declare bankruptcy within the first year.
2. Naturally, Draguta didn't mean hang the baskets up, she meant hang up the contents of the baskets.

# Chapter 17

1. Most of us make do with two-hundred-thread-count cotton; that is, two hundred strands of cotton per square inch of fabric, counting the up and downy threads and the side to sidey threads. Most weavers claim it's impossible to create true one-thousand-thread-count cotton, as there is simply no way to squeeze five hundred threads vertically and horizontally into one square inch. These weavers have yet to meet the incredible craftsmen and women of Venzelemma, who achieve the impossible on a daily basis.
2. Balloon – somebody with an inflated ego.
3. Atspish – a less than stellar result.

# Chapter 18

1. During plagues in Brugel's middle ages, morticians would haul a wagon through town calling, "Bring out your dead." Passed-out drunks were sometimes mistaken for corpses and flung on the wagons. They would sober up rapidly and give up drink. Hence the phrase, "on the wagon".
2. A television talent program, where many contestants receive their first honest criticism. It's often so emotionally crippling it sends them back to school so they can get a proper education and do something they might actually be good at.

# Chapter 19

1. Yia-sou is a friendly 'hello' in Greek. Say it to just about anyone and you'll go places, either in Athens, Greece, or in Melbourne, Australia.

# Chapter 21

1. It's called "circular breathing" and is especially useful when playing the didgeridoo.
2. Aren't flip-top lids on toothpaste wonderful? It's so easy to snap the lid back in place. In the days when you had to screw the lid on, many time-poor people would forget to replace the lid. Because clearly, it was soooo much effort to screw one tiny little lid back on the tube. It's enough to drive you completely insane.

   It's no coincidence that the introduction of flip-top lids on toothpaste tubes in the early 1990s dovetails neatly with Brugel's plummeting divorce rates.

# Chapter 22

1. What Ondine is relying on here is the "double coincidence": the idea that the information she gives the Duke has the same value as the information he needs to hear. She's also relying on the information she will subsequently be able to give Draguta being of the same value as any information Draguta may give to Ondine (about why she's padding her teddy with precious objects rather than fluffy stuff). So really, she's relying on the "quadruple coincidence", and the chances of that happening are virtually zero.
2. "Keeping stump" is an old Brugel idiom about staying quiet and being clever, and your deepest desires will come to you. It refers to the classic Brugel fable of "the Fox in Disguise", who strapped branches on his limbs and sat on a tree stump with his mouth wide open for so long, the forest creatures couldn't help but get closer and closer to get a better look at the strange tree. Eventually the dim forest sweeties walked straight into the fox's mouth and he got everything he wanted. It may also be a mishearing of the phrase "keeping stumm", but nobody in Brugel would know what you were talking about.

# Chapter 24

1. Pedants love to point out that bananas plants are herbs. This is true. However, the fruit is still fruit. Like many fruits, bananas are sweet and go nicely with ice cream and chocolate, which is not something you can say for parsley.
2. Someone with excellent lineage who turns out bad. The combination of caramel, being golden and scrumpy; and yoghurt, being so lovely and delicious, should be fabulous, but instead it's horrible.

# Chapter 27

1. Except she probably would have said, "You will be let down by Hamish," because of her penchant for the passive voice.

# Chapter 28

1. The Dentate is Brugel's equivalent of Parliament. Dentate means "the place with teeth".

# The Winter of Magic

## Chapter 1

1. In Brugel, name days are not birthdays. They are far more important than that. It's the day you celebrate the saint you are named after, rather than the accidental day on which you were born. If you're not directly named after a saint, you'll be given one as a middle name. One of Ondine's middle names is Benedicte, named after the patron saint of spelunking. Benedicte is also the patron saint against witchcraft, which is pretty convenient considering the situations Ondine has been in.
2. Venzelemma is the capital city of Brugel, a country in Eastern Europe that still hasn't made a dent in the Eurovision Song Contest.
3. In Brugel, eating is the new black.
4. They do have a dishwasher, which is brilliant for crockery, but everything else has to be done by hand. Beer goes flat if detergent residue is left on the glass. Flat beer may be all the rage in neighbouring Slaegal, but in Brugel it just won't do.
5. Something that is incredibly unlikely to happen. A fish can dance on the table, but few of them want to.
6. At the risk of becoming bogged down in footnotes before the story can gain momentum, there have been huge ructions in Brugel lately. Duke Pavla is too sick to rule, his wife Kerala is responsible for that sickness and is being kept under high security lock and key. As a result, the Duke's sister the Infanta Anathea is only too happy to take control.
7. Lord Vincent is almost as gorgeous as Hamish on the outside, but under the skin he's rotten right through.
8. Let's face it, Hamish is a trouble magnet.

9.  In neighbouring Slaegal, bread rolls on the table are not complimentary. Nor are they all that edible. They are, however, very effective for stabilising a wonky table leg.
10.  A ravishingly demented drink made from sozzled peaches. The consumer feels no ill effects for the first few minutes, then they stand up to find their knees don't work.

## Chapter 2

1.  Mustn't forget Old Col. AKA, Miss Colette Romano, Ondine's great-aunt and all round fabulously batty witch. And lousy chaperone. See *ONDINE: The Autumn Palace*.
2.  See *ONDINE: The Summer of Shambles*. Look, we could get bogged down in backstory if we're not careful. You *have* read the first two books, haven't you? Oh for goodness sake. Go read them. I'll wait . . . OK, you're back? You're fast!
    Are you sure you didn't skim?
3.  Because this is a family pub, all tips are shared. If people enjoy their meal, they're not simply tipping Hamish for being gorgeous and attentive, they're tipping Henrik and Cybelle for the sumptuous food and Ondine for the sparkling clean plates they're eating from. And for Da for keeping such a well-stocked bar. And Ma for keeping it all running smoothly.
4.  Isn't it nice when they do this? "Mind your head, that's it, watch how you go, gentle."
    It's all part of the Courtesy in Custody program, which began in neighbouring Craviç and has spread throughout the world.
5.  "Dorian Grey" is a camera filter setting used to make ageing movie stars look like ingénues, to convince the public that anti-wrinkle creams work. Or a devilishly good novella by Oscar Wilde, about a dashing youth whose portrait ages instead of the man.
6.  Bellreeve is where the Autumn Palechia is located. It's also the setting for a fair amount of trauma in the previous book. No wonder Ondine felt sick at the thought of going back there. They won't be – going back to the palechia that is – just in case you were thought this third novel would push the reset button.

## Chapter 3

1.  At this time of year, Brugel's tiny strip of territory along the Black Sea would be deserted, the beach chairs and umbrellas covered in snow. The Venzelemma Tourist Bureau And Committee For The Prettyment of Brugel leaves the chairs on the beach all year round, but they are chained together to prevent thefts. They also have 'anti-towel-technology' fabric, which makes towels slide right off them, so tourists can't reserve a chair and then wander off for the rest of the day. However, the fabric is so slippery tourists have also been known to slide right off them, especially if they put a towel down first.
2.  Orschlappen is the Brugelish term for earflaps. The huge coats and warm hats made Ondine feel like she was wearing a duvet, but at least she didn't look as silly as those people who wear blankets with sleeves.
3.  In the old days, they used to throw acorns at the bride and groom, but they hurt!
4.  Because of the huge spike in weddings, every service provider opens their doors super-early to cope with the onslaught of customers.

5.  In many western countries, people wear their wedding bands on the fourth finger of the left hand, but in much of Eastern Europe it's on the right. In Brugel, it doesn't matter, as long as it fits one of the fingers and doesn't slip off.
6.  Breakfast should be an uncomplicated affair, or as they say in Brugel, "It's not roquette salad."

# Chapter 4

1.  These are Ondine's thoughts, in bracketed italics. Just in case you weren't sure.
2.  Unless you are Linda Lou Wolfe from Indiana, USA, who has married 23 times, making Elizabeth Taylor look like an amateur.
3.  In Brugel, it's traditional for weddings to be held on a Wednesday. Linguists claim Wednesday derives from the Norse god *Woden*, but Bruglers are positive it's derived from the Olde Brugelish word for *Wedding*. Being a superstitious country, it's considered good luck to marry within the same calendar year as your engagement. Nobody has a clue why, but nobody is brave enough to buck convention. Hence the sudden rush of marriages in December and very few of them in January.

# Chapter 5

1.  The filter we all have in our brains, that stops us – just in time – from saying the wrong thing. Unfortunately, it's not always possible to find the 'on' switch in time.
2.  When the granite stones turn cold, they can be used for a curling match, which is a popular form of post-wedding entertainment.
3.  Pleather looks just like real leather, but is much kinder on cows.
4.  Few Brugelish cars have airbags.

# Chapter 6

1.  Boak = "Oh dear, something I have eaten does not agree with me."
2.  Ducking the paper is the local expression for avoiding filling out forms or completing other brain-drainingly horrid paperwork. It's usually achieved by signing the blank paper at the bottom of the page, then handing it back to the official with a crisp ßr100 bill at the top.
3.  Despite the name, Slaegalpines are not native to Slaegal, the country that neighbours Brugel. They are however, in plentiful supply in that country, and feature heavily in Norange, that country's capital. Legend has it that the first families brought the pines with them, when they arrived from somewhere much further east.

# Chapter 7

1. Across Brugel, the Wednesday laundry curfew is strictly adhered to, so that those getting married (on a Wednesday, of course) will not have the blight of people's smalls lowering the tone of their day.
2. Something huge and puzzling that everyone knows is right there but nobody wants to talk about.

    Pachyderms are not native to Brugel, so the expression, 'The elephant in the room' never caught on.
3. In Brugel, a finger sandwich is a dainty morsel that you can hold in your fingers. This is not always the case in Slaegal.
4. "No offence". The two words uttered before the speaker always says something truly offensive.
5. Anything that has exceeding its statute of limitations. Whether a civil court case for negligence, or a decades-old feud between two women who fought for the affections of the same handsome lad.
6. Similar to a waltz, but less poncing and more snuggling.
7. Only sparkling wine from the Champagne region of France can be called Champagne. In Brugel, locals call it 'bubbles' or 'sparkling'. The really cheap stuff is called 'tart fuel'.

# Chapter 8

1. She hasn't been to Melbourne, Australia, where the entire citizenry wears fashionable mourning clothes all the time, even though Rock'n'Roll died years ago.
2. Brugel has two commercial networks that broadcast nationally, and the non-profit BNB, the Brugel National Broadcaster funded by the sale of Brugel-Made televisions. BNB is commercial free and broadcasts every second Sunday, and on special occasions.
3. It's not called Savo Square, because it's shaped like a hexagon.
4. In Brugel, Christmas proper doesn't begin until Christmas Eve, December 24. It's also illegal for anyone to put up Christmas decorations before December 1. This is one of the drawcards for people migrating to Brugel. Absolute guarantee, you will never read a tweet from a Brugeler complaining of Christmas merch in stores in September.
5. It's not a waste of food throwing cheese balls, because the myriad stray dogs hanging around will eat them up. In many parts of the world people employ a "five second rule" for eating dropped food – if the food has been on the ground for less than five seconds, it's still safe to eat. No such rule exists in Brugel because the dogs get it first.
6. Old Col had removed them, with a spell (which may or may not have included anaesthetic!) during a fraught time under the table at the Autumn Palace. And while it is terribly cruel to remove all a dog's teeth in one swoop – with or without magic, with or without anaesthetic – those same teeth were about to chomp Shambles in half, and Old Col simply wasn't going to let that happen. The teeth had begun to grow back since that incident, but the dog wasn't back to full bitey-ness at this point.
7. Fried cheese balls are banned at football matches in Brugel, as cold ones are used as weapons.

# Chapter 9

1. The jewels and pretty shiny things they'd found under the floorboards in book one were well and truly spent on renovations and the wedding. The ones Ma had been able to keep, of course. The rest she'd taken back to the creators at the Hera Collection.
2. Brugel is one of many countries in Europe that has intermittent power supply during winter, on account of large amounts of snow, frozen connections and people being unceremoniously disconnected because they cannot trudge through the snow to get to the bank to pay their bills on time. They could try internet banking, but this requires a reliable electricity supply.
3. The first dinner, followed soon after by the second.
4. Cybelle is the Banksy of Brugel.

# Chapter 10

1. People who are not-yet-witches, but believe they one day will be.
2. A funicular rail line is so steep the carriages must be hauled up the incline with sturdy cables. The two carriages are always attached to each other, so while one goes up, the other comes down, thus minimizing the energy required to reach the top.
3. Which is one reason why Brugel has so few mountains of any repute. But they do have some wonderful castles.
4. Literal translation is, "Welcome to Brugel, don't mind the mess the maid has the day off."
5. Just like the way politicians wear a cattleman's hat and blue work shirt when they visit 'the country folk'.
6. The official story was that the hotel in Norange, Slaegal's capital, had run into 'financial difficulties', what with the economy and employees stealing from their workplace. A pen and notepad here, a complete 1,000-thread sheet set there. But in this case, management was stealing from staff, stripping their homes while they were at work and selling the ill-gotten goods online. The real reason was that there was so much whacky magic happening around Brugel, they simply had to move to that magical epicentre.
7. Brugel has been on the receiving end of great waves of migration as life in other parts of the world became unbearable.

   In the fifteenth century, witches and warlocks fled the Spanish Inquisition; in the seventeenth century, people escaped the Salem Witch Trials, and in the late 20th Century, it was music lovers deserting the Eurovision Song Contest.

# Chapter 11

1. In Brugel, there is no right to remain silent if you are arrested. There is, however, the right to respond to all questions in haiku.
2. Your Lordship is the correct address to the head of Brugel, whether Duke or Duchess.

# Chapter 12

1.  A coffee substitute that came into its own during the Soviet Coffee Crisis of 1976–79. International price hikes made it near impossible for Bruglers to get their hands on the proper stuff. Farmers in Slaegal and Craviç sowed thousands of acres of chicory, in the hope of satisfying local demand. By 1980, fresh supplies of coffee beans from Vietnam made its way west, and the crisis was over. This in turn lead to precisely zero demand for local chicory and the crops ran to seed. To this day, their blue flowers grow rampant across the landscape.
2.  And potatoes have eyes.
3.  Everyone except the chicory farmers would be happy. They are still trying to claw back their decades-old losses.
4.  D is the second letter in the old Brugelish alphabet. In Soviet days, if plan 'D' failed, there were thirty-one more letters to fall back on.
5.  Listening with your mouth open does widen the ear canals so you can hear more clearly. Alas, it makes you look like a slack-jawed yokel.

# Chapter 13

1.  Around 1346, Black Plague spread from Asia to the Crimea, which is very near Brugel. Sonja of Yersina was a tea and spice merchant whose travels brought her into contact with the plague. Although she did not develop any symptoms herself, she passed it on to her customers and then some. This could have been terrible for business if not for the fact her parents were undertakers. She inherited the thriving family trade in 1348 when her parents popped their clogs
2.  At Bruglish fat farms, you go in thin and come out looking normal. As opposed to the ones elsewhere in the world, where you go in fat and come out a little less fat, before abandoning all your promises at the first plate of hot chips. Mmmmm, hot chips.
3.  At CovenCon, they allow non-witches and non-seers to call themselves pre-witches and pre-seers, so that those on the way to witching and seeing feel as if they are really on their way.
4.  It's a lay-down misère, if you tick the 'vegan' box on your conference registration, you'll get an eggplant stack.

# Chapter 14

1.  The correct temperature for making espresso is between 88 and 95 degrees Celsius (at sea level). Tea, of course, needs to be made with boiling water that is 100 degrees Celsius (at sea level). It's not about being fussy, it's about doing things properly. We must uphold our standards or the savages will win (at sea level).
2.  The last time Biscuit had taken a bite out of Hamish, he'd had all his teeth and Hamish was a Shambles ferret. And Ondine hadn't been there to protect him. Some quick thinking from Col saved the moment. She had magicked all of the dog's teeth out, so he couldn't do any harm.

# Chapter 15

1.  Be nice to animals, because you never know when you'll be turned into one.

# Chapter 16

1.  An incredibly popular tofu substitute, made from chicken.
2.  The infamous Debutante Ball so many decades ago, where Hamish had taken his first taste of plütz, tripped on Col's dress, ripped her hem and called her a witch. Oh, and Col had then turned him into a ferret.
3.  Old Brugelish Latin meaning, "pound for pound".

# Chapter 17

1.  In any conference there will be at least three workshops you really want to attend. And as fate will have it, two of them will be on at the same time.
2.  Brugelish currency.

# Chapter 18

1.  The Brugelish translation of the classic line: "Keep your friends close, but your enemies closer". A good half hour of Google searching will show this quote is usually misattributed to Sun Tzu or Niccolò Machiavelli, yet the first record of it is from Michael Corleone in *The Godfather Pt II*, (1974).

# Chapter 19

1.  Lions are not native to Brugel, so Ondine has nothing with which to compare the noises in her head.

# Chapter 20

1.  With extra thick fur on the earflaps.

# Chapter 21

1.  A resort on the Black Sea, built inside an enormous bubble-dome, with sunlamps glowing fourteen hours a day. It's the one holiday destination where a 'sun guarantee' actually means what it says.

# Chapter 22

1. In some parts of the world, you can give your camera to another tourist and ask them if they wouldn't mind taking your picture. In Brugel, if you give your camera to a passer-by they will say, "thanks very much" and walk off with it.
2. In some sections of neighbouring Craviç they have "caravan only" roads so that the only drivers they hold up are other caravan drivers. Their prettiest roads are reserved for cars, motorbikes and bicycles. Trucks and white vans are restricted to motorways. It's a form of motoring apartheid other countries can only dream of.
3. Otherwise known as God's waiting room.

# Chapter 23

1. Figurative mice, not literal ones. Ondine's mutating magic isn't that far out of control. Yet.
2. The literal translation of Martisor is, "March better be here soon, I can't feel my feet any more."
3. Lactose intolerant Bruglers often migrate to Slaegal, where they are much happier.
4. Similar to cotton candy or fairy floss, this confection is made from silky strands of spun sugar, which you eat with a crochet hook.

# Chapter 24

1. How weird? The moment they'd stepped over the flagstones in *The Autumn Palace* a tornado had appeared. Then it had rained fish. That's how weird.
2. The Brugel equivalent of hating someone's guts.

# Chapter 25

1. The Brugel Bannermen's Guild takes credit for the series of festivals all lined up in a row, having spearheaded a campaign for such events. They erect banners for "festival z" while taking down the banner for "festival y", thus saving time – but not money, as they are paid only for banners they erect, but not take down.
2. Barry means good. Or puke. If you have a really good night out, you have a Barry good Barry at the end of it.
3. Massive insult, in both Scotland and Brugel.

# Chapter 26

1. Do not try this at home. The turning yourself into a shadow and leaping into someone else's body bit. The battery on the tongue? Go ahead, loads of fun. *Bzzt!* You're welcome.

2. They hadn't made it all the way through the snow maze, because it was enormous and could take hours to get through. They'd simply waited around the corner, had a chat, explored a little, then used cheat codes to find their way out again.
3. She still had to behave herself and do the right thing by Brugel.

## Chapter 27

1. The literal translation of "nincs" is "No way José". Someone who says "no" to everything is known as a "nincompoop".

## Epilogue

1. Stop fussing, lassie, there's not much you can do about it now anyway.

# The Spring Revolution

## Chapter 1

1. Did you think I'd forgotten about the footnotes? Not a chance! Vincent's mother was previously known as Duchess Kerala. However, now that Kerala's husband Duke Pavla is no more, mostly because Kerala fed him pastries made from poisonous rhubarb leaves, she is known as The Dowager Duchess Kerala.
2. If none of this is making any sense, it's most likely because you've accidentally picked up the fourth book in the series instead of the first.
3. "It's fun to stay at the DYMA," is a popular Brugelish refrain when someone starts acting loopy.

## Chapter 2

1. Considering the magic had caused so much mayhem only a season earlier, and continues to cause mayhem around the country if recent news reports are anything to go by, Ma should still be worried about this. As should Ondine and Hamish.
2. Brugel's answer to Instagram. You thought it was going to be YouTube, but nobody in Brugel knows what that is.
3. Fabulously sweet Romanian wine, which is hugely popular in Brugel because of its peachy overtones, which reminds them of plütz.
4. Slagging off means saying things that are uncomplimentary. Even if they are true.
5. The Slaegal Tourism Bureau never lets facts get in the way of a good marketing campaign.
6. Fret not. This is not a Slaegal book, but somebody from Brugel – that would be Lord Vincent – is spending time in Slaegal, and we need to know what he's up to.
7. Norange has no height restrictions on buildings per se, but the roof of the house cannot be taller than the tree in the atrium. Therefore if you want a multi-storey house, choose a very tall tree and build your house around it.

8. The Zendgraf (literal translation; *Sent Lord*) is the lord ruler of Norange, dating back to the days when the Holy Roman Emperor would send his lords to keep an unruly mob in line. The wife of a Zendgraf is a Zendgravine. In modern times it has become a hereditary but purely honorary title. Like Brugel, Slaegal embraced democracy, with mixed results, after the fall of the USSR in 1991.

9. Vincent and the Zendgraf are only cousins by marriage, and second cousins at that. It's the Zendgravine's mother, Lady Nelly, and Vincent's father, the Late Duke Pavla (may his soul rest in peace) who are first cousins. Don't stress, there won't be a test.

10. Over many years, exposure to cold weather extremes breaks the capillaries under the skin, leaving the cheeks and nose red and blotch-ridden. The same effect can be achieved much sooner from drinking hard liquor.

11. The full idiom is, "When in Norange, do as the Noranges." In other words, when you're in a strange place, do your best to blend in.

12. Vincent has always been a bucket-half-full kind of person. Or as they say in Brugel, "You can be sad that a goat has horns, or be grateful the horns have goats on them, and the goats give you milk."

13. Crashing cups or glasses together is a tradition as old as time. Less about friendship and more about self-preservation, the act helps the drinkers avoid an early grave. If one or more glasses is tainted with poison, crashing them together slops the toxin into all drinks, thus putting everyone on an equal footing.

# Chapter 3

1. Sletto is Slaegal's own chain of deeply discounted supermarkets, where you not only bring your own bags, you bring your own trolley.

2. Merely talking about a problem doesn't solve it. You've got to take action.

3. A user-edited database for all things Eastern European, www.cantbelieve_it-snotwikipedia.br.

4. Several former Soviet Bloc countries, including Brugel and Slaegal, have formed their own song competition to rival Eurovision. That's not to say they are exclusive, as some countries *cough* Craviç *cough* are known to enter both.

5. Tradies is the non-sexist way to describe tradesmen and women. Women are highly represented amongst Slaegal bricklayers and are amongst the most sought after in the world.

6. Gaspado is Slaegalese for 'honourable man', which is their equivalent of the western honorific of Mister. Gaspada is 'honourable woman' and is used for both 'Miss' and 'Mrs', because all women are honourable, whether married or not.

7. The full expression is, "When the gale is blowing and the plütz is flowing, we shall meet under the table." This harks back to the days of poor building regulations, where shoddy tradieship often resulted in collapsed walls and roofs. The safest place to be was with a bottle of plütz (for its warming properties on a cold night) underneath a table (for its stability and security).

# Chapter 4

1. The ballroom is a short walk from Savo Plaza, which will prove incredibly convenient later on.
2. If we gave the instructors names, they'd take on far too much importance in the story. In reality they did have names and their parents loved them very much, but they're little more than extras in Ondine's story.
3. A payphone is a public telephone secured to a fixed position, which is connected to a landline. A rarity in most modern countries, Brugel's plethora of public phones is a source of national pride. And a reminder of how unreliable mobile phone coverage is.
4. If Ondine had things her way, this latest adventure would come to a swift conclusion and she could get back to borrowing Da's eyebrow dye to fix Hamish's hair.
5. The Broaku markets on the Caspian Sea are clandestine traders' yards where excess munitions from government stockpiles are bought and sold. Cash only. No time wasters.

# Chapter 5

1. Lunatic soup is two or more types of alcohol mixed together.
2. "I'll be right down in a minute," means, "When I get around to it".
3. *BrugelMelody* is the local competition, held in early spring each year, to choose a song to represent Brugel at the PopEuroTube Song Contest in May. Some years the songs are even half good, but most years the competition is held in secret to spare viewers and participants from pain and humiliation.
4. Every marketplace in the world has donut vans, it's the law. Dolphin-shaped jam injectors are optional.
5. They were on stage, separating Mrs Howser's control from Lord Vincent, then separating Mrs Howser's soul from her body, with the help of Duchess Anathea's intervention with a vacuum cleaner.

# Chapter 6

1. Sure everyone has email and Snapchat accounts now, but this is Brugel before the turn of the century. (Which is to say, the turn into the 21st century.) The first novel was about events that happened "exactly twelve years ago today."
2. Mt Verka Serduchka is one of Brugel's highest points, being almost four hundred meters above sea level and one of the last remaining hills that hasn't been excavated into a castle or fort of some kind. Hiking to the summit is popular all year, as is having your photo taken 'holding up' the leaning broadcast towers of VTV6 and BrugStereoFM. The towers were constructed in the early 1950s and began leaning almost straight away. They were straightened in the 1970s, with much fanfare and even greater expense. However this resulted in weaker transmission signals and a reduction in tourism, so they leaned the towers back to the way they were.

3. Other countries in PopEuroTube Song Contest have no such qualms about their performers or composers being from another country, but Brugel is fiercely Brugelish. If the performers don't meet this criteria, visa arrangements are quickly made.
4. Botflies are hideous parasites that grow under an animal's skin. You really don't want to look it up on a search engine. No please don't. OK, fine, I'm not your mother.
5. Five years out of date in Brugel is the equivalent to fifteen for the rest of us.
6. Anyone familiar with the PopEuroTube Song Contest rules knows that the maximum number of performers on stage is six, so if the rock outfit gets through, they'll have to cull performers. There is, however, no limit on the number of drum kits allowed on stage.
7. Any more than one phone call per household and the BrugelTel system will collapse under the onslaught.

# Chapter 7

1. Anything couched with an "I don't need to be rude, but," is apt to be rude.
2. Pleather is a wonderful substitute for leather and earns a bovine stamp of approval from the BBB, the Brugel Board of Bovines. Not actually chaired by bovines but humans, obviously. Cows cannot sign documents, as they lack opposable thumbs.
3. It's not barging in unannounced, as long as you make two firm knocks first before you barge in.
4. Even thieves need a night off from time to time.
5. With marshmallows = hot chocolate. No marshmallows = hot cocoa. It's the rules.

# Chapter 8

1. If you've ever rubbed any brand of mentholated gel on an aching muscle, then accidentally rubbed your eyes, you'll know the pain.
2. Brugel and Slaegal have had a frosty relationship at the best of times, which often manifests into 'nemesis status' during times of national competitions.
3. That ball. Where Hamish (as a young lad) had offended Old Col (as a young Colette Romano) and she'd turned him into a ferret (the evergreen Shambles).
4. Most people these days would simply grab their phone, which comes with a camera on it, but this is Brugel, and technology takes a while to arrive. If Ondine had grabbed her phone, the cord wouldn't have reached the doorway.
5. An enormous party to celebrate something big, like a wedding or your team winning a football game. When your team loses, you have a wake.
6. Elmaree the First had broken the quill she used to sign a marriage agreement with Prince Faddei of Slaegal. The phrase 'Elmaree's Stain' refers to the blue ink spilled over her writing hand, and the 'stain' on her reputation for reneging on a deal. It was never going to be a good deal for Elmaree anyway, but historians can be so cruel. For more details, read *All For Love: The Life and Times of Elmaree, the First Grand Duchess of Brugel*.
7. Hygienically cautious people endeavour not to touch anything with their palms or finger pads, as this is the fastest way to transmit bacteria and viruses, which adore warm, moist conditions. Comparatively, the knuckles are usually drier and less

conducive to harboring germs. This dovetails neatly with Brugel's public health announcement series: "Stop Touching Your Face!"

8. Trieze-points (pronounced 'trez-pwa') is thirteen points, the highest score any country can give a contestant on PopEuroTube.

9. Blagger is Brugelish for telling very big fibs, which are very similar to the things that come out of the back-end of a bull. Blagger is not to be confused with Blogger, although the results can often be the same.

# Chapter 9

1. There was a half-hour wait to gain an audience. Because even though Ondine considered herself a friend of the duchess, she was still a member of the public and she didn't have a prior appointment.

2. 'Loosely based' in that Black Sonja was responsible for the spread of Bubonic Plague, not cholera, throughout the Black Sea region. People caught cholera from drinking contaminated water, whereas the plague was spread from person to person from sneezing, shaking hands and touching one's face.

3. Sure, Margibelle's performance is about the song, but it's also about putting on a show. Margi doesn't want to stand on stage like a lump if she can help it.

# Chapter 10

1. Snarfled is the act of stifling a laugh while coughing a little. Spluttering may also be involved.

2. A fraudulent slip is where you accidentally blurt out the truth. This is completely different from a Freudian slip, named after the enthusiastic 'father' of psychology, Sigmund Freud, who spent his lifetime reading naughty subtexts into everything.

# Chapter 11

1. As with Eurovision, The World Cup (in either football, rugby or curling) is something Brugel has also failed to win.

2. Sponduletise means to talk utter rubbish and be a right proper pain. Closely related to, spondylitis, which is a horrible affliction of the spine and muscles.

# Chapter 12

1. This is a lovely trick, which cafes and restaurants often deploy. Customers feel less inclined to order the cheapest item on the menu, for fear of being judged a tight-wad. Clever establishments set their prices to make the second-cheapest item the most profitable for them.

2. In Brugel, a samovari is one who works behind the samovar; in the same way a barista (bar tender) works behind a bar. A samovari may be male or female, and their skills of

brewing tea and cultivating a disdainful attitude towards customers takes years to cultivate.

3. Brugel's debutante balls are so old fashioned, guests must follow exacting rules of propriety. Only men may ask women for a dance, not the other way around. If a woman is asked for a dance, she may politely decline, although this seldom happens.
4. The maximum song length on PopEuroTube is four minutes. When the song is particularly terrible, it feels longer.


# Chapter 14

1. Whirlypits means nothing is making any sense, which is par for the course in Brugel.


# Chapter 15

1. Da's idea of Margi having a 'bun in the oven', proving that 'Dad Jokes' afflict fathers the world over.
2. The blue flowers of the chicory plant, which grow wild across the Craviçian landscape.
3. Timetabling isn't even a proper word, let alone a verbing of a noun. But of course Birgit and Babak let Vincent get away with it, because he's the Duke.


# Chapter 16

1. At a restaurant, if you have around half the meal left on your plate, the establishment may give you a 'doggy bag', which is code for 'let's pretend it's for the dog but it's really for me'.
2. As has been mentioned before, all of this took place at least a decade ago, so the laptop took up the space of two large coffee table books, and sucked electricity out of the wall like a vacuum aimed at a pile of confetti. It wasn't that unusual to take a portable computer out during the day. That was the point of them being portable. However, Brugelers were slow adopters to technology, so it was out of place.
3. Restaurants put attractive couples in the window, in an attempt to attract more attractive people.
4. Brugelish Blend is a combination of Peppermint, Black and Green tea.


# Chapter 17

1. An idiom peculiar to former Soviet Bloc countries. Because of supply shortages, local roasters regularly mixed coffee with higher and higher percentages of chicory until one day, at breakfast, the locals 'woke up' to the scam and could smell only the lie that was chicory.

# Chapter 18

1. Thin and delicious crepes, which are excellent with all manner of savory or sweet fillings. Or both if you're pressed for time.
2. Closing universities during a coup d'état is a rookie mistake, and one I expect none of you to make.

# Chapter 19

1. A 'backie' is a passenger on a bicycle, who is not always at the back, as the handlebars are often more comfortable. It is, however, dangerous and often illegal.

# Chapter 20

1. Ribbentrop cocktails are named after Joachim von Ribbentrop, who signed the Molotov-Ribbentrop Pact between Nazi Germany and Soviet Russia in August, 1939.